A DISTANT THUNDER

TERESA de LUCA

20426

AVON BOOKS ◆ NEW YORK

In memory of Maria and Anthony

Originally published as *By Truth Divided* in Great Britain in 1989 by
The Bodley Head Limited

AVON BOOKS
A division of
The Hearst Corporation
105 Madison Avenue
New York, New York 10016

Copyright © 1990 by Teresa de Luca
Published by arrangement with the author
Library of Congress Catalog Card Number: 89-24154
ISBN: 0-380-71086-2

Published in hardcover by William Morrow and Company, Inc.; for
information address Permissions Department, William Morrow and
Company, Inc., 105 Madison Avenue, New York, New York 10016.

First Avon Books Printing: March 1991

AVON TRADEMARK REG. U.S. PAT. OFF. AND IN OTHER COUNTRIES, MARCA
REGISTRADA, HECHO EN U.S.A.

Printed in the U.S.A.

RA   10 9 8 7 6 5 4 3 2 1

AUTHOR'S FOREWORD

The Spanish Civil War is a vast and complex subject; this novel merely scratches the surface of it. It is not necessary to know anything about the period to understand the book, but for the benefit of those readers who would like some background details, I am setting these out below for reference.

A Distant Thunder begins in July 1930. At this time Spain was in political turmoil. Power remained in the hands of the rich, the Church, and the Army; the poor were poor on a feudal scale. Increasing social unrest had led to the resignation of General Primo de Rivera, Spain's long-standing military dictator. Free elections were held the following year, and a democracy was established. King Alfonso went into exile, and Spain had its first Republic.

There followed five tumultuous years of conflict between the parties of the right and left. In February 1936 a general election resulted in a narrow majority for the Popular Front, an uneasy coalition of left-wing parties. It was strenuously opposed by the parties of the right, who feared it would preside over a workers' revolution and the establishment of a Marxist state. In addition, the new government soon found itself under pressure from militant groups of workers, particularly the Anarchists, who felt that it was too moderate and had defaulted on its pledge to implement drastic social reforms.

A coup by Army officers took place in July 1936 with the aim of overthrowing the government and replacing it with a right-wing military dictatorship. The rebellion broke out in Spanish Morocco and triggered off simultaneous uprisings all over the mainland; the rebels were met by troops remaining loyal to the Republic, supported by *ad hoc* workers' militias. Within days, Spain was divided almost in two, with about half the country falling to, or supporting, the rebels, and the rest remaining under government control. The situation rapidly escalated into full-scale civil war.

The war, in simple terms, was between the Right and Left. The

Right opposed the elected government and called themselves Nationalists, but were also referred to variously as Insurgents, Rebels, or Fascists. They were supported by the landowners, the well-to-do, the majority of Army officers, and the Church. The Left, who supported the elected government, were known as Republicans, or Loyalists, and were popularly referred to by the other side as "Reds." They were supported by the proletariat, socialist intellectuals, and those regions of the country wishing to establish or preserve separatist home rule (Catalonia and the Basque country). The Republican side was profoundly anticlerical; the destruction of churches and the persecution of priests and nuns quickly became a major propaganda issue.

Fearful of provoking a second world war, Britain and France promulgated an international nonintervention agreement. This was soon flouted by Germany and Italy, which went to the aid of the Nationalists/Fascists (soon to be led by General Francisco Franco, also known as the *Caudillo,* or Leader). The Soviet Union responded by allying itself with the Republic and organized the recruitment of the famous International Brigades. The war incurred appalling loss of life and did not end until February 1939, with a victory for the Fascists. General Franco remained dictator of Spain until his death in 1975.

This is not a history book but a work of fiction. I have simplified, condensed, omitted, and distilled in the interests of readability. I have chosen not so much to chronicle what did happen, as to imagine what might have happened. This is particularly true of the events taking place inside the Alcázar; I would like to point out that these are entirely speculative, and that no disrespect is intended to surviving veterans of either side. No one would deny that dreadful wrongs were perpetrated by both sides in this war, as in any other war, but any similarities to any real persons, living or dead, are entirely coincidental. It is testimony to the tenacity and spirit of the Spanish people that they have survived this terrible struggle and its consequences to create a successful and prosperous democracy.

TERESA DE LUCA

GLOSSARY

Bracero	Laborer, farmhand
Casa del Pueblo	Workers' club/meeting place
Caudillo	Leader (Franco)
Chorizo	Preserved sausage
Churro	Fritter
CNT	(Confederación Nacional de Trabajo) Anarchist Trade Union
Latifundista	Owner of a large estate
NKVD	Communist Secret Police
Novio/Novia	Fiancé(e)
Paseo	Evening stroll/(figuratively) assassination
POUM	(Partido Obrero de Unificación Marxista) Far left neo-Trotskyist party
Pronunciamiento	Military coup
Pueblo	Village, township
Puta	Whore
Regulares	Moroccan troops
Requeté	Carlist militiaman
Señorito	Young gentleman
SIM	Servicio de Investigación Militar (Republican counterespionage agency)
Tapas	Snack/hors d'oeuvres
UGT	(Unión General de Trabajadores) Socialist Trade Union

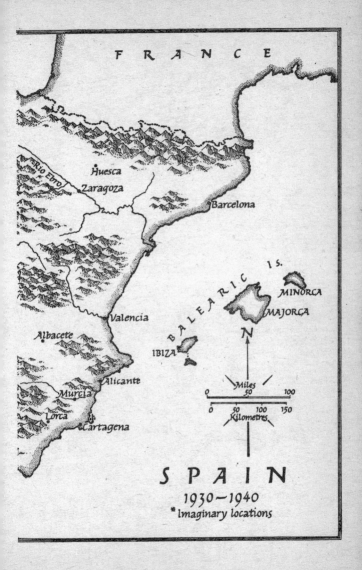

FRANCE

Rio Ebro

Huesca

Zaragoza

Barcelona

Valencia

Albacete

Alicante

Murcia

Lorca

Cartagena

BALEARIC IS.

IBIZA

MAJORCA

MINORCA

N

Miles
0   50   100

0   50   100   150
Kilometres

SPAIN
1930–1940
* Imaginary locations

PROLOGUE

SPAIN, JULY 1936

Dolores loaded her gun and waited. She had been assigned to an upper window, at the front of the house. The lookout in her father's watchtower had sighted enemy troops less than five kilometers away. There had been no resistance to slow them down and white flags fluttered over every chimney. The attack would start soon, very soon.

Holding the rifle Lorenzo had taught her to use, she felt close to him again, she knew something of what he was feeling. What difference did it make that they were fighting on different sides? They were both outnumbered by people who wanted to kill them, both caught up in events beyond their control. As long as their son survived, nothing else mattered . . .

And now, while there was still a little time, she must remember Jack. Jack, frozen in time and space with his bunch of bright red flowers whispering, "I love you, Dolly." A love less worthy than Lorenzo's, certainly, a love she should have shrugged off years ago, but a love that had branded her, changed her, left her not the same, taken something away from her and kept it out of reach, beckoning her somewhere she could not follow, except, perhaps, through death.

Except that she would not die. She would live to find it for herself and snatch it back again. There must be more to come. There must be more . . .

PART ONE
JULY–DECEMBER
1930

1

SPAIN, JULY 1930

"Welcome!" sang the seagulls. "Welcome back, Dolores!"

Dolores leaned against the rail of the *Leontes* and watched Lisbon harbor slide slowly toward her, savoring the experience for the very last time. Never again would those seagulls shriek a treacherous farewell. Just a few more hours along dusty, sunbaked roads and she would be safely across the border, she would be home again, for good.

Home. Meaning Spain, her family, Lorenzo. Most of all Lorenzo. Soon she would see Lorenzo again, no longer a humble cadet but a fully fledged officer. And soon she would be his wife. His *wife!*

She laughed out loud, broadcasting her delight to the hills above her, but the sea breeze swallowed the sound and reduced it to silent vapor, as if warning her to be discreet. Undaunted, she laughed on, loudly, mutely, into the wind. Her love must remain a secret, for the moment, but she need not hide her joy at coming home.

The estuary broadened and spread into the big, bright, glistening bay of Lisbon. Tiers of terra-cotta roofs reached up to a cloudless sky, basking in the hot July sun. It was still a foreign country, but it was redolent of home, glowing with warmth and welcome. Dolores had conveniently forgotten that she had set sail from Southampton on a perfect English summer's day. Southampton was frozen forever in her memory as a dull, gray, threatening place, shrouded in autumn mist and misery, heralding yet another year of exile. Five long, English years of chilly convent and flavorless food and dripping skies. But now another Spanish summer beckoned, ablaze with light and love.

Her lips curved in a wicked smile as she thought of Lorenzo's letters, nestling safely in a neatly hollowed-out volume of *Lives of*

3

the Great Saints—a mammoth tome now purged of its former piety and packed with illicit passion. It lay innocently at the bottom of her cabin trunk, soon to reclaim pride of place on the topmost shelf of her bookcase. The routine censorship of mail at the Ursuline Convent in Hampshire would have made the exchange of love letters impossible, but by great good fortune none of the holy sisters understood Spanish, and this ardent correspondence had been Dolores's lifeline. Lorenzo dared not write to her at home, and so those well-thumbed pages would have to sustain her until his longed-for leave, next month. Next month they would have two precious, furtive days together. No, not furtive. Now that she had finished school, now that Lorenzo had received his commission, he would surely speak to her father . . . wouldn't he?

Her eyes scanned the quayside as it bobbed and swayed toward her. Her mother and Ramón, her elder brother, would be there to meet her, as always. Josep, the eldest of the three Carrasquez children, would be missing; he was in a seminary in the north, studying for the priesthood. Her father never troubled to come, thank goodness. His stern, irascible presence would only put a damper on the reunion.

"Mamá!" yelled Dolores, spotting the fair, slim figure on her brother's arm. "Ramón!" She wrenched her straw hat off her head and waved it in excitement and saw them raise their hands in return. She continued her waving and shouting as the ship docked, bouncing up and down in her blue sailor suit while the wind whipped through her hastily pinned-up hair, loosening several long, dark strands and blowing them into her eyes, blurring her view.

How near and how far away they seemed! This last, static part of the voyage always seemed interminable. All she wanted to do now was to race down the gangplank and straight into her mother's arms. But she was obliged to curb her impatience while port officials boarded the ship and supervised the unloading of the baggage; only then would the passengers be released. It took forever. It was like being back at school, back in prison, standing in line, waiting your turn, doing what you were told. But never again. When she walked off this ship, she would be free at last. Her days of being locked up were finally over . . .

A thousand questions boiled and bubbled in her mind. Was there any news from Josep? Had there been any more trouble with the workers on the estate? Had the Doberman bitch had her puppies? How was her horse? Most of all, what was for dinner?

By the time she was allowed to disembark and finally emerged from the gloom of the customs shed, she was ready to burst with excitement. Forgetting that she was a well-bred young lady of eighteen, she broke into a run, losing her hat in the process, and hurled herself at her mother and brother, throwing her arms round both of them at once.

"Really, Dolly," scolded Pamela Carrasquez, in her own language. She never spoke Spanish if she could help it. "Just look at the state of you. Wasn't there a maid on board to iron your clothes? And your hair's all over the place . . . Careful, darling, you're ruining my face. . . ."

Pamela Carrasquez had retained the exquisite beauty of a china doll—baby-smooth, lily-white skin, golden hair and huge, vacant eyes. Pale blue English eyes that hid from the hostile foreign sun under a vast collection of broad-brimmed hats.

Undeterred, Dolores continued to ruin her mother's face, hugging her into laughing breathlessness. Then she launched a similar attack on her brother, who leaned languidly on his stick and accepted her embrace with a smile of seraphic cynicism. He was an extraordinarily beautiful young man, with the perfect profile of a god, the soulful eyes of a saint, and the innocent charm of a cherub, the purity of his features gloriously sullied by a smile that was full of sin.

"Sweet, silly sister," he chided her, bestowing a regal kiss on her forehead. "You look like a little peasant, as usual. You had better tidy yourself up before our dear father sees you. He's in a filthy mood today. . . ."

He broke off his speech and began coughing violently into a monogrammed handkerchief. His mother looked at him anxiously.

"Ramón has not been at all well," she whispered to Dolores. "I tried to make him stay in bed today, but he would not hear of it."

"Don't fuss, Mother," said Ramón sharply, recovering his breath. He turned to the porter, waiting patiently with Dolores's trunk. "This way," he barked with an imperious twirl of his cane, and limped off briskly toward the waiting car. The built-up boot on his withered leg had not robbed him of his princely demeanor; he flourished his stick as a monarch might wield a scepter.

"What's been happening?" asked Dolores as they climbed into the back of the luxurious Hispano Suiza. "Your letters never tell me anything."

"Happening? What ever happens in Albavera?" said Ramón, signaling to the chauffeur to drive off. "Nothing, that's what's been happening. Nothing." His voice retreated into a snarl; the first wave of unease dampened Dolores's high spirits.

"Darling, please don't upset yourself again," said his mother, fearing yet another eruption. Dolores provided a new and captive audience; in a moment he would be ranting and raving again. "Remember what the doctor said. Breathe deeply and keep calm."

Ramón's childhood polio had left him with a perennially weak chest, and his rage-induced asthma attacks were terrifying to watch.

"Meanness, that's all it is," continued Ramón to his sister. "What would it cost the old miser to let me study in Madrid? A mere pittance. Just because my tutors have all been brainless idiots, he dares to accuse me of a lack of application. He dares to suggest that I would waste my worthless time and his precious money!"

"Nonsense, darling," soothed his mother helplessly. "He doesn't want to lose you, that's all. He looks to you to take over the estate one day. With Josep gone, he needs you by his side . . ."

"Pah! I already know all there is to know about running the estate. A strong steward to keep the workers in line, and a fat bribe each month to the Civil Guard. I could run the estate with my eyes shut. I could run the estate from Madrid. So could he, if he had a mind. Thanks to him and his eternal meanness, we are prisoners, all of us, condemned to rot in that godforsaken place until the day he dies!"

Dolores felt her bubble of elation burst. It was strange how exile concentrated the mind, allowing it to remember only the good things. She remembered Ramón's ready wit and devastating charm, but not his vile temper and childish rages. She remembered her mother's gentleness and vulnerability, but not her vapid air of discontent, her lethargy. She remembered the stunning beauty of the countryside and forgot the hungry, hollow eyes of the workers who starved in the midst of plenty. She remembered the taste of Lorenzo's last kiss and shut her mind to the impossibility of their intended union. But she seldom thought of her father, her father who was the cause of everything she strove to forget. Her father, Don Felipe Carrasquez, the most feared, the most hated landowner in the entire province of Badajoz.

She sat between her mother and brother, linking arms with both of them, chattering about her doings at school in an attempt to change the subject. For years now, Ramón had been pressing his father to send him to Madrid to study . . . law, medicine, classics, literature, anything. Anything that got him away from rural Albavera and into the swim of city life. But unlike Josep, the scholar of the family, Ramón's academic record was abysmal. His delicate health, and his mother's overprotectiveness, had prevented him from attending school, and he thus escaped the Jesuit education that might otherwise have harnessed his quick brain. Despite many hours of enforced idleness, Ramón had shown no aptitude for study, and a succession of tutors had proved unable either to discipline or instruct him. His father had threatened to beat him, to no avail. Even Don Felipe, with his savage temper, had hesitated to belabor that crippled, diseased body, for fear he might dispatch it to its maker for good.

"He's stopped my allowance," continued Ramón, interrupting his sister. "Can you believe it? Because I dare to run up a few paltry debts, he has turned me into a pauper! What pleasures do I have, other than good wine and the occasional game of cards? A gentleman does not play to win. And if I choose to visit certain ladies in Badajoz, it is no more than the old goat does himself . . ."

"Please, Ramón," hissed Pamela. "Not in front of your sister. Tell me, darling, how are your cousins?"

"Edmund came to see me at half term," said Dolores, seeing the vein throb in her brother's temple, knowing he was on the brink of one of his tantrums. "We went for a picnic. Auntie Margaret couldn't come, because it was Flora's half term at Everdean, and she had to go there instead. Everybody sends their love."

Dolores's English cousins, the children of Pamela's sister Margaret, suddenly seemed unreal, remote, invented. When Dolores was in Spain, she could scarcely believe that England existed, and vice versa. They were two such different worlds, and yet she belonged to both of them. The Townsend family had been part of her life for the last five years. She had spent her Easters and Christmases at their London home, and they had treated her with unreserved, unfussy, unfailing affection. Edmund, now twenty-six, had become a surrogate Josep. Like Josep he was wise, kind, patient, clever; like Josep he commanded absolute trust. Flora, who was eighteen, like Dolores, was cheerfully empty-headed, not a thought in her head bar clothes and getting a husband—very much as Dolores's mother had been as a girl. Auntie Margaret and Uncle Norman were terribly English and sensible; Dolores had never heard a cross word pass between them. The Townsend house in Holland Park was tranquil, ordered, dull. The Carrasquez mansion in Albavera seethed with love and hate. But it was home. It was still home.

"I wish you could have stayed on in England," sighed Pamela. "If only you could have done the season. Your aunt and I had such fun as girls. So many parties, so many nice young men, such lovely clothes . . . I must get a seamstress in to make you some new things . . ."

She ran her hand absently through Dolores's dark hair. She looked so like her father, all three children did. The same black eyes, the same stubborn jaw, the same tawny complexion. How handsome Felipe had been, in those far off days, how jealous poor Margaret had been of her wealthy marriage. And how she envied Margaret now. England had come to represent all Pamela had lost—youth, laughter, freedom, hope. Her children had been her only solace—but now Josep was lost forever to the arms of Mother Church, and poor Ramón would surely not make old bones. If she had any hope left, it was vested in Dolores. How hard she had fought to save her daughter from sharing her fate! How relieved she had been when Felipe had finally agreed to let her have an English education—an act of perversity rather than benevolence: Dolores, by rebelling and weeping and pleading not to go, had effectively sealed her fate.

Pamela had hoped that Dolores would learn to prefer England, that she would choose to continue her studies there, or ask to stay on with her English cousins in London and perhaps meet some eligible young men. But Dolores had proved stubbornly Spanish, she could not wait to leave school and come home again. And for what? What was there for her here but some ghastly arranged marriage and a lifetime of unremitting boredom?

"Auntie Margaret wishes you'd visit," said Dolores. "She says the change would do you good."

Pamela smiled wanly. She could just imagine Felipe's reaction if she ventured to suggest such an expedition. A wife's place was in the home, docile, decorative and dumb. For years now, he had ignored her while watching her every move. His love had become a kind of possessive indifference; hers had turned to fear. Pamela had lived to regret her family's decision to visit San Sebastian in 1903, and their readiness to deliver her into the arms of the dashing young Spaniard who had fallen in love with her at first sight and wooed her extravagantly in halting French. Felipe had never forgiven her for producing a sickly child, and for preferring that sickly child to him. She had nursed Ramón through that dreadful illness, prayed for his survival, and all the time Felipe had wished him dead . . .

Poor Ramón. It was cruel to deny him his few diversions; wine and cards and loose women were legitimate entertainments for a young man of his class. But secretly, selfishly, Pamela was relieved that Felipe had refused to set him up in Madrid. He still needed a mother's care. More honestly, his mother needed someone to care for.

"Perhaps Papá will change his mind," said Dolores, ever the optimist, squeezing her scowling brother's arm. "We'll have to work out a way of persuading him."

Ramón greeted this fatuous remark with a derisory grunt. Pamela sighed in despair. Years ago she had begged her husband to take a house in the capital, in the hope that he might eventually move his family there and become an absentee landlord, like any other self-respecting *latifundista*. But Felipe viewed Madrid as a hotbed of left-wing intellectuals and preferred his isolated status as lord of all he surveyed. His poisonous hatred of the workers had bred the obsessive belief that the minute his back was turned his land would be invaded. Such revolts had occurred elsewhere in the country, to be suppressed brutally by the Civil Guard.

"We must get you a personal maid," murmured Pamela, ruffling her daughter's long, unkempt hair. "You really must take more care with your appearance, Dolly. Remember, you're a young woman now."

"Much good may it do her to spend time on her appearance," snapped Ramón. "For whose benefit will it be? My father never lets *you* visit or entertain. The same fate will befall my poor sister. She will sit at home in her finery all day, staring at the four walls, until our father marries her off to some fat old widower."

"I most certainly won't sit at home all day," said Dolores with spirit. "I can't wait to go riding again. I can't wait to take the dogs out. I can't wait for—"

She stopped herself just in time. She had nearly said "for Lorenzo to come home on leave," and this was neither the time nor the place to blurt out her secret. Lorenzo had warned her time and again to be discreet, a quality that came naturally to him, but not to her.

As the son of the obsequious family lawyer, Lorenzo Montanis was a familiar figure in the Carrasquez household and his visits aroused no suspicion. He and Josep had served as altar boys together, and he regularly joined Don Felipe's hunting parties, being a spectacularly good shot. Felipe admired his horsemanship and had permitted his tomboy daughter to go riding with him—a joint activity that had been established many years before. He had lacked the foresight to review the situation; Lorenzo was quiet, respectful, unobtrusive, and he knew his place. As for Dolores, she was just a child.

Lorenzo himself knew better. A hesitant, furtive, sixteenth-birthday kiss had produced a devastatingly eager response which had shocked and excited him. With some difficulty, he had restrained both himself and her. Was there anything more erotic than uninhibited innocence?

"Such rustic pleasures will quickly pall," Ramón assured his sister knowingly. "Not that you're home for good, you'll see what I've had to put up with all these years . . ."

". . . a nice quiet girl," continued Pamela vaguely, her thoughts still on the question of a maid. "Not somebody local, of course. Angelina has a niece, in Castile—"

"Why not somebody local?" said Dolores. "Heaven knows, there are enough people in need of work."

"You know how your father feels, Dolores."

"He fears that a local would murder us in our beds," sneered Ramón, in the contemptuous manner of one who fears nothing.

"Then we won't tell him," said Dolores. "He won't notice one more servant around the place. The workers are so hungry, Mamá, it could make all the difference to a girl from the *pueblo* to have a regular wage . . . What about little Rosa García? She's very young, but she's strong and cheerful . . ."

Pamela smiled and shook her head. It was typical of Dolores to know this wretched girl by name. She was incapable of riding past the miserable shanty dwellings on the edge of the estate without jumping down from the saddle and dangling some verminous child and accidentally dropping a handful of coins into the dust.

"We'll see," she said indulgently. Pamela was glad to have her daughter home, and yet she couldn't seem to *feel* it, perhaps because her emotions were stunted from lack of use, perhaps because she would happily have given Dolores up forever, in the hope of giving her a better life. She patted her hand and Dolores took hers, squeezed it tight and kissed her on the cheek. Poor Mamá. Poor, dear Mamá . . .

The rest of the journey was strained. Pamela fell into one of her reveries, as if retreating into some inner space beyond her family's reach. Ramón's mordant mood persisted, and his carping soon became tedious. As always, Dolores's impatience with her brother was tempered by pity. She could well understand why he got depressed and bitter. It must be bad enough to be born crippled, but Ramón had to live with the memory of being able to jump and run. No wonder he envied his siblings their mobility and freedom, no wonder he chafed at his lack of independence. Overindulged by his mother and shunned by his father, he seemed condemned to eternal, whining babyhood.

And yet, when it suited him, he could be a delightful companion. He was a born raconteur, and had held Dolores spellbound as a child with fantastic stories of his own devising. Josep, five years older than Dolores, had always seemed like a grown-up. Ramón, although three years her senior, had long since become her little brother.

The journey seemed longer than usual, but at last they crossed the Spanish frontier and Dolores felt the familiar thrill of delight to find herself once again in Estremadura, with its forests of oak and its rust-red earth, its rolling hills and glittering streams, its wild cactus and almond trees, its irregular patterns of ancient drystone walls.

As the car veered south at Badajoz and bumped along the narrow country lane, Dolores craned her neck and watched for the first glimpse of her father's watchtower. The isolated position of the house, built on high ground and surrounded by trees, was calculated to give it both seclusion and security. It had been built by Dolores's grandfather, a prosperous tradesman who had married a wealthy Catalan bride and subsequently purchased vast tracts of Church land under the so-called reforms of the previous century. When new, the dazzling white, Moorish-style villa, with its graceful arches and porticos, had been visible for miles around. Since then the trees had grown up all around it, and Don Felipe had added a superstructure, a high tower from which he could view the farthest reaches of his empire.

At last the car swept up the driveway and the watchdogs came bounding toward it, trailed by two yelping puppies. Following their mother's example, they allowed Dolores to pet them and licked her face. Then she ran straight for the stables with the dogs in hot pursuit. Her spirits lifted again, shedding their burden with the boundless resilience of youth. She was home at last. She was home.

"She's so dirty," said Pamela in English, wrinkling her nose in distaste. Little Rosa García smiled nervously, unable to understand.

"Then we'll give her a bath," said Dolores. "Would you like to work for me, Rosa? Angelina, my mother's maid, will show you what to do. It's very easy. There's no heavy work."

Rosa nodded eagerly. An orphan, and the youngest of a litter, she was dependent on her elder brother, Tomás, who could barely afford to feed his own family.

"Darling, she'd be fine for washing and cleaning and so forth, but she'll never make a lady's maid. Just look at her hands, they're like raw hams. Let's give her a job in the kitchens and get you someone else. We can't possibly let a girl like this live in."

"I like her," said Dolores stubbornly. "She's young, she'll learn. We'll have to get her brother's permission, of course. I'll speak to Tomás myself."

Tomás García was a giant of a man, a union leader and the uncrowned king of the *pueblo*. It might be that his pride and principles would balk at allowing his sister to consort quite so openly with the oppressor.

"But your father . . ."

"We won't tell him!" repeated Dolores, exasperated now. It frustrated her to see her mother so bludgeoned into obedience. Her father lived in a world of his own, his time fully occupied with masculine pursuits and local politics. The servants were Pamela's department, they all looked alike to him.

"Very well," sighed Pamela, adding hopefully, "but I don't suppose her brother will agree."

Rosa grinned uncomprehendingly and looked all around her in wonderment. She had never seen such splendor as the Carrasquez house, everything about it seemed to shine—the marble floors, the polished furniture, the watered-silk upholstery, the innumerable china and silver ornaments. She had never thought to step inside this place, she had been quite bewildered when Dolores had accosted her, laundering by a stream, and sat down on the bank beside her, careless of her fine clothes. She had talked to her gently, kindly, and then brought her back here, on horseback, holding her tight around the waist with one hand while she wielded the reins with the other.

"Don't be frightened," she had said, and she hadn't been. She hated Don Felipe, all the workers did, and she mistrusted his pale, foreign wife, but like Tomás, she had always admired Dolores, if for different reasons.

"All right," said Dolores, before her mother could raise further objections. "Angelina will get you some clothes and show you your quarters. And as soon as your brother has finished work, I'll speak to him."

Tomás was more fortunate than most. His prodigious strength guaranteed him regular work, whenever there was work to be had. Don Felipe's vast army of landless laborers were hired by the day for the merest pittance and lived on the brink of starvation; they were denied the right to grow their own food and found themselves liable to prosecution if they so much as gathered firewood. Vast tracts of arable land were kept wantonly uncultivated as a sanctuary for game; poachers were shot on sight. There had been futile strikes in the past, but hunger had proved a harsher taskmaster than even Don Felipe.

Dolores hesitated to visit the shack where Tomás lived with his family. His wife, Ignacia, was a formidable creature with flashing hostile eyes, one of the few workers whom Dolores instinctively feared. According to Rosa, Tomás had been hired that morning to help erect Don Felipe's new pigsties—pigsties far better appointed than the miserable hovels occupied by those who built them. The pedigree herd grew fat on the local acorns and yielded the finest *chorizos* in the province.

As the sun went down Dolores slipped out of the house and waited behind a tree, by the roadside, so that she could talk to Tomás on his way home, unobserved by her father's foreman. The tall, bearded figure was easy to spot. He towered over his fellow workers as they trudged wearily back to their shacks, with only a few miserable coins to show for their hard day's labor.

"Tomás!" called Dolores boldly, emerging from her hiding place. "Can I speak to you, please?"

There was a chorus of ribald laughter as an embarrassed Tomás complied with this outlandish request. Dolores blushed, aware of her own impropriety.

"Is it all right if Rosa works at the house as my maid?" she blurted out, overawed as always by the sheer size of the man. She gabbled on, stressing that Rosa would be well fed and paid, making her offer sound an abject plea.

Tomás didn't answer right away. When he did, it was with his usual surly courtesy.

"I work for your father," he said bitterly. "How should I object to my sister working for you? You have no need to ask my permission."

"She is only fourteen," mumbled Dolores. "And she has no father."

"Thank you for your respect," said Tomás with dignity. "I know you will treat her well."

"Oh, I will," said Dolores, smiling earnestly. "I'll take great care of her."

Tomás knew the discussion was at an end, but he stood rooted to the spot, bewitched as always by her grace and beauty. It was the nearest he had ever stood to her, he was close enough to reach out and touch her . . .

She held out her hand, as if for all the world she had read his thoughts. Tomás looked at it blankly. The daughter of a landowner did not shake hands with a laborer.

But she grasped his huge, filthy paw without flinching. Her hand was smooth and soft, but firm, it felt like a ripe peach.

"Good night, Tomás. And don't worry about Rosa. I'll look after her for you, I promise."

He nodded and released his hand and walked quickly away. He could feel the sweat breaking out all over his body. But his shirt was soaked through already, so at least it didn't show.

Rosa was so used to hard work, she could barely find enough to do. Dolores made few demands on her, and spent much of her time outdoors, unlike her brother, who lounged in bed all morning and hung around the house like a caged animal, snarling at anyone who came near him. He often took his meals upstairs, on a tray, washed down with an excessive amount of wine, and rang his bell incessantly, too idle even to cross the room to take a book from the shelf.

Despite its grandeur, Rosa found the house a gloomy place. The other servants were all imported from other provinces, and openly regarded her as inferior. Doña Pamela rarely spoke to her, or anyone else for that matter, she seemed to drift around aimlessly, like a reluctant guest in her own house.

But the young master had treated her kindly. He had a nice smile, and when occasionally it had fallen to Rosa to answer his bell—she was relentlessly put upon, when Dolores was not there—he always spoke to her nicely, even though he was generally considered to be ill-tempered and abusive. Indeed, she had often heard him shouting and swearing. If his food was not to his liking, or his shirts were less than perfectly ironed, then woe betide the unfortunate culprit. So she regarded herself as very lucky to have escaped the young tyrant's wrath. And besides, she felt sorry for him. So rich, and yet a cripple. Rosa associated health and strength with money; for that reason he seemed more pitiable to her than a poor man would have been.

She enjoyed her new life. It was luxury to eat the succulent crumbs from the Carrasquez table, sleep in a bed, draw water from a tap, wear clean new clothes. In all her fourteen years she had never known such ease. Happiness, always an abstract word, began to have some meaning . . .

One Sunday morning, the family set off for High Mass as usual, leaving Ramón lying abed, pleading a wheezy chest. Rosa, like most of the peasants, never went to church. The Church was a luxury only the rich could afford.

It was noon when Ramón rang for his breakfast. Rosa happened to be in the kitchen, foraging as usual. She often helped the cook in exchange for a length of sausage or some eggs, which she passed on to her brother for the children.

The cook sighed noisily and clattered a tray together with fragrant fresh-baked rolls, butter, honey and strong, sweet coffee.

"Take that lot up to the young lord and master," she barked at Rosa. "And be quick about it."

Rosa hurried up the stairs with her burden, enjoying the tantalizing mixture of appetizing smells. She put it down on the table outside Ramón's room and tapped on the door.

"Come in!" barked Ramón. She entered, neat and nervous as always, demure in her starched apron. She averted her eyes from the caliper splint and built-up boot lying by the bed and approached timidly with her tray.

Ramón flashed her a lazy smile and looked her up and down. Since his father had stopped his allowance he had not had the price of a whore in Badajoz, and wine was a poor substitute for women.

"Sit down, Rosa," he said kindly. "You must share my breakfast with me. I hate to eat alone."

She hesitated, puzzled, but he smiled again, boyishly, pleadingly, innocently.

"Let me pour you some coffee. Sit down, Rosa. Sit here, on the bed, beside me."

And she obeyed him, as trusting as a child.

Fasting had never agreed with Pamela, and it was not the first time she had fainted before she could take communion, She slumped forward, banging her head, and had to be carried out by her husband, Dolores following anxiously.

Felipe, as usual, showed scant concern for his wife's condition. Women were forever fainting in church. By the time they got home, she was quite revived, and able to walk unaided. Felipe stayed in the car and ordered the chauffeur to turn around again. He was lunching with the local police chief and magistrate, both of whom he had safely in his pocket; together they rigged the local elections, dispensed rough justice and maintained their feudal notions of law and order.

Felipe sank back into the leather upholstery, preoccupied as always. The current political instability troubled him greatly. Now that Primo de Rivera, the long-standing military dictator, had resigned, all manner of Marxists and demagogues were inciting the workers to revolt, demanding land reforms and free elections and other seditious nonsense. Until now the unions had been impotent, and so they must remain. His power was under threat, he must take steps to protect himself.

Power was all that mattered to him now. Power was proof of his success; his family was a constant reminder of his failure. Pamela's thin, English blood had diluted and weakened his own. One son a cripple and wastrel, the other a miserable priest. As for Dolores, she was a mere female, and thus even more contemptible than either of them. He must set about finding her a husband, sooner or later. Someone with money and land and sound politics, someone who could be useful to him . . .

As the sound of the car engine died away, Dolores, in the drive-way, heard another noise. Pamela heard it too, but she was still too lightheaded to take it for more than some servants' squabble.

It was not weeping, not screaming, but a dreadful primitive howl, like the cry of a wounded animal. Letting go of her mother's arm, Dolores raced indoors and up the stairs, overtaking the cook and Angelina, and burst without knocking into Ramón's room, already knowing with some dreadful sixth sense what she would find.

Rosa was lying on the floor, moaning hysterically, her face buried in her hands. Her skirt was torn and twisted and a thin trickle of blood crept slowly down her leg. Ramón was prostrate on the bed, still in his nightshirt, fighting for breath, his face already blue. Pamela, galvanized out of her torpor, began barking instructions at the servants and administering first aid to her son, quite oblivious to poor sobbing Rosa. Soon Ramón was propped up on half a dozen pillows, with three women fussing around him, while Dolores sat on the floor, rocking Rosa in her arms, speechless with rage. Blood was pouring from the girl's mouth; a front tooth hung by a thread.

Dolores felt the tears of anger boil up and overflow. She was angrier with herself than with her brother. It was as futile to blame Ramón for raping a servant as to blame a prowling tomcat. She should have foreseen this danger, she should have warned Rosa to be careful. She had promised Tomás that she would look after his little sister. She had promised and broken her word . . .

Ramón affected total amnesia. He had never touched the girl, she was lying, trying to blackmail him. Would he sully himself on a girl of that class? The idea was preposterous.

But the brutal evidence of his attack told its own story, and the incident was soon the talk of the village. Rosa had fled from the house, still weeping, accompanied by Dolores, and had refused to return. Tomás, as it happened, was not at home and Dolores had had to explain matters to Ignacia, who had hissed like an angry snake and sworn to exact a terrible revenge.

The threats were hollow, of course; reprisals would have provoked swift and bloody retaliation by the Civil Guard, and Tomás knew it. Don Felipe's fury was terrible to behold, and much of it fell upon his wife and daughter for having employed the little slut behind his back. While Pamela whimpered and Dolores looked on stonily, he formally disowned his son.

"No longer will you bring disgrace upon the family!" he roared. "No longer will you hang around your mother's neck like a spoiled child! You will get your wish at last. You will get your wish with a vengeance. You will go to Madrid, but not to live in luxury. You will learn the value of money the hard way, you will live on a fixed allowance which will allow you no scope for gambling or drunkenness or lechery. And God help you if you dare ask for more or show your face in Albavera ever again! Now get out of my sight!"

Wisely, Ramón had begged, on his knees, to be allowed to stay. Pamela was granted one week's leave of absence to install him in a suitable apartment; within two days of the incident they were gone, leaving Dolores lonely.

It took all her courage to ride into the *pueblo* alone and make her apologies to Tomás, while Ignacia spat venom and Rosa cowered in a corner, her nervous smile brutally disfigured by the missing tooth.

"I will make it up to Rosa, Tomás," vowed Dolores. "When I marry and have a home of my own, I will make it up to her. Meanwhile, this is all the money I have. Please, please take it, to make up for the wages she would have had."

Ignacia snatched the bills and counted them. How hideous this miserable hut was, with its dirt floor, corrugated iron roof and rough, adobe walls! And now Rosa was condemned to live in squalor again, having known better.

"I take full responsibility," continued Dolores doggedly. "As soon as I have money of my own, I will take care of her. I swear it."

They didn't believe her, she could tell. Tomás, inhibited by his wife, refused to meet her eye and Ignacia's hatred buzzed in the air like a wasp. Head bowed, Dolores rode sadly back to the house, locked herself in her room, took down *The Lives of the Great Saints* and spent the rest of the day reading it.

"So you will speak to my father?" pleaded Dolores between kisses. They had tethered their horses and hidden themselves in a bushy hollow surrounded by infant oaks.

Lorenzo hesitated. She looked so lovely in the dappled sunlight, with her hair tumbling around her face and her eyes bright with love. It had been all he could do to prevent himself from taking her, here and now. But as always, his kisses had been chaste, his embraces respectful and restrained. Not only because she was a pure, if passionate, young girl, but because he knew he could not trust himself. And the sordid story of Ramón and Rosa had been like a dreadful warning.

"Soon I will speak to him. But not yet. It's a bad time. Your father's still angry because of your brother. And your mother's still upset."

Upset was an understatement. Since her return from Madrid, Pamela had been behaving like one bereaved—dressing in black, attending Mass twice a day, not sleeping, not eating, kneeling for hours on her prie-dieu begging God for a miracle. Her conversion to the faith had been circumstantial, but it served to fill the emptiness of her life and Father Luis, the grasping parish priest, had profited handsomely by it.

"I'm sure Ramón is enjoying himself," Dolores had chivied her, helplessly. "It's what he wanted, after all. And the apartment sounds lovely. Perhaps we can visit him together, when Papá has calmed down."

But Pamela had just shaken her head and wept anew. Ramón's allowance was minimal, she knew in her heart he would soon be in thrall to creditors, unable even to afford a doctor when he needed one. He would neglect himself cruelly, and next time the asthma struck, he would be all alone, he would choke to death . . .

"But *when* will you speak to him?" demanded Dolores yet again, winding her arms around Lorenzo tightly, trying to hug him into decisiveness. The embrace was childlike, but seductive. She was so innocent, so trusting, he knew she would deny him nothing. How could he deny her anything?

Dolores looked up at him adoringly. How tall he was, how strong, how handsome! His hair was the color of her chestnut mare, a wonderful golden brown, and his eyes were like hazelnuts. What beautiful children they would have together! How proud she would be to be his wife!

"I only have my Army pay," Lorenzo reminded her. "And my first posting is not what I'd hoped for. Just a small garrison, with little chance of promotion . . ."

"But you graduated with honors!"

"But I have no connections. No connections, no money, no land . . ."

"But I have!" protested Dolores, impatient with him now. "Or rather, my father has. He'll fix things for you! Lorenzo, you *promised*—"

Lorenzo shut his eyes in despair. How badly he wanted her! And yet how terrified he was of losing her altogether . . .

"You must speak to him tonight," continued Dolores, imperceptibly taking charge, as always. "You are invited with your father for dinner, it's the ideal moment. Tomorrow you'll be gone and then I won't see you again for months! You *must* speak to him tonight. If you don't . . . then I will!"

She was so determined, so fearless, so confident, she had all the qualities he lacked. A lack she failed to perceive, because she loved him . . .

"Very well," said Lorenzo, heart hammering. She was right, things couldn't drag on like this. If he delayed any longer she would take him for a coward. He had gone into the Army to prove himself a man, but the Army had never tested his courage as she did.

He untethered her horse and lifted her on to the saddle. She smiled in delight, she gloried in simple, physical strength. They rode together to the top of the clearing and then kissed again and went their separate ways, Dolores, jubilant, toward her father's house, Lorenzo, brooding, into Albavera. He had better confide in his father. He had been Don Felipe's lawyer for twenty years, perhaps he would intercede for him. But more likely he would curse him for a fool.

Dolores spurred her horse on. Her father, she reasoned, cared little for her and would be glad to get her off his hands. Granted Lorenzo had no fortune, but since her father already had more money than he could spend, it couldn't possibly make any difference to him whether she married a rich man or not. With her father's influence, Lorenzo would be guaranteed a good posting and swift promotion. And then once she was married, she would send for Rosa. Mamá would miss her, of course, but she would visit her often. Mamá had wanted her to stay in England, after all. Surely Mamá would be glad for her?

She handed her horse over to the groom and sauntered into the house, singing.

"Dolores!"

The song died in her throat. The voice was her father's, cold, hard and sibilant with anger. Dolores's heart sank. She so badly wanted him to be in a good mood tonight. What had she done to fall foul of him this time?

She put her head meekly around the door of her father's study and felt the blood freeze in her veins. Her mother was sitting rigid in a corner, staring straight ahead of her, sightlessly. Her father was standing with his legs apart and his hands behind his back, surrounded by litter. There were scraps of paper all around him, torn into tiny pieces, and *The Lives of the Great Saints* lay gaping and empty on the floor.

"So," thundered her father. "You take after your vile brother after all. Never have I read such filth, such obscenity!"

The stinging blow to her cheek knocked her sideways.

"Felipe . . ." whimpered Pamela.

"Be quiet! Answer me, girl! When, and where, and how often has this man defiled you?"

"Defiled me?" Dolores stared at him stupidly.

"Don't act the innocent with me, young lady! Has Ramón not already brought enough disgrace on my name? To think that this man has sat at my table, to think that I trusted him! All this talk of horses and riding! I'll wager he rode more than a horse!"

"Papá! Lorenzo wants to marry me! We're engaged to be married! He wants me to be his wife!"

Her father let out a roar of satanic mirth.

"Naturally he wants you for his wife! Why else would he seduce you? You little imbecile! A life of luxury at my expense would suit him very well!"

He picked up the hollow book from the floor and threw it at her. The vicious blow sent Dolores reeling to the floor.

"You may thank your pious mother over there that your secret has been exposed. Father Luis thought she might take some comfort from the life of Saint Teresa of Avila. Ha! Such comfort! And in front of Angelina too, that tattletale! Soon the whole province will know that my daughter is no better than a whore! Go to your room and stay there! I will see that this man is ruined and his fawning father with him. I'll teach you to make a fool out of me!"

He grabbed her roughly by the arm, all but wrenching it from its socket, and frog-marched her up the stairs, hurling her into her room and slamming the door behind him.

Dolores lay rigid on her bed, too horrified to cry. Not horrified for herself, but for Lorenzo, and his poor blameless father, who would lose both his income and livelihood. And it was all her fault, her own stupid fault. Oh why had she not destroyed those letters, kept their secret safe? Had Lorenzo not warned her to do so, time and again? She lay immobile, oblivious to the swelling bruise on her jaw and the pain of the torn muscle in her shoulder. All she could feel was a sense of shame, shame that she had betrayed the man she loved.

"Dolores!" said Josep calmly. "Open the door and let me in."
Silence.
"Dolores, if you kill yourself, I'll never make archbishop. Not with a sister in hell. Take that noose from your neck, get down from your chair, and let me in."
"Is there anyone else there?" said a small voice.
"Only me."
"Has Father Luis gone?"
"He's downstairs, giving spiritual succor to Mamá. I'm getting bored with this, Dolores, I'm going to break the door down."
"If you do, I'll—"
"Go ahead. Jump to it. Hang yourself with my blessing. If you can. I don't believe you're standing on a chair, I don't believe there's a noose. I don't believe you know how to tie a noose."
"You swear there's nobody else there?"
"Have I ever lied to you?"

There was a great deal of commotion as Dolores dismantled her makeshift barricade—first the chest of drawers, then the dressing table, then the bed. Josep suppressed a smile. For three days now Father Luis had intoned mortal sin at her through the keyhole. But Josep knew his sister far too well to threaten her with hellfire.

The key turned in the lock, and Dolores opened the door, looking sheepish, as well she might. There was no noose dangling from the ceiling, no chair beneath it. The shutters were tightly closed to keep out prying eyes, and the room reeked of chamber pot.

"Here," said Josep, handing her an apple and a piece of sausage. She took a hasty bite of each and locked the door again.

"This is silly, you know," he said mildly, opening the shutters and letting some air in.

"I won't go back to England. I'd rather die. If I can't marry Lorenzo, I'll kill myself. You don't need a noose. You can do it by holding your breath or refusing to eat." She wolfed another mouthful of apple. "You can do it by cutting your wrists."

Josep felt in his pocket for his penknife and handed it to her.

"I brought it to cut you down," he said, lips twitching.

"You don't believe me, do you? You think I don't mean it."

"I'm sure you mean it. But I don't think you'll do it."

"Well, they did, or they wouldn't have sent for you," said Dolores with some satisfaction.

"The summons didn't go down too well, I can tell you. I'm in quite enough trouble as it is."

"Trouble?"

"They've threatened to throw me out." Josep lay back on the bed and put his hands behind his head.

"Throw you out?" echoed Dolores, amazed. "What did you do?"

"Opened my big mouth once too often. Imagine if you had to sit and listen to Father Luis all day long. That's what it's like. They slander God, that's what they do, they make Him as mean and petty as themselves."

"Oh Josep! Not you too. Another disgrace will put the lid on it, Papá will go absolutely beserk. Oh God! I was so looking forward to coming home and now everything's going wrong!"

Her sangfroid collapsed quite suddenly and two large teardrops ran silently down her cheeks.

"Oh, I'll talk my way out of it somehow," said Josep, softening. She looked so absurdly tragic, it was difficult not to laugh. "But they've only given me forty-eight hours' grace. I've got to go straight back again, today, and I won't thank you if you make me late, or if Mamá has to send for me again."

Dolores wiped her eyes with her sleeve. Just the sight of Josep made her feel silly and immature.

"Think of Mamá," he continued. "It was her idea to send you to London, to save you from something worse. It won't be forever, and it's better surely than staying at home, with Papá breathing down your neck."

"But Lorenzo—"

"Don't you think you've caused him enough trouble already? The quicker the dust dies down, the better it will be for him. You might have had the sense to burn those letters. Or to hide them somewhere more intelligent. Come here."

He patted the bed. Mutely, she lay down beside him. He put his arm around her and held her like that for a moment without speaking, without needing to. She knew he was right. He had told her nothing she didn't know already, and yet she had needed to hear the words from someone she could trust.

"They think I'll forget him," muttered Dolores, sniffing. "They think he'll forget me."

"Then prove them wrong," said Josep, smiling, not knowing what he said.

2

LONDON, NOVEMBER 1930

"Did you hear what I said?"

No answer. Dolores sat staring into space, nibbling the top of her pen, deaf to her cousin's chatter. Half a dozen sheets of notepaper lay scattered over the bed, covered with bold, black handwriting. There was ink all over her fingers.

"Which do you think?" persisted Flora, twirling in front of the glass. "The blue marocain or the cinnamon crepe de Chine? Dolly!"

Dolores blinked.

"Sorry, Flo. What was that?"

"Oh, for heaven's sake. What on earth do you find to say to the poor fellow?" She picked up a sheet and squinted at it. "It's enough to make one want to learn Spanish."

Dolores snatched it back.

"I'm nearly done. I wanted to get it finished before tea. And I think all your dresses look absolutely fine. I don't know why you worry so much. You always look nice, whatever you wear."

Not quite as nice as you, though, thought Flora. Dolly would throw on any old thing and still manage to upstage her. Dolly would arrive at the Moulton-Blairs' looking vague and exotic and faintly disheveled, and affect not to notice men staring at her when they should have been staring at Flora. And one couldn't even hate her for it, which only made it worse.

Flora took off her dress, still undecided, and turned her attention to the serious question of earrings. Dolores reimmersed herself in her letter, surfacing abruptly to the magic sound of the song.

"Tea!" she said, scrawling a flamboyant signature. "I'm famished." She gave the envelope a smacking kiss and stuffed it into her handbag to await a surreptitious stroll past the postbox. Flora's mother was under strict instructions to vet her niece's mail—not that she would ever have dreamed of doing so. But Dolores preferred to take no chances. Subterfuge had gotten to be a habit.

Flora sipped China tea sedately and kept her mind firmly on her figure while her cousin piled nervously into the fruitcake. Dolores put her insatiable appetite down to years of iron rations at the Ursuline Convent, and certainly the nuns' abhorrence of waste had left her with an ill-bred compulsion to clear her plate. When Flora had teased her about it, she had become quite prickly and started to get all intense about the dreary old starving peasants back home in Spain, a topic that left Flora yawning. Please God she didn't bring it up at the Moulton-Blairs' tonight. Dolly was always saying things that made one cringe.

"And what were you planning to wear this evening, Dolly?" quizzed her aunt as Dolores licked her fingers greedily, a deplorable but incorrigible habit.

"Oh, whatever you think," mumbled Dolores with her mouth full. "What about that new pink thing?"

Margaret Townsend exchanged long-suffering glances with her daughter. That new pink thing was an exquisite organza evening gown trimmed with henna-colored French lace and paid for out of a clothes allowance that fairly broke poor Flora's heart. Dolores had been fitted for it like a recalcitrant child, with her usual lack of vanity, while Flora sulked and sniffed. Such a shame that they weren't the same size . . .

Transforming Dolores into a fashionable young lady was proving to be uphill work, which was hardly surprising after five years in a nunnery. It was a pity she couldn't have gone to Everdean with Flora and learned a modicum of social graces, but of course her father wouldn't hear of it, Everdean being Church of England and therefore beyond the pale. These Spaniards were fixated on religion. No wonder she had run wild the minute she got home to Spain and formed this undesirable attachment. Still, three months' separation had not yet cooled her ardor. She had spurned the attentions of several perfectly charming young men, and insisted on telling everyone that she was "engaged." Clearly, it was to be a long haul.

"That new pink thing, then," said Mrs. Townsend, adding pointedly, "That won't clash with you, will it, Flo?"

"Heavens no," said Flora. "Pink's so passé. Is Edmund deigning to escort us tonight or not?"

"He said he would, for once. Luckily Clara's at one of her political meetings. You know how she hates him to be sociable, people must think him horribly rude.''

"Thank God we don't have to worry about him marrying her," commented Flora, with a sly nibble at a biscuit. "Long live Free Love."

"Really, Flo."

"Imagine having Clara for a sister-in-law," continued Flora, shuddering.

"She's extremely well connected and rather rich," pointed out her mother.

"And ugly," snorted Flora.

"That's not her fault," said Dolores.

"Certainly it is. She doesn't give a fig what she looks like."

"So what? Edmund seems to like her the way she is."

"Only because he feels sorry for her. You know how Edmund is about lame ducks. If she cared for him at all, she'd make an effort to look her best for him and get on with his family and friends. Still, thank God the Moulton-Blairs are too sinfully bourgeois for her. Talk about the skeleton at the feast."

Dolores usually made a halfhearted effort to stick up for Clara during Flora's routine diatribes, but the image was so apt to the occasion that she joined her in an uncharitable giggle, assailed by a vision of the angular Clara scowling balefully at the canapés. Lucky Clara, to have better things to do.

The Moulton-Blair dinner party was her aunt's latest attempt to introduce her to some suitable young men, a project with which she had stubbornly refused to cooperate. She had made it quite clear that she had no desire to marry some stuffy Englishman, nor to live in England. Five interminable years of school had been more than enough. A life sentence was unthinkable.

Still, nobody ever listened to her. She would be left in England, for years if necessary, until she finally gave in to pressure and married someone else. Or so they thought. They thought that it was just infatuation, they thought she didn't know her own mind, they thought that Lorenzo would get tired of waiting. Well, so he had. And so had she. As they would soon find out . . .

"I think I'll go for a walk," said Dolores innocently, eager to catch the next post. "Are you coming, Flo?"

"Good Lord no. I've got to get ready for tonight."

Three hours was the bare minimum for the niceties of Flora's toilette.

"A walk?" echoed Mrs. Townsend. "At this hour? It's getting

foggy. You know how easily you catch cold. Besides, you can't go wandering about on your own in the dark."

"I'll take Bounder with me," said Dolly, eyeing the indolent spaniel lounging on the hearthrug.

"Bounder! Walkies!"

Bounder stretched luxuriously and showed no inclination to bound. Undeterred, Dolores hauled the sluggish canine to its feet and attached its leash without further ado.

"If you must go out," said Mrs. Townsend despairingly, "would you mind popping this in the post for me?" She got up and fetched a letter from her bureau. Dolores went rather pink. Flora smirked.

"And for goodness' sake don't be long. You've got to put your hair up, remember."

Dolores grabbed a finger of shortbread and made a determined exit, leaving her aunt sighing.

"Giles Moulton-Blair is such a pleasant young man," she reflected. "Just the sort of boy poor Pamela would approve of. One can but hope."

"Giles Moulton-Blair has bat ears," observed Flora witheringly. "Not that Dolly notices what any of them look like. I must go and have my bath."

She left her mother pondering over a second cup of tea, regretting yet again that she had saddled herself with the thankless task of finding her niece a husband, let alone one likely to satisfy her sister's expectations. Upstaged by Pamela's glamorous marriage, Margaret had tended to overstate her own social standing, never expecting it to be put to the test. Norman Townsend, as a senior civil servant with an unspectacular private income, was moderately well-to-do, but by no means wealthy. There had never been any question of Flora doing the season, and the family had no dealings with the aristocracy, with the unlikely exception of Edmund, whose mistress was the daughter of an earl.

Of course, Pamela was completely out of touch, and still nurtured prewar notions of gracious living. She had not been back to England since her marriage, tied down by the demands of her xenophobic husband and ailing younger son, and according to her letters, she lived the life of a recluse, ignored by her husband, isolated by her poor Spanish, and enjoying no social life beyond an excessive attendance at Mass. She had languished through twenty-six hot summers and cold winters, dreaming of Madrid the way the three sisters dreamed of Moscow, spending her days dressing, resting and praying, consumed with exhausting inertia. Her ambitions for her daughter had expanded, year by year, to fill her interminable leisure. Dolores would one day marry a titled English gentleman and attend an endless round of house parties and garden parties and dinner parties. She would shop in Harrods and take tea in Fortnums and wear hats at Ascot and read about herself in *Tatler*.

"The boy is penniless," Pamela had written, "and Felipe is convinced he is a fortune hunter. Knowing how headstrong Dolores is, I dread to think what may happen if she stays here. She is quite capable of running off with this boy and thereby ruining herself. Having married hastily myself, I know what it is to repent at leisure. Help me prevent her from wasting her life. Unlike her brothers, she is English through and through, however much she tries to deny it. She does not belong here, and I will happily give her up to see her safe."

She doesn't belong here either, thought Margaret, sighing. But at least she was safe.

"Will you be home before me?" asked Edmund, struggling with his tie. Clara made no attempt to help him.

"Probably not. If it goes on late, I might well stay at Irene's. So don't rush home early on my account. I'd hate to drag you away from such scintillating company."

"You know I'm only going to give Dolly moral support. Flora never bothers to look out for her and she invariably gets stuck with the party bore."

"Poor, poor Dolly."

"Why is it you can't take to her? You ought to have a lot in common. You both care about the same things."

"Nonsense. She's politically ignorant."

"That's hardly her fault. She was educated in a convent."

"So was I."

Edmund turned away from the mirror to look at her the right way around.

"Look, Clara, she's only a child and she's my first cousin."

"Meaning what, exactly?"

"That you've really no need to be jealous."

"Don't be ridiculous." The line of her mouth softened, and weakening, she undid his tie and deftly arranged it into a perfect bow. She was still flushed, her normally colorless skin tautly reflecting the rosy tint of her hair. She looked almost the way women were supposed to look after lovemaking, not that Edmund was that easily deceived. He put his arms around her protectively and whispered some nonsense in her ear, forcing a smile. She was like one of those little birds they eat in Italy, bones and all. One unrestrained squeeze would have crushed her to pulp.

"I was thinking perhaps you might take Dolly along to one of your meetings," continued Edmund doggedly. "She isn't ignorant by choice and I'm sure she'd find it interesting."

"She'd be bored," said Clara. "Besides, she thinks one puts the world to rights by good works and charity. A budding lady bountiful, the most reactionary breed there is."

"Then reeducate her."

"I haven't managed to reeducate you yet."

"The study of literature ruins one for politics, Clara my love. One becomes too aware of the intractability of human nature. It's greed and envy that make the world go around, you know. And none of us is immune, reeducated or not."

"Oh go to your stupid party," sighed Clara. "Go on."

Edmund set off for his stupid party, walking briskly toward Whitechapel tube station, his mind still on his cousin. Perhaps Clara had good reason to be jealous. He had been Dolly's trusted mentor and best friend throughout her lonely school days, a welcome visitor at half term and a regular correspondent. His resolutely avuncular manner masked a possessiveness he was loath to admit, even to himself. Since her return to England, he had been torn between relief that her half-baked engagement had been aborted, and unease at his mother's attempt to pair her off. Dolly certainly ought to do more with her life than marry some boy next door, but Edmund shared Clara's prejudice against the chinless wonders paraded for her benefit. She deserved something better than that . . .

"You look ravishing," complimented Edmund wryly, as his sister let him in.

"And you look heartbreakingly eligible," countered Flora, proffering a powdered cheek. "Dolly isn't ready yet. She went for a walk after tea and forgot the time."

At that moment, footsteps were heard on the stair, heralding Dolores's belated appearance. She looked, as usual, untidily striking, her long, dark, heavy hair coiled with haphazard artistry on top of her head. Flora kept nagging her to have it cut and waved, but Dolly had insisted that Lorenzo wouldn't like it, as if men knew what they liked.

"Edmund," she panted, kissing him on each cheek. "What a relief you're coming with us." She treated him to her dazzling sunny smile. Edmund felt suddenly lighthearted.

"I only came to give you moral support and save you from harassment by Archie Prendergast," he said with a sideways glance at his sister. Archie Prendergast was generally considered to be Flora's exclusive property.

"Archie's not quite poor enough for Dolly," said Flora. "Luckily for me. We can't all afford to despise money."

"Archie's very sweet," said Dolly tactfully. Privately she thought Archie a bore, but Flora was very proud of him. "But he's attached. The best men always are. Including Edmund."

"More's the pity," said Flora. "And where is the lovely Clara this evening?"

"At one of her meetings," said Edmund curtly, "as I told Mother, and as she no doubt told you. She's staying overnight with a friend in Bloomsbury."

"While that huge house of hers in Curzon Street stands empty. What I could do with a place like that . . . Still, Whitechapel's so much cozier than Mayfair, isn't it? I bet she simply worships your smelly neighbors."

"Do stop bitching, Flo," said Edmund mildly. The exchange of insults was purely routine. Flora adored her brother and resented Clara for displacing her in his affections. "Save it up for later. You and Alice Monro can whisper scandal in a corner and tear everyone else to shreds. Are we ready?"

"Will you be coming back here afterward, Edmund?" inquired his mother hopefully. "I had your bed aired."

Edmund hesitated, seduced by visions of solid comfort and a hearty breakfast. If Clara was staying with Irene, there was surely no harm in indulging himself for once and letting his mother fuss around him. His father would rail at him over the kippers about the usual things, but a grudging, growling respect had replaced his former outrage, and Edmund bore his perfunctory rantings with a stolid good humor. He was enduringly fond of his family, and increasingly eager to share them with Clara, who had none, who had only her inheritance to remember hers by.

"That's very thoughtful of you, Mother. Thank you, I will."

"Then will you come riding with me tomorrow morning before you go back?" pleaded Dolores, who trotted an old hack along Rotten Row once a week and dreamed of the wide open spaces of Estremadura. Flora loathed horses.

"Certainly," Edmund beamed, and then Dolores gave him one of those special looks that meant she had something to tell him.

But at that moment the cab arrived, and he knew he would have to be patient.

Dolores could not wait to tell Edmund of Lorenzo's plan. While knowing his reservations about her intended marriage, she put these down to his never having met Lorenzo. How could anyone who knew Lorenzo not think her the luckiest girl in the world?

Dolores had written to him from London, bemoaning her forced banishment, swearing eternal fidelity, and telling him to write care of Edmund. Lorenzo, with his father all but ruined and his career prospects blighted, had decided he had nothing more to lose.

His plan, hammered out on the white-hot anvil of his love and loathing, had been bold but simple. He had hesitated at first to put it to Dolores, knowing that she would agree immediately, and that the burden of responsibility must remain squarely with him. But as each dreary day passed, his despair burned deeper and deeper into his soul. He must, for once, show himself her match in courage and determination. He must, for once, take their future into his own hands.

Dolores knew his latest letter by heart and had written back immediately applauding his plan, hence her hurry to catch the post. She looked across the supper table at Edmund, longing to share her secret, as if by sharing it she could hasten the interminable wait until the dream became reality. She remained lost in thought, oblivious to her surroundings. Mrs. Moulton-Blair had placed her between her son, Giles, a dentist, and the dreaded Archie Prendergast, who did something incomprehensible in the City, and mercifully chose to ignore Dolores, concentrating his attentions on the ever-flirtatious Flora. Meanwhile Giles sought to make Dolores feel at home by embarking on a gore-by-gore account of a bullfight he had once attended in Pamplona. He had the tone of an anthropologist describing primitive tribal rites and she could almost hear him thinking: bloodthirsty lot, the Spanish.

Aunt Margaret was right, she had no social graces, if social graces meant the ability to engage in meaningless conversation with people you had nothing in common with. Her own mother set great store by social graces, except that there was no one at home to practice them on. Dolores felt sorrier than ever for Mamá. Sorry for her because she was married to her father, and sorry for her because she obviously didn't understand anything about love. She had married for money, as far as Dolores could see, and wanted her to do the same. But at least she had learned from her mother's mistakes. She would marry for love, and for life.

* * *

Jack had just had his best week ever. Thirty-three mops, twenty-nine dust brushes, and no fewer than eight vacuum cleaners. He wished he'd gone into selling months ago instead of slaving away at the Empire Court, washing stacks of greasy dishes and scavenging unsold dishes of the day and getting home too tired to read, let alone write.

As it was, he should finish his third novel well ahead of schedule. *Unending Rapture* by Griselda Latymer (author of *Sold to a Sheik* and *Gypsy Bride*) was shaping up nicely. Like its predecessors, it obligingly wrote itself while Jack thought about more interesting things. His article for *Red Rag,* for example. The most difficult thousand words he had ever produced, even though the pittance they paid for it wouldn't have kept Griselda in smelling salts. But at least there was some pride in seeing something published under his own name, even if there wasn't much to choose between the two genres in the sincerity stakes. In fact, writing was not so very different from selling brushes, given the common necessity to suspend disbelief, and Jack, mindful of the likely sensibilities of *Red Rag's* editor, had felt it wise to gloss over the means by which he made ends meet.

He had not troubled to lie, only to edit. It was perfectly true that he had once worked an honest lathe at Truscott's in Lincoln, it was perfectly true that he had been laid off—thank God—and it was perfectly true that he was now a self-educated, struggling writer who financed his craft by the sweat of his brow. All of which had served to make exactly the right impression on the gullible Harry Martindale, with his patronizing awe of the workingman. So why spoil the illusion of grit and integrity with talk of dust brushes and penny romances? Martindale's left-wing posturing had served only to reinforce Jack's contempt for the ruling classes, a contempt almost as great as that which he felt for his own class, but one couldn't explain such a paradox to an intellectual.

Until recently, Jack had been too intent on escaping his origins to think of exploiting them. His gift of gab, both the spoken and written variety, was a means of obliterating the past, not of glorifying it. Certainly he felt no nostalgia for the grimy cottage, for the siblings too numerous to name, for his worn-out virago of a mother, for his bronchitic father, for the stench of squalor, for the smug stoicism of those who took a pride in being poor. He despised those writers who sentimentalized such scenarios, unless they did it cold-bloodedly, for gain. Nevertheless, his piece on *Sweated Labour in Hotel Kitchens,* attacking the current arguments against a much-needed minimum wage, had undoubtedly found more favor as the

work of an angry victim of the Depression than that of a thriving
foot-in-the-door salesman or prolific lady novelist, both of whom
had generously subsidized the article, and both of whom Jack resented as one does any benefactor.

And so tonight he would be aggressively working class, prod the
oversensitive consciences of the apologetic rich, shame Harry Martindale into giving him a proper job, or at least a commission for
future work. It was a piddling little paper that nobody read, but it
was a start. He would write about any subject he cared to name, in
whatever terms he wanted—ideally something he didn't care about—
next time. Emotion got in the way of creativity, and journalism had
always struck Jack as being far more creative than fiction.

The meeting of the Twenty-Six Club, to which Martindale had
so kindly invited him, was being held at some very fancy address
in Bloomsbury. It was a three-story Georgian house, and the heavy
brass-encrusted door was opened by a maid, who showed him into
a vast, ill-lit room done up like an Oriental bazaar: carpets on the
wall, but not the floor—which was strewn with raffia mats—strange
lantern-shaped lamps all over the place, and cushions, not chairs,
to sit on. There were tieless men wearing sandals and some quite
old women with long hair hanging down their backs, all of them
talking very loudly.

Jack took an instant dislike to everybody there. To his mind, they
were typical middle-class socialists, full of inverted snobbery, cliqu-
ishness and self-congratulation. He was acutely aware of his cheap,
smart clothes, his uncertain status as a social exhibit, his license to
behave boorishly and be excused for it. Then he reminded himself
that these people were here to be exploited, used, conned . . .

He held back, watching, waiting, until some ugly bitch stood up
and talked a lot of hot air, which interested him not one whit. He
was too busy sizing up the strange-looking redhead, sitting rapt and
pensive on the other side of the room . . .

Clara, unaware of his scrutiny, sat listening to Irene Derbyshire's
tremulous exhortations, nodding and clapping automatically. Tonight's meeting focused on a prospective campaign for mother and
infant health centers to be set up by Local Authorities, financed by
local taxes and subsidized by the Exchequer. All children and pregnant women should be entitled to unlimited free medical care. Too
many of them were still dying of poverty and ignorance . . .

The subject should have been dear to Clara's heart, given that
her own entry into the world had killed not just her mother, but in
due course her father as well. In fact, she had little feeling for

children and scant sympathy for feckless creatures who became pregnant once a year, willy-nilly. Better to give them birth control than encourage them to breed. Not that she would have dreamed of voicing such a thought out loud. In any case, she mistrusted her own thoughts. Other people's were much more likely to be sound.

These gatherings gave her a sense of being needed, even if it was chiefly for her money. What else did she have to offer? If money could buy love, then she was more than happy to spend it. On the other hand, it was prudent not to be too generous. And just as a beautiful woman will take care of her face and figure, anxious to preserve her looks, so Clara husbanded her wealth, her only power, which she would have traded willingly for beauty if beauty were for sale.

Love. Meaning comradeship, not with one person, but with all people in a just, equal society. That was love. The other kind was too intense, too painful, too dangerous. She had grown to love Edmund far too much for her own good, or for his. How could he be so tolerant, so patient, so eternally forgiving? Could he not see that she didn't deserve him? How relentlessly she had tested him with her bad humor and her spite and her sarcasm, how stubbornly he bore it all. What gave the edge to their confrontations was the fear that one day she might push him too far, that he might finally desert her for the beautiful woman he was entitled to, one who would make him happy, as she never could.

Irene stepped down to polite applause and there was a leisurely, well-bred drift toward the refreshments. She was a tall, big-boned, full-figured woman of thirty, with piercing black eyes and heavy brows and an unashamed disregard for fashion. Clara was fascinated by her apparently effortless ability to attract men, given that she wasn't in the least bit attractive. Her current lover was Harry Martindale, part-time poet and editor of *Red Rag*, a self-styled, iconoclastic weekly which ran at an unapologetic loss, offset by hefty subscriptions from the faithful.

"Clara," boomed Irene, hugging her. Irene could not speak to people without touching them. "Lovely to see you. No Edmund this evening?"

Irene wooed Edmund relentlessly, appalled at his refusal to back up his egalitarian ideals with political commitment, and besides he was rather good-looking.

"He had some marking to do," said Clara. "I couldn't drag him away. I liked your speech."

"Early days yet, I'm afraid. As we know, pushing for an act is only half the battle. Harry's going to give our housing march a big

spread in *Rag*. Congratulations on getting so many signatures for
the petition, Clara. I know how busy you are with the Whitechapel
by-election, you must have been working all hours. Excuse me,
won't you, I've just spotted Ronald Carmichael . . .''

"Clara," acknowledged Harry Martindale, extending a fleshy
hand and arranging his thick sensual lips into a carnivorous smile.
It never ceased to frustrate Clara that men were allowed to be ugly.

"Hello, Harry. How's circulation?"

"Steady. I hope you've read this week's issue?"

"Naturally," said Clara, thrown by Harry's interrogative manner
and fearful that her mind would go a complete blank. "I liked that
piece on the Coal Dispute."

"Did you? I thought it was rather uninspired, but I didn't like to
offend the contributor, naming no names. At least I didn't have
to pay for it, you know how tight our budget is. But I'm trying to
broaden the content a bit, get away from the standard tracts. Readability, you know. No use preaching to the converted all the time.
Or boring them, for that matter. Popularization, that's the key to
communication, don't you agree?"

"As long as one doesn't trivialize," put in Clara earnestly. "That's
the danger. Sugaring the truth just to make it more palatable."

"You make truth sound like medicine," observed Harry, a shade
reprovingly. "I prefer to regard it as a prophylactic. Prevention is
better than cure."

Clara fell silent. She had twice submitted articles to *Red Rag*,
the products of desperate conviction, not to say hours of unrelenting
effort, without so much as a letter of rejection to show for her pains.
The suspicion that they would surely have been accepted—albeit
after studious editing—had she put her own name to them, made
her failure harder to bear. She couldn't write either, any more than
she could paint, her first unrequited love. The act of creation eluded
her at all levels.

"If we want to reach the man in the street," pontificated Harry,
"we have to speak to him in a language he can understand, break
down the verbal barriers that make him mistrustful of us left-wing
intellectuals—without talking down to him, of course."

"Yes," mumbled Clara, chastened. Her own pieces had been
rife with multisyllabic jargon. "Yes, I'm sure you're right."

"For example, I decided to take an unsolicited piece from a
disgruntled young hotel worker for next week's edition. A bit un-
sophisticated, of course, but straight to the point. Grass roots stuff.
No waffle. And terribly topical with the Trade Board Inquiry com-

ing up. Normally one's tempted to spruce that kind of thing up, but I decided to leave well enough alone, let it speak for itself . . .''

Clara was no longer listening. With a sixth sense, she had felt somebody staring at her and looked to see who it was. It was a man she had not seen before, and he was definitely staring at her and not bothering to pretend otherwise. She blushed, aware as always of the peculiar color of her hated saffron hair, her skeletal figure, her overlarge hands and feet. Although he himself was gaunt and sallow and badly dressed in an ill-fitting suit set off by a frayed collar and excessively shiny shoes.

Noticing her lack of attention, Harry looked over his shoulder to see what had diverted it.

"Talk of the devil," he said. "Jack, so glad you could make it. Clara Neville, meet Jack Austin, our newest contributor."

Jack Austin continued to stare, unabashed, and said how-d'you-do in an unidentifiable regional accent. Clara found herself tongue-tied, succumbing helplessly to the crippling shyness that always made her seem standoffish.

"Harry's been telling me about your article," she ventured stiffly. "I look forward to reading it."

"Not as much as I do," said Jack. "First time I'll have seen my name in print."

"But not the last, I hope." Harry beamed. "Will you excuse me? I'll be in touch, Jack."

Jack nodded in the surly style these people expected of him and turned his attention back to the redhead. In a room full of loud, overbearing women, she had seemed the most likely prospect.

"You a friend of Mr. Martindale, then?" queried Jack, wondering who she was with, if anybody.

"In a way. That is, we're both friends of Irene Derbyshire, the woman who spoke earlier."

For no reason at all, she blushed again, and then he saw just how to play it.

"I don't mind telling you," he said, with deliberate, shuffling awkwardness, "I don't understand too much about politics. As a matter of fact, I feel right out of my depth here. D'you know all these people, then?"

It worked like a charm.

"Excuse the mess," said Jack politely, not that there was any. The room was as bare as a cell. Clara was breathless after the long cold walk from Archway tube station. She had hesitated to suggest a taxi, thinking he might be embarrassed at letting her pay.

She sat down stiffly on the narrow bed while Jack rifled through the piles of papers on the table, surreptitiously burying *Unending Rapture* in the process.

"Here it is," he said, producing a dog-eared copy of his article. "Sorry about the writing. The fair copy's with Mr. Martindale, of course."

He handed it over, glad that he had checked the spelling so rigorously. His painstaking obsession with grammar and punctuation was rooted in a dread of being thought stupid and uneducated and ignorant. He had never paid any attention at school, knowing he had no chance of staying on, and had bullied teacher's pets with sadistic relish, taking a pride in his reputation as a troublemaker, his glib line in cheek, his contempt for corporal punishment, which wasn't a patch on what his mother could dish out.

Clara peered myopically at the lined pages while Jack observed her. She was an odd-looking girl, unreal, otherworldly, with eyes that changed color with the light, sometimes hazel, sometimes green. The jacket of her heavy tweed suit gaped forward emptily at the chest as she bent forward, and one long-fingered bony hand plucked nervously at the lapel. She wore no wedding ring. Her opinion wasn't worth having of course. She was too well-bred to say what she really thought. Besides, he didn't care a whit for her opinion. It had been an excuse, that was all, and she knew it.

"I shall never eat in a hotel restaurant again," she said finally, looking up at him. "I should think you'll get the sack if they read this."

"Someone had to say it," Jack shrugged, filing this remark for future reference. "Not that it'll make any difference. I can tell you now what'll happen at the Commissioner's Inquiry. All the employers'll stand up and say that we'd be worse off with a Trade Board, that all we catering workers do so well for ourselves, what will all the tips and free meals, that we like things just the way they are. And of course there's no union to argue with them, which proves that we don't need a union, otherwise we'd have one, wouldn't we? And the chap from TUC will do his best but he'll be outnumbered by all the smooth-talking objectors. Still, what use is a union if people are scared of joining it? Not that a union's the answer to everything. Can't stop you getting laid off, can it?"

"Is that what happened to you?"

"That's right. Not much call for agricultural machinery once the farmers start going bust. Last I heard the whole works had shut down. Well, I wasn't about to join any dole line, so as soon as I got my cards I came straight down to London. I've had a few jobs since then, I can tell you. There's always work in London, if you don't care what you do. But I've always wanted to write. Not that I've had much in the way of education, as you can see. But I read a lot. I get hold of books from the secondhand shops and the public library. So I'm learning."

He tried to look diffident and waited for the inevitable praise.

"But your style is so direct, so natural," insisted Clara. "You mustn't try to change it. You know, most of the stuff in *Red Rag* is terribly pretentious. This will be a breath of fresh air. Firsthand observation is much more powerful than theory. You must keep on writing. What's that over there?" She pointed at the stack of paper weighed down beneath *The Concise Oxford English Dictionary* and a battered library edition of *Gulliver's Travels*.

"I'm writing a novel," admitted Jack, truthfully enough.

"A novel? How interesting. What's it about?"

"I'd rather not say"—again, truthfully.

"Of course. Sorry. Well, I look forward to seeing it in print. Let me know when you've finished it. I . . . know a couple of publishers. Most of them don't read unsolicited manuscripts, you see. I'd be delighted to help, if you'd let me . . ." She blushed again, fearful of sounding condescending.

"Thanks, I'll remember that. But it's journalism I'm really interested in. I know people like me are supposed to start as the tea boy and work their way up, but I've always had ideas above my station. What I'm after is a shortcut."

"I'm sure Harry will want more of your work," said Clara. "I shall make sure everybody reads your piece. The trouble with *Red Rag* is that not enough people read it."

"Well, it's pretty boring, isn't it? The only good thing about it is its name, only it doesn't live up to it. It's supposed to be independent and controversial, but everything it says is just what you'd expect. And then, most ordinary working people wouldn't understand a word of it. I mean, look at the folks who were at the do tonight. Too pleased with themselves by half. 'Jack, m'boy,' " he mimicked, in a booming, plum-in-mouth rendition of Harry Martindale in full throttle, " 'Jolly well done and we'll be in touch.' "

And she laughed, not a polite laugh, but a genuine reaction, for once. You could tell she didn't make much of a habit out of laughing. It made her eyes change color again.

"And what do you do?" asked Jack while she had her defenses down, knowing perfectly well that she most likely didn't do anything.

"Not much," Clara shrugged. The question should have put her on the defensive, but it provoked instead a need to invite his scorn. "I'm a dilettante. I tried painting, and wasn't any good at it, and writing, and I wasn't any good at that either, and now I dabble in politics, which doesn't require any talent."

"You can say that again," said Jack. "Not if Ramsay Mac-Donald's anything to go by."

"He's not a true socialist," agreed Clara carefully. "But it's hard for him, without an overall majority. And of course Labour's become a scapegoat for the Depression. We'll never solve the problems of poverty and unemployment until we've got the political muscle to destroy capitalism and redistribute wealth."

Jack got the impression that she had learned this little speech by heart.

"You got plenty of money, then?" he asked.

"Enough," said Clara.

"Thought so. You want to watch those friends of yours. They'll have it off you if they can."

"Don't worry," said Clara, amused. "I'm really quite mean."

"Good. Hang on to what you've got, that's my motto. So apart from the politics, what else?"

"Nothing really. I keep house, of course," she added with a touch of pride.

"What, you mean cooking and cleaning and such?"

"That's right," confirmed Clara, rather thrown by his accusatory tone.

"Why, when you could afford to pay someone else to do it? You're doing someone out of a job."

She plucked at her collar again and tilted her head placatingly.

"Cooking occasionally for two people and cleaning a very small house is hardly a job."

"Two people?"

"Me and my . . . my . . ."

"You mean, you're not married to him?"

"That's right."

"Why not? Is he married already?"

"I don't believe in marriage, that's all."

"Children?"

"I don't believe in them either."

"You're a funny girl, aren't you. So what does your fellow do?"

"He teaches at the local school. He used to lecture, at Oxford, but he gave it up. We live in Whitechapel."

Jack stared at her in exaggerated disbelief, and then nodded knowingly.

"You mean you're slumming it."

"If you insist on putting it like that."

"People like you make me sick," said Jack. His voice was matter-of-fact, unemotional. It was impossible to take offense. In fact, the insult was like a balm, it was curiously soothing.

"Sicker than the people who eat in the Empire Court?"

"You know where you are with the people who eat in the Empire Court."

"And of course they do give people a job."

"If I was rich I'd eat in the Empire Court every day and I wouldn't give a bother for the people who worked there. If I was rich I'd live in a nice house and have servants and do as I pleased. Your trouble is, you don't know when you're well off. You're spoiled rotten."

"You're very quick to sit in judgment."

"You mean I haven't got any manners. You mean I'm rude and uncouth and I don't know my place."

"Of course I don't mean that! I only meant—"

"So you won't mind seeing me again, then?" said Jack, interrupting her.

"Er . . . of course not. I shall be at the next meeting of the club. I do hope you'll keep coming. I can nominate you, if you'd like to become a member. The people aren't so bad when you get to know them."

"It's you I want to see . . . Clara."

He pronounced it Clare-a, not Clah-ra, as if making it his own. She went very red and didn't answer.

"I was thinking, a Sunday," continued Jack innocently. "We could go to Speaker's Corner and heckle."

"Heckle? Yes . . . that might be fun."

"So, tomorrow week, then?"

"Tomorrow week? Um . . . all right then. Look at the time. I must go."

"I'll walk you to the tube. I really appreciate you coming around, Clara. I don't know many people in London. I enjoyed our talk."

He had reverted to the sly bashfulness that had brought down her guard at the start. It was all put on, of course, she knew that now, which only made it that much more seductive.

* * *

Dolores had breakfasted early, only to have her rise-and-shine eagerness dampened by a cloudburst, which would put an end to her longed-for ride with Edmund. Her high spirits took in water and duly sank. March. How would she ever survive till March? Would she ever stop wishing her life away? How glorious it must be to be together all the time, not to be doomed to endless separations and subterfuge, not to have every encounter rushed, not to write one's love but to act it, every day, forever.

"Good morning, Dolly," said Edmund, joining her. "I might have known you'd be first up. The rain looks set, I'm afraid."

He helped himself to coffee. Dolores got up and shut the dining room door.

"I must tell you this quickly, before the others come down. Listen. Lorenzo and I have decided to elope."

So that was what she had been bursting to tell him. Edmund suppressed a smile.

"How romantic. When?"

But Dolly was deadly serious.

"In March. Lorenzo is due three whole weeks' leave in March. He's going to come to London and then we shall take the train to Scotland and get married."

"In Gretna Green?"

"You're not taking me seriously, are you? It's all planned. I was relying on you to help us."

"Dolly, I hate to be a bore, but I have to tell you I don't think an elopement is a terribly good idea. It will only make things even worse with your family."

"How could they be worse? You don't understand how things are at home. My father will never *let* us get married. He's already threatened Lorenzo, and as for me, he'd keep me under lock and key forever, if necessary! But once we're *married,* once I'm Lorenzo's *wife,* he can't unmarry us, can he? Specially once there's a grandchild on the way. But it all has to be carried out with the utmost *secrecy.* If he found out what we were planning, Lorenzo's very *life* could be at risk!"

"You make it sound like a Gothic novel, Dolly. This is the twentieth century."

Dolores's eyes flashed melodramatically.

"Not in Spain it's not! How horribly English you are sometimes! And I thought I could count on you. You won't help us, then?"

"I won't give you away, if that's what you mean. But I don't see how I can help. What exactly was it you wanted me to do?"

"Nothing drastic. Just to say I'm staying with you and Clara for a while, so Auntie Margaret doesn't suspect anything. I'll phone her from Scotland and tell her the truth, once we're safely married."

"You want me to lie for you?"

"Edmund, I can't just *disappear.*"

"Very considerate of you. Had you thought of leaving a note, for example?"

"They might come after me if I do that. It happens. I've read about it in the papers, you know, when the heiress runs off with the undergardener."

"March," mused Edmund.

"March. And it's only November. Nearly five months. It's an eternity."

"Suppose we talk again nearer the time," said Edmund pleasantly. "As you said, it's a long way off. A lot could happen between now and March."

"I had to tell *somebody,*" insisted Dolores plaintively, crestfallen, giving herself away completely. It was approval she craved, and the thrill of conspiracy. Edmund felt suddenly old.

"And how did you enjoy last night?" he asked cheerfully, in an attempt to bring the discussion down to earth. "Giles Moulton-Blair seemed rather keen on you, I thought."

Dolores made a face.

"I hate Englishmen," she asserted sweepingly. "They're so stuffy."

"I was thinking," continued Edmund, "that you might meet a more interesting type of person if you went along to one of Clara's meetings. You'd find the atmosphere more informal, and the conversation a good deal less trivial."

"Why, you're every bit as bad as Auntie Margaret." Dolores grinned, seeing through him.

Edmund had the grace to look sheepish.

"All Englishmen are not stuffy, although I agree the ones you've met so far tend to be, including myself. My motive, I assure you, is not to marry you off, just to broaden your experience a little. I hate to sound pompous, but you are only eighteen."

"My mother was married at eighteen."

"Exactly. Will you pass the marmalade, please?"

Dolores made patterns on the tablecloth with her knife.

"Clara doesn't like me," she pointed out without rancor.

"You're quite wrong. She's just shy, that's all, it makes her seem unapproachable. She repays a bit of effort, believe me. Look, give it a try. They call themselves the Twenty-Six Club. There's nothing exclusive or extreme about them, they're just a group of middle-of-the-road, middle-class socialists who drum up money and publicity for various hobbyhorses and occasionally manage to achieve something worthwhile. The new Housing Act is their pride and joy, they've been lobbying for slum clearance for years. You'll find most of the members are women and they feel strongly that women have more to do in life than just get married and have babies. Flora would loathe them.''

He could see that his last remark had hit home.

''If it's all so terribly interesting, why don't you go along to these meetings too?''

''Because it's something Clara needs to keep separate. She hates being seen as half of a couple, which I can quite understand. And besides, I'm too much of a cynic for that kind of thing.''

''How can you call yourself a cynic? You wouldn't be working in that school if you were. You're more of an idealist than Clara. I mean to say, she doesn't actually *like* people much, does she? Not like you.''

''Beware the idealistic cynic,'' said Edmund. ''He likes the things he knows are bad for him. So, shall I speak to Clara?''

''If you like.'' Dolores shrugged. ''But it won't make any difference. I'm not going to go falling in love with anyone else.''

''My dear Dolly,' said Edmund, folding his napkin, ''the very last thing I want is for you to go falling in love.''

He arrived home to find Clara still in bed, which was unusual for her. She had had one of her restless nights, the scattered bedclothes bearing testimony to some nocturnal struggle. Edmund covered her up carefully and went to light the fire.

He filled a scuttle from the coal shed, crumpled newspaper, laid firewood. It was bitterly cold. But the house was dry and in good repair, a far cry from the hovel of Flora's imagination. He lived in luxury, compared with most of his pupils, and to live in luxury near the school had seemed the least he could do.

An idealist indeed. Had Dolores witnessed his dour, schoolmasterly manner, the iron-hand discipline he imposed, his unwavering readiness to wield the cane as necessary, his determination not to be seen as soft, to resist the temptation to court popularity, to put the children's interests first and not his own, she would have called him a realist instead. Tough kids they were, used to a clip around the ear for the slightest thing and wary of kindness. Much more of a challenge than Oxford undergraduates, who were more than capable of teaching themselves. Much more of a challenge than churning out abstruse papers that did nobody any good. Fifty hostile pairs of eyes staring at him, snickering at his posh accent, mistrusting him. His predecessor had been a small, wiry, elderly woman who had taught their parents before them, a no-nonsense spinster they had loved as well as feared. They had seen him as a usurper, a scapegoat for her premature demise, and two years on and eight free grammar school places later—the first Parratt Green Primary had ever laid claim to—he still walked a tightrope between respect and rejection. Ever aware of his own shortcomings, he was not happy in his work, but to have been happy in his work would have been, to his mind, a danger sign, an early symptom of the self-satisfaction that was an occupational hazard of his trade.

The fire spat and spluttered into life and he warmed his numbed hands in front of the thin flames, thinking about his cousin and her half-baked elopement project, trying to be objective. He would have liked to have met this Lorenzo, to have talked to him man to man, to have berated him for his selfishness and irresponsibility in suggesting such a plan. And yet one couldn't in conscience blame him. He himself could never have resisted such passionate devotion. And Dolores was right, things were different in Spain, perhaps her fears were not quite as absurd as they sounded to English ears. But what troubled him most was that she seemed to confuse marriage with freedom, not realizing that the two conditions were poles apart, that marriage would demand the sacrifice of what little freedom she had so far known.

"Hello," said Clara sleepily behind him. "How long have you been home?"

"Half an hour. I thought you would be staying with Irene, so I spent the night at Mother's."

"I left the meeting early. It wasn't particularly interesting. But I couldn't sleep, I was awake till three."

"Go back to bed," said Edmund. She shook her head, kneeling in front of the hearth and holding out her hands.

"How was your evening?" She seemed drowsy and compliant.

"Deadly dull. Can I ask you a favor?"

"You can ask."

"I've asked you once already. Make friends with Dolores."

"Oh for goodness' sake." Her mood threatened to snap.

"No, listen. I'm concerned about her. Her head's full of nonsense, and yet she's got a good quick mind and bags of energy that are all going to waste. She's so busy rebelling against what she doesn't want that she doesn't know what she *does* want. I want you to help her find out."

"Why me? Do you suppose *I* know what I want?"

"A good teacher doesn't claim to have all the answers."

"So you'd like me to play auntie."

"She's had enough of that from my mother. I'd rather you played big sister. She could do with one of those. One she can confide in."

"If it will please you." She shrugged, allowing him to kiss her. Her response was warmer than expected, it had something of the languid indolence he sometimes caught between waking and sleeping, magically elusive, titillating. But as if short of kindling, the flame flared and fell.

"You're cold," said Edmund. "You had better get dressed. Oh, and by the way, Mother has asked us for lunch next Sunday. It will give you and Dolly a chance to talk."

"I'm doing something next Sunday," she said too quickly. "I'm . . . I'm collecting signatures for the LCC petition, with Irene and Charlotte. I promised."

"Very well. Which evenings are you free? We'll go to dinner instead."

"Is it absolutely necessary for me to endure these endless family vettings? It's not as if we're getting married."

"Your choice, not mine."

"I don't recall a proposal."

"You've always made it perfectly clear that you wouldn't accept one. Are you saying you've changed your mind?"

"Edmund, you're giving me a headache. Ever since I woke up you've been badgering me."

"You're being particularly testy, that's all. Go back to bed and sleep off your bad humor. I've got work to do."

If he had shouted the words, they would have been gratifying. But he spoke calmly, as he always did. "You're a perfect vixen, Clara," he would say, evenly, unmoved by her abuse, her tantrums, her vile moods. She felt utterly powerless.

"Better make it Wednesday, then," she said humbly.

Sunday was a bitterly cold day. Clara sat fidgeting nervously in the taxi, which was parked so as to give her an unobtrusive view of their agreed meeting place. She would wait for Jack Austin to arrive and then give it ten minutes or so before joining him. Her stomach fluttered nervously as it had done as a child while she waited to go into the dark tunnel of the confessional; she was seized with the same horror of imminent exposure, of the spiritual nakedness which was even worse than the physical kind.

She had half decided not to come, but hope and fear and curiosity had made such hesitation a matter of form. Not that she was taken in for a minute. Jack Austin was hardly the first man to have courted her money. Having inherited enormous wealth at the tender age of two, following her father's suicide, she could have bought herself a personable, well-educated, well-bred husband several times over, and might well have done so, if only out of loneliness, had even one of her suitors had the courage to be honest with her. But instead they had pretended sincerity, feigned admiration, insulted her intelligence, taking her for a fool, hardened her heart, brought her to the bitter knowledge that it was better to be predator than prey. And a predator she had become, and it was better, until Edmund . . . She must not think about Edmund now.

Jack contrived mysteriously to evade her surveillance, appearing at his post quite suddenly, out of nowhere, dressed in his Sunday best again, although he wore no coat. Clara shivered. She had swaddled her thinness in a heavy woollen overcoat and stuffed her orange hair into a hat with a deep mushroom brim which came down low over her eyes. She wound down her window, scrutinizing him, her shortsightedness blinding her to distracting detail, enabling her to spot a hitherto unseen swagger, a provocative insolence in his posture that was at once alluring and hostile. It was as if he had staked out a patch of territory around him, like some wild animal. He lit a cigarette, cupping his match against the wind, and inhaled luxuriously with the crass flamboyance of a gangster puffing a fat cigar. There was a tawdry glamour about him she had not noticed before, ever too conscious of herself to study others closely. Hypnotized by the glowing blur between his lips, she sat immobile, fascinated, until he addressed a passerby, who glanced at his left wrist obligingly and moved on. She blinked and scrambled hurriedly out of the cab, assailed by sudden guilt at having deliberately imposed an unnecessary wait on a man who didn't own a match.

She paid the fare and waited for the cab to drive off before she crossed the road and joined him. He dropped the stub and ground it out with his heel.

"Thought you weren't coming," he said easily, as if he didn't much care either way.

"Sorry I'm late. I got held up."

"I thought we'd start with the Bible thumpers," said Jack, pointing, "seeing as it's a Sunday. You're not religious, are you?"

"Heavens no," said Clara.

"At least they're harmless."

"I don't agree. Bribery and threats, that's all religion is. It degrades people so."

"Same as politics. Give me a half-cracked nut any day rather than a politician. They're the ones I save my rotten eggs for. Lousy amateurs, most of them. Can't sell for toffee."

"They aren't *all* hypocrites," protested Clara uncomfortably. "Some politicians are very sincere people. The Labour candidate at the Whitechapel by-election certainly is. I wouldn't be canvassing for him otherwise. And politics *is* fundamentally amateur, that's what democracy is all about. It's about people wanting to share their beliefs, not about crooks trying to make you buy something."

So she thought salesmen were crooks. Well, she would do.

" 'Course, sincere's not the same thing as honest," said Jack. "And dishonest's not the same as telling lies. I mean to say, telling lies is honest enough, as long as you know you're lying and why you're lying. It's dishonest if the only way you can tell lies is by believing them yourself. That's what sincere people do. Lie to themselves."

"That's a rather unorthodox theory. Which are you, then, honest or sincere?"

"That's for you to decide."

"What about your article in *Red Rag?*"

"What about it?"

"Was it sincere, and did you tell any lies?"

"The real question is, did you believe it?"

"Well yes. Your facts were very precise and you argued your case logically and with conviction."

"Then I must have told the truth. The truth is what people believe. There's no other kind. That's why it's so bloody dangerous. Ever read that story about the Emperor's new clothes?"

"Of course I have."

"Naturally. Your nanny read it aloud to you after tea in the nursery when you were five years old. I only got around to reading it last week. Ignorant, that's me."

He smiled unexpectedly and offered her his arm. Clara took it, and smiled back without wanting to, already half-bewitched.

They toured the soapboxes sedately enough, Clara envying and Jack mocking those who had the nerve to stand up in public and risk ridicule and abuse. They listened to pleas for electoral reform, to grouses about war pensions, to an impassioned speech from a Russian exile about Stalin's latest purge. Clara seemed unduly interested in some ranting Spaniard, who lisped through his speech to a chorus of jeering *olés*.

"Support the Spanish people in their struggle!" he yelled. "Support us in our fight for democracy! No more dictators! No more

monarchs! We demand free elections and justice for all! Refuse to
buy Spanish goods except from a new republic! Write to your MP!
Demand trade sanctions now . . .''

"Let's find somewhere to sit down and talk," hissed Jack into
her ear, making her shiver. "I've heard all this before, I come most
weeks. It was only an excuse to see each other again."

"Each other," he had said, not "you," as if it was their secret,
something already shared, almost as if he were inviting her to make
the next move, to acknowledge his words by action.

She suggested some tea. "My treat," she said firmly, back on
safe ground now. "As you said yourself, I can afford it."

They went into a Lyons Corner house, humid and smelling of
soup. Jack saturated his tea with sugar and said easily, "Could you
afford to lend me some money? A fiver would do it."

"Of course," she said too quickly. She would have expected him
to be more subtle. "More if you need it. Are you in difficulty?"

"I got the sack," he said, "like you said I would. And I was
already behind with the rent. So I'm in a bit of a fix. You know
what it's like, trying to get to work. No, of course you don't know
what it's like. But don't worry. I'll find something. There's always
work for them that's not fussy, isn't there? I'll pay you back."

"No hurry," said Clara, fumbling inside her bag. She reached
her hand out underneath the table.

"No need to hide it," said Jack, taking the note and holding it
up to the light. "Worried folk'll think I'm your gigolo? I expect
you get lots of fellows trying to sponge off you."

"Naturally," said Clara stiffly. "I wasn't trying to be furtive,
just tactful."

"Don't be tactful on my account," said Jack, pouring spilled tea
from his saucer into his cup. "I'm not the sensitive type. Can't
afford to be. Look, do you want me to be honest with you, or
sincere? I can't manage both at once."

His manner was perfectly straightforward, forcing an answer.

"Honest, I suppose," muttered Clara, cornered.

"That doesn't mean telling the truth, remember."

"I remember."

"Right then. It's not just your money," said Jack. "I expect with
most of them, you thought it was just your money and it probably
was. But with me, the money's only part of it."

"What are you saying?"

"Do you like me?"

Clara flushed brick red.

"Do you like me enough to want to help me? Even if I hadn't really lost my job and wasn't really behind with the rent? Do you like me enough? There's not much in it for you, bar the obvious, and I wouldn't expect you to put much of a price on *that,* being as it's the cheapest thing in the world."

"Don't be offensive," said Clara, standing up.

"You asked me to be honest. Now you're complaining because I'm not being polite, like you're used to. Do you like a bit of flattery first? I could have given you that, no trouble at all. Do you think I don't know how to flatter?"

"You can flatter and still be honest, by your own account, as long as you know that you're lying and why you're doing it. Was it just too much trouble?"

"Not flattering you was a compliment."

"A sincere one?"

"One that didn't involve an unnecessary lie. Lies are currency, I don't believe in wasting them."

She sat down again.

"Have you really got sacked?"

"No. I just needed an excuse. For you, not me."

"An excuse for what?"

"For you to give me the fiver, for a start. To bring up the subject, natural-like. You've got money and no talent, you said so, not me. I've got talent and no money."

"There are plenty of people with money and no talent. Why me? And why should I choose to help you?"

"That's why I asked if you liked me."

"I hardly know you."

"Not surprising, when you won't even look me in the eyes. Why won't you look me in the eyes, Clara? Scared to, are you?"

Her head jerked up stubbornly and she looked at them. For the first time she saw that they were blue and refreshingly cold. No lukewarm lechery, no clammy cunning, just icy challenge and the promise of pain.

"I must go home," she said.

"To Whitechapel? Or to Curzon Street?"

"How did you know about Curzon Street?"

"I wouldn't mind seeing it, actually, if that's not being too cheeky. Can I walk you home?"

"How did it go?" asked Edmund, jumping up to greet Clara. "Poor darling, you must be frozen."

"Hello, Clara," said Dolores shyly. "You said on Wednesday to drop in sometime, so I'm afraid I took you literally. I was so bored at home. Everybody's got a cold. I've been helping Edmund mark some books. I hope that's all right."

"If she'd arrived earlier, she could have helped you take around the petition," said Edmund. "Pity we didn't think of it before."

"We were supposed to have loads of people to luncheon," continued Dolores, "and of course it had to be canceled. That's how I managed to get away, but I spent too long riding first. Perhaps I can help next time."

Clara took off her hat. Edmund hung up her coat, kissed her, gave her an odd look, and went to put on the kettle.

"Did you get lots and lots of signatures?" went on Dolores. "I think it's such a terrific idea. Edmund was explaining to me about the slum clearance act and all about the march and everything. It sounds so exciting, I'd love to help. Specially on the infant welfare campaign. I mean, having a baby's worrying enough if you're rich, let alone if you've got no money. There's one woman in the *pueblo* who lost three babies, one after the other. She'd got no milk to feed them, you see. And her other three children are all skin and bone. Nobody cares. Father Luis told her she was blessed by God to have her sufferings here on earth."

"How *frightfully* tactless of him," said Clara rather loudly.

"Her husband told Father Luis he had the evil eye and tried to drag her out of the church but she wanted the baby baptized before it died so it wouldn't go to limbo. Babies can't go to heaven unless they're baptized, you see, and . . ."

"Spare your breath, Dolores. The entry qualifications for heaven are well known to me. Having once debarred myself by missing Mass, I now commit mortal sins with gay abandon."

Clara made an extravagant, devil-may-care gesture. "Did you hear that, God?" she bellowed at the ceiling.

Dolores laughed uncertainly. It was obviously meant to be a joke, not that Clara normally went in for jokes.

"You should talk to my brother Josep," she continued, undaunted. "He's going to be a priest."

Clara gave a mirthless bark.

"I hardly think we'd have a great deal to talk about."

"Oh, you're quite wrong. Josep isn't like an ordinary priest. Or won't be, if he ever gets ordained. I think Josep has a true vocation. He says—"

Clara's lip curled in disdain and she gave an unladylike snort. Dolores faltered.

"Sorry. Am I being a bore?"

"Not at all," said Edmund, rejoining them and giving Clara a warning look.

"I apologize, Dolly," said Clara with excessive formality. "I didn't mean to be rude. I'm just a teeny-weeny bit *tired,* that's all."

"Let me fetch the tea," said Dolores, jumping up. "You sit down. This is such a treat for me, you've no idea."

She ran off to the kitchen.

"Just watching that child wears me out," said Clara, hiccupping.

"You can see what I mean about wasted energy," said Edmund, his heart sinking. "You could dump any amount of donkeywork on to her, you know. She's quite tireless. You take too much on yourself."

"Nonsense. I'm one of your idle rich. I haven't got enough to do. I can't even take a job without depriving someone else of it. Do you think we ought to have a woman in to cook and clean? Just to give her a job?"

"I can't afford to employ a woman to come in," said Edmund shortly.

"For goodness' sake. *I'd* be paying for it."

"I refuse point blank to be subsidized by you and your eternal money. There must be plenty of other good causes. Sometimes I wish you'd just give the lot away and be done with it."

"Don't be ridiculous." Clara's voice rose shrilly and her mouth began to wobble.

"Let's not argue," said Edmund. "Not while Dolly's here. Why don't you have a rest before tea?"

"I hope this baby-sitting isn't going to become a regular thing," continued Clara, not troubling to speak quietly. "One needs some privacy."

"Don't be mean," soothed Edmund, humoring her desperately, his eyes flying to the kitchen door. "She's so excited at the thought of joining your march, she's talked of nothing else all afternoon."

Dolores kneed open the door with much rattling of the tea tray.

"I'm so excited about going on the march," she said, pouring busily. "Poor Edmund is quite worn out with it. It will be all right if I come, won't it? Edmund said the more the merrier. Do tell me if I start to get on your nerves, by the way. Sister Perpetua used to say I would try the patience of a saint. Clara! Are you all right?"

"I'm fine. Please excuse me. I must lie down."

She got up and walked unsteadily out of the room.

"Oh Lord. Was it something I said?" said Dolores, perturbed. "After Wednesday, I thought she wouldn't mind if I . . ."

"Dolly," said Edmund. "Would you think me terribly rude if I asked you to leave? It's just that . . ."

"Of course not," said Dolores, taking a hasty gulp of tea. "I'm on my way. Sorry. Do say sorry to Clara for me."

"Stop saying sorry. It's not your fault."

He stood on the doorstep while Dolores mounted her bicycle and hurtled off down the street at breakneck speed. Then he walked back inside, slowly, and stood for a few moments collecting himself before he tapped on the bedroom door and went in.

Clara was lying on her back, arms spread wide, exhaling fumes of gin.

Edmund pulled her up into a sitting position and put her head between her knees, fearing that she might vomit while asleep and choke herself. She groaned and swore at him. Five months, it had been, since the last time she had drunk. Five whole months. As Dolores had said, five months was an eternity, and he had been foolish enough to regard them as such, foolish enough to congratulate himself, foolish enough to have faith, to show he trusted her, to invite deceit, to tempt fate. He would have shared her more willingly with another man than with that one false friend.

All in all, it had all been a lot easier than Jack had dared to hope, even if he had got rather more than he bargained for. It had all happened so fast. He had expected to have to loosen her up a bit first, get her tiddly even. Heaven knows, there was enough booze in that place. But she had told him she was a teetotaler, and it had seemed bad manners to drink alone. Afterward she had made out she was angry with him, probably just to cover her embarrassment. Well might she be embarrassed, thought Jack, grinning. He might have guessed she liked a bit of rough. And she gave as good as she got.

No wonder she had kicked him out as soon as it was over. Which had suited him very well.

3

Young Señor Carrasquez was still fast asleep, it being not yet noon. Consuela gathered up the debris in the sour-smelling drawing room and let in the light. She noticed that the fine, chiming clock had disappeared from the mantelpiece, in settlement of some gambling debt or to grace the pawnbroker's window—hopefully the latter, given that her wages were overdue. Her husband disapproved of the type of work she did, even more so when it went unpaid, and failing settlement, this would be her last visit. There was, admittedly, no shortage of more congenial domestic posts in the Salamanca district of Madrid, where the well-to-do segregated themselves from the lower classes, and perhaps she was indeed a fool to remain in the service of an impecunious young drunkard and put up with his numerous filthy habits. Not that she had ever shrunk from dirt. And as she argued with her husband—not that there was any arguing with her husband—the boy knew no better. If being born into money was a crime, it should surely be laid at the door of the father, not the son. And then where would they all be without the rich to pay their wages? An argument which foundered when wages went unpaid.

She flung the windows open, making the dust motes spin, and set to work, letting the cold, clean air disperse the fetid excesses of the night, her activity intruding cruelly into Ramón's slumber. The beating of the rug over the balcony rail, the squeak of the window latch, and the rhythmic rasp of the carpet sweeper penetrated his consciousness as distant sounds of approaching violence, while he lay immobile, trapped, powerless against the threat of attack. Then his dream burst and he shuddered into wakefulness and reality and relief, rolling over thankfully and spreading his arms across the double bed, glad now that he had slept alone, that he did not have to face sly pretense or bovine indifference.

Consuela rapped loudly on the door and marched in without

ceremony. He opened one eye and curled his features into a winsome smile. Consuela did not smile back. Her manner with him was always surly to the point of belligerence. But Ramón was not troubled by this semblance of hostility. He knew real hatred when he saw it, he had grown up surrounded by it, and Consuela's urban arrogance seemed harmless and superficial in comparison.

"Cheer up, Consuela," he chivied her lazily. "I was extraordinarily lucky at cards last night, although unlucky in love as you can see. I put my winnings in the usual place, you know what thieves I entertain here."

He sat up in bed and yawned voluptuously. Consuela parted the shutters, making him blink. Then without waiting to be asked she knelt, brought out the built-up boot from under the bed, and handed it to him.

He pried open the insole with a quick, practiced squeeze and removed a bundle of notes from the hollow space within. Consuela counted out what she was owed and handed back the rest, half of which he tossed carelessly to one side, redepositing the rest in its hiding place. Then he threw aside the bedclothes and dangled his withered limb over the edge of the bed while Consuela strapped on the caliper splint and helped him with his trousers and imprisoned his foot. An act of homage disguised as duty, though neither were deceived. She felt the familiar frisson that came from their formalized intimacy, his slight irritation making her fumble as always.

Consuela's ill-concealed devotion amused Ramón and touched him and repelled him. It was a pity that the poor woman was so gross, her body ravaged by childbirth, her hands roughened by work, her face lined by poverty, or she might have had other uses. He sent her out to fetch his breakfast while he shaved meticulously, splashed himself with French cologne and put on a clean white shirt and silk cravat. His black hair gleamed under the tortoiseshell comb as he smoothed it flat with brilliantine, his reflection mocking him with its beauty. Here, as at home, all the mirrors were positioned above waist height and tilted upward. Following a near-fatal bout of asthma, after he had caught sight of himself in his sister's full-length mirror, his mother and Dolores had learned to manage without one.

Consuela returned with a jug of coffee and fresh, sweet rolls. Ramón poured brandy into the steaming brew with the delicate precision of an English lady adding milk to tea. He inhaled as he sipped, taking the vaporized alcohol straight into his lungs, letting it do its inestimable work. After breakfast, he must write to his mother, and explain that a recent bout of asthma had generated yet more doctor's fees, and thus left him short of funds; happily, he had made a speedy recovery, thanks to a prescription for a very expensive new drug available only in Madrid. The medical care available in the city was far superior to that in Albavera, so she was on no account to worry about him . . .

Ramón always put his asthma attacks firmly in the past tense, ever fearful that his mother might defy her husband and hasten to his bedside, thereby discovering the conspicuous absence of the silver, crystal, table linen and other such essentials with which she had so lovingly equipped the apartment less than six months before.

His sudden banishment had been like a gift. After years of virtual incarceration, he had at last found release in the guise of punishment. If he had realized that seducing a servant would have brought him his longed-for liberty, he would have employed this tactic long ago. It was lucky for him that the girl had screamed the place down and tried to fight him off. Very lucky indeed . . .

As for the brat she was expecting, he flatly refused to believe that it was his. The pregnancy had no doubt been contrived before or since, in an attempt to blackmail him. Still, the more trouble García stirred up, the better. Ramón dreaded nothing more than his father's forgiveness and a welcome back to the fold.

His letter was soon finished, devoid as it was of any content other than a list of his mounting expenses and florid assurances of filial affection. His work for the day complete, Ramón put on his hat and fur-lined coat, picked up his ebony walking stick, and hobbled forth in search of recreation.

As the crowd assembled for the march from Stepney Green to County Hall, Jack hung back from the rest of the crowd, watching. They were just another bunch of do-gooders to his mind, and he for one was unimpressed by their ostentatious concern for the lot of the working, or more often nonworking, man. This afternoon was an exercise in exhibitionism, as invigorating as any other voluntary exertion, to whet their appetite for tea and crumpets. But Harry Martindale was paying for a story and a story he would get.

He pulled up his collar and pocketed his hands against his lack of gloves or muffler, stamping impatiently from foot to foot, his eyes watering against the wind and the bright white light of the winter sky. The party was not due to set off for another twenty minutes, but he would have expected Clara to be the early type, marshaling her forces with sullen energy and reveling in the bitter weather. He had thought about her often since last Sunday, and thinking about her gave him a sense of power. He could feel it now, smoldering deep inside his frozen body.

Jack had never done any courting, having lacked the means or the susceptibilities to engage in conventional amorous pursuits. The girls of his hometown were all hell-bent on marriage, and he had seen too many of his contemporaries tricked into premature middle age to find their charms beguiling. He had received his sexual education, such as it was, at the hands of faithless wives. It had been Eva Dumford, a friend of his mother's and old enough to be his own, who had introduced him to her somewhat dilapidated delights, for the eventual benefit of others younger and more desirable and just as miserable as herself. In consequence, Jack had learned to spot a miserable woman a mile off. And miserable women were invariably married, just as Clara was in all but name. Not that he had any illusions about his ability to make such women happier. That was not his intention, nor theirs, if they were honest. They seemed to him to be addicted to their misery, they craved abuse, they thrived on guilt and self-pity. His contempt for them found expression in a controlled, calculated cruelty, provoking in his victims the luxury of self-indulgent fear.

Clara had kept her side of the bargain, quite apart from the money, which had cost her nothing. Two days later he had heard from Harry Martindale, who had asked him to write up today's event in a "direct, down-to-earth style," a style that would have been better suited to more direct down-to-earth material than a bunch of bored, moneyed women advertising their social conscience. They would never achieve anything, except in principle. And Jack was deeply suspicious of those who trafficked in principles. It was a form of moral parasitism; he felt diminished by the patronage of such people. But they were crying out to be used, and he would use them, as he had used Clara. She had badgered Harry Martindale not as a supplicant, as Jack would have, but as an equal. And even that had cost her little enough, even though his talent was all of one penny in the pound, and her influence all the rest.

He saw her before she saw him, but the second their eyes met he knew she would not acknowledge him. A lot of exaggerated embracing ensued as the faithful hailed one another. Clara had a new recruit with her, a tall, striking, foreign-looking girl, whom she introduced rather frostily to a chorus of sisterly squawks before leaving her awkwardly alone. The girl fell back, as if wishing to be unobtrusive, until someone sang out to her to take one end of a banner emblazoned HOMES NOT SLUMS, which she did enthusiastically, holding it aloft like a flag.

Jack counted sixty-seven people as the march straggled away. Local residents looked on lethargically, displaying little inclination to associate themselves with their well-housed benefactors. No doubt they had more pressing demands upon their time and energy.

Jack accosted a sad-eyed woman leaning by the remains of a gate in front of a decaying tenement, much like the one he had grown up in. She held a crying baby in her arms while two unhealthy-looking offspring sniveled around her skirts.

"What d'you think of this lot, then?" he asked her jauntily, provoking a baleful shrug.

"Who's going to pay the rent on these new places, then?" she asked rhetorically. "And who's going to get them? There won't be enough for everyone, that's for sure. So who's going to get them?"

"The people who need them most?" ventured Jack, embarrassed at his own enforced fatuousness. She would take him for one of them.

She sneered. "And there's always someone worse off than yourself, ain't there? I'd sooner they picked names out of a hat. It's fairer."

Perhaps a lottery was fairer than a competition. She was right, there was never enough to go around, whatever the commodity, and privation inspired a certain pride when it was perceived as universal, the universe automatically excluding Clara and her kind. But envy undermined that pride, and people felt more envious of their peers than ever they did of their betters. Dividing the poor with envy was good social policy, it stripped them of their dignity and stopped them joining forces against the rich. Petty reform was a cheap deterrent against revolution. Feed a dog and it will no longer hunt in packs, it will be your grateful servant . . .

Walking briskly, he joined the tail end of the procession, where a couple of local youths were making themselves obnoxious.

"Whass your name, darlin'?" one of them jeered at Clara's young protégée. "Doin' anyfink tonight, then?" She ignored them. Jack held back watching.

"Too posh for the likes of us, she is," observed the other mournfully. "That's a lady, that is. Good legs, mind."

The other standard bearer, a matron of military bearing, turned around.

"If you can't be polite, then please amuse yourselves elsewhere," she intoned humorlessly.

"Did you 'ear that, my man? If you can't be per-lite, then you've gotta amoos yourself elsewhere."

"Any ideas where I might amoos myself, old bean?"

"Yeah. Not with 'er, though. Talk about the back of a bleedin' bus."

"Here," said Jack. "Mind your language. Go on, off with you."

"'Oo are you, then? The bleeding footman?"

Jack seized the speaker by the scruff of the neck.

"Apologize, then clear off," he said, twisting his arm behind his back. The lad yelped in pain. Jack twisted a bit harder, whereupon the other one ran away.

"Please," said Clara's friend apologetically. "You're hurting him. He was only being silly."

Jack let go and pushed.

"Thank you," she said as the youth beat a hasty retreat. "I know you were trying to help."

"Here," said Jack. "Let me carry that for a bit."

He took the pole, dragging his eyes away from her with difficulty. He had long ago categorized all women into types, but this one defied classification. There was something bright and exotic about her, she stood out against the dull English afternoon like an orchid blooming in a privet hedge.

"If you like," she said. "But I was rather enjoying it. Are you one of the Twenty-Six Club too?"

"I'm a journalist," said Jack, liking the sound of the word. "I'm doing a piece on this for *Red Rag*."

"*Red Rag?* Oh, Clara gets that, I shall have to make sure I read it."

"Clara Neville, you mean? Are you a friend of hers?"

"She's . . . engaged to my cousin," she said ingenuously. "Do you know Clara too? Well, of course, everybody does. She's terribly active, isn't she?"

"Terribly," said Jack. "I'm Jack Austin."

She reached out sideways for his right hand and shook it energetically.

"I'm Dolores Carrasquez," she said.

"You mean you're Thpanish?" mimicked Jack, intrigued, using this as an excuse to look at her again. "Pleathed to make your acquaintanth."

It was more than just her looks that fascinated him. Her accent was perfect, upper-crust English, but the way she spoke didn't suit it—it was too warm, too direct, too natural, it didn't go with her class. It was as if her nationality set her apart, lifted her out of the system, made her somehow accessible.

"Half Spanish. My mother's English," she said in the manner of one who has explained it all many times before. "And since you're afflicted with such an unfortunate lisp, you had better call me Dolly. Everybody does."

The nickname suddenly made her seem homegrown. It was like an optical illusion, he found himself staring at her again. But she didn't seem to notice.

"So," he said, recovering himself. "You're a new recruit are you?"

"Only a very ignorant one. I don't know anything much about politics. But I do feel strongly that everyone should have decent housing. In Spain, the workers live in the most dreadful squalor, much worse than here. And a lot of them are starving. You wouldn't believe what it's like. Rich people have things all their own way and poor people don't have any rights at all."

Jack remembered the impassioned Spaniard at Speaker's Corner and wished he'd listened more attentively.

"Aren't they agitating to get rid of the king and start up a democracy?"

"Easier said than done," she said. "The people with money and land want to use the king as a sort of puppet, to keep them in power. You don't know how lucky you are in England. At home the Civil Guard would be standing by, with guns, ready to break this demonstration up. Although I must say I thought there were going to be a lot more people than this."

"Ah, but look at the quality," said Jack.

She looked at him curiously.

"What I mean is," he continued, "these people may not have any firsthand experience of poverty, but they're well-dressed and articulate and they have direct access to the right people. So a hundred of them can get more done than a thousand shabby, inarticulate people with nothing but a personal grievance. I mean to say, who takes any notice of hunger marchers? And then a mob of angry workers is so uncivilized, so undemocratic. Look at the suffragettes, for example. A handful of well-bred ladies, they were, not an army of downtrodden women. But the downtrodden women still got the benefit, even though they couldn't have cared less."

"What are you saying exactly? I can't make out whether you approve of these people or not."

"What difference does it make?"

"Well, how you think will affect how you write about it, won't it?"

"Why should it? I'm writing for *Red Rag.*"

"And that makes a difference?"

"Well, it's bound to, isn't it?"

"You mean, if you were writing for, say, the *Tory Trumpet,* or whatever, you'd give a different account of things?"

"I wouldn't write for the *Tory Trumpet.*"

"On principle, you mean?"

"I don't have principles, just prejudices."

She fell silent for a moment.

"So what do you think will happen when we get to County Hall?"

"Not much. A couple of people, Clara and somebody else, I should think, will go forward to meet some stuffed shirt and hand him the petition. He'll assure them that the relevant committee is already giving the matter its full and urgent attention, and then we can all pat ourselves on the back and go back home for tea. Where's home, by the way?"

"Home? Oh, you won't have heard of it. Albavera's just a small town about twenty kilometers south of Badajoz."

"Badaho*th?* Sounds a long way to go for tea."

"Oh, you mean in London? My aunt and uncle live in Holland Park. Where do you live?"

"I've got a room in Holloway. It's a dump, but better than the lodging house I was in before. And at least I can come and go as I please. The landlord keeps well away—with good reason."

"Well, that's the most important thing, isn't it? Freedom. Independence."

"I'd rather be free and independent in Holland Park."

"I'm neither, as it happens. Women rarely are. I'd rather be a man in Holloway."

"You'd be wasted as a man."

Jack bit his tongue, furious with himself. He hadn't meant to think that, let alone say it. Was there anything more banal than an unpremeditated compliment?

"I most certainly wouldn't be," she retorted, taking him literally. "I should make the most of it. But since I'm not, there's not much point in complaining. Perhaps I should just settle for being one of these middle-class ladies that get things done. Better than being one of the downtrodden ones who couldn't care less."

She grinned philosophically and reclaimed her half of the banner. Jack didn't let go straightway. She looked at him quizzically and he opened his mouth to say something and didn't. Then he relaxed his grip.

"Thank you," said Dolores Carrasquez.

"My pleasure," said Jack.

The next day Jack received a note. It was very much as he had expected.

"Thursday, four o'clock" it said succinctly. The venue, implicitly, was the house in Curzon Street.

Infuriatingly, he had arranged to meet Dolly on the very same day at three o'clock at the National Gallery which, incredibly, she had never visited, and which had the advantage of being free. He would have to leave her by three-thirty to make the rendezvous with Clara, which was a pity, but perhaps just as well.

"That's most awfully *kind* of you," Dolores had said, when he had nobly volunteered to show her the city's art treasures. "I'm terribly ignorant about art. The nuns didn't much approve of it." He smiled at the memory of it. Her naïveté was so cheerful, so robust, so devoid of the coy bashfulness or sly coquetry that usually went with it. There was something irrepressible about her, a wholesome springtime earthiness, a hybrid vigor, a contagious enthusiasm. She had the pure, perfect sexuality of apple blossom. He had forced himself to risk a rebuff, rather than curse himself afterward for cowardice. And luckily she had proved too politely innocent—or ignorant—to refuse him.

His article for Harry Martindale had taken shape nicely. Over a hundred demonstrators, cheered on by well-wishers along the route, had met thousands of fellow marchers from all over London outside County Hall, and had been assured that speedy implementation of the new Housing Act was receiving top priority. Those who had never doubted the ability of the Labour government to force through social reform would await developments with confidence. Those who saw the act as placatory whitewash might yet be proved wrong. And those who felt that true socialism had already been betrayed would, as true socialists, welcome any evidence to the contrary.

Jack prided himself on having pitched the tone just right. *Red Rag* regarded itself as dissenting from the anodyne government of the day without embracing the more extreme factions of the left. It combined cautious optimism with a reformist zeal which, as Jack had so rightly noted, had touching faith in democracy and abhorred civil disorder. It sought to reshape society with a chisel, not a pickax. More artistic, and far less messy. He might use that phrase one day. But not just yet.

Dear Josep,
I pray daily that your studies continue well and that I will soon have the great joy of attending your ordination. (This flowery opening was for the benefit of the censors.) The endless round of social engagements continues, but I think that at last Aunt Margaret is learning to despair of me. Last weekend I went to Edmund's house for the first time, although I had to cut my visit short as Clara was not well. But she very kindly invited me to join her on a march from Stepney Green to County Hall, which was great fun. Lots of marchers set out simultaneously from all over London, all carrying petitions for quick action on slum clearance—although the slums are nowhere near as bad as the shacks Papá's workers live in. Clara says that whole streets of terrible old houses will have to be condemned and demolished under the new act and replaced with modern council flats, but it will take forever unless we keep up the pressure on the LCC. Clara says that a Labour government is no guarantee of social reform while they do not have an overall majority in parliament, and that there is still a lot of work to be done to achieve true socialism. I don't exactly understand what she means by true socialism, but I don't like to appear too boringly ignorant, and as long as it is to do with making everybody equal, then I am naturally in favor of it. Edmund says it's best if I don't make remarks about such matters in company and I daresay he is right, as after all, I am a guest here, and make enough nuisance of myself as it is.

It wasn't what she was longing to tell him, it wasn't what was on her mind, but it would have to do. Discretion must be her watchword. It pained her to withhold her plans from Josep, whom she trusted absolutely, but there was always the faint, disastrous possibility that he, or even the person who read his letters, might regard it as his duty to betray her. Disobeying one's parents was a sin, after all.

She left her letter on the post tray in the hall and set off for her appointment with Jack Austin. Knowing that Flora wasn't remotely interested in art, Dolores had glibly suggested that she accompany her on this cultural outing, and her invitation duly spurned, she aroused no suspicion in going on her own. This preliminary had added to the fun. She was pretty sure that Auntie Margaret would disapprove of Jack Austin, and not just because he was poor.

She hadn't bothered to change, as a matter of principle. Flora's eternal obsession with clothes wearied her, and she greatly admired Clara's lack of vanity, so different from her own less honest variety. Dolores had enough self-knowledge to know that she looked presentable whatever she wore. She had never known the misery of wishing herself different, without being any great admirer of her own looks. It seemed petty to complain about minor details, when she knew what it was to have a real physical deformity like Ramón's. If Clara did have a dreadful complex about her looks, as Flora so unkindly asserted, then that was rather self-indulgent of her. Dolores prided herself on not judging by appearances. Look at Jack Austin, for example.

His clothes had been cheap and shabby, indicating his low social status, but he had carried them with a certain panache, which she had admired. And he had said unusual, quirky things, and made her laugh. Edmund would be delighted that she was engaging in an illicit rendezvous with an unsuitable young man, even if he wasn't anywhere near as tall and dark and handsome as Lorenzo. The attraction was hardly physical. He was a haphazard-looking individual, nothing about him matched. Bright blue eyes with nondescript, midbrown hair, a sharp, thin face that suggested height, though he was short for a man—not much taller than she—and then again his fingers were long and tapering, artist's hands in an artisan's body. But there was nothing haphazard about the way he spoke. His speech was as fast and fluent as moving water, and just as elusive to close examination. She wondered if he wrote like he spoke. He didn't look like someone who wrote, he looked like someone who did things. He was like a coiled spring, full of suddenness. And throughout this disjointed analysis she did not once stop to wonder what he had made of her.

It was a bright, blustery afternoon, the clouds trimmed with black and gold, oozing sunshine. But by the time she emerged from the Charing Cross underground station, they had collapsed into gray drizzle, against which her flimsy umbrella was scant protection. It blew inside out as soon as she opened it, snapping a strut, and cursing it, she ran as fast as she could across Trafalgar Square, joining several other drenched passersby who had acquired a sudden appetite for art.

Jack caught sight of her, damp and disheveled, strands of hair sticking to her forehead, her legs splashed with mud, her umbrella dripping limply, and laughed out loud. She looked delightfully be-draggled, like a dog too polite to shake itself dry.

"Very funny," she said, depositing her soggy umbrella. "All I did was cross the road."

"Serves you right for not taking a cab."

"I like the tube. I like watching the other people and imagining what they do."

"What would you imagine I did, if you saw me on the tube?"

"I was wondering that myself. You don't look like a writer."

She followed him into the gallery, not looking to the right or left, happy to talk rather than look at the pictures. She certainly liked to talk.

"What's a writer supposed to look like?" asked Jack.

"Oh, soulful and sensitive, I suppose."

"Soulful and sensitive journalists get ground up for newsprint. And you shouldn't judge by appearances. Think how different I'd look spiffy."

"I don't judge by appearances," said Dolly defensively, won-dering if she had, and then, forgetting to be tactful, "Are you very poor?"

"Stony. That's why I suggested the National Gallery. It's free. I'd rather have gone to the cinema. To tell you the truth, this lot leaves me cold."

"Oh, let's go then. I'd much prefer the cinema myself. I've got plenty of money on me. I can pay."

"No thanks," said Jack. "It wouldn't be the same."

Dolores made a face and sighed.

"Everything always boils down to money, doesn't it? My family is obsessed with it. Everyone in Spain is. They say one half of the country works but doesn't eat, and the other half eats but doesn't work. It's not that much of an exaggeration."

"Then you must be glad to be living in just, equitable, caring Britain with its rich philanthropists and its Labour government and its incorruptible politicians."

"No. I'd rather live in a just, equitable, caring Spain. There are plenty of people at home who would like to see change. Once we have a democratically elected government, then everyone will get a fair crack of the whip."

"Like they do in Britain?"

"We could do a lot worse. Look at you. In Spain, once you're poor, you're poor for life. There's no way people can move up. Not like you will."

"What makes you think I'll move up?"

"Because *you* think it. It shows."

"So you're in favor of people moving up? How right-wing of you."

"Right-wing?"

"Yes. Once your worker's got money in his pocket and a nice place to live in, he won't want to share it with anybody else. Once he's got what he wants, he'll start voting Tory. If you want him to vote Labour, you have to keep him where he is."

"I thought you were anti-Tory."

"I am. I've got no money."

"But *I've* got money, and I wouldn't mind sharing it."

"Only because you were born with it and you didn't have to earn it and you feel guilty about it. If you'd fought for it and sweated for it you wouldn't let it go."

"But there are lots of people who are born with money and who *don't* want to share it, like my father."

"I never said there weren't. Most of them don't feel guilty, see. I wouldn't, that's for sure."

"You're very given to sweeping statements."

"Occupational hazard. But they're terribly effective. The dictionary of quotations is full of them. All contradictory. You can move anything with words. That's why I like them."

Dolores stopped short.

"I haven't looked at a single picture," she said, staring haplessly at the nearest exhibit.

"Then we'll have to come back another day. Actually, I have to go in a minute. A job cropped up unexpectedly. When can I see you again?"

"Oh, whenever you like. I've got time on my hands."

"Let's go to the cinema next time, shall we? Will they let you out for long enough?"

"Oh, I shall tell them I'm visiting Clara. She'll back me up all right."

"Don't offer to pay again, will you? I'm expecting some money in soon, so I can afford it."

"If you insist. I didn't mean to offend you."

"What about Saturday?"

"No, there's bound to be something happening on Saturday, there always is. Nothing ever happens on a Monday, though. What about Monday afternoon?"

"Monday afternoon would be fine."

"Oh, good. That will give me something to look forward to. Pity you've got to go so soon."

A great pity, thought Jack.

"Dolly!" Edmund smiled, spying his drenched cousin waiting by the school gate. "I wasn't expecting to see you today."

"They're not expecting me back for tea," said Dolly. "They think I'm at the National Gallery."

"And why aren't you?"

"I was. But the person I was meeting had to leave early, and rather than wander around on my own, I thought I'd pop over and see Clara. But she's not in."

"No, she had things to do in town today. Well, let's get you into the dry. You're positively sodden. I'll give you a key so you can let yourself in in the future. You should have taken a cab."

"I tried, but with the rain it was hopeless. Are there any letters for me?"

Edmund opened his front door to a hungry cat. Dolores bent down and picked it up, with pretty-pussy coos. It was a Siamese, a singularly unaffectionate creature, which responded only to Clara. It arched its back angrily and Dolores set it down again.

"Here you are," said Edmund, handing over the envelope. Dolores ripped it open and read the letter greedily. She went rather pink, then sat down to read it again.

"Any news?" said Edmund, lighting the gas under the kettle.

"Not really. Just looking forward to when we get married, you know."

It was an untypically explicit letter, inspired by wine and frustration and the imminent reality of their union, frankly, almost crudely expressed, quite unlike Lorenzo's usual flowery style. Dolores never thought of physical love in verbal terms. Such tame romantic fiction as she had read, covertly, had left her unmoved, unconvinced, preferring her own private fantasies to off-the-rack substitutes. But they were fantasies of emotion and sensation, untrammeled by clumsy words. And Lorenzo's words were clumsy, unworthy of the act they glorified, reducing the sublime to the prosaic. Dolores herself dreamed healthily of sexual rapture in a vague, instinctive sort of way. Lorenzo's newly rampant phraseology left her disturbed, dissatisfied, disenchanted.

"Something wrong?" queried Edmund, bringing tea.

"No. Nothing. Listen, can you tell Clara for me that I'm supposed to be here all of next Monday afternoon? I'm going to the pictures with someone Auntie Margaret wouldn't consider *eligible*. If he was, I wouldn't be going.''

''I'll tell her. Did you meet him on the march?''

''Yes.'' Dolores helped herself to stale Madeira cake. ''He's a journalist. A bit seedy and not the least bit attractive.''

''But you liked him?''

''I thought he was interesting, that's all. He's terribly poor and working his way up the hard way.''

''Careful, Dolly,'' said Edmund. ''There's a type of chap who smells out rich young ladies and spins them hard luck stories. Clara can tell you all about those. London is full of them.''

''Oh, don't worry. I offered to pay for the cinema seats and he wouldn't hear of it.''

''Mmm. He sounds like a seasoned operator.''

''Really, Edmund. You're so horribly suspicious. I've only got my allowance, after all.''

''Which is more than he earns, undoubtedly.''

''And which I'm saving for when I'm married. You must think I'm awfully stupid.''

''No. Just incorrigibly softhearted.''

''Well, *you* were the one who wanted me to get out and meet people and grow up, so if your suspicions are right it should be an education, shouldn't it? In any case, I shall be telling him I'm engaged.''

Edmund felt a stab of sympathy for the luckless scribbler, and then a pang of anxiety.

''Dolly, you've led a very sheltered life. Do watch out for yourself. There's no point mincing words. Don't go back to his digs for tea or anything silly like that, now will you? I feel responsible for you.''

''If I went back to his digs,'' said Dolly, teasing him, ''it most certainly wouldn't be for tea.''

Edmund lit his pipe and puffed patriarchally.

''You have a great potential for folly, young lady. It's part of your charm, and highly spottable to the male of the species. When I first invited Clara to a terribly respectable concert at the Wigmore Hall, I confess I had only one thing on my mind. All men have only one thing on their minds, and you would do well to remember it.''

Dolores giggled through a mouthful of cake.

''What first attracted you to Clara?'' she asked.

''I don't exactly know,'' said Edmund honestly enough. The attraction had been immediate, instinctive, overpowering. She had touched him like a piece of grit begging to be made into a pearl. "Something in her eyes. Her vulnerability, I suppose. And she has her own kind of beauty, even if most people choose not to see it."

"And what happened after the concert at the Wigmore Hall? Did she come back to your digs for tea?"

"That's none of your business, young lady," said Edmund, camouflaging his confusion in a cloud of tobacco smoke. "And in any case, it's irrelevant. Clara was twenty-one when I met her and she's cautious and reserved by nature. You are a good deal younger and inclined to be somewhat rash."

"Oh I do so love it when you're pompous, Edmund. It suits you so. You'll make the most wonderful father."

"Don't say that in front of Clara, will you."

"Why not?"

"Because she doesn't want children."

"But you do, surely?"

"I respect her wishes. So don't go dropping one of your famous remarks."

"Oh. No, of course not." Dolly stirred her tea sympathetically. "I can't wait to have children," she blurted out well-meaningly. "I would like at least four, two boys first, and then two girls. I'm going to call the boys Andrés and Eduardo, and the girls Magdalena and Francisca. What do you think?"

"That you have touching faith in the future."

"Is that a bad thing?"

"Not if it's tempered with determination. Optimism's fine as a stimulant but deadly as an opiate. It's first cousin to complacency and fecklessness. I've never gone in for it much myself. I'm a natural plodder, flat feet firmly on the ground, one step at a time."

"I think Clara's very lucky to have you," said Dolores, squeezing his hand, and then, impulsively, "Maybe she'll change her mind. About the children, I mean."

"Have another piece of cake and shut up," said Edmund. "You talk too much."

"No thanks, I'd better let you get on. It looks like the rain's let up a bit. Remember to tell Clara about Monday. And don't worry about me."

She bent to kiss him and opened the door to let herself out.

"Haven't you forgotten something?" Edmund smiled, picking up Lorenzo's letter which had fallen from her lap. Tea had dripped from the bottom of her cup and smudged the ink.

"Heavens," said Dolly. "I'll forget my head next."

"Don't do that," said Edmund.

"Do I disgust you?" taunted Clara.

"Utterly," Jack assured her, picking up his cue, wondering absently what time it was. He had had more than enough for one day. She was insatiable as only a totally frigid woman can be.

She rolled off the bed, still in her slip, which she never took off, cherishing her one absurd inhibition like a cannibal with a pet goldfish. He had never seen her naked and had no desire to.

"I think you can go now," she said coldly. "I don't think you've earned any dirty money today. Go on, get out."

Jack grabbed hold of her wrist, and pulled her down roughly, whereupon she bit hard into his arm with startling viciousness.

"You rabid bitch," snarled Jack wearily. "God, you're repulsive."

"Then show me how repulsive I am."

"Not until I've had my dirty money."

She leered grotesquely, and fetched a note out of her purse, waving it tauntingly in front of his face. Jack snatched it out of her hand, losing a small corner in the process, turned his back on her and began dressing.

"Get out, then," hissed Clara. "You're despicable. You're no better than a whore."

"And shall I show you what a whore thinks of her client?" asked Jack, watching her twitch in anticipation.

But to spit in her face, as required, proved momentarily beyond him, and he left her howling the kind of profanities she could only have learned from far rougher trade than he.

In his haste to get away, he hailed a cab. Last time it had been easy, easier than expected. But this time he had had no stomach for it. It was seeing Dolly, thinking about Dolly, that had done it. He would have to arrange his timetable better in the future, or else Clara would send him packing. And he couldn't afford to let that happen yet.

It should have been a relief to get back to *Unending Rapture,* but Dolly got in the way of that as well, wrecking his concentration, making him feel ashamed.

Elvira looking into Sebastian's eyes, smoldering like her own with unconsummated desire . . .

Which was the more degrading? Ministering to Clara's perversions or writing genteel pornography? Selling brushes or washing other people's greasy plates?

"Forever, my darling," she breathed, feeling his manly chest hard against the softness of her surrender . . .

Everyone sold themselves if they were poor. And women had always sold themselves: marriage was nothing but legalized prostitution for most of them, which was why they were all so keen on conning themselves about love. Love was the detergent that washed the contract clean.

He swung her into strong arms as if she were a feather, and murmured in her ear, his voice hoarse with passion . . .

When he married, it would assuredly not be for love. It would be for money and power and influence, and to make other men envy him. But a rich, high-class, beautiful wife was still well out of his league. A few Claras would do nicely until then. Might as well poke her and get paid for it as spend time and money and energy buying bargain-basement sex. Not that he would have bothered. Sex was not that important, except as a means to an end . . .

Dolly didn't fit in with any of it. Dolly was something extra, that was all. A self-indulgence, an incentive, a reward, something to spend a bit of Clara's money on, something to enjoy for its own sake. A long, cool pint after a hard day's work, a scent of flowers after a day down the sewer. And real. Not a substitute. Real.

Stuffing the finished manuscript into a manila envelope, Jack pondered the manner of Griselda's imminent demise. Her editress knew her to be elderly and arthritic but it seemed banal to let her die of natural causes. He favored a fall down the stairs and a broken neck. After she had received her standard fee.

Clara emptied the last of the bottles down the kitchen sink. She flung open the windows to release the fumes, breathing in the noise of traffic and starlings. Jack. He had understood her immediately, as Edmund never would. What glorious relief there had been in that obscene pantomime, that soaring flight into blessed degradation, her evil spirit free to repollute her sterile body. She would not hurt Edmund, she told herself, because Edmund would never know. She would hurt only herself, which was what she wanted to do.

She remained subdued over dinner that night, which wasn't unusual in itself, except that her quietness was conciliatory rather than sullen. She was attentive to Edmund's account of a perfectly ordinary day, served and cleared the meal with wifely solicitude, and sewed a button on his shirt while he smoked his pipe in luxorious contentment.

He felt almost guilty about her present mood. Ever since her gin-sodden lapse, she had been trying to show her contrition, as if the crime were against him rather than herself. How proudly she had concealed her addiction, how bravely she had struggled to overcome it, how endlessly self-critical she was, how impossible it was to compensate her for all she had suffered. Better for her to have grown up starved of food rather than of affection. The body recovered and renewed itself faster than the soul. She had never known love except, briefly, from her pervert of an uncle, she had been born into the role of scapegoat, the instrument of both her parents' deaths. A confused, lonely childhood steeped in religious mumbo jumbo had increased her crushing sense of guilt, which she had tried in vain to exorcise by deliberate, defiant sin.

How could he have begun to tell an innocent like Dolly the sordid overtures to their love affair? That when he had first met Clara she had been on the very brink of a nervous breakdown, pleading with him to punish her for imaginary transgressions, confessing to all manner of exaggerated vices, relentlessly courting his disgust and scorn? She had been like a man-eating bird with a broken wing, he had nursed her back to health and been endlessly savaged in the process, and finally, after much bloodshed, won her trust, and love. Not the cozy humdrum sort that made the world go around, but something unique, irreplaceable, sometimes painful but always precious . . .

It would seem a strange kind of love to one who still believed in hearts and flowers. Perhaps he was wrong to want more than that for Dolly, wrong to push back-street kids into grammar schools, wrong to abhor ignorance and waste. Enlightenment often did more harm than good, in the long run. But Dolly was so strong, she radiated strength. It would be a crime to let it atrophy.

"By the way," he puffed casually, as Clara peered shortsightedly at her needlework. "Dolly is having a small adventure. She's telling my mother she'll be here with you next Monday afternoon so that she can go to the cinema with some undesirable young man."

"Good gracious," said Clara. "I thought she was true to the gun-toting boyfriend back home."

"So she is. I think she's trying to prove something or other. She made great play of telling me how unattractive she finds this chap."

"Which means the reverse, of course," said Clara. "Why is he so undesirable?"

"Penniless and presumably left-wing to boot. That is, she met him on your march. A journalist, she said."

Clara started, jabbing the needle into her finger as an after-thought. She watched the red blob soak into her handkerchief.

"There will be the most dreadful to-do, Edmund, if she gets herself into any kind of trouble. You encouraged this, remember."

"The only person Dolly needs to be protected from is Dolly, and that's precisely what I am trying to do. But by all means have a sisterly chat with her yourself."

"And just how much of my experience do you think would be useful to her?"

"I leave that to you to decide."

Clara bit off the cotton thread between her teeth.

"Let her make her own mistakes," she said. "She might as well learn the hard way that men only want sex or money or preferably both. Including soldier boy, no doubt."

"Do you include me in that blanket condemnation?"

"I wish I could. You're perfect, damn you." Her voice cracked. "God only knows what you see in me."

Edmund took the workbasket off her lap and pulled her to her feet. The look in his eyes sent a nauseous wave of love and guilt rippling through her guts.

"I wish I didn't love you, Edmund," she muttered almost angrily. "If I didn't love you I could let you go. I hate myself for what I do to you. I wish you'd throw me out."

But the way she clung to him belied her words. And it always reassured him when she wept. There was love in the blessed loss of control, love in the self-recrimination that heralded surrender. And afterward, they would be an inch closer. Just an inch, but closer.

Jack did Dolly proud. The best seats and a box of chocolates and tea and scones afterward at a prissy little café with a silver cake stand and starched aprons and china cups. She was wearing a red silk blouse that looked ready to ignite the dark woolen fabric of her coat, and she seemed genuinely unaware of the heads that turned to look at her, at them. What does she see in *him?* they were wondering, much to Jack's discomfiture and delight.

She had begged to see the Marx Brothers in *Animal Crackers,* and Jack had found it puerile, but Dolly had literally laughed till she cried, she laughed uproariously at the slightest thing. Jack wondered if all her emotions were bubbling, lavalike, just beneath the surface, waiting to be tapped. But despite that, or perhaps because of it, he was reluctant to make the usual boy-meets-girl overtures under cover of darkness and flickering fantasy. He didn't want to share her with some idiotic film. He wanted her all to himself.

Meanwhile, he sought to disarm his troublesome libido by describing her à la Griselda. Sparkling black eyes, hair like a raven's wing, tip-tilted nose, honey-colored skin with the bloom of a fresh peach, luscious lips ripe for passion, a high, full bosom, long slender legs, and a waist that could be spanned by two manly hands. A warm, fluid voice and a laugh like silver. God. How useless words were. Overused, inadequate, threadbare. It ought to be possible to invent new words, to create a unique, precise, pristine language dedicated to its chosen subject.

"Do you prefer the top or the bottom of a scone?" asked Dolly, cutting one apart and spreading both halves liberally with raspberry jam and cream.

"I've never thought about it," said Jack. "They're not something I eat all that often."

"Oh good, in that case you can eat the tops and I'll have the bottoms. I do prefer them, that's why I always eat the top bits first."

She put the top of her scone upside down on his plate.

"Excuse my fingers."

"Not at all."

"I do wish you'd let me pay for this. I'm not playing Lady Bountiful, you know. In fact, in a few months' time I'm going to be cut off without a shilling, so I'm actually saving quite hard. It's just that you paid for the cinema seats and chocolates."

"Why are you being cut off?"

"The usual reason. I'm getting married to someone my father disapproves of. We're going to elope, as a matter of fact, on March twenty-third. It's a secret, of course."

"If it's a secret, then why are you telling me? I'm not in the least trustworthy."

"I thought I should, just to avoid any misunderstandings. That is, I didn't want you spending money on me thinking anything might come of it, if you know what I mean."

"I know exactly what you mean."

"Oh dear. I suppose that sounded a bit conceited, but I prefer to get things absolutely straight, don't you?"

"It's not conceited. Why else would I take you to the pictures except to seduce you?"

"You're laughing at me."

"Yes. And at me. I had a cheek asking you out in the first place. I thought you'd make some excuse. I should be in the pub, priming some shopgirl on shandies, not sitting in a select tearoom with a lady like you. You're right out of my class, and you know it. It was very kind of you to deign to come out with me.''

''Oh *don't!*''

''Why not? Now you'll have to agree to see me again, just to prove you're not a snob. As for you being engaged, that doesn't bother me at all. Don't give it a second thought.''

He picked up another scone, sliced it, and handed her its nether portion. She took it from him, her fingers still damp from being licked. He felt an almost unbearable urge to put them in his mouth and taste them.

''The other thing I wanted to say,'' she continued irrepressibly, ''is that my cousin Edmund warned me that you might think me stupid and gullible and, you know, a soft touch, and I wouldn't like us to meet again without telling you that I'm not at all, even if I seem that way. I'm actually very tough and extremely selfish.''

''You mean he thought I was planning to scrounge off you?''

''That's right. His fiancée, Clara, you know, has had a few bad experiences. I suppose when you're female and rich and a socialist people think you're just panting to give all your money away to the first person who asks for it. Because of feeling guilty and not having had to work for it, like you said.''

''Your cousin was quite right to warn you. But I'm only interested in money I can earn. I've never taken a penny I didn't work for.''

''Right then. I'm so glad that's all sorted out.''

''Wait a minute. I don't think it is.''

''It isn't?''

''Not quite. I'm . . . still going to try and seduce you. I don't expect you to succumb, of course, why should you? But knowing how you like everything out in the open, I thought I'd say my piece right now and risk my marching orders rather than deceive you. I hope my being honest hasn't frightened you. But then, you don't scare easy, do you?''

He was painfully aware of the sound of his own voice, complete with uncultured vowels. He knew he had just been either incredibly stupid or positively inspired.

She sat back in her chair and folded her arms and stared at him in saucy disbelief. He stared back, with a creditable display of sangfroid. He wasn't totally in control of this and he didn't like it, or perhaps he did like it, which was even more worrying.

''I'm Spanish, remember?'' she said at last. ''You know, virtuous and volatile. I carry a dagger in my handbag of tempered Toledo steel with which to defend my honor. My fiancé is also Spanish. You know, valiant and violent. He happens to be a crack shot and quite a lot bigger than you.''

''You don't say,'' said Jack, feigning terror. ''What else should I know about him?''

''What do you want to know?''

''Enough to work out the secret of his charm.''

''Oh very well. He's called Lorenzo and I've known him all my life. He's very handsome. Tall, broad shoulders, very strong. He can pick me up just like that. His father is—or rather used to be—the family lawyer and Lorenzo joined the Army because he didn't want to study law. He's not much of a one for books, he loves activity, you know, riding and shooting. He really is a crack shot, he wants to be an instructor one day. He showed me how to use a rifle once, but it was terribly heavy and I hurt my shoulder and he wouldn't let me try again.''

''So why doesn't your father approve of him?''

''Because he's only got his Army pay and Papá thinks he's after my money. But that's not true.''

''How do you know?''

She glared.

''Lorenzo doesn't care about money. He's very idealistic. He hates the way the rich control the country, he'd like to see the land reallocated and the Army reformed. He says none of that can happen till we have a republic. My brother Josep thinks the same way. He's training to be a priest. He thinks the Church is very corrupt and ought to do more to help the poor.''

''Have you just got the one brother?''

''No, two. My other brother, Ramón, is very right-wing, like Papá. He says that if the workers aren't kept down they'll run amok and start a revolution. It probably sounds ridiculous to you, but that's the way people think in Spain, if they own land, it's normal. Papá thinks that everyone who disagrees with him is a Marxist.''

''So does he think your fiancé is a Marxist?''

''Oh, Lorenzo always kept his views to himself, not to antagonize Papá, so that he'd let us get married. Much good that did. The money thing was enough in itself. When Papá found out that we were engaged, he sacked Lorenzo's father and said he'd make sure Lorenzo never got promoted. Then he sent me away to England to keep us apart. So he's bound to cut me off when we get married, but I'm sure he'll relent once I have a baby, especially if it's a boy.''

''You'd better have a baby right away then.''

"Oh, I shall. I love children, don't you?"

Jack shrugged.

"They're okay if you've got plenty of money. They're a life sentence if you're poor."

Dolores got out her purse.

"I'll see you again if you let me pay my share."

"No. Don't patronize me. And *I'm* not saving up to get married. Perish the thought."

"Why perish the thought? Don't you want to get married?"

"Certainly I do. But saving up doesn't come into it. I intend to find myself a rich wife."

"You mean, marry for money?"

"Naturally. Women have always done it, so why not me? Look at Cinderella. No one thought any the worse of her."

"I thought you only wanted money you could earn."

"I'd earn it. You ought to find my ambitions reassuring, being as you're about to be cut off. Ulterior motives would be a waste of time. My intentions are purely dishonorable."

"Just seduction?"

"Just seduction."

"And you seriously think I would let you seduce me?"

"You're the one who's done all the seducing so far. You're quite enjoying leading me on, aren't you? Not that I'm complaining."

She sat silent for a moment while she digested this, lips pursed primly. Then she stood up to go.

"Thank you for the cinema and the chocolates and the tea," she said with steely politeness.

"My pleasure. When can I see you again?"

"I'm not sure. I'm very busy this week. Christmas shopping, you know."

"We could stroll around Harrods together."

"I prefer to shop alone."

"The main entrance. Wednesday, two o'clock."

"I shouldn't think so."

"Till Wednesday, then."

Dolly flounced out of the tearoom, nettled. Leading him on indeed. Wednesday, two o'clock. Two o'clock, Wednesday.

Jack went out the next morning in search of *Red Rag*. The local outlets didn't carry it, of course, there being no demand for it in such a hand-to-mouth district, but they had one copy at the King's Cross station bookstall where he had bought his first issue.

His story was on page three, and he read it through at the speed of thought. It had been cut by about a hundred words, the best hundred words of course. And they had misspelled his name as Austen, as in Jane. But it was in print and he would get paid for it and it would go in his portfolio and a year from now he'd be writing for a proper paper and five years from now he'd pick and choose his assignments. And then they'd leave his copy alone and they'd spell his name correctly and it would be him doing them the favor and not the other way around. And pigs might fly, for a change.

He walked on to Harry Martindale's office, which occupied self-consciously plebeian premises above a bakery in Camden Town. The smell of new bread was cozy and wholesome.

"Jack, m'boy," boomed Martindale, pumping his hand. "Seen your piece this week, have you? I thought the layout was rather good."

"You spelled my name wrong," said Jack.

"Oh, just a printer's error, you know. How can I help you?"

"I need a job," said Jack. "Regular work. I got sacked from the Empire Court after they saw my piece."

"Did you indeed? Now that's too bad. The price of principles, eh? Perhaps we should have used a pseudonym."

"I write under my own name or not at all."

"Then perhaps you should write under your real name and work under a different name." Martindale obviously shared the common view that writing wasn't work. "As for a job, I'd suggest you try a local paper. That's the way people start, you know." He beamed encouragingly.

"I don't want to write about weddings and church bazaars. Look, you wouldn't have to pay me very much. I could fill that paper for you every week, so you wouldn't have to fall back on free contributions from people who can't write. You could pay me according to circulation. I guarantee you I can double it in six months. You want to get yourself on the newsstands, get ordinary people buying your paper and reading it and learning from it. A paper that doesn't toe the line, that lives up to its title, that makes people think, not a broadsheet for intellectuals, and not a talk-down-to-'em comic, either. A paper for action, for change. This government's sold out already, it's got both hands tied behind its back. It's conning people. It's no more socialist than a vicar's tea party. The whole country is living in cloud cuckoo land while the politicians bury their heads in the sand. They won't wake up to what's happening until it's too damn late. *That's* what I want to write about. That's what you ought to want to print. You want to open people's eyes to what's coming to them. Fascism. War. In a few years it'll be obvious. You want to be saying it now, today, instead of churning out intellectualized waffle that nobody bothers to read.''

"Jack, my dear chap, I wouldn't disagree with anything you've said, but one has to be realistic. I—''

"I'm being *realistic*. You can get a week's work out of me for less than the rent on that posh flat of yours in Hampstead, because where I live only costs twelve bob a week. You can get a *year's* work out of me for half what you paid for your nice new Rover Meteor, because I can always walk or take a tram. I know my place, don't worry. All I want is a breadline wage and a chance. It's not that much to ask, is it? Or aren't you serious about the paper? Don't tell me you're another flaming dilettante. I'd convinced myself you were different from the rest of them.''

Martindale opened his mouth and shut it again. At that moment he would willingly have bought half a dozen vacuum cleaners to get this aggressive young troublemaker out of his nice quiet office. Who the hell did he think he was, challenging the bona fides of a founder member of the Twenty-Six Club, the selfless proprietor of an independent socialist weekly whose heavy losses were subsidized out of his own pocket? How dare he call him a dilettante when he could have lived in idleness off his private income? Did he think he was made of money?

"Just pay me what I was getting at the Empire Court,'' said Jack, "and I'll write more than you can print.''

"You couldn't have a byline on everything,'' began Martindale feebly.

"It's a deal. I'll start today then. I thought I could do a post-mortem on the Whitechapel by-election next week. Why the Labour majority was cut from nine thousand to nine hundred. Oh yes it will be, you'll see. And everyone will just blame it on unemployment. Well, that's just an excuse. I've already started writing it, actually. Don't worry, I'll work a week in hand, so you don't end up out of pocket. That's what they do at the Empire Court. Well, I'm glad we've sorted all that out.''

He seized Harry Martindale's soft chubby hand and subjected it mercilessly to a working-class grip.

"A month's trial,'' Martindale managed to say.

"That's more than generous of you, *sir,*'' said Jack obsequiously, touching an imaginary forelock and walking backward out of the room.

* * *

Ramón was sublimely happy. Like the good steward of the parable, he had taken his mother's money and made it multiply. The sole of his shoe was stuffed with security, his bloodstream with soothing absinthe, his mouth with some anonymous piece of flesh. He liked to be the passive partner, enjoyed the sultan-like indolence of seeing a woman sweat. She was older than he would have liked, although she had seemed young under the streetlight, but she knew her trade and when she was finished she would take her pittance and go.

His associates had warned him against his practice of buying cheap. They had tried to inveigle him into select establishments where one paid for the privilege of avoiding disease, where one could pick and choose and have the benefit of a regular partner. And where he would be patronized as a rich, young cripple, cooed at to order by some beautiful girl who found him repulsive. No, better, the casual encounter with one as damaged as he. A congress of shared contempt was purer than one of hypocrisy.

She grunted in relief, her task complete, dressed herself quickly and went back out into the street, leaving behind her the comforting, pungent odor of a cheap lodging house. And Ramón slept.

He dreamed of beauty and fear and power and pain, of glory and impotence and bliss and death, the scattered components of despair. And he woke again to the sound of creaking windows and beaten rugs and another day's remission.

There was a letter from his sister, enclosing the requested contribution toward his doctor's bills. Dolores knew nothing of Rosa's pregnancy, thank God. Ramón had assured Dolores of his abject contrition for his inexcusable behavior; he had promised faithfully, if nebulously, to make amends to Rosa at some future date. But at the moment, alas, he was a pauper, barely able to keep body and soul together. If Mamá knew of his privations, she would be sick with worry . . .

Dolores had proved unable to refuse him. She was absurdly soft-hearted, even as a child she had been a compulsive sharer, unable to enjoy the smallest treat unless she divided it in two. Ramón folded the crisp English notes and put them in his pocketbook while he idly perused her letter.

She prattled of some pointless project to help the poor—such things diverted her—inquired solicitously after his health, and said how much she looked forward to coming home and visiting them, as if their father would ever allow such an expedition.

. . . I am sorry to hear that Papá is being so mean about money, but you are quite right not to trouble Mamá, especially as I have enough to spare at the moment and would rather she did not worry. I wish I could send more, but everything is much more expensive here than it is at home and Aunt Margaret makes me go to the hairdresser all the time and fusses if I don't buy clothes. However, I am hoping that if all goes well I shall be home sooner than you think. How's that for a little mystery?

It grieves me to think of you poor and lonely and miserable. I wish you could have come to London with me. You would enjoy all the socializing so much more than I do. Take care to keep warm and to eat properly.

Much love,
Dolores

What a dreary place London sounded. Full of cold, civilized people anxious to do good, with a government that scooped off scum and called it cream. A soft, effeminate country, lacking in pride, in thrall to its grubby proletariat, its former splendor fled. It was a country for women to be happy in, not men. His sister would undoubtedly forget Lorenzo in the arms of some flabby philanthropist, and indulge herself in a lifetime of visiting hospitals and hovels. Still, Lorenzo would be no loss. Married to him she would be reduced to penury, and English do-gooders invariably had plenty of money. He was fond of his silly little sister, and wished her well, or at least wealth.

He picked up his pen and wrote back in his elegant, italic script:

Dear little sister,

Thank you for your sweet letter and your generous aid to a brother in distress. You know how these Jews chase their debts. I would rejoice in your intention to return home early, and to visit me in my solitude, but out of love and concern I must urge you to abandon such plans. Madrid is no longer a safe place for young women of good family. There is a growing hatred here for anyone with clean hands, and the rabble continue to agitate for so-called reforms in the hope of driving decent people out of the country. You would do well to stay in England. Believe me, if the Left have their way, all our father's land will be confiscated and you and I forced to break our backs in the fields while the peasants sit idly watching. The king, alas, is too weak and fearful to stand up to those who plot against him, and therefore our best hope is for another pronunciamento, as only military rule can restore peace and stability. Your romantic ideals of equality for all are charming but misguided, and I share our mother's relief that you are in a country that, although already corrupt in its own way, eschews revolution. A republic would be nothing more than a license for legalized sedition, masterminded by Marxists, homosexuals and atheists who pollute this city and plot the subjugation of our once noble country. Wait until Right has prevailed before returning, whereupon a warm welcome will await you from us all. Lorenzo will no doubt have the chance to advance his military career if the Army is called to power; your presence would only be a worry and a distraction to him. Believe in the wisdom of a cripple; I have many lonely hours in which to think.

Your loving Ramón

Democracy was humbug. What right had illiterates to a vote on anything, what hope was there for any government elected by vermin and led by traitors? At least the elections of old had been controlled, the delegates approved by those who had a vested interest in a strong, unified, ordered Spain. Free elections would merely pave the way for thieves and opportunists and demagogues to loot and destroy the country's assets, to harass and exile its heirs.

Much as he hated his father, on such issues they were of one accord. As for his holy, peasant-loving brother, he would soon change his tune once history repeated itself, once he witnessed a reenactment of the Tragic Week of Barcelona, twenty years before, when their grandmother had witnessed churches burned and nuns' corpses disinterred at the hands of murderous anarchists. Without the Army to restrain them, the infection would have spread unchecked, and it still lurked everywhere like some deadly virus, waiting for a moment of weakness to lay the national body low, to cripple the country just as viciously as polio had crippled him. Before long his simpleminded brother would be consecrating blood, not wine, and be hounded into hiding by heathens.

Sometimes, in alcohol-hazed daydreams, Ramón liked to imagine that his leg had been damaged in battle, that he had a row of medals on his chest to honor his disability. He was an ardent admirer of General Millán Astray, gallant patriot and founder of the Foreign Legion, who had lost both an arm and an eye defending the empire and wore his wounds with pride not shame. But his wretched boot was proof that he had been the victim of fate, not a hero of war, someone to be pitied, not admired. And yet perhaps one day the time would come when he too could serve his country, earn the recognition and respect that should have been his due. His destiny had been thwarted, not curtailed. Every man had his purpose, and perhaps his adversity had been visited on him by providence, to prepare him for some grand design.

Poor foolish Dolores, poor foolish Josep. Even yet, it might fall to their poor, clever brother to save them from themselves.

"I hear you have a new admirer," said Clara. Her tone was almost friendly. They had spent a busy afternoon delivering by-election propaganda door-to-door, and Dolly had braved both hostile Tories and savage dogs in her determination to get the job done.

"Oh, I wouldn't call him an *admirer*. I think he finds me a bit of an oddity. He's one himself, come to that. But at least he's not boring and I don't have to make small talk. Edmund was right, about getting out and meeting some new people. Flora and I don't have a lot in common, even though she's been terribly kind, and I really don't enjoy all those parties and dinners much. I can never think of anything to say to people."

"I find that hard to believe. You never stop talking."

"Oh, it's different with you and Edmund. I don't have to get dressed up and be polite and worry about embarrassing Aunt Margaret with my lack of social graces. I feel about fourteen years old next to Flora. She puts it down to my convent education."

"You should have contrived to get expelled, like me," said Clara. "Mind you, my guardians packed me off to a finishing school in Lucerne, for my sins, which was even worse. I thought I should go mad from boredom."

"What did you do to get expelled?"

Clara hesitated.

"I don't think I ought to tell you that."

"Why not? Is it terribly shocking?"

"They seemed to think so at the time."

"Oh *please* tell me," begged Dolly, no doubt expecting some ripping exploit straight out of a romance novel.

"I had a love affair. I was discovered in flagrante."

Dolly opened her mouth in awe.

"With a *man?*" she asked, fascinated.

"Of course not."

"Sorry, silly question. I meant—"

"It wasn't a silly question. There were no men available. They discovered us in a compromising position in the hockey building. She was expelled too, of course."

"Oh," said Dolly. "Oh."

"Are you shocked?"

"Um . . . not exactly. But I don't understand . . . What I mean is . . ."

"Didn't anything like that ever happen in your school? Of course, they hushed it up. They always do. Since it can't effect procreation, I suppose it's an even greater sin than ordinary sex."

"Oh, I don't think the Church says that sex is a *sin,* exactly."

"Why do you suppose priests have to be celibate? Because sex, and women, are seen as vile and corrupting."

"Oh no. Josep says that . . ."

"Oh spare me your saintly brother," said Clara. "Sorry, I'm always rude." Dolly fell silent.

"And were you . . . in love with her?"

"Oh, I shouldn't think so. She took an interest in me, and I didn't have any friends. I didn't realize what her interest was until it was too late and then I didn't like to offend her. She was a bit like me, a misfit. Weren't you ever lonely and miserable at school?"

"Oh absolutely. All the time. I never wanted to leave home at all, but my mother has always been obsessed with my having an English education. I used to live for the holidays. If it hadn't been for Lorenzo's letters, I should have *died.* He was my lifeline. He still is, of course."

"Have you told him about your new gentleman friend?"

"No. I mean, I wouldn't like him to get the wrong impression. In any case, he's hardly a gentleman, and I wouldn't call him a friend either."

"So why bother with him?"

Dolly furrowed her brow as if trying to work it out.

"Curiosity," she said. "He intrigues me, that's all. There's nothing in it."

"As long as he realizes that."

"Oh. I told him I was engaged. He didn't seem to care. You know him actually, at least he knows you. He's called Jack Austin and he's a journalist."

"The name rings a bell," said Clara. "But then I meet so many people."

"He's quite ordinary-looking. Difficult to describe. You wouldn't notice him in a crowd. Anyway, I said I'd see him again, just to kill time, you know. And I know all about not going around to his digs. Edmund has been doing his big brother act.''

"I'm glad to hear it.''

"Clara . . . how old were you when you . . . I mean, you were twenty-one when you met Edmund, weren't you?''

Clara cast her mind back two years, remembering that dreadful, miraculous evening. She had picked a violent public quarrel with her escort in the middle of a dinner party; a dozen guests, including Edmund, had seen her at her spectacular worst—drunk and disgusting and depressed. Especially depressed. If Edmund hadn't taken her home with him and looked after her till morning, she might have succumbed to the ultimate temptation, the one irredeemable sin. And he had been her hold on life ever since.

"Oh, Edmund wasn't the first," said Clara. "I must have been about your age, I suppose. It seems a long time ago.''

"I often wonder what it'll be like.''

"Impure thoughts. Remember next time you go to confession.''

"Sometimes I wish Lorenzo and I had anticipated our vows. Still, it's not much longer to wait now.''

"Mmm. Well, if temptation rears its ugly head before March, do be sensible. My man in Harley Street can fix you up with a dear little diaphragm so you don't go home with any unwanted baggage.'' She smiled brightly, enjoying Dolores's horrified expression.

"Honestly, Clara," said Dolly. "You must be joking. I couldn't do *that* even if I was married. I mean, it's a mortal sin. And I told you, I'm saving myself for Lorenzo.''

"Just doing my duty.'' Clara shrugged. "I take it you do know the facts of life?''

"Of course," said Dolly with more dignity than conviction. There were a great many things she didn't know, but Clara thought her enough of a fool already. And besides, soon she would know everything there was to know. And then nine months later, she would have her firstborn in her arms, little Andrés, looking up at her with his father's eyes.

4

Two o'clock, Wednesday, arrived almost too quickly for Jack. He felt ill prepared, and uncommonly tired. Two further encounters with Clara had seen to that, they had left him exhausted. Not physically, despite her excessive demands, nor mentally, as he conducted their sessions on instinct, not intellect. It was a sluggish, spiritual fatigue, a liverish inertia that was unrelated to the effort expended. It was as if she fed off his energy parasitically, draining him like a leech, drawing strength from their meetings, as if she knew she had robbed him of something.

Still, thanks to Clara, he now possessed a respectable ready-made suit, two new shirts, a decent pair of shoes and a raincoat, all of which he wore with as little vanity as a soldier wearing camouflage, ever aware of his own nakedness beneath. As for his brand-new, secondhand Remington, he nursed it as lovingly as a rifle.

It had already fired off the article on tomorrow's by-election result, bar minor details like the actual voting figures. He had managed to interview all four candidates, which had given him enough material to slant the story any way he liked. As it was, he should manage to upset all of them, always supposing Martindale didn't lose his nerve. Luckily, Martindale was scared of seeming scared, and given his claimed commitment to controversy, he'd look feeble if he objected. After all, there was nothing technically libelous and nothing that wasn't true, in its way. There had been no need to invent anything. Facts were an infinitely malleable commodity, and Jack took a professional pride in knocking them into shape. And what was omission but a necessary discipline, a form of self-editing? There was nothing worse than long-winded pedantry.

What was it about the printed word that inspired trust? If he, Jack Austin, were to stand up in public and say his piece out loud, every word he uttered would be colored by his accent, his appearance, the sublanguage of voice and mannerisms. But the very same words in print were purified, depersonalized, invested with the sanctity of silence. Reading was thought-to-thought communication, which broke down only if the reader stopped reading or failed to understand the words. Jack was determined that his readers would do neither, and the conciseness and clarity of his writing, its lack of abstruse references, its woefully unpretentious style, were geared to his readers' needs rather than his editor's foibles. Jack craved success, not prestige. Prestige didn't pay the rent, prestige was the province of those who already had enough success or those who despised it as common. And Jack was far too common himself to despise success just yet.

The next item on Jack's shopping list was a bath. His lodgings gave him access to a cold tap in the corridor and a malodorous lavatory, which he had to share with umpteen strangers, not just family. The first-floor bathroom at Curzon Street had been old-fashioned but opulent by Jack's standards. Its freezing temperature—the house being unoccupied save for the housekeeper's quarters—and its lack of hot water were of no importance to him; it was private, and it was clean. On his second visit, he had helped himself to a cold bath before leaving, while Clara jingled her keys impatiently in the hallway. He never felt clean after a visit to the public baths with their cracked, abrasive, limestone-stained tubs and their smell of carbolic, for all that the water was scalding. And then, yesterday, he had kept his appointment with Clara to find that the boiler had been lit. The house was warm, hissing with hot water, and he had left it slightly groggy, corrupted by comfort, compromised by this gift as he had never been by wages.

So at least he was clean for Dolly. The second of his two new shirts, both white, was full of fold lines and pinholes and felt stiff and papery next to his skin. His new shoes were rubbing against his heels and the unaccustomed protection of a coat made him feel almost feverish.

The windows of Harrods were decked out for Christmas with elaborate Yuletide displays. Santa Claus sat smugly in a sled packed full of fripperies and an elaborate crib gave center stage to the three wise men holding their gifts aloft, like patron saints of shopping. Jack stood by the main entrance, feeling uncomfortably like an off-duty doorman, jostled by perfumed furs, his normally acute powers of observation shut right down, subjugated to the empty process of waiting. Waiting was like a toothache, it robbed the mind of its flexibility. After half an hour he was sure she wasn't coming and still he waited, a triumph of experience over pessimism. He knew her just well enough to know that she would come.

When she did, flushed and breathless, he didn't recognize her at first. She had had all her beautiful hair cut off, it was short and crimped and waved and fashionable and it didn't suit her at all. Her skin was pink from the dryer and peppered with tiny black fragments of hair.

"I'm sorry I'm late," she panted. She had obviously been running. "I went to the hairdresser and it took forever. I thought if I got rid of it I needn't go so often. My aunt was making me spend a fortune having it put up for parties. It looks dreadful, I knew it would, but it'll grow again. I itch all over. I've got hair all down my back. I'm dying to go home and have a bath but I thought I'd better check if you were still here first."

"Don't move," said Jack.

A sharp-looking remnant was hanging from her right brow, threatening to fall into her eye. He picked it off like a flea.

"Here," he said, holding out the corner of his brand-new handkerchief. "Spit."

She did so, as unquestioningly as a child, and he proceeded to clean the debris from her face like a nanny, licking the handkerchief himself as he went.

"Thank you," she said. "It was so hot, too. I almost wish I hadn't done it, but at least now that it's short I shouldn't need to go again for ages. It's a permanent wave, you know."

"What did they do with the hair?" asked Jack wistfully.

"Swept it up. I didn't realize it weighed so much. I feel quite light-headed."

As she spoke she put her hand to her back and scratched and couldn't quite reach the spot and had to turn around and let Jack do it for her.

"No there, *there*. Oh bliss. Thank you."

"Don't mention it," said Jack, his toothache fled, the waiting gone, full of a sense of now.

"I can't go shopping like this. I really must go home for a bath. I'm sorry."

"Don't be. Can I come too?"

She hesitated infinitesimally.

"I'm looking quite respectable today," continued Jack provocatively, "and I can even talk posh if I put my mind to it."

"It's not that. It's just that you don't exist. That is, who do I say you are? They keep me on a bit of a leash, I told you."

"Well, can't you introduce me as a friend of Clara's? I know her quite well."

"Do you? She doesn't seem to know you. But then she knows so many people."

"It wouldn't be a lie. We are acquainted."

"Well . . . I know, we could go to Edmund's instead. It would be much easier. I can have a bath there, he gave me a key, and he gets home at four. Have you met Edmund? You'll like him."

"What about Clara? Won't she be there?"

"I don't know. But it won't matter if she is. She knows I've been meeting you and she certainly won't mind me having a bath."

"Right then," said Jack. "Whitechapel, didn't you say?" She didn't realize she hadn't and before she could change her mind he had hailed a cab.

She wriggled uncomfortably throughout the journey and kept searching under her collar removing stray tufts. She talked incessantly of Edmund. She sounded half in love with the chap. He was gentle, kind, good-humored, patient, funny and just a little bit pompous. He was adorable. Her enthusiasm irritated Jack, who had already formed the view that Edmund must be a fool. Either he knew of Clara's adventures and tolerated them, or he was unaware of them, and either way he was a fool. And yet he was curious to meet Edmund, if mildly apprehensive at the thought of running into Clara. Dolly had clearly mentioned him to her, and she had kept her mouth shut, aware, no doubt, that any sabotage would backfire upon herself. It amused him to think of Dolly ingenuously telling her sour-faced friend of their meetings and using her as an alibi. And yet if Clara hadn't tried, albeit subtly, to warn Dolly off him, then she was no kind of friend. He found himself wishing that she had. He would like Dolly to think he was dangerous. Her trust inhibited him, it protected her more than fear could ever do.

It was a small but genteel end-of-terrace house next door to a school. The children were having their afternoon break, careering around the playground, yelling raucous abuse at one another. Dolly tapped on the door, and when no one answered, used her latchkey.

Inside it was full of pretend-poverty. The furniture was hand-me-down but good quality. The floor was covered with well-worn Wilton, not cheap lino. There were fresh flowers in a vase, and a pedigree cat, and the curtains had been made by a seamstress.

"Would you like to start the fire and make some tea?" said Dolly. "No, I need the matches first to light the water heater. I'll throw them down to you."

"Let me do it," said Jack, but she insisted she knew how and before long there was a roar from above as the gas ignited, and she tossed the matchbox at him before shutting herself in the bathroom.

The fire was already made up in the grate. Jack put a match to the newspapers and watched them catch. It seemed to sum up the ephemeral, inflammatory nature of his craft. Then he put the kettle on and found two bone china cups with matching teapot. He wondered if Clara had bought these items specially, like a child decorating a doll's house, or whether they were simply Curzon Street surplus. He found the nuances of quality difficult to gauge without a price ticket to guide him. He had spent more than he needed to have done on his clothes, for precisely that reason. He had wanted a bit of class, however invisible, and had been willing to pay for it.

His mind strayed inevitably to Dolly in her bathtub. His fear of frightening her—she was a virgin, after all, a species of which he had absolutely no experience—was marginally less than his fear of having her laugh at him. The coy, step-by-step tactics no doubt appropriate in such circumstances were untried and untested and didn't suit his style. Frustrated women of a certain age liked the direct approach, and had Dolly been one of that eager breed, he could simply have marched into the bathroom, lifted her dripping from the tub, and got on with it, knowing her protests were purely a matter of form, to kid herself rather than him. But Dolly, damnit, was a Nice Girl, saving herself for her wedding night, an event that was scheduled for March 23, so that every day wasted would be time irretrievably lost. He went upstairs and stood outside the bathroom, seeking inspiration. She was singing something in Spanish, and after a few minutes he heard an Archimedes-size splash as she got out of the water.

"Dolly," he called through the door. "Don't run the water away. I'd like to have a bath too."

"Don't be silly," she shouted back. "The water heats up as it goes over the jets. I can run you another one straightaway."

"Not unless you let me pay for it."

She opened the door a fraction, releasing a puff of warm steam into the chilly hallway. She was wearing a pale blue chenille dressing gown, presumably Clara's, which was too small for her.

"I've got no idea how much hot water costs," she said.

"Neither have I, so I'll use yours, thanks," said Jack, pushing past her. He sat on the edge of the bath in front of the taps, guarding the plug, and set about removing his shoes and socks.

"You're not serious?"

"If you had to live in a place with no hot water you'd know I was serious. You're embarrassing me by making such a fuss. No one likes to admit they hardly ever have a bath. Can I trouble you for a hanger?"

He handed her his jacket and slipped off his suspenders. She picked up her pile of clothes and fled, and a moment later an arm appeared around the door with a hanger, and he put his trousers over it and it disappeared again.

There was a jar of bath salts on a shelf and Dolly had used them liberally. He would smell rather sweeter than he had intended, but no matter. He got into the tub and lay back and looked sadly at the huge, wasted erection that poked up above the surface of the water, mocking him, and wondered whether, if Dolly could see it, she would have the slightest idea what it was for. He soaped his hands and did what was necessary, and afterward he lay backward with his knees in the air, burying his face in the water, holding his breath to make his baptism last as long as possible. Then he sat up and washed himself all over for the second time in two days. Little bits of her shorn locks clung to the side of the tub and he picked them off and dropped them back into the water and imagined burying his fingers in the dark curly mop she hid between her legs, and then he felt himself swelling again and cursed her and let all the water out and ran in the cold like a regular boy scout until he was shriveled, shriven.

He used her damp towel and called for his suit, which was produced instantly by a disembodied arm, almost as if she had been skulking outside ready with it.

When he rejoined her in the sitting room she was presiding primly over the tea tray. Her face was very red.

"I wish you hadn't done that," she said. "The water must have been disgusting."

"Hardly. I bet you have two baths a day at least."

"That's not the point."

"The way I was brought up, we all used the same water. A tub once a week in front of the fire, Dad first, then us kids. The water was as black as ink by the end. Revolting, isn't it, the way some people live?"

"Don't. Don't do that to me. I don't deserve it."

"Don't do what?"

"Throw your class in my face. Besides, you only took a bath to make me feel uncomfortable. It's not as if it was necessary."

"It was to me. And not because I was dirty, either. And not just to make you feel uncomfortable, even though I knew you would."

"What then?"

"It was the nearest I could get to you, that's all. It was a physical thing. It was the nicest bath I've ever had, with bits of you floating about in it. I could have done without the bath salts, though. They spoiled the taste."

"Stop it." She shoved a plate at him. "Have a biscuit."

He selected a ginger nut and dipped it into his tea. She immediately did the same, as if to legitimize his lack of manners. A semicircle of biscuit broke off and sank, and she started fishing around for it with her spoon.

"You disapprove of me quite a lot, don't you?" said Jack, goading her. "Why don't you say so? It's condescending to spare my feelings. I bet you'd have told me my fortune long ago if we'd met at some ritzy party."

"Not at all. I'm very polite to everyone."

"Don't be polite with me," said Jack.

"You'd rather I was rude to you?"

"It would be a start."

"A start to what?"

Jack took hold of her hand, extracted her half-finished biscuit and replaced it with his own. Then he began eating and gesturing at her to do the same. She looked at the biscuit uncertainly and then at him, trying to hide her distaste.

"It won't bite," he said.

"Not like you," said Dolly. "You bite, I'll bet." And she illustrated her words with a defiant demonstration, like a child executing a dare. "There," she said. "What was that supposed to prove?"

"That you'll do things you don't want to do, rather than give offense. Poor Jack, if I don't eat this revolting soggy biscuit he'll think I'm afraid of catching something. I mustn't hurt his feelings, because he's so poor."

"Don't be ridiculous."

"So you'd have nothing to lose by kissing me, because that biscuit was simply crawling with genuine lower-class germs. Millions of them. Do you kiss your fiancé?"

"Naturally. And only him, thank you very much."

"You mean, you've never kissed anyone else?"

"Well . . . no."

"What a waste," said Jack. "You're as mean as your father, aren't you? Except that you're soft on beggars. If I begged and

begged, you'd give in, wouldn't you? You like to patronize people,
to feel you're doing them a favor. You'd kiss me soon enough if you
felt sorry enough for me.''

"That isn't true!'' She stood up, angry now.

"Then don't make me beg. Do it anyway, just to prove me
wrong.''

He pulled her down onto his lap, knowing now that he had preempted her protests. She had a crumb in the corner of her mouth
and he pushed it back between her closed lips with a quick, lizard-
like movement of his tongue and then he pulled his head back and
waited while she stared at him, fuming, cornered.

"You're frightened to kiss me,'' he taunted smugly. "You do
scare easy after all. What exactly are you frightened of, Dolly?''

"I'm not frightened. Oh for goodness' sake. What a silly fuss
about nothing.''

She pressed her mouth purposefully against his, as if determined
to retain the initiative, and he willed himself not to respond. She
pressed a bit harder and parted her lips just a fraction, but he jerked
his head backward, thwarting her.

"What's the matter?'' she said, rattled now. "I'm kissing you,
aren't I?''

"Not so I'd notice,'' said Jack, letting go of her. "You're not
much good at it, are you? Oh well, thanks anyway. And for the
bath. And for the biscuits.''

He looked around vaguely for his coat.

"I think you're very rude,'' said Dolly, very pink now. And then,
with angry curiosity, "What do you mean, I'm not much good at
it?''

"Oh, it's not something you can explain in words. I'd have to
show you, but I'd better not, seeing as you're so green.''

She hated that, he could tell. She wore her pride very close to
the surface, he knew her weak spot now.

"I'm sorry, Dolly,'' he went on with feigned remorse. "I didn't
realize you were such an innocent, being engaged and all. If I had
I wouldn't have been so forward. My mistake. I was forgetting
you'd been in a convent. You're quite right to save yourself for your
husband. I'm sorry I tried to seduce you. Will you forgive me?''

But she treated this false apology with the contempt it deserved,
threw back her head in a terribly Spanish way and said, "Suppose
you show me, then.''

She stood very straight, stiff as a board, as if waiting to be shot.
Jack couldn't bear it any longer. For the first time, here was a

woman who knew less than he, who knew nothing beyond what he would teach her. And having spent all his life feeling ignorant, learning avidly, greedy for any kind of knowledge, the sense of superior wisdom was alien, intoxicating. He kissed her, hesitantly at first, and then impatiently, unable to maintain his unfamiliar, pedagogic role, rushing her, devouring her, using her mouth as a shallow substitute for what he really wanted, making no allowances, asking too much of her, getting it.

Her response was passionately naïve, she simply imitated what he did with devastating accuracy, as innocently as a child repeating swear words. Only when he tried to touch her did she balk at reciprocation, pushing his hand away. He suppressed a wave of irritation. He was huge again, painfully so, he was not used to restraining himself, he had no experience of being refused.

"Please, Dolly," he said, "I promise I won't hurt you. I promise."

She relaxed again and he carried on kissing her and then he tried again to unbutton her blouse, and she swatted his hand away again.

"No," she said. "Don't touch me there."

"Why not?"

"Because I don't want to have a baby, that's why."

"You can't get a baby from me touching you there."

She wriggled free.

"Thank you," she said, suddenly all polite again, "for showing me. I did ask you to, after all. But I only meant for you to kiss me, nothing else."

Jack grabbed hold of her hand.

"Nothing else?" he said. "Nothing else? It doesn't work that way, Dolly. There's always something *else.*"

He made her feel the something else and she tried to pull away and he wouldn't let her.

"I only kissed you," said Jack. "This is what *you* did to me. Don't talk to me about *nothing else.*"

He unbuttoned his fly, pushed her hand roughly inside it and held it there, cursing himself for a fool, anticipating her horror. But this time she didn't resist, robbing him of control, succumbing to her own curiosity rather than to his will. There was no lust in the cool, exploring fingers, just fascination, it was as if he had shown her some helpless suffering animal, a hamster or a pet mouse, that aroused a natural, tactile sympathy. He closed his hand around hers and guided it, cursing the earlier self-administered relief that would make this second monster harder to subdue, dreading the moment she would pull away, savoring each delicious second as if it were the last.

"That's right," he said. "Keep doing that. Please, Dolly."

She continued to caress the poor distressed creature, inexpertly but sympathetically, trying to soothe its anguish, making it worse. And yet it seemed a shame to enlighten her, to replace her simple, fumbling instincts with the ability to do what any whore could do, what he could have done better by himself. Better to enjoy the exquisite agony of being teased, titillated, tortured, than to reduce magic to mere manipulation. Her very ignorance was bliss.

But then he heard a key in the latch, and Dolly let go abruptly and clapped her hand to her mouth in horror. "Oh my God," she spluttered. "There's Edmund."

And she giggled, the little minx, leaving him to rearrange himself hastily while she ran out into the hall to great her beloved cousin.

She kept him talking out there for a moment, twittering about her visit to the hairdresser as if to delay his entrance and then breezed back in with the sunny innocence of a born dissembler.

"Edmund Townsend, Jack Austin," she sang out brightly.

"Jack," said Edmund, grasping his hand, and then, with barely perceptible irony, "Dolly's told me so much about you."

"I was about to say the same to you," said Jack, disarmed. Edmund was not quite what he had expected. His mind had fused Dolly's hero worship and Clara's infidelity to produce an image of an upper-class twit with the temperament of a rather battered teddy bear. But there was a physical forcefulness about him, a natural authority, combined with that elusive, intangible quality popularly called charm. Reluctantly, Jack liked him on sight.

"I daresay. Dolly's the world's worst chatterbox. She makes people sick to death of each other before they've even met, not that she ever says a bad word about anyone."

Dolly made a face and ran to brew fresh tea. Edmund flopped into an armchair and gestured at Jack to sit down.

"Actually, it's time I was off," said Jack, and then, on a calculated impulse, "Dolly was kind enough to make free with your hot water. I've just had a bath at your expense. I hope you don't mind. I don't have a bathroom where I live."

"Don't mention it," said Edmund, stuffing his pipe. "I thought I could smell Chanel."

"Er . . . Dolly had a bath too," said Jack, looking Edmund straight in the eye. "She'd been to the hairdresser and was feeling itchy."

"Yes," said Edmund. "Pity, that. Such beautiful hair. The fiancé will be devastated."

"She's told me all about him as well."

"I don't doubt it. Dolly has a knack of making all the men in her life rather jealous of each other, don't you agree?"

"Not half," said Jack. "Though I must be about as far down the pecking order as you are up it."

"We're first cousins, unfortunately," said Edmund, "or perhaps I should say, fortunately. She's a lovely girl."

He gave Jack an unequivocal look.

"The sooner she's safely married the better, eh?" said Jack.

"She seems to think so," said Edmund dryly. "She's very young. Clara showed me your piece in *Red Rag*. I enjoyed it. Made a change from their usual sermons, anyway. At least you can write."

"Thanks," said Jack. "They've given me more work since then. 'Course, they don't pay much."

Edmund looked appraisingly at Jack's stiff new clothes and raised a quizzical eyebrow, leaving the question unspoken but implicit.

"But I've come into a bit of money lately," continued Jack, "so I can manage for a bit. I'm not after Dolly's if that's what you're thinking. She told me you were bothered."

"Don't take it personally. I'm very glad she arranged for us to meet. Better the devil you know."

So he wasn't a fool, after all. For whatever reason he put up with Clara, it wasn't because he was a fool.

"More biscuits, Jack?" said Dolly archly, returning with a tray. There was a new insolence about her manner that pleased and irritated him. "*Half* a biscuit, perhaps?" She snapped one in two.

"No thanks. I must be going." he turned to Edmund. "Thanks again for the bath." He looked defiantly at Dolly, who had the grace to go slightly pink. Edmund gave her a sharp look.

"Anytime, old man," said Edmund casually, lighting up. "Come around again, for a bath and a meal. Clara's not a bad cook. Dolly can fix up a date to suit us all."

"Oh. I wouldn't want to put Clara to any trouble. I know how busy she is."

"She likes going to trouble. I warn you, we'll be made to wash up afterward. Clara is very emancipated."

"I'm used to washing up," said Jack.

"That's what worries me. I'd hate to find myself cited as a fellow-exploitee in some future exposé. You have what it takes to be a dangerous enemy, Jack. Please take that as a guarded compliment.''

"I'm not a bad friend, either, when I've got a mind," said Jack. "Good-bye, then. Good-bye, Dolly."

And she smiled and nodded at him privately, mockingly, as if suddenly aware of a shift in power and sat there like a duchess while Edmund saw him out.

Dolly braced herself for a lecture, but Edmund didn't deliver one. He finished his tea without comment, produced a pile of exercise books from his briefcase, put on his glasses and got on with his work while she cleared away the tea things and went to clean the bath, only to find that Jack had already done a meticulous job. He had even polished it dry and put the wet towel in the linen basket.

"I'll fix up a time with Clara, then," she said, kissing the top of Edmund's head as he bent over his books, red pencil poised.

"Yes, do," said Edmund. And then, sharply. "That's a very clever young man, Dolly."

"Is that meant to be a warning?"

"Of course. I won't insult you by spelling it out. Talk to Clara, won't you?"

"Don't fret," said Dolly gaily, putting on her coat. "I brought him here to meet you so you wouldn't fret."

"Well, I'm fretting more than ever. Go home now, I've work to do."

She missed her stop, forgetting to change trains at Paddington and daydreaming all the way to Hammersmith, where she raced across the bridge and hopped breathlessly onto a train going the opposite way. She felt exhilarated, mischievous, wicked, assembling all the half-understood fragments in line with her newfound knowledge, rereading Lorenzo's last letter in her mind, translating the clumsy words into something enticingly real.

There had been a constant admonition in Lorenzo's kisses, a reverent restraint, they had been rationed, brief, full of procrastination. She had felt like an impatient child demanding a treat, bought off with promises, made to feel greedy. Lorenzo set great store by waiting. He was a perfect gentleman, he respected her. He had been bolder in word than ever he had in deed, but Jack was right, there were some things words were no good for. He should have shown her, not left it to another man to do so. Why hadn't he shown her?

It was true, she had been a little bit frightened of Jack, obscurely, intuitively so. His words rang in her ears. "I only kissed you, this is what *you* did to me," and she was filled again with an unfamiliar, heady sense of power. It was almost as if their roles had been reversed, as if he had betrayed a fear greater than her own.

She ought not to see him again. She ought not to kiss him again, given what it did to him, and it had done something similar to her, invisibly so, she could still feel it like an insistent, throbbing ache that sent shooting tremors right down to her feet. Lorenzo would be hurt to know what she had done, but then he didn't know, so how could he be hurt? Flora did similar things, she was sure. Flora had dropped several mocking hints about the things she did, challenging her to ask for details, and Dolly had always changed the subject, ashamed to admit her ignorance. In fact, all English girls probably did as much and more, it was normal and harmless as long as you didn't get a baby, and there was no question but that she wouldn't let him do *that* to her. *That* was sacred, that was what Flora meant by doing "everything but." Everything but. As long as she remembered the but, and as long as Lorenzo didn't know, and wasn't hurt, there would be no harm in it.

But that night, the half-fled throbbing reasserted itself and she quelled it as instinctively as an itch, and finally recognized temptation.

The mood in the garrison had reached fever pitch. Lorenzo started as he heard a voice in his ear.

"You're still with us, are you not, Montanis?"

The words were crackling with conspiracy. Lorenzo nodded, heart beating wildly.

"It could be any day now," murmured his fellow lieutenant. "But we must wait for the sign. There are to be risings all over the country. We must act simultaneously, to be sure of victory."

The moment he had longed for, at last. Any day now, a left-wing military coup would finally depose both the monarchy and its ministers, and pave the way for a new republic. Discontent among junior officers had reached boiling point; ill-paid, bored and frustrated, they were ripe for revolt and eager for the chance to overthrow the old guard who kept a stranglehold both on the country and the Army itself.

"The men are bound to side with us, and the NCOs," continued his comrade. "The senior officers will be well outnumbered, they are certain to surrender. If they resist, we will kill them."

Lorenzo nodded. He had never killed before, never, thank God, been called upon to help the Civil Guard crush some ill-armed peasant revolt, the only active service most soldiers ever saw. He could hit a target with unerring accuracy, he was trained to kill, and yet killing had always been an abstract concept, a technical exercise. He was a marksman, not a murderer. Much as he hated his commanding officer, a corrupt, diehard right-winger, the thought of shooting him appalled him. But of course, he wouldn't have to shoot him. That would be the privilege of one of the ring-leaders. With luck, he wouldn't have to shoot anyone. With luck, it would be over quickly.

He waited anxiously for the sign. Mutiny was in the air, making it thick, making him short of breath. Soon there would be an end to dictators and monarchs, a new era of justice and freedom would begin. All the misery of Spain cried out for relief. The Army would be midwife to democracy and set the laboring people free . . .

Dolores would be glad. Dolores would be proud that he had struck a blow for liberty and equality. No longer would the likes of Don Felipe treat workers like serfs and grow rich on human suffer- ing. The land would be redistributed, starvation and poverty would be a thing of the past. Best of all, the Army would be rid of its top- heavy bureaucracy, promotion would be based on merit, not family connections, no longer would he have to resort to part-time book- keeping to supplement his miserable pay. He would be able to support Dolores in comfort, and his aging, impoverished father. Suddenly all things seemed possible . . .

His optimism was short-lived. Within hours he was to hear the terrible news that the garrison at Jaca had lost patience and revolted prematurely, with disastrous results. The young officers who had led the rising had been shot, and the advantage of surprise had been irretrievably lost. The rebellion would have to be abandoned; it would be suicidal to proceed.

Lorenzo took it harder than most. Somehow it seemed like an omen, a denial of all his most personal and precious dreams.

"We can't give up now," he protested. "If we act together, surely we can still win."

"Caution, my friend," admonished his fellow conspirators. "Better that we live to fight another day. And our comrades have not died in vain. Already there are calls for strikes and demonstra- tions in protest against their murder. Public opinion is now firmly against the king, there will have to be elections. And if all else fails, our time will come again."

But when? thought Lorenzo. Hope was like wine, it dulled the mind. It was despair that bred determination, not hope. It was despair, not hope, that hardened his resolve to prove himself. In a few more months, he would strike his own blow against oppression, he would make Dolores his wife. An act not just of love, but of revenge.

"I hear I'm expected to cook for you," said Clara, briskly repairing her lipstick. Jack had been waiting for her to bring up the subject.

He straightened his tie in a spare corner of the dressing-table mirror. It was an oddly matrimonial scenario. The tone of her voice was perfectly civil, perhaps the heating had made her indolent as well. Their play-acting had acquired the ease of familiarity, her stage fright a thing of the past, and afterward she had become abruptly normal, conversational even.

"I hear you're a very good cook."

"Rubbish. Edmund is very easily pleased. He's not fussy, obviously."

"You're a bitch to do this to him. What if he finds out?"

"Don't worry about it. He won't challenge you to pistols at dawn. He's a pacifist. Turns the other cheek better than any Christian."

"I've found a new flat in Bayswater," said Jack, getting down to business. "It's eighteen-and-six a week. They want a month's rent in advance and a deposit on fixtures and fittings and a reference."

"Mmm. Well, if you must deflower Dolly I'd rather you didn't do it in our house. Edmund would feel horribly compromised. He's in love with her himself, of course, incestuously or not."

"You're jealous."

"Naturally. Of her, not of you. You can do what you like with her as far as I'm concerned. I tried to give her the benefit of some sisterly advice but the poor child didn't understand a word I said. You should find it almost too easy. She's fairly bursting with youthful sensuality, isn't she? Well-covered as well. I daresay you could do with a bit of variety."

"Shut up," said Jack coldly, hating her. "She's only a kid. I can get sex anytime I like without seducing Dolly. I like her, that's all."

Clara emitted a hoot of hollow laughter.

"Very *sincerely* put. How much do you need?"

Jack helped himself from her handbag as instructed. It was stuffed with pamphlets headed "Free Medical Care Now!" and he pulled them out to find her purse, dislodging a small booklet.

"What's this?"

"A prospectus. I thought it was high time I got a proper job. One that wouldn't do anyone else out of a living."

"Nursing? That won't leave you much spare time for politics."

"Perhaps the by-election result has convinced me that my services are expendable."

Jack helped himself to the exact amount he had asked for.

"What does Edmund think about it? You'd have to live in, wouldn't you?"

"Oh, absolutely. He'd hardly ever see me. I haven't said anything to him yet, let's wait and see if they deign to accept me first. But he won't try to stop me, it's not his way. And at least it'll give him a chance to meet somebody else."

"And if he did, wouldn't you be jealous?"

"Of course I would. I love him, in case you didn't realize. I know I'm bad for him, that's why I'm doing it. I know myself better than you think. Nursing's ugly work, it should suit me. I'm not afraid of blood."

"I want to do a piece on hospitals," said Jack. "The history of two patients in need of identical treatment, one on the dole and the other a nob. Can you get me some introductions?"

"I'll send you a couple with the reference for your new landlord," said Clara, brightening. "Harry's bragging about you, you know. Setting himself up as some kind of Svengali. Watch out. He'll take all the credit, you'll get all the blame."

"He's a publisher." Jack shrugged.

"Of a tin-pot journal nobody reads."

"They will, though," said Jack. "They will."

"What are you doing for Christmas, Jack?" asked Edmund, handing him a glass of sherry. Clara and Dolores were crashing about in the kitchen, there was an air of imminent disaster about the catering. "Visiting family?"

"No fear," said Jack. "There are enough of them not to notice one missing. I'm the oldest of ten. Could be eleven by now."

"But you're surely not going to spend the day alone?"

Edmund adored Christmas, loved choosing gifts and finding sixpences in the pudding and singing carols, never mind about the words, the tunes were splendid. A large tree dwarfed the room. Clara had thought it frivolous, but had decorated it nonetheless to please him.

"No. I'm going alone to a soup kitchen down by the Embankment. For a story, you know."

"But that won't take all day, surely? I wish you'd join us, if you've nothing better to do. Us being Clara, my parents, sister and Dolly. People will be dropping in and out all the time."

"Well . . . thanks. I might just take you up on it."

Clara and Dolly appeared in tandem. There was a faint smell of burning.

"Shouldn't be long," said Dolly cheerfully, accepting a glass of sherry. Edmund poured out some mineral water for Clara. There was an awkward silence. Edmund seemed much less at his ease with Clara in the room, she changed its chemical composition like some sinister catalyst. Apart from anything else, Jack felt wretchedly overdressed in his suit. Edmund was in his shirtsleeves and pullover, sporting a pair of well-worn tweeds, and the girls were both in workaday dressed underneath their aprons. He had assumed such people always dressed for dinner, had worried over his lack of more formal attire. He tried to catch Dolly's eye and failed, and caught Clara's instead and wished again he hadn't come.

"I've just suggested that Jack join the family gathering on Christmas Day," said Edmund. "The more the merrier."

"I thought you were spending the day down at the Embankment," said Clara.

"Some of it," said Jack, draining his glass, still looking at Dolly.

"We're going to a party in the evening," said Dolly suddenly, addressing her feet. "You could always escort me if you've nothing better to do."

"I don't dance," said Jack categorically.

"You don't have to dance."

"All right then."

And then she smiled, almost imperceptibly, a smile that excluded Edmund and Clara, a smile smiled purely for him.

"Can I take my jacket and tie off?" said Jack. He felt damp all over, hot and cold at once. "I feel like a stuffed shirt."

"Please make yourself at home. Jack will need a dinner jacket for the Prendergast do, Dolly."

"Right," said Jack, grateful for the tip-off. "I'll rent one."

"That'll set you back a few bob," said Clara slyly.

"I'll manage. I had a check from Martindale this morning. Got to open a bank account before I can cash it, though. It's crossed."

"You can endorse it over to me if you like," said Edmund. "But I haven't got any cash on me at the moment. Do you have any cash, Clara?"

Clara got up, fetched her handbag, and handed it to Jack, her lip curling in amusement.

"Help yourself," she said.

"That's all right," said Jack, coloring. "Got to have a bank account sooner or later. It doesn't feel like money, though. I'm used to being paid in cash."

"Of course," clucked Clara, snapping her bag shut again. "That's typical of Harry, of course. He doesn't concern himself with practicalities."

"Talking of which, how much longer, Clara? Our guest is faint from lack of nourishment."

"I'm sorry, Jack," said Clara, feigning mortification. "I'm afraid I'm no one's idea of a housewife. My upbringing, you know. Being domestic has to be learned at one's mother's knee. The Jesuit approach."

"Be fair, Clara," remonstrated Edmund with rather forced joviality. "I did offer to cook it myself."

"You see? Pathetic, isn't it, the way we play at keeping house. Much better for us all to have gone out to the Empire Court. More *honest* anyway."

"Shall I go and have a look at the meat?" volunteered Dolly. "The book said to baste it."

She got up.

"I'll help you," said Jack, following her. "Give Clara a rest."

He closed the door behind them.

"There goes a lad who knows all about basting meat," observed Clara. "They make a delightful couple, don't they?"

"Don't start bitching, Clara. If Dolly's going to have a young man while she's here, we ought to make him welcome. He's much more likely to act responsibly if he knows the family."

"Ah, all the frustrated paternal instincts coming out."

"I don't feel parental about Dolly, as you very well know. But at least I have the grace not to flirt with her."

"I wasn't flirting with him. I don't flirt with people."

"Every remark you've made to him has been loaded. Not the words, the way you say them. For God's sake, Clara. Not in front of Dolly. Not in our own house."

"Your house. Not our house. I've got my own house, thank you."

"If you humiliate me tonight, you can go back there. I mean it, Clara."

He said it quietly, unemphatically. The threat would have been a small victory had he spoken in anger, angry threats were nothing but pleas in disguise. But why should Edmund stoop to pleading when he had all the power?

She walked over to where he sat and knelt down at his feet and put her head on his lap, saying nothing, while he stroked her hair, and they were still locked in this unlikely tableau when Jack and Dolly returned, bearing soup plates. Dolly looked pleased and Jack curious, and for the rest of the evening Clara behaved like a lamb.

"I'm sorry about the meat," said Dolly yet again as soon as they were inside the cab. The meat had indeed been a disaster, burned to a frazzle on the outside and raw within. Clara had blamed the oven and Dolly the recipe and Edmund the butcher, Jack alone had managed to eat it, oblivious to its flavor or texture, his mouth still full of Dolly. No half measures with Dolly, no going back to the beginning. They had carried on exactly where they had left off, no messing around, and then she had briskly checked to see whether she had produced the desired effect and laughed in delight and left him blushing.

"Forget about the meat," he said. "Listen, what time are they expecting you home?"

"If you're about to invite me back to your digs, the answer's no. But I don't mind you kissing me again."

"You know what you are? You're nothing but a rotten little tease. It's easy for you to stop, isn't it? It's just a game for you. You're like a kid, playing with a new toy. Be careful, Dolly. It's more dangerous than you think. Don't trust me, will you? I'm telling you now not to trust me, so you can't say I didn't warn you."

Her eyes sparkled in the darkness, watching him, waiting. She felt safe in a taxi, he ought to take advantage of that. And so he did. Ignoring his own need, he concentrated on leaving her in the same state as she had left him, and after a bit of token hand slapping she gave him an inch and he took a mile, or rather less, leaving her just short of full measure, leaving her in agony, teaching her a lesson, enjoying her wide-eyed confusion as he tipped her out of the cab at Lansdowne Gardens and blew her a mocking kiss and drove on in style to Bayswater.

Flora was still up, lounging over cocoa and a romantic novel in the living room.

"*Buenas tardes*," she called as Dolly crept up the stairs. "There's still come cocoa in the thermos. Don't go rushing off. I've got some news."

Dolly hesitated. She was simply dying to shut herself in her room and put an end to her discomfort. He had done it deliberately. And she had let him. She was angrier with herself than with him.

"I'm terribly tired, Flo."

"Don't be a bore. Look."

She held out her hand and showed off her ring.

"Archie proposed!"

"Oh, Flora, congratulations!" Dolly retraced her steps and gave her cousin a hug. "I'm so pleased for you."

"You missed the champagne. We came back early to tell the parents. Daddy's terrified at what the wedding will cost, poor lamb. Archie has simply shoals of relations. Think of all the presents! I'm going out tomorrow with Mummy to make a list. Come and sit down."

Flora regaled her for the best part of an hour with talk of brides-maids and wedding breakfasts and flowers and honeymoons, all the things that Dolly's forced elopement would deny her. It would take at least six months, Flora declared, to make all the preparations. She would be a June bride.

"Can I ask you something?" blurted out Dolly, unable to bear it any longer. "Now that you're engaged, will it still be . . . everything *but?* For the next six months?"

"Why do you ask?" said Flora, picking up the tremor in her voice, fascinated. The question was so untypical of Dolly. Dolly was such a funny little prude.

"Well . . . it must be difficult, mustn't it, not . . . not giving in?"

"Difficult for Archie, perhaps. That's the whole point. You don't think he'd be marrying me if I'd let him go the whole way, do you? Besides, I'm wearing white. What a funny question."

"But aren't you just *dying* to know what it's like? I mean Lorenzo and I are miles and miles apart, which makes it easier, in a way, but you'll be seeing Archie every day. I don't know that I could bear to see someone I loved every day for six months and not . . . not . . ." She faltered, unsure of her vocabulary.

"Good heavens. One gets pestered enough once one's married, by all accounts. Plenty of time for all that. Besides, Archie re-spects me. He knows just how far he's allowed to go. Why are you asking me all this? You're usually so coy."

"Oh . . . I'm just missing Lorenzo, you know."

"That's entirely your own fault. I've stood on my head trying to introduce you to all the eligible men I know. You could have come out with us tonight and met some interesting new people instead of dining with Edmund and Clara in their dreary little hovel. You *are* coming to Archie's Christmas party, aren't you, because now it's going to be our engagement party as well.''

"Oh yes. In fact, I shall have an escort. One of Clara's friends. I . . . met him there tonight.''

"Good Lord. Well, what's he like? If he's one of Clara's friends he must be perfectly dreadful.''

"He's not perfectly dreadful. He doesn't have any friends or family in London and would have spent Christmas Day all on his own, so Edmund thought it would be a nice gesture to include him in everything. He's quite ordinary-looking. I don't suppose you'll like him. He's very intelligent.''

"Thanks very much.''

"I didn't mean it like that. I meant—''

"Never mind.'' Flora yawned luxuriously. "Look at the time. I shall sleep like a top tonight. Are you coming up?''

"I think I'll sit for a bit, thanks,'' said Dolly. "I'm still wide awake. I think I'll write a letter to Lorenzo.''

And she did, pouring out everything she was feeling, misdirecting it, legitimizing her lapse, convincing herself that Jack was nothing but a surrogate, a scavenger, an embezzler. And believing it made her feel forewarned, if not forearmed.

Lorenzo's new posting was the best Christmas present he could have hoped for. He was not the only young officer to receive sudden marching orders—thanks to the failed coup, immediate steps had been taken to thwart further conspiracy, and an inordinately high number of junior officers found themselves suddenly cut off from their former associates and sent to opposite sides of the country in a nationwide game of tactical military chairs.

Lorenzo was one of the lucky ones; fortuitously he had got exactly what he wanted. Zaragoza, at the foothills of the Pyrenees, was a long, long way from Badajoz. Don Felipe's tentacles surely did not stretch that far, and city life would be more congenial for Dolores than his present remote outpost. It seemed almost too good to be true, there had to be a catch . . .

His leave. This unexpected move might mean a change in the date, or the length, of his leave. He hoped it would be brought forward rather than put back. Dolores would be devasted if their wedding plans had to be deferred; best not to worry her, or raise her hopes, until he knew for certain. She seemed to long for the date of their union even more intensely than he. He knew her latest letter by heart, it had leapt off the page, assaulting him with its vigor, its promise, its frankness. It was an almost improper letter for a young girl to have written, and yet what kind of man would he be to carp at such protestations of devotion, such unalloyed impatience to be his? From the moment she had left for England, he had feared usurpment, suffered imagined betrayal. He felt ashamed of his lack of faith in her. She was the kind of woman who could only love one man, who would love that man for life or not at all.

"I don't believe it. It's Jack Austin, isn't it? Jack!"

A big, shabby man abandoned his place in the soup line and hailed Jack like a long-lost friend.

"Billie Grant! What brings you down these parts?"

"Same as what brought you. No work, what else? They're wondering if you're dead, your ma and pa, asked me to look out for you. Well, well, well. You're not here for soup, that's for sure. Very posh."

"I've been lucky," said Jack shortly, the fleeting feeling of camaraderie giving way to vexation. He had no wish to explain himself to someone who had known him all his life. "And they know very well I'm not dead. I've sent them something most weeks, not that I expected any thanks for it."

"Without an address. You ma's upset. She was hoping you might come home for Christmas."

"Don't break my heart, will you. They never had no time for me when I was at home. I told them straight I'd not be back. She'd probably had a few."

"Talking of which," said Billie, "you look like a bloke who could stand a mate a round or two."

"I can't stay," said Jack. "Got another job after this one."

"Job? What, with the Salvation Army?"

"No, I'm a journalist," said Jack, feeling ridiculous. "You can tell them that if you like. Not what my dad would call man's work. Here, have a few on me."

"No thanks, lad. I can manage. But if you hear of any work, tip me off. I come here most days."

"For Christ's sake," said Jack, irritated, stuffing the money into Billie's pocket. "Don't come over all proud and poor on me. I can afford it."

"I'll pay you back," said Billie. "Soon as I get work."

"With interest," said Jack. "Merry Christmas then."

"Merry Christmas!" bellowed Billie, beaming, meaning it, poor bastard.

Jack quickened his step, eager to get away. He liked to feel anonymous on a job, his fluency depended on it. And now he would write a lousy, stilted, hackneyed piece, tainted with Billie's unspoken accusation that he had sold out, crossed the lines, betrayed his origins. He should have flung his arm around him and filled him up with beer and waxed nostalgic for the grime, he should have impressed him with talk of socialism and *Red Rag* to prove he was still working-class at heart. And yet such hypocrisy stuck in his craw. Why dress ambition up as a vocation? His only vocation was to succeed, he exploited the Billies of this world with every word he wrote. The day he forgot that he would become soft, self-congratulatory, useless, he might as well chuck his typewriter in the river and take over the soup ladle instead. He felt contaminated, compromised, exposed, diminished. The strains of cheerful carols rang in his ears. Peace on earth, goodwill to all men Humbug.

"Time to open the presents!" announced Edmund.

"Not until we've pulled our poppers!" protested Dolly. She was flushed and very mildly tiddly. She had barely touched her Christmas dinner, a fact that was palpably significant to Edmund, although Jack, unused to her prodigious appetite, had failed to note it.

They had seated him opposite her, between Clara and Flora. Clara had pointedly ignored him throughout the meal, engrossed in conversation with Edmund's father, whose sister had been a nurse in the Great War. His approval of her new choice of career was entirely genuine, as well as providing a good opportunity to try to make the girl feel accepted. If she persisted in her role as an outsider, Edmund would eventually be lost to the family for good, and Mr. Townsend was inordinately fond of his son, a fact that he concealed assiduously, especially from Edmund. Margaret would have been happier, of course, if Edmund had picked a more affectionate kind of girl, but they had both known their son too well to try to interfere. Edmund seemed to thrive on challenges and appeared to be content; perhaps Clara, like his teaching job, satisfied some inner need known only to himself.

Jack could feel occasional vibrations under the tablecloth as Flora played footsie with Archie Prendergast, whose effete moustache and affected drawl filled him with unadulterated loathing. Dolly had been rather subdued at first, before finally taking pity on him in his isolation and talking to him with her eyes in a way that Jack

feared could be overheard by the entire table. It took him a while
to realize that she wasn't doing it deliberately, it was a speechless
variant of the garrulousness she had not yet learned to control.

The whole question of presents had bothered him, filled him with
a wretched feeling of not knowing the form, of being an outsider.
He had brought flowers for Mrs. Townsend, which had seemed to
go down well, and he had a present for Dolly in his pocket which
he preferred to give her in private. He hoped fervently that no one
gave him anything: it would smack unbearably of kindness and put
him in their debt. Despite Edmund's airy assertion that people would
be dropping in and out all day, he was so far, not counting Archie
and Clara, the only guest.

Still, the atmosphere was relaxed enough, the house smaller and
humbler than he had expected, well below the standards of Curzon
Street. The housekeeper had Christmas off, and Mrs. Townsend
had served the meal herself, with help from Flora, Clara and Dolly.
Jack who had braced himself for butlers and candelabra, was heartily relieved.

"Popper?" offered Dolly, extending her arm across the table.

"Don't pull them sitting down, Dolly dear," remonstrated Mrs.
Townsend. "Something will get knocked over. Stand to one side."

Everyone got up and started tugging madly.

"You're not pulling hard enough," said Dolly. "It won't bang."

Jack yanked suddenly, pulling her against him.

"Do we have to go to this party?" he hissed in her ear. "I've
been invited to another one, and I'd rather take you there instead."

"Of course we have to go. It's to celebrate Flora's engagement.
We can't not go."

"That's a pity. My friend will be very offended. Look, could we
drop in there, afterward, just to show our faces? It's not far, only
Bayswater."

"I didn't know you had any friends. I thought you were a little
boy lost, boohoo."

"There are lots of things you don't know about me. Look, I'll
stand still and you pull, okay?"

Dolly managed to fall over backward in the attempt and had to
be picked up, giggling, by Edmund.

"Dolly, I do believe you're slightly tipsy," said Edmund. "You
should have had some Christmas pudding. It acts like a sponge."

He unfolded the paper hat and crowned her poor shorn locks
with it. Dolly scrabbled on the floor for the trinket. It was a miniature brass bell. Jack bent to pick it up.

"You should wear it around your neck," he said, "to warn folks you're coming." He ting-a-linged it and put it in his pocket.

"Presents!" announced Flora. Jack tried to make himself invisible while the parcels were unwrapped to reveal bottles of perfume and handkerchiefs and ties and books and fountain pens and scarves and bits of china and jewelry galore. It made his own small offering seem meager, paltry, even though it had cost him far more than it seemed to be worth. Something to do with the number of carats, and he had thought it best to buy something small, of good quality, than a larger piece that might look cheap to her.

"Poor Jack," murmured Clara. "Didn't Santa bring you anything? You must have been a naughty boy."

Edmund had bought her a nursing textbook, as if to prove he didn't mind her latest hobbyhorse, although of course he did. She knew he was counting on her not being able to stick it, and was determined to prove him wrong. She had given him a John Donne first edition. She had written something on the flyleaf, and Jack had tried to sneak a glimpse at it, but Edmund had turned the page over instantly, looking pleased as punch.

"Still," continued Clara, "perhaps Dolly will feel sorry for you."

Dolly was in fact in tears, hugging her benefactors one by one and sobbing that they had been too, too kind.

"Poor Dolly," clucked Mrs. Townsend, turning to Jack. "Such an emotional child. She misses her family."

"And her fiancé, I suppose," said Jack, fishing.

"*Faute de mieux,*" murmured Edmund, overhearing, and fearing that he had excluded Jack by his remark: "That is, for lack of anything better," and then, to conversationalize his tactless assumption of ignorance, "It's pure infatuation. Entirely circumstantial. And of course he's been labeled forbidden fruit, a grave tactical error, in my view . . ."

He tailed off, having said more than he meant to, aware that these remarks might be taken as covert encouragement, and yet, perhaps, subliminally, he had intended them as such, taking vicarious satisfaction in thwarting his unseen, unacknowledged rival, in half hoping Jack might do what he himself could not.

"Fancy a game of billiards?" he said. "I think they can manage without us for a bit. Flora will want to play charades in a minute. Best escape while we can."

"Thanks," said Jack gratefully. "I'd enjoy that."

* * *

Archie's public school accent was a second-generation acquisition; the Prendergasts were nouveaux riches with the accent on the *nouveau*. Nothing hand-me-down found its way past their door; such antiques as they possessed had been haggled for, not inherited, so that their value was known to the last guinea. Mr. Prendergast was a builder, throwing up mean little semidetached houses in the suburbs while occupying a substantial residence in Wimbledon, built solidly in a bygone age to far higher standards than his own.

Jack, having no appreciation of aristocratic taste, found the Prendergast house a great deal more impressive than Clara's in Curzon Street. The whole of the ground floor had been thrown open for the party, which centered on a huge living room the size of a barn, complete with orchestra and a groaning buffet table manned by waiters as stiff and erect as penguins. The Prendergast motto was never to use a lampshade where a chandelier would do, and every wall was lined with either new, leather-bound, unread books or heavily framed pictures, most of them hunting scenes or costumed portraits, providing a ready-made illusion of ancestry. The vast number of braying guests were evidently Archie's friends; his parents had no doubt been prevailed upon not to show him up by a parade of low-class relations and business associates. There was talk of a honeymoon in Monte Carlo and an architect-designed house in Thames Ditton, the four parents talking stiltedly at one another, repeating themselves endlessly on the limited common ground available while the ''young people enjoyed themselves.''

Jack, who was quite unable to dance and had no intention of learning in public, was forced to stand on the sidelines while Dolly was whisked around the floor by a succession of slick young men-about-town. It annoyed him to see their soft palms spread against her back, their manicured fingers entwined with hers. For someone who claimed to hate social gatherings she appeared to be enjoying herself quite immoderately, and if it was true that she found all Englishmen boring then she was certainly polite enough not to show it.

Jack eavesdropped his way around the house, transcribing remarks into his mental notebook, the snatched, alcohol-loosened fragments revealing that most of those present despised their hosts— for their bogus gentility, for their ostentatious taste, for the way in which old Pa Prenderghastly earned his living, building rabbit hutches for plebs. Jack knew now what had been in Edmund's mind when he had flatly refused to come.

"Clara wouldn't enjoy it," he said simply. "She had enough for one day. I've made my excuses to Flora. It'll give you something to write about, I daresay."

He was a master of understatement, Edmund, thought Jack, full of strong feelings kept rigorously in check, conveyed only through a filter of dry cryptic wit. They had talked of anything but Dolly . . . or rather Jack had talked and Edmund listened. He hadn't meant to talk so much; despite his natural fluency he seldom said anything without an objective in view, he had no habit of idle chat. Jack had never been gregarious, his schoolboy rebelliousness had graduated into brooding unsociability, a stubborn pride in being a misfit, an aggressive need to pick a fight with anyone who dared to challenge his ascetic eschewal of the public bar, his belated pursuit of book learning, his cynical mistrust of the sacred cow of a union. Jack had never had a friend, certainly never felt a positive liking for another man, and it was odd, looking back, that throughout their peaceful game, soothed by the rhythmic clicking of the balls, insulated from the shrieks of laughter from the living room, he had not once felt compromised, not once felt guilty. Twice a week he defiled and abused Clara Neville, for money; made her beg and scream and curse, for money; exploited her sick, sad self-disgust, for money. And he should surely have felt guilty and compromised, because now he knew and liked Edmund, Edmund who loved Clara, God alone knew why. Perhaps he would have felt guilty if he had loved Clara too, and he was glad he did it for money. The money exonerated him, and Clara too, because she didn't love Jack any more than he loved her. She loved Edmund, in her own warped way, he was sure of that now. His contract with Clara was strictly business, nothing more, he saw no reason to go back to being poor just because he liked Edmund. Clara would only do the same with somebody else, and at least she was safe with him, he was sane even if she wasn't, she was better off with him than with some half-crazed fellow pervert. And so Jack refused to feel guilty, at least as far as Clara was concerned. The annoying thing was that Edmund had succeeded, without one direct reference, in making him feel guilty about Dolly.

Of course, Edmund underestimated Dolly. Edmund had no idea of the hot, Spanish temperament that lay beneath that demure, English schoolgirl façade. Whatever happened it would be by her choice, it would be what *she* wanted. There was a reckless streak in her, an innate hedonism, she played life by ear, pleasure came naturally to her. And Jack blessed the nuns who had curbed her joie de vivre, the strict upbringing that had denied her experience, the naïve obsession that had kept her loyal to Lorenzo. It was as if family, schooling and fiancé had conspired together to save her for him, deliver her to him, and afterward she would never be the same again and it would be all his doing, an act as fundamental as life, as irrevocable as death.

No, he would not feel guilty about Dolly. He had warned her not to trust him, so his transparent lie about the party in Bayswater was fair play. He would not feel guilty about Dolly because he would not force her. It was she who compelled him, not the other way around. It was he, Jack, who was possessed, not she, by a desire that transcended the sexual. The sexual part of it was undeniable but incidental. He would never go through all this pantomime just for sex—a grossly overrated pastime in Jack's view, he had always had a certain indifference to it, viewed it as a diversion, not a need, an activity that bypassed the heart, or rather the mind, which for Jack were synonymous. Yes, she had got into his mind, like a good book, affording him more than entertainment, coloring his thoughts, leaving a marker on his memory.

Jack had ordered a cab for eleven o'clock, and at a quarter to he accosted Dolly in midtango and mouthed at her to be ready to leave shortly. She laughed gaily, whether in acceptance or rebuffal he couldn't tell. Edmund's parents had already taken their leave, and the Prendergasts had followed suit soon afterward, retiring upstairs to a chorus of relieved good-nights.

"I must wish Flora and Archie well before we go," said Dolly breathlessly, sliding her arms into the proffered coat.

"I did it for both of us," said Jack. "Come on, the taxi's waiting."

She didn't protest, as if preoccupied with something else, and as soon as they were inside the cab, she said, "Are we really going to Bayswater?"

"Yes."

"Not to Holloway, by any chance?"

"I've moved from Holloway."

"Moved to where? Bayswater, I suppose."

"Of course."

"So there's no party."

"Only in a manner of speaking."

"I ought to insist you take me home."

"If you insist, I will."

He had not meant to tell the truth just yet, but there were occasions when the truth deceived better than lies. The truth could invest the worst of intentions with a wholly spurious integrity. And besides, she had guessed already. Confession disarmed the accuser far more effectively than denial.

"And what do you plan to do when we get there?"

"When we get there? I thought you wanted to go home. I was about to ask the driver to take you home. Would you prefer to go to my place, then?"

"It all depends on what you plan to do when we get there."

"Whatever you want. I'm at your disposal. We won't do anything you don't want to do. That's a promise."

"I don't trust your promises. You warned me not to."

"So I did."

"Well . . . perhaps for half an hour or so. I don't want Christmas to end just yet."

Jack felt in his pocket.

"I got you a present," he said, producing a small box and thrusting it at her.

It was a very simple gold chain, and Jack had threaded it through the wire loop of the little brass bell that had fallen out of the cracker. It jingled tinnily as she picked up the chain and admired it.

"Thank you," she said uncertainly. "But I wish you hadn't. I didn't buy anything for you. That is, I wanted to, but I thought you might be embarrassed. I wish I had now."

"You can buy me something for my birthday instead," said Jack.

"Of course. When is it?"

"In April."

"Oh. I'll be gone by then."

"Then you'd better give me something before you go."

She didn't comment, removing a rope of amber beads from her neck and replacing it with the chain, fastening the clasp unaided.

"I won't ask what you want," she said, "because I already know. I want you to know that I already know. I can't bear for you to think I'm silly and green. I'd rather you thought I was a loose woman. Perhaps I am, letting you do the things you did."

"Everyone does them, Dolly."

"Not when they're engaged to someone else, they don't."

"So what? Is he faithful to you, this fiancé?"

"Faithful? Why yes, of course."

"I bet he's not. No disrespect. It wouldn't make any difference to the way he feels about you, I'm sure. No more than I make any difference to the way you feel about him. I'm not expecting you to love me. It would only matter if you loved me. Then he'd have something to complain about. You don't love me, do you Dolly?''

"No, of course not.'' Her voice trembled.

"Then that's all right then, isn't it? Look, I just wanted you to myself for a little while, that's all. We can talk for a bit, and then I'll take you home . . . don't get upset.''

He hadn't expected tears. He had been prepared for mischief, prevarication, anger even, but not for her to get upset. What on earth had he done to upset her?

"Oh please, Dolly, don't cry. Don't cry. What's the matter?''

He cradled her against him, awkwardly, unable to take advantage of her distress. It was as if she were exercising her power over him in reverse, unmanning him. She sobbed quietly all the way to Bayswater, dabbing away with his handkerchief, removing every last vestige of powder and rouge, leaving her face scrubbed of artifice. But she didn't say what was the matter and he didn't ask her again.

It was a self-contained basement flat, comprising one room, a tiny kitchen-cum-bathroom, and a lavatory. It was poorly furnished and decorated but spotlessly clean, still smelling of soap and bleach. Jack had spent all Christmas Eve on his hands and knees, scrubbing every crevice, and had slept between blankets since moving in so that the brand-new linen sheets he had bought would be still fresh and crisp. Of course, there was no question of that now. Not with Dolly looking so pale and sad and wan. More than anything he needed her vitality, her laughter, her devilment. Her misery was more than he could bear. She sat down on a hard chair and looked around listlessly.

"This isn't too bad,'' she remarked politely. "Is it better than your previous room?''

"A lot better,'' said Jack, and then, almost upbraidingly, giving way to helpless disappointment, "I only moved here because of you. Because I couldn't have taken you to the other place. It was filthy and stank. I wanted somewhere I could bring you to, somewhere we could be private, somewhere where your cousin wouldn't walk in and spoil everything.''

"Oh don't,'' she said through another sob. "Don't. Can't you see, I feel bad enough already? Oh, I wish Lorenzo were here. I wish I were already married. I wish he had seduced me before they sent me away. Then I wouldn't be in this mess. Then I wouldn't want to do things with you.''

''You don't have to do them,'' said Jack desperately, trying to pinpoint just where he had gone wrong, cursing himself for mismanaging her, for triggering a reaction he hadn't foreseen, for thinking her predictable, for being stupid enough to imagine himself in control.

''I'm sorry, Dolly. Look, I wish I'd never brought you here. It was wrong of me. I'll take you home.''

It was nothing to do with scruples, he told himself. Once you got scruples, you were done for. He just didn't want to anymore, that was all. Not yet, not now. After days and nights of wanting nothing else, not yet, not now. And even as he thought it, he knew he was afraid of it, denying scruples in order to obfuscate the real reason, a sudden, paralyzing indecision, a loss of confidence, a fear of failure. It was as if the real Jack had suddenly taken it into his head to unnerve the imposter, to remind him that he only existed at the whim of his creator, that he could be displaced at any time by one weaker and yet stronger than he.

''Take me home?'' echoed Dolly. ''What am I supposed to say now? Yes please? Why must you make it so difficult for me? Why must you make me say I don't want to go? If I wanted to go it would be easy, if I wanted to go I wouldn't be sitting here crying and making a fool of myself. After all it cost me to come here, you're just going to let me go? Well, don't expect me to come back again, damn you!''

She stood up, the rigid dignity of her posture at odds with her wobbling, twitching features as pride and humiliation and fear and desire and guilt and anger fought open battle all over her face. She meant it, about not coming back. No second chance. Not yet, not now, meant never.

''Dolly, I . . .''

''Don't touch me! Take your hands off me!''

''Don't go. Please, please, don't go.''

''Too bloody late!'' shrieked Dolly. The word sounded comical in her mouth. ''I want to go back to how I was. I was happy before I met you. I loved Lorenzo and I was perfectly, perfectly happy. And now . . . and now . . .''

And he thought how incredibly sweet it would be to hear her say ''I love *you*,'' and felt an insane desire to say it first, and didn't say it.

''. . . I don't know anymore. I suppose you think I'm easy, someone you can amuse yourself with for a few weeks, and I'm not easy, I'm not, because you wouldn't believe the number of people who've tried to . . . to take liberties, and I didn't let any of them. I'm a standing joke, you know, a little convent prude. People make fun of me to Flora. And it wasn't just because of Lorenzo, it was because I never *wanted* to before, and I want you to know that!'' And then, almost as if she realized that she had just paid him a huge, if oblique, compliment, she ran abruptly out of steam, finishing lamely with, ''I'd better go now.''

Jack walked over to the door, turned the key in the lock, and put it in his pocket.

''I'm not going to let you,'' he said. ''Not after all that.''

She sat down again limply, as if relieved, still in her coat. Underneath it she was wearing a long, peach-colored dress in some flimsy, shimmering fabric that made different parts of her body catch the light as she danced. He had been dreaming of taking it off all evening and now he was scared to. Locking the door had been an act of faith, a gesture of defiance against fear. Why had he not anticipated fear? Lust was bold, fearless, carefree stuff. Love was full of pitfalls, love was risk.

He took off his dinner jacket, knelt down and lit the gas fire. It was freezing, and she wouldn't be used to the cold. He wished he had thought to buy some brandy, it seemed feeble to offer her tea. Griselda snickered at him from the shadows. Where was the bucket of champagne, the crystal glasses, the flickering candlelight, the baronial hearth? Why did he not speak honeyed words in low, throbbing whispers, mold Dolores's soft curves against his manly chest, bring her to the very brink of ecstasy with fiery, bruising kisses? Failing that, where was the line of glib chat, where was the sexual swagger, where was the self-assurance born of indifference? It was as if he were the shrinking virgin, not she. Perhaps he was a virgin, of sorts, afraid of losing part of himself forever. He put his hands around her neck from behind and tinkled the little bell, tongue-tied. He wanted to tell her she was beautiful, but the word wasn't good enough. She shivered in the aftermath of a sob.

''Sorry to make a scene,'' she muttered, sniffing. ''I said too much, as usual. Yap, yap, yap.''

She put her hand up to his. It was ice-cold. ''Take your coat off,'' said Jack. ''You'll feel warmer.''

She stood up and let him slip it off her shoulders and then, before the moment lapsed again, he felt for the tiny buttons down her back and started to unpick them, holding his breath, waiting for her to stop him. But she sighed in something like resignation, and just stood there patiently while he fumbled endlessly, and at last the dress fell to the floor to reveal not gossamer, lace-trimmed lingerie, not sensuous silk, but an all-enveloping underskirt and a flannel petticoat, both of which, had he but known it, still had embroidered name tapes stitched inside them.

"I feel the cold terribly," she explained, while he fought not to smile. "Don't you?"

"I can't afford to," said Jack, grinning, whisking off shirt and tie to display a Spartan lack of vest. The rented trousers were too big for him around the waist, and rather than hold on to the suspenders he got it over with and took them off, feeling uncharacteristically shy, fully expecting her to laugh at him.

"Do be careful to hang those up properly," fussed Dolly, picking them up off the floor. "They're not yours, remember. Fold them on the crease. Here, let me do it."

Bemused, he let her. He sat on the bed in his underpants, watching her move briskly around the room in her woolly underwear while she hung the suit up carefully and folded her dress over the back of a chair, filling the mean little room with grace and business, hiding her nerves behind a brave display of persnickety tidiness. And yet the sight of her performing these humdrum tasks was unbelievably erotic, he could feel his growing power like a blessed visitation.

"Dolly," he said. "Stop that. That's enough."

She finished what she was doing and sat down uncertainly beside him.

"I haven't much of a clue what to do, as you know," she mumbled, pulling one of her faces. "So . . . I think you'd better be quick, before I change my mind."

Be quick, she said, not knowing what she was saying. He hoped he wouldn't be quick. He wanted to make it slow and sweet and memorable, to make it last forever, to spoil her for anyone else. Be quick, she said, and yet he hesitated, fearful of frightening her, abashed at the prospect of hurting her. He wondered if it hurt a lot. How much easier it was when you didn't care.

But how could he not be quick? She made it impossible for him to be otherwise, destroying him with her eagerness, her generosity, her greediness, her artless lack of inhibition. She hadn't much of a clue what to do, but she did it all the same, in her own original, inexpert way, investing the whole cold, calculating process with passion and spontaneity and joy, pushing him well beyond his limits, heedless of the consequences.

He felt almost angry with her for rushing him, for rushing herself, and yet he was glad of her impatience, flattered by it, dizzy with being wanted, like a demented bee hovering over an open well of nectar. He felt angry with himself for letting her down, for letting himself down, because it was the first time, and special, and now it would be over much too soon, he would not want to remember it and he had wanted to remember it forever, and he concentrated on his anger, hoping it would save him, and pushed her legs apart almost roughly, and tried to forget she was Dolly, Dolly who made him care.

But she reminded him who she was, eager now, trusting, ignorant, at his mercy.

"Jack," he heard her whisper from beneath him, "Jack, I won't get a baby, will I?"

"No, of course not," said Jack, hoping suddenly, savagely, selfishly, that she would, resolving to spill every last drop of himself inside her, blinded by an overwhelming need to immortalize the moment, to make himself indelible.

He thrust harder than he needed to, expecting resistance, but it was like stepping into water. He felt it fall away beneath him, fathomless, roaring, and floating prematurely to the surface, leaving her still floundering.

And fingers seemed too coarse to soothe her pain, and so he gently licked her clean of virgin blood until she sighed and slept.

After an hour he woke her. They dressed hurriedly in silence, stepped out into the bitter cold and walked the dark streets in the direction of Holland Park until Jack finally sighted a cab. She leaned her head on his shoulder drowsily and kissed her hair and squeezed her hand, dreading the moment of leaving her, and when the moment came all he could manage was "Good night, darling Dolly," the unfamiliar endearment sounding strange on his tongue, his voice thick with the prospect of loss, heavy with a terrifying urge to weep.

"Good night, darling Jack," she said, and then irrepressibly. "Tomorrow? No, I forgot, we're going to Granny Townsend's in Sittingbourne. The day after tomorrow. I'll come the day after tomorrow, in the afternoon. Write your address down for me, quick."

"No, no, I'll come and fetch you."

"But I don't know when I'll be able to get away."

"Whenever you get away, I'll be here."

"I can't wait. Can you?"

"I can wait. I'm good at waiting. Hurry up, you'll catch cold."

She unlocked the front door and stood there, waving, shivering, until the taxi turned the corner of the street, leaving Jack more happy and more sad than he had ever been in his life.

Dolly proved almost impossible to rouse next morning. She missed breakfast, which was unheard of, appearing in the hallway flushed, bleary-eyed, and ten minutes late for the projected departure for Kent, much to her uncle's annoyance. Flora, an inveterate late riser, had been up with the lark, and had already left separately with Archie, eager to charm irascible old Granny Townsend into parting with a substantial engagement present.

Mr. Townsend couldn't abide prattle while he was driving, and Dolly was therefore obliged to keep her peace, not that she was feeling very talkative. Not only was her throat dry and sore, but her mind was fully occupied with thoughts of yesterday, and tomorrow. The memory of what had happened was even more vivid than the reality. The reality had been blurred, dreamlike, except that dreams were hard to remember afterward, and this wasn't. Most of all she remembered feeling him pulsate inside her like a second, palpitating heart, and the terrible look of sadness in his eyes as he said, "Oh God, Dolly, I'm so sorry." She had thought he meant sorry for hurting her, except that it hadn't hurt much and it had stopped hurting almost straightaway and she had just begun to enjoy the feeling of opening up and sucking in and feeling fuller and fuller of him when it had stopped, and then she gradually understood that it wasn't supposed to stop, that the bursting open was meant to happen for both of them, and she had been horrified to have failed him, to see the anguish in his eyes, and then touched deeply, deeply touched, it had been like an act of worship, the most exquisite kiss imaginable; not that she could have imagined it, it was like trying to imagine heaven, you could only use things you knew, like harps and clouds and choirs, as ciphers for the things you couldn't know until you got there.

Tomorrow they would have more time, tomorrow she could explore him properly, he was like a box full of secrets, full of surprises, full of knowledge. She had not had time to look at him properly, she wanted to feel every part of him with every part of herself, what she wanted was limitless, it would take forever.

Not forever. March 23 hovered like a specter. Lorenzo. She had betrayed Lorenzo, she had done that ultimate thing with another man, and she had done it willingly, knowingly, wantonly, she had lied to her own conscience, disguising her intention even from her-

self until it unmasked itself and demanded recognition. She had
known, she must have known from the beginning. It had been like
a seed germinating in the dark, no less alive for being hidden,
invisible.

She would have to write to Lorenzo, confess her crime, tell him
she was a fallen woman no longer fit to be his wife. Lorenzo would
be hurt and appalled, and would write back breaking off their engagement, which was all she deserved. And yet she didn't feel like
a fallen woman. She felt elevated, honored, even though she had
committed a sin. Or had she? She couldn't distinctly remember
being taught it was a sin, it wasn't in the Catechism or the Ten
Commandments, the Ten Commandments were only concerned
with adultery and coveting they neighbor's wife, which were sins
for married people, and she wasn't married, and neither was Jack.
There was fornication, of course, fornication and lechery and li-
centiousness, works that were linked with Sodom and Gomorrah
and revelry and idolatry, works that had no relevance to the exchange of mysteries, the shared celebration of delight. But it was
still a sin to hurt another person, and she would hurt Lorenzo and
he would punish her for it by no longer wanting to marry her, as
was his right, and that would hurt, because she didn't love Lorenzo
less because of what had happened, she felt exactly the same about
him as before. It was silly to say she loved Jack more than Lorenzo,
because they weren't comparable kinds of love . . .

She wouldn't write just yet. Lorenzo's leave wasn't for weeks and
weeks, it wasn't necessary for her to write just yet. Besides, Lorenzo might tell his father of their broken engagement and perhaps
even the reason for it, and then the news would get back to Papá,
and once Papá knew that she was a fallen woman he would have
them send her home and then she wouldn't be able to see Jack
anymore, or Lorenzo, or anyone else, ever. Perhaps she could break
it off with Lorenzo without telling him the real reason. Then her
father would be pleased not furious, and she would be allowed to
stay. But it seemed low, base, to lie to him, to make him feel he
was the one at fault, when the fault was all hers. She must at least
allow him the privilege of dismissing her, she must at least spare
him any sense of blame.

Best not to do anything just yet. Best to live for today, or rather
tomorrow. Tomorrow.

Tomorrow found Dolores with a throat like sandpaper and a temperature of 102°. She got up regardless, determined not to miss her
rendezvous with Jack, only to faint, at the breakfast table, for the

first time in her life. She was obliged to confide in Flora, who was
charged to look out for Jack from the bedroom window and deliver
a hastily scribbled note, in a pointedly sealed envelope, saying that
she had caught a chill but would be better in a couple of days.

The couple of days passed in a blur. All her limbs ached, she
shivered and sweated by turns, and it hurt her chest to breathe. She
dreamed incessantly, feverishly, not knowing what was real and
what was fantasy. One minute Jack would be sitting there, beside
her bed, and then Lorenzo, and then they would both be there at
once, one on either side of her, Jack, Lorenzo, Jack . . .

Jack. Was it really Jack, or was she delirious? He was holding a
huge bunch of hothouse roses, red as blood, hot as coals. He was
leaning over her, squeezing her hand, whispering, "I love you, Dolly.
Get well soon, for me." He was kissing her burning forehead with
lips as cold and as soothing as ice. And then he was gone.

She was sure she had dreamed it until she read the letter he had
left for her, written on her aunt's headed paper.

Tuesday, December 29

Dear Dolly,

    *I was very sorry to hear that you were ill and hope these
flowers will cheer you up.*

    *I have to go to Leeds to do a job for Harry Martindale and will
be gone a few days, which is why I persuaded Mrs. Townsend to
let me see you, even though you were still dopey from the drugs
and probably won't remember. But Flora assured me you were
getting better, which was a great relief.*

    *I will telephone as soon as I get back, to see how you are. Get
well soon.*

Happy New Year,
Jack

It seethed with unsaid words, it was almost as if he had known that
her aunt would read it first, and been careful not to compromise
her. Dolores was rereading it for the hundredth time when Flora
marched in, wearing an apron over her new lilac silk evening dress
and bearing a bowl of beef tea on a tray.

"Mummy's orders," she said. "She made me promise to see
you had some of this before I went out."

Mrs. Townsend had been fussing nonstop throughout her niece's
illness, and had been reluctant to go out and leave her on New
Year's Eve, but Dolly had insisted that she was perfectly all right

and would let the housekeeper know if she needed anything. Her aunt and uncle had already left for an overnight house party in the country; Flora and Archie were attending a New Year's ball in town.

Dolores obediently consumed a couple of spoonfuls under Flora's watchful eye. The effort exhausted her.

"I wonder what Lorenzo would think about these," said Flora slyly, fingering one of the long-stemmed roses on the bedside table. "You should have *seen* Jack's face when he saw you lying there. You're going to have your work cut out getting rid of him, you know. He looks the persistent type."

Dolores pushed the tray to one side. "I'm sorry, Flo. I don't think I can manage any more."

"Poor lamb. You look terrible. What a bore to be stuck in bed on New Year's Eve while we're all out enjoying ourselves."

"I don't mind. I'm not feeling very partyish."

"Still, Mrs. Baines will be here, if you want anything."

"I won't want anything," said Dolores. "I shall be fast asleep. You look lovely, by the way."

Flora bent to kiss her.

"At least you won't be outshining me, for once. Happy New Year, Dolly."

"Happy New Year, Flora. And to Archie."

Flora rustled out on a cloud of scent, and not long afterward Dolores heard a car horn hoot outside and the front door slam. She fell into a restless sleep again, dreaming, dreaming. Jack, Lorenzo, Jack, Lorenzo . . .

"Miss? Sorry to wake you miss."

"That's all right Mrs. Baines. What time is it?"

"Just going on ten. There's a telephone call for you, miss. It sounds urgent or I wouldn't have bothered you."

Dolores sat up.

"Is it Mr. Austin?" she said, scrambling out of bed, suddenly full of energy.

"It's a gentleman speaking in Spanish, miss. I can't understand what he's saying."

"In Spanish? Oh my God."

Panic-stricken, Dolores ran down the stairs, barefoot. No one ever phoned from home. The telephone was kept in Papá's study, used solely by him, and kept exclusively for business. Somebody must have died. Mamá, Ramón. Something terrible has happened, she could feel it in her bones . . .

Mrs. Baines hovered anxiously while Dolores took the call. The young lady was as white as a sheet and shivering, she looked ready to faint any minute, gabbling away in Spanish as fast as she could, getting herself all worked up. Mrs. Baines bustled back upstairs to fetch her dressing gown and slippers, and when she returned she found Dolores sitting rigidly by the telephone, trembling all over.

"What's the matter, miss? Not bad news, I hope?"

Dolores didn't answer. Mrs. Baines put the dressing gown around her shoulders.

"Can I help you, miss? Is something wrong?"

Dolores came to with a start.

"Wrong? Oh no, nothing's wrong. That was just . . . just my brother, phoning from Madrid to wish me a Happy New Year."

"From Madrid? Fancy that now. You look dreadful, miss. You'd best get straight back into bed."

Dolores walked upstairs again, on Mrs. Baines's arm, her limbs as heavy as lead, and allowed herself to be tucked in like a child.

"Good night, miss. Can I fetch you a hot drink? You're still shivering."

"No thank you, Mrs. Baines. I just want to go to sleep. I shan't be wanting anything else tonight."

"Good night, then, miss. And Happy New Year."

"Happy New Year, Mrs. Baines."

Dolores heard the bedroom door click shut and buried her face in the pillows, head spinning, heart beating wildly. It was like a judgment on her. How stupid she had been to think she could choose. She had no choice, no choice at all . . .

Numbly, slowly, she heaved herself out of bed, got dressed, and packed a small bag. Then she parted the curtains a fraction, sat by the window, and waited.

The time passed slowly, inexorably. The grandfather clock in the hall chimed eleven, and then midnight, January 1, 1931, the beginning of the rest of her life. She could hear distant roars of revelry in the street, and then the house sank into perfect silence. Mrs. Baines, having had her solitary tipple, would now be safely in bed.

At half past twelve precisely, as arranged, a taxi drew up, opposite the house, and stood waiting for her like some phantom carriage.

Dolores crept down the stairs, giddy with anguish, and opened and shut the front door very quietly. Then she ran across the street and into Lorenzo's arms.

PART TWO

FIVE YEARS LATER

JULY–OCTOBER
1936

5

TOLEDO, SPAIN, JULY 1936

"Papá, when will Mamá be home?"

Every day the same question, every day the same answer.

"Once your grandmama is better, Andrés." One couldn't say, once your grandmama is dead, without having to explain death, and Lorenzo had hoped that his son wouldn't have to understand death for a few more years yet. But the latest letter from Dolores had not been encouraging, or rather had been encouraging, given his selfish haste to see her home again.

Pamela Carrasquez was slipping fast, and Lorenzo could only hope yet again that her undiagnosed condition was not catching. Dolores had dismissed the possibility, but the fact that she had left Andrés behind in Toledo spoke for itself. She was the most devoted and affectionate of mothers, and having nearly lost her son at birth, she had remained perennially overanxious about his health, even though he had turned out a sturdy little boy, Lorenzo's pride and joy.

He missed his mother fiercely. He missed her reading aloud to him at bedtime, he missed the way she tickled his toes, he missed the infinite reassurance of her smile. Every time Dolores wrote, she included a note for him, written in large clear letters and covered in kisses, cheerfully worded to make him laugh rather than cry. Only Dolores could wipe away his tears—tears he was already too proud to shed in front of anyone else. Luckily he was fond of Rosa, his nursemaid, whose own small son gave him the company he would otherwise have lacked. It had grieved Lorenzo to know there would be no more children, but that had been a small price to pay for Dolores's life, the news had barely registered against his relief that he had not lost her. He would never have dared make love to her again but for the knowledge that he could do so without risk, which was a comfort to him, if not to her.

"Time for bed, you two," called Rosa from the kitchen. "Both of you in the bath, straightaway!"

They did not look like cousins, not that they knew they were cousins. It had been typical of Dolores to want to provide a home for her bastard nephew and his unfortunate mother, given Ramón's singular failure to accept even nominal responsibility. Not that he could manage to maintain himself, let alone a family. Dolores made regular duty visits to Madrid, to find him in ever more reduced circumstances. Afterward she would report back to her mother that Ramón was well, quite well, soothing the poor woman's distress that she could no longer respond to the begging letters he still wrote without compunction. Lorenzo was for once in his life in whole-hearted agreement with Don Felipe. He didn't see why Ramón should receive further subsidy. The mire he wallowed in was of his own making; it infuriated him that Dolores made sacrifices in order to help him. Thanks to Lorenzo's recent appointment as an instructor in firearms at the Toledo Military Academy, they were better off than they had been in the early days of their marriage, but they still had precious little to spare. He would not shed a tear for his brother-in-law when his wretched, parasitic life came to its long-awaited, premature end. Either the asthma or the absinthe or the syphilis must surely finish him soon, the sooner the better.

Still, Lorenzo was deeply attached to little Rafael, if only because he was the image of Dolores, far more so than her own son. Andrés did not take after either of them. Andrés looked more like Dolores's mother, with his English coloring and startling blue eyes. The poor woman had never seen her grandchild; his birth had served only to harden her husband's heart.

Don Felipe had refused to acknowledge their illicit union, and had done everything possible to have it declared null and void. For one thing, they had married in France under blatantly false pretenses. For another, Lorenzo had not obtained his commanding officer's permission to marry, fearing that any such request might be either denied or betrayed. In addition, Dolores had allegedly been abducted from London against her will. Lorenzo had inveigled her from her sickbed while her guardians were attending a party, removed her to the boat train, and thence to some cheap French hotel, where he had no doubt taken advantage of her enfeebled state to violate her in advance of the so-called marriage . . .

And there was the rub. By the time Margaret Townsend's anguished cable reached her sister, the so-called marriage had already been consummated, and no sooner had Felipe completed his negotiations with the judiciary—who had driven a long-windedly hard bargain—than an untypically subdued Dolores had played her trump card. One bastard in the family was quite enough, although by the time Andrés was born in late September, he might as well have been the second.

This visit home, Dolores's first since her marriage, had required considerable courage. She had written:

My father still refuses to speak to me. I eat my meals and sleep in my mother's room. He says if I am seen elsewhere he will have me ejected as a trespasser. Only the dogs dared risk his wrath by seeming pleased to see me. If it is true that poor Ramón is insane, I know now where he gets it from.

Tomás sends his best to Rosa. I visited him yesterday, while Papá was out on business. How good it is to see the workers cultivating their own land at last! Even though the yields have been very poor they are at least no longer starving. Papá of course is furious. He swears he'll get his land back, by fair means or foul . . .

Lorenzo sighed. One could hardly blame the peasants for seizing the land illegally, nor the new socialist government for allowing them to keep it, but it was still the wrong way to go about things. Such things should be done by due process. More and more the workers were taking the law into their own hands while the government looked on. Where would it all end?

It is true that feelings are running high, but you are quite wrong to worry about my safety. Tomás would never let anything happen to me, on account of Rosa and Rafael. I know you fear revolution, but if you were here with me you would understand why the workers are so frustrated. They expected great things of this new government, but so far it has been slow to make the reforms it promised them. God forgive me, I have found myself wishing my father dead, except that I know that Josep would be forced to hand over his inheritance to Holy Mother Church, the greediest landlord of them all. I have missed Mass now for three weeks. I cannot abide to hear it sung out of such a gluttonous mouth . . .

Revolution. Dolores could not begin to understand what that would mean. The bourgeoisie murdered in their beds, culpable or not, the country ruled by a squabbling consortium of Marxists, anarchists, and separatists masterminded by imperialist Soviet infiltrators. For her it was all so simple, she still believed in a utopia where everyone would be equal, where everything would be shared. Five years ago, when the new republic had been established, Lorenzo had shared that dream. True democracy, an end to injustice and corruption. The future had seemed bright and full of hope, a long-awaited era had begun.

But the dream had shattered. The new government had failed to satisfy the anarchists, who had boycotted the next elections, thus enabling the right wing to come to power and undo all its good work. There had been two turbulent years of riots, strikes, repression, and violence. And now the pendulum had swung again. The left-wing parties had joined forces and achieved a majority in the recent elections. But the situation was far from stable.

It could only be a matter of time before the new Popular Front government was overthrown by its own extremists; the moderates whom Lorenzo had supported were outnumbered, powerless against the furies they themselves had unleashed. Before much longer there was likely to be civil disorder on an unprecedented scale, and it would be his duty as a soldier to enforce law and order.

Feelings among his students at the military academy had reached flash point. Many cadets had joined the Falange, a thriving neo-Fascist group of extreme right-wingers. Lorenzo had once had considerable sympathy for José Antonio de Rivera, imprisoned leader of the Falange and son of the deposed dictator, but his declared desire to improve the lot of the common people was evidently not shared by most of his supporters. Class hatred seemed to be their driving force; rich young activists demonstrated their beliefs by driving through the streets of Madrid taking potshots at passing workers and engaging in violent demonstrations. The knowledge that both Don Felipe and the worthy Ramón now sported Falange membership cards came as no surprise.

As for the left-wing officers' faction, they seemed equally blinded in their own way, and just as inimical to Lorenzo's moderate views. He no longer felt able to support any party, and when asked his politics, he would reply simply that he was a Republican, which by now meant all things to all men.

He wished Dolores's mother would die quickly. He wanted her safely home again. It was true that Tomás, Rosa's giant of a brother, had taken responsibility for her safety, but even Tomás could not protect her against crossfire. Don Felipe went everywhere with an armed bodyguard; his house was rumored to be fortified as if for a siege; if it came to a workers' revolution, he would surely head the list of enemies of the people, and Dolores, as his daughter, would be in danger.

Lorenzo's stomach knotted with anxiety. She had been gone for nearly a month now, the longest month of his life.

"Don't go," he had pleaded. "Not with all this trouble brewing."

But she had smiled and put her arms around him and hugged him tight, determined and optimistic as always.

"You're such a worrier, darling. I shall be perfectly all right. Why should anyone want to hurt me? Besides, the workers have no arms. What chance would they have against my father? You take all these rumors too seriously."

"Then let me come with you."

"No!" She shuddered. "You know how my father hates you. It will be quite hard enough for me without you there. And besides, we can't leave Rosa alone with the children. What if there was some emergency? Please understand. Mamá's dying. She needs me. Who else is there? Josep can't leave his parish and Ramón would do more harm than good."

"I need you too. We all need you."

"I'll write every day. And I'll come home as quickly as I can. I shall miss you dreadfully."

She had clung to him and wept on the day of her departure, and for one blessed moment he had thought she was about to weaken. But she had proved unshakable. He had put her on the train with a heart as heavy as lead, and ever since then he had sunk into one of the black depressions that only she could relieve. Her generosity, her laughter, her unfailing good humor, were as vital to him as the air he breathed. Only Dolores could relieve his frustration and anxiety. Only Dolores could make his fears for the future seem exaggerated, absurd.

"You take life too seriously, my love," she would tease him. "You always have." She made light of their relative poverty, she claimed to like the humble apartment they lived in, she swore to this day she had never regretted their marriage.

"We have each other and Andrés, not to mention Rafael and Rosa. So we're rich. It's my father who's poor. Forget about yesterday and stop worrying about tomorrow. Today's what matters . . . "

And today was yet another day without her. The privilege of living outside the barracks, the luxury of privacy, the illusion of civilian freedom, made her absence harder to bear. He dreaded coming back to a home unilluminated by her presence, despite the noise of two lively children and their cheerful, good-natured nanny. It was worst at night, missing her soft, warm weight in the bed beside him. It was not sexual frustration—affection was their bond, rather than passion—more an empty feeling of isolation. He had not realized how dependent he had become on her, how much he relied on her for strength, for confidence. Dolores was more than just a wife, she was his only friend. He wished she loved him as exclusively as he did her, he wished she understood how hard he tried to deserve her. But Dolores loved far too many people, whether they deserved it or not.

Dolores's absence from Mass had not gone unnoticed. Her sentimental attitude toward the *braceros* was well known, and their godlessness was obviously catching. She would have been sorry to miss Father Luis's sermon, which was based on the Beatitudes, a favorite theme of his. Blessed are the *poor* (in heart), he intoned, blessed are the meek, blessed are they who *hunger* and *thirst* (after righteousness). These sentiments went down well with the well-heeled and well-fed bourgeoisie of Albavera; meanwhile the more blessed occupants of the district hungered and thirsted without benefit of Father Luis's encouragement.

After Mass the good father was to dine with Don Felipe, who kept the best table in the province. The old priest had recently moved into the Carrasquez household, following repeated threats against his person, and had been glad to find that the wayward daughter was banned from all but her mother's bedroom. He remembered only too well that summer Sunday several years before when he and Don Felipe and Doña Pamela had returned from church in expectation of a hearty meal, washed down by good wine, only to find the table set with nothing but bread and water. The servants were nowhere to be seen, and Dolores had been wearing an apron, ready to serve them.

She claimed sweetly to have been much impressed by the good father's ennoblement of hunger, and had taken the liberty of evacuating the enormous kitchen of all unnecessary foodstuffs. She had disposed of sundry extraneous items such as sides of beef, whole cheeses, sausages and hams, barrels of olives, casks of wine, sacks of rice, flour and beans—and rather than destroy them she had sent them by donkey cart to the squalid colony of shacks where the laborers lived in stubborn sinfulness. Given that they faced certain damnation on account of their lack of piety, they might as well indulge in gluttony while they could.

All this had been said with saintly sincerity and been accompanied by repeated endorsements of the good padre's extreme wisdom, so much so that her father had not dared beat her until the priest had left in search of a better dinner. He had blamed it on her English education, on her English blood, on her English friends, and at first Dolores had hoped that her misdemeanor might prevent a return to school, but perversely it had reinforced his view that her presence at home invited almost as much trouble as her good-for-nothing brother's.

Fearful of making himself a laughingstock, Don Felipe had not sought to reclaim the lost food, which had in any case been distributed with the speed of light and hidden like pirate's gold. He had, however, refused to sow crops for the following spring, claiming that the peasants had no need of further charity and could look to his daughter in the future to feed them.

There was no doubt, in the priest's opinion, that there was bad blood in the Carrasquez family. The daughter wild and willful, the younger son a drunken lecher, the elder a renegade who should never have been ordained, in Father Luis's view, although his parish, among the anarchist scum of Andalucía, was one calculated to reform his misguided views. Of course, the wife was English, an ailing, neurotic woman who had converted on marriage but never properly understood the faith, who had failed to instill in her children the true values of the Church. Such mixed marriages were doomed to failure, and this one had only been solemnized by gracious dispensation of the archbishop himself, inspired by a large contribution toward various worthy causes calculated not to jeopardize the blessedness of the poor.

Father Luis had already administered extreme unction to Doña Pamela, rather than find himself roused from his bed or called away from the table. She might go at any moment or she might drag on for weeks. Either way she was too incoherent to make her confession and likely to remain so. He had noticed that her hands were still thick with rings, of no possible use to a dying woman, but he had caught the daughter looking at him oddly as he closed his chubby fist around her emaciated fingers, no doubt because she had her eye on them herself, as a posthumous and undeserved dowry.

Dolores had spent her sinful Sunday morning writing to Josep again, having had no reply to her previous letter. Communications with Fontenar, a small village in Andalucía, were notoriously bad, but in any case, there was nothing he could do, there was nothing any of them could do. Brain fever had at first been diagnosed, but now there was talk of a tumor; the suggestion that she should be removed to Badajoz for hospital observation had sent Don Felipe into a rage, which Dolores's pleas served only to exacerbate. The doctor had been philosophical; the action of moving her might in itself prove fatal, and in his opinion her condition was undoubtedly terminal. And so Dolores sat, day after day, alone with her thoughts, waiting for her mother to die.

Dolores was unused to inactivity, unused to being alone with her thoughts. At home she occupied herself with the needs of her family, and did voluntary work for the Sisters of the Annunciation, who ran the local school. The new Popular Front government was proposing to remove the children from their care and substitute a state-run establishment, a prospect that appalled the nuns.

"Marxist tracts will replace the Catechism!" the mother superior had declared indignantly. "Young souls will be lost forever to the devil!"

"But think of all the children who don't come to school at the moment," Dolores had remonstrated, thinking of Rafael. Rosa, who hated and mistrusted the Church, kept her son at home. "It's not their fault if their parents aren't Catholics. Surely they deserve an education too?"

"And why are their parents not Catholics? It is all part of a Red conspiracy to outlaw the Church. Soon we shall be persecuted for the faith, like the martyrs of old . . ."

But Dolores found the holy sisters harmless enough. The long years in the convent had accustomed her to their funny ways, and the priests themselves made sure they had no power. There were precious few worker-priests like Josep.

In any event, the nuns seemed glad of her industry, and all the while she was busy she was content, able to count her blessings. A healthy child, a substitute brother for him, a good husband. A better husband than she deserved. The gentlest and most considerate of husbands, who asked nothing more than her occasional passive acquiescence, who had never attempted to seduce her, before or after marriage . . .

But here, sitting by her dying mother, there was nothing to do, except think, and remember, and regret. The memory was capriciously selective, it got stuck in certain grooves, like with a warped record, repeating the same episodes over and over again at the expense of others that might have been less painful. It had never allowed her to forget Jack standing beside her bed with that huge bunch of flowers and whispering, "I love you, Dolly."

She had written to him, care of *Red Rag*. She had made no allusions, no excuses, she had just stated facts, that Lorenzo arrived unexpectedly; that they had eloped a few months ahead of schedule; that she wished him well in the future. It had been formal, polite, very like the one she had written Auntie Margaret, except that she had apologized to Auntie Margaret and she hadn't apologized to Jack. He hadn't replied, thank God, and that had been the end of it. She had neglected all her English relatives shamefully ever since in an attempt to forget what had happened, as if she could ever forget. She hadn't even answered Edmund's letters. She would only have had to tell him lies.

How foolish and shortsighted and immature she had been in those far-off days. She had lived in a world of her own, she had yet to learn that there is no such thing as free will, that one is always thrown off course by the will of other people. How could she possibly have foreseen that Lorenzo would arrive out of the blue like that? It had never occurred to her that he might get a new posting and be obliged to take his leave early. His sudden appearance had been like a judgment on her, it had proved utterly impossible to jilt him to his face. Writing him a letter, from afar, was one thing, but direct confrontation had been quite another. All her courage had been swamped by the most agonizing guilt, and besides, she had had no time to think, to prepare her words. He had been so bold, so resourceful, so romantic, so full of faith! What chance had disloyalty and doubt against so much love and strength and resolution?

Her mother muttered incoherently, thirstily, and Dolores helped her suck some water from a sponge. The effort of swallowing exhausted her, the liquid converting itself instantly into beads of sweat. Then she fell back into a tormented doze.

"Ramón," she murmured, pitifully, yet again. "Ramón. My baby . . ."

Dolores wiped her mother's forehead, wondering yet again if she had done wrong to keep the news from Ramón, whether she should have sent him the fare and trusted him not to squander it, whether she should have subjected her mother to the dubious comfort of Ramón's presence, risked letting her see how haggard he had become, risked subjecting her to one of his distress-triggered asthma attacks, half-real, half-histrionic, risked having two patients on her hands instead of one. And she told herself yet again that Mamá was well past recognizing anyone, that Ramón was with her in her mind, whole and perfect and unscarred by disability, doing her more good than ever he could have done in the flesh. And she tried to accept that one must rejoice for those who die, that grieving was selfish, that death was a liberation, not a loss. For this was the first death she had ever known.

Ramón was not drunk in the normal sense of the word. Drunkenness belonged to an age of innocence. Total oblivion eluded him cruelly, however much alcohol he consumed; the effect it produced was a negative relief, a masking of pain, not a source of pleasure.

Of course, his days of fine wines and cognac were long gone; he no longer entertained fellow señoritos in the smart bars and the restaurants of Madrid, no longer kept an apartment in the exclusive Salamanca district, no longer had the benefit of Consuela's housekeeping. She had worked for several weeks without wages until her husband had put a stop to it and press-ganged her into the CNT like the good anarchist he was. Now Consuela worked in some shoe factory, happy as a pig in shit as long as there were plenty of strikes to be struck, looking forward to the day of revolution when the workers would run amok in the streets and tear their betters limb from limb. And Ramón was alone.

He now lived among the rabble he had despised for so long, in a wretched slum dwelling off the Plaza de Chueca, where his senses were constantly assaulted by the noise of domestic strife and shrieking babies, and by the stink of rancid cooking oil and decaying rubbish and fermenting sewage, all of which he endured with haughty stoicism. Even in the filth and squalor of his room—an attic he referred to as his studio—Ramón inhabited a world of private grandeur, of glorious isolation, immune to the intrusion of lesser mortals. He retained a sense of superiority, of separateness, of devastated splendor. His face, though prematurely lined, still had a certain dignity; pride and pathos sat upon it with equal grace.

Poverty was the cross that all great artists had to bear. It was a noble fate. Would that he had discovered his talent earlier, when he still had money for such luxuries as paints and canvas! The revelation of his gift had come to him too late, soon after his debtors and his father's intransigence had driven him out of his elegant apartment and forced him into these miserable, unworthy lodgings. Perhaps hunger had inspired him. Mystics fasted deliberately, in search of truth.

His routine had become a ritual. Each day he would dress himself in his tattered finery, and hobble either to the Parque del Retiro or the Puerta del Sol, depending on the weather and the time of year, there to sit with his latest masterpiece chalked on the ground before him, receiving contributions from his patrons like a god accepting worship.

No wonder the other pavement artists gave him a wide berth, fearing unfavorable comparison. At first they had thought to drive him away, mocking his brilliant, innovative, abstract style, a style well beyond their puny comprehension, but soon, seeing him eat into their profits, they had wisely found other pitches farther away. Ramón had displayed a lofty disdain for their insults, the piqued accusations that he was not a true artist, that he was no more than a common beggar, that people gave because he was a cripple, not because they admired his work. Ramón was no common beggar. Why, everyone knew that a beggar must kneel. Madrid was full of kneeling beggars, with arms outstretched in supplication. Ramón knelt before no man. His disability precluded kneeling. He sat proudly beside his work, his good leg tucked under his body, his wasted limb exposed, his boot unlaced and open in dumb receptiveness.

It was the poor who gave. The rich for the most part passed by, unmoved. They preferred, in their arrogance, to look for works of art in the Prado. Doubtless if Goya or Velázquez had spread their works at their feet, they would have been similarly shunned. Yes, it was the poor who gave. Not that Ramón credited the poor with appreciation of his genius, it was merely that some of them still instinctively recognized a being superior to themselves. In any case, it was right that the poor should give. It was they, after all, who were draining the country of its substance, their mouths ever open to suck the teat of the state. The new government was like a wet nurse with an overgrown infant that clamored to be weaned, that was becoming greedy for bread. But for the ravening hordes of the poor the country would prosper and be strong again, and he, Ramón, restored to his former place in society. Had not his downfall been engineered by that ungrateful little bitch of a Rosa and her blackmailing brother, who had dared to besmirch his character by claiming that he had sired her brat? Why, his seed would have died instantly on such inferior soil, no child of his could have grown in such a worthless womb. That was typical of the poor. Lying, scheming and avaricious. So if some wizened old woman or young man in overalls threw him the odd *céntimo*, they were just contributing toward the common debt, he owed them no thanks for such just compensation.

These days he managed his finances with care, having outgrown his youthful taste for gambling. Gambling was a gentleman's pursuit; as practiced in the evil bars around the Plaza de Chueca, it was debased to the level of theft. Ramón had been robbed too often by greasy marked cards and loaded dice. Even if he had succeeded in winning, he would doubtless have been stripped of his assets before he had a chance to hide them. He had by this time forgotten what an accomplished cheat he had been in his heyday, telling himself that his wits were just as sharp as ever, but that one gambled for amusement, not for gain, and certainly not for loss. After all, he had to eat. And drink.

Night was the most lucrative time. Cheap wine inspired carelessness and generosity, and many of the workers had bulging pockets, thanks to the unfettered power of unions, which were busy exacting revenge for the last two years of right-wing rule. One *peseta* bought ten liters of rough wine, but Ramón was afflicted with a weak bladder, and to leave his post was to lose income. Absinthe was dearer, but more discreet, it bypassed his troublesome urinary tract, heading straight for the bloodstream and the brain.

Today was a fine summer's day. Ramón had enjoyed a profitable morning by the Sol and dined in a worker's café on a coarse stew of beans and sausage. The buxom proprietress felt sorry for him, melted at his beatific smile, and frequently forgot to charge him. She was a very stupid woman, but a passable cook and, understanding his shyness, she let him draw up his chair against a protruding window ledge and eat his meal alone, where he was safe from the jibes of her less sensitive clientele.

As Ramón limped slowly into the park to take his siesta in the shade of a horse chestnut tree, he was incensed to see that his usual pitch, by the fountain, had been invaded by a stranger, who was kneeling, arms outstretched, in front of his avant-garde portrayal of Don Quixote, a brilliant, blurring spiral of blues and grays and yellow. After nearly three years of solid tenure this was an unprecedented outrage, and Ramón steeled himself to beat off the interloper with his stick.

He was almost on top of the despicable creature before he realized it was female, and some long-buried streak of gallantry made him drop his arm. She looked up at him pathetically and held out both her hands, palm upward.

"Please, señor," she murmured plaintively, in a strong Southern accent, "I have not eaten for two days, señor."

She saw only his face, too consumed with her own wretchedness to notice his leg.

"What is your name, child?" he said, almost kindly, adapting graciously to the unaccustomed role of benefactor.

"Marisa, señor, please, señor."

"And where do you come from, Marisa? You are not a Madrileña."

"No, señor, I am from Andalucía. I have come to Madrid to work. There is no money and no food in my village."

"And how did you get here?"

"I walked, señor."

"You walked all the way from Andalucía?"

"Yes, señor."

"And why have you not found work? The unions will find you work."

"I arrived here only today. I want only food for today, señor, tomorrow I will work, I am no beggar, truly."

She was trembling, almost as if she expected to be hit, adopting the cowering posture of a badly treated animal.

"Here," said Ramón grandly, extracting a coin from his pocket and holding it out in front of her face, letting it catch the sun. "Go to the *pastelería* on the other side of the square and ask for two *rosquillas del santo,* which are a speciality of our city, one for yourself and one for me, and I will instruct you in the ways of Madrid. Well, what are you waiting for?"

She sprang to her feet and did exactly as she was told, not having sufficient wit to disappear with the money and spend it on more sustaining nourishment. Ramón watched her run out of the gates, weave her way across the Plaza de la Independencia, dodging hooting traffic, and disappear inside the pastry shop. She returned on the double with the two minute, bite-sized delicacies, for which Ramón had retained a well-bred weakness, and a handful of small change which was right to the last *céntimo.*

"What, are you mad?" he chided. She had been stuffing herself avidly, even as she crossed the road, her mouth working like a piston, licking every elusive crumb, every precious smear of icing from her lips. "No one will give you money if they see you eating. Let us go and sit down, out of sight, and if you are a good child perhaps I will buy you an ice."

The tiny cake was but a tantalizing memory by the time they

reached the bench. She sat watching him eat his, eyes huge with hunger. It amused Ramón to torment her in this fashion. He ate slowly, savoring every morsel, chewing luxuriously. The money would have filled her to bursting with bread. She was obviously a complete simpleton to do his bidding so unquestioningly. But she was pretty enough, with black, curly hair and large peasant breasts which jutted pathetically out of her bony rib cage, as if robbing the rest of her body of flesh. Her skin was horribly brown, of course, but it was young enough not to have wrinkled yet. She could not be more than fifteen or sixteen, such women were haggard crones by the time they were twenty. No point in asking her her age, she would not know.

"So, Marisa," said Ramón, wiping his mouth on a monogrammed rag. "Perhaps I can help you find work. I am a very influential man in these parts."

Involuntarily, her eyes flew to his boot. Ramón felt a surge of irritation.

"Does my shoe interest you, child? Well it might, I see you yourself are unshod. Would you like some shoes, Marisa?"

"I have no need of shoes, señor. It is summer. But I would be grateful for any work."

"Any work, eh? And what can you do?"

"I am strong, señor. I can do any work. I can scrub floors, wash clothes . . ."

"Excellent, excellent. I am sure I will be able to find you a place without difficulty. I will talk to my associates tomorrow. And where will you sleep tonight?"

"Why, here, señor, in the park."

"In the park? Without shelter?"

"I have no need of shelter, señor. It is summer."

"My child, there are many evil people in this city. A young girl alone at night, penniless and without shelter . . ." He shook his head reprovingly. "But you will be safe as my guest, in my studio. Yes, indeed, I am an artist, it was my work you were admiring when we met. You have nothing to fear from me. I am, alas, a cripple, as you observe. But perhaps you are too proud to accept hospitality from a cripple. Not too proud to let him share his food with you, but too proud to share his roof. Did you say you wanted an ice cream?"

He hailed a vendor on a tricycle and purchased two ices, one chocolate, one lemon.

"Which would you prefer?" he asked, amused at her noncom-

prehension. The little idiot had never seen an ice before. She held
out her hand for the lemon one, which was the slightly larger of the
two, and her tongue shot out with reptilian speed, recoiling at the
sensation of cold. Undeterred, she consumed it with ravenous haste,
and Ramón, whose weak bladder had long since robbed him of his
predilection for ices, generously handed her his as well, which she
gobbled as unquestioningly as a sow. No, not a sow, she was more
like a stray dog, ready to follow the first person who tossed her a
crumb, and whatever native cunning she might have had had been
blunted by the sight of his leg. People assumed that all cripples
were eunuchs. She was his for the taking.

Josep no longer preached to an empty church. For a long time now
the Church of Santa Maria, in Fontenar, near Córdoba, had remained empty (except on Sundays, when those without transport
grudgingly avoided mortal sin), but he preached nonetheless, after
a fashion. He preached in the olive groves under the burning, Andalucian sun, he preached by the stream, dangling his feet in the
water while the women did their washing, he preached while he
dug the grave for a stillborn child.

The church had not been empty at first, but he had effectively
evacuated it of its former congregation. The local landowners and
bourgeoisie now drove fifteen kilometers up and down narrow hilly
tracks in order to hear Mass in neighboring Baenilla, and called
upon Josep's services only in the direst emergency. Inevitably he
had been summoned to Córdoba soon after taking up his ministry,
and threatened with an indefinite period of spiritual renewal at a
closed monastery in the north. Since then he had learned a degree
of discretion as the price of his survival, but it was not often put to
the test. Those who had complained to the bishop had been permanently frightened off by his persistent demands for money to
help the poor rather than buy new altar cloths or repair the church
roof; neither were they eager to have their confessions heard by one
who was not satisfied with routine peccadilloes, who prompted
them in the most presumptuous fashion to examine their consciences for the deadly sins of avarice, sloth and defrauding laborers
of their wages, who had reminded them of his right to withhold
absolution unless satisfied of their desire to repent.

Afterward he had cursed himself for his lack of caution. Better
to have wooed the rich with flattery, to have wheedled their money
out of them by stealth, to have promised them specific rewards in

heaven. And yet to court the rich would have been to alienate the poor, to brand himself a lackey, as his predecessors had been.

Christ had preached in the open air, and Josep saw no reason not to follow His example. Christ himself had been a rebel, Christ himself had been executed for sedition, Josep took comfort in the conviction that Christ would doubtless have been banished to the monastery in Pamplona for life, always supposing He had survived the seminary.

Josep had spent his childhood listening to Father Luis's sermons and had endured a Jesuit education of the most ferocious discipline, and yet these deterrents had served only to strengthen his vocation. It was a desire to surpass, not to emulate, that inspired him, he had always had more pride than piety. His chief characteristics as a child had been a quick temper and an unquashable willfulness, which had proved resistant to repeated beatings with the buckle end of his father's belt. He had been sent away to school to have the spirit knocked out of him, but the spirit had burrowed deep within him instead, the fire had become a furnace, all the hotter for being contained, controlled.

Josep gloried in being a priest of the people, one whose church, despite its vulnerable location, still stood untouched and unburned. The anticlerical violence that raged throughout the province had passed him by, perhaps because he was deemed to be "not a proper priest," a halfmocking epithet which he cherished as a compliment. Little by little, he was winning. One day these people would come to Mass, see the church as a haven, not as a symbol of oppression . . .

But meanwhile, the collection plate stayed all but empty, and Josep went hungry. He never dined in the houses of the rich, not that they invited him anymore, nor would he accept hospitality from people who had barely enough to feed themselves, though when anonymous gifts of food were left on the porch he accepted them gratefully and tried not to think about who had gone without to give them. True, the people were better off since coordinated strikes had forced up wages, but the intimidated landowners still lived like princes in comparison. He had taken an unholy delight in seeing the recent transference of fear from worker to employer, and although he preached moderation and restraint, he sometimes felt as if he were shielding the enemy.

He prepared to say a lonely weekday Mass as usual, to consecrate the bread and wine for his sole consumption. Once a week, without fail, he walked into Baenilla—two hours there, and three back, uphill—to join his former congregation outside the confessional, forced himself to lay his soul bare before the priest who had usurped him, forced himself to listen humbly to the oily, self-righteous tones asking "How many times?"

"Bless me, Father, for I have sinned. It is a week since my last confession. I have been lazy in rising. I have been guilty of the sin of pride. I ate meat on Friday." (Cold rabbit, the only food in the house.) "I have had . . . impure thoughts."

"How many times?"

A pause.

"Twice. No, three times."

"At night or during the day?"

"At night, Father. While I am asleep, and I wake and see the evidence of my sin and I am ashamed."

"This fault of yours is persistent, my son. Every week you confess the same sin. You must mortify the flesh. Read the lives of the saints, who scourged themselves and wore belts of thorns under their garments, who fasted and forced their bodies into submission. You must mortify the flesh."

Privately Josep regarded mortification of the flesh as a dangerous and unnatural exercise, a warped form of sexuality, with pain a substitute for ecstasy. As for fasting, he did that anyway, willy-nilly, and his problem had not proved tractable to hunger. He wondered if all priests had the same trouble, or whether he was particularly afflicted. It was not a subject that had ever been discussed in the seminary, except in the most oblique terms, and when he had sought guidance from his superiors, he had received the same old advice about fasting and mortification of the flesh and had been told, in so many words, that matters would improve as he got older. And here he was at twenty-eight with the problem unresolved.

As if knowing his secret problem, the more nubile members of Josep's flock subjected him to persistent, coordinated, merciless teasing, and he had learned to rebuff such advances in the kind of crude language they understood, letting them know that he was no fool, that they hitched their skirts and unbuttoned their blouses in vain. There had never been any danger that he would forget himself. It was as if he recognized his own susceptibility to the drug, his own potential for addiction.

He had just begun the Mass when he heard a slight noise behind him and turned, startled, to see that he had a congregation of one. The woman was wearing a black mantilla and had buried her face in her hands, so he could not tell at first who she was. She mumbled the opening responses correctly, if almost inaudibly, but he recognized her by her speech as María Ortúz.

María was an exile from the Basque Country. Her husband, Juan, had run away to sea as a boy and met and married her when on shore leave in Bilbao, and some years later he had returned to his native province, bringing his wife with him.

Juan, a union militant, was profoundly anticlerical. He had expressly forbidden his wife to attend church ever since Josep's much-hated predecessor had banned her from High Mass on Sundays, as some of the ladies present had complained that she smelled. Juan himself had turned up on the following Sunday in her stead, the first time he had set foot in a church since boyhood, wearing boots and clothes that had been liberally anointed with dung, and had sat not at the back of the church, as befitted his lowly station, but right at the front, placing himself next to the daughter of the local olive baron. The next day he had been sacked, and the day after that there had been a strike, and the day after that workers had been imported from the next village to break it, too hungry to care about the plight of their neighbors. Fighting had broken out, worker against worker, and eventually the Civil Guard had fired shots to restore order. Two men had been wounded and one child accidentally killed, and in the end everyone had gone back to work rather than starve.

Since then María had obediently avoided the church, and her presence today was a milestone, not that Josep could take credit for converting her, because she had always been, despite her enforced absence from Mass, extremely devout in the Basque tradition. He knew she pined for her beloved homeland, where the land was lush and green and the peasants prospered and the priests were seen as friends. Sometimes, listening to her reminiscences, Josep had found himself wishing that he too could work alongside like-minded colleagues, with a willing congregation, in peace and harmony instead of being harangued by the hour and having to strive to put the Gospel in the context of union doctrine. But then, of course, he would have missed out on the triumph of this particular moment. He was suddenly consumed with the sheer joy of being who and where he was.

"*Dominus vobiscum,*" he chanted, his strong voice echoing in the emptiness.

"*Et in spiritum tuum,*" she whimpered.

And that night Josep's dreams were untroubled and he slept as innocently as a child.

* * *

Clara woke to the silent reproach of a cold cup of tea and a fire already lit. It was twenty past eleven and she had slept for almost twelve hours. Her mouth was dry as a bone and her head ached viciously. But as hangovers went, she'd known worse. Much worse.

Edmund had poured the drinks out for her, filling the glasses to the brim, giving her one measure less than the night before, making her swallow them one after the other. She had been perfectly foul to him, ignoring the hard look of love in his eyes, almost frightened by his cruel determination, his lack of pity. Edmund knew that she wanted to go back to work as soon as possible, and had forced her to admit that a nurse with a drinking habit was a danger to her patients. And so she had agreed to his plan, a kind, lenient ruthless plan whereby she would drink only at an appointed hour and under strict supervision, a little bit less each day. That way she did not have to fear strange insects in the shadows, she would be spared the awful agonies of sudden, total abstention.

She hadn't actually wanted that final drink last night, so soon after the previous one, but Edmund had forced her to swallow it straight away and then held her over the basin while she was sick. He had not been in the least sympathetic. He loved her too much for that, damn him. And because she loved Edmund more than she hated herself, she was determined not to let him down. She had let him down quite enough already.

She had paid the price of those nine months of secret joy. With hindsight, she should have known from the start that her pregnancy was doomed. After the stillbirth, Reverend Wilcox, the hospital chaplain, had called to see her and offered quavering condolences. He had spoken of God's will and suggested that her dead baby was extraordinarily blessed to have been called to its maker so soon and thus evade this vale of tears. Clara had asked him to kindly leave her in peace as she was a Roman Catholic anyway and if she ever decided she wanted spiritual help it certainly wouldn't be from a namby-pamby outfit like the Church of England. Reverend Wilcox had apologized, saying he had no idea, she was down as an agnostic, and he always saw the agnostics, but of course he would ask Father O'Mally to come in to see her. The next day she had discharged herself and had drunk herself into the first of many stupors.

She heaved herself out of bed, put on her dressing gown, and went down to fetch the mail. It was all addressed to Edmund, apart from a Communist party circular for Clara enclosing a full program of events for the forthcoming People's Olympiad, a left-wing fes-

tival being held in Barcelona in opposition to the Berlin Olympic
Games. Edmund had been relieved when she had finally agreed to
go on holiday, if less than delighted at her choice of destination.
He had, however, refused point blank to join the party tour bus;
they were to travel alone, by train, and make their own hotel arrangements.

It would be the first time they had been away together, other than
for a few days. Idleness held no charm for Clara, she relaxed best
when working double shifts or listening virtuously to some party
hack. This anti-Fascist pilgrimage gave her a motive for self-
indulgence; her renewed political fervor was a sign of recovery
which Edmund was loath to discourage.

Edmund's *Times* and *Red Rag* were still on the breakfast table;
Clara's copy of *The Daily Worker* lay folded by her plate. Clara
drew a glass of water from the tap and drained it thirstily. Then she
emptied some sugar into a cup, flopped down into Edmund's chair,
and began eating it with a teaspoon, while she flicked irritably
through *Red Rag*.

"Mass strikes and factory occupations throughout France," she
read, crunching the granules noisily. "An eyewitness report from
our foreign correspondent."

The account was as vivid as a novel. Edmund had joked that Jack
ought to be in Hollywood writing film scripts. His controversial
coverage of the invasion of Abyssinia had sent ripples of disquiet
throughout the Foreign Office, and according to Edmund's father,
Jack was simply begging to encounter insuperable bureaucratic
problems next time he tried to renew his passport.

Red Rag had changed beyond all recognition, for the worse, in
Clara's view, an opinion that was evidently not shared by the staggering number of people who actually bought it. The days of predictable dogma were long gone; no one was safe from attack
anymore, whatever their political color; controversy was its watchword, all the way to the bank. It contrived to be both serious and
satirical, populist and chic, achieving a cross-class, cross-party
readership unprecedented in a political journal. It was passed
around factory floors and could be found in the smoking rooms of
respectable London clubs. It was the smart thing to be seen reading.
It could not be dismissed. A copy was delivered every week to Ten
Downing Street.

"Only in Britain," Jack had written recently, "could I tell the
truth without fear or favor, protected by our enviable tradition of
free speech and our abhorrence of state censorship. Only in Britain

could a totally independent newspaper such as this survive without selling its soul to political or commercial interests. I am indeed the envy, if occasionally the unwitting enemy, of fellow journalists from other less privileged publications. I do not ask you to disbelieve what you read in the *Mail* or even the *News Chronicle*. I do not seek to convince you that this paper has the monopoly on truth. I ask you only to read, and compare, and judge for yourself, and to be thankful that our country is still free enough for you to do so. But for how much longer? A contagion is spreading across Europe. Once contracted, it is incurable. Fascism is the moral rabies of our time. Throwing crumbs to this mad dog does not rob it of its taste for flesh. We feed it, thinking it will thank us and not bite us, even though its jaws are still dripping with the blood of innocent children. But I still have faith in this government to recognize the danger and act. I have suffered ridicule for this, and look forward to being proved right.''

Jack was still a salesman at heart, and Harry no better than an entrepreneur. But what exactly were they selling? Reading Jack's pieces, which were often unashamedly contradictory, was like trying to solve a huge riddle. God only knew what he really thought behind all the verbal dexterity.

Two years before, he had sent her a check equal to the exact amount he had received from her during their brief relationship—not that she had kept a tally, although he obviously had—from the very first day.

"Don't take this as an insult," the note had read. "I'm sure you'll donate it to party funds in any case. Just don't tear it up for spite.''

Preempted, she hadn't. She knew very well why he had done it. He had done it because of Edmund, because he wanted in some small measure to blot out his guilt. The friendship between the two men had stuck in her gullet at first; she had been insanely jealous. She would almost rather Edmund had taken a lover than formed such an unlikely and threatening bond with another man. As far as Clara could see they had nothing in common, it was like a conspiracy to make her feel superfluous. Several times she had been tempted to blow the whistle on Jack, to expose him for what he was, but she couldn't do it without implicating herself, and for all she knew Jack had beaten her to it, and so she held her peace.

She had always known that Jack would abandon her as soon as he could afford to, and so he had. At the end he had repeated that early lie—or was it?—"I want you to know that it wasn't just the money. I expect with most of them you thought it wasn't just the money, and it probably was. But with me, the money was only part of it.'' If it was a lie, it seemed a pointless one, after the event. But Jack said things for his own reasons.

She had not attempted to replace him. Not because he was irreplaceable, but because by that time the rigors of her day were punishment enough. She had never expected to have to work so hard, never in her vilest fantasies had she felt herself so totally abused. The hierarchy of the Coronation Hospital was even more rigid than that of the outside world, and Clara had wallowed in being the lowest of the low, haughtily ignored by doctors, patronized by qualified nurses, treated like a scullery maid by Matron. Better still, the patients did not smile wanly in their beds and bless her. The no-hope ward to which she was assigned contained an assortment of rotting bodies with voracious appetites and defective bowels who gibbered and drooled and shouted abuse. The ward stank permanently of physical decay. At first Clara had gagged on it and been sick and decided not to eat before she went on duty in the future, until once she had turned up for the early shift on an empty stomach and fainted, sending a full bedpan crashing onto the newly scrubbed floor, spilling its contents all over herself, and feeling unutterably foolish when a fresh-faced fellow probationer had brought her around and called her love and made her sit in the rest room sipping sweet tea while she did her chores for her.

Academically, her choice of career had been a disaster. The low intellectual self-esteem that had made her so susceptible to processed dogma made her equally resistant to undigested fact. She had wept over her medical textbooks, while girls younger, brighter and less privileged than she devoured knowledge as naturally as children, and after dismally failing her first-year exams she had had to start all over again, wondering all the while if she would have been given a second chance if she hadn't donated a thousand pounds to hospital funds as a gesture of apology for having wasted everybody's time.

In the end she had qualified by the skin of her teeth, and they had let her know it. It had been their way of telling her she would never be given more than minimal responsibility, never be given more than an average reference, that she would always end up in the most unpopular wards, with no hope of promotion. But she had found this oddly soothing. ''Not much up top with Neville, but God, what a worker!'' she had overheard Sister say one day. And afterward she had mulled this over and felt uncommonly satisfied.

Nursing was far more than just a job of work. It was a living, active penance that suited her temperament perfectly, and Clara had no desire to alleviate its effect. She had finally proved herself and achieved some measure of self-respect, enough to reject the flaccid politics of her youth, enough to eschew compromise, enough to throw herself on the mercy of the Communist party, an accredited worker now, and not a phony.

And Edmund had proved himself too. He had survived every test she had set him. He had let her move out, he had let her be free, he had learned to make do on the little bit of herself she had to spare. Unexpectedly, their relationship had thrived on separation, their time together had been precious, tranquil. Edmund had welcomed the genuine exhaustion that drained her destructive hyperactivity; Edmund had admired the strength of character that had led her to achieve her ambition. Edmund had known her well enough never to flatter her, never to tell her how proud he was of her, knowing praise would only compel her to run herself down. For a while she had been almost content. And then she had pushed her luck. She had wanted a baby to love as well as Edmund, and God had duly punished her for her greed.

She heard Edmund's key in the latch and got up jerkily to greet him.

"How are you feeling?"

"Smell my breath. That's how I'm feeling. Did you get the tickets?"

"First-class. And I booked a room with bath at the most expensive hotel available. The comrades will be appalled."

"Edmund!"

"Poor darling. It would be much more fun to travel a thousand miles by coach chanting the *Internationale*. It would be much cozier staying in some flea-bitten hostel. It would be much more edifying to—"

"All right, all right, I give in." She took the tickets from him and sat down to examine them.

"What's this?" she said.

"Onward tickets to Rome. Via Venice and Florence. Fair's fair."

"But we'll be gone weeks!"

"Term doesn't start again till September. If I can put up with two weeks of sport and politics for you, both of which bore me to tears . . ."

"You know how I hate faits accomplis. You might have consulted me."

"You wouldn't have agreed." Edmund sawed a chunk of bread and wrapped it around some cheese. He offered it to her first and she shook her head in disgust and he shrugged and ate it himself.

"Anything interesting in this week's *Rag?*"

"Just the usual distortions and exaggerations. You know how Jack goes in for cheap effects."

"Jack's exaggerations have an uncanny knack of coming true. Let's hope he's wrong about the next war, though."

"Jack's simply dying for a war. A war would make his name nicely."

"He's doing quite well for himself without one," said Edmund. "And in any case, all journalists overstate their case, like barristers."

"Except that Jack won't risk losing a case by being properly partisan. He likes to play with words to keep his options open. He's a natural turncoat, a pure opportunist."

"If you ate something you'd be less ill-humored."

"Stop nagging. I'm only eating for one now, after all."

Edmund bit back the words of comfort. Sympathy only made her worse. But the sight of her anguish tore him apart, made the pose of callous practicality ever harder to maintain. Hopefully a few weeks away from home would give her the breathing space she needed, build a barrier between the past and the future, above all, get her away from his well-meaning family. His mother and Flora had rallied around and done their best to comfort her, and Clara had put on a brave face in their presence. But the visits had been an ordeal rather than a solace; their very normality seemed to intensify her own sense of failure. Flora, who had bloomed her way through both her pregnancies and produced two perfect offspring, had robustly counseled "trying again," driving Clara to the limits of her precarious self-control.

Never once had she shown him up in front of his family, not without considerable effort. They had done their best over the years to make her feel accepted, and even Archie, who wisely did what Flora told him, had learned to swallow his politics in Clara's presence and tolerate her Communist proselytizing with a semblance of genuine interest. It pained Edmund to know that they did it for him, rather than for her, but it reassured him that she went along with the charade for his benefit, not theirs. The love that shone from Clara had always been refracted, lighting up unlikely corners, diverting the eye, defying expectation, none the less dazzling for being oblique.

"Perhaps I will have something to eat after all," she said, and then, yet again, "I'm sorry, Edmund. Why do you put up with me?"

"Pure selfishness. The only reason anybody ever does anything."

And the tone of voice was Edmund's, but the words might just as well have been Jack's.

Tomás called the meeting at the *Casa del Pueblo* to order, uncertain as always of his ability to control it. Since that glorious March dawn when workers throughout the province had invaded the land with impunity, the mood of elation had evaporated. The harvest already showed signs of being poor, jeopardizing the purchase of seed and fertilizer for next year. And what use was land to a poor man without credit? The government talked and talked but did not act. It had been left to the people to take the law into their own hands. Meanwhile Don Felipe brooded in his mansion, consulting daily with his fat associates, and although the Civil Guard's activities had been curtailed by government decree, there was nothing to stop private acts of sabotage. Whole fields of workers' grain had shriveled and died, bloated fish bobbed in the rivers, wells had been fouled and mysterious fires had destroyed homes and crops.

While other landowners had fled to the cities, Don Felipe obstinately refused to budge. It was rumored that the huge house was stuffed full of men and guns, that he was waiting daily for an attack so that he could mow his enemies down and reclaim his losses. But guns or no guns, there were those who wished to storm his stronghold like the Bastille, seeing him as the evil force that was thwarting their grand endeavor. And Tomás had argued that this would be suicide, that they would be walking straight into a death trap, that in time the moment of revolution would come, when the workers would be armed and rise up in unison all over the country, and then and only then would they take their revenge.

"They are few and we are many," declared a young hothead, rising to his feet. "I for one am willing to die to rid ourselves of this tyrant. He sits in his fine house and laughs at us. And why does he laugh at us? Why does he not flee, like so many of his kind? I'll tell you. Because he knows that we are weak-willed, and led by a coward!"

He strode angrily toward Tomás, who towered over him. Tomás could not but admire the lad's audacity.

"Not only that," continued his critic, gesturing wildly, "he thinks that now he has his precious daughter to protect him, Tomás here would see all our crops burned and all the rivers poisoned and all the wells filled with shit before he would risk hurting one hair on that beautiful head!"

There was a rumbling murmur throughout the room.

"Go then," said Tomás quietly. "Go with your pitchfork and die for your cause. Be assured, you will not die alone. No, your grave will be watered gloriously with the blood of our wives and children. There are many heroes like you in Spain. Such heroism is a form of murder. As for Dolores, by all means kill her too, and prove beyond all doubt how brave you are. Kill her dying mother while you are about it. Kill me. Kill, kill, kill. And then die avenged. Make haste. What are you waiting for?"

There was an audible sigh. Tomás could have felled his opponent with his bare hands, but he was always slow to anger. His size and strength and quiet dignity had made him a natural leader, one who had never needed to raise his voice or impose his will.

"Sit down, José," muttered the boy's grandfather. "Tomás is right. I have lived longer than you, and I know he speaks the truth. The last fifty years are littered with the corpses of young fools like you. The hour of revolution is near, when we will strike together from a position of strength. Why play into the hands of the enemy? As for the young woman, she is blameless. Has she not taken Tomás's sister and nephew into her own family?"

"She adopted her brother's bastard because she is barren and uses Rosa as a servant," spat José. "I for one am not deceived. It is her *beauty* that protects her, not her goodness." He made an obscene gesture.

Tomás took the boy by the scruff of the neck and lifted him one-handed clean off the floor.

"Show some respect for your grandpa, boy," he said mildly. "We have listened patiently to what you have to say. Who else wishes to speak?"

He dropped José without ceremony and sent him stumbling to his seat.

"But when will the hour of revolution come?" called someone else. "How much longer must we wait for justice?"

There was a murmur of support from the audience.

"The union will call us to act when the time comes," said Tomás firmly. "We are just a small part of the whole, a whole that must act together or not at all."

"Together with whom?" called someone else. "The anarchists?

I'm a socialist, so are we all. Is it to be a socialist revolution, Tomás, or an anarchist one? I'll not fight alongside anarchists. I want my own spread, one I can pass on to my sons. The anarchists will collectivize everything, we'll get enough to eat and no more. They think people are to be kept happy like pigs in a sty. And the Communists are no better. We want land, not just bread!''

"We are socialists and we will remain socialists," said Tomás. "Let the anarchists have their way in Andalucía and Catalonia. And the Communists are few and far between. Here we have nothing to fear from either of them. Let each party follow its own path to freedom. Let us not waste energy railing against our fellow workers."

"But can we have revolution and government too?" came the question. "Our leader, Caballero, said that socialism cannot work within a democracy. Five years ago we saluted democracy, we hailed it as our savior. And now our own leader speaks out against it. After the revolution, then what, without democracy?"

Tomás sighed. He was no politician, these endless debates wearied him.

"We will create a new workers' democracy, once the wealth has been redistributed and the Church disestablished. There can be no true democracy until that happens. One thing at a time, my friend."

"The sooner the better," shouted someone at the back. "Let's start with the Church. It's so well greased it would only take one match!"

There was a rumble of approval for this suggestion. Next to Don Felipe and his brutal stewards, Father Luis was the most hated man in the district. Tomás could not immediately think of a counterargument to this suggestion, and it might at least release some of the pent-up frustration to let them destroy that hated monument to greed and corruption. On the other hand, it might intoxicate young men like Juan to wreak further destruction on the homes of the bourgeoisie. Many of them lived in fear but had nowhere else to go, and believed that all the while Don Felipe and his henchmen remained, all might be well. To leave one's property unattended was to lose it, perhaps forever.

"Wait till the dying woman is buried," said Tomás finally. "Let the fat priest say his words over her grave. Then let the church be her funeral pyre."

He chose his words carefully, aware that young José was not alone in thinking him more than a little enamored of Dolores. His wife, Ignacia, a passionately jealous creature, had accused him repeatedly of lusting after her, and it was true, he did, without the slightest hope of ever consummating his desire. Tomás's sexual prowess had become legendary, thanks to the indiscretions of his wife, a coarse, sensual woman who openly solicited other women's envy with explicit tales of his strength and stamina. Ignacia was herself a big, heavy-boned creature and more than a match for the silly young girls who were foolish enough to try to tempt her husband. One saucy look in his direction and the looker was likely to find herself flat on her back, straddled by Ignacia's huge bulk, losing hair by the handful. Only once had Tomás been unfaithful, during the most recent of his wife's pregnancies. No sooner had she given birth than she had accosted the guilty young widow in the fields and stripped her naked in full view of everyone before raping her repeatedly with an unpeeled ear of maize, leaving her bloodstained weapon fully inserted for someone else to remove. What she had done to her husband remained a subject for lewd speculation, but Tomás had never looked at the girl since, nor she at him.

"The old woman has been dying for weeks," shouted someone. "Why should we wait?"

"Give it a week, then." Tomás shrugged. "She will be dead within the week, the daughter says."

A grumble of consent went around the room.

"We will take a vote on it this time next week," said Tomás. "Agreed?" A chorus of grunts and nods.

"*¡Viva la revolución!*" finished Tomás. "*¡Viva la República!*"

And his congregation chanted their response and filed out of their pews.

Ramón was feeling a great deal better. It was luxury indeed to have a nurse again. Providence had obviously smiled on him, bringing this humble creature to his aid at his hour of need. He had thought he was about to die, not realizing that she had been sent as God's chosen instrument, to preserve him as part of some grand design. She had known exactly what to do, her brother, as it turned out, being similarly afflicted. And then, as his airways cleared in the thin light of daybreak, she had wrapped him in a blanket and made him sit on a chair while she hung the sweat- and urine-soaked sheets out of the window to dry, and turned the evil-smelling mattress.

He had given her some coins to buy bread and coffee, and while she was out had checked that his shoe was intact. He could imagine her wide-eyed fascination at seeing so much money at once. He counted it, as he did every day of his life, and replaced it lovingly. Now that it took him a year to earn what he used to spend in an evening, he had turned from spendthrift to miser; he worshipped money as never before. Today there was nothing worth spending it on, but tomorrow or the next day, or the next, his father would die, God rot him, and he would buy a fine set of new clothes and return home in splendor to reclaim his inheritance.

Then he checked under the loose floorboard for his other treasure and found the revolver happily nesting in the sawdust. He blew down the barrel and took aim at a man in overalls, in the street below. Lacking a fast car to get away in, he did not shoot, but imagining the bang and the crumpled body was nearly as good. Better in a way. Recently he had attended a public rally called by the Falange in the hope of seeing a few miserable workers bite the dust. But he had been shocked and terrified at the size of the counterdemonstration, the ferocity with which it fought back, and after witnessing a fellow Falangist not twenty yards away fall backward with a bullet in his skull, he had taken cover and hidden himself till the trouble was over.

Where were the workers getting their weapons from? Was that not proof that a huge plot was brewing, that the Reds were arming them in readiness for revolution? He was glad he had a gun to defend himself. A gentleman was not safe in such a district. It required great courage to live among these people, to spy on them and gather information about their habits. He must make a note of everything he saw and heard, in preparation for the day when he would be called upon to defend Spain from those who conspired to overthrow it. It was his sacred duty, his divine purpose; he had been plucked from the jaws of death to this end.

He replaced the gun quickly as he heard the girl's footsteps running up the stair. The cracked jug was filled with thin, bitter coffee made from barley, and the loaf already had a gouge out of it, where she had torn into it hungrily, dipping it into the steaming liquid as she ran along the street.

Ramón broke off a piece of bread delicately and gestured for her to fill a grimy china cup. He had little appetite these days and viewed her greed with fastidious distaste.

"When do I begin work, señor?" she inquired tentatively, gathering the crumbs off her skirt into her palm and tipping them into her mouth.

"Once you have proper clothes, my child. You cannot go to work dressed in rags."

"Proper clothes?"

"My associates will not be impressed by your appearance. You are not in the olive groves of Andalucía now. You are in the city and must dress accordingly."

Marisa looked puzzled. From what she had seen in the street below, she was no shabbier than most, and considerably cleaner than her new protector. But she was grateful to this poor, sick cripple for befriending her and did not like to contradict him.

"I will buy new clothes as soon as I get my wages," she said humbly. "I have no money for clothes."

"Then I will give you one week's wages in advance. You may work for me for one week, and one week only, so that you may buy new clothes and prepare yourself for your new life. Then I will be able to recommend you to my associates with confidence. A reference from me will assure you of a good position."

"But a woman in the *panadería* told me there was work to be had in the garment factory. I can sew, señor. I forget to tell you, I can sew."

"Pah! There you will work like a dog and the union will help themselves from your wages. There you will work till your dying day with no hope of improving yourself. You must use your talents, Marisa, not turn yourself into a slave of the union. I can insure you earn double, treble, what you can earn in the garment factory. How many brothers and sisters do you have?"

"Six, señor. And my brother is sick, like you."

"Six." These people bred like rats. "Well, by all means go to work in a factory. Then you will have enough to keep yourself alive. Why bother to earn more? Let your family starve, by all means. Why should you think of them? After a month you will have forgotten their plight. You are young, and the young are selfish. Be off with you."

"But I do care about my family, señor. I am sorry if I have offended you. I—"

"Very well. I accept your apology and I will allow you to work for me until I find you a suitable position. I am a very sick man, Marisa. I would like to do some good before I die. You may wait downstairs in the street for me. I will join you directly."

Red would suit her, he thought, as he extracted the notes from his hoard. Cheap red cotton, cut low at the neck, and cheap red lipstick to match. Not that he desired her for himself. He had learned his lesson the hard way. No gentleman ever touched a worker's whore.

6

"How is Clara?" asked Jack, signaling to the waiter for the bill.

"A lot better," said Edmund. "She's really looking forward to this trip. The prospect of a few demonstrations and anti-Fascist rallies seems to have bucked her up no end."

"You might get more than you bargained for," said Jack. "If I didn't know Clara so well, I'd tell you to call it off. The right and the left in Spain are very dangerous animals, and they're both baying for each other's blood. A rally could easily turn into a riot, with armed police firing in all directions. If you must go, for God's sake be careful."

Edmund did not need telling twice. He remembered only too clearly how Clara had got herself arrested in 1931 for assaulting a policeman during the hunger march, how she had demonstrated against Mosley in 1934, returning home with a torn lapel and a bruised jaw. He intended to keep Clara on a very tight rein.

"Thanks for the tip, old man. I won't let Clara out of my sight, believe me. But I can't possibly call it off now, she'd be devastated. It's hardly my idea of fun, but you know how important her politics are to her. Anything to bring her out of herself. She's been through hell these last few weeks. In any case, I'm quite curious to see a bit of Spain. Because of Dolly, you know."

"And how's Flora these days?" said Jack, changing the subject abruptly.

"Flora? Oh, same as ever. Always on the go, organizing everybody and everything. I don't know where she gets all her energy from. She's dying to have you decorate one of her dinner parties. How's Angela?"

"You mean Elizabeth, don't you?"

"Do I? I suppose I must, then. How's Elizabeth?"

"Haven't a clue. She doesn't know I'm back yet, thank God. Let's go back to my place and sink another bottle."

155

"Sorry, Jack, I ought to be making tracks. It's eleven already, Clara will be getting worried. You must come over for a meal one night, when we get back.''

"Does that mean Clara's forgiven me for last time?''

Edmund smiled. Sympathy wasn't Jack's style. Far from offering tactful condolences he had lost no time in engaging Clara in a heated political quarrel which had quite brought her back to life.

"Oh, no hard feelings, I'm sure. I think Clara rather enjoys arguing with you, it's become a ritual. You know how protective she is about the party line. She likes to have things cut and dried. It's her Catholic upbringing, I suppose.''

"Poor Clara. Tell her I'd dearly love to write the party line, it would save me no end of time and trouble, except that no one would take me seriously ever again, least of all *The Daily Worker*. Well, if you must desert me . . .''

Jack paid the bill languidly. It amused Edmund to see how utterly at home Jack made himself in this prestigious gentleman's club, how eclectically he fitted in against the dark wood and dark leather despite his lack of old school tie, his untutored vowels, his studied raffishness. He had gone one better than conforming. He had made his failure to conform seem enviable, a privilege denied to those who sought to reject their inherited values, who had to strive self-consciously toward something which to Jack came naturally, effortlessly.

"Did you have that bet on Running Water, then, Phipps?'' Jack inquired of the poker-faced waiter.

"Yes, sir. Thank you very much for the tip, sir.''

"Didn't have anything on it myself. You owe me one.''

"Yes, sir. Thank you, sir. A very good night, sir.''

He was clearly inhibited by Edmund's presence, unsure whether to lapse into his usual sotto voce bonhomie in the presence of such a solemn-looking gentleman, who might consider him to be taking liberties.

"Good-bye, then,'' said Edmund, shaking Jack's hand.

"Have a good holiday,'' said Jack. "And remember what I said.''

"I will, don't worry. See you soon, I hope.''

Edmund hurried off in the direction of Temple tube station. Jack hailed a cab and rode from the Strand to Eaton Square, where he now occupied a service flat with easy access to Victoria. He pondered whether to call Elizabeth, who would be languishing by the phone in Cheyne Walk, working herself up into a petulant state of aphrodisiac rage. He had given her his solemn promise to call her from Geneva, just for the pleasure of breaking it. Like all women reared on flattery, she adored being badly treated. She would complain bitterly, endlessly, that he never listened to her, never told her things, showed her no respect, treated her like a whore, when in fact all she really wanted was to be systematically and comprehensively fucked out of her spoiled little skull. And the next day she would tell one of her shrill little friends what a swine he was and start working herself up toward their next soulless encounter. Her confidantes were invariably eager to meet the beast in person, and frequently contrived to do so. In fact, there was nothing to beat personal recommendation. Elizabeth had been Angela's best friend.

Years ago Jack had fantasized about the luxurious apartment he would one day inhabit, the expensive objects with which he would fill it, the beautiful women who would succumb to him in it. The reality was small, functional and Philistine. It could have belonged to anyone, there was no stamp of personality upon it. No photographs, no keepsakes, no evidence of the past. He could have moved into it yesterday, rather than three years ago, and he never entertained in it. Edmund was the only person who had ever set foot inside it, bar his cleaning woman. The thought of bringing a woman here was anathema to him, an invasion of privacy which he could not have tolerated. To have some woman touching things, lying between his sheets, leaving her scent on the air would have violated the perfect vacuum he had sought to create.

He flopped back on the bed with his shoes still on, lit a cigarette and smoked it gloomily in the dark. The scathing dispatch he had sent from Geneva, denouncing the League of Nations as a monument to cowardice, hypocrisy and injustice, had mirrored his present bitter mood, and yet his disgust had drained him, leaving him bored, lethargic, desperately low on adrenaline. The war in Europe he had been predicting for so long was stultifyingly slow in coming, and yet there was no sense of suspense, everyone had been lulled by compromise, fooled by caution. Hitler was getting away with murder, Mussolini was still a figure of fun, and Japan was simply too far away. He had begun to feel part of the conspiracy. People read his pieces smugly, reassured by detail, brutalized by fact. It was as if they thought they could stop things happening just by being well informed and discussing them to death. Not since the Griselda days had he despised his readership more.

Still, the troubles in Spain might liven things up; there was a good story brewing there. The right and left had polarized into two extreme camps; fascism versus Marxism should be a struggle worth watching. Martindale had insisted that the readers weren't interested in Spain, and Jack looked forward to proving him wrong. All his instincts told him that the balloon was about to go up, and he was determined to be there when that happened, with or without Harry's blessing.

Any antidote to his present apathy would be a relief. He needed something new to get his teeth into, something to convince himself he wasn't played out, a suspicion that had begun to haunt him. Recently he had begun to toy with the idea of packing it all in, of disappearing without warning, of spending a year or two wandering incognito, searching. Quite what he was searching for he did not know, but it wasn't money or fame or success or a rich wife or any of the other things that had lost the charm of inaccessibility. Perhaps he was searching for what Edmund had. A sense of purpose, however unrewarding the goal might seem to anybody else. A purpose spiced with danger and the imminence of loss, a single-minded zeal uncomplicated by rational thought. He envied Edmund. Edmund knew exactly what he wanted and didn't care if everyone else thought him mad for wanting it. Whereas he, Jack, had always wanted what other people would respect and envy, until he got it. Was there anything less rewarding than a cold-blooded wish come true?

And yet the one time his blood had run hot, he had been cheated. It had been like a warning never to want anything for its own sake ever again, never to pay for anything in advance.

Damn her. Damn her, damn her, damn her.

Pamela Carrasquez was buried on a Sunday, having breathed her last the night before. Dolores was surprised to see Tomás standing humbly outside the church, but news traveled fast in Albavera. Had it not been for her grief and her preoccupation with catching the first available train home and surprising her waiting family, she might have sensed something portentous about the giant figure lurking awkwardly in the square, watching her from a distance. As it was, she assumed that he was waiting to catch her before she left, with some message for his sister.

Father Luis sprinkled the coffin with holy water and began intoning the *De Profundis*. The congregation was small, many people being too nervous to attend church these days. Dolores's father remained silent throughout the responses. Like many ardent supporters of the Church, he was not in the least devout and no doubt believed that when the hour of judgment came, matters could be arranged in the usual way.

He had met Dolores that morning at the door of her mother's room, her prison for more than a month, and escorted her down the stairs and through the kitchen and out of the back door, claiming that she was only fit to use the servants' entrance and could not be trusted. Once again, Dolores had been assailed by the suspicion that her father was plotting something, something he did not wish her to discover, but her normal curiosity had been blunted by exhaustion and grief. According to Angelina, her mother's elderly maid, Dolores's former bedroom was currently occupied by houseguests, as were many other spare rooms in the house. She had complained grouchily of all the extra work, but when asked who the guests were and how long they were staying she had shrugged and pleaded ignorance and changed the subject, as if aware she had spoken out of turn.

Since then Dolores had been too abstracted to give the subject further thought. She knew that Father Luis had recently moved in, ostensibly to be on call for her mother's last hours, but more likely because he was too afraid to remain alone in his former quarters. No doubt there were others who, like him, looked to her father for refuge and protection against the gathering storm.

Dolores nodded at Tomás, who was still waiting outside, head respectfully bowed, as the small procession moved out into the sunlight and made its way slowly toward the white-walled graveyard, set just outside the town. The family vault was open to receive the alien corpse, now trapped forever in the land it had never learned to love.

The formalities were brisk, there was little evidence of mourning around the gaping tomb. Dolores wanted to cry and could not, while her father stood ramrod straight, dry-eyed and evidently impatient to get away. She wished that her brothers were here. Ramón, at least, would have wept. And although Josep would not have wept, having enough belief to rejoice, his vigorous faith would have been a comfort. But there was no Ramón, no Josep. And Dolores blinked back the tears which finally welled up, recognizing them for tears of self-pity. She longed ferociously for home, for Lorenzo and Andrés, for Rosa and Rafael. Soon she would be with them again. She should not begrudge a few minutes more of her time, a few more minutes of sharing the awful loneliness her mother had known for so long.

As the mourners shuffled off toward the waiting cars, Dolores knelt on the ground and crossed herself and shut her eyes, wishing to be left alone for a while with her thoughts. She had no doubt she would be excluded from the funeral wake, and in any case she would have found it distasteful to witness her father carousing with the usual bunch of hangers-on, none of whom had ever given her mother a second thought. She felt curiously numb, having dreaded and yet longed for this moment for six interminable weeks; she was aware only of the warmth of the sun on her back and her impatience to be gone, to leave that house of sadness once and for all.

She tried in vain to concentrate her thoughts in prayer, shutting her eyes, clutching her rosary beads for inspiration. She could hear the sound of the cars driving off, hear the heartless birdsong, hear the silence. And she tried to hear her mother's voice, speaking to her from beyond the grave. What would her mother say to her, now that she had the benefit of infinite wisdom? Surely she would say, you are blessed, Dolores. Blessed that you did not marry for love and in haste, as I did. Blessed that you married out of duty and respect, even though you received and deserved no credit for it. Blessed that providence has protected you, seen fit to spare you the sufferings of your foolish, headstrong, passionate mother . . .

But I am cursed, Mother. Cursed with memory and guilt and endless wondering. Blessed are those like you, whose illusions were cruelly shattered, cursed are they who daydream still . . .

The tears flowed again, shamefully. This was not prayer. This was self-indulgence. How easy it was to listen to her mother now, to talk to her now, too late, how tempting to harass her poor departed spirit, still weary from its journey. Rest in peace, Mother. The blessedness of death is to forget, to cease to care, to find all life's tribulations supremely petty. And bending to her will, the inner voices sighed and said no more.

Dolores swayed on her knees, eyes closed. It was very quiet now, blissfully quiet. She sat back on her heels and buried her head in her hands, plunging into the dark pool of soothing silence, a silence that exploded suddenly into a huge, gushing roar, coming from the direction of the church.

She scrambled to her feet and ran to the gate of the cemetery. And then she saw why Tomás had been waiting outside the church. He had a message for his sister all right. Rosa would laugh when she heard the news, and Lorenzo would rebuke her for it, and she, Dolores would say nothing, hopelessly able to see both points of view.

The wind was blowing the smoke toward her, clouding the column of fire that spiraled heavenward in mock oblation. Dolores thought of Josep and shuddered, and thought of Father Luis and felt nothing at all. Drawn by morbid curiosity, she hastened her steps and ran along the narrow pathway back toward Albavera.

The Church of Santa Eulalia stood in the middle of the main square, surrounded by the homes of the bourgeoisie. Lorenzo's late father had once lived close by, in a substantial house with graceful, wrought-iron balconies, now occupied by the local miller. But the church itself was modest enough, an unprepossessing brownstone building with a humility and charm sorely lacking in its present incumbent. Josep had always managed to find peace inside it, the cool echoing hush of its thick walls and Moorish tiled floor had calmed his clamoring spirit. He had loved the multiplicity of tiny altars lining both walls, with their ornate wooden carvings and smiling, friendly statues, just as he had loved the stark austerity of the central altar, which was bereft of gold leaf or other unnecessary extravagance—for Father Luis was the thriftiest of stewards.

Josep would be sorry to see the carvings curl into cinders, to see the statues crack and crumble, to see his chilly haven of tranquillity blister with heat and vibrate with infernal noise. Josep would be angry. Angry with Father Luis, not with Tomás.

The wind was blowing the smoke straight down the main street, like a horizontal chimney, sparing the neighboring houses, whose inhabitants poured out of their homes in terror and ran for cover, fearing not so much the fire as the huge throng of workers who had assembled in the square, admiring their handiwork. There was an atmosphere of fiesta, young men running to and fro with flaming batons held triumphantly aloft, children being held high for a better view of the impromptu fireworks display, couples embracing, enjoying their moment of exhilaration, while others passed buckets of water hand to hand and doused the adjoining buildings, to prevent the flames spreading, laughing and joking all the while. Dolores stood speechless, torn between horror and fascination, too bound up with her own thoughts to feel herself observed.

And then, belatedly, she realized that people were looking at her and pointing at her and snickering and shouting provocative abuse, and she felt a sudden moment of fear, remembering that they still saw her as an enemy, in spite of, or perhaps because of, her efforts to prove herself a friend. She looked round, panic-stricken, for Tomás, and not seeing him, turned on her heels and ran, driven by some instinct of self-preservation, aware of the bitter irony of seeking sanctuary in her father's house.

But no one troubled to pursue her, and as she reached the miserable makeshift dwellings on the edge of the village, signifying the start of her father's land, she slowed her pace, panting, reminding herself that all this was nearly over, that as soon as she got back her father's chauffeur would drive her to the station at Badajoz, that thereafter she would never return, that Albavera and its burning church and its vengeful peasants would be part of her life no longer.

The first kilometer was uphill. The sun beat down relentlessly, and Dolores began to sweat. It was as if the heat from the burning church pursued her in her flight. She was relieved, at first, to see her father's car appear on the brow of the hill, thinking it had been sent to collect her. But when she saw two others close behind it, belonging to neighboring landowners, she realized, with a sickening lurch of fear, that their mission was something else altogether.

She turned and ran back the way she had come, as if all the furies of hell were pursuing her, and saw, through the smoke, Tomás marching toward her at the head of his tattered army, leading them in triumph back to their hovels, leaving those with soft hands to clean up as best they might.

"Tomás!" she shrieked, still too far away for him to hear her. "Tomás!"

She ran faster now, not knowing whether she was running into danger or away from it, knowing only that she must warn them, tell them to take cover. They were laughing and cheering and chanting slogans, fists held high in the Republican salute, naïvely unaware of the wrath they had ignited along with the holy timbers. The whole of Albavera was visible from her father's watchtower, the sight of the flames had brought him back like an avenging devil.

None of the people was armed. It was more a carnival procession than a military one. Children sat astride their father's shoulders, old men and women hobbled with their sticks. No one looked afraid. Why should they? Churches were being burned with impunity all over Spain, the Civil Guard had been forbidden by government decree to intervene. Not all the churches in Spain, the president had declared, were worth one Republican life. Father Luis had taken a wise precaution in evacuating himself. The only wonder was that it had not happened weeks ago . . .

Many of them were still coughing and spluttering, eyes watering with the smoke, so that they heard the approaching threat before they saw it, as the engines hummed ever closer like a swarm of angry bees.

Dolores turned her back on the crowd to face the oncoming vehicles, as if by so doing she could stop their progress. She stood rooted to the spot, aware of a sudden babble of alarm in the distance behind her, paralyzed by fear, and just as she thought her father's car would run her over, it screeched to a halt. And then her limbs came back to life and she turned again and ran.

She was used to the sound of guns. Her father had shot hundreds of thousands of game birds over the years, she had watched their bodies drop from the sky, bright with plumage, heavy with death. And now he had discovered better sport.

She saw a young man's face burst open like a watermelon, and then she saw another clutch his chest and fall onto his knees. And then she saw nothing at all.

"When will Mamá be home, Papá? Will she be home for my birthday?"

"Of course, Andrés. She will be home soon, very soon."

Lorenzo had received another letter that morning, saying that his mother-in-law remained much the same but was barely able to swallow water, let alone food. Her suffering was terrible and Dolores prayed for her release. There followed endless inquiries about the children and instructions for Rosa and reminders about domestic matters of no importance. She seemed unaware of recent events in Toledo, much to Lorenzo's relief. She had enough to worry about already . . .

In the last few days the town had been witness to unprecedented acts of violence, sparked off by similar events in Madrid and other major cities. A leading official of the steelworkers' union had been found with a bullet in his back, and the next day a much-hated factory owner had been multiply stabbed in the men's room in a restaurant and left with his head immersed in a washbasin full of blood. Riots threatened to break out at any moment, and it was only a matter of time before some innocent passerby was injured. Rosa had been given strict instructions not to let the children stray beyond the walled courtyard at the front of the house.

The government had lost all authority. Every day there were resignations and new appointments and huge public meetings whipped into frenzy by demagogues of rival parties. Everyone, to the right and to the left, was plotting to overthrow it. Its former supporters, the workers, accused it of betraying them and claimed that only a revolution could set the people free. Its long-standing enemies—the Church, the landowners, and the bourgeoisie—now looked to the right-wing Army officers to stage a coup and impose martial law.

Lorenzo remembered only too clearly that abortive coup of five years ago, when he had been prepared to risk all to set up a new republic. How much had changed since then! Democracy had been discredited, it had become synonymous with chaos . . .

"Don't look so worried, señor," said Rosa cheerfully, dishing out a bowl of rabbit stew. "She will get here faster than any letter. One day you will come home and she will be here waiting for you."

"Thank you, Rosa, I am sure you are right. Are the children asleep?"

"Like two little angels. Can I go out now?" Her cheeks were flushed in anticipation. Her *novio*, Roberto, was a pleasant enough youth despite the fact that he was a leading light of the local CNT and word-perfect on anarchist dogma, which Rosa parroted unquestioningly, much to Lorenzo's despair. "Your socialist brother wouldn't agree with a word of that," he had told her sourly one evening when she was driving him to distraction, and she had looked confused and not known what he meant, and Dolores had squeezed his arm and shamed him into silence.

How easily people were swayed by words, how accidental their allegiances were. How many Rosas were there in Spain, how many were there following the few, docile as sheep, angry as wolves? And if it ever came to a war, as some predicted, how many sides would there be? More than two, that was for sure.

At this very moment Tomás's and Roberto's respective unions were firing shots at each other in street battles in Madrid. And at the academy there was endless squabbling between monarchists, Falangists, Carlists, right Republicans, left Republicans. And then what about the Communists, the Trotskyites, the Basque nationalists, the Catalan separatists, all with their own axes to grind, axes that split and splintered each group into further warring factions? If and when it came to a choice, which side would he, Lorenzo, be on? And he pondered the question restlessly while knowing in his heart that freedom of choice was an illusion, that choice was anything but free.

After receiving absolution and stifling his glee at his confessor's perceptible disappointment ("Anything else, my son?" "No, Father."), Josep called in at the post office to ask if there was any mail for him. There were three letters, one from an old seminary friend, and two from his sister, the most recent one dated some two

weeks before, its journey dogged by the prevailing chaos of strikes
and bureaucratic subversion. Both were postmarked not Toledo as
usual, but Badajoz. Josep knew before he began to read that there
could be only one reason for his sister to visit the family home, and
hoped with sinful fervor that it was his father who was dying and
not his mother.

Dolores's style was factual and unemotional as always. Such a
change from her adolescent missives from school, all those years
ago, full of underlinings and exclamation marks and hyperbole.

> Dear Josep,
>
> I assume you did not receive my earlier letter. This one may
> well not reach you in time. Mamá is seriously ill, it is thought
> there is a growth on the brain. She cannot see and her mind
> appears to be completely gone, so any visit would be for your
> own benefit rather than hers. I have not told Ramón, for if she
> were to return to consciousness his presence would undoubtedly
> distress her. So I write to make you aware, not to beg you to
> come, so that you may offer Mass for her. I cannot believe God
> listens to Father Luis, and my own ability to pray is sorely in
> need of your encouragement. If you write back, write to Toledo
> as I doubt if I will be here much longer. I would like to know that
> you are safe and that your church is still standing. I think of you
> often in these troubled times.
>
> Your loving sister

She made no mention of his father, an omission that spoke for
itself. The other letter was in an identical vein, written a week
earlier. He felt guilty. It was true, he seldom wrote, he had neglected his old family shamefully since embracing his new one. But
there was no point in rushing to Dolores's side without knowing
whether she was still there, and it seemed likely that his poor mother
was already dead. He walked back into the post office and asked
to make a call to his father's house.

He waited for over an hour, reading and rereading the letter from
his old friend Eduardo, who was now established in a large prosperous parish in Navarre, a Catholic and conservative stronghold,
another country. He had been the only fellow seminarian for whom
Josep had felt any comradeship, and his letters, full of wry observations, were always welcome.

This one was written in a more serious vein. Eduardo described
how the Carlists, the dominant right-wing group in the province,

were forming militias and parading through the streets in readiness for a religious crusade against the atheistic and anticlerical government. Eduardo had been called upon to bless the troops of volunteers, known as *requetés,* many of them only boys, the new soldiers of Christ. He hoped that it would not come to war, but feared it would, and if this happened he was proposing to enlist as a military chaplain.

> *What else can I do? I am young and strong. Why should I sit in safety while others fight to defend me, and indeed you? It seems to me that you must be in great danger. The newspapers here are full of tales of atrocities in the south, and it seems that many priests have already abandoned their parishes. Will you be forced to do likewise? Surely you cannot ally yourself with those who seek to destroy the Church? Or will you abandon your cassock altogether? How will you reconcile your two vocations?*

War. What kind of war? Rich against poor, right against left, Church against State? Could one support the poor and the Church as well? Who was his enemy? Who was friend and who foe? As for danger . . . he had never felt himself in danger. The idea of fleeing his parish seemed absurd . . .

His reflections were interrupted by a tap on the counter as the clerk gestured him toward her. There was no connection available to the number he had requested. There was a fault, as yet unspecified. Or there could be a strike at the exchange. There were many strikes at the moment, and many faults went unrepaired. He should try again tomorrow. Or perhaps in a few days' time. And Josep began the long walk home to say Mass for his mother's soul.

Tomás had seen them lift Dolores's body into her father's car and drive off, hooting wildly. All around him was weeping and confusion. A dozen men had sprung forward to avenge their comrades and been spattered with bullets and Tomás had yelled at people to lie down flat on their faces. Mothers had lain on top of their children, husbands on top of their wives, tears and blood had soaked into the dust and for one dreadful minute, looking at Don Felipe standing there like Satan, training his sights on the recumbent bodies as if deciding in which order to shoot them, Tomás had thought that they were all about to be massacred. But he had fired only one more shot, a coup de grace at the still twitching figure of José, making the lad's grandfather jump in terror as he bent over the

body, his old face distorted with grief and terror. Then, apparently
uninterested in finding out if his daughter were dead or alive, he
had ordered his men to pick up her body, turned his back on his
enemies, knowing he could do so without risk, and driven proudly
away.

Eight people had been killed, six men, a woman and a baby.
There was no question of reporting the deaths to the police. Don
Felipe would produce a dozen witnesses to say the shots had been
fired in self-defense, his daughter would be declared a victim of
mob violence, and someone would be arrested for her alleged murder. No, there was nothing to do but bury their dead and wait.

There were those who had wanted to storm Don Felipe's house
by night, despite the vicious dogs that stood sentinel. Tomás, heavyhearted, had pleaded caution. But he had to agree that the crime
must not go unavenged. They must get arms from somewhere.
Perhaps the union would find them arms. Tomás agreed to send
word to union headquarters seeking support, with little hope of
success. Even if the union had access to arms, why would it send
them to a humble outpost of the Landworker's Federation, when
arms were needed for the struggle against the anarchists in Madrid?
The only hope was the revolution. The revolution must come soon.
And then they would avenge their fellow workers. Then he would
avenge Dolores . . .

Dolores was lying in the bed where her mother had died. She was
aware of the peculiar odor of the sickroom, the smell of putrefac-
tion, and thought momentarily that she was with her mother again,
in heaven, or more likely purgatory because she was in pain. Not
burning pain, just a dreadful headache, so she could not be in hell.
She wondered how long she would be here.

"Mamá?" she called into the darkness. "Mamá?"

But the voice that answered was not her mother's. It was Angelina, her mother's maid.

"Angelina? Why is it dark?" Panicking, she put her hand up to
her eyes. They were bandaged.

"Angelina? Am I blind? What has happened to my eyes?" And
then her memory started jerking the fragments into place, piecemeal, out of order, she was kneeling on the ground next to her
mother's grave, and then she saw a face explode into flames, setting
fire to the church. And her eyes were full of smoke and dust and
she could not see. She began tearing at the bandages and Angelina
went scuttling off in search of assistance.

They were wound tightly, she could not find the knot and her arms were heavy, too heavy. Then she heard her father's voice.

"Lie still! You must lie still!" There seemed to be commotion all around her, she was made to lie down again and drink some bitter liquid. And then she knew she was asleep again, in that she was paralyzed, her body beyond the reach of her mind. But her mind did not sleep. How could it, above the din of her dreams and the pain in her head and the crying of her baby in his cot beside her, alive? She had thought she was dead then, too, and the noise of her wailing infant had left her with the same feeling of power-lessness. She had wanted to pick him up and stop him crying and put him to her breast, but she had had no control over her limbs, she could hear people speaking all around her as if she were not there. And now it had happened again. Andrés was crying for her in Toledo, her mother was in her grave, Lorenzo did not even know if she was dead, or sleeping. But there was the pain. If she was not dead, then the pain was her hold on life. She concentrated on the pain amid the noise and confusion and swirling colors, fighting the peace and quiet of blessed oblivion, refusing to let her feeble body seduce her soul into sleep.

Marisa called in at the *panadería* while Ramón hobbled back to the apartment. The proprietress looked at her sourly, as did the other drab women in the line. This pleased her. They were jealous of her fine red dress and her glittering earrings and the string of beads around her neck. No one had ever been jealous of Marisa before. It made her feel important.

She had been apprehensive at first, when Ramón had explained what was required of her, but he had spoken to her with such kindness and courtesy she had not liked to refuse. It seemed a lot of money for very little work, and it had all sounded quite easy. All she had had to do was to let the man do to her what her father had been doing for years. And then afterward, when she had fol-lowed him out of the room above the café and down into the street, Ramón had been waiting for her, and he had bowed and kissed her hand and given her the most beautiful smile, as beautiful as a baby's, and then he had whispered in her ear and called her the most desirable and most clever girl in the world and ushered her into an alleyway where another man was waiting. Ramón had told her she would be paid even more this time, as long as she did exactly as she was asked, and the man had gone with her up to the room again.

This man had not done the same things as her father or the other man. She had not understood what he wanted at first and he had become angry and shouted at her, but Marisa did not mind men shouting at her, all men shouted at women. When eventually she understood, she had complied, remembering what Ramón had said.

It was easier, if anything, and very quickly over, and she had been surprised, because she would have expected to be paid less for that, not more. But Ramón had said, not at all, and there were other things that were even easier and even more expensive, as she would soon discover.

Ramón had great plans for her, he said. There were rich men visiting Madrid, foreigners who would pay ten, twenty, fifty times as much, but before he could introduce her to any of them she would have to work hard to perfect her art.

"Remember, you are an artiste," he told her. "And as you develop your talents, under my guidance, you will become more and more sought after. One day you will be able to buy fine clothes and visit the hairdresser and work in the grandest hotels in the city and kings and princes will be begging me for your favors. I am very pleased with your first day, you have a natural talent. But you must on no account reveal what you do. My associates come to you in confidence. Their wives are often sick or old or ugly, you understand."

Marisa nodded eagerly.

"These left-wing puritans are all hypocrites," he continued, as if to himself. "Their preaching is pure cant. But by all means let them shut down the brothels, as they propose to do. This will only make your services even more sought after."

Marisa understood nothing of this, but she nodded again, ever attentive.

"The Reds preach free love and attack matrimony," sneered Ramón. "And why? It is because they hold women cheap, they believe that women should be made available to all, that no value should be put upon their favors. Such people are fools, Marisa. Remember that a man will only value what he must pay for. And now we must give a thought to your poor mother in Andalucía. I myself will write to her for you and send her part of your wages every week."

"Thank you, señor," said Marisa. "And how much money have I earned today?"

He took hold of her hand, rested it palm upward on the table and counted out some coins.

"I retain the rest for safekeeping," he said. "And for the purchase of more clothes. Would you like a pair of silk stockings, Marisa? And a pair of red shoes with high heels? Look, I have a present for you."

He brought out of his pocket a tiny box of bonbons, wrapped up in a little gold box with fine silver ribbon. Marisa looked at it speechlessly, the first present she had ever received in her life.

"Oh thank you, señor, thank you," she said, her face lighting up with the beauty of pure happiness. Why, she had never been so happy. "You are the kindest person in the world." And so he was, for her world was small and mean.

Lorenzo had left Rosa and the children still sleeping. He woke earlier and earlier these days. It was normally Dolores who was up with the lark, who would bully him gently out of bed, but since she had been away, that perfect early-morning sleep, the most delicious kind there was, had been denied him.

His students were all on holiday, his time taken up by routine, by long-winded meetings, by paperwork, by boredom spiced with unease, punctuated by quarrels. Still, he was spared the greater cut-and-thrust of life in the Toledo barracks, commuting as he did between his house and the military academy, which was isolated inside the Alcázar, the huge fortress that crowned the city. It sat high on a hilltop, overlooking the narrow cobbled streets, its impregnable position evidenced by the number of sieges it had withstood over the centuries. Four mighty towers stood at each corner of the vast square building, its high walls concealing a cloistered courtyard, beneath which ran a maze of cellars set in solid rock. Bathed in morning mist, it had the air of a sleeping giant secure in its lair. It seemed remote from the sordid strife that beset the city, an enduring symbol of chivalry and history and permanence, a witness to more noble conflicts than the one that lay ahead, a bastion of honor, still redolent of the spirit of El Cid, the home of kings and heroes. How sadly times had changed. The glory of Spain's imperial city had dissipated, its proud traditions seemed anachronistic, relics of a vanished past.

The Army had taken a hammering from the new left-wing government, who had sought to subjugate rather than modernize it. No one had benefited from the so-called reforms, except senior officers, who had been bought off with massive pensions and now indulged in politics at leisure. Lorenzo, while sharing in the general mood of discontent, was at least no longer ambitious. He had come to think of himself as a teacher, not a soldier, he had come to know his strengths and limitations. The Army was his job, not his life. His life was Dolores and the children and his guns. That guns were instruments of war was hardly relevant, they might just as well have been any other precision instrument, working only as well as the hand and eye of the operator, demanding care and practice and dedication.

Lorenzo's melancholy mood was not improved by the memorandum lying on his desk, which brusquely dismissed the tentative suggestions he had made for extensions to the next term's syllabus. Surely weapons instruction mattered more than gymnastics? In Lorenzo's view the colonel's passion for sports was indulged to the detriment of far more important subjects like his own. It was symptomatic of an effete, peacetime army.

He fell to brooding, covering the same old ground over and over again. It seemed to him that there were too many divisions within the Army for it ever to unite behind the government, or against it, or behind the workers or against them, or behind or against whatever other force tried to assert its will over the prevailing chaos. The Army had split into factions, just as the workers had done. These days every man was a law unto himself.

What if part of the Army rose up against the government while the rest defended it? What if soldier had to fight against soldier? Then it would be not so much a *pronunciamiento*, more a civil war, or rather an attempt at one, with both sides similarly ill-equipped and inefficient, both sides encumbered by undisciplined civilians. Inevitably the numerically stronger side would win the day, something that would doubtless become apparent almost immediately, reducing the conflict to a short-lived, domestic squabble, not a real war.

He sighed, still unconvinced by his own cynicism, knowing in his heart that he was dodging the real issues, wishing Dolores were here to confide in. She had always been a tower of strength, discreetly so, never seeking to dominate him, never reproaching him with his lack of material success. He knew she still clung to the idealistic notions he had long since abandoned, but in politics, as in everything else, she had urged him to be true to himself.

"Whatever happens, I will stand by you," she had said, time and again. And she had. She had been disinherited for him, she had nearly died bearing his son, she had endured five years of harsh economy. She had been a loyal and generous wife. Now, as always, he felt unworthy of her. He still had to prove himself, still had to make her proud of him.

"You must follow your own conscience," Dolores would say, if she were here. "My first loyalty is to you, not to abstract principles."

There was nothing abstract about the principles that tormented him now, they were becoming terrifyingly real . . .

Josep had hoped to see María at Mass again, but she did not appear. He wondered if Juan had found out about her previous visit and subsequently beaten her for it. He was known for his violent temper; María was often to be seen sporting a black eye or a thick lip.

Still, according to his rival priest in neighboring Baenilla, attendance at Mass had dropped sharply everywhere. Anarchist attacks against churches and clergy were spreading unchecked throughout Andalucía; some priests had gone into hiding, fearing persecution, and many people now prayed at home, rather than risk violent abuse.

"That church of yours cannot escape much longer," his father confessor warned him. "It will be burned by these murderous anarchists, like so many others before it, and you with it, if you are not careful. Here in Baenilla, at least we have the military garrison close at hand to protect us. Up there in Fontenar, you could all be murdered in your beds . . ."

Indeed, many of the neighboring landlords had decamped, feeling increasingly insecure in their isolated estates now that they had been bullied and terrorized into paying grossly inflated wages while the government looked on.

"My church is quite safe," Josep assured him. "If they had wanted to burn it, they would have done so long ago."

"Pah! You flatter yourself. You think that because you have allied yourself with the workers, they will spare you. But I know these people of old. Be assured, they despise you in their hearts, they laugh at you behind your back."

"Thank you for your advice, Father," said Josep, stiffly. "But time will tell."

"Soon you will have to choose," continued his mentor, warming to his theme. "The Church has already begun a holy crusade in Navarre against this wicked, atheist government of ours. Mark my words, these Marxists will not rest until the Church is officially outlawed. Is that what you want?"

"No, of course not, but—"

"Well, that is what you will get, if the left have their way. They think the government is too moderate. Moderate! They yearn for revolution. They would like to see every priest and nun murdered, every church desecrated and destroyed! Open your eyes, my son, before it is too late!"

Josep let him rant on, knowing that it was futile to quarrel. He would only be misunderstood and misquoted. Politically, he was in an impossible position. The Church was firmly opposed to the Popular Front government, which sought to strip it of centuries of unfettered power. The Church expected and required all priests, all Catholics, to support the campaign it was currently spearheading to discredit the government and ultimately bring it down.

As a priest, his allegiances had been decided for him. But as a man he would always support the worker against the oppressor, the poor against the rich. Was he a man first, or a priest?

He had tried to be both. He had taught children to read, he had dispensed iodine and bandages, he had rolled up his sleeves and labored in the sun and joined in Andalucian folk songs and allowed foolish, adolescent girls to flirt with him. He had driven the rich out of his church to demonstrate his good faith. These people did not see him as their enemy, they respected him and liked him. They might not attend Mass, that was still in the future, but assuredly they would not persecute him, they would not drive him away.

As for his church, it was a humble enough affair, despite its lofty location. The village of Fontenar had been built on a hilltop, like most other towns in the province, to protect it from former foes, and the church was perched dizzily on its highest point, the bell tower a useful lookout against attack. The adjoining houses were inhabited by Josep's vanished flock, those who grew fat on olives. Olives were Fontenar's livelihood, every cobbled corner exuded the thick, pungent smell of the crushed fruit. But those who tended the noble crop, who harvested, processed and pressed it, who packed and transported it, did not grow fat on olives. Bread spread with oil and garlic was a diet that kept a man thin, as Josep knew to his cost.

Concerned at María's continuing absence, Joseph set out to visit her. She lived in a rough hillside shack just outside the town, and in the past she had always seemed pleased to see him. But today he found her tongue-tied and reluctant to meet his eye.

"I was sorry not to see you at Mass," began Josep. "I was hoping you would come again."

"I'm sorry, Father, but . . ."

She turned her back on him and continued spreading her wet washing over the bushes to dry.

"Did Juan forbid you to come?"

She nodded without turning around.

"Then perhaps I should be speaking to him, rather than to you."

"Father . . . say nothing to Juan." Her thick accent was as usual hard to penetrate, she had spoken only Basque until her marriage. "You ought to leave, Father. You ought to leave this place."

"Leave? I am not at liberty to leave, María. This is where I must work until I am sent elsewhere. Where would I go? And how would I explain myself to the good bishop?"

"Soon there will be nowhere for you to work," she said gruffly. "Soon you will have no church."

Josep stared at her for a moment in disbelief. Then he shrugged and smiled, refusing to take her seriously.

"Then I must stay indoors for a while," he said, "and protect myself from the sun. For not even Juan would burn my church while I am inside it."

María did not return his smile.

"You are in danger, Father," she repeated. "You must go. There is no place for you here. I cannot say more. I cannot."

She turned her back on him again, dismissing him, shoulders trembling.

Josep began speaking again, but she walked quickly away from him, without looking back. The rejection was like a slap in the face. The poor woman was only trying to warn him, and yet he felt angry, humiliated, betrayed. His fellow priest's predictions rang in his ears, mocking him. "I know these people of old. Be assured, they despise you in their hearts . . ."

"My church is quite safe," he had said proudly. Never for one moment, in his sublime arrogance, had he thought this could happen to him. It was a denial of everything he had achieved so far, a final, savage insult. He imagined the satisfaction of those who had exiled him to this place, the smug I-told-you-sos of his superiors. There would be no clucking sympathy for him, this would be seen as a judgment on him, a fitting punishment for his renegade views, proof that they had been wise and he young and foolish . . .

How gullible he had been! He had believed that his church was inviolable, he had thought that he was different, special, he had put his trust in these people and tried to earn their trust in return, never dreaming that they were just using him, humoring him, *tolerating* him. And now he had become tiresome, now they proposed to dismiss him, like an importunate lover . . .

No. He would not let them do it. He would not be made to look a fool. Arsonists they might be, but murderers never. He would refuse to leave the church, and they would have to burn it with him inside it, and this they would not do. It never occurred to him that he might be courting martyrdom—he loved life too much for that. If he stood up to them, if he showed them he was not afraid, they would back off. He would protect his church with his life. No, not protect his church. Protect his self-respect.

Angelina was snoring. It must be night. Dolores put her hands up to her head and began working at the knot on the bandage. She felt dizzy and nauseous and she knew she must be quick. The bandage had stuck to her hair just above her right ear, glued by dried blood, and she winced as she pulled it free. Then Angelina stopped snoring. Dolores held her breath and rested her aching arms for a moment, waiting, but soon the shuddering gasps resumed and in a few more moments she was free.

And she could see. She felt her head and eyes all over, and apart from the throbbing bullet wound above her ear, she could find no other damage. She had not been blind at all. She had just been prevented from seeing.

She could see the moonlight leaking through the gap in the shutters and a thin band of light under the door. Slowly she eased herself out of bed, the springs miaowing like hungry cats. She felt sick and giddy and light-headed and euphoric. She knew only that she must leave this house immediately and go home. Her mother was dead, and she was not blind, there was no reason for her to stay. It occurred to her with startling clarity that she had been kept a prisoner. It was like some mystic revelation that had come to her in her sleep, requiring no analysis, perfect in its elemental truth.

She dressed clumsily in what clothes she could find and stumbled around the room till she found her handbag. She had the money she had brought with her, which would be enough to get her home, and she had thought to take two of her mother's rings as keepsakes, the only inheritance she would ever have. She felt full of reckless confidence, intoxicated by adrenaline. She would slip out of the house by the back door, walk into Badajoz and catch the next train home. She would outwit her father, thwart his evil plot. She knew now beyond doubt that he was mad, quite mad. Clearly he was determined that she should never see her husband and son again.

Six years on, he was trying yet again to keep her away from Lorenzo. He had threatened to lock her up all those years ago, and now he was carrying out his threat, settling his old score. He had shot her and drugged her and blindfolded her and put Angelina to guard her. He was planning to keep her in the house forever. He was mad. But she would escape him.

The grounds of the house were guarded by a brace of vicious watchdogs, trained to tear any intruder limb from limb. They were pedigree homebred Dobermans, and Dolores had played with them as puppies. Hopefully they should give her no trouble, but just to be on the safe side she had better take some sugar with her.

She crept downstairs, holding her shoes, looking furtively to the right and left, and quietly shut herself into the kitchen, which was an immense, stone-floored room, hung with elaborate ironwork like some ancient torture chamber and leading out into the vegetable plots and orchards. The estate grew or raised all its own food; vast amounts of it went to waste each day.

Dolores filled her pockets with some rough lumps of sugar broken off the large loaf in the pantry. As an afterthought she also took some stale rolls, *chorizo*, and a few figs to sustain her on her journey, wrapping them in a napkin and stuffing them into her handbag.

She stood on a chair and slid the topmost of the three heavy, iron bolts that secured the back door. Then she climbed down again, too quickly, making the blood rush to her head, and paused giddily before sliding the center one. And then the third. She turned the key in the lock very slowly, anxious not to make any noise. Still nobody stirred.

She opened the door a fraction, wincing as the hinges squeaked. She must make sure that the dogs did not bark. If the dogs barked they would wake up the whole house. She put her fingers in her mouth and blew into the warm night air, musical with crickets. It was a quieter whistle than her father's, higher pitched than either of her brothers'. The dogs' instant recognition of her whistle, the first day she had come home, had been the only welcome she had received.

She sighed with relief as they came bounding toward her out of the darkness, making low whimpers of pleasure, knowing that to bark was to set off the alarm. Dolores patted them and fed them sugar and let them accompany her down the long, winding driveway that led to the fields and freedom.

The railings surrounding the house were a recent embellishment, added since Dolores had left home. They had come to seem like prison bars, designed to keep her in rather than to repel invaders. But in her dazed state she had quite forgotten about them and the heavy iron gate, secured with a huge padlock. Somehow she would have to climb over the top. And then the dogs started to bark.

She ordered them to be quiet, and they obeyed unhappily, growling. They were right, of course, no one was permitted to climb over the gate. Not she, Dolores, and certainly not Tomás. *Tomás!*

He was standing on another man's shoulders, preparing to hoist himself over the top, and the sight of the dogs had frozen him in this unnatural posture. He looked almost comical. Dolores felt an insane desire to laugh.

"Stay," she hissed at the dogs, pointing at Tomás. "It's a friend. Stay."

Sullenly, the dogs obeyed her, glaring silently at the trespasser, as if knowing they had received a false command. Dolores distributed more sugar.

"Tomás, what are you doing?" she sang out gaily. "Can you help me get out? Why are you trying to get *in?*"

How funny it was, she trying to get out and Tomás trying to get in. Why on earth anyone should want to get in was momentarily beyond her comprehension. And she started to laugh, not aware that she was laughing, drunk on danger, ecstatic at the prospect of freedom, dizzy still from the pain in her head and the strange buzzing noises in her ears.

Tomás jumped down beside her. The dogs growled deep in their throats, ever suspicious.

"Dolores," he hissed, shaking her gently, while she continued to laugh helplessly. "Dolores, you must do as I say." He squatted on the ground. "Put your legs round my neck. Hurry."

She sat astride him, piggyback, still giggling. Tomás stood up straight.

"Now hold on to the railing and stand on my shoulders. Don't be afraid."

She did as bidden, to find her waist level with the top of the gate, and looked down giddily over the other side where another man had his arms outstretched, waiting to catch her.

"Now sit on the top of the gate and then jump," hissed Tomás. "Julio will break your fall."

Julio was Tomás's younger brother, as short as Tomás was tall. Dolores waved at him skittishly, consumed with a reckless sense of the ridiculous. Only then did she see the other men, too many men to count, lurking in the shadows behind him. They were car-

rying pitchforks and scythes and hoes and sticks. Her hand froze
in midair, her laughter died in her throat.

"Jump!" ordered Tomás urgently, and she flew and fell and
flattened poor Julio. Two other men dragged her to her feet. And
then the dogs started barking.

She called out to stop them, but she was too late. Tomás's shirt
was already soaked with blood. She heard a loud crack as he straddled one of them like a donkey and jerked its head back. Then he
got up and wrenched his knife out of the other dog's throat.

"The dogs!" screamed Dolores. "You killed the dogs!"

Julio tied a rag around her mouth to silence her and tied her
roughly to a tree. Helplessly, she watched the men toss their im-
plements over the railings and hoist each other across, disappearing
one by one into the darkness.

Julio helped the last man over, cut the rope and tied her hands
together with it, leaving the gag around her mouth. It smelled disgusting, she could feel the acid from her empty stomach rising up
in her throat, and unable to expel it, she began choking. Julio
dragged her down the hill, well out of earshot, before taking it off,
and let go of her briefly while she retched painfully onto the grass.

And after that she could remember running and falling over and
then children eating sugar lumps and *chorizo* and figs, and then
nothing.

Edmund insisted they take the journey in easy stages; Clara was
still anemic and painfully thin, and he was anxious not to overtire
her. As they traveled south, her spirits seemed to stretch toward the
sun. Gradually her nervous exhaustion gave way to a convalescent
languor; the dark circles under her eyes were fading, and a new,
healing pinkness glowed beneath her pallor. By the time they arrived in Barcelona, on the eve of the festival, she was almost cheerful, and Edmund had begun to hope again.

The city was thronged with visitors; the hot summer evening was
thick with noise. They went for a stroll before dinner along the
Ramblas, the long, leafy walkway running from the main square
down to the harbor. According to Baedeker, it was a delightful
promenade, famed for its stalls selling books and birds and flowers,
and lined with bars and charming pavement cafés. But tonight it
seemed lacking in the carefree atmosphere described in Edmund's
guidebook; it reminded him of Piccadilly Circus in the rush hour.

"What a lot of people," said Clara. "Do you suppose they've
all come for the Olympiad?"

"They look like locals to me," said Edmund uneasily. Large groups of men were amassing all along the route, talking and gesticulating wildly. Loudspeakers attached to the trees on each side of the avenue blared out music, interrupted by incomprehensible public announcements. People hung out of upper windows watching the goings-on below.

"Is there going to be an anti-Fascist demonstration?" asked Clara, excited. "What's it all about?"

"I don't know," said Edmund. "Perhaps the hotel manager can enlighten us." Remembering Jack's warning he inveigled a reluctant Clara back to their hotel, where he sent her upstairs to change for dinner while he spoke to the proprietor in a garbled mixture of French and English which left him none the wiser.

"Well?" said Clara when he rejoined her. "What did you find out?"

"Not much. As far as I could understand, there's some dispute brewing between the anarchist trade union and the government. The manager advised us to stay well away from the Ramblas and the Plaza de Catalunya."

"Why?"

"I presume because there's going to be some kind of trouble. But it's definitely nothing to do with the Olympiad, so there's no earthly reason for us to get involved. Now let's have some dinner."

Clara chafed a bit at this, but certainly the street outside their hotel seemed quiet enough, and by the time they had finished their meal, which was served with interminable slowness, it was late enough to preclude any further expeditions.

Clara found it difficult to sleep, but she refrained from tossing and turning, anxious not to disturb Edmund. She hadn't had a drink all day, having promised herself that Barcelona would mark a new beginning, and now she was paying the price of her premature pride. She breathed deeply, trying to quell the restless craving that tormented her, watching Edmund sleep.

Watching him sleep was always soothing, watching him sleep was her secret vice. Watching him sleep she could touch his face with her eyes, trace every line she had put there since that Oxford supper party where they had first met, eight years before.

At the time she had been having an affair with Teddy Lovell, a postgraduate student in politics, a fellow defector from the aristocracy whom she had briefly admired. She had been aggressively clad in green silk trousers, a man's dress shirt and a purple bow tie and bandeau, a bohemian ensemble which she had neither the confidence nor the wit to carry off successfully. It had been a warm, humid evening, and she had become very hot in her ridiculous outfit, having drunk too much Chablis and eaten hardly anything at all. She remembered highbrow conversation going on all around her and feeling stupid and uninformed and tongue-tied, unable even to regurgitate the secondhand views of people who *were* intelligent. She had started to feel rather drunk and then Teddy, who was also rather drunk, had made some terribly crude remark about it being high time he got Clara tucked up safely in bed, and he had rolled his eyes and everyone had laughed. They had carried on laughing when Clara started picking up crockery and cutlery and throwing them at him. But they had stopped laughing soon enough. She had caught his eye with a spinning teaspoon, producing howls of anguish, and people had rushed to his aid while she continued to hurl random items around the room. She remembered thinking, these people are all afraid of me, these people think I'm mad, and wanting to give them a run for their money, and wanting to make a fool of Teddy Lovell with his hot breath and his hot hands and his hot, throbbing instrument of torture. God, he had been so proud of it, strutting around the room admiring its naked tumescence, telling her proudly how many women he had satisfied with it while she lay there thinking how unspeakably ugly it was, bright red and twitching crookedly in its nest of coarse, dark hair.

"Good for you," a voice had murmured in her ear, and she had turned and looked and fallen into something like love.

She had spent the night in Edmund's rooms, sleeping illicitly if innocently in his bed while he dozed gallantly in an armchair. She had woken with a blinding migraine, and he had forced her to drink a disgusting concoction of eggs and brandy and honey. She had been subdued at first, ashamed of her behavior and disoriented by his beauty. It seemed to shine out of him and over him like an aureole, even though there was nothing unusual about the steady gray eyes or the hair the color of damp sand or the narrow, straight nose or the thin, wide mouth. He was conventionally handsome, no more, and would not have stood out in a crowd but for his exceptional height. She guessed he had shot up late in life—he had none of the round-shouldered stoop of the tallest child in the class. No, his beauty was in her eyes, not in his looks, and that disturbed her.

She had reverted abruptly to her usual waspishness but he had grinned good-naturedly and offered to take her back to London on the back of his motorcycle, a reconditioned Norton which he rode at terrifying speed. She had pressed her face into his back in an ecstasy of terror, reveling in her own cowardice. She had always hated skiing, swimming, riding, sex and heights, had always forced herself to confront these physical threats with a convincing show of bravado, more afraid of showing her fear than of the thing itself. But this time she had wallowed in her fear, not troubling to hide it, knowing for once that she was safe, quite safe.

He had dropped her off at Curzon Street and raced straight back to Oxford in time to take a two o'clock tutorial, leaving her peevish with a sense of anticlimax. He had not suggested that they meet again, he had merely engineered it, innocuously, through mutual acquaintance, as if to lull her with propriety, knowing that it was something she despised.

At the time she had been in transition between painting and politics. A humiliating year in Paris had taught her that she had no talent and she had been looking for another peg on which to hang her identity. She had jumped in at the deep end by going along to a Communist party meeting, bearing an introduction from a fellow art student who, like the rest of her Left Bank acquaintances, had no idea of her background and had been glad to vouch for her. She had duly presented herself at the shabby flat in Paddington as plain Clara Neville, not Lady Clara Neville, landlord and capitalist, who had never done a day's work in her life, who was so rich that she could afford to despise money.

The trade unionists and party activists who spoke talked long and loud of the need to eliminate parasites like herself, who lived off the sweat of others. An unemployed miner from Wales had been brought to London to tell of starvation and children without shoes and desperate men who risked their lives for slave wages. He had every right to be angry, he deserved the cheers from the floor, and Clara would have been happy to put fifty pounds in the hat that was passed around, but had not dared give more then ten shillings. She had looked around the room furtively, feeling conspicuous in her handmade clothes, trying to identify other class renegades. There were two teachers, a nurse and a doctor present, all of whom would have despised her even more than the angry Welshman. She had never gone back.

Had she been an intellectual, perhaps she might have talked her way in, as others had done before her. As matters were, she had abandoned her two-hour fling with Marx in favor of a cozier, more complacent brand of socialism, where others like herself made her welcome, where her money was an asset, not a barrier, where she was applauded for her readiness to part with some of it, where she did not have to apologize for having it in the first place, where it could buy her a pardon for what she was, where it could compensate for her lack of words, her lack of beauty, her lack of everything.

Even then she had felt superfluous, insignificant, if marginally less culpable than before. Edmund was the first person who had ever taken her seriously, if seriously was the right word. He treated her with a cheerfully courteous irreverence, humored her with just the right degree of intractability. She found herself giving in to him on everything, albeit with the worst possible grace. He found politics a bore and politicians sinister and their followers gullible, and yet he encouraged her to dabble, to find what solace and support she could from people he himself had little time for. All summer long he had made no reference to his own decision to reject the intellectual cocoon of academe—rife as it as with middle-class socialists—for the dubious satisfaction of teaching in a run-down, East End school. When she had voiced her approval, he had pointed out almost irritably that *politics* had nothing to do with it, as if politics contaminated everything it touched. She had admired him hopelessly for his moral self-sufficiency, an admiration tempered by mistrust. There was no possible reason for such a man to love her, his misplaced love served to heighten her sense of worthlessness, and she had set out to prove she didn't deserve it, to him and to herself.

She had been nothing if not honest, brutally so, parading her vices, wallowing in shame, in an orgy of provocative self-disgust. But he had proved impossible to shock, humbling her into voluntary virtue. It had been almost too easy.

Deceit had been the turning point. Deceit and Jack, Jack and deceit. A new and unforgivable sin against him, one that engendered fear and superstition and a belated need to mollify her much-insulted God. And so she had gone into nursing to redeem herself, to earn Edmund's respect, to make herself independent of him. By living apart from him she had tried to live up to him. And thanks to him she had succeeded, and still she had failed. She had rejected all half measures, all soft options, she had got her diploma and joined the party and overcome her morbid fear of childbirth; for a while she had been almost too happy, happy enough to tempt fate, only to find that she had been fooling herself, she was as much of a failure as ever. And now she had to begin all over again . . .

"Clara?" Edmund woke up abruptly. "What time is it?"

Clara swallowed the sob that had disturbed him.

"Just after midnight. Sorry if I woke you."

"Haven't you been to sleep yet?"

"No."

Edmund put his arm around her.

"Poor darling. What's the matter?"

"Nothing."

"You seem tense. Would you like to talk for a bit?"

"I don't want to talk." She clung to him, shivering, assailed by a sudden awful vision of unimaginable loss. "I don't want to think. Edmund . . . make love to me."

Edmund felt his heart leap.

"Are you sure it's all right?"

"It's all right. It's been all right for ages, except in my head. I'm sorry I've been so selfish. I'm so sorry, Edmund . . ."

It was, as always, a gift, in that she took nothing for herself, too intent on pleasing him to allow him the one reward he wanted. It was her peculiar way of proving to herself how much she loved him. One could do such things for pleasure, such as it was, with anyone, anyone at all. And because she associated self-gratification with guilt, she held back from it, seeing it as a shoddy substitute for something infinitely more precious. She knew that he understood, that he would never belittle her by claiming to understand, that he would continue to strive, on the surface, for the humbler physical objectives of love, using her body as a decoy for the surreptitious penetration of her soul.

Afterward they slept, but not for long. They were brutally awakened at dawn by a cacophony of factory hooters, all blasting in unison, followed by a massive explosion and a deafening eruption of gunfire.

Clara ran to the window and Edmund pulled her away, "Keep away from there!" he shouted, alarmed. "Get back into bed and stay there while I find out what's happening."

Edmund ran down to the lobby in his dressing gown and found the hotel manager besieged by a gaggle of demented guests, all demanding to know what was going on in half a dozen different languages.

The poor man was no linguist, but then he didn't need to be. The word was international enough to require no translation. The word was revolution.

Marisa was delighted with her new shoes and stockings and the big bottle of cologne and most of all her radio. It had been kind of

Ramón to buy her a radio. She had enjoyed listening to the dance music until she realized that dance music displeased him. She kept forgetting that he was a cripple.

She lived like a princess. Instead of getting up at sunrise, as she had done all her life, she went to bed at sunrise. Bed being Ramón's bed, where she slept head to foot, her arm around his poor withered leg, her feet against his chest. It was the way she had always slept at home, with a pair of feet either side of her head, one male, one female, and she was perfectly comfortable, much more comfortable than she had been lying on the floor. After a week of lying on the floor she had crept under the covers while Ramón was asleep, knowing that he slept heavily, and when he woke up he had been angry at first, and tried to pull his leg free of her grasp. She had understood why, it was only natural, and she had kissed and stroked it and then he had lain back again and started to cry, and she had kept cradling his poor damaged limb until the sobs subsided and gradually he dozed off again.

And so they had slept ever since. At first Marisa had been troubled that he did not attempt to take matters further, and wondered if she should explain to him that she would not expect him to pay her as the others had done. But she was afraid of saying the wrong thing and making him angry or sad, and so she said nothing, deciding that being a cripple had made him shy of women and that she must wait until he was no longer shy.

They would sleep until noon. Then Marisa would put on one of her new dresses and help Ramón with his caliper splint and boot and he would do her hair for her, standing behind her as she sat on a three-legged stool in front of a spotted square of mirror propped up on the window ledge. She had thick, curly, gypsy hair, long and unkempt, and he would arrange it extravagantly with fancy buckles and combs and ribbons as if every day was a fiesta. She hoped that one day he would offer to paint her portrait, or even draw her in chalks, on the pavement, for all the world to see. He had explained that his fragile health prevented him undertaking commissions these days, and indeed he had been too busy looking after her to pursue his normal outdoor activities, a sacrifice for which she was duly grateful.

Marisa did not enjoy her new job, any more than she would have enjoyed scrubbing floors or working in the garment factory; any more than she had enjoyed laboring in the olive groves. Work was not something to be enjoyed. Work was a means of earning money, and this was assuredly the only work that would ever make her rich.

In moments of weakness, when a man disgusted her, she would numb her perceptions with daydreams, and remind herself that she was no longer starving, that already she possessed fine clothes, that this was only the beginning.

After rising Marisa would visit the *panadería*, decked out in her finery, enjoying the envious mutterings, and they would breakfast on bread dipped in unsweetened coffee. And then they would leave the narrow, squalid streets and enter another world, strolling along the wide pavements of the Calle de Alcala toward the Plaza de la Independencia and into the Retiro Park, Marisa taking Ramón's arm with all the proud possessiveness of a new bride, Ramón stiff and haughty and peevish as always, but with such beautiful manners. He treated her with elaborate, formal courtesy when they were out-of-doors, as if she were a real lady. He taught her how to sit elegantly and how to smoke a cigarette out of a holder, and lectured her on the social graces she would require to succeed in her new career. He spoke of restaurants and bars and food and wine and roulette and vingt-et-un. He spoke of Biarritz and Paris and Monte Carlo and Rome and London. He had visited every city of the world and said that one day she would accompany him on a grand tour. They would board a liner at Lisbon for New York and have a cabin of white and gold and silk, and she would wear evening dresses and diamonds and there would be flowers and candles and every night an English prince or an American millionaire or an Arab sheik would visit her in her stateroom and bring her the most wonderful presents. These rich and powerful men would be her slaves. The dingy café in the Calle de San Lucas was the anteroom to a life of power and opulence and magic. And Ramón was the sorcerer who would make her dreams come true.

They would sit in the park by the boating lake and watch the world go by while Ramón talked and she listened, her head protected by the wide-brimmed hat he had bought to keep the sun off her face. Ladies had white skin, and if she kept out of the sun for a whole season hers would grow white as well.

After an hour or two they would take their siesta in the shade of a tree, Ramón dozing with his head in her lap and later he would buy two ices and she would eat both of them, and then they would visit the shops in the Gran Via and Marisa would choose whatever Ramón dictated. A lipstick, a necklace, a scarf, a frilly garter, a little box of marzipan fruits. Every day he bought her something. Marisa herself had no money in her newly acquired handbag. Ramón said that ladies never carried money, because a real lady always had a gentleman there to pay for everything she needed. This troubled Marisa because she would have liked to buy a present for Ramón, to thank him for all his kindness. She longed to be able to produce that wonderful smile at will, she imagined giving him fine cigars and a gold watch and a handsome black walking stick, but he never bought anything for himself, although he liked to listen to her radio.

But today they had not gone to the park. Today she had not been allowed to go out to buy bread. Today Ramón was not speaking to her, gesturing at her to be quiet while he twiddled the knobs on the radio incessantly.

There was a lot of noise in the street below. Marisa had hung out of the window and seen groups of men marching with their fists held high and chanting, ''Arms, arms, arms! Arm the workers! *¡Viva la Revolución!''*

She had asked Ramón if the revolution was beginning but he had become angry and told her to shut up. Her father had spoken incessantly of the revolution. He hated anyone who lived in a house and wore a tie; when he was full of wine he would shout angrily of the day when Spain would be washed clean with the blood of the vampires who had fed on her for so long. Their wives would be forced to bear the sons of workers, their children would be made to toil in the fields, their property would belong to everyone. Money would be abolished, food and goods would be distributed by committees of workers according to everyone's needs, there would be no more rich and no more poor and everyone would be equal. There would be no government and no state; each collective would run its own affairs. There would be no more churches and no more priests, no more parasites of any description. Every man would be completely free. All the enemies of the people would be shot.

Marisa had not properly understood the things her father said. But she had never been moved by his talk of equality. For as long as she could remember she had dreamed of being rich. She had dreamed that one day while she was working in the fields some son of a rich grandee would scoop her up onto his horse and carry her away. She had dreamed that her parents were not really her parents at all, that she was the daughter of an aristocrat and had been lost in a shipwreck, that her bogus mother and father had found her washed up on the beach and put her on the back of a donkey and taken her back to their village, and that one day she would be recognized by the mole on her left ankle and be taken away to live in a fine house with servants to wait on her and a motorcar to ride

in and she would marry a man of noble birth and have beautiful
children and live happily ever after.

Her father, she knew, would disapprove of the life Ramón had
planned for her. Her father despised money and luxury and fine
clothes and idleness. Such things were indeed unfair. That was
what made them worth having. She hoped that the revolution would
not spoil everything. The men who gave her money were not rich,
it was true, but Ramón had promised her that her future clients
soon would be. What would become of her if there were no more
rich men?

She would have liked to have asked Ramón, who knew everything, but he kept shushing her to be quiet, and then he got out a
pencil and some paper and began writing. He had promised to teach
her to read. Ladies read fashion magazines at the hairdresser's and
menus in restaurants and romantic novels on the sun deck. She
longed to be able to read.

The voice on the radio kept repeating the same things over and
over again.

"There is no truth whatsoever in the rumors of a military rebellion . . . A minor uprising has occurred in Morocco, but this has
already been crushed . . . The Army has not, repeat not, rebelled
on the mainland. The Army remains loyal to the Republic . . .
Ignore all reports to the contrary . . . The government is fully in
control of the situation . . . There is no need for panic . . ."

Then there would be strident music and Ramón would turn the
knobs again and listen to other voices speaking in different languages, which she assumed he could understand. He spoke English, she knew, and some French, and Latin too. She wondered
which language he was writing in.

By evening the noise in the street had grown so loud that Ramón
had to turn up the volume. Crowds were mustering, rival union
banners held aloft. There was a scuffle between the UGT and the
CNT before they retired to opposite camps, chanting slogans and
hurling occasional volleys of abuse at each other.

Marisa was very hungry, but when she had mentioned this Ramón had shouted at her to be quiet and eat her marzipan fruits.
Marisa had not done so, they were much too pretty to eat, and
besides she had noticed that the bottle Ramón drank from was
almost empty. Soon she would be sent out to replace it, which
would give her a chance to buy some food. Ramón was hardly ever
hungry, he was too well-bred.

Marisa had ventured downstairs once to empty the slops and

been accosted by some toothless old hag of a neighbor who had jabbed her in the ribs and said that there would be no more *putas* in the new Spain, she had better watch out, and Marisa had jabbed her back and told her she was an ugly old bitch and then a man had looked out of his door and yelled at the old woman to be quiet, and then he had put his arms around Marisa and kissed her wetly on both cheeks and said that she was his sister and that soon the workers were to be given arms to take over the city in the name of the proletariat.

When she had gone back upstairs and related these encounters to Ramón he had become irritable and started to shake and then pant and she had burned some newspaper in a saucer and made him inhale the smoke until he felt better. And then, a new voice came through, from Radio Seville, which seemed to cheer him up. An old general was saying that Spain had been saved by its glorious Army.

"The days of Marxists and atheists are numbered!" he roared. "Soon this evil Red government will be overthrown and martial law will restore peace and order to our troubled homeland. Those traitors who oppose us will be shot like dogs! *¡Arriba España!*"

Then Ramón's eyes had grown bright and he had laughed and muttered to himself. And all the time the noise in the street outside grew louder.

"We-want-arms! We-want-arms!"

Marisa had to remind Ramón twice that it was time for her to go to the café. She asked him what the voices on the radio meant and he said that she should not concern herself with politics, ladies should show no interest in politics. She was never to mention politics to any of her clients except to agree with everything they said, whatever that might be.

At last he stood up unsteadily, kicking over the empty bottle, and gripped Marisa's arm tightly as they descended the narrow stairway with its decaying plasterwork and creaking timbers. All the neighbors had taken to the streets; the doorway was barred by a mass of bodies.

"Here comes the cripple and the whore!" yelled a man wearing an anarchist armband. And then, rhythmically, at Marisa, *"Puta, puta, puta!"* And gradually everyone joined in, like howling wolves, *"Puta, puta, puta!"*

Marisa felt a shudder of fear run through Ramón's arm and knew she must defend him. Summoning up all her gypsy blood she spat in the face of one of the haranguers and brought down a torrent of obscenities upon his miserable head, shaking her fist and denouncing him as a miserable traitor to his class. Were there no lawyers, no policemen, no nuns left in the city, that he stooped to threaten a cripple and a woman who lived for the day of revolution when all the workers would be free?

"Beware of that man!" shouted Marisa. "Do not listen to his bourgeois moralizing! Why, to me he sounds just like a priest!" She knelt at the man's feet and crossed herself.

"Bless me, Father, for I have sinned . . ."

There was a roar of raucous laughter which spread through the crowd like a chorus of sheep. The man muttered angrily and melted away. Marisa rose to her feet, took Ramón's arm proudly, and let him lead her out of danger.

"You did well, Marisa," he said, rather breathlessly, as they turned the corner safely. "But now you know why I dress like a pauper. These people are prone to jealousy. Beauty and breeding frighten them, you see."

And Marisa was glad of her breeding, which had indeed frightened them. She had been ready to fight, with her elbows and feet and teeth and nails if any of them had dared to touch Ramón. These city people were pale and puny, no match for a true Andalucian such as she. She had nothing to fear from them.

"Harry? Can you hear me? It's a bloody awful line."

"Jack? I've been trying to reach you for days. Where the hell are you?"

"Sitting on a time bomb in Madrid."

"Madrid? What's happening in Madrid?"

"Civil war, I think," said Jack.

7

Jack poured himself another whiskey and read through his draft dispatch and knew it wouldn't do. It was the literal truth all right, but the literal truth wasn't what he was paid to write. Any fool could write the literal truth and leave the reader to do all the work. It was lazy and amateurish and worst of all misleading; he would have to rewrite it, and fast. He was leaving shortly for Barcelona, ostensibly to cover the story there, although his real reason was to track down Edmund and Clara and make sure they were all right. Concern for them tainted his satisfaction at having been proved right . . .

It was his first visit to Madrid, though not to Spain. He had covered the miners' uprisings in the north the previous October, a minirevolution that had been brutally suppressed by the right-wing government of the day, with the help of Moorish troops directed by one General Francisco Franco. Then, as now, he had been conscious of a pulse in the air. He had not felt it in France, or Abyssinia, or anywhere else; it was something unique to Spain. That throbbing energy was heady, evocative, infectious, reminding him of things best forgotten, reminding him of Dolly. It made him feel threatened, vulnerable. A hotel room was a hotel room, whatever the view from the window, a limbo between reality and artifice, a place to feel detached in. But in Spain he couldn't feel detached— and it showed. He had written:

Madrid, July 20. There is jubilation in the streets of the capital today as workers celebrate the birth of their long-awaited revolution.

Yesterday a panic-stricken Popular Front government finally acquiesced to the people's demands for arms. It acted not a moment too soon.

While rival unions fought one another for control of some

5,000 rifles, rebel soldiers were being briefed for action inside the Montana Barracks. No doubt they anticipated an easy victory. For three days the government had played into their hands by refusing to arm the workers. For three days the Fascists had been gathering strength, expecting little resistance. But, like the government, they underestimated the combined will of the people.

Although relatively small in numbers, Fascist troops marched boldly out of their stronghold and prepared to take the city. This foolhardy move was swiftly repulsed by a huge mob of angry Madrileños, who forced them to retreat and take cover back inside the barracks. There they remained under siege all night, offering only sporadic machine-gun fire against trigger-happy civilian militias. Meanwhile groups of workers ran amok throughout the city and reduced more than fifty churches to smoldering ruins.

From dawn onward the Fascists were subjected to continuous aircraft and artillery bombardment by troops remaining loyal to the Republic, and eventually a white flag was sighted. Amid shouts of triumph, the crowd advanced to occupy the barracks, only to be met by renewed bursts of machine-gun fire.

Enraged by this foul play, the workers surged forward en masse, breaking down the mighty doors of the barracks by sheer force of numbers. Their revenge was bloodthirsty indeed. The enemy were hurled from the parapets onto the cobbled courtyard below, where their smashed and mutilated bodies were trampled underfoot.

The workers' militias are even now rejoicing in their victory. A victory that they shared with their brave comrades in Barcelona, Valencia and Toledo. A victory for the revolution, not for the Republican government. A victory in spite of the government.

The government must now concede that it has lost all authority and bend to the will of the masses. Its first priority must be the suppression of the military coup and the defeat of fascism. And the price of that defeat is a workers' revolution. If the revolution is suppressed, the military uprising will succeed and fascism will triumph.

The people must be armed and given their head before it is too late. It is already too late in many parts of Spain that have fallen without a shot to the fascists. And why? Because the government fears revolution more than it fears the generals. The Republic is dead! Long live the Revolution!

* * *

No, it definitely wouldn't do. He had written it knowing that he couldn't possibly send it out. For one thing it wouldn't get past the censors and for another Harry wouldn't print it, and for another it would scare the gentle readers half to death. *Red Rag* could not afford to condone revolution. That tired old word "democracy" would have to do.

Still, he always liked to write the truth down first, so that he could hold it up to the light, like a photographer scrutinizing a negative, deciding what should be cropped and what touched up to achieve the best result. The camera did not lie, of course, but what was a darkroom for? Jack lay on the bed and shut his eyes and locked himself into the lonely darkroom of his mind. Then he fed some fresh paper into the typewriter and got down to work.

Dolores fell out of a long, dark tunnel straight into blinding light with a shock as sudden and cruel as birth. There were no shutters at the unglazed hole in the wall, and the sun shone through it like a searchlight, straight into her eyes.

She was lying on a straw mattress, on a dirt floor, on a spine that ached, her head heavy with pain. She shut her eyes against the dazzle and tried to sit up, hearing herself groan.

An old woman stooped at the low doorway, looked inside, and disappeared again. Dolores lay back dizzily. She passed her hand across her forehead and noticed her mother's rings, cutting into her swollen fingers. She pulled at them, making her knuckles sore, trying to provoke her memory into action, knowing that she didn't want to remember, that she was afraid to. Fear. Fear was in the air all around her like some poisonous gas. She felt as if she would choke on it.

Then another woman came in and lifted her head roughly saying, "Drink."

It was cognac. Not the local grape brandy, but fine French cognac. And then she started to remember. She could see Tomás covered in blood and men running across the grass toward her father's house, and the fear burned deep into her throat as she swallowed.

The ministering angel was Tomás's wife, Ignacia, a big, strapping woman with muscular arms and thick, sensual lips surrounded by a shadow of coarse, dark hair. A pungent, musky, sexual odor hung over her like some primitive aura, aggressively unfeminine, aggressively female. Dolores had always been nervous of Ignacia.

She had never been able to bridge the barrier of her hostility, little suspecting the reason for it.

Dolores lay back again, head swimming. It seemed unnaturally quiet outside. The normal everyday sounds were lacking, it was like nighttime with sunshine.

"I will bring you food," said Ignacia, adding, "Fine food. The kind of food you are used to." She laughed unpleasantly and left the hut.

After what seemed like hours, she reappeared, with a plate of fine Serrano ham and a loaf of bread. Meat formed no part of a laborer's daily diet, and Dolores knew immediately where it must have come from. The thought of eating made her feel nauseous. And then she saw Tomás in the doorway, watching her.

He touched his wife's arm and indicated with a gesture that she should leave them. She hesitated, as if on the point of disobeying him, but not even Ignacia disobeyed Tomás.

Dolores looked up at him, trying to focus in the splintered gloom.

"Have you killed my father?" she asked. And then, "Will you kill me too?" And she remembered the hatred in Ignacia's eyes and knew that Tomás had saved her life.

"Without you, we would have failed," said Tomás gruffly. "I thought we were going to our deaths. But we lost eight people on the day we fired the church, we lost a woman and a child, and revenge knows no fear. How could I stay behind while others went forward? I knew there were dogs, I knew the doors were barred. I knew the house was full of men and guns. But you deceived your poor dogs, you left the door unbolted. If I believed in God I would think you were His instrument. We lost three men and killed twenty. We killed all your father's friends, we spared their women and children, though not from mercy. It was I who killed your father, Dolores. I cut his throat while he slept. He stank of drink, so did they all. They thought they were safe. And so they would have been, but for you."

Dolores lay back. She felt nothing. If only she could feel something. Anger, sorrow, relief, fear. But even the fear was gone, leaving nothing, nothing at all.

"They thought that we would not attack all the while you remained," continued Tomás quickly, with a glance behind him. "My own people taunted me with this. I had to prove it was not true. I was ready to kill you too. Innocence is not protection. The innocent will always outnumber the guilty, in death as in life. It was not I who saved you. It was Julio who brought you back here and protected you.''

Dolores nodded. Julio, Tomás's brother, Rosa's brother. It was Rosa who had saved her. *Rosa.* Her thoughts swarmed together suddenly, violently.

"Home," she said. "I must get home. I must get word to my husband. How long have I been here?"

The hollow feeling was flooded with panic. She scrambled to her feet clumsily, stumbling against him. He gripped her elbow, immobilizing her.

"You cannot go home," he said quietly. "Not yet."

"Why not? I must go home. I must."

"Listen to me, Dolores. Your father's house is now our stronghold. We have guns, ammunition, grenades. The place was an armory for the Falange. The others came to join your father, together with their families, seeking safety in numbers. They were preparing for war. Do you understand?''

Dolores looked at him in horror.

"They knew the revolution was coming, and now it has. All over Spain the workers are taking control. All over Spain the Army is in revolt against them, and against the Republic . . ."

"The Army? In revolt? But my husband—"

"Some of the Army has stayed loyal to the Republic. But many garrisons have rebelled, led by Fascist officers. All over Spain workers are fighting to protect their villages, and so must we, to the death if need be. But if we die, we take the wives and children of your father's friends with us. If we die, we take you with us. Do you understand me?''

"But what has happened to my husband?' shrieked Dolores. "What has happened to the children? Oh God!"

"Would your husband have rebelled against the government? Or would he have stayed loyal?''

Dolores began weeping.

"I don't know!" she lied desperately. How many times had Lorenzo railed against the government, how many times had he hinted that an Army coup was the only way to restore law and order? How many times had she shut her ears, not wanting to argue with him, never dreaming that it would come to this!

"Well, now your husband has had to choose," said Tomás, his voice hard. "He's either with the Fascists or against them. There is no middle path.'

And then she flew at him, her eyes full of rage and terror.

"Whatever my husband has chosen to do, he is no Fascist! *Whatever* my husband has chosen to do he is no murderer, as you are! *Whatever* my husband has chosen to do, he would never take women and children hostage, as you have done! Whatever he has done, he will have done it bravely, he will have done what he thought was right!"

The repeated whatevers told him she already knew the answer in her heart. Her loyalty was tearing her apart, and the love in her eyes made him vicious.

"The Fascists in Toledo have been overpowered," he informed her cruelly. "They have taken refuge inside the Alcázar, where they remain besieged. Soon it will be their tomb."

Dolores let out a gasp of horror. Tomás pulled her roughly out of the hut and lifted her on to one of her father's horses, holding her fast so that she could not move, while Ignacia smiled grimly, arms akimbo. In the cornfields on both sides of the narrow road, people watched, giving Tomás the Republican salute, which he returned, guiding the reins with his left hand. And a part of her wanted to do likewise, to acknowledge the justness of their cause. But now she could not. How could she?

"Rosa, when will Papá be home? When will Mamá be home?"

"Mamá, why are you crying?"

"Be quiet, both of you. Finish your supper, and then you must go to bed. I'm tired."

Rosa wiped her eyes with the corner of her apron. She no longer knew whom she was crying for. Herself, the children, Dolores, Lorenzo, Roberto, the baby inside her womb. How could she be crying for all of them? How could she cry for Lorenzo and Roberto too? Lorenzo was Roberto's enemy. Lorenzo was a Fascist. Lorenzo was defending the Alcázar, where Roberto, as an anarchist militant, was being held hostage. If the Alcázar fell, the Fascists would kill their hostages first. If it was relieved, they would kill the hostages afterward. Lorenzo had a chance of life, while Roberto would certainly die. Her second child would be born without a father, just as her first had been. And yet, Lorenzo had always been a father to Rafael. Lorenzo was a kind, gentle, generous man. Both children loved him. Dolores loved him. And she loved Dolores. So how could she wish Lorenzo dead? How could she not weep for him?

Dolores. What had happened to Dolores? So many rumors, which of them were true? Triumphant tales of landowners made to dig their own graves, hideous accounts of revenge and retribution.

Surely no one would want to hurt Dolores? Surely she would not
be made to pay for her father's crimes? Surely Tomás would protect
her with his life?

She had feared for little Andrés. She had told the anarchist militiaman who had visited the house that both the children were hers,
she had indicated her fervent hope that Lorenzo would perish as
befits all enemies of the workers. And as Roberto's *novia,* she had
been believed. But after the militiaman had gone she had found
herself shaking with terror. She was afraid of everybody, afraid for
everybody. Everybody she cared for was in danger. Whoever won
the day, people she loved would die.

She had wanted the revolution when Roberto spoke of it. She
had wanted it when Tomás spoke of it. She had wanted freedom
and justice and equality. Of course she had. But now she was not
so sure. The dream had seemed different from the reality. In the
dream only enemies were killed, not friends. In reality it was hard
to tell the difference.

Josep's church was full, for once. Full of people who had formerly
shunned it, hiding in fear of their lives.

Ever since the anarchists had taken control of the town late last
night, wholesale panic had prevailed. Juan and his men had
screeched into Fontenar in a truck, bristling with weapons and
burning with revolutionary zeal. Leading "reactionaries" had been
manhandled into the vehicle and taken away to be "executed,"
while patrols set fire to the premises of anyone who had exploited
the poor.

Throughout the night people had slipped under cover of darkness
into Josep's church. It should have been the first building to be
burned, and yet it stood untouched, like a citadel, because he had
refused to leave it. Juan had held a gun to his head and told him to
leave the church immediately. Josep had told him to go ahead and
shoot, and Juan had cursed and spat, and walked away.

His unforseen responsibility weighed heavily on his shoulders.
These people thought that his church was safer than their own
homes. Suddenly its priest, that much-shunned anarchist sympathizer, was hailed as a savior, a go-between, someone whose presence guaranteed protection from the mob. Frightened women
sobbed and babies cried. Josep wanted to tell them to return to their
homes, to assure them that the militia would not harm them, that
the people who had been taken away and shot had been known
Falangists and enemies of the people. But he dared not. He dared

not have one life on his head. How could he know what Juan's men might do? How could he know who was deemed to be an enemy of the people? To have voted for the Catholic CEDA party was rumored to be enough to guarantee certain death.

Josep had tried to negotiate with Juan, to no avail.

"Give these people safe passage back to their homes," he shouted. "Then I too will leave the church and you can burn it."

It was thanks to his infernal stubbornness that these people were holed up like rats in a cage. Better a hundred, a thousand burned churches than one avoidable death.

"We do not bargain with priests," came the answer. "The Church has no more power, no more say. Let them take their chances. No one innocent of crimes against the people has anything to fear. Only those who are guilty need to hide. Those who are guilty are wise to hide."

A large number of people inside obviously felt guilty. To have sacked a servant for stealing stale bread, to have beaten a child for taking fruit from an orchard, to have dined with a right-wing politician, to have refused credit or withheld wages or charged interest against those who lived from hand to mouth—all these were crimes against the people. Collective guilt hung in the air like thick fog. One elderly man and his ailing wife were brave—or foolish—enough to leave. Ten minutes later a shot had rung out, no doubt completely unconnected with their departure, but it was enough to lead to the hysterical assertion that the husband had been executed for giving evidence against a poacher some five years before.

"If you stay here," Josep had told them, "I cannot guarantee your safety." But they were all too terrified to leave. Only the continuous whining of the children reassured him. Juan had children of his own. Juan would not attack a church full of children. The Church could not protect these people, but perhaps the children could.

His congregation complained yet again that the children were hungry, as if expecting a miracle, and lacking either loaves or fishes Josep went outside again to beg some food for them.

"Let them go hungry a bit longer," responded Juan. "Let their children know hunger, as ours have always known it. Let them live off their fat. Let them feed on the body of Christ." There was a shout of laughter from his companions and one of them fired a shot in the air, making everybody inside jump and start gibbering prayers.

Josep was asked to offer Mass for the victory of the generals and swift redemption from the powers of darkness.

"I will pray for no generals," he said. "I will pray for right to triumph over evil and for all men to live together in peace and equality. You have known hunger for one day and you pray for generals to redeem you. These people have known hunger for generations. Who will redeem them? Let us pray for all the hungry people in Spain."

Their murmured responses were halfhearted and resentful. He tried to feel sympathy for them. Most of them were ignorant, if not innocent. None of them deserved to die, least of all the children. But neither did peasant children deserve to die from malnutrition. His sympathies were with Juan and his men, his sympathies had been with them even as Juan had held the gun to his head.

His thoughts returned to Dolores. None of the people in this town had committed crimes against the people on anything like the scale of his own father. People like his father had already fled the country, if they had any sense, leaving their minions to bear the brunt of their wrongdoing, people who had not the means to flee, who had nowhere else to go, who had thought the Civil Guard would protect them forever, who had never dreamed that they would defect.

But against all expectations the Civil Guard did defect, sensibly enough, when clearly outnumbered, as they had defected in Baenilla. The worthy burghers of Baenilla could not have guessed that the nearby military garrison would waver at the sight of an angry mob of workers, that they would hurriedly declare their loyalty to the Republic, that an anxious Civil Guard would be quick to follow suit. Loyalty was circumstantial stuff. Everyone wanted to be on the winning side. It was a wise man who had kept his options open. Those who bore the stamp of party membership were dying to the right and to the left, and killing to the right and to the left, and who was doing the dying and who the killing now seemed a minor detail.

Was his father dying or killing? Nothing was predictable, nothing was certain. Had the revolution sparked off the rebellion, or the other way around? Which was the earthquake and which the tidal wave? Which would claim the most lives?

As Josep walked down the altar steps and genuflected, a man tugged his surplice and asked that they barricade themselves in, in case the anarchists stormed the church.

"The church is open to anyone who seeks refuge," said Josep coldly. "And its doors remain open to anyone who wishes to leave.

Besides, there is no barricade that those men could not destroy.
You are only alive by God's grace and theirs. Be quiet and give
thanks.''

He disappeared into the vestry, shutting his ears to the mutterings. He had not realized how much he valued the time he spent
alone, how important silence and privacy were to his well-being.
He felt stifled by the demands of the horde in his church looking to
him for salvation, he wished they would all go away and leave him
in peace. The whole situation was ludicrous, his position was untenable at any level. If only he had taken heed of María's warning
his church would now be a ruin and these people safe, for the most
part, in their own homes. Their presence here was inflammatory,
in all senses of the word. As for their blind conviction that redemption was at hand, did they not believe the evidence of their eyes and
ears? Why could they not accept that the inevitable had happened
at last, that the old order was being swept away, that ancient scores
were at last being settled, that there could be no redemption until the
sins of the past were expunged? And yet they clung to the past like
flotsam, not realizing that the current was carrying them out to sea.

He slipped out of the side door of the church and walked up to a
militiaman, a raw young lad dwarfed by an antique rifle.

"Tell Juan I want to speak to him," said Josep. The boy yelled
for Juan at the top of his voice, not taking his eyes off Josep for a
moment.

"Yes?" barked Juan irritably. "What do the fat pigs want this
time? Aren't they happy in their holy sty?"

"Come inside with me now," said Josep. "Show them you are
not a common murderer. Give guarantees for the women and children. Keep us men as hostages, if you like. Prove to them you are
fighting for a just cause, that you have no wish to terrorize innocent
people."

Juan dropped his rifle, seized Josep by the collar and shook him
violently.

"Hostages?" he bellowed. "Hostages? I should kill everyone in
that church. Reprisals. *Reprisals!*" He was spitting with rage. "I
should kill them all now, while we are still alive to do it! Has your
merciful God not told you, priest, of his servants' work in Seville?
Has he not told you how the priests there are offering thanks for
the massacre in Triana? Has he not told you how mothers fought
to protect their children with brooms and boiling oil? Has he not
told you how the brave soldiers of Christ hacked them to pieces
with their babies in their arms? Do not talk to me of women and

children and innocence!'' Juan spat in Josep's face. ''The day Fascist troops march into Fontenar, we shall light a beacon to welcome them. Your congregation will burn brightly in salutation. You had better lead them in prayers, priest, praying that our armies repel the Fascists in time. Meanwhile, anyone who tries to leave the church will be shot, and the body returned to you to say grace over. Pray that this is somebody fat, priest. Then that scum in there may die as they have lived, gorging themselves on human flesh!''

He pushed Josep violently backward and picked up his rifle. He caught Josep looking at it and waved it at him.

''You thought we had no arms!'' he sneered. ''For years now the union has been gathering arms in readiness for this day. You think we would be foolish enough to confide in *you?* We kept them well hidden from anyone who might betray us!''

Josep recoiled as if struck and walked quietly back into the church. All eyes were on him as he made his way to the foot of the altar.

''Let us pray,'' he began. There was a concerted thump of knees hitting the ground. ''Let us pray . . . for the workers of Triana, who have been massacred by Fascist troops.''

A wild cheer went up. Josep gritted his teeth.

''And then let us pray for ourselves,'' he continued grimly, ''who are shortly to be executed in retribution.''

The cheer turned into a thin wail, succeeded by sobs of terror.

''Our only hope,'' continued Josep, ''is that government forces put a speedy end to the military rebellion, so that the workers' militias may be disbanded and order be restored.''

He turned to face them and they gaped at him openmouthed, ready now to pray for anything that might save their skins. He should have felt pity for them, but he was filled with sudden cruelty, a delight in frightening them. They had not been frightened of hellfire, but they were frightened of gunfire, they were frightened of dying. They would sell their souls to the devil for the chance of life. He felt a sudden respect for those who had no truck with either God or the devil, whose souls were not for sale.

''If we die, we will not be martyrs,'' he went on, as if to deprive them of this chilly comfort. ''If we die we will be merely casualties of war. We will not be heroes, merely victims. We will not have fought and lost, merely lost. If we are to die, therefore let us die humbly, begging forgiveness for our sins. Let us purge our hearts of thoughts of vengeance.''

Vengeance. Where did justice end and vengeance begin?

* * *

"To be opened in the event of my death."

Lorenzo had addressed the envelope before beginning his letter to Dolores, as if to remind himself that he was writing his own epitaph. He must choose his words carefully, to give Dolores the maximum comfort, to give Andrés something noble to remember him by.

My darling wife,

I pray constantly that you are safe in your father's house and that by the time you read this letter peace and order will have been restored to our divided country.

I scarcely need to tell you why I have taken up arms against this feeble and diseased government of ours. I have done it for my family and for Spain. I have been true to myself, as you have always urged me to be. Five years ago I was ready to mutiny and risk everything in the cause of democracy; now I must do so again.

The Popular Front government has betrayed its duty to democracy. It is a travesty of everything a true republic should be. It is dominated by extremists who publicly call for revolution, who persecute the Church, who condone terrorism, who have no control over their own masses. The moderates for whom we voted have lost their voice; there is, I am convinced, a plot to impose a Marxist state.

I am confident that our struggle will end in victory; right must surely prevail. But I do not expect to live to see that day. Here in Toledo we are grossly outnumbered by government troops and workers' militias. At the time of writing this, we are holding out in the Alcázar, our last stronghold against those who demand our surrender.

We number a mere thousand—a hundred officers, a couple of hundred civilians, and the rest Civil Guard. There are also women and children in our care, families of the defenders, who are here for their own safety, fearing persecution if they remain at home. Our son is not among them. Please God I have done right in not bringing him to this place.

Dolores, I left Andrés with Rosa because I truly believed, at the time, that he would be safer with her than here with me. As Roberto's novia, she will be well looked after by his union and be able to defend Andrés from a position of strength. She loves him as her own and will hopefully reunite him with you as soon as may be. Even now I worry that I made the wrong decision, and yet how could I condemn an innocent child to be incarcer-

ated in squalor and darkness? Colonel Moscardo, our commanding officer, has wisely ordered that the families be confined to the cellars, to keep them safe, but it is terrible to see small children denied light and liberty, and forced to share the fate of their elders. I would rather my son lived in a Red Spain than died defending my beliefs.

We are well armed and have prepared ourselves to hold out to the last. The poor cavalry horses supply our food, and we draw water from our own well. Who would have thought it would ever be put to such use again, as in the sieges of old! These resources we share with some fifty or sixty hostages, political activists who must now pay the price of their convictions. Such is war. The colonel's own son was taken hostage by the Reds. Today he received word by telephone that if we did not surrender within ten minutes, the lad would be shot. He spoke to him and told him to die bravely and then repeated that we will never surrender. I myself could not have done what he did if it had been Andrés's life at stake.

I am no Fascist, Dolores. I am a Spaniard, and a Catholic, and a Republican. It is the Reds who wish to destroy the Republic, and I have rebelled not against the Republic but against the spineless government that has betrayed it. Explain this to Andrés for me, if history should ever try to brand his father as a traitor.

I must end by trying to tell you how much I have loved you, more with every day of our marriage, for your calm, your wisdom, your forbearance. Five years with you and the gift of our son have given me more than my share of happiness. I pray constantly for you and the children and Rosa, and that soon you will live in peace and harmony in a strong, united Spain.

God bless you.

Your loving husband,
Lorenzo

Fine sentiments, he thought, folding the letter. Dying for one's beliefs was easy; it was living up to them that was hard. Who knew what the next days or weeks might bring? Victory might carry its own disillusionment. The price of victory might be thousands of innocent lives. He could not deceive himself about that, could not stifle an awesome sense of responsibility. Blessed are the fanatics, for they shall not know doubt. Blessed are the simpletons, for they

shall have no understanding. Cursed are they who think, for they
shall find no peace . . .

Jack reread the final draft of his piece on the Montana Barracks and
decided it would have to do.

TRIUMPH IN MADRID
Fascists beaten back

There is singing in the streets of Madrid tonight as workers occupy the site of the Montana Barracks, fallen fortress of fascism,
chanting triumphantly, *"No pasaran."* They did not pass today.

That they did not pass was thanks to spontaneous action by
virtually unarmed men, women and children, who braved continuous machine-gun fire to storm one of the best-defended
strongholds in Spain. They proved the impossible, that even Fascist troops armed to the teeth are no match for the united will of
the people.

After hoisting a false white flag and mowing down the unsuspecting workers who advanced to accept surrender, the Fascists
paid the price of their treachery. Undeterred by a hail of bullets
from the parapets, the workers surged together, shoulder to
shoulder, and succeeded in the cost of many lives in breaking
down the doors of the barracks.

This time the surrender was swift and genuine. While workers
occupied the barracks and laid claim to sorely needed arms and
ammunition, trembling Fascist troops were taken prisoner and
escorted under guard to the city's Model prison.

No sooner had the barracks surrendered than the triumphant
militia rallied its forces to repeat its triumph in Toledo, where
the Fascists have been driven back into the mighty hilltop fortress
known as the Alcázar. Armed workers are flooding toward the
city, transported by fleets of private cars, taxis and trucks, freely
volunteered by ecstatic Madrileños, eager to contribute toward
the common struggle.

But amid all this rejoicing, let us not forget one thing. Courage
is no substitute for arms. Never again should workers have to
rely on their own suicidal bravery or the abject cowardice of the
enemy. Let us not be deceived by what has happened here today,
let us see it as an inspiration, not as an example. An unarmed
Republican is a dead Republican. By rights the workers of Madrid should have been massacred here today, as they are being
massacred elsewhere in Spain, armed with only pitchforks and

shotguns. The Fascists have been planning this coup for many months and are well prepared; unless the Republic secures a supply of arms to match its enemy's, it cannot hope to survive.

The Republic's struggle must be our struggle. Without swift and unconditional help from other surviving democracies, Spain will be delivered bleeding into the hungry jaws of fascism . . .

Rousing stuff, thought Jack. Much good would it do. When had Britain ever lifted a finger to defend democracy against fascism? Especially when democracy was just a nom de guerre for a workers' revolution. Even fascism had to be better than that . . .

Jack stepped out of the hotel and walked briskly along the Gran Via toward the telephone building to file his dispatch. It was a tall tower which had already become a kind of club for foreign journalists, and Jack was obliged to be sociable while waiting for his piece to be cleared by the censors, a tall thin man and a cheery little woman. Neither of them were linguists, nor were they politically sophisticated. They were only there for form's sake, and Jack wondered how long it would be before they were replaced by something more efficient and sinister, how long it would be before smuggled-out copy became the only kind worth writing.

He returned to the hotel by the back streets, narrow, litter-strewn, foul-smelling alleyways, a world away from the art nouveau elegance of the city's wide walkways, splendid still despite the accumulating piles of refuse and the garish, proselytizing banners.

The wretched slums had acquired an air of tattered gaiety, their doorways and balconies decked out with Republican flags, their grimy walls adorned with slogans. Behind closed doors the left-wing *checas,* or committees, would be busy drawing up the latest death lists. Already some of their earlier victims were on public display, left to rot where they had fallen, with notices around their necks proclaiming their former Fascist sympathies.

Jack got his dictionary out of his pocket to check the meaning of some graffiti. His grasp of foreign languages was ungrammatical, but he absorbed vocabulary like a sponge. His first foreign assignment, four years ago, had filled him with the old, familiar feelings of ignorance and inadequacy, and since then he had taken his usual pains to educate himself, ever mistrustful of the interpreters and press releases so generously provided by hospitable foreign governments.

His interest in the anarchist graffiti duly attracted the attention of a patrolling militiaman.

"Papers," he demanded, eyeing Jack suspiciously.

Wise visitors did not stray into the working-class quarters of the city, and Jack had fully expected to be stopped. It was a hot day and he would normally have been in shirt sleeves, but today he had put on a suit and tie to test out the rumor for himself, the rumor being that anyone wearing a suit and tie would be suspected of being a Fascist and taken off for questioning.

"Viva la República," said Jack, endorsing this sentiment with a rather cavalier Republican salute. He waited patiently while his passport, his press card, and a couple of restaurant bills were subjected to minute scrutiny. After a respectable delay the young man finally grunted and waved him on. He couldn't have been more than sixteen and more than likely couldn't read, he had just wanted to get near enough to smell out any incriminating fear. Jack had been in awkward spots before, and had learned the importance of not showing fear. This time it had been easy, because he hadn't actually been afraid, even though perhaps he should have been. There was a quality of amateur dramatics about the whole affair, with people posturing uncertainly in their allocated roles, leadenly repeating the lines they had learned with little understanding of what the play was about, investing the whole tragic business with an element of farce, like a badly acted *Macbeth*.

The bar of the Florida Hotel was crowded with fellow journalists, the bar being the front line from which most of their dispatches would be written. They were pooling information noisily in the interests of convincing eye-witness copy and speculating on likely developments. Their collective assumptions made a good story, something the folks back home would understand, nice and simple, easy to write. There was always an occupational tendency to think in journalese, to reduce any eventuality to the scale of the space available, to enlarge any triviality to the potential size of the headline.

Bloodthirsty lot, the Spanish, they all agreed. The Latin temperament and all that. A bunch of bloody foreigners killing one another. It would be a nine-day wonder back home, of course. One dead Englishman would always be bigger news than a thousand dead dagos . . .

Yes, thought Jack. That's what Spain needs. A few dead Englishmen.

Ramón had been cruelly thwarted by the sudden takeover of most of the city's hotels. He had been on the point of introducing Marisa to a modest establishment overlooking the Sol, where she would number minor businessmen and traveling salesmen among her up-graded clientele. Unfortunately the Residencia Rey Alfonso III, in common with many similar hostelries, had now been requisitioned by a workers' committee. Even first-class hotels had been taken over by the unions or converted into billets for the militia and only a handful still functioned normally, by special dispensation, in or-der to cater to the sudden influx of foreign visitors.

His plans for Marisa had been ambitious but not extravagant, involving a gradual climb up the ladder of her profession. But these recent developments called for a change in strategy. He must seek to exploit the potential of the current increase in tourism, he must be bold and fearless, as befits a successful entrepreneur . . .

This new bout of scheming served in some measure to distract him from the constant broadcasts of Red demagogues, inciting the workers to further atrocities and praising them for their latest mur-ders. Teeth gritted, Ramón forced himself to listen carefully to everything they said, making the appropriate entries in his note-book, and rewarding himself for this penance by tuning in to Radio Seville, on which General Queipo de Llano assured him daily that the rabble would soon be liquidated.

Since Marisa's outburst on the stairway, they had both been left in peace, if only because there were plenty of other targets for harassment. There were many scores to be settled, people were too busy denouncing old enemies and troublesome creditors to the *che-cas* to spare a thought for the likes of them. But trade had been poor. Many people were afraid to go out at night and risk interro-gation by marauding militiamen, and those who were not afraid were too busy terrorizing others to have time for more innocent entertainment. Yes, business was bad.

Ramón hated the thought of sharing his profits with a middleman who simply exploited the efforts of others, but the time was right and if he did not act soon, others would beat him to it. And so, while Marisa slept off a miserable two clients, weeping with anger that she had not earned her daily present, Ramón extracted nearly all the money from his shoe and set off for the big hotel on the corner of the Gran Via and Calle de Carmen, an imposing building reputedly full of foreign journalists.

The doorman was an odious individual, with ideas above his station, and proved intractable about his terms. Their conversation was couched in circumlocutions that left no room for misunder-standing. A lump sum and a daily retainer, whether she showed up or not. The hotel guests thought in pounds and dollars, not in miserable pesetas, he was getting a bargain.

Even after haggling, the so-called bargain left his lovingly hoarded resources at almost zero. He returned home to find Marisa still sulking.

"You have had your present," snapped Ramón, fighting the constriction in his throat, trembling with the thrill of the enormous gamble he had taken. "I have just invested my entire fortune in your future, even though you are ill prepared. You will be dealing now with foreigners, gentlemen, wealthy people, who will expect more of you than the riffraff you have entertained so far. There will be other girls more beautiful than you vying for their favors. Therefore you must give them more for their money, so that they wish to see you again. Do you understand me?"

She understood in essence, if not in detail, and the detail was simple to relay, she accepted instructions unquestioningly. And Ramón blessed the excesses of his youth, the fortune he had squandered in the pursuit of vice, the voracious appetite which had destroyed his health and left him able to discuss such things without the slightest tremor of discomfort.

Marisa had no modesty and had no sense of humor. What use had she ever had for such inessentials? She took everything literally, everything seriously. She was infinitely amenable, requiring only the assurance of reward, she was as obedient as her father's dogs without the impediment of intelligence. Cunning yes, intelligence no. Her peasant cunning would protect her, her survival instinct would keep her safe. Ramón had left prostitutes black and blue, one he had all but strangled in a drunken rage, but the only face he could remember was that of the gypsy girl who had drawn blood and left him screaming. And so, more as a talisman than a tool, he bought Marisa a present after all. He spent his last pesetas on a very small, very sharp knife.

As a prison, the Carrasquez mansion was congenial enough. The widows and children of Don Felipe's private army were not, as Dolores had expected, bound and gagged, nor were they engaged in menial labor, nor where they being fed on bread and water.

She found a dozen women and as many children confined to the upper floor of the house, where they lived in fractious idleness, waited on as usual by the household servants. By the time their unwilling hostess joined them, they had progressed from gibbering terror to petulant inertia, punctuated by hysterical weeping, which was mimicked instantly by their offspring, producing sound effects that would have credited a torture chamber. Dolores's initial fellow feeling—they had fallen on her neck like old friends—wore off remarkably quickly; she was astonished at her own callousness, the way her own problems had eroded her capacity for sympathy and tolerance, the speed at which contempt displaced pity.

"These animals show no respect for their betters!" complained the widow of her father's steward. "They refused to let me use the telephone! They won't even allow us to listen to the radio!"

"They don't want us to know that the generals are almost here, that's why!" put in her elderly mother. "Soon we will be rescued and these barbarians will all be shot! I for one will enjoy watching . . ."

". . . and they expect us all to eat with only fingers and spoons!" added another portly dowager, quivering with indignation. "It's outrageous! I refuse to have one of those horrible men standing outside the bathroom door! It's indecent! You must speak to them and tell them we won't tolerate it a moment longer!"

For three days Dolores endured their endless carping. As daughter of the house and a known Red sympathizer she was expected to use her twofold influence to improve their living conditions, and was subjected to a continuous barrage of demands and imprecations. Before long she found herself the villain of the piece, the butt of all the anger and resentment the women dared not express before their jailers.

"Your poor father would turn in his grave!" she was accused repeatedly. "Why don't you do something? Perhaps these savages will listen to you. Do they not realize how severely they will be punished for what they have done?"

Dolores reminded herself that these women had just been bereaved and traumatized, and tried to curb her irritation.

"This is no time to worry about trivialities," she said. "We must think of ways to try to escape. Perhaps when it is dark, we could—"

"Escape? Escape? Why give them the pleasure of killing us, when the generals are almost here?"

"They might do more than kill us!" wailed another woman. "They might tie us up, torture us, for our children to watch while they rape us . . . !"

Despite such lurid speculation, which was greeted by a chorus of shrieks and sobs, the women still clung to a blind, novelettish faith in their ultimate rescue and the summary execution of their warders. It never occurred to them that any attempted rescue would guarantee them certain death.

Meanwhile, Dolores thought of little but escape. Every door was guarded and she had no doubt that Tomás's men would not hesitate to shoot. Escape would clearly be impossible without an accomplice.

Seeing that Rosa's brother Julio was on bathroom duty one morning, she indicated her desire to relieve herself, and once they were alone on the landing she grasped his arm and hissed in his ear, "Julio, I am so worried about Rosa and the children. I must get home. You must help me. What difference does it make whether I am here or not? You have all these other people as hostages."

"Rosa and the children are safe," said Julio shortly. "You have no need to worry about them."

"You mean you have had news? Tell me! What has happened?"

"Nothing has happened," said Julio. "They are safe at home, with Rosa. What should have happened? Toledo is held by Republican troops. No harm will come to them in Toledo."

"Then let me join them. Please. Just let me out of here and I will make my own way home. Please, Julio. For Rosa."

"It is not up to me," said Julio woodenly. "If it was up to me, or up to Tomás, you could go. But the others, they want you here. They think you give us something to bargain with. They think your life could buy many other lives."

"But they're wrong, Julio, surely you can see that? If this house is attacked by the Fascists, we must either surrender or we will all be killed. They won't stop to bargain with us!"

Dolores made a gesture of despair. The peasant mind was so parochial. Could they not see that Albavera was just a dot on the map, a stopping-off point between Seville and Badajoz, her father's house a mere ant to be crushed under the boot of an advancing army?

"It is we who will kill them," said Julio stolidly. "We will see them coming from the watchtower and we will shoot them from the windows as they approach. They will only kill us at great loss to themselves. Even if we are defeated, we shall have advanced the cause by their deaths."

The words were as stiff and stilted as a recital of the Catechism. Normally Julio was quite unable to string two words together, but these words were not his own.

"It's not about victory, is it?" said Dolores, exasperated. "It's about defeat. It's about vengeance. That's why you're keeping us here, as ready-made vengeance for your defeat. So that you can die honorably, as you see it, die happy, because you've taken me and those stupid women and their wretched children with you! What harm have they ever done you? It was their husbands who harmed you and they are dead!''

''No one has harmed them,'' said Julio. ''No one is threatening to harm them. It is the enemy they have to fear, not us. Once victory is ours we will let them go. We treat them better than the Civil Guard has ever treated us. We are civilized people, not savages.''

It was the longest speech she had ever heard Julio utter. A squat little fellow with bad teeth and a squint, he was suddenly tall with new dignity and self-respect, his tongue-tied cheerfulness had fled forever.

''Then I will have to try to escape without your help,'' said Dolores. ''And you will have to shoot me in the attempt.''

''You can't escape,'' repeated Julio. ''It's impossible.''

Dolores put her handkerchief to her eyes and sat down despondently on the window ledge. She sniffed plaintively while Julio shifted from foot to foot in acute embarrassment.

''My baby,'' she lamented. ''My husband. When shall I ever see them again? Tell me, Julio, what news is there of my husband?''

''Ask Tomás,'' he mumbled awkwardly, his features twitching at her distress. ''I'm not supposed to talk to the prisoners.''

Dolores began sobbing quietly, watching Julio over the top of her handkerchief. He was bright red with discomfiture, unable to meet her eye. Poor Julio.

''Please, Julio, some water. I feel faint. Some water, please.''

She knew it was only a gesture. She would never have had the courage to jump, but the threat would serve at least to release her frustration, it would mark her out from her flaccid fellows. She had spent long periods of her youth locked in her room, the victim of her father's displeasure; she had spent years incarcerated in the Ursuline Convent, and she had just spent more than a month confined to her mother's bedroom. Enough was enough. She had lost the habit of rebellion in the last five years, placid, uneventful, humdrum years, but the rebelliousness was still there, bursting for a chance to express itself. It was a moment of pure, exhilarating madness.

The second Julio's back was turned she clenched her fist behind her handkerchief and punched the window with all her strength, sending glass showering like hailstones onto the walkway below. Again and again she punched, beating out the pane, seeing the handkerchief change from white to red.

After a moment of frozen inaction, Julio dropped his rifle and began pulling her away from the window. Dolores flung herself forward and kneed him, hard, in the groin, winding him, gaining enough time to straddle the window ledge, with her skirt up to her waist and one leg hanging into the void.

She felt a brief moment of pity for the hapless Julio as he recovered himself and retrieved his rifle. He pointed it at her desperately.

"Jump and I'll shoot," he panted. "Come back inside or I'll shoot!"

Dolores turned her back on him, and dangled both legs over the ledge. Julio would not shoot her in the back. She looked down and then shut her eyes as a wave of vertigo overpowered her. She was still clinging to the sill for dear life when Tomás, hearing his brother's shouts, raced to the scene and dragged her roughly from her perch. Dolores struggled wildly, screaming and yelling.

"Let me go home!" she shouted. "I want my baby! Let me go!"

A terrible din ensued from the prisoners, who assumed no doubt that she was being murdered. Other workers joined the fray.

"Kill her," hissed Ignacia. "Kill her, or she will try again."

"She will not try again," said Tomás.

"Yes I will!" sobbed Dolores recklessly. "Kill me, then! Go on, kill me!"

"The girl has courage," said somebody else. "She is not like the others. Put her in a room by herself and tie her up."

"No need to tie her up." said Tomás. "We will put her in the cellar."

Ignacia smiled nastily.

"Yes," she jeered. "Put her in the cellar. Then she can pretend she's with her precious husband, inside the Alcázar!"

The words echoed in Dolores's ears all the way down the stairs and into the cold dark basement of the house. For days now she had been hoping against hope, trying to convince herself that her fears were groundless, that Lorenzo might yet be safe . . .

"I sent a messenger to Toledo," said Tomás. "Your son is well. Rosa and both the children are well."

"And my husband?"

Tomás didn't answer. Dolores sat down on the stone floor and buried her face in her hands.

"Rosa's *novio*, Roberto, is also inside the Alcázar," said Tomás. "The Fascists took him hostage. Your husband may have to kill him, even as I may have to kill you."

Dolores began weeping quietly. Tomás turned away.

"Rosa sends her love," he said, and left her.

* * *

Ramón watched Marisa cross the road into the foyer of the Florida Hotel with the anxiety of a mother abandoning a child on its first day at school. He felt bereft, redundant, as if this day marked the passing of an era; he was filled with a maudlin sense of loss.

He had spent nearly an hour dressing her hair and deciding exactly what she should wear. Her complete lack of lingerie couldn't be helped for the moment, her nakedness under the thin dress was to be passed off as deliberate. The black lace she craved was expensive, she would have to earn it.

The doorman nodded at him dismissively, as if to indicate that his ragged presence was no longer required, and Ramón bit his lip and shuffled off. As instructed by the doorman, Marisa seated herself on a velvet plush banquette by the entrance to the hotel bar. There was a crowd of men standing at the counter, drinking and smoking and talking loudly to each other in a foreign language. Marisa eyed them appraisingly through the clouds of tobacco fumes. She had no preferences of any sort, her romantic fantasies were centered on wealth, not looks. Ramón had assured her all these men would be wealthy. They could be as ugly as sin for all she cared.

The men ignored her, engrossed in their conversation. She was hopeful that one of them would invite her to dinner. She longed to sit at a table with a white cloth and be waited on, to drink wine out of a crystal glass, to eat meat with silver cutlery off a china plate. Ramón had impressed on her the importance of not taking anything that did not belong to her, however tempted she might be. If she stole anything belonging to the hotel she would never be allowed inside it, ever again. And on no account was she to steal from any of the gentlemen either, even if they left their money or watches or cigarette cases lying around, even if they were asleep or drunk.

She sat patiently and waited. Eventually one of the men left the group and walked past her on his way to the lobby.

"*Buenas tardes,* señor," said Marisa, plucking at the hem of his jacket.

He stopped and looked at her with a pair of bright blue eyes, returned her greeting in Spanish, and made to move on.

"It is so hot," continued Marisa, touching her throat. "I am very thirsty."

The man stopped again and said politely, "What would you like to drink?"

Ramón had told her always to ask for lemonade, never for alcohol.

"Lemonade, please, señor."

He gestured to the waiter and ordered her a drink and she thanked him and smiled and crossed her legs, barring his way. He made a sign that it was nothing, stepped over the obstruction, and walked on.

Marisa drank her lemonade, disappointed, wondering what she had done wrong. Her flimsy purple dress was cut very low, right down to her nipples, and she had hitched her skirt up to her thighs the way Ramón had told her. And she had smiled and shown her good teeth, and she was drenched in cologne.

The other men were still talking, talking. Men together would always ignore women. She looked around the lounge for rivals, but there were no other women to be seen. She was suddenly afraid that she had been cheated, that the doorman had deceived her, that she should be sitting somewhere else. She wished Ramón were here to advise her.

She took the little square of mirror out of her handbag to powder her nose, and saw the doorman reflected in it, coming toward her.

He bent and whispered in her ear. "Room three-oh-five," he said. "Hurry up."

Ramón had taught her numbers specially. The doorman indicated the elevator but she shook her head. Not for the richest man in Spain would Marisa have walked into an elevator. She ran up the stairs to the third floor, found room 305, tapped on the door and went in as bidden.

The man was foreign, and very fat. He asked her immediately how much, and Marisa swallowed hard and named the sum Ramón had decreed, adding, parrotlike, "Unless you want something extra. I can do whatever you want."

Ramón had said she was to do whatever they wanted, without question, as the more bizarre the request, the more she would be paid. Lacking imagination, she had accepted this instruction with equanimity.

"How much to do . . . whatever I want?" said the man.

She was prepared for that too, and answered him with the glib immediacy of a shopgirl.

He took out his wallet and peeled the bills off a wad, and watched her count them and put them in her handbag. Then he gestured at her to remove her dress, and she did so, revealing her lack of underclothes. Her ribs had receded behind a layer of new flesh, and Ramón had already begun to scold her about getting fat. This man was very fat indeed. But he removed his clothes nimbly enough, revealing a huge belly that hung down obscenely, quivering under his own weight. Marisa couldn't imagine how much he must have eaten to get as fat as that.

She lay on her back as instructed while he knelt astride her, his penis drooping flaccidly between her breasts. But he pushed her hands away, telling her to lie still, while he drank noisily from a bottle of Manzanilla, and muttered to himself in his own language. His flesh wobbled as he swallowed. It was very white, like raw dough, except for his bloated lips which were red like a clown's. His breathing was labored and once or twice he burped noisily, emitting a smell of boiled turnip. Then at last he heaved himself off her, parted her legs and inserted two short stubby fingers. Marisa moaned on cue, indicating her appreciation, and this seemed to please him, so she moaned a bit louder.

And then as she took breath to moan again the air rushed out of her lungs as her legs were jerked upward and backward toward the bedhead and something was jammed inside her from above, something hard and cold, and then there was a gurgling noise and a sticky liquid dripped down her stomach and onto her breasts and the man began giggling shrilly.

Before she had time to work out what had happened he removed the empty bottle, lay down and made her sit on his face while he drank what trickled out of her. Then he licked the residue off her breasts and belly, grunting like a pig and letting out occasional high-pitched squeals, before presenting her with a limp erection which exploded feebly the instant she closed her mouth around it.

He shuddered, broke wind, and promptly passed out. For a horrible moment Marisa thought he must be dead, until his snores reassured her. She went into the bathroom, fiddled with the taps, and filled the bath full of hot water. Then she climbed into it up to her neck, the first bath of her life, luxuriating in this oft-imagined treat, enjoying the sensation of feeling like a real lady. There was a silver shaving mug and an ivory-handled cutthroat razor by the washbasin, but remembering Ramón's strictures, she left these alone. She drained the water away regretfully, dressed quickly and left the room, anxious not to miss any waiting customers.

Marisa could not wait to tell Ramón about her first engagement. It had all been very easy, and Ramón would be pleased with her, and she hoped very much that the rich foreign gentleman would ask for her again.

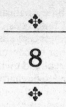

The People's Olympiad had to be canceled due to *force majeure*, but most of the visitors stayed on anyway, as war tourists. Wild horses wouldn't have dragged Clara away, and Edmund knew better than to try.

For a whole day Barcelona had been torn apart by street fighting. The anarchist workers, alerted to the Fascist conspiracy, had seized arms illegally; rebels and revolutionaries had met head-on. The resulting battle was bloody indeed; it was all Edmund could do to prevent Clara from rushing out and joining in the fray.

The ensuing rout of the Fascists filled her with wild elation. The sight of her waving a Republican flag and cheering the victory parade made Edmund's heart turn over; it was the first time in months he had seen her happy. He sent a cable to his parents to assure them they were safe, and prepared to sit it out.

Theoretically, the "Republic" had triumphed over fascism; in actual fact the revolutionaries had taken control of the city. Overnight, the moneyed classes and clergy disappeared from view, anticipating a reign of terror. Capitalism was to be abolished, the Church disestablished, and all business collectivized; henceforth everyone would be equal. Just how all this would be achieved remained unclear, and the immediate cessation of the hotel's hot-water supply struck Edmund as a sign of things to come. But where Edmund saw chaos, Clara saw only utopia.

Utopia was full of smoldering churches and armed patrols and rotting corpses. The sight of a dead priest, hoisted onto a cross bearing the words "I was a Jesuit," had made Edmund feel nauseous, but Clara had gaped at it in morbid fascination, going so far as to raise her camera until a passing militiaman deterred her from contaminating her film. Despite a complete lack of Spanish, let alone the local Catalan dialect, she seemed to pick up the official line remarkably quickly.

"These aren't harmless little Anglican vicars," she told Edmund
earnestly. "The Catholic Church has oppressed the poor for centuries. It's the richest, greediest capitalist in Spain. It preaches poverty and steals from the poor by conspiring with the employers to
keep wages down. It's corrupt and evil. And in any case, if he's a
Jesuit he should be delighted to be martyred, shouldn't he? They've
done him a favor."

Long after the fighting was over, they continued to hear erratic
bursts of gunfire, which Clara ascribed to Fascist sympathizers who
had taken to the rooftops and were firing randomly on the workers
below. When Edmund suggested dryly that the shots might be em-
anating from the routine slaughter of the bourgeoisie in back alleys,
she accused him of reading right-wing propaganda, as if such a
commodity was to be found in Barcelona.

"This is how it should be everywhere," she kept saying. "This
is how it should be at home."

Try as he might, Edmund could not imagine the citizens of
Whitechapel murdering the local vicar and occupying the telephone
office in the name of the proletariat. Neither could he imagine Clara
rejoicing in the forced requisition of the house in Curzon Street for
use by armed militia. Of all things, Clara had always despised
anything remotely military. She had always claimed that if she had
been a man in the last war she would have been a conscientious
objector; she had always sneered at those who avowed willingness
to fight for their country. Anyone who fought for his country was
either a dupe of the state, to be used as cannon fodder, or a bloodthirsty hooligan looking for a license to kill.

He reminded her of this, mildly enough, being a pacifist himself.
He himself would doubtless have ended up in prison in the last war,
but as for the next . . . about the next he wasn't so sure.

"What's the difference between fighting the Fascists in Spain and
rearming at home against Hitler? How can the party be antirear-
mament and anti-Fascist as well?"

"You don't *understand*," sighed Clara, meaning that she didn't
understand either. But then Clara didn't need to understand. Clara
was a natural fanatic, a hundred years ago she would have been a
Carmelite nun. Edmund felt obscurely guilty that he remained so
disaffected, so skeptical, that his principal preoccupation was not
the defeat of fascism or the fate of democracy, but the safety of his
cousin . . .

"I wonder what's happened to Dolly," he said. He had written
to her, care of her parents, but she had never replied. Dolly's elope-

ment had put a severe strain on the relationship between Edmund's
mother and her sister, and they had finally ceased to correspond.
He knew that Dolly had had a child and moved to Zaragoza, but
that had been some years ago and there had been no recent news.

"Her husband was an Army officer, wasn't he?" said Clara. "Do
you suppose he joined the uprising? Poor old Dolly. Imagine finding oneself married to a Fascist."

"Let's hope she's safe, that's all," said Edmund shortly.
"Whichever side her husband's on. Though I don't suppose anywhere's safe."

The news from the rest of Spain was patchy. As far as they could
gather, the military coup had started in Morocco, triggering coordinated outbreaks in garrisons all over Spain. Parts of the country
had fallen to Fascist generals and were now under martial law;
elsewhere the rebels had either surrendered or been overpowered.
As yet few details were available, and the final outcome was very
far from clear.

Hearing that the press were billeted in the Hotel Majestic, Edmund called in there hoping to find Jack, without success. He left
a note with the desk clerk, in case he turned up later. *Dear Jack,
We're at the Hotel Atlantis until I can persuade Clara to move on.
What the hell is going on? I can't make sense of it; presumably you
can?*

Jack would make sense of it all right. Jack would deliver some
tersely preedited account of events, full of filtered facts and tidied
truth, a left-wing tract written slightly askew, dogma flamboyantly
rearranged to suit his purpose and confound his critics. His professional pride was curiously bound up with a determined contempt
for his craft, a dry rejection of its more pretentious claims.

"Journalists have to write to please their editors and their readers," he had told Edmund once, "so they either find a paper that
matches their prejudices, or they change their prejudices to order.
In my case, I changed the paper instead, that's all. Morally, there's
no difference."

"Well?" said Clara unenthusiastically when Edmund returned
to the hotel. "Any sign of him?"

"Not yet. I left a note telling him where we were. Let's hope he
arrives before we leave next week."

Clara didn't answer.

"Unless you'd like to move on before that," continued Edmund
carefully.

"No. I'd like to stay a bit longer . . . till we see how things work out in the rest of Spain."

"Clara . . ."

"It isn't over, Edmund, not by a long shot. I can't possibly go wandering off on holiday while part of Spain is in Fascist hands. Especially not to another Fascist country!"

"Why does everything have to boil down to politics? What's Michaelangelo got to do with Mussolini?"

"I only agreed to go to please you. Don't make me feel I'm being selfish. This is important, Edmund. The Republic will need all the help it can get. The party wanted to mobilize everybody to—"

"If it's mobilizing everybody, it can manage without you. We agreed that you were run down and that you needed a holiday. You're in no fit state to start campaigning."

"But I feel so much better! I haven't had a drink since we got here, have I? I haven't even *wanted* a drink. I'm perfectly all right. How can I go on holiday when there's important work to do? Edmund you *know* how I feel about fascism. People at home will be told all sorts of lies. It's vitally important that some of us can say we've seen it for ourselves. At home they'll hear all about a dead priest or two, but they won't hear anything about a real workers' democracy in action, because the British government is terrified of a real workers' democracy. There's more to democracy than buying people off with a bloody vote so they can choose Labour or Tory, not that there's any difference anymore. Edmund, don't you *care?*"

"I care about you," said Edmund stubbornly, envisioning the endless round of meetings, lobbying, leafleting, fund-raising and general donkeywork. "When I was in Barcelona," she would say, to those who normally talked down to her. And everyone would listen. And because everyone would listen, she would be lost to him again, caught up in a world of strangers who called her comrade, people who did not care.

"Let's wait and see," said Edmund. "If Barcelona's anything to go by, the Fascists got a lot more than they bargained for. It may not come to a war."

They returned to their hotel the following afternoon to find a message from Jack: *I was relieved to find your note waiting for me. I just arrived in Barcelona this morning but you were out when I called. Join me for dinner tonight at my hotel.*

"I expect he'll subject us to his usual warped view of things," said Clara peevishly. "Don't expect me to sit there and agree with him."

"I'd be seriously worried if you did," teased Edmund, undaunted. He was inured to their political disputes; Jack and Clara got on best when they were arguing. "But at least Jack's got his ear to the ground. If anyone can understand this mess, he can."

Jack was waiting for them in the hotel lobby, which was thronged with foreign journalists. Clara forced a smile and allowed him to kiss her on the cheek.

"I was in Madrid when it started," he said as he led them into the dining room. "I had a hunch that things were about to break. Not on this scale, though. Worrying about you two spoiled the fun. Thank God you're both all right."

"Only just," said Edmund. "I had to tie Clara down. Good thing one of us is a coward. So, what's the news?"

"Here in Catalonia? Or the rest of Spain? They're two different countries, you realize. And hostile ones, at that. In Catalonia the war's all over, and the local hate committee's now in charge. The socialists hate the anarchists, the anarchists hate the Communists, and the Communists hate everybody else."

"Especially the Fascists," put in Clara.

"Especially the government in Madrid," Jack corrected her. "The Fascists can march into Madrid tomorrow for all the Catalans care."

Clara began drumming her fingers on the tabletop.

"Of course we can't tell that to the folks back home," continued Jack imperturbably. "It's too complicated. So we have to reduce it to a kind of football match: Republicans versus Fascists. The truth of the matter is that there's more than one war going on in Spain and more than two sides fighting it. But there's no point confusing the readers, is there?"

He signaled to the waiter for a bottle of wine. Clara covered her glass with her hand.

"You mean you're going to lie?" she said.

Jack shrugged enigmatically and Edmund fell to wondering how often fact was predigested, rendered intelligible, abridged, how much was deliberately left out and how much misunderstood in the first place, how much was impressionistic, how much hearsay, how much collaborative effort. According to Jack, journalists pooled their resources and agreed basic facts in the interests of common credibility; it was not a conspiracy to deceive, more an attempt to make sense out of conflicting information. And having agreed, they would go away and slant their own pieces in the relevant direction, and every one would come out the same yet different. And the reader read. How vulnerable the reader was! Despite Jack's cynical disclaimers, Edmund still nurtured a certain reverence for the printed word, a basic respect for its integrity, and yet print was nothing but a gelling agent: it had no substance of its own.

"Roll on press control, eh, Clara?" said Jack. "Like they have in Mother Russia."

"It's better than letting the newspaper barons brainwash people!"

"Oh, the party washes whiter, I agree . . ."

Edmund held back from the ensuing debate, bemused. Was the right to lie a basic human freedom? Since when had censorship safeguarded truth? If misinformation was inevitable, then let it be freely written, let it adapt itself to varying shapes in the interests of controversy. Controversy created an illusion of choice, of freedom of thought. At the end of the day people would always believe what they wanted to believe . . .

"Trotskyite!" exploded Clara, jolting Edmund out of his reverie. It was the dirtiest word in her vocabulary. He flung Jack a pleading look. Jack made a gesture of truce.

"Let's not prove my point by squabbling. The Fascists' greatest strength is that they're united. Unless the parties of the left can sort out their differences, unless all the Jacks and Claras stick together, the Fascists will walk all over them." He raised his glass. "To a united Republic."

"To a united Republic," echoed Edmund and Clara. Clara took a swig of mineral water, somewhat appeased.

"So what's been happening in the rest of Spain?" she asked, her curiosity getting the better of her belligerence. "Who's winning?"

"So far the Fascists have taken about half the country, and they won't stop there, believe me. In most places there was no resistance. If the government had armed the workers, it might have been a different story."

"So why didn't it arm the workers?" said Edmund.

"Because it was scared of starting a revolution. Look what's happening here in Barcelona. But if the workers *hadn't* seized arms, the Fascists would have taken Barcelona too. The Republic's biggest asset is the revolution, the combined strength of the people. Its biggest weakness is poor organization and a shortage of trained men and equipment. It's lost over half its army, remember, and most of its experienced officers. Not a very good basis for winning a war."

"We never realized things were as bad as that," said Edmund, looking at Clara uneasily.

"You weren't meant to. On the one hand the government's desperate to keep up morale. Domestic propaganda is full of fleeing Fascists and triumphant workers' militias. At the same time, it wants to convince us foreign journalists that democracy will be destroyed unless the Republic gets aid from abroad—aid meaning arms, of course."

"That's what I keep trying to tell Edmund," put in Clara. "People at home have to be made to care."

"Enough to take on Hitler? I'll believe that when I see it."

"Hitler?"

"The Army of Africa is on its way over from Morocco, courtesy of Air Adolf. It's the Spanish Army's crack corps—top-notch officers plus Moorish mercenaries. More than a match for what's left of the Republican army. The workers' militias are all very well when it comes to beating back a few rebel officers, but Moorish troops are a very different kettle of fish."

"Good God," said Clara. "This will start another world war."

"Don't count on it," said Jack. "Britain and France will shut their eyes and pretend it's not happening, precisely because they don't want another world war. Hitler can do what the hell he likes, and he knows it."

He replenished Edmund's glass.

"So, how long are you two planning on staying?"

Edmund looked at Clara and Clara looked away.

"Another week or two, probably. What about you?"

"I've got some interviews lined up in Madrid the day after tomorrow. Then I'll probably take a trip to Toledo. About a thousand Fascists plus wives and children are under siege inside the military academy. Sounds like quite a good story. After that I'm not sure."

"Do you know what's happened in Zaragoza?" asked Edmund. "The last I heard, Dolly's husband was garrisoned there."

"It's gone over to the Fascists," said Jack. "The rebels caught the workers napping and took it without a shot."

"Oh. She'd be all right, then. Still, soldiers get moved around a lot. I suppose she could be anywhere by now."

"Let's hope she ends up on the winning side," said Jack.

"I'll drink to that," said Edmund.

It was cold and dark in the cellar, and deathly quiet. Dolores lost count of the number of days she had been there. Her idleness left her exhausted; not even in sleep could she escape the constant treadmill of her thoughts.

"The children are safe," she would repeat out loud into the listening gloom, over and over again. It was the only comfort she had, the only thing that kept her sane. But she refused to voice the only other certainty, as if to deprive it of substance. Lorenzo's survival now depended on a Fascist victory. And a Fascist victory would mean death for everyone in this house, herself included. Either way, she would lose. She would lose either her life or her husband, perhaps even both . . .

If only she had been at home when it happened! How hard it must have been for Lorenzo to make his decision all alone! Or perhaps not. Perhaps it had been easier for him. If she had been there, she would have put his safety before anything else. She would have counseled him, no, begged him, to ally himself with the stronger side, whichever that might be. She would have fought tooth and nail to prevent him going to his death. And loving her, he might well have given in, and later despised himself for it. Duty and honor were so important to him. She had underestimated that, failed to realize where his unshakable sense of duty and honor might lead him . . .

"Dolores. Wake up, Dolores."

It was Tomás, standing over her in the dim light of the oil lamp. His face was drawn, gray, his voice hard.

"Is something wrong?" she said, alarmed. "What's happened?"

"Ask me rather what will happen," said Tomás. "Ask me what will happen when the Moors get here. Moorish troops from Africa, brought by German airplanes. They are twenty kilometers south of here. They have killed every Republican between here and Seville."

Dolores rubbed her eyes in confusion. Troops from Africa, here, in Spain? Repeatedly she had been told that Republican forces were nearby, that rebel troops were being beaten back, that the entire province would soon be under workers' control.

"Do you know anything of the Moors, Dolores? The Moors who are now Christ's comrades, invading our country yet again in the name of Mother Church? They take no prisoners. They show no mercy. They kill and torture for pleasure. They will castrate the men, rape the women, gouge out the eyes of the children, while they shout '¡Viva el muerte! Long live death!' "

"But surely you can't fight Moorish troops?" said Dolores, suddenly flooded with hope. Perhaps Tomás was going to release her, perhaps everyone was going to flee, before the enemy arrived . . .

"Others have fought them with sticks, and died for the cause. But we have arms and ammunition. If we flee, what hope is there for the Republic? If we flee we betray those who have died already."

"But surely—"

"For years we have waited for arms, for years we have waited for the revolution. We will not abandon it now. If we are to die, then we will die fighting. I tell you all this because the hostages are to be shot before the house is taken. But there will be great confusion. Here in the cellar, you may be overlooked, you may survive to greet your Moorish liberators. If you can convince them that you are both the wife and the daughter of *Fascists*"—he spat on the ground—"then perhaps they will spare you. It is your only chance."

The offer of life was more terrifying than the threat of death. She imagined waiting, waiting, trapped and helpless, while the battle raged above her. She could almost hear the sound of heavy boots and raucous voices, almost see the bloodstained bayonets and smoking rifles, almost smell the animal sweat of mercenaries faced with a young, attractive, helpless woman begging them for mercy . . . She shuddered.

"No," she said. "No."

"Do not ask me for your life. I cannot let you go. This is as much as I can offer you."

"I'm not asking for my life. I can fire a rifle, my husband taught me how. Let me fight."

"You, fight the Fascists? Think what you are saying. The others would not agree. How do we know you would not turn your weapon against us?"

"For what purpose? I might as well turn it upon myself! Tomás, please. Don't leave me here in the dark! I would rather your people shot me now, than haggle for my life with Moorish soldiers! Tell them I want to fight! Tell them now!"

Tomás told them. She could hear him telling them, her ear pressed up against the cellar door, her heart hammering.

"She is not to be trusted!" barked Ignacia. "She takes you for a fool, Tomás!"

"Be quiet, woman," said another voice. "We all know why you hate her. At least the girl has courage."

"She is not like the others." It was Julio speaking. "She doesn't deserve to die."

"Her father was our enemy!" Ignacia's voice again. "Her husband is a Fascist. Of course she deserves to die. Let's kill her and be done with it!"

A babble of squabbling voices ensued.

"What has happened to the revolution?" shouted one of the men. "When we took this house we were sure of victory! There was no mention then of Moors! What's the point in trying to fight them? We should flee now, before it is too late!"

"Coward!" snarled somebody else. "Traitor! Fascist!" There was the sound of a scuffle and then Tomás's voice rose above the din.

"Those who have no stomach for the fight are free to run away. They will be shot from the air as they flee, in any event, as so many others have been. Let each man choose his own way to die. Those who wish to die fighting should be allowed to fight."

"But not a *hostage,*" hissed Ignacia. "Why should we arm the enemy? You keep your brain between your legs, Tomás, now as always! Aah!"

Her speech ended in a yelp of pain.

"Let us take a vote," continued Tomás calmly. "There is no time for dispute. The Fascists will be here in a matter of hours. Either we agree to arm Dolores or we kill her. Either we arm her or *I* kill her, here, now, in front of you. We have argued long enough."

Dolores sank to her knees on the cold stone steps. She knew in her heart the vote would go against her. They hated her, they saw her as the enemy. Ignacia hated her, and now, at last she understood why . . .

Tomás would kill her quickly, kindly. There was no need to be afraid. She crept down to the bottom of the stairs again and waited for the door to open and flood the dismal cellar with light. In a moment, she would know her fate. Either way, she would soon be free.

Lorenzo was as weary of politics as he was of horsemeat. A raid on a nearby granary had supplemented the daily diet with a small ration of unleavened rye bread, hard and tasteless as rock, but his own part in this daring sortie had done little to relieve the tedium. Every day he was reminded that they were making history, embracing a heroic crusade against the forces of evil. And yet the prevailing mood was one of boredom.

The continuous bombardment against the fortress walls was as ineffective as a peashooter, as were the hordes of untrained militiamen taking inexpert aim over the tops of their makeshift barricades.

Walls four meters thick would withstand all but the heaviest artillery. Yet the shooting went on, monotonously, broken only by a
mutually agreed cease-fire to enable a local blind beggar to pursue
his daily route unmolested while insults were fired across the lines,
far more satisfying than bullets.

Meanwhile, for lack of other bloodshed, those trapped inside the
Alcázar had begun to turn on one another.

"The Civil Guard are planning a takeover," asserted Captain
Sanpedro, a leading light among the younger officers. "The Army
has got to make a stand."

"Surely solidarity is all that matters now?" said Lorenzo. "The
Civil Guard outnumber us by eight to one. We're lucky to have their
support. And in any case, the colonel's still in charge."

"Not for much longer," predicted one of Sanpedro's fellow Falangists. "Not if the Civil Guard have their way. We've got to show
them who's boss."

"Montanis doesn't care who's boss, do you Montanis?" sneered
Sanpedro, jabbing Lorenzo in the ribs. "Montanis thinks that everybody's equal. God help us from lily-livered liberals!"

"God help us from fanatics and extremists," said Lorenzo,
clenching his fists. "If you want a fight, let's have one."

"A fight? I thought solidarity was all that mattered. You confuse
me, Montanis. Tell me, what exactly are your politics? Evidently
you don't expect your wife and child to share them."

"I've told you before, my wife and child are visiting relatives,
in Albavera."

"How very convenient . . ."

And so it went on, day after day. Lorenzo controlled his temper
with an effort. Fighting with a fellow officer was degrading and
would solve nothing, much as he itched to do so. Physically, Sanpedro was no match for him. Physically, he could have beaten him
black and blue. But words had never been Lorenzo's forte: in any
argument he would hang himself, leaving Sanpedro smirking.

"Montanis is right, unity is all," declared his antagonist. "Why
else would we have shot those traitors who wanted to surrender?
We should shoot all traitors, don't you agree, Montanis?"

"We have already shot them," said Lorenzo curtly. "So what's
the point in discussing it?"

"Ah, but have we? Who knows what other traitors lurk among
us? Stragglers, who have held their peace to save their skins, who
secretly wish themselves on the other side of the lines. Such people

must be tracked down and weeded out, before they spread the poison of defeatism.''

''Haven't you anything better to do than to start a witch-hunt?''

''What's the matter, Montanis? What's it to you? Why should you take it personally? Where exactly do you stand?''

''I oppose anarchy and revolution. I support law and order and democracy. I am a patriot . . .''

Time and again he allowed himself to be lured into heated arguments, one against many, and inevitably he protested too much. He knew that there were others who shared his views, and yet they held back, reluctant to be misjudged. Sanpedro had built up a powerful clique around himself and regarded so-called moderates as little better than Reds.

''Sanpedro's got his eye on you,'' a colleague warned Lorenzo sotto voce. ''Be careful what you say.''

Lorenzo felt the first wave of unease and despised himself for it. Confinement and inactivity were breeding paranoia and mistrust. Both he and Sanpedro were victims of the same disease. A collective claustrophobia was affecting them all.

Constant worry about Dolores and Andrés did nothing to improve his state of mind. He devoured the daily newsheet avidly in search of reassurance, wracked by doubt and hope. According to Union Radio broadcasts, the Army of Africa was advancing on Badajoz. If Dolores was still in her father's fortress of a house, then all might yet be well. But what if she had returned to Toledo? Toledo was not a safe place for the wife of a rebel officer, but Dolores would know no fear in her eagerness to be reunited with her son . . .

Guilt rose up in his throat like acid. He had placed them both at risk, put his principles before his family's welfare, failed to consider the consequences of his actions. He should have played safe, held back, and then sided with the majority, as many others had doubtless done. Perhaps Sanpedro's jibes had a grain of truth in them. Perhaps he did wish himself on the other side of the lines . . . No, that was weakness, vacillation. He had not come this far to lose heart now. He had not come this far to allow himself to be baited and demoralized by narrow-minded bigots. Henceforth he would ignore Sanpedro, treat him with dignified contempt . . .

Lorenzo's duties involved a regular inventory of ammunition and weapons, including the growing supply of homemade grenades, metal doorstuds sandwiched together with explosive. On his way to the stores one morning, he noticed a group of prisoners being brought out for exercise into the central courtyard. The hostages were housed in the stable block, where they were segregated into small groups and watched over by the Civil Guard in eight-hour shifts. Those deemed to be the most likely troublemakers were put in the care of selected men who excelled at this type of work and who needed an outlet for their sadistic streak to keep them happy.

As Lorenzo approached, his thoughts far away, he was appalled to see one of the Guard trip up a prisoner and send him sprawling on the cobbles. The man struck his head on the ground as he fell and before he could get up again his assailant kicked him viciously in the ribs while the other prisoners stood by in growling impotence and the guards hooted with laughter.

Lorenzo would have intervened as a matter of principle, even if the injured hostage had not been Rosa's *novio*. He did not pause to ascertain the man's identity, and indeed, was not even aware that Roberto had been taken hostage. But Lorenzo did not see Roberto; all he saw was a defenseless man being attacked by a bully who dishonored their joint cause.

"What's going on here?" he demanded, accosting a burly NCO.

"The prisoner tripped and fell, sir. He's a clumsy oaf of an anarchist, sir."

"If I see any prisoners tripping in future, I shall regard your supervision as inadequate," said Lorenzo coldly. "See that he gets medical attention immediately."

"Gracias," murmured the prisoner, giving the Republican salute, as if daring the guard to manhandle him again, and Lorenzo turned to look at him and saw the quick, twisted smile of recognition.

"Good day, Roberto," he said heavily. "I daresay you would sooner be manning those barricades."

"I would sooner you were manning them with me," said Roberto. "As it is we are enemies. *Salud.*"

Lorenzo walked on, stiffly, without looking back. Roberto bore him no ill will, nor should he, except that they were enemies. Ill will was not the prerogative of enemies. At least you knew where you were with an enemy. Allies were another matter altogether.

Josep was awoken at dawn by a loud rumble of thunder, as a tremor shuddered through the church from its stone floor right up to its vaulted ceiling. People started out of their uneasy sleep, resumed their whimpering and praying, and then the babble assumed a note of frantic hope. Their deliverers were at hand.

Josep ran out of the church. A cluster of militiamen were staring up anxiously at the lookout, the first glimmers of sunrise just picking out his shadowy shape against the darkened sky. He was transfixed by the second sinister flash spurting out of the olive groves below, the lightning to the next clap of thunder. And then a shrieking missile flew harmlessly over their heads and spent its fury somewhere far behind them.

"Get back inside, priest," shouted Juan, pushing Josep roughly, "and pray the next shell hits your church. It will be a quick, holy death for you. We will leave no Fascists here to greet the Moors. Sing your own requiem, or offer prayers for our victory."

His words were drowned as another shell exploded, falling short against the hillside below. The next one would find its mark. And what use were rusty rifles against artillery?

Nevertheless Juan and his men took up their firing positions and began shooting uselessly at the unseen enemy, oblivious to the risk of shrapnel, protected only by rudimentary cover from sacks of earth and farm carts. They had not dug any trenches. Trenches were anathema to the proud militiaman: one could not fight from a hole in the ground.

"For God's sake, take cover," yelled Josep. "All the while they're bombarding us they won't advance. Get into the cellars, the basements, until it stops and *then* come out and fight. It's suicide to stay above ground. There's room in the church crypt. I'm going to move all these people into the crypt, but there's room for a few more."

"I will hide in no church," spat Juan, and at that moment a gaping hole appeared in a house at the end of the street, sending rubble flying like bullets. Josep threw himself on the ground.

"If you stay above ground, you'll all be killed!" he shouted desperately. "Then they'll just walk in and take the town without a shot. You might as well hoist a white flag now and be done with it. If you want to fight, take cover!"

A further explosion finally convinced Juan, even if Josep's words had failed to. Amid great confusion and vociferous dispute, word was spread to get below ground. It was not an order, as such: anarchists neither took nor gave orders, but there was no time to take a vote on the suggestion or discuss its political validity. Before long every cellar contained both bourgeoisie and revolutionaries and those who did not care, united only by the will to survive.

The walls of the church were a good meter thick, its occupants undoubtedly safer than anyone else. Had Juan and his followers had any notion of modern warfare, they would have fortified it for their own use. But they were simple peasants who had never seen battle, who knew nothing of military strategy, who had no organization, no discipline, no training, who had relied on their hilltop position to protect them, their tactics several centuries out of date. How many little armies were there like that in Spain, blinded by courage and ignorance?

The mood inside the church was increasingly jubilant. Again Josep was asked to lead prayers for deliverance. Again he refused. Perhaps he had been wrong to urge Juan to take refuge. Better for the militia to be killed instantly, better that the Fascists march in without a shot. Resistance would only lead to unnecessary slaughter, with innocent people getting killed in the crossfire. Juan and his men would all die anyway, Josep was sure of that. Why should they succeed where the workers of Seville had failed?

Josep ushered everyone into the disused crypt, despite protests from one of the women that it would be full of rats and other vermin. He distributed candles and kept telling them to be quick. There was always the risk, however remote, that a shell might penetrate a window.

There was nowhere to sit and the floor was damp and cold, which punctured their euphoria somewhat. They had just rearranged themselves into positions of squabbling discomfort when Josep heard another noise, a different noise from before. It was a high-pitched whining shriek from above and it was followed by the most thunderous crash, and then another, and then another. They were being bombed from the air.

"Don't be afraid," someone yelled above the cries of terror. "We're quite safe. They're our planes. They're *our* planes."

And Josep nearly laughed out loud, but at least the man had faith. And who was he to sneer at faith, in any shape or form?

Harry Martindale had enclosed a bundle of newspaper cuttings with his latest letter. Jack found it useful to know what the right-wing press were saying, not to mention the good old *Daily Worker*, even if it was all entirely predictable.

According to the *Observer* and the *Mail*, whose correspondents had been sent to the Nationalist side, the workers were running amok all over Spain, murdering indiscriminately, violating nuns and expropriating everything in sight. Total anarchy prevailed, allegedly masterminded by the Communist party. Meanwhile, Nationalist forces (they never used the term "Fascist" any more than the left-wing used the term "Red") were busy reestablishing law and order and were being greeted ecstatically by the poor, beleaguered middle classes, the backbone of any country, who had been relentlessly victimized by power-crazed revolutionaries.

The Daily Worker told a different story. There was no mention of a workers' revolution, no hint that the elected government had been on the verge of collapse; democracy was the key word. The Fascists were murdering innocent, unarmed civilians and building barricades out of dead babies; the workers were repelling them with an unbridled heroism straight out of *Boy's Own Paper.* The colorful and inventive narrative was punctuated by chunks of undiluted dogma and paranoid invective against those who dared to doubt Republican solidarity.

There was nothing that inclined Jack to modify his latest copy.

Today France struck democracy a mortal blow. Prime Minister Blum's fine promises have been broken and a unilateral policy of nonintervention has been declared.

There are those who would attribute this change of heart to Mr. Blum's recent visit to London. But who can blame Mr. Eden for counseling caution or for banning arms shipments to Spain? The peace must be preserved at all costs.

Mr. Eden is sincere in his devotion to peace. After all, we can decline to help the Republic in the comforting knowledge that there are others who will fill the breach.

Others will not stand by, as we do, and see Hitler's Junkers 52 bombing civilian targets. Mr. Stalin will assuredly find himself moved to act on behalf of all peace-loving nations. Yes, if we do not intervene, and leave it to him to do it for us, we can rest assured of one thing: whichever side is victorious, Spain will be one day be safe in either Fascist or Communist hands . . .

According to Harry, the Labour party was urging for formal nonintervention, while the Communists were agitating against it. The little piece he had just written should wrong-foot everybody nicely.

Jack rearranged the colored pins on his map to show the latest Nationalist advances.

Badajoz. It was doomed. The Army of Africa was mowing down everything that stood in its path. What use were armed militia when they hadn't a clue how to fight? The so-called training being done in Madrid was criminally inadequate. Badahoth, home, a long way to go for tea. Like Edmund, he wondered where she was living now. She had put no address on the letter she had sent care of Martindale a month after her elopement, and even if she had he wouldn't have replied. It had annoyed him that she had thought he might, that he had so little pride. But he had kept her note, not out of sentimentality, but as a fetish against future folly, a reminder that he was weaker than he thought.

> *Dear Jack,*
>
> *I told you I was going to elope on March 23. But Lorenzo's leave was brought forward unexpectedly and he arrived without warning on New Year's Eve. So I didn't get a chance to say good-bye to you.*
>
> *I wish you success and happiness and will always remember you kindly. I hope you will do the same for me.*
>
> *Dolores*

It was ridiculous that he should have suffered so much. She was right, he had always known she was engaged, known she was due to marry on March 23, 1931, and by March 23, 1931, he might have been ready for it to happen. By then he would have reached the final page, and sad or happy, there would have been an ending, the story would have been complete. But he had not been allowed to finish it, and the unread chapters haunted him still. He had invented them endlessly in his mind, tormenting himself with fiction. The book had seemed so full of knowledge, he had been so greedy for its secrets. It was the not knowing that had made him suffer. He had been ready for loss, but not for deprivation.

He would have liked to have heard that she had grown fat or turned into a shrew. He would have liked to have met her again and found her trivial. Failing that, he had fooled himself he had forgotten her, resisted the temptation to pump Edmund for news. Not that he had needed to. Edmund had freely volunteered what little news he had, sighing over her failure to keep in touch. His mother rarely heard from her ailing sister, but apparently Dolly had been disinherited with a vengeance. There was at least one child, he gathered. And there was never any more to tell, which perhaps was just as well.

And yet every day he had been in Spain he had thought of her and hoped that she was safe. It hardly mattered which side she was on. Fascist or Republican, what difference did it make? Such tags were meaningless in human terms, they were just abbreviations, a way of identifying the goodies and the baddies for home consumption. There must be no good Fascists and no bad Republicans, or vice versa, according to your prejudices. And even if Dolly had grown fat and shrewish and trivial, he could not believe her bad, and hoped her safe.

He left his piece to cook a bit longer and strolled down to the bar. A couple of chaps were back from the Sierra front, and would be sharing out the goods. Jack found battles tedious, standing on some hill somewhere, being allowed to see what they wanted you to see, most of it boring and confused and occasionally horrific, just for the sake of saying "I saw," as if it mattered what you saw, as if what you saw affected what you wrote. And of course it made you sound heroic. Journalists loved to escape bombs and bullets by the skin of their teeth. It was a miracle how they always survived, unlike photographers who cheerfully got themselves killed for the sake of some lousy picture they could have faked.

Jack listened without comment, making occasional notes. There had been a closely supervised visit to allow the press to see the newly formed 5th Regiment in action. It was composed entirely of workers, newly trained under Communist supervision, and drilled in ideology as well as weaponry. Morale was good, apparently, and discipline impressive. The Communists could teach the anarchists a thing or two about discipline.

Jack accepted one of the labor-saving press handouts and glowing recruiting leaflets, and once he had heard what he wanted to hear, he went off in search of dinner. He avoided the hotel dining room, preferring cheap workers' restaurants, where he might see or hear something interesting. He had always filled up lonely hours abroad with the help of a dictionary and a friendly local, eager to chat for the price of a drink.

He smiled at the lemonade girl who was sitting in her usual place, awaiting a customer, dressed in a black satin dress that was far too tight around the bodice. She was extraordinarily pretty, aggressively voluptuous, and totally sexless. He felt a sudden need for company.

She smiled back expectantly.

"Are you hungry?" asked Jack, aware too late that the question sounded coy.

She nodded eagerly.

"Let's have dinner, then," said Jack, offering her an arm, and grinning to himself at what the others would be thinking. Jack never slept with prostitutes. Nor did he intend to now, but he felt curiously benevolent toward this poor kid, sitting patiently in the bar each night waiting to be abused. She was an enemy of the people of course—prostitution had been officially outlawed by the revolutionary committees—and when she stepped uncertainly into the street, having donned a shabby raincoat and scarf to hide her tawdry finery, he realized it would be cruel to take her to his usual place where she would be forced to eat dinner wearing her coat.

He pulled it off her shoulders again, untied the scarf, and led her into the hotel dining room, where she visibly relaxed, even though she obviously had little idea of how to conduct herself. Jack found it amusing to watch her watching him, copying everything he did. He ordered soup and fish and chicken—the shortages besetting the rest of the city did not affect approved hotels—and she ate with devastatingly ingenuous greed, very fast, like a sparrow gobbling an oversized crust, fearful of bigger birds.

Jack had often gone hungry, both while growing up and during his first months in London, and he had coped with the humiliation of it by denying his appetite, by cultivating an indifference to food that had outlived the lack of it. But the girl had evidently been a great deal hungrier than he.

The conversation during dinner was limited to Jack itemizing everything he could see, while she gravely corrected his pronunciation and told him the words he did not know. But during the coffee she relaxed a little and began to prattle artlessly, asking him his name and what he did and how old he was and did he have a wife and children and was it very cold in England. Her Spanish was a thick, singsong variety and from her looks he guessed she was from the south, and when he asked if she was a Madrileña she shook her head and said that she came from Andalucía. She had a mother and father and six brothers and sisters who were very, very poor and had only the money she sent them every week. And her brother was very, very sick. It was a standard sob story aimed at extorting the maximum fee, but it was probably true enough, in essence if not in fact. Jack asked her if she had a husband in Madrid and she said she had a *novio*, but he too was sick, very, very sick. And then, as if to remind him tactfully that time was money, she touched his hand across the table and asked him if he was tired.

"Very, very tired," said Jack, suppressing a smile, and then, "How much?"

She bent forward discreetly and recited her terms extra slowly and clearly for his benefit. She had a strange twisted innocence, like a child hawking dirty postcards. Her services were pathetically cheap, and this was an expensive pitch. It seemed almost churlish to turn her down. And yet he could no more have made love to her than to his little sister.

He signed the bill and gestured at her to follow him. She balked at getting into the elevator, but he chivied her inside and she shut her eyes and clung to him in terror as it creaked and lurched its way upwards.

As soon as they got inside his room she began taking her clothes off. She was wearing absurdly fancy underwear, a black boned corset that thrust her breasts upward, a pair of black frilly panties and black lacy garters. She kept these on for the moment, as if eager to show them off. Jack didn't like to offend her by asking her to put the dress back on, but he didn't want to see her naked and feel like a pedophile.

"Sit down, Marisa," he said kindly, searching his vocabulary. "I just want to talk to you. Nothing else. Just to talk. Do you understand?"

"Are you sick?" she asked, concerned, feeling his forehead.

"No," said Jack, "not sick," though perhaps he was.

"Oh," said the girl. And then, perplexed, "You are homosexual?"

The word was the same in Spanish. Jack smiled and shook his head.

"You do not like me?" She sounded more worried than offended, as if she had done something wrong.

"Yes, yes, I like you. Of course I like you. But I never . . . make love . . . to women I like."

"What, never?"

"Only once. So, because I like you, I prefer to talk. You can teach me Spanish. I will pay you just the same."

There was a pause.

"How much?" she said, anxious now.

"You are doing . . . whatever I want. Talking."

He counted out the money so that she could relax.

"Just for talking?" she repeated, looking at the bills, assailed by either scruples or suspicion.

"Talking is what I want," said Jack. And he wondered why he was doing this, for charity was not in his nature: it must be because this girl reminded him of Dolly.

Quite why she should remind him of Dolly was not immediately apparent. She didn't look like Dolly and certainly she didn't attract him sexually in the way that Dolly had done. Perhaps it was the evocative air of wayward innocence, the preoccupation with essentials, the lack of artifice, the fundamental honesty. She wore her whorehouse lingerie like a child with a new dress, and yet her vulnerability had a sharp edge of wariness, a guileless mistrust. She was naïve, but not stupid. Yes, she must remind him somehow of Dolly. And the reminder had been enough to make him feel lonely, which was different from being alone. He had always been alone but never lonely, until Dolly.

Jack patted the bed and told her to lie down. Just lying down on the bed in her underwear would make her feel she was doing something. He poured two glasses of whiskey and gave her one. She sat up, took a big swallow and promptly choked.

"Tell me about your life," he said, thumping her on the back. "I will ask when I cannot understand."

Her life was all present and future tense. There was no more mention of the starving family, now that his money was safe in her handbag. She spoke incessantly of her *novio*.

"He is very clever, very refined," she said, acting out each word. "He is so kind to me, so generous. Every day he buys me a present. Every day. He chooses all my clothes for me, he arranges my hair. My hair is beautiful, yes?"

"Your hair is very beautiful," agreed Jack.

"He is teaching me to be a lady. His father is very, very rich and one day he will inherit all his money, and a beautiful big house, and we will live there and have many, many children. Beautiful children. My *novio* is very, very handsome. He smiles like an angel . . ."

Jack wondered if this pimp cared anything for her, and how much of the money in her bag would go to keep him in drink and gambling. Then she showed him the bracelet jingling around her skinny little arm. It looked like real gold, which surprised him, and there were three gold charms dangling from it, a heart, a fish, and a key. Tomorrow her *novio* had promised her a little bell that tinkled, from a shop in the Gran Via. He never bought anything for himself, he thought only of her.

She seemed genuinely in love with him, although it was a child-like love, she was like a little girl telling him she had the best daddy in the world. Her devotion was robust and unsentimental and touching and he could only hope the pimp appreciated it. He had been planning to buy Dolly a real gold bell that tinkled, to replace the worthless trinket from the popper, and would have earned the money to pay for it in exactly the same way. It seemed ironic that he should be buying one for this girl instead and yet it was curiously comforting.

Marisa pulled back his cuff and peered at his watch.

''Do you want me to stay all night?'' she asked, in a manner that suggested his time would shortly be up.

''No. Do you have another . . .'' He didn't know the word for appointment. But she finished his sentence for him.

''It is Saturday. Every Saturday I visit the same gentleman, here in the hotel. I have to see him at eleven o'clock, after he has eaten. But afterward he sleeps. I can come back afterward.''

''No, no need.''

''I can see you again tomorrow. I come here every night, except when I bleed.''

Jack stifled a laugh. She had all the outrageous solemnity of an infant.

''Perhaps. But often I work at night. Perhaps we will talk again in a few days.''

''Your Spanish is good. I would like to learn English. My *novio* speaks English, and French, and Latin. He is very educated. Do you speak French and Latin also?''

''Not Latin,'' said Jack. ''I am not educated.''

''Nor I,'' said Marisa sympathetically. ''But I am learning. I am learning to read.''

And then Jack realized that Dolly was just an excuse. This girl reminded him of himself.

The vote for Dolores's life had been evenly divided, and Tomás had had the deciding vote, much to Ignacia's chagrin. She had taken it upon herself to watch Dolores like a hawk, still expecting treachery, and Dolores could feel her eyes on her all the time, burning with hatred.

They were manning three upper windows at the front of the house, together with Tomás's elder son. Dolores loaded her rifle and showed Ignacia and the boy how to do likewise. It was a Lee Enfield 42, well maintained and oiled, and there was plenty of ammunition. The lookout in the watchtower had reported troop movements in Albavera, less than five kilometers away. There had been no resistance to slow them down; white flags had been sighted over every chimney. It would start soon, very soon.

Dolores was beyond fear. She was strangely elated, her earlier fatalism had been displaced by reckless defiance. Ignacia was more realistic. In a fit of belligerent camaraderie she asked Dolores to shoot her before the Moors entered the house. They could shoot each other simultaneously. She poked her rifle between Dolores's ribs to demonstrate her goodwill. She had already regaled her, in gruesome detail, with tales of what the Moors did to women.

Some of the women and children had been evacuated, others had wanted to stay and fight. Tomás's two sons, aged eleven and twelve, had remained. His only other surviving child, a girl of eight, had been sent to join Rosa in Toledo.

To Dolores it seemed outrageous that the Moors, the oppressors of old, should be fighting alongside Spaniard against Spaniard, and she was sure Lorenzo would respect her wish to fight. It no longer seemed anomalous that Lorenzo should be defending the Alcázar while she fought for the Republic. They were both in exactly the same position, they were both outnumbered by people who meant to kill them. Holding the rifle he had taught her to use, she felt close to him again, she knew something of what he was feeling. What difference did it make that they found themselves on opposing sides? Had she not prayed every day for his deliverance? And if he could see her now would he not wish her victorious? And would they not both willingly embrace defeat if their defeat could help Andrés survive?

"I will shoot you if you wish, Ignacia," said Dolores. "But if I want to die I shall choose my own moment. Please don't point the gun at me like that when it is loaded."

Ignacia had little chance of hitting anything other than at point-blank range. Like most of the others, she had never handled a gun before and the recoil would ruin what little aim she had. Dolores was easily the best shot in the house. She had grown up with guns, she had watched her father clean them and load them and use them—not that she had ever been allowed to shoot as her brothers had. Josep had shown little enthusiasm, but Ramón would practice endlessly with a pistol, sitting in a chair while Dolores set up targets for him, shrieking with glee every time he scored a hit, much to his sister's admiration and envy. But under her husband's expert tuition she had developed a good eye and quick reflexes and Lorenzo liked to joke that she was his best cadet.

The thought of killing did not distress her as much as she would have thought. She ought to have been appalled at the prospect of killing. Perhaps killing was a natural reflex, suppressed by civilization. Killing was stealing life, killing was a blow against death, for every man she killed she would live a few seconds longer. If she could kill enough of them she might survive. How dreadful to be with those women upstairs, or locked up in the cellar below, denied the reprieve of killing.

The waiting seemed endless. The horizon was invisible from her window, lost behind the trees, the waiting would be easier to bear once they could see their enemy. How Ramón had always admired the Foreign Legion! He loved to read of the African campaigns, he reveled in tales of gore and glory. Poor Ramón. At least he would not be called upon to fight, his disability might yet save his life. Unlike God knew how many others, he would not find himself press-ganged onto the wrong side; he would not be forced to risk his life for a cause he did not believe in.

The same applied to Josep. Priests could not fight at all. She shuddered. Perhaps he had met the same fate as Father Luis, perhaps his anarchist flock had finally shown their teeth. No, not the same fate. Father Luis's belly had been slit from neck to groin, spilling out years of sloth and gluttony. They had spread his body naked on the grass and urinated into the gaping mess and left the corpse for birds to peck at until it heaved with maggots. No, they might kill Josep, but they surely could not bring themselves to hate him. And if Josep died at least he would go to heaven. For herself she was not so sure. Every day she renewed the sin of deceit, out of love, but love did not absolve her. Every day of her marriage she had lied to her husband, out of love. And out of love, he did not suspect her, out of love he could look into Andrés's bright blue eyes and see only himself reflected. She would take that secret with her to her grave, and go to hell for it with head held high.   -

And now, while there was still a little time, she must remember Jack. She could not imagine him today, or here, she could only imagine him then, there, frozen in time and space with his bunch of bright red flowers, whispering, "I love you, Dolly." He *had* said it. A love less worthy than Lorenzo's certainly, a love she should have shrugged off years ago, but a love that had branded her, changed her, left her not the same, taken something away from her and kept it out of reach, beckoning her somewhere she could not follow, except perhaps through death. Perhaps it would come again at the last, perhaps that missing piece of her would be waiting, perhaps she would be whole again.

Except that she would not die. Better to live to find it for herself and snatch it back again. There must be more to come. There must be more.

There was more. They did not wait for the demand for surrender, did not wait for the attack. A volley of shots rang out from the watchtower above, and was instantly mimicked throughout the rest of the house. There was no discipline, no coordination, no strategy, no hope.

The response was swift and savage. Dolores could not see the enemy, who had taken cover behind the trees; but she soon heard them, and felt them, as a burst of synchronized gunfire showered against the house. There were screams of terror from the prisoners, and more erratic, staccato shots from above and below. Dolores shut her mind to the futility of it all and kept firing and firing, unable to see but forcing herself to imagine an enemy struck down with every squeeze of the trigger, counting out loud to herself as she fired. Twenty-five dead, twenty-six dead, twenty-seven—

She was jolted out of her trance by a sudden earsplitting noise louder than all the rest of it put together, a bloodcurdling shriek from Ignacia. Dolores turned to look, thinking she must have been hit, but she was bending over the crumpled body of her younger son.

He was already dead, from a bullet in the neck. Ignacia flung herself across the body, beating the floor with her fists, cursing and weeping uncontrollably. Dolores knelt down beside her helplessly and tried to offer comfort, but Ignacia swore at her and pushed her roughly away. Dolores returned to her window and began firing again. There was nothing she could do. She did not want to think about the dead child, not wanting to imagine what Ignacia must be feeling. Suppose it was Andrés lying there . . .

Gradually Ignacia's sobs subsided. She scrambled to her feet, picked up her rifle, and ran out of the room. Dolores did not attempt to follow her. It was Tomás she wanted, only Tomás could comfort her.

Noise, noise, noise. Noise bludgeoned the brain, and that was a blessing. Death would surely be like one final deafening thud, one last long scream . . .

And then she heard a huge, collective scream of terror from the prisoners upstairs. A scream that had that last, long quality of death. And then the roar of a lioness. Ignacia . . .

Dolores raced up the stairs, rifle in hand, but she got there too late. The shots rang out in quick succession before she reached the landing, and she burst into the prisoners' room just in time to see Ignacia discharge her sixth bullet into the skull of a tiny baby, spilling its brains into its dead mother's lap. Women and children cowered behind the furniture. Ignacia's eyes were wild, she was insane with grief and hatred.

Dolores walked up to her, and touched her arm.

"Ignacia," she said. "Come with me. You are needed below. Tomás wants you. Hurry now."

Ignacia looked at her blankly and fell silent, weeping quietly, pathetically, leaning on her rifle, her fury apparently spent. Dolores took her by the elbow and tried to inveigle her toward the door, but she was paralyzed, immovable.

"Tomás wants you," repeated Dolores. "Come with me. Let us find Tomás together."

Ignacia took a step backward and shook her arm free. Dolores held her breath and forced herself to stand very still, to stay very calm, not to show any fear. But then there was another cry of terror from the prisoners as Ignacia abruptly came out of her trance, jerked back her head, and pointed her weapon at Dolores, waving the barrel in a rabid circle, pulling the trigger repeatedly, uselessly.

"Fascist!" she hissed. "Dirty spy. *Whore!*"

"You must reload your gun, Ignacia," said Dolores coldly. "And then you must come with me and avenge your son. It was the Moors who killed him, not these women and children. We are wasting time."

Ignacia took another step back and let the rifle butt slip to the floor, holding it by the barrel. Then she grimaced hideously and raised it high above her head like a club.

"Fascist *whore!*" she spat, bringing down her weapon with manic force, and toppling forward like a felled tree as Dolores shot her dead.

The wailing from the women and children was terrible, the floor littered with bleeding corpses. Dolores felt her stomach heave. She turned and fled from the carnage, concerned only to get as far away as possible, running blindly down the stairs and down more stairs into the huge kitchen, hot and noisy as hell itself. The air was thick with the smell of frying: women were boiling pans of oil to hurl at the invaders. Tomás was crouched at a window, firing solidly.

Dolores tried to find her voice. His son and now his wife. His wife, killed not by the Fascists but by the woman whose life he had saved . . . No. She would not tell him. She would not need to tell him . . .

Her will to live had spent itself, she was ready now. She had wanted to kill and now she had. She had seen her victim die before her eyes, she had destroyed an attacking enemy, she had done what she had sworn to do. And now she had better die.

She did not trouble to take cover between shots. She rested her head on the sill, like a sitting target, eyes streaming, unable to see, not wanting to see anymore. She had been shot before. It wasn't so bad. There was no pain, not at first. So dying shouldn't hurt at all. It shouldn't hurt more than living.

Captain Sanpedro had been proved right. There were indeed traitors inside the Alcázar, Red agents, intent on assailing its impregnability from within. A giant might withstand the attacks of midgets, but not a spreading cancer. The tumor must be cut out quickly, before it was too late.

The treachery was beyond doubt. A woman hostage was missing. It was impossible for anyone to escape, therefore she had been smuggled out, God alone knew how. A hunt had been made for her body, to rule out murder or suicide, without result. A wall of silence surrounded the event. The Reds were laughing up their sleeves, anticipating the next escape, no doubt.

"The colonel has lost all authority," declared Sanpedro to his henchmen. "He is burying his head in the sand. He fails to see the need for drastic action. And the Civil Guard will make the most of it, believe me. Soon we will be taking orders from their commander instead of our own. Something's got to be done, before it's too late."

The colonel, a chivalrous old man, seemed to view the escape with a certain equanimity. The missing hostage was only a woman, a victim of circumstance, the wife of a Republican deputy who had been captured in his stead, the husband being absent in Madrid. And she was sick. Compassion was not necessarily treachery . . . Yes, by all means mount an investigation as to how she got out, for what it was worth, but it was doubtless an isolated incident . . .

Sanpedro had duly mounted his investigation. He questioned all the men on guard that night, and all the other hostages in the stable area, where the woman had been confined. His interrogations revealed nothing, except that siege conditions were already sapping vigilance and commitment. A creeping inertia was already getting a grip, some jolt was badly needed to restore discipline and morale. He began to see treason smoldering in every eye, suspecting everyone of sabotage.

Lieutenant Montanis was just the type to have connived this woman's escape, with his cockeyed notions of right and wrong. But unfortunately he turned out to have an alibi. He had been malingering in the infirmary all week, assailed by some mysterious stomach ailment, and had reportedly not left his bed except to evacuate his festering bowels. Which was a pity, because Sanpedro had heard with great interest of his mysterious association with the anarchist hostage and his unwarranted intrusion in a matter that did not con-

cern him. Routine brutality had always been the province of the
Civil Guard, and the boneheads had to be allowed some sport.
Montanis was a weak sort of soldier, not that he was really a
soldier. He was merely an instructor, a glorified bureaucrat, he
shouldn't even be in uniform.

After reporting that all his inquiries had proved fruitless, Sanpedro sought authority for his next move. It was refused. The colonel would not hear of it, and that was the end of the matter.
Sanpedro was dismissed with a flea in his ear, and was quick to
confide in his followers that he had begun to have suspicions about
the colonel himself.

Three days later another hostage disappeared. And not a harmless woman this time. This time it was a Red politician, who would
even now be regaling his comrades with his triumph.

"How many other escapes are planned?" demanded Sanpedro
of his cohorts. "The traitor must be identified, and quickly. Already we must be a laughingstock . . ."

General Franco would be furious, justifiably so. Had he not urged
them in his daily broadcasts to hold out to the last, not to weaken,
to remember that they had become a symbol, an inspiration to the
rest of Spain? Would he not be gravely disappointed to learn that
the colonel had not been up to the noble task entrusted to him, that
he had been too weak to take the necessary action?

After another exhaustive and abortive inquiry, Sanpedro's request was finally granted. The order went out for all defenders and
prisoners to assemble in the central courtyard. Lorenzo, still pale
and weak from his gastric upset, had been summoned from his
sickbed to attend.

Sanpedro looked in his element as he strutted to and fro in front
of the dejected group of filthy, ill-fed prisoners. A number of them
were bruised or cut about the face or limped painfully. Lorenzo felt
a wave of disgust, and then reminded himself that the other side
undoubtedly treated its hostages with similar brutality, which made
him feel even worse. His own intervention to help Roberto had
probably guaranteed the fellow further maltreatment at the hands
of his thwarted guards.

The group of shabby prisoners contrasted sharply with the well-
turned-out parade of soldiers and Civil Guard. The sporadic firing
in the background had become routine, men had been called down
from their positions to join the assembly. There was an air of almost
festive interest, anything to relieve the grinding monotony. The

colonel himself was absent. This was clearly to be Sanpedro's personal show.

"As you must all be aware," he began self-importantly, "two hostages have escaped. It has fallen to me to conduct a full inquiry, which has produced no information.

"Clearly no one could have escaped without the collusion of a traitor. Either that traitor steps forward now and admits his crime, or a hostage will be executed in his place. Tomorrow two hostages will be executed, the next day three, and so on. Meanwhile, we shall continue to hunt down the culprit, however many lives are sacrificed in the meantime. No traitor shall be allowed to escape justice. Let him not think that by craven silence he can buy his own miserable life with that of others. Sooner or later he too will die with these deaths on his conscience, and we have no priest here to absolve him. I am waiting."

Lorenzo was appalled. How many "traitors" would they find this time? Over twenty waverers had been shot three weeks before, in the first days of the siege; those who had lost their nerve and wanted to surrender, those who had acted in haste and repented at leisure, those who had not been clear what issues were at stake. The confusion of those hours! There had been no unity of purpose, no time for discussion, just panic and haste and muddle.

For the committed right-wingers, it had made no difference; for others the wrong decision had led them to their deaths. And yet some had apparently survived the purge by stealth. Treacherous cowards or secret heroes, depending on your point of view. But whoever was guilty, why had he not fled himself, instead of letting a hostage go? Perhaps the traitor was a hero after all. Perhaps all traitors were heroes in the wrong place.

There was complete silence underlying the din of shells exploding against the fortress walls. No one stepped forward.

"One more minute," said Sanpedro. "In one more minute the first hostage will be shot. There will be no firing squad. I will nominate an officer to carry out the execution."

Lorenzo's heart started hammering violently at this sinister departure from military etiquette, its purpose only too painfully clear. He was assailed by the helpless feeling he used to have at school, the dreadful moment of hollow certainty when he knew he would be selected to demonstrate his ineptitude before the whole class. He had no doubt that it was his name that was about to be called. He fancied he could see Sanpedro looking at him out of the corner of his eye, mockingly, enjoying his horror. But he would have to do it. If he refused, it would undoubtedly be seen as proof that he was one of that hidden nest of traitors . . .

And then, just as the suspense was becoming intolerable, a huge weight fell from his shoulders, leaving him dizzy, as he heard Sanpedro bark, ''Very well. Lieutenant Vasquez, you will carry out the execution. The hostages who are to be shot have already been selected in order of political culpability. Fetch the prisoner.''

Lieutenant Vasquez stepped forward. He looked very pale, well aware that his selection labeled him a suspect. His avowed hatred of the Popular Front government was entirely on religious grounds, his sister being a nun and all his family devout Catholics. But he was no lover of the Falange and Sanpedro knew it.

As he stepped forward without flinching, as if to demonstrate his innocence, Sanpedro gave the order for the prisoner to be fetched from the straggling group of hostages, standing apart on the other side of the square, helplessly awaiting their fate.

Lorenzo began to breathe freely again. Not today. It would not be today that he had to do it. Tomorrow, perhaps, if no one confessed. But not today. Until that day came, he was nothing but a bystander, powerless to intervene, there would be no blood on his hands. And yet to kill a man who was not armed, who had not been tried or convicted, that was no job for a firing squad, let alone an officer. Except when the officer himself was the one on trial . . .

A big, bearded man was jostled forward. Lorenzo shut his eyes and felt himself sway forward. He heard Sanpedro give the order, and braced himself for the shot, but he never heard it.

When he recovered consciousness he was back in the subterranean gloom of the infirmary, his jacket streaked with incriminating vomit. And yet, he had been vomiting all week. Why should today be an exception?

Jack's predictions had been proved right. Untrained militias and the rump of the Republican army were no match for shock troops. The Army of Africa was advancing relentlessly, destroying everything in its path, and the outlook for the Republic seemed bleak. Clara was more anxious than ever to go home.

''We've got to get public opinion behind the Republic, make people realize how much is at stake, lobby politicians, raise money . . . You could help, Edmund. You don't have to join the party to fight fascism . . .''

So there was nothing to be done but give in with a good grace; she was restless now, and no longer happy. Her early euphoria had hardened off, the fire in her eyes had been banked down with slow-burning hatred. Despite Jack's lecture on unity, or perhaps because of it, she had begun to rail constantly against the non-Communist parties of the left; the lack of unity was clearly all their fault. Edmund could only hope she would recover her good spirits once she felt herself back among friends.

There was a long wait at the frontier while their passports were scrutinized minutely. The guards were on the lookout for Fascists with false papers attempting to flee the country. While Edmund looked unquestionably like a bona fide tourist, Clara had affected Spanish working-class garb which did her no favors on either side of the border and provoked unnecessary suspicion. But knowing Clara, she would glory in her rope-soled sandals until they fell apart, wearing them to her party meetings well into an English winter.

Still, it was better than sharing her with a bottle, and as she kept pointing out, this could be something they could do together, for once, if only he would stop sitting on the fence. Clara liked to blame Edmund's incorrigible skepticism on Jack, who was politically totally promiscuous and sneered at anyone with convictions. Edmund could have been a great asset to the party if Jack hadn't filled his head full of rubbish . . .

Still, her energy had returned with a vengeance. She showed no signs of fatigue on the journey home and did not even wait to unpack before going straight around to see Bert Winterman to find out what plans were already afoot, leaving Edmund to collect her cat from a neighbor and cut the pocket-handkerchief lawn and make the necessary pleasantries over the garden fence. He was asked polite questions about his holiday and answered them with routine descriptions of the food and weather and plumbing. He found himself unable to utter a single word about the war that didn't sound absurd in an English back garden. It seemed so remote. How could you possibly summarize what was going on out there without making some perfectly crass generalization? Mr. Fisher, the retired grocer who lived next door, remarked chattily that Spain seemed "a rum place to go for a holiday, what with a load of bloody foreigners killing each other all over the place" and Edmund found himself quite unable to disagree. Yes, it had been a rum place to go for a holiday, and there were indeed a load of foreigners, many of them distinctly bloody, killing one another all over the place. And he knew he ought to make some reference to the threat of fascism and the importance of combating it, but it seemed so false, it smacked of salving his conscience with self-righteous cant. It was so easy to talk.

And yet what else could he do except talk? And how could he talk with any conviction? Whose side was he supposed to be on? The Communists, when he didn't believe in communism? The anarchists, when he didn't believe in anarchism either? The socialists, he supposed, if only because they weren't Communist, weren't anarchist, though what they actually were remained unclear. You couldn't just be anti-Fascist in Spain, you had to be anti other anti-Fascists to fight on two fronts at once. No, to say anything was sheer hypocrisy. In any event, he was a pacifist, as indeed all left-wing intellectuals—how he hated that phrase—were officially pacifist. As a pacifist he had no option but to support nonintervention. Except that he didn't support it.

Having discharged his domestic duties, Edmund set off to visit his mother, craving tea and scones and trivia. He had cabled her to expect him home, and hopefully she would have banished her normal coterie for the day.

He found her dressed in black. But she smiled happily and hugged him and didn't look unduly distressed. Edmund wondered which of his elderly relatives had died.

She told him over tea, producing Dolly's letter with a sigh. It had been written nearly three weeks before.

Dear Aunt Margaret,

Forgive my long silence over all these years. As you will have guessed already, it is bad news that leads me to write to you. My mother died today, after an illness of several weeks, although as you know she has been ailing for some years.

The postal services here are beset by strikes, but I am sending this letter off immediately so that the news reaches you with the least possible delay. After the funeral tomorrow I am returning immediately to Toledo, so if you wish to reply please write care of my husband, Lieutenant Montanis, at the military academy. I do hope Edmund and Flora are well. I'm sorry yet again that I put you in such a dreadful position all those years ago. I did mean to keep in touch, but the first few weeks at home were very difficult for me, and then I was very ill with my pregnancy. Anyway, I apologize again for abusing your hospitality and for seeming so ungrateful. I'm afraid I was rather wild and headstrong as a girl. No longer, I assure you.

> *Much love,*
> *Your niece Dolores*

Edmund looked troubled and his mother patted his arm.

"Don't be upset, darling. It's not as if you ever knew her. We weren't even close. Poor Pamela. Such a disastrous marriage. And then deprived of all her children just when a mother needs them most. How lucky I am in you and Flora and Daddy. I used to envy her being so rich, you know. It seems so silly now. Edmund . . . what is it?''

"I didn't know Dolly was in Toledo," said Edmund uneasily. Seeing his mother's blank expression, he explained, as simply as he could, what was going on there.

"There's presumably a fifty-fifty chance that her husband's joined the uprising, and if he has then she's probably with him, holed up inside the military academy. Jack mentioned it when we met. There are any number of women and children there, families of the rebel officers. They've been besieged by Republican militia ever since the troubles started, and so far they've refused to surrender."

"But . . . the people inside. They're the Fascists, aren't they? Surely Dolly's husband wouldn't be a Fascist? She was always so frantically left-wing, poor child."

"I don't think it's quite as simple as we've been led to believe," said Edmund. "And frankly, I don't care what she is. She probably had no choice in any case. I just don't want Dolly to get hurt, that's all. I'll write to Jack and tell him straightaway. Perhaps he can find out what's become of her."

"Oh, Edmund! You know, it never occurred to me that *Dolly* might be in danger. Once I knew that you and Clara were safe, I stopped worrying. Politics are so boring and you know I never read the newspapers . . ."

Her artlessness was like a breath of fresh air.

"I shouldn't think you'd be any the wiser if you did," said Edmund.

"I do hope she's all right. What a dreadful business! Your father says that the Communists were plotting to take over the government and that the Army always sorts out these things in countries like Spain. What does Jack think?"

"I'm never sure what Jack really thinks. You know how he likes to play devil's advocate."

"Such an odd boy," sighed Mrs. Townsend, forcing another tea cake on her son. "I felt so sorry for him that Christmas. He looked so desperately out of place. You know, I think he was quite smitten with poor Dolly."

"Yes," said Edmund, "I rather think he was."

9

Dolores woke up cramped and stiff. It had not been sleep, more a trance of terror, some primitive state of suspended animation to conserve what strength and sanity she had left.

She was still alive, then.

She had thought herself ready to die, seeing death as a liberation. But she had missed her chance, she had fled from its deliverance, clinging to life like a coward. Her courage had failed her, such as it was. It hadn't been courage at all, it had just been a craven death wish that passed for courage, the specious courage of a suicide.

She had been crouching at her post, reloading her rifle, when the first enemy shell burst through the kitchen wall, showering rubble and shrapnel. She had covered her head against the blast, pressing herself into a corner. She had not seen the pans of boiling oil topple and ignite; she had been aware only of the roar and then the intense heat and then screams and the smell of roasting flesh as the room became a lake of burning oil, with bodies dancing like dervishes in the flames, and ammunition going off like fireworks, fueling its splendor, the huge wooden table an island of glowing charcoal rising above the lapping waves of fire. The flames and debris barred the only exit save the cellar. Dolores had no other thought than to leap into that quenching well of darkness, almost falling down the stairs with the weight of following bodies.

One of them was Tomás, dazed and wild-eyed, his left sleeve completely burned off, his arm ruptured and bleeding. As her eyes adjusted to the gloom she could pick out two other people crouching in the darkness, an old man and a boy who was whimpering in pain. She ran up the stairs again to see if anyone else was coming, but the air was black, and the sound of another explosion made her shut the door against the flames.

It was all over. It was only a matter of time before the house would be overrun and searched, only a matter of time until they were discovered, and yet the instinct to hide was all-powerful. Dolores felt her way in the dark toward the meat safe, heaved open the door and pushed the two others inside, where they sat cowering under the swinging carcasses, gruesome reminders of butchery and death.

"Quickly, Tomás," urged Dolores. "Get inside. It's our only hope. Please, Tomás."

Tomás shook his head violently, as if rousing himself from sleep and began stumbling toward the stairway.

"No," he said. "I must find Ignacia. I must find my boys."

Dolores tried to catch hold of him and sank her fingers unintentionally into the raw flesh of his arm, making him yelp with pain.

"Tomás . . . Ignacia is dead. So is Federico. I saw it happen. And Marco was in the kitchen. He can't have survived. Live to avenge them, Tomás. Live to avenge them. Tomás, please don't go. I'm so afraid. I need you. Please don't leave me, Tomás!"

He wavered and she gritted her teeth and sank her nails viciously into his bleeding arm, trying to rob him of resolution. He sank to his knees, trembling, and let her drag him to his feet and toward the storeroom.

Dolores shut the door, and they waited in utter blackness, deafened by the continuing explosions from above, squashed together with whole sides of pork and beef and the dangling, rotting corpses of game, which her father liked to hang until the intestines had turned green and dropped out of their own accord. They would all be dead meat soon, thought Dolores, as the blood from Tomás's arm seeped through her sleeve and the vibrations from the boy's quivering body sent shudders through her own. Then the old man made a gurgling noise and the air was filled with the stench of excrement and his body slumped to one side.

Dolores buried her head in Tomás's shoulder, unable to weep, for she felt no pity, only envy for his merciful escape. Oh to have a heart that was old and weak instead of one that bruised her ribs with savage, stubborn vigor. But Tomás still seemed oblivious, rigid with shock and grief and shame. The same shock and grief and shame she would have felt if Lorenzo and Andrés lay smoldering upstairs while she squatted in sunken safety. Except that she wasn't safe. Sooner or later they would be discovered. The thing she had dreaded more than death, the thing she had thought to avoid, would happen after all. She would be tied to a tree and raped repeatedly, her breasts would be sliced away from her like hams . . . The litany of horror had been recited so often it had become as routinely real as the torments of purgatory. And she had already started to think the automatic words of supplication before she heard them uttered, before she heard the thin, frantic whisper of the boy, before she heard Tomás join in tonelessly, before she found her own muted voice. "Holy Mary, mother of God, pray for us sinners now and at the hour of our death, amen. Now and at the hour of our death, amen. Now, at the hour of our death. The hour of our death. Death. Death . . ."

How long had they been here? It was silent now. The blackness and cold and immobility had finally reduced her to a semiconscious stupor, some instinctive, possumlike mimicry of death. Dolores had no idea how much time had passed; she knew only that she was cramped and stiff and still alive.

"Ssh," hissed Tomás into her ear. "Be very quiet."

There was a noise above them as the door of the cellar was thrown open amid a jabber of coarse voices. She felt her throat close with terror, robbing her of breath.

There were heavy footsteps on the stair, followed by the rasp of boots on the stone floor. A wavering pattern of light flickered through the ventilation grill above their heads, as a torch beam explored the gloom. Then more unintelligible speech and the general sound of exploration, of a barrel being kicked over and a sack being ripped and dried beans bouncing like hailstones. And as death stalked nearer and nearer Tomás's arm encircled her more and more tightly, pressing her against him, pressing the young lad against him, a hand across each mouth to stifle any cry of fear. Dolores clenched her teeth together to stop them chattering, hoping now only that it would be over quickly, certain only of discovery, craving no more than an end to waiting.

But the footsteps receded and it was suddenly very quiet again. Her suspended breath started to come in gasps and she was aware of the pain of her full bladder and the nauseating smell of the dead old man and the sour taste of thirst as the numbing power of fear gave away to the squalid sufferings of survival.

Tomás removed his hand from her mouth. A thin white light shone through the grill, constant, natural light. Tomás stood on tiptoe and peered through the opening.

"They've left the door open," he said. "Stay here while I look."

The hinges shrieked as he emerged and shut Dolores back in her prison. He was gone for what seemed like a long time. Dolores tried to rouse the boy, but he did not respond, and Dolores felt his skin for death, but it was warm, hot even, and she could feel his shallow breath damp against her hand.

Eventually she could bear the waiting no longer and reached out to open the door, starting with horror as it pulled away from her. It was Tomás, signaling silence.

"We must stay here till night," he whispered, shutting himself back in. "The kitchen is open, one wall completely gone. If we wait till dark we can try to get away. They will have destroyed at least part of the railings in the advance. If we can get out into the fields under cover of darkness we can head for the river and try to get back across the lines. Assuredly the troops will have taken all your father's fine horses. Can you walk?"

Dolores nodded.

"I don't know about the boy," she said, "I can't wake him."

Tomás struck a match. The lad's legs were raw from ankle to thigh.

"He will die," said Tomás shortly. "Let us hope he will be dead by nightfall. Best for him. Better to die in here than at the hands of the Moors. I am glad you saw Ignacia dead, Dolores. She feared the Moors greatly. Did you truly see her dead?"

"Truly," said Dolores, swallowing her secret, feeling it stick like a fish bone in her throat. "I saw here dead from a bullet in the chest. It was quick."

"I am glad," said Tomás.

"And Federico too. In the neck."

"I would wish death for myself, except that you are alive. While you are alive I will protect you. I would have broken your neck, just now, before they could have taken you."

"Thank you, Tomás."

"There would have been no pain. For myself, I had my knife, but it is difficult to die quickly by a knife. There is a lot of blood in me."

Dolores heard the sob in his voice, cradled his head in her arms while his body throbbed with silent anguish. And she tried to weep too, to shed some of her pain, and could not. It was as if her tears had all been counted and she had to save them for a greater grief.

Jack stretched back luxuriously in the back of the open-top Bugatti, the erstwhile property of a royalist nobleman who had bequeathed it hurriedly to the people of Toledo before taking off for cooler climes. It had served today to transport a visiting Labour MP to the scenic hilltop that housed the city's principal tourist attraction. The siege of the Alcázar had become a focus for day-trippers from

Madrid and visitors from abroad, all eager to take a safe, if useless, potshot at the enemy.

Harry Martindale had wired Jack to interview Bill Arnold about his stand against Labour's policy of nonintervention, and Jack had to admire the chap, out-and-out phony that he was, for being one jump ahead of the game. He could go back home now and say how he had taken part in the siege—nay, *fought* in the siege—having personally fired several brave bullets against the Fascists. Yes, he had certainly done his bit for Spain, not to mention his own ego. And he would have the snapshots to prove it.

"Hold it!" barked the photographer, clicking the shutter. "Perfect. Shall we have one with the lady now?"

The lady obliged, simpering, gasping at the weight of the rifle and letting her husband position it for her.

"Don't fire it, lovey. It kicks."

She took aim charmingly while the photographer did likewise.

"Perfect," he enthused. "Now if I could just have one of you together, with the Alcázar in the background. Lovely, lovely . . ."

The siege was rapidly becoming a fiasco. Colonel Lister, a Spaniard trained in Moscow, had wanted to exercise his newly formed Communist 5th Regiment by taking the Alcázar by storm. But the Alcázar was the anarchists' baby; the government had duly declined his offer, fearful of unleashing further internecine strife, and Lister had withdrawn in disgust.

The anarchists were conducting the operation with their usual lack of method. Groups of militiamen laughed and joked behind the old mattresses which served as barricades, cuddling with their girlfriends and enjoying the attention of the spectators. Right enough, it was a better billet than joining the beleaguered Republican army which was currently beating off, or rather not beating off, the relentless Fascist advance. But then you'd never get an anarchist to serve in an army battalion, to wear a uniform or obey orders or salute an officer. Of all the parties of the left the anarchist faction was the one that Jack admired the most, and the one he had least faith in. Couldn't they see that they were playing straight into the Communists' hands?

"Have a shot, Jack lad," said the honorable member, with gritty northern bonhomie, handing him the rifle.

"No thanks," said Jack. "Until you persuade the rest of your party to see things your way, I'd rather not waste the Republic's ammunition. In any case, I'm a lousy shot. I might miss."

"They should drop half a dozen bombs on the place. Blow it sky high. Why don't they? They've got the planes. What's that French chap up to?''

"I think Monsieur Malraux is rather tied up fighting the Arm of Africa. A rather more dangerous animal than the poor bastards in the Alcázar, who aren't actually killing anyone much, apart from each other by now, I shouldn't wonder. And remember the place is full of women and children. It's hardly worth wasting bombs on. It's just a symbol, that's all. It doesn't rate all this ballyhoo. If you want to know what the war's really about, I suggest we take a little drive out to the front. Bit riskier than this, of course, but a much better story for the people back home. I'd be glad to arrange it for you.''

"Er . . . thanks, Jack lad, but duty calls. Got to be back in the constituency by the end of the week. These pictures will give folks the flavor of what it's all about. Life behind the barricades, the people's army against a Fascist stronghold, held up by lack of equipment and arms.''

"Pity," mused Jack. "I had it all arranged. Earplugs, tin hat, the lot. You could get some wonderful snaps." Jack flashed a lazy smile at the honorable member's lady. She touched the brim of her hat and winked under cover of her hand.

"Well, back to the hotel, then," sighed Jack. "Got to write my copy before I leave tomorrow. Pity you won't be coming with me. Another time perhaps."

"It must be very dangerous," cooed the lady. "War correspondents must have to be terribly brave. Doesn't your wife worry about you?"

"I'm not married." Jack smiled. "If I was I'd find better things to do at home."

"Um . . . You wouldn't happen to know of a good *hairdresser* by any chance? The one I went to yesterday made such a mess, I daren't take off my hat. Willie, I simply must get it done before dinner tonight."

"I did happen to notice a place near my hotel, if that's any use to you," said Jack helpfully, picking up the hint. "I can show you where, if the driver drops us off."

"How kind of you. Willie, would you mind? I feel such a wreck."

"Eh? Oh, all right, love. Thanks a lot, Jack lad. Er . . . let me see what you've written, won't you?"

"Oh naturally. I'll bring it with me this evening. Of course, it'll get all carved up by the subs, not to mention Harry, so I can't guarantee the final result. You know how it is. Well, we'd better be off then, if your good lady wants her hair done in time for dinner.''

The car set them down as directed and Arnold drove on. The lady began twittering her thanks again.

''My pleasure,'' said Jack, understanding her nervous manner perfectly. ''Tell me, how long does it take to have your hair done?''

''Oh . . . at least an hour. Probably two. Or even longer. You know how slow the service is out here.''

''You'll probably need a drink by then,'' said Jack, indicating his hotel. ''Perhaps we could have one together, when you've finished. Room twenty-three.''

''Room twenty-three,'' said the lady.

While he waited, Jack put the finishing touches to his article.

Today I talked to Bill Arnold, Labour MP for Ilkley North, as he laughed and joked with Republican militiamen behind the barricades. Bill shouldered a rifle to good effect for several hours, and assured Spanish workers of the growing support in England for their assault on this fortress of fascism.

But Mr. Arnold would be the first to agree with me that the siege has reached a stalemate. The Alcázar has become little more than a symbol, while the real struggle is going on in the devastated villages around Badajoz, the last remaining Republican stronghold dividing the enemy-occupied territory to the north and south. While Colonel Lister's redoubtable 5th Regiment equips and trains its men to modern battle standards, and drills them in Communist ideology, other Republican battalions are fighting for survival with out-of-date and malfunctioning equipment, and with only the most basic of training.

Colonel Lister is fortunate, for he has powerful friends abroad who have a personal interest in his success. Meanwhile less privileged militias are being butchered by the Fascists for lack of arms.

I had to dissuade Mr. Arnold from his wish to visit the front personally, in deference to the interests of his constituents at home, but he assured me that he is now more convinced than ever that continued nonintervention will not only assist a Fascist victory, but will leave the Republican forces increasingly dominated by Communists, the only faction with the support and arms to succeed, and one that has no wish to share its glory with the socialists and anarchists whom it regards not as comrades but as deadly rivals . . .

Jack sealed the envelope, which would be reaching Martindale anonymously via the innocuous luggage of an obliging fellow countryman. He scribbled an edited version to show Arnold over dinner, and poured himself a whiskey. She was no catch and no chicken, but she would do. Thank God for miserable married women.

She was practiced enough at her hobby to have had her hair convincingly rearranged, and all in less than half an hour. Hearing the coy knock at the door, Jack drained his drink, let her in and began unbuttoning his cuffs without preamble. He always left women to undress themselves, and after a second's hesitation she did so, with a grotesque degree of coquetry, as if she were proud of her sagging breasts and her stretch marks and her orange-peel thighs. Still, she was scrawny enough, and didn't look as if she weighed much.

Jack lifted her off her feet, pinned her up against the wall, and plunged straight in, making her gasp, although she was more than ready for him, having spent the last forty-five minutes in mental masturbation. She wrapped her legs around him and started the inevitable groaning and moaning and foul language, and then she bit his ear, quite viciously, the bitch.

It was hard work. He was fed up with her by the time she uttered her final guttural cry, arching her neck and showing her fillings and dragging her nails across his back. He finished her quickly and dropped her without ceremony, and only then did he smile at her, a practiced smile that would feed her foolish memory with the fantasies she craved. He thought, not for the first time, that there was a lot to be said for Clara, who knew when she was acting, who had never for one moment fooled herself.

Jack had learned the value of afterplay. It made up for his dislike of preliminaries, for his depersonalization of the act itself, it was the secret of his wholly unjustified reputation as a good lover. And it required no effort on his part. So he poured her a drink and let her talk. They all loved to talk. Sex provoked chatter, true passion blissful silence. He remembered that perfect silence still, the glorious freedom from the need to speak, with everything said and unsaid and untrammeled by useless words.

After she had gone, he bathed and changed for dinner, and reread the letter Edmund had sent to Madrid.

. . . so it seems Dolly has ended up in Toledo. Her married name is Montanis and her husband a lieutenant who instructs at the academy, which she gave as a care-of address. If you can find

*out what has become of her, it would put my mind at rest, or not,
but it would at least put an end to wondering. All the things I
saw in Barcelona seemed unreal, like watching a film, but Dolly's
real and she makes the war real too . . .*

It hadn't taken much detective work to find out that Lieutenant
Montanis had indeed joined the uprising, although the military
authorities had not been helpful about the whereabouts of his wife.
It was to be *assumed* that she was with him inside the Alcázar. Jack
had felt a stab of fear at the implication. It was to be assumed,
because she would be mad to remain in the city and risk arrest or
victimization. Why else would so many of the defenders have taken
their families with them? But undoubtedly some of the wives and
children were elsewhere, by chance or design, in hiding, or closely
watched, and in any case Jack preferred not to work on assumptions.

That evening he was due to dine with Arnold and the government
minister who was hosting his visit—a member of the war cabinet
with a special responsibility for public relations. Jack saw this encounter as the ideal opportunity for some string pulling, not to say
blackmail. The Republic was losing the propaganda war, and
needed all the good publicity it could get.

Dolores was half English; she could be passed off as a relative
of one of Arnold's constituents about whom the family was anxious.
Hardly her fault if her husband had joined the uprising, nothing
beyond the scope of a caring Labour MP, nor of a humanitarian
Spanish socialist . . .

Arnold had proved a bit difficult at first about associating himself
with the relative of a wife of a Fascist—bad for the image that—
until he realized that Jack meant business and would not hesitate
to pay him back if thwarted. Damned journalists. He duly brought
the subject up after the meal, telling the lie convincingly enough.
The man was a politician after all.

The minister was at pains to deny the rumors Jack had heard
about Republican atrocities. It was true, he admitted, that certain
extremists had acted disgracefully in the name of the revolution,
but such factions were now firmly in check.

"All kinds of smears are being promulgated by Fascist sympathizers," he said. "Especially abroad. Do not be deceived by right-
wing propaganda, Mr. Austin."

"Right-wing propaganda has it that the defenders took their
families with them for their own safety. Right-wing propaganda has

it that families left behind in Toledo have been harassed, arrested, imprisoned, killed—''

"Preposterous. Absolutely preposterous."

"Quite. Still, you know how gullible the public is. At the moment I'm afraid the right-wing press have got things all their own way. I'd like to expose these Fascist lies for what they are. For example, if I were able to interview Señora Montanis and tell my readers that she is safe and well and unafraid in Toledo, that would prove your point nicely, wouldn't it? I found it rather suspicious that no one's prepared to tell me where she lives. The family wrote to her care of the academy, you see. If what you say is true, then hopefully I'll find her safely at home."

"Interview her? I'm sorry to say the unfortunate lady is almost certainly with her husband. Not by choice, you understand. Many wives and children have been incarcerated in the Alcázar against their will."

"Against their will? How can you possibly know that?"

The minister paused before answering.

"Military intelligence," he said shortly.

"From inside the Alcázar?"

"Naturally we have agents working behind Fascist lines, and the Alcázar is no exception. We infiltrated the Falange long ago, in the interests of national security. We are informed that both the families, and many of the defenders themselves, would dearly like to surrender but are too afraid to say so, for fear of instant execution. A militant minority of fanatics is determined to sacrifice hundreds of lives, including those of their own wives and children, to a lost cause. One can only sympathize with the fate of such innocent victims."

"How interesting," said Jack. "I'd love to quote you, of course, but it does sound suspiciously like Republican propaganda. Can you prove it?"

"Certain information remains classified, Mr. Austin. But already our infiltrators have effected the escape of two key hostages."

Jack sat up.

"Escaped hostages? Can I speak to them?"

"They are currently receiving medical treatment and will not be available for press interviews until fully recovered."

Jack smiled cynically. So they hadn't learned their lines yet.

"Of course. So presumably, if Señora Montanis has been imprisoned against her will, your people might also help her to escape?"

"Mr. Austin, you are being fanciful. The fate of Señora Montanis, although lamentable, is scarcely a matter of national importance. There is a limit to the number of escapes that can be achieved. The principal function of our agents is to pass us information and to promote surrender. Morale is pitifully low already. The only reason we have not taken the Alcázar by storm is because we are reluctant to kill the innocent along with the guilty. Otherwise we would have made short work of it weeks ago.''

"No doubt. So, presumably you're in regular wireless communication?''

"Evidently. Naturally I cannot jeopardize such a delicate operation by going into detail.''

"You have my word that I will be discreet. Believe me, I am eager to help the Republic in any way I can. My paper has a very wide circulation. Very wide. And Señora Montanis has very influential relatives in England, doesn't she Bill?''

"Um . . . very influential,'' muttered Bill, unhappily.

Jack sighed and shook his head.

"Such a pity you can't give me any definite information on her whereabouts. Everyone will assume the worst. Other journalists might get hold of the story and try to portray the lady and her husband as heroic—gallant officer and loyal wife sticking together against the barbarian hordes—that kind of thing. Or they might try to convince their readers that she and her child are rotting in some Republican jail. All fantasy, of course. But in the absence of fact, one has to write something . . .''

"Jack . . .'' began Arnold warningly as the minister's brow darkened. Jack ignored him.

"Still, I fully understand your position,'' he continued, lighting another cigarette. "What with the anarchists running the war, and all the revolutionary chaos, I suppose you can't afford to upset anyone. Don't worry. I'll make my own inquiries. Sorry to have bothered you with such a trifle.''

The minister was no fool and got the message loud and clear.

"The anarchists may be running the siege, Mr. Austin, but they are most certainly not running the war. As you are aware, there are no anarchist cabinet ministers, and as for revolutionary chaos, I can assure you that government and military departments are in full control of the situation. Naturally I will be glad to make the necessary inquiries. This was always my intention. Rest assured, Mr. Austin, that the Republic has no quarrel with women and children. Kindly write that down.''

Jack scribbled obligingly while the minister waxed eloquent on the chivalry and compassion of Republican troops, the high level of military discipline and commitment, and the heroic work of agents working behind the lines. Then Jack read his words back to him, slowly and precisely, as if reciting the terms of a contract.

"Rhetoric is no substitute for news." Jack smiled as he put the top back on his pen. "And bad news is no substitute for good news. I do hope you'll be able to give me some good news soon."

"That sounded like a threat," grumbled Arnold later.

"It was meant to," said Jack.

"¡Viva Cristo Rey!" came the shout from above as the doors of Josep's church were flung wide open. "Long live Christ the King!"

There were cheers and sobs, people crossing themselves frantically and scrambling to their feet, pushing and jostling their way out of the crypt and into daylight.

Josep found his church full of troops, a mixed bag of Foreign Legionaries and Moorish *regulares,* resplendent in their blue djellabas and red caps. A Spanish officer saluted him in the name of General Queipo de Llano and declared Fontenar liberated in the name of God and Spain. He congratulated Josep on his heroism in protecting his congregation against the anarchist mob and invited him cordially to bless his troops. He was charming, civilized and urbane, evidently unperturbed that the town had just been bombed indiscriminately, and that the elimination of the anarchist militia had involved the haphazard slaughter of a large number of civilians.

Josep ignored the extended hand, shook his head and walked out into the morning sunlight. Death was everywhere. Juan's men, who had come out of hiding to meet the advancing troops, were lying in the blood-spattered dust, while the townsfolk clustered around them in groups, some of them sobbing at their own losses and taking great solace in the sight of these enemy corpses. Josep knelt down beside Juan's body, made the sign of the cross over him, and murmured the absolution given to the dead and dying who cannot confess. Then he did the same for another body, and another, many of them unrecognizable, shot to pulp by machine-gun fire, not that it mattered who they were. And another, and another, ignoring the angry mutterings all around him. How dare he absolve the souls of unbelievers? How dare he try to obstruct their passage to hell?

Josep felt a tap on his shoulder.

"You may say Mass if you wish, Father, over the common grave, which my men will start digging immediately. Your present actions are not appropriate and are causing distress to the bereaved. I would

ask you again to give my men your blessing and to lead prayers for
those we have lost in today's battle. You are free once more, Father,
to practice your ministry unhampered by Marxists and atheists. No
one will burn your church now, you need walk in fear no longer.
Every day we are ridding Spain of those who challenge the authority
of God."

The officer extended his arm in the Fascist salute, convinced of
the righteousness of his cause, seeing himself as an exterminator
of vermin, of disease, of crime, with a sacred mission to replace
freedom with order. And Josep clenched his fist tightly and felt an
overwhelming urge to raise it and strike the air in a gesture of
secular blessing for those who had died in vain. But he unclasped
it again and tried to look at the man with charity. He had done what
he thought was right. That was the pity of it.

He went back into the church and blessed the dusty soldiers and
then said Mass for the dead to a packed congregation. Army trucks
set about transporting the injured to the nearest field hospital. The
few anarchist wounded were given the coup de grace and consigned
to a mass grave. Josep did not attempt to intervene. They were
undoubtedly better off dead from a single shot than they would be
nursed back to health only to be imprisoned and executed later.

The civilian dead were buried individually, mourned by weeping
families, who saw them not as the victims of a Fascist air raid, but
as martyrs of Christ, heroes who had died for their beliefs. There
were no recriminations toward the troops. A rearguard contingent
was to be left behind, billeted with great hospitality, to give the
town protection and to mop up any lurking Reds.

"You have nothing to fear now, Father," repeated the captain,
pleased with his good day's work. "As you can see, the anarchist
rabble are no match for trained men. They have no discipline, they
are merely the pathetic tools of those who incite them to revolution."

The good captain proved a mine of information. He was happy
to reply to Josep's questions and to draw a rough map showing the
progress of the Nationalist troops.

"The battle will soon be won, Father," he assured him. "We
have met with little resistance. We have been welcomed everywhere
as the army of liberation. Soon Badajoz will fall, and then Madrid
and Barcelona . . ."

Josep was anxious for news of his family, but the information
was inconclusive. His father's land was now behind Nationalist
lines, much to the old man's relief, no doubt, and his poor mother
was presumably dead by now. But there was no way of knowing

whether Dolores was still in Albavera, or back in Toledo; neither could he be sure of her husband's loyalties.

"Soon our troops will relieve the Alcázar," predicted the captain. "What a heroic struggle! A handful of brave souls against thousands of Reds. What a glorious day it will be when we take the city!"

Josep had known Lorenzo since boyhood, and had always found him dull, a pleasant but unoriginal fellow who had the good fortune to be extremely handsome and thus turn his silly little sister's head. Still, the marriage seemed happy enough; certainly it was hard to imagine Lorenzo allying himself with the far right—or the far left, if it came to that. But now there was no more middle ground. Suddenly no one could sit on the fence any longer, least of all himself.

His sympathies lay, now as always, with the poor, with the workers. As a man he belonged on the other side of the lines with the Republicans. But if he crossed over, he could no longer be a priest. The captain confirmed what he already suspected; priests in the Republic were now in hiding, in fear of their lives, they were hunted down as enemies of the people to face imprisonment or even death. If he crossed the lines, he would have to abandon his cassock. He would have to enlist as a soldier, be prepared to kill. The Republican army had no chaplains.

The Nationalist army, of course, did. He could offer his services, bless Fascist troops for battle, join the bloody crusade against the godless government, endorse a cause he could not believe in, become a holy hypocrite.

Or he could remain here, try to reconcile himself with his former congregation, perform an endless, boring round of meaningless ministry, selling tickets to heaven, achieving nothing. Those whom he cared to serve were dead or fled, any who were found would be rounded up and shot. The families of Juan and his men would even now be fleeing east and north, seeking refuge in Madrid and Valencia. He would never see them again.

In any event, he would not be allowed to remain in his parish. His remarks about the workers of Triana, his refusal to pray for the victory of the generals, his blatant revolutionary sympathies, would undoubtedly reach the ears of his bishop and result in a summons to Córdoba. And this time he might well be threatened with more than a spell in the monastery . . .

He must act quickly. But before he did anything else, he must find out if Dolores was safe. If she had found herself in Albavera when the troubles broke out, she would not have been able to return to Toledo without crossing the lines, at enormous risk. Possibly she was stranded, without news of her husband, perhaps she needed help . . .

As for Ramón . . . Josep tried hard to think of his brother with compassion, but for years now he had not thought about him at all. The two brothers had never been friends. Ramón had always been envious of Josep and openly derided his voluntary celibacy, taunting him about being a secret homosexual. During his early days in Madrid, Ramón had pestered his brother for money; when Josep failed to oblige him, Ramón had written obscene, abusive letters. Soon afterward he had been evicted from his apartment in Salamanca, and Josep had not heard from him since.

There was nothing left for him in Fontenar. He was a moral outcast, without allies, everyone was his enemy. His first duty now must be to his neglected family, and to himself. He must leave this place before he was driven out. He must choose before choice was denied him.

Marisa tinkled her little bell happily, swinging her thin brown arm to and fro, wishing that she were not dressed in the shabby old frock that failed to do her jewelry justice. But Ramón was right to be cautious; she had no wish to have her new wardrobe ripped off her back.

Ramón had purchased the item without comment, other than to say she was a foolish child to want such a tasteless object. But she knew he delighted in buying things for her, try as he might to hide it, and she longed to give him something in return.

She longed to buy him some fine new handmade boots. The soles of his existing pair flapped as he walked and yesterday she had noticed a widening gap between the uppers and the built-up base of the right foot, but when she had pointed this out to him he had become irritable.

"My boots are comfortable," he snapped. "If I need new ones I shall buy them for myself. You think of nothing but spending money! You are on no account to meddle with my possessions or try to mend them or presume to replace them. Do you hear me?"

And so she had dropped the subject, although it pained her even now to see him so poorly shod when she possessed a fine pair of red high-heeled sandals and silk stockings to go with them.

All he ever bought for himself were his bottles of spirits to soothe his bad chest, and after paying for food and rent he sent all the rest of her earnings to her mother with his weekly letter. Her mother had never written back, of course, because she couldn't write, and lately Marisa had begun to feel resentful that her brothers and sisters had new shoes when Ramón did not.

The solution had been simple enough. She had started to keep back a little of what she earned. The Englishman had paid her far too much, and she had felt justified in retaining half of it, in order to buy Ramón a present and have a little left to spare. One day they might be in need of extra money and be glad of a few savings. Ramón was much too generous with money. She would rather he had kept it for himself than sent it to her mother. Indeed her affection for her distant family diminished by the day; she had even suggested that perhaps they could begin to manage without her help, but he had called her a wicked girl to be so selfish and would not hear of it. Occasionally, without any warning, Ramón would get very, very angry with her, and once or twice she had felt almost frightened, but she always remained passive and silent until his rage had run its course, and then afterward he would send her out to fetch an ice or a bag of bonbons, or spend an hour teaching her her letters, or allow her to massage his leg for him, and the murderous frenzy would be forgotten in the ensuing perfect happiness. It was odd that he had never once struck her. Men always struck women, in Marisa's experience—she was not afraid of that. Her one fear was that he would banish her, or leave her, that she would be alone. And so she was careful not to make him angry.

Ramón was exhausted by their walk to the shops and back, and Marisa encouraged him to lie down and rest for an hour or two. She waited until he was fast asleep before retrieving her savings, which she had rolled inside an empty lipstick case and secreted inside herself. She knew that Ramón would be angry if he found money in her bag and she had nowhere else to hide it. She counted out what she needed, replaced the nest, reinserted the tube and slipped out quietly to make her purchase.

She knew how much Ramón adored the *corrida,* and there had been a sad lack of bullfights since the troubles, most of the matadors were on the other side and the anarchists opposed the sport on principle. But this one had been organized and supported by the anarchists themselves to raise funds for their militias, and Marisa had seized her chance to give Ramón a little pleasure.

Tickets were on sale in the familiar café on the corner of the Calle San Lucas. Marisa counted out her money at the bar and put the tickets safely in her handbag. She was just turning to go when she felt a hand on her shoulder.

It was her very first client. He grinned unpleasantly, put his arm around her and murmured a suggestion in her ear, jerking his head ceilingward to the room where she had learned her trade. Marisa looked at him with disdain. His clothes smelled and his fingernails were dirty and the room upstairs had bare floorboards and a hard bed and no sheets, and all for the sake of a few miserable coins.

"No," she said, tossing her head haughtily. "I'm too busy." And for two centimos she would have named her new conditions, her new price, her new worth, and watched his eyes dilate in disbelief, but she knew better.

"Too busy?" said the man. "Too busy?" He caught hold of her arm roughly and she wrenched it away. "You never used to be too busy. Where's your crippled boyfriend? Does he know you're too busy?"

There was a babble of voices as heads turned to look.

"He's sick," said Marisa quickly. "I must go."

"Sick, eh?" roared the man, adding to the world in general, "She's just found out her pimp is sick. He's sick all right, and so are you and now I'm sick as well. How many men are sick because of you, because of him? Pox-ridden whore!"

He hit her savagely across the face, Marisa jerking her head back just in time. Then she kneed him in the groin and turned and ran and didn't stop running till she was safely home, puffing with outrage.

She wasn't sick! She was full of health. There was nothing wrong with her. Ramón had taught her how to use the rubber bag and pump herself full of disinfectant so that she would not get sick. It would also prevent her from having babies, he said. She had used the bag every single day, and she was perfectly, perfectly well. How dare the man say she was sick in that way, that Ramón was sick in that way, and even if he had been sick in that way she could not have caught it from Ramón because Ramón had never made love to her . . . because he was too sick, he said. She had asked him once, why not, and he had said he was too sick, and she had thought he meant his chest and his bad leg . . .

Some dirty *puta* had made him sick, and the other man as well, and she, Marisa, was being blamed! She would have liked to scratch the filthy bitch's eyes out. Poor Ramón. He often said he was a very sick man, that he was not long for this world, and she had never dreamed he meant *that* . . .

Marisa never cried, there had never been any point. But the tears came now, unbidden. Poor Ramón. She would work and work and save and save and take him to the finest doctors who would make him well again, and once he was well again they could get married and have children and the doctors would cure his chest and mend his leg as well, and he would be perfect again, as perfect as his face. And she wiped her foolish eyes and smiled again.

When she got in he was still sleeping, lying on his stomach, his face pressed into the pillow, his shoes and caliper splint on the floor. Recently she had begun to notice the squalor of the room and the filthiness of the sheets, which contrasted with the luxury of the hotel; but she would always prefer new clothes to clean linen and gold trinkets to new furniture. And she could continue to have her finery as long as she saved a little bit each day so that one day Ramón might be well again. She added this fantasy to her collection, cherishing it, believing it, knowing that believing things made them come true.

When he woke she rubbed his leg for him and reimprisoned it.

"Hurry up," she said. "The *corrida* begins in an hour. One of my gentlemen gave me two tickets."

"The *corrida?* What are you talking about? There is no *corrida*. Leave me in peace. I am tired."

"There is! Look, I have the tickets here! Hurry, or we will be late . . ."

He continued to grumble, but eventually gave in.

"What do the anarchists know of the *corrida?*" he muttered crossly. "It will be a fiasco. I come only to boo, you understand. I have seen the best matadors in my time. I remember once . . ."

Ramón continued to reminisce as they made their way, arm in arm, toward the metro station and joined the crowds converging on Las Ventas, the site of the city's splendid new bullring. He had been a regular patron in his early days in Madrid, sitting with his fellow señoritos in the best seats, in the shade. Its elaborate, Moorish architecture had appealed to his sense of grandeur—he had loved to imagine himself in the role of matador, making the crowds gasp in admiration at his daring, grace and skill.

The vast arena was packed to capacity, and Marisa was glad that she had bought her tickets in advance. There was a festive, high-spirited atmosphere, like a workers' holiday, with no fat bourgeois hogging the best view. Marisa's contempt for the bourgeoisie had come with her mother's milk; she had no aspirations to be middle-class—her dream was to be rich and well-bred.

Ramón sneered at the unconventional regalia of the matador and his henchmen as they paraded around the ring to enthusiastic cheers.

They were all wearing red and black scarves, and the matador's cape was also black and red, the anarchist colors. Once the first performance started, it was all too clear that they had been lured here on false pretences.

"I told you it was not a real *corrida,*" hissed Ramón, as the so-called matador baited his aging quarry to a chorus of partisan cheers. "They might as well bring on a nanny goat." The bull was indeed a decrepit creature, some farmyard reject fit only for a stew-pot. "This fellow is obviously a bumbling amateur. Let's go."

"They always bring the best bull on last," pleaded Marisa, squeezing his arm. "And the best matador. Be patient."

Ramón fumed throughout the first two fights, while his uncouth fellow spectators cheerfully applauded each clumsy move. Marisa, whose knowledge of bullfighting was rudimentary, seemed to find the spectacle vastly entertaining; each new rush of blood excited her, she had no concept of artistry, just a plebeian taste for gore . . .

But Marisa was right about one thing. They saved the best bull for the last. The star attraction was led into the arena to a roar of surprise and delight, and even Ramón gasped at the sight of it. This bull had two legs and was wearing a cassock and its horns were strapped to its head with a red and black ribbon. Marisa shrieked in amazement while Ramón sat speechless, horrified at this travesty of the torero's noble art.

A wave of outrage rose up in him, more at the lack of respect for the *corrida* than out of any religious scruples. He stood up to leave. No gentleman could sit and watch such barbarous sport, listen to the blasphemous cheers of this filthy rabble. He would not wait for the picadors to pierce the priestly neck with their lances; he would not wait for the matador to torment him and play with him and exhaust him before finally delivering the death blow. It was horrific, obscene, irresistible . . . He sat down again.

Marisa squealed fastidiously and hid her face behind her hands, leaving her fingers wide enough apart for the odd peek, looking nervously at Ramón, fearful now of his displeasure. But his initial shock seemed to have given way to detached disgust. His attention was absolute, his eyes unblinking, he stared at the arena in the manner of a giant viewing the antics of midgets.

The bull, alas, proved to be yet another miserable specimen, who showed no respect for the honorable traditions of the bullfight. At first he refused to charge, cowering while the crowd booed loudly, and it required highly unorthodox encouragement from the picadors to induce the feeble wretch to run at the matador's cape. Neither was the pathetic animal capable of tossing the horses. When forced to run at one of them, horns down, he received a hefty kick from an angry hoof, sending up shouts of "¡Olé!" from the spectators. He had to be dragged to his feet and held upright to receive the *banderillas*, but his scrawny shoulders, streaming with blood from the picadors' lances, lacked sufficient flesh to retain the colorful darts.

But fortunately the spectators were no purists, and good-naturedly tolerated these departures from normal procedure. With each new blow they bellowed their bravos while Marisa, having overcome her earlier scruples, joined in, jumping up and down in a frenzy of ghoulish excitement, luxuriating in horror. Ramón sat speechless, rigid, wincing in involuntary delight every time steel pierced flesh, wishing only that he could see the face contort in anguish, that he could hear the cries of fear.

But the pitiful creature had no stamina, and all too soon he collapsed in a twitching heap. With a flourish the matador drove his sword down vertically into the back of his neck, removed the mock horns, and held them aloft to frantic applause. And then, with a final theatrical gesture, he made a deft sweeping cut and removed his trophy, impaling it on the end of his blade for all to see.

"The ear!" shrieked Marisa while Ramón blinked myopically. "He's cut off the ear!" She clung tightly to Ramón, intoxicated by the roar of the crowd, existing only as part of it. "*¡Bravo! Bravo!*"

"*¡Bravo!*" whispered Ramón, discharging the contents of his swollen penis with a shudder of purest ecstasy. It had been better than any woman. Or any man.

They worked by the light of candles. Dolores found a roll of cheesecloth, which she used to bandage Tomás's burned arm. Tomás emptied a sack of chick-peas and filled it with supplies for the journey. The troops had not returned to the cellar, having found better spoils of war than humble foodstuffs. The license to loot was the Moor's only pay and the Carrasquez silver plate and jewelry had probably saved their lives.

The young boy had died, sparing Tomás the need to stop his breath. There had been no noise from above for several hours, but they had not dared make a move till nightfall. Now, as they reached the top of the staircase and looked around the gutted shell of the kitchen and listened to the silence, it seemed clear that the soldiers had moved on, there being nothing left to take and no one left to kill.

There were charred, unrecognizable remains curled up amid the blackened debris and everywhere the stench of burned flesh. Tomás hesitated, tempted to try to find the bodies of his wife and children, but there was always the risk that a couple of guards had been left behind and he did not want to put Dolores in danger.

They planned to make their way cross-country under cover of darkness, toward the Rio Guadiana. Once they were safely across the river, they would proceed cautiously until they were sure they were back behind Republican lines, after which they would continue their journey, by whatever means available, to Toledo, some two hundred and fifty kilometers away. Tomás was anxious to find his daughter and sister, and Dolores frantic to be reunited with Andrés. The practicalities of their escape had served to occupy their minds. All Dolores could think about was getting home; she ceased to brood upon the massacre or the part she had played in it. She could scarcely remember shooting Ignacia now—the memory had been buried beneath a surge of fresh hope and determination—she had been brutalized beyond guilt.

No problems with a locked door this time, they were able to walk through the wall. Tomás darted from tree to tree, Dolores following, until they found a wide gap in the railings, which had been ripped out of the ground like bean poles, the grass gouged out and flattened by boots and artillery. The troops would have continued their march northwest, toward Badajoz, and so they cut across the road and took a zigzag route northeastward, under cover of trees wherever possible, avoiding the Toledo road until they could be sure of safety.

At sunrise they stopped to sleep, after breakfasting in a ditch. Tomás knew he ought to be thinking of his dead wife and children, but it was too ugly and too painful, and as the sun rose over the horizon he was increasingly tormented by the old familiar feelings of inadmissible lust. Several times she seemed to notice him staring at her, and averted her eyes, embarrassed. No doubt she thought him gross and repulsive, although she treated him with the same respect and courtesy as always, reminding him of those far-off days when he had first desired her, without hope of possession.

But those times were surely past. The social gulf that had always divided them existed no longer. The revolution had made them equals. It angered him that he should still feel inferior to her, humble before her, unworthy of her, that years of worshiping her from afar had left him weakened and dependent, like a dupe of religion.

Dolores caught the brooding look in his eye and looked away, mortified by Tomás's terrible grief, his inability even to speak civilly, the dreadful agony of bereavement that excluded her. She felt inadequate and ashamed of her own callousness, her determined denial of her crime. How could she possibly burden him with a confession and then insult him by saying she was sorry? Besides, he might abandon her, kill her even, crazed by grief, and who could blame him? She was a murderess, of sorts, and a liar, certainly, but not a fool. She would never make the journey on her own. She needed him to get her to Toledo.

He had walked too fast for her and still she kept up, panting but uncomplaining. When they had reached the river, shallow with summer heat, he had let her walk across it unaided when he could have carried her, he had let her slip and stumble, which she put down to his sorrow and preoccupation. By morning they had already traveled some thirty kilometers, at a punishing pace, and she was fairly sure they must be safely behind the lines, but she did not like to pester him with questions.

Her hunger satisfied, Dolores finally gave way to crippling fatigue, all her limbs suddenly weak and useless. She felt her eyes closing against the brightening light and put her head down on the wine-red earth and slept instantly, a sleep of pure exhaustion, while Tomás lay pensive, watching her.

He was glad that his wife had died quickly, and he wished that his sons could have lived. And yet all he could think about was that soft, sleeping body that denied him both healing sleep and decent grief. He despised himself as nothing more than a rutting animal without a mind or soul, the creature his wife had made him. Their lovemaking had been frequent, crude and savage, devoid of tenderness or beauty, with Ignacia clawing at him and cursing him and shouting for more, always more, while he labored long and angrily to silence her, leaving her ever dissatisfied, ever complaining, ever jealous, ever demanding, robbing him of his power, challenging his strength, using his pride to enslave him. And now, God forgive him, he was free. Free and frustrated and angry, wanting not to subdue but be subdued, to have one taste of sweetness in a bitter life, to forget his huge, coarse body and find the peace that lay within hers. But she was a virtuous, married woman, she was no adulteress. And from the bottom of his heart he wished her husband dead.

He was woken by the sound of Dolores screaming in her sleep, sitting bolt upright, her eyes wide open, staring sightlessly at the sun. He tried to rouse her but she was locked in the horror of her dream and fought him back until he slapped her repeatedly on both cheeks and she fell into his arms, sobbing.

"Please forgive me, Tomás," she wept. "Please forgive me." And he did not question why she should ask forgiveness, and gave it freely, ashamed of his former churlishness. He cradled her in his arms and comforted her and pulled her close as if to keep her safe; and with proximity came peace, the torment passed.

Six hostages had been shot in three days. Three suspects had demonstrated their loyalty to the cause. Lorenzo knew his turn must be drawing near.

The ritual had become the focal point of the day. He wondered if Sanpedro was spinning it out to provide entertainment for the troops. The pattern was always the same. The same question was asked to the same lack of response, the executioner was selected and the prisoners fetched.

The quivering suspects' lack of aim had been spectacular, even at point-blank range. Lorenzo knew he would only need one shot, that he could hit the heart of a sitting target almost with his eyes shut, and he wished he could keep his eyes shut, that they would offer him the blindfold instead. None of the hostages had accepted a blindfold; they had died with eyes full of pride and hatred, shouting "¡Viva la República!" and Lorenzo had envied them their courage. When his turn came his hand must not shake, he must show respect for his victims by delivering instant death, the sort of death he would wish for himself.

He waited numbly for his name to be called and yet again he was disappointed. Yes, disappointed, he was past relief. Sanpedro was clearly enjoying keeping him in suspense. Every day Lorenzo fancied he could see him laughing at him behind his hand, whispering with his cronies, sharing the joke.

And so he stood rejected and watched another officer step forward. No, not another officer. It was a Falangist civilian, one of Sanpedro's personal clique. Lorenzo was puzzled. He could hardly believe that Buesco was under suspicion. Buesco would never help a hostage to escape, his hatred of all Reds was vociferously beyond doubt. What on earth had he said or done to bring doubt upon himself?

But he smiled as he stepped forward, and nodded. It was a smile of anticipation. Sanpedro smiled back and barked the order for the prisoners to be fetched.

And then Lorenzo understood. This was reward, not punishment. Buesco was evidently delighted at the prospect of personally eliminating four unarmed enemies of Spain. Lorenzo had an insane urge to volunteer in his stead. Better to kill the prisoners himself, cleanly, a reluctant soldier obeying orders, than to watch a sadist slaughter them for sport. But he could not do it, he would not be allowed to do it, and he stood frozen to the spot, powerless, as he saw that one of the four prisoners was Roberto.

The first victim was a big, strong ox of a man who towered over the strapping Roberto, the next in line. His hands were tied behind his back and as he stepped forward he spat at Buesco to show his contempt. His face showed no fear, but he was shaking from head to foot, shaking so much he could not stand still.

Sanpedro gave the order to fire and Buesco raised his pistol. He was no marksman, or perhaps he was. The bullet hit the man squarely between the legs and he sank to his knees, blood gushing from his testicles.

Buesco took aim again, as if to finish him off. Then he hesitated, smirked to himself, and left the big man writhing in agony while he turned his attention to his next victim.

Roberto was a great, gawky lad of barely twenty. Rosa had confided in Dolores, giggling, that he was very shy and knew little about women. And now he was to be butchered too, first a foot, perhaps, or a kneecap, or an elbow, a young man who was shy with women.

Buesco took careful aim and blew off one of Roberto's ears. And then Lorenzo started to run.

No one tried to stop him. He was aware of all eyes riveted on him as he threw himself between Buesco and Roberto, pulled out his pistol, and put the first hostage out of his misery, shooting him cleanly through the head. And as half a dozen officers leapt forward to restrain him he shouted his confession at the top of his voice, so that everyone might hear it.

"I am the traitor!" he yelled over and over again. "I am the traitor!" And there was such relief in saying the words which were, in their way, no lie.

Following their return to London, Clara was surprised and pleased at Edmund's sudden urge to participate, his unprecedented willingness to stand up at fund-raising meetings and talk about what he had seen, even if what he said was somewhat unorthodox and had caused her some initial embarrassment.

"There is a war in Spain whether we like it or not. And I speak as a pacifist. As a pacifist I want to see the war over quickly. As a pacifist I do not want to see Hitler get a foothold in Spain for the price of a few airplanes, because I firmly believe that will lead to a much greater war, a war in Europe. I don't pretend to know much about politics, although of course I'm anti-Fascist, or I wouldn't be standing here. But as someone who doesn't know much about politics, I ask you to remember what the newspapers won't tell you, because it isn't news, that behind *both* sides of the lines there are thousands, millions of ordinary Spaniards, people like you and me, who don't know much about politics and yet have been *forced* to take sides in a war not of their choosing.

"No doubt there are some people here today who think the Republic has got a lot to answer for and that the Nationalists, or Fascists, whichever you choose to call them, are not all bad. Well, I'm not going to try to convince you otherwise. What I want to say is that it really doesn't *matter* which side you support, it doesn't even matter if you don't take sides, because by giving money to this fund today you'll be helping the innocent victims of war, not those who perpetrate it. Not a penny of your money will go to buy arms, not a penny of your money will go toward killing. It will provide relief for the homeless, the hungry, the wounded, the widows and orphans who are suffering and dying needlessly. Would any of you watch a baby die because you didn't share the politics of its parents?"

The odd thing was, it worked. It worked better than when Tony Price or Bert Winterman stood up and bellowed the party line and got a lot of people's backs up. Edmund had even got money out of Catholic hecklers who turned out to be soft on starving children.

The first time Edmund had spoken Tony and Bert had been furious. They had accused him of cheap sentimentality and not being anti-Fascist enough, but they had shut up when they counted the takings, perhaps realizing that the ordinary citizens of East London were more inclined to listen to the diffident local schoolmaster than a bunch of flaming bolshies.

Edmund had flatly refused to join the party—not that they would have had him—and Clara hadn't pressed him. He insisted that his interest was purely humanitarian, and refused to be drawn into discussions for fear of embarrassing her in front of her friends. And he was honest with himself about his motives. Yes, of course he meant what he had said in public, but his interest was more personal than he cared to admit to Clara.

Thinking about Dolly, and how her loyalties might have changed, had forced him to put himself in her shoes, to wonder what it must be like to be a nonintellectual, middle-class Spaniard faced with the prospect of a workers' revolution. What it must be like to be a Catholic Spaniard seeing churches destroyed and priests martyred. What it must be like to be a landowning peasant with a humble smallholding, terrified of collectivization. And he had to admit to himself what he dared not admit to Clara: that he could quite well imagine how those Spaniards felt. They felt that the government had lost control, that the social fabric was about to be destroyed, that groups of militant workers were about to take over the country, rob them of their property, destroy their heritage, abolish God.

He tried to imagine his parents as Spaniards, Flora and Archie as Spaniards, Archie's arriviste parents as Spaniards, and there was no doubt in his mind as to which side they would be on if they were Spaniards. And they might be ignorant, or acquisitive, or insensitive, or lacking in social conscience, but they were not evil, they were not Fascists, they did not deserve to die or to have to kill. Spain must be full of people like his parents, people like the Prendergasts. He tried to imagine Archie in a Nationalist army, himself in a Republican one; he tried to imagine himself having to shoot his sister's husband, or vice versa. Or perhaps he was fooling himself, perhaps he wouldn't be a Republican if he were a Spaniard. It was so wonderfully easy to be anti-Fascist in England, in public and in private, the term was irreproachable, and yet it was grossly inadequate and misleading and self-congratulatory. It irritated him to hear Clara's comrades brandishing the term for their own vainglory, indulging themselves in virtuous belligerence, using the war as a political platform without any insight into how half the Spanish people felt.

But he kept such thoughts to himself, certain that they would be misunderstood, that they would brand him as a Fascist and thus disgrace Clara. Clara had become less strident now that she felt him less aloof, and she tolerated his heresies as being well-intentioned. The comrades were forced into a position of grudging respect, if only because he had been there and they hadn't, although many were planning to go to Spain to kill their share of Fascists. Clara's caucus consisted mainly of refugees from the middle classes, peppered with union activists. There were few ordinary working people present at the meetings, other than a cluster of exiles from branches in the provinces who had been driven south by unemployment. Clara respectfully avoided this contingent, ever wary of their scorn. Some of them were virtually homeless, living in seedy lodging houses, and she was acutely aware of the house in Curzon

Street standing empty, and glad that it was tied up in trust and could not be sold and guilty that she did not open it up as a free hotel for all the unemployed comrades in London. Sometimes Edmund wondered why she didn't find some philanthropic use for it, why she employed people to maintain it and keep it ready for occupation, why she occasionally chose to stay there, always alone. He concluded that it was a kind of citadel, bleak, empty, but nonetheless her past, somewhere that excluded him and others, something that kept her conscience pricking, her own peculiar hair shirt.

He quarreled more with his father than the comrades. Edmund had always respected his father's intelligence, despite their ideological differences, and never until now had he suspected him of bigotry. It irritated him when he would withdraw from their discussions by implying that if Edmund knew what *he* knew, if Edmund had access to certain incommunicable, confidential information, then he would think quite, quite differently.

Edmund was deeply fond of his father as a man who loved fishing, Shakespeare and Gothic architecture, Mozart and sticky gingerbread, who spoiled his wife and daughter, who was kind to his son's mistress, a patient, sensitive, generous man hiding behind a self-consciously touchy exterior. He did not like to think of him as a right-wing bureaucrat parroting a party line even narrower than Clara's. But the old boy insisted on missing the point, wouldn't listen, refused to budge from the view that intervention would lead to escalation and provoke a second world war, rather than help prevent one. Spain was a politically primitive country not yet ready for democracy. There was much too much hysteria about so-called fascism. It was certainly no worse than anarchy or Communism. The left was using it as a bandwagon, he was amazed at Edmund for being so easily taken in.

"I could convince you that I know what I am talking about," he said, rustling his newspaper, "but I am not at liberty to do so." And then, sharply, "And if we *were* to intervene and that *were* to start another war, you'd still conscientiously object, I trust?"

The question was anxious rather than provocative. Mr. Townsend's brother had been killed in action and he himself had been wounded at Passchendaele. He had always respected Edmund's pacifism.

Edmund shrugged.

"In principle, certainly," he said. "In practice, one can never know until the time comes."

"Then let's prevent a war, not cause one," said Mr. Townsend, inhaling stertorously, a sure sign that he was upset. And Edmund finally understood that his right-wing, bigoted bureaucrat of a kind, caring father just didn't want to see him get killed.

Jack hung around his hotel for two days, waiting for news, curbing his impatience, enduring agonies of doubt. He had played the minister like a fish, relying on his anxiety to prove his point, his desperate need for favorable publicity, his eagerness to show off. Jack had left him in no doubt that no news would be construed as bad news, and that he would not be bought off with fairy tales. But manipulation was at best an inexact science, and there was always the risk he had overplayed his hand.

If Dolly was anywhere in the city, they would surely find her and deliver her up to him as living proof of Republican fair-mindedness . . . wouldn't they? If she was in the Alcázar, perhaps, if he hammered away at it long enough, they might just decide to get her out in the interests of pulling off a major and much-needed propaganda coup. Either way, she was in terrible danger and he could hardly make that danger worse . . .

He felt a cold chill of fear and self-mistrust. This exercise wasn't solely for her benefit; his motives were selfish, as always. He wanted to see her again. He wanted to be the knight on a white charger, to earn her gratitude and respect, to make her *sorry*. He tried to imagine her distressed, bereft, helpless, the way he had been when she had left him. But he could only remember her strong and confident and determined. More than anything he wanted to reverse those roles, to see her weak, to feel himself strong again, to exorcise the ever-present ghost of failure. He wanted to delve deeply, blindly, into the pit of the past and find gold among the rubble of regrets. And in doing so he might well have done more harm than good . . .

When the summons finally came from the minister's office, he went fully prepared for lies and evasion, expecting obfuscation and empty reassurances, determined to turn the screws.

"A visit was made to the Montanis apartment," the minister informed him. "A servant girl answered the door. She said that Señora Montanis went to visit relatives with her child some weeks ago, she claims to have no idea where. A routine search was made but there was no sign of occupation by any other adults. The girl has two children and is pregnant; her *novio* is a hostage. She voiced great hatred for both Señor and Señora Montanis. She is an anarchist, which speaks for itself."

He made an apologetic gesture. The anarchists were, as always, an embarrassment.

Jack's mind raced ahead. If she was with relatives, then perhaps she was still in Albavera, which was now behind Fascist lines . . .

"I knew this information would not satisfy you," continued the minister. "Such a girl is hardly a reliable informant. I therefore sought confirmation as to whether Señora Montanis is known to be in the Alcázar. I have today received word from our people inside that she is definitely not with her husband . . ."

Jack let out a gasp of relief.

". . . who has in any event been killed."

"Killed?"

"A record of the casualties sustained is naturally of great value to us. Lieutenant Montanis apparently intervened in the sadistic killing of a hostage and was shot. The horror at this event has greatly increased the general desire for surrender. We fully expect a mutiny to occur. The Fascists would have you believe that the Alcázar is a symbol of their courage and unity. But as you can see it is a citadel of cruelty and coercion."

"How do I know this is true?"

"Mr. Austin, if I wanted to lie I could easily have told you that Señora Montanis was in the Alcázar and dead of typhoid fever, or worse. If I wanted to lie, I would scarcely have credited her Fascist husband with a heroic act. You should know when people are lying. You are a journalist. I give you my solemn word as a Spaniard and a socialist that this information is true. I have acted in good faith and now you must do the same." He gestured toward Jack's notebook, reminding him of their tacit agreement. Jack looked at him for a long time. He met his gaze unwaveringly, and in the end it was Jack who looked away. Her husband was dead. The thought gave him a hideous, inadmissible thrill. Yes, he believed that much, if only because he wanted to believe it . . .

Jack wrote for a few minutes, his mind buzzing. There was a good chance that she was safe. Her father was presumably a Fascist, if she was still in Albavera she would be all right, safe behind the Nationalist lines. But what if she wasn't still in Albavera? Perhaps the servant girl was lying . . .

"This is just to give you a rough idea of the kind of thing I'd like to say," said Jack at length. " 'Republican military intelligence reports diminishing morale among the defenders of the Alcázar, who are known to have suffered heavy casualties. Although the fortress could easily be taken by storm, the siege has been protracted in an attempt to induce surrender and thus spare innocent lives. Sources close to the government assure me that no harm will come to the women and children who have been so cruelly forced to share the fate of their menfolk. They were pleased to confirm that Señora Montanis was fortunately not in Toledo at the time of the uprising. She will be distressed to learn that her husband has been killed in action and I will continue in my efforts to trace her and assure her that the Republic will be glad to allow her an exit permit to enable her to visit anxious relatives in England.' ''

The minister beamed. Jack did not return his smile.

"Can I have the address of the Montanis apartment? I'd like to speak to this servant girl myself."

"You will find her unhelpful and aggressive. She is an anarchist."

Jack handed over his notebook and watched him write down the address. The minister sighed.

"This war is not as simple, Mr. Austin, as it may seem to foreign eyes. Here in this very city you will find socialists harboring priests; on the other side you will find Falangists protecting Red intellectuals. We are not all bloodthirsty extremists. If you find Señora Montanis, please trust me, please let me know. I myself have a wife and child. I would like to deal with the matter . . . *personally*. Do you understand me? I would like to reassure the lady that she has nothing to fear."

But you do, thought Jack, shaking his hand. If he was really as moderate as he claimed, his days were surely numbered.

The Montanis home turned out to be a humble enough place, a first-floor apartment set in a small, walled courtyard, in a run-down quarter of Toledo. Dolly had undoubtedly come down in the world and Jack couldn't resist the fleeting thought that he could have done much better by her.

He looked up at the tiny balcony, where several pots of leggy geraniums straggled brightly, and tried to picture her watering them, opening and closing the shutters, leaning against the wrought-iron railings. He must have been standing there for several minutes, lost in thought, when he saw a ball flying toward him and instinctively put out his hand to catch it.

Three children stood looking at him warily, a swarthy little girl of eight or nine and two younger boys, one of them the absolute spitting image of Dolly. He had her black eyes and her full mouth and her dark luxuriant hair. The resemblance took Jack's breath away. He threw the ball back at him, making him run for it, staring, fascinated.

"What's your name?" asked Jack, crouching down beside him, flooded with sudden hope that she was here.

The child was very bashful and didn't answer, staring back at him mistrustfully.

"Why do you want to know?" demanded the other boy bumptiously. "Who are you?"

He was a cheeky little brat, thought Jack, as his questioner appraised him boldly with a pair of bright blue eyes. Ignoring him, Jack addressed the little dark boy again.

"Is your Mamá at home?" he asked cajolingly, but the child turned on his heels and ran into the house, to be followed immediately by his two companions, the girl giggling, the boy scowling.

After a minute a young woman came out, obviously the servant. She was rosy-faced and gap-toothed and surly, and around her neck she wore a red and black scarf.

"*Salud*," said Jack. No one said *buenos días* anymore in Republican Spain. The girl looked at him suspiciously and didn't return the greeting.

"Is Señora Montanis in?" inquired Jack. "I am a friend of hers, from England."

"She is not here. She has gone away. I don't know where she is. I told them this already."

"Gone away?" repeated Jack, looking puzzled. "Without telling you where she was going?" The girl nodded belligerently. "Then . . . why did she leave her son here with you? I saw him playing outside with his friends. She sent me a photograph of the little fellow, so I recognized him straightaway."

The girl opened her mouth and shut it again.

"I know you told them yesterday that her child was with her," continued Jack smoothly. "It was right of you to protect him. Where is Dolores?"

He extracted a bill from his wallet and held it out to her.

"I don't want your money," said the girl vehemently. "How do I know you are her friend? If you are her friend . . . then you must be a Fascist!"

"I know she was at home in Albavera, with her mother," Jack went on patiently, still smiling. "She wrote and told me of her mother's death. But that was some weeks ago, and she said she was coming back to Toledo. Please tell me the truth. I assure you I am not a Fascist, just a friend from England. All of us in England are very worried about Dolores. And I know you wish her well, because you lied to protect her little boy."

He took out another bill.

"Have you had your wages?" he asked. "Who is paying your wages?"

"I have had none for a month!" declared the girl. "I am not to be bought for wages. I work here because I choose to work. I choose it."

She sniffed noisily and Jack realized she was very near to tears. She struggled with herself for a moment while Jack produced his passport.

"Can you read?" he asked. "This is proof that I am English. Also my bad Spanish is proof."

He tilted her chin to make her look at him and felt a pang of pity for her. She was little more than a child herself.

The girl sniffed and blew her nose, looking from right to left nervously. The door to the house was ajar, and Jack ushered her inside. It was dark and cool in the hallway and he could hear the children shouting at one another in the apartment above.

"I promise no harm will come to you or the children or to Señora Montanis. Please take your wages. Dolores would want you to have your wages. You have to buy food, you need money."

The girl took the money with a singular lack of enthusiasm and stuffed it in the pocket of her apron. She didn't speak for a long time and Jack stayed silent, waiting.

"Dolores is dead," she said at last, almost inaudibly. "She must be dead. How do I tell the child? The father a Fascist and the mother dead. How can I tell him that?" Her plump shoulders began vibrating. "And my *novio* a hostage. And my brother and all my family dead. All dead."

Her voice rose to a wail and sank to a whisper all in the same breath.

"How do you know she is dead?" said Jack. She was a very simple girl, she was hysterical. He did not believe Dolores was dead. He wanted to argue with her and call her a fool, he felt his anger and impatience bubbling up and kept his voice calm, cool. "How do you know?"

"My brother Tomás works on her father's land. Last week he sent his daughter to me, because the Fascists were only two days away. The workers had killed the old man and taken Dolores hostage, my brother could not prevent it. And now the Fascists have reached Badajoz, so they must have taken Albavera, and if they have taken Albavera then all my people will be dead, and Dolores with them. The Moors take no prisoners. When Tomás sent Petra to me, I knew how it would be. I knew how it would be.''

Jack shut his mind to the images he had painted so vividly in his dispatches, tales of butchery and mutilation and wholesale carnage, atrocities so appalling they required no embellishment, atrocities even worse than the ones perpetrated by the Republic. Whether she had been killed by the Moors or the peasants, her fate would have been hideous. It wasn't true. It couldn't be true.

''What about the child?'' said Jack hoarsely, recovering his composure. Perhaps he could get the boy to England. Edmund would surely want to adopt him, he was desperate for a child. ''If it is true that Dolores is dead, her child is now an orphan. Lieutenant Montanis has been killed.''

The girl's eyes opened wide in horror, and filled up with fresh tears. If she really hated her employer, she had a strange way of showing it.

''How can you know this?''

''I am a journalist. I know certain people in the government who got word from inside the Alcázar. I came to tell Dolores this, and to take her back to England.''

''He died in action?''

''Struck by an enemy bullet,'' said Jack, not wishing to tell her the whole story. The girl bowed her head. ''The boy has relatives who will be glad to care for him. I am sure this is what Dolores would want.''

''No!'' Her voice rose to a shriek. ''I will provide for him! He is like my own son, they grew up as brothers! No one will take Andrés away from me. No one!''

Jack would never understand the Spanish. By her own account this girl's brother had taken Dolores hostage and possibly even had a hand in killing her and yet she was clearly ready to defend Dolores's child with her life. It didn't make sense and yet it made perfect sense, in a civil war, or possibly any kind of war.

''No one will take him away from you,'' said Jack gently, helpless in the face of such lionesslike fervor. ''What is your name?''

''Rosa,'' she muttered. ''Rosa García.''

''Well, Rosa, I will leave you some money now, for the boy, and I will come again, from time to time, with more. I am like his uncle, you understand. And if by any chance Dolores should return, I want you to give her this.''

He wrote for a few moments on his notepad, tore out the page, and sealed it inside an envelope.

"I have explained about her husband and asked her to contact me urgently," said Jack. "Please tell her that her friends and relations are worried about her. Please tell her I will arrange to take both her and the child back to England if she wishes. Will you tell her all that? And will you contact me if you need help? I will be in Madrid. Here is my address and telephone number. If you leave your name, I will come immediately."

He handed her his card, and she put it with the envelope in her pocket. This time she didn't argue about the money. Jack was eager to get this over with now, anxious to get out of the house Dolly had lived in, anxious not to see the little boy again with his mother's huge dark eyes. What a filthy, stupid, evil war this was. The war that provided such good copy, the war that let him fly so many controversial kites, the war he had almost welcomed. Dolly dead. It wasn't possible. Dolly, young and beautiful and dead, and all for nothing. It was like a judgment on him for his lack of compassion, his opportunism, his callous, journalistic eye. Damn Edmund and his letter. Dolly had died five years ago, and now he would have to go through it all again.

The girl began weeping anew. Half of him wanted to comfort her, if only to comfort himself, and half of him wanted to walk away and deny that this was happening. Impulsively, he put his arms around the sobbing girl and hugged her.

"There's still hope," he said. "There's always hope. She may have got away." But she shook her head violently, and then the children came running down the stairs and he walked quickly away.

When he got back to the hotel, he began a letter to Edmund but his hand shook so much he had to tear it up and begin again on his typewriter, the one he had bought with Clara's money a hundred years ago.

. . . I gave the girl my card and left a note for Dolly, so if she turns out to be alive, hopefully we'll hear from her. I'll go back to Toledo in any case, to check. Albavera is now Fascist territory; there's no possible way I can get behind the lines, and even if I tried it, it would be like looking for a needle in a haystack. If Dolly did survive the troubles she will have had the sense either to present herself to the authorities as the wife of a rebel officer— assuming she knew her husband had joined the uprising—or to flee. One thing's for sure. If she's still alive, she'll turn up in Toledo sooner or later, because of the child.

I saw her little boy, who looks uncannily like her, and made

*sure the servant girl was all right for cash. When I suggested
exporting him to England she nearly threw a fit, but it seems an
obvious solution. Can such things be arranged through the con-
sul? Perhaps your father would know.*

He had meant to end it there, but he weakened, burdened with too
much thought, too much disgust.

*Suddenly I'm ashamed of the way I earn my living, I feel like a
war profiteer and perhaps I am. I always used to think I understood why you're a pacifist, but I didn't understand at all, until
now. I used to think I understood why people fight in wars, but I
didn't understand that either, until now . . .*

A small village twenty kilometers from Badajoz. He remembered
her saying it on that gray November day, a place he'd never heard
of, a place he'd never thought to see. And now he never would. It
would be suicidal and fruitless to attempt to cross the lines. The
Fascists would never grant him a visa, and even if they did, the
Republic would never let him back in. The best thing he could do
would be to sit tight in Madrid, stay in touch with Rosa, pray for
Dolores to turn up, and persuade her to come back to England.

The situation on the Estremadura front was dire, so dire that the
government had prohibited all journalists from going there, fearful
of further reducing Republican morale. This ban had made Jack all
the more determined to take a look for himself. The Republic would
do better to advertise its defeats rather than its victories, not that it
had had any victories to speak of. So far it had been a pushover for
the Fascists. The Army of Africa had proved unstoppable, a brilliant, ruthless fighting machine, backed up by first-class air cover,
with German planes and German pilots knocking the Republican
air force for six. As for Malraux and his much-publicized squadron,
the would-be saviors of Spain, Jack thought they might as well have
stayed at home. He had interviewed several of the French pilots,
who were billeted at the Florida Hotel, together with the usual
retinue of hangers-on, and had found them overly pleased with
themselves considering their poor track record to date. People who
regarded war as an adventure invariably lost interest once the novelty wore off, and Jack avoided their company, preferring that of
honest mercenaries like himself.

He had teamed up with two photographers who were also eager

to defy the ban, and in an hour they were due to set off in a hired
car and see how far they could get. Laszlo, a Hungarian, and his
girlfriend, Thérèse, a stunning Parisian redhead, were both working for a French magazine, and had shown themselves to be grittily
realistic and totally professional, with none of the smug amateurism
that Jack found such an irritant. They were honest about their ambition, hungry for success, and totally dismissive about their suicidal courage. And after surviving a stint in the trenches, they would
feel exhilarated enough for some of it to rub off onto Jack. He didn't
begrudge them their elation, because it was ingenuous; they didn't
strut around patting themselves on the back and acting as if they
were doing Spain a favor. And they had both been poor, even
poorer than Jack, poor in Paris, where the poverty had a different,
more glamorous flavor. They were outrageous and tough and
charming and Jack worried today, as always, that they would take
one risk too many. He envied them, as always, their passion for life
and for each other, their lack of shame in it, their ability to feel and
show their feelings.

But today he was oblivious to their ribald humor and dry repartee
as the vehicle lurched its way from pothole to pothole. On the way
they passed several groups of refugees, mostly women and children, heading for Madrid. They trailed along wearily, carrying bun-
dles of possessions, their feet bleeding, their faces blank with
bereavement and loss. They made graphic pictures but increasingly
banal copy; it had all been said already and how much impact had
it made?

Every so often Jack would leap out of his seat, imagining he saw
Dolly, and once he made the car stop and ran after a young woman
who of course wasn't Dolly. Jack couldn't think what to say to her,
so he thrust some money at her instead, feeling patronizing and
inadequate and angry that she wasn't Dolly, as if it were her fault.

Which would be worse for Spain in the long run, a quick Fascist
victory, or a long drawn-out Republican defeat? Because there could
be no Republican victory. Not without a sudden massive injection
of trained men and arms. And trained men and arms had their own
price, a high price. They could only be bought by mortgaging the
revolution, or what was left of it.

Better buy them then, from the best salesman in the business,
the only one prepared to do the deal. Good old Joe Stalin knew all
about selling. Get a foot in the door, the rest was easy.

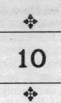

10

Tomás and Dolores made their way to Toledo on foot. Such transport as was available had been commandeered for military use and only those refugees who were wounded had any hope of being picked up. They walked for a week across ever-changing countryside, through vast yellow fields of grain, silvery-green olive groves, hills of wild pasture dotted with sheep, streaked with poppies, bright with wild rose and honeysuckle. They slept when the sun was high to avoid the blazing furnace of the open road by day, resting wherever they could find shade, eking out their provisions from the hedgerows. Dolores lost track of time, suspended in a cloud of constant pain, not only from her blistered, bleeding feet but from excruciating headaches, the result of her recent injury. The wound above her ear had healed, but the bullet had grazed her skull, and in her darker moments she feared that it had done some deeper, unseen damage, that she was doomed to die before she saw her son again—a fear that served to propel her body long after its reserves of strength had been exhausted.

When Toledo finally came into view, high on its perch, wearing the Alcázar like a crown, it seemed like a vision of heaven, and Dolores quickened her pace, revitalized by her eagerness to reach her journey's end. But Tomás held her back and reminded her that they must wait until dark so that her arrival home would not be observed by neighbors. They would present themselves to the militia patrols as man and wife, but otherwise tell the truth. There could be no question of Dolores remaining in her home, where she would be recognized as the wife of a rebel officer. This would put herself, the children, and Rosa at great risk.

Dolores nodded, unable to think beyond the moment when she would see Andrés again. The practicalities of finding other accommodation, after eight days in the open air, scarcely registered. Hunger and fatigue merely heightened her euphoria. In a few hours she would be home, she would hold her child in her arms and then soon, God willing, the Alcázar would be relieved and Lorenzo safely restored to her . . .

"Not long now, Lole. Not long now," murmured Tomás as the sun slipped closer to the horizon. "Try to rest now." It pleased him to call her by this diminutive, something nobody else called her, as if to banish her old identity, to remind her that they were equals now.

Dolores sank down onto the grass. Obeying Tomás had become second nature. Ever since the night of her terrible dream, when he had lulled her back to sleep, he had been unfailingly gentle, strong, wise, reassuring, unselfishly putting his own grief aside, thinking only of her. Guilt and gratitude had made Dolores submissive, humble. There was something awesome and dignified about this man; she had grown to admire and trust him absolutely. Remembering Ignacia's angry accusations, she had wondered at first whether he expected some reward for his services; several times she caught him looking at her, and once or twice, when they had touched accidentally, she had feared he might make some physical advance, feared it not for its own sake, but because she dreaded to cause him the pain of rebuff. But her worries had proved groundless. He maintained a respectful distance; only his eyes gave him away.

As they sat watching the sun go down and finished the last of their food, Dolores seized her moment to ask him for yet more help.

"Thank you for all you have done for me, Tomás."

"There is no need for thanks. You have always been kind to my family. I killed your father, I might have killed you. So now my debt is partly paid."

And I killed your wife, thought Dolores. I killed your wife and I will be in your debt forever.

"I want to ask another favor of you," she said. "I know it is not safe for me to remain in Toledo. But I cannot leave until I have news of my husband. I cannot leave without letting him know that we are safe. He must be in torment, worrying what has become of us."

"He could be dead," said Tomás gruffly. "And either way, he would not want you to draw attention to yourself. In any case, it's impossible to get messages across the lines."

"How do you know? Can't you talk to the militia?"

"And admit that I am shielding the wife of a rebel officer? Think what you are saying."

"But surely one of Roberto's friends would help? Rosa would know who to speak to. Perhaps we could trade news of Lorenzo for news of Roberto. Then neither side could object, surely?"

"You are raving, Lole. The idea is madness."

She took a deep breath before saying quietly, "Then I'll have to stay in Toledo. I'll have to go into hiding and wait till the Alcázar is relieved, or until it falls. I can't just desert my husband. If I'd been at home when it happened, I wouldn't have run away. I would have waited for him."

"You think that Fascist troops will arrive to save him? This will not happen. Soon the Alcázar will be a heap of rubble. Mourn your husband now, Lole. Save your own life and that of your son. We will collect Andrés and Petra and take them to Madrid. Have I brought you this far to leave you in terrible danger? Think of your son. Will you condemn him to share your fate? Why do you suppose your husband left him with Rosa? In fairness to him you must take your child and flee. This is what he would want."

"Then help me. Help me get word to him. Just a short message. Just 'Dolores and Andrés safe with Ramón.' No one else will understand what that means. Then at least he'll know where I've gone."

"You still dream of a Fascist victory?"

"I still hope for my husband's life. What kind of wife would I be otherwise? Please help me, Tomás. Please."

It moved him to hear her beg. If only her husband could see her now, pleading before a humble laborer, with her long hair dirty and unkempt, her eyes red and swollen from dust and heat and tears, her body no longer fragrant but smelling of sweat and soiled clothes. She was still beautiful, more beautiful, because she was no longer inaccessible.

"Very well," he said at length. "I will see what can be done. But I will claim the message comes from your husband's ailing sister in Madrid, that she sent Rosa a letter asking for news. No one must connect this with you. We can trust no one. No one."

"Thank you," she said, and he watched her anxious expression melt into relief and gratitude and hope. It made him feel powerful; it made him feel weak.

"Meanwhile," he continued gruffly, "you must give me your mother's rings. They incriminate you and we need to sell them. I may have to offer bribes."

He had made her take the rings off soon after their escape, and their removal had involved a great deal of saliva and sore knuckles. Dolores pulled a handkerchief out of her pocket and unwrapped them, handing them over without question, giving him all her worldly goods, her inheritance, her dowry.

"Of course. Rosa will need money, but I've no idea what they are worth. I only took them as keepsakes."

Tomás had no interest in their value. Without them, she was destitute, without them she could not escape him. She had never been poor enough to know the foolishness of what she had done.

At nightfall they entered Toledo and were duly accosted and interrogated by armed sentries, truculent youths shabbily dressed in blue overalls. Tomás did all the talking and produced his union card, which cut little ice with the anarchist militiamen but at least served to allay suspicion. They were directed brusquely toward the municipal building, where they would be issued with papers and allocated food and temporary shelter. But the accent was on the temporary. Toledo had no room for refugees. They would have to move on.

The narrow, winding streets of the city were obstructed by barbed wire and barricades, and Dolores was obliged to take a detour, hampered by the blackout. The apartment looked deserted, with no welcoming light peeping through the shutters to greet them, and Dolores endured agonies waiting alone in the dark while Tomás climbed the stairs and tapped lightly on the door.

It seemed a long time before anyone answered, but then at last she heard low voices and a muted squeak of joy and raced up the stairs and through the open door and past a speechless Rosa and into the children's bedroom.

"Leave her," said Tomás to his sister. "Leave her alone with her son."

Rosa clung to him, weeping, while he told her what had happened.

"I thought you were dead," she babbled, incoherent with emotion. "I thought Dolores was dead. I told the Englishman that she was dead."

"The Englishman?"

"He came to give her the news that Lorenzo was killed."

"Her husband has been killed?"

"He said he knew this from someone in the government who got word from behind the lines. He said he had come to tell her this and take her and Andrés to England. He said if she should ever

return I was to give her this. He said he would come back.'' She
pulled the envelope and card out of her apron. ''He recognized
Andrés from a photograph, so I could not lie. He wanted to take
him away, but I would not let him. Oh, Tomás! How do I tell her
her husband is dead?''

"Say nothing!" said Tomás sharply. "Say nothing of this Englishman.'' He took the letter and card from her.

"But she would be safe in England,'' continued Rosa, perplexed.
"She is in danger here. And she is a widow now.''

She gasped, horrified, as Tomás struck a match and set fire to
the letter and card, letting them burn down to his fingers without
wincing.

"Yes,'' he said. "She is a widow now.''

It was stifling hot with the shutters closed and Ramón longed for
morning, when Marisa would be home and he could have air and
daylight again. Last night he had opened them just a finger's width
while he scribbled in his notebook by candlelight, and within minutes some Communist bully from the house committee had been
banging on his door cursing and shouting at him to put the light
out.

The bombs had fallen on the War Ministry, near enough for
Ramón to think his hour had come but not quite near enough to
make the blackout seem tolerable in the stifling August heat. They
had been German planes, and the raid had led to angry demonstrations outside the embassy. Ramón had a low opinion of the Germans, in fact he hated all foreigners, but now he was forced to
concede that they had their uses.

The Communists and socialists had organized the civil defense
system, given that the anarchists were incapable of organizing anything. Ramón had been informed at a meeting of the block that he
would have to take his turn as a listener for the sirens, the signal
for everyone to make their way into the shelters. The more able-
bodied residents were detailed to paint the streetlights blue. Marisa
had been glad she worked at night in well-ventilated premises, and
Ramón had wished he could sleep through the threatening hours of
darkness. But he could never sleep till Marisa was safely home.

As it was, he had to work by candles with the shutters closed—
stronger light seeped through the gaps—which gave him a headache
and made him feel breathless. As for taking refuge in a cellar, he
would rather die underneath a bomb than submit to such claustro-
phobic torture. Besides, there was no danger. The bombs would

surely be dropped on government buildings, on the airports, on factories, not on a dingy residential area such as this.

He took another drink, wiped the sweat from his brow and sharpened the pencil with his razor, taking refuge in fantasy.

As I had already been advised by X, bombing proceeds on target, and I am reliably informed by my contacts that the city is scheduled to fall within the month. As instructed, I continue to keep a detailed daily record of events and to pass information on through the usual channels. Today I made the following observations . . .

He chuckled to himself as he imagined how many of his odious neighbors would be rounded up and shot on the strength of his evidence against them. He could see it now: as soon as the city was saved these scum would change sides and affect support for the Nationalist cause, to save their own miserable skins. But they would not escape him. He had their names and whereabouts and verbatim quotes all written down. Out of their own mouths they had damned themselves, day after day. Now they laughed and jeered at him for a cripple; they had always refused to believe that he was of exalted birth, bowing to him in the street and calling him ''Your Highness'' and occasionally tripping him up or knocking him sprawling on the pavement. But soon, very soon, they would realize that he was not only of good family, he was a secret agent as well, reporting their every move. They would kneel and weep and beg his intercession while he stood proudly and watched them die . . .

His writing was minute and spidery. He wrote on both sides of the paper, embellishing each page with his initials. There was no room in the boot for money anymore, the wad of bills was with the gun under the floorboards, his notebook having become infinitely more precious than money. On the day of liberation his notebook would be his passport to reward and glory, one day his memoirs would be published, children would learn in schools of his resourcefulness and courage, his years of living incognito among the rabble for the sake of his beloved country. And Marisa would be elevated with him. He had concluded that she must indeed be right in her suspicion that she was the child of an aristocrat, who had been abducted by peasants. Were this not the case, he would find her company intolerable. She had been brought up as an animal, of course, but he had come to her rescue just in time, before the damage became irreversible. One day she would be his consort, one day he would make her his heiress.

The news was always garbled and distorted by lies and propaganda but he understood from the broadcasts of General Queipo de Llano, that great patriot, that Moorish troops had claimed another heroic victory at Badajoz, liberating it from workers' control, which must mean that his father's estate was now safely behind Nationalist lines. He hoped from the bottom of his heart that the rabble had killed his father first, before they themselves were slaughtered. What a delicious irony, to have the peasant hordes release his inheritance. For he would surely inherit now. His holy elder brother had probably been burned alive in his church by this time, a fitting end for one who thought that *braceros* possessed souls. As for his sister . . . well, naturally he would take care of Dolores. She had married a pauper and would need his help. He would share his wealth with her, make sure that she had fine dresses and servants and a motorcar; and he would be generous to his little nephew, who would respect him and love him far more than his own buffoon of a father. Yes, Dolores would one day have cause to be grateful to him; she was a foolish child but he was fond of her.

He initialed the final page with a flourish and packed the notebook, together with his Falange membership card, back into his boot. Marisa was right, it needed mending. Tomorrow he would buy some glue; it would be disastrous if it came apart while he was walking and his notebook fell out and passed into the wrong hands. What danger he lived in!

He had no watch, but he calculated it must be near enough midnight. Formerly he had relied on the chimes of the nearby San Domingo Church, but they had long since been silenced, and now he had only the clock in the local workers' café, which was always slow. Marisa had begged to buy him a watch. The girl was obsessed with spending and did not understand the value of money: she was young and extravagant as he had once been. But at least she had someone to defend her interests, and she was not beset by cheats and robbers such as had preyed on him, not condemned to live all alone and friendless in this evil, hostile city.

He could expect her home anytime between daybreak and midmorning, depending on whether she had been required to spend the night. If a man were drunk she often stayed the night anyway, if she had nothing else to do, and would tell him next morning that he had asked her to. She would then demand breakfast on a tray— she had a great weakness for the hotel's strong coffee which she drank very sweet—and despite all Ramón's strictures, she always managed to filch a teaspoon or a linen napkin along with a pastry or two to bring home, and would take more delight in these misappropriations than in the money she had earned legitimately. But she was adamant that she never stole from her gentlemen, although she often wheedled things out of them. She had brought Ramón a silver tie clip—not that he dared wear a tie—a silk handkerchief, a bottle of cologne, all of which she swore had been given to her freely, as gifts, on top of, not in lieu of, her fee.

Certainly she seemed to have established a regular clientele and Ramón no longer feared that she would lose her pitch. There was the lucrative weekly rendezvous with the overweight Russian, known only as "Gregory," and his bottle of Manzanilla. There was the French pilot who wanted her every night and was finished with her in less than five minutes. There was the impotent Englishman who paid her just to talk. Ramón obliged her to relate all her activities to him in minute detail: how long for, with whom, and what exactly had been required of her, a clinical debriefing conducted with the utmost seriousness and with a certain amount of anxiety. Of all the things he dreaded, it was that she would not come home one night, that some rich foreigner would take her for his mistress, set her up in an apartment somewhere, rob him of his only asset and his only comfort. That, and his recurring nightmare of physical abuse, as the memory of his own misdeeds haunted the lonely hours of waiting. Once when she had returned with welts on her back and thighs he had raged at her and all but wept, cursing her for a fool, but she had shrugged and said that it hadn't hurt much and the man had paid her well. And however tired she was, he made her use the douche before she slept, and every day he inspected her black lace panties for symptoms of disease. She was a slovenly creature, and required constant nagging. To deploy such domestic skills as she possessed would have ruined her hands, so he was obliged to send her clothes out to be laundered. Ramón's own clothes were too threadbare to withstand boiling water, but he flatly refused to replace them. His rags were his uniform, his disguise, the means by which he survived. New clothes would merely arouse suspicion, but he could not explain that to Marisa: she was only a woman and could not be trusted.

His reverie was interrupted by a distant whine, followed by a commotion below and the shout to proceed to the shelters. Ramón blew out his candle, trembling, and slid under the bed. It was almost certainly yet another false alarm, perhaps even a deliberate one. The Communists were never happy unless they were giving orders and bossing people about; nonetheless he felt a stab of fear, for Marisa, of course, not for himself.

The blackness was terrifying. As a child he had always had a nightlight and once he had woken up and found it extinguished and thought he was dead and his throat had closed so quickly and so tightly he could not even scream. He felt himself begin to pant and cursed the miserable body that constrained his spirit, that made him a weakling and a laughingstock, that denied him freedom and respect. And he remembered his hero, General Millán Astray, founder of the Foreign Legion, with his one arm and his one eye, his butchered body living proof of heroism. So it would be with him one day. Neither his wretched caliper splint nor his laboring lungs nor his putrefying organs would deny him his moment of glory. Rather, they would enhance it, proclaim him as a man for whom such handicaps were as nothing, for whom pain was a mere trifle.

Marisa heard the siren shriek and cursed it. It would lose her a good hour's work and all for nothing. And then she thought of Ramón and wondered whether she should go home early to look after him, and decided it would only make him angry.

She had just had her bath and Gregory was comatose as usual. She had better shake him awake and warn him to take cover. He was a good client, every week a wad of money for a few minutes of cold bottle and hot tongue. He lay on his back, snoring, with his huge belly rising and falling and his blubbery lips still wet and sticky. Yes, he was a good client, but she had other clients now. And so she tiptoed out of the room and left him to take his chance.

Josep disappeared from Fontenar by night, and was picked up by an Army truck early next morning. The soldiers assumed immediately that he had crossed the lines, fleeing from persecution, as innumerable other priests had done.

"I wish to return to my home parish in Albavera," Josep told them. "The priest there knows me well and will vouch for me."

"We can take you as far as Córdoba, Father," they said. "There they will give you food and shelter and money. You should present yourself at the bishop's palace."

Josep hurriedly declined this offer, saying that his elderly mother was gravely ill, and he was anxious to reach his home village before she died.

"I have been in hiding for many weeks now," he said. "I have delayed too long already."

They set him down, as requested, at a military hospital outside the city, where he would be able to pick up another lift. There he told the same story all over again, with appropriate embellishments, claiming that his church had been razed to the ground. The nurses, who were all nuns, treated him like a hero. They gave him a meal, washed and ironed his clothes, and pressed money and provisions on him before he continued his journey. Another truck was delivering supplies to a hospital in Vallemora, eighty kilometers south of Badajoz, where they would be happy to give him a bed for the night . . .

It all seemed too easy. But as yet his disappearance from Fontenar would not have been reported; once it was, he would assuredly be classed as a defector, and put on the wanted list of missing Reds. Soon it would be folly to use his real name. Soon his identity papers would be of no use to him . . .

If Dolores was not in Albavera, if his mother was already dead, what next? What next, God? He tried to imagine himself back in the Republic, joining the militia, fighting, killing, dying unshriven, and knew he could not contemplate it. The Republican army had no use for priests, it needed only soldiers, soldiers to join its fight against the Fascists, against the Church. But surely there must be others who believed in both God and in democracy, like himself? Surely there was a role for him somewhere?

As the army vehicle bore him toward Vallemora, he looked to the right and left for signs of devastation, but the countryside seemed tranquil enough, with white flags fluttering over every chimney and peasants working in the fields as normal. Yet again he was assured that the war would soon be over.

"Vallemora fell in minutes," the driver told him cheerfully. "A gang of workers occupied the town hall with a few shotguns and started hurling stones at the troops. Pathetic, isn't it? A couple of grenades made short work of *them*. Hell must be getting pretty crowded, eh, Father?"

Vallemora was a prosperous market town, the domain of tradesmen and artisans and small shopkeepers who grew fat on the produce of local estates run by slave labor. Apart from its ruined municipal building, it bore no battle scars. Its small local hospital had been requisitioned for army use, and Josep was welcomed by its chaplain, who proved eager to hear all about his escape and regaled him with his own adventures.

"I myself fled from Madrid," he told Josep, "disguised as a peasant woman. What a journey! Madrid is an evil place. Full of Communist agitators. Thank God for our brave generals!"

He took Josep to his quarters, chattering all the while. "We must take our evening *paseo* together," he said hospitably. "You have arrived at an opportune moment. You will be able to witness tonight's execution in the Plaza d'España. Afterward we are invited to dine with the civil governor and with Father Sánchez, the parish priest."

"A public execution?" said Josep, appalled.

"Why certainly. Part of the purge, you understand. These Reds are like vermin, they are everywhere. By making an example of them, we can discourage further sedition and save innocent lives. Hurry now, or we shall be late."

He led Josep briskly out into the street and toward the main square, which was already thronged, as if for a fiesta. Children sat astride their fathers' backs, waving Nationalist flags, while vendors plied the crowd with refreshments. People stood to one side to let the two priests pass, and in moments Josep found himself in a front-row position, a privileged guest at this civic celebration.

Three prisoners were lined up before a firing squad. Josep had expected them to be peasants or workers, who had been rounded up as revolutionaries, but the men were clearly middle-class, they looked very much like the respectable burghers Juan and his men had terrorized in Fontenar.

"Red intellectuals," murmured Josep's companion, by way of explanation. "A journalist, a doctor, and a poet. Educated men who should know better."

The civil governor mounted the podium and began his address, pausing frequently for applause.

"Let this be a warning to those subversives still lurking among the honest citizens of Vallemora. Let us all be vigilant in identifying the enemies of Spain. Remember, the enemy have spies and agitators everywhere, and only the combined will of the people can flush them out and bring them to justice. I congratulate those who have already proved their patriotism by tracking down and denouncing the miserable wretches you see before you. No traitor shall escape the wrath of God!"

A loud cheer greeted this speech, and then there was a good deal of shoving and stretching as everyone jostled for a better view. Father Sánchez then took the stage.

"Two of these men have confessed their sins and been granted absolution. After many millennia in purgatory they will, by the infinite mercy of God, find their way to salvation. Let us pray for them. The third man," he pointed at the sinner accusingly, "remains by choice unpurged, condemned to everlasting hellfire. Atheism is a cancer that must be cut out and burned, even as his soul will be cut from his body and burned. ¡*Viva Cristo Rey!*"

"¡*Viva Cristo Rey!*" echoed the crowd, switching their *churros* to their left hands and crossing themselves devoutly.

Josep gaped at the surrealism of it all, the hideous distortion of everything he understood God to be. Two thousand years ago this crowd would have cheered the Crucifixion. He forced himself to watch as the shots rang out and the prisoners pitched forward and toppled and twitched. The captain of the Civil Guard strolled along the line of bodies administering the coup de grace before the corpses were lifted like sacks of potatoes and tossed on the back of a waiting truck. Another cheer went up and then the band struck up military music and people began mingling and laughing and joking, well pleased with their evening's free entertainment.

Josep remained silent throughout dinner. After many months of hunger he had no appetite for the succulent tortilla or the fat river trout or the roast sucking pig or the luscious pastry, stuffed with custard and glistening with sugar.

"You seem preoccupied, Father," said the civil governor heartily, draining another glass of fine wine. "You must surely be relieved to have found safe harbor at last, and to have escaped with your life. Many priests were not so fortunate. Hundreds, no thousands, have already died horrible deaths at the hands of the mob."

"I am concerned for my family, that is all," said Josep. "My father's workers were militants, and my mother has been very ill."

The civil governor assured him that all was well in Albavera.

"I do not know the area personally," he said. "But I hear that the town offered no resistance. The workers met the troops in open country and were soon disposed of. Everywhere it is the same story. Believe me, once we take Madrid, it will be all over. All the eastern provinces will surrender, and then the Basque country will follow suit."

Josep looked surprised.

"I thought the Basques were staunch Catholics," he said, remembering Maria's tales of her homeland.

"So they are," said Father Sánchez. "It is a scandal. They have sold their souls to an atheist state to preserve Basque independence."

"The Nationalist cause is committed to uniting Spain under one central government," explained the civil governor. "The Basques have a parochial, peasant mentality, they fear to lose home rule. Hence they have allied themselves with a Marxist Republic, and soon Catholic will be fighting Catholic on the northern front. A tragedy . . ."

A tragedy, everyone agreed.

"So . . . their army has chaplains, I suppose?" said Josep.

"Presumably, of a sort. The Basque priests are a seditious breed, the absolution they give will surely be worthless in the eyes of God. Let us hope the Holy Father will see fit to excommunicate them."

Josep remained lost in thought throughout the rest of the meal. He retired early, claiming fatigue, but he did not sleep.

"Edmund? I'm ho-ome," sang out Clara, flinging her hat over the banister. She carried a roll of posters under one arm and began undoing the string. They were to be put all over town early the next morning, and she had been detailed to decorate every spare bit of wall she could find.

"Aid for Spain now! End Fascist butchery! Speak out against nonintervention!"

The crude drawing showed a map of Spain overprinted with a huge swastika, with Eden and Hitler shaking hands across it, both faces locked in an obscene rictus of friendship.

"Edmund?"

He was sitting in the living room, just staring into space. He looked up absently. The radio was switched off, and he was not reading. He was doing absolutely nothing, which was ominously unusual.

"What on earth's the matter?" asked Clara sharply, putting her posters down on the table. "You look as if somebody's died."

A letter was lying, open, on his lap. He handed it to her wordlessly. It was from Jack.

"Oh, " said Clara at length. And then, "So which side was she on in the end? Same as the Fascist husband, I suppose."

"What the fuck does it matter what side she was bloody on?" hissed Edmund with sudden venom. Clara recoiled as if slapped. Edmund never used bad language.

"Kindly don't swear at me," said Clara frostily, flouncing into the kitchen. "Personally, I think it makes a great deal of difference."

"Shut up," said Edmund curtly. "Just don't say another word."

He snatched back the letter and marched out of the house, slamming the front door behind him, an unprecedented display of bad temper.

Clara wished, belatedly, that she had been less tactless, but she was annoyed with Edmund nonetheless. Presumably it was all right to be a Fascist as long as you were pretty with a nice smile and you flattered a man's ego. As for Jack's sanctimonious postscript, that was just proof of what she had always suspected. He had never been the same after Dolly had disappeared, for weeks he had been far moodier and more savage than his role required, abusing her not for show but for real, as if he really hated her. And now Edmund was going to behave the same way. If Dolly had been fat with warts and a prickly chin neither of them would have given a damn. If she'd been thin with a big nose and ginger hair, she would have been expendable. Bloody men.

Still, she reflected, as she brewed tea and switched on the radio for the news, at least it had made the war come alive for him at last, if that wasn't a contradiction in terms. More alive than it had ever been in Barcelona. And *he* accused *her* of being overemotional!

Not that she had anything personal against Dolly. She had liked her well enough, and if she did turn out to be dead, then that was a great pity, but it was hardly more earth-shattering than all the rest of the war put together, just because Edmund and Jack still carried a torch for her. As for bringing the child back to England, who was supposed to take care of it? Not Jack, that was for sure. She could hear Edmund now. A child to replace the one they'd lost. Some adorable little replica of Dolly, much better than anything *she* could hope to produce. Just let him dare suggest it . . .

An hour later he came back. Clara braced herself to receive the apology, but he didn't give one. Instead he said, "I was fond of Dolly. You might at least respect that. And kindly don't ever refer to her as a Fascist. Whatever damn side she was on, and God knows there are at least a dozen, she wasn't a Fascist in the way *you* mean it. There but for the grace of God go I, and probably you as well. Remember that next time you sit in judgment."

He flopped down on the sofa, as if exhausted by this prerehearsed speech, indicating that he had said his piece and that was the end of it unless she was unwise enough to prolong the quarrel. There was never any point in quarreling with Edmund and having the last word by default.

"I'm sorry," said Clara. "If I'd known you still cared so pas-

sionately about her I would have kept my mouth shut. I may sim-
plify things, but you deliberately complicate them because you've
got an inbuilt compulsion to make excuses for people. Have some
tea.''

She rattled crockery as a token of truce. Edmund sighed and
inspected one of the posters. Clara tipped some flour into a bowl.

"You pour the boiling water while I stir," she said. "I'm sticking
these up in the morning. What happened to that brush?''

She wielded a wooden spoon busily while Edmund added the
contents of the kettle.

"I was hoping you'd come along to the meeting with me tonight," she continued briskly, as if nothing had happened. "Dr.
Peabody of the Spanish Medical Aid Committee is coming to give
a talk. Apparently the Republic is short of dressings, syringes,
drugs, everything. Do you realize the front is over two thousand
miles long? Think how many field hospitals they're going to need
once things really get hot.''

Edmund looked at her through a cloud of steam, feeling suddenly
cold all over.

"Of course," continued Clara, "there isn't much point in sending medical supplies to the Republic if they haven't got enough
trained staff to administer them.''

Edmund put down the kettle.

"Are you saying what I think you're saying?''

"I was planning to go back to work in September anyway. I'm
beginning to feel like a malingerer. And even you can't deny I'm
better.''

Better. Yes, she was better. She was eating, sleeping, not drinking. She had stopped having nightmares. She was already working
a twelve-hour day without any apparent signs of exhaustion, hawking leaflets, touting petitions, rattling tins, organizing rallies, doing
anything and everything that was asked of her, glorying in her new
"I was in Spain" status. And now that wasn't enough. Like any
other drug, like alcohol, her latest palliative required stronger and
stronger doses to have the required effect. Stronger and stronger
doses until it killed her.

"I won't let you go," said Edmund.

"You could always come too. They're crying out for volunteers.
You could drive an ambulance.''

"Don't try to blackmail me, Clara.''

"Don't try to blackmail *me*. Which do you think is more important, treating hernias in Mile End or saving lives in Spain?''

"You mean, which is more glamorous, don't you? There are plenty of lives to be saved in Mile End without risking your own. Charity begins at home."

"Glamorous? There's nothing glamorous about war. You of all people should know that. I refuse to argue with you, Edmund. I just want to apply, that's all. Don't worry, I daresay they won't want me anyway. I know you think I'm not up to it. I don't need you to remind me what a mediocre kind of nurse I am."

Her mouth began to wobble and Edmund was assailed by a sudden vision of her as a child, doomed ever to be sold short, to be rewarded for nothing and denied her heart's desire.

"Stop running yourself down," he said shortly. "You're a perfectly competent nurse and you know it. You're no good at exams, that's all. I'm not trying to lay down the law, you know that's not my way. I just don't want to lose you."

"I want to do something *special* with my life, can't you see? It's so easy for people who are beautiful or clever, it's so easy for women with children. They don't have to prove anything. I do."

"Not to me you don't."

"Especially to you. I'm sorry about Dolly, Edmund. I didn't mean to be unkind. I know I'm a bitch. But I'm not as weak and useless as you think. I feel like a leech, sucking you dry. You've got to let me be myself. Don't let's quarrel. Please."

By unspoken consent, they dropped the subject there. Edmund remained subdued for the rest of the evening, their roles reversed for once as Clara tried to humor him, troubled to see him in such low spirits. She told herself that he was just brooding about Dolly, rather than worrying about her plans to nurse in Spain. No doubt he was banking on them turning her down. But nearly six years' practical nursing experience must count for something, not to mention her party membership . . .

Yes, she had a lot to prove. To Edmund, to herself, to Jack. Jack knew the very worst of her, and she had never quite forgiven him for it. Jack refused to take her seriously, he thought she was just a hanger-on, regurgitating dogma, and made no bones about saying so.

"You're a great credit to the party, Clara," he had told her once, in the course of one of their routine quarrels. "Word-perfect, brain switched off, blinders firmly on. The Nazis must be kicking themselves that they didn't get to you first . . ."

She would show Jack she wasn't just a talker. She would show Edmund she wasn't a failure. So what if she was only an average nurse, somebody had to do the donkeywork. Glamorous indeed. It would be horrific, there would be people with their arms and legs blown off, men screaming in agony, and they thought she couldn't take it, they thought she would have another nervous breakdown, as if the sufferings of others ever gave anyone a nervous breakdown. Wasn't other people's suffering the perfect antidote to self-pity? She would surprise them all yet.

"Mamá, when will Papá be home?" said Andrés.

It was daybreak, and they were preparing to leave.

"Is it true Papá has gone away to fight? Rosa said I must wait and ask you."

"Yes, it's true," said Dolores, searching for words he would understand. "He is fighting for his beliefs. Your father is a brave man and whatever he does he does it for you and for me. Listen to me, Andrés. We must leave this house in a minute and go with Tomás to find somewhere else to live until your Papá comes home again. We have to pretend that you are Tomás's little boy, just for a little while. It's a sort of game, because your Papá's enemies might want to hurt us if they knew who we were. So if anyone asks you, Tomás is your Papá. Do you understand?"

What bitter irony it seemed, asking her son to deny a father who wasn't even his father . . .

The thought came to her unbidden, perhaps because she hadn't seen her son for weeks, perhaps because he had grown, changed, in her absence, but suddenly he reminded her so palpably and so painfully of Jack that she found herself transfixed, tongue-tied, staring her past in the face.

"I understand," said Andrés solemnly, even though he couldn't possibly. "Why can't Rafael come too?"

"Because Rosa needs him, just like I need you, just like Tomás needs Petra. You must make your Papá proud of you," she continued, "by being a good boy and not complaining and doing what Tomás tells you."

She hugged him tightly, thinking of Tomás's dead children, bitterly aware of her own good fortune. She would do anything to keep Andrés safe. Anything. Kill, steal, lie, betray, prostitute herself. She had already proved herself capable of any crime. She rejoiced in her own selfishness, the stuff of survival. She might be damned, but she was still alive.

"Are you ready, Dolores?" said Tomás, from the hallway. "It is getting light."

Rosa clung to Tomás, weeping. Petra clung to Rosa, weeping. And then, Rafael joined the fray and clung to Dolores, weeping. Andrés stood to one side, dry-eyed, only the occasional sniff betraying his confusion.

In the end, Tomás became impatient and agreed to let Petra stay behind with Rosa and Rafael. Every time he looked at his stocky, swarthy little daughter he could see Ignacia glaring at him through her eyes, reading his thoughts, unmanning him, filling him with guilt. He did not want Ignacia's eyes upon him now, he wanted to forget. He wished they could leave the boy behind as well. He wished they could leave all the past behind and start afresh . . .

"We must go," he said yet again. "I will come again tomorrow, Rosa." He gave her a meaningful look. While Dolores slept, Tomás had impressed on his sister over and over again that she must say nothing of the Englishman's visit. He himself would tell Dolores of her husband's death, but in his own way.

Rosa had listened unhappily, understanding him only too well. She knew her brother of old as a man of huge appetites, and now he was without a wife. He had always been in love with Dolores, an absurd, hopeless love, and now at last his chance had come. He would not let any Englishman rob him of his prize . . .

Rosa was left to calm Rafael and put him back to bed, with Petra's help. She felt drained by all the excitement, her joy at seeing her brother and Dolores safe was marred by self-pity, a feeling that they had abandoned her. If only Roberto were here!

"You'll stay with me, Petra, won't you?" said Rosa, sniffing, setting her niece on her lap. "You'll stay and help me with the baby when it comes? Like I helped your mother when you were born? Your mother would like that . . ."

Petra clung to her tightly. She needed a mother more than a father now. And Ignacia would surely turn in her grave at the thought of her daughter calling Dolores mother. Tomás knew that. Rosa had seen it in his face. Surely Dolores could see it too? No, perhaps not. She thought only of her husband, not knowing him to be dead. Rosa had no wish to break the news herself, but her enforced duplicity troubled her; she found it hard to look Dolores in the eye. Dolores had assumed she was just worried about Roberto and had tried to comfort her.

"Tomás is going to talk to one of Roberto's friends," she said. "To see if we can trade news of him for news of Lorenzo. We won't leave till we have word. Oh, I wish I could stay here with you! Poor Rosa. Don't cry."

Tomás had looked on balefully, silencing her with his very presence. It was Tomás who had betrayed Dolores, her own hands were clean. The card and letter were burned now, there was nothing she could do. If only the Englishman would return in time!

Dolores had deliberately dirtied Andrés's clothes and had not washed or changed or taken any luggage away with her, for fear of undermining their claim to be newly arrived refugees. There was an interminable wait and innumerable questions before Tomás was finally allocated temporary lodgings, a room in the former home of a factory owner, who had been "taken for a drive," in anarchist parlance, never to be seen again.

The house, a large stone mansion with magnificent views over the Tagus Valley, bore a large banner over its front door proclaiming it to be communal property. The walls, both inside and out, were covered in revolutionary posters, and the late owner's possessions had been strewn all over the floors like rubbish—books torn from their bindings, religious statues smashed to smithereens, fine clothes ripped to shreds, and, chillingly, broken toys and mutilated dolls.

Dolores watched her menfolk devour bread and sardines, too anxious to be hungry.

"Will you speak to someone today?" she asked.

Tomás nodded and she smiled gratefully, filling him with shame. The thing he wanted most in all the world, and now it was within his grasp. All he had to do was tell the truth. All he had to do was lie . . .

"She will not stay with you," his sister had warned him. "Whatever she says or does. Do not be deceived, Tomás. She will use you, that is all. She loves her child and she needs a protector. And so she will use you, as I would, as any mother would in her place. If you really loved her, you would let her go. In England she would be safe . . ."

She would still be safe, with him. He would guard her with his life. He would earn her love and trust and respect. They would come together in the spirit of the revolution, they would live together in freedom and equality.

Tomorrow he would tell her he had got news of her husband. Tomorrow he would tell her her husband was dead. He would comfort her in her distress, offer her protection, take her to Madrid. Then the war would be won and they would start a new life . . .

His heart sank. He was a fool, a fool to think she would ever want one as gross as he. But no matter. He would take her on any terms, content only to give. He would give, and give and give, but he would not give her up.

Catching sight of his father's watchtower, Josep asked the driver to set him down, saying that he would walk the rest of the way. He waited until the vehicle was safely out of sight before proceeding. He proposed to tell his family, and any local townsfolk, that he had been granted leave of absence from Fontenar. He could scarcely admit the truth before his father, who was more than capable of turning him in.

The trees seemed higher than ever. He was almost at the top of the hill before the house came into view and stopped him in his tracks.

The railings that remained were bent and twisted; every window had been blown out and the white walls were black and pitted. There was a gaping hole where the front door had once been, a part of the upper story had collapsed.

Josep heard himself calling for his mother and sister, his voice echoing uselessly in the strange, still, sinister silence. As if in a trance, he went inside, bracing himself for the sight of their dead bodies. Every surface was covered thickly with soot and debris, the air was still acrid with the smell of smoke. Charred remnants of furniture lay strewn like firewood, the marble floors were cracked from wall to wall, as if pulled apart by an earthquake. The back wall of the house was all but demolished, the door of the cellar open to the sky.

Those rooms that had escaped the blaze were empty, ransacked, with the contents of drawers and cupboards scattered everywhere. Stupidly, he searched every inch of the house, shouting "Dolores! Mamá! Dolores!" narrowly escaping a heavy fall as part of the staircase gave way beneath him. There was nothing to show what might have become of his family, no human remains among the wreckage.

Cautiously, he climbed the narrow stone steps up to the watch-tower and looked all around him, squinting his eyes against the sun. There was no sign of anyone working on his father's land. Albavera appeared to be intact, but for its church spire, which was black . . .

He ran as if pursued toward the town, cutting across the fields in his haste. Please God his mother was already dead when this happened. Please God Dolores was back in Toledo. Please God the whole family had fled in time . . .

The church door was open. All the carvings and statues were missing, all the stained glass had gone, but candles were burning and rows of chairs stood where the pews had once been. The thick walls had survived the conflagration, only the trappings had been lost. An old woman was crouched in the gloom, arranging flowers on a simple, makeshift altar. Josep knocked on the vestry door.

"Father Luis!" he called. "It's me, Josep!"

A priest appeared, a young, ruddy-faced individual.

"I am Father Alvaro," he said, looking curiously at Josep's grimy cassock and blackened hands and face. "Forgive me if I do not know you. I have been in this parish less than a week. How can I help you?"

He ushered Josep inside.

"There is much work still to be done, as you can see," he continued. "The tabernacle was desecrated and the holy relics destroyed. New ones had to be consecrated and sent from Avila. A shocking business . . ."

"My family," panted Josep. "What has happened to my family?"

The young priest sighed and bowed his head.

"I regret to say that over fifteen families perished at the hands of the mob. Yours was among them, perhaps. The workers stormed the Carrasquez house, where they had taken refuge."

"That's my father's house," said Josep urgently. "What happened to my sister, my mother?"

"Everyone in the house was killed," repeated the young priest sadly. "I myself was not here at the time. I have been recently transferred from Cacáres. I shall offer Mass for them. My sincere condolences."

"Oh for God's sake!" exploded Josep. "My sister doesn't live here, she was visiting from Toledo. I'm trying to find out if she was here when this happened. Where's Father Luis?"

"Martyred," said his fellow priest, shaking his head. "He is with the angels. *Requiat in pace!*" He crossed himself.

Josep sprang to his feet, exasperated.

"Excuse me. I must find someone who knows me. I must—" There was a gentle tap on the door and a head peeped around it. It was an elderly woman, her arms still full of flowers. She took one look at Josep, dropped her burden, and burst into tears.

"Angelina!" said Josep, embracing her. "Angelina, what has happened to my family?"

She mumbled incoherently, gripping his hands tightly and shaking her head and moaning, her plump body quivering with distress. Then she whispered something in Josep's ear.

"May I speak to this lady in private?" he asked. "She was my mother's personal maid and is very upset."

The priest left them alone.

"Is it true?" said Josep. "Did the workers kill them all? Tell me, Angelina!"

"They let me go," she mumbled. "I was so frightened. The big man, Tomás, let me go, because I was old. He wanted to let Dolores go too, but the others would not let him. They would not release the other servants, they said they were lackeys who had betrayed their class. Thank God your poor mother died when she did. She could not have borne it. She was buried the day it all started, the day they burned the church. Your father and his men attacked the workers and killed many of them. Dolores was shot by accident, in the head. I nursed her, I feared she would die. The house was full of your father's friends, and their families. So many guns! I was afraid, all the servants were, but we had nowhere else to go . . ."

"My sister!" prompted Josep urgently. "Tell me what happened to my sister."

"The workers stormed the house by night. I woke up to find Dolores gone, taken prisoner. They killed your father and all the men, and kept the women and children hostage. They said the Revolution had come, and that once the generals had been defeated we could all go free. But then they heard the Moors were coming, and the big man let me go."

"He let you go and not Dolores? What harm had she ever done to him?"

"He wanted to free her. All the time there were arguments. But the others said she was a Fascist because her father and her husband were Fascists."

"Lorenzo?"

"Tomás got word from Toledo that her husband had rebelled. But for Tomás they would have killed her then. Tomás told me to take refuge in Albavera. He said I would be safe there because all the bourgeosie had raised white flags. But he said the workers would fight to the death and take their prisoners with them. And then . . . and then . . ."

She collapsed into more sobs.

"The house was shelled," said Josep for her. "It caught fire."

"No one survived," whimpered Angelina. "Many of the bodies were burned, unrecognizable. The soldiers looted the house, they took everything. All the silver, all your mother's jewelry. The people here say the workers took it and sold it before the troops arrived." Her voice sank to a whisper. "But it's not true. The people here say that the workers raped the women and put the babies' eyes out, but that's not true either." She clung to him. "Don't tell them I said it wasn't true! I'm so frightened!"

"There's nothing to be frightened of, Angelina," said Josep, his voice choked. "You're safe."

"Afterward the Civil Guard questioned me," she babbled. "They accused me of letting the workers into the house. They said someone must have unlocked the door for them and drugged the watchdogs. I told them, never, never! I have served your family for forty years! Why would I bite the hand that fed me? They showed me a paper saying that the workers had disposed of all your father's valuables and tortured the women and children before killing them. I signed it. I had to sign it! Was that a sin, Father? I dare not confess it . . ."

"Ssh. You are blameless. What happened to my sister's little boy?"

Angelina sniffed and wiped her eyes.

"Dolores left him with Rosa, in Toledo. Tomás got word that he was safe. He said Rosa loved the child as her own, she would never let anyone harm him."

"And my brother?"

Angelina shook her head.

"Still in some slum in Madrid. That is what killed your poor mother, assuredly. That and losing her daughter. Both of them cut off and banned from the house! You are a rich man now, Father, you will inherit the estate. Please God the Reds do not win the war! They will confiscate all land, all property. No one will be allowed to own anything. Everyone will have to work without wages and live in a collective. Father Alvaro says . . ."

Josep put his arms around the poor, confused old woman and hugged her into silence.

"Angelina, I must go soon. I must see the graves, and then go."

"Your mother is in the family vault. The workers buried your father and all his friends behind the house. Your sister . . . they could not identify her. Many bodies were burned. There is to be a monument . . .''

He left her still weeping and walked alone toward the white-walled cemetery, thinking of his sister as a little girl, as a young woman, as a wife and mother. She had never harmed a living soul, she had brought nothing but joy to everyone who knew her, and now the sins of their father had been visited upon her. Poor Lorenzo. Poor Andrés. Thank God his mother had been spared this dreadful pain. How futile it seemed to take sides! There was no more right, only wrong. Both sides were evil. War was evil. He wanted no part of it. And yet he had to do *something*. And to do anything at all, he had to remain free.

His time was running out. Already his unauthorized absence would have been reported, already his bishop would have received a verbatim account of his latest heresies, heresies that would no longer be tolerated. Already patrols would have been alerted that another Red intellectual was on the loose . . .

He remembered the civil governor's words over dinner. The Basque country was both Catholic and Republican, the only possible safe harbor for a pariah such as he, the only part of the Republic where a priest was not an enemy of the people. But the Basque country was five hundred kilometers north, perilously far away. In all likelihood he would be stopped long before he reached it. He would be questioned, identified, arrested, tried, he would end up before a firing squad, like the one in Vallemora. But what were the alternatives? Better to die than to have to kill. Better to die than to recant.

Dolores would have understood. His role as the older, wiser brother had never blinded him to the truth; they were birds of a feather. Like her he was imprudent, impetuous, proud, like her he believed in instincts, let his heart rule his head.

He knelt down before the family vault and picked a flower out of the vase placed there by poor Angelina.

"Explain this to Mamá for me, Dolores," he said out loud. "Tell her I don't condone those who killed Papá; tell her I can't forgive those who killed you. Tell her there's nothing I can do to help Ramón, or your little boy, other than to pray for them. Tell her this is the only thing I can think of to do. Help me get there, help me be brave. Watch over me, sweet little sister."

The white carnation was flecked with red, like tiny drops of blood. He kissed it and pressed it inside his breviary. Then he walked quickly out of the cemetery and took a long deep breath of danger.

"It's not true!" shouted Dolores. "I don't believe you!"

"Calm yourself. The boy will hear you."

Tomás could see Andrés through the window, playing war games in the courtyard below with a gang of scruffy little boys, happily killing Fascists with the best of them.

"I would never lie to you about such a thing, Lole," he said. "I was there during the cease-fire, I heard the parley myself. The lines are only a few meters apart, the words were quite clear. Rosa was with me. Ask her. She will tell you the same thing. Your husband died bravely, Dolores. He died in action. You should be proud of him."

"Rosa heard this too?"

"Ask her. If you do not trust me, ask her."

She looked deep into his eyes, boring them for truth, and he returned her gaze unflinchingly. The cruelest thing he could do would be to fail to convince her. He could not bear to see her cling to hope when there was none.

"Why would they lie?" he continued. "They would never admit that they had lost a man unless it was true."

He wished she would weep. Her eyes were dry, unnaturally bright.

"I am happy for Rosa," she said at last.

"They are probably lying about Roberto," said Tomás gruffly, unhappy with this enforced invention. "They probably killed all the hostages long ago."

"Don't tell Rosa that," said Dolores sharply. "Let her hope. I wish they had lied to me! I wish you had lied to me! What will I tell Andrés? How will I tell him?"

She was trembling all over.

"You must be careful what you tell Andrés. He is only a child, he will repeat whatever you say. You must tell him that your husband died for the Republic."

"So he did! He believed in democracy! He died for what he thought was right!"

"I meant no disrespect. I meant—"

She sank to her knees and buried her face in her arms. At that moment he would have done anything to bring her husband back to life, anything to make her happy again.

"Don't be afraid, Lole," he said. "I will look after you. I will see that no harm comes to you or the boy. We will go to Madrid. There nobody knows you. There you will be safe."

Dolores continued to weep, tears of guilt as well as grief. He was so strong, so gentle, so kind, so brave. He had risked his life for her, and she had used him relentlessly, given him nothing in return. On the contrary, she had killed his wife. And now Lorenzo, too, was dead. It was like a retribution for her crime.

She reached out for his hand.

"Don't leave me, Tomás."

"I will never leave you. I swear it. I would die for you, Lole."

"Thank you," she murmured. He embraced her awkwardly and she clung to him tightly, like someone drowning. "Thank you."

But the words were no longer enough. It was not just gratitude that drove her on, it was a conscious bid to ensure he kept his word, a way of binding him to her, a reward, a plea, a promise. There was so much comfort in his arms, so much warmth in his solid bulk. He seemed to embody strength and life and hope. Surely she owed him this much? And besides, she had nothing else to give . . .

Afterward, in the damp, sad quiet of shared loneliness, she wept again for Lorenzo. And for the first time in years, she wept for Jack.

Jack sat bolt upright in bed and switched on the light. He rubbed his eyes and looked at his watch. Three in the morning. He had suffered recurring nightmares ever since his visit to Toledo, for the last week he had woken up shouting and sweating, unable to remember the bloody images, but knowing he must have seen her mutilated, fractured, hacked to bits. But tonight he had dreamed she was alive, and he had started running toward her, but she had been in a crowd of people, and he had lost sight of her and the sheer relief and frustration of it had jolted him awake, and for a few precious seconds he had clung to the vanishing fantasy, willing it to be true.

It haunted him for the rest of the day, ruining his concentration, reducing an interview with Prime Minister Caballero to a page of doodles. Afterward his mind had gone completely blank and he had to make the whole thing up, not that it made any difference, given that he didn't propose to quote him. The old man's mistrust of the Communists was undoubtedly obstructing the provision of much-needed Soviet arms, and he would have been astonished at the new friendship Jack had laid claim to on his behalf. Nonetheless, a steady influx of foreign observers into the capital, of mixed nationalities and undoubtedly bogus identities, indicated that plans were already afoot, with or without Caballero's approval. Stalin never did anybody any favors. If he came into this war, it would be to suit himself, not to oblige anyone as insignificant as the Spanish premier.

The next day, unable to face another night of dreams, good or bad, he returned to Toledo and went back to Dolly's apartment. The servant girl was in the courtyard, hanging out washing, with Dolly's child clinging to her skirts, bashful as ever.

"*Salud*, Rosa," he said. "Have you any more news of Señora Montanis?"

She hesitated for a moment, then said something in the child's ear, and it scampered away. The little girl, who had a mouthful of clothespins, did likewise, looking back twice as if reluctant to leave her aunt alone.

"Yes," she said, not looking at him, her voice sinking to a rapid whisper. "I have news. But it was as I told you before. My brother arrived from Albavera, he escaped from the Fascists. He has gone to Madrid now. Everyone was killed. My older brother, my sister-in-law, my nephews. Everybody. Dolores also. She died bravely, defending the house against the Fascists. She died for the Republic. My brother was with her when she died. Her last wish was that I should look after her child. You cannot take him to England. You cannot."

Jack sat down on the cobbles.

"I am sorry," said the girl, perplexed to have the stranger at her feet. "But many have died. I have lost nearly all my family. Many have died." Jack covered his face with his hands, no longer listening, no longer wanting to listen. She disappeared into the house again and came back with something in a glass.

"Drink," she said gently, crouching down beside him and handing it to him. Jack looked at it blankly. The expression on his face quite frightened her.

He hadn't believed it before. Not for a minute. And because he hadn't believed it, because there was room for doubt, he had come to terms with it, carried on working, been able to hope in secret. He had thought he had believed it, and congratulated himself at being able to bear it. After all, he had known her only briefly, and it was over five years ago, and he had toughened up a lot since then, and he had neither forgiven nor forgotten . . . especially not forgotten. And so he had been able to tell Edmund, he had written it down to make it real and still not believed it. He wrote things down all the time to make them real, not believing them. Had he thought to cheat death like that, by writing it down so that he didn't have to believe it?

Rosa stood watching him, wringing her hands, troubled at the effects of her deceit. Lying had become a habit lately, but if Tomás had not told her exactly what to say, perhaps she would have faltered, perhaps even now she would have tried to comfort him with some crumb of hope.

But she dared not. This man was no friend. This man was a lover. Had Tomás guessed as much, perhaps, fearing some English sweetheart of long ago?

She felt sorry for the poor man in his sorrow, and guilty at her part in it, she would have liked to take him inside and let him rest in the cool and quiet until he felt better, but he might ask to see Andrés, and she had not rehearsed a reason for his absence and could not think of one, and so she left him sitting in the dirt, watching the brandy trickle away where he had knocked the glass over. Then, quite suddenly, he jerked himself upright, covered in dust, pulled out his wallet and groped blindly in it, handing her a bundle of bills.

"Look after her child for me," he said hoarsely. "And contact me if you need help." He coughed to clear his throat and blew his nose.

"If you ever have to leave this place, if you are ever in trouble, leave a message for me. You still have my card?"

"Yes." Rosa nodded, confused. "I still have your card."

"*Adios.* Forgive me, I mean, *salud.* Thank you, Rosa."

Yes, he must be a lover, thought Rosa, transfixed by the look in his eyes. His grief was as savage as Dolores's had been for her poor husband. How she had wept the day she left for Madrid! At that moment she very nearly blurted out the truth, Tomás or no Tomás. And then she noticed something else about his eyes. They were blue, bright blue.

"Do not worry, señor," she said sadly, understanding at last. "Do not worry about Andrés. Never was a child more loved."

He smiled his thanks, a strained, uneven smile, exactly the same as Andrés's smile after he had been crying. Tomás had been right to be jealous of this man. Tomás could not give her a child.

11

Granazán, near Huesca
October 25, 1936

Dearest Edmund,

Thank you for your letter. Just the shortest possible note in reply before I go back on duty. There is only time for work and sleep, but I send you thoughts often, which I hope you receive. Last week was a fearful rush. Two hundred new cases in three days. Not just soldiers, but refugees from bombed villages, with feet cut to ribbons from their journeys over the mountains. And a few of the enemy, you'll be glad to hear. We spent four hours yesterday operating on a Moorish soldier with a gangrenous leg. Just as well he died, as I think the villagers would have lynched him. They don't understand medical ethics, and I can't say I blame them.

Any news would be welcome, though I daresay the English press is full of the usual lies. The censors took away our radio, which leads one to assume that the news is mostly bad. I'm sure you can find some cryptic and scholarly way of bamboozling the poor wretches who have to read our letters.

Despite the dreadful lack of everything—do keep up the fund-raising, we need it more than ever—morale is good, among party members at least. There are still a few saboteurs about—one of our ambulances was "liberated" the other day by the local anarchists, who run this part of the world, and I'm pretty sure the anti-CP factions connived at it.

More tea please, next time you send a parcel. Tessa is leaving us tomorrow, so I've asked her to look you up and deliver this letter for me. She won't be coming back, more's the pity, because her foot is now permanently damaged, but she's going to be fully occupied at home, helping to recruit volunteers for the International Brigades. The first contingent have already arrived at Al-

*bacete and are being trained for the defense of Madrid. Men from
all over the world, can you imagine? And not just party members
either.*

Much love,
C.

Edmund folded the letter and smiled rather fixedly at his visitor.
The significance of Clara's last sentence was not lost on him. She
needn't have bothered to underline it, but the lack of subtlety was
no doubt deliberate. It was a reproach, not a plea.

"More tea, Tessa?" he said stiffly. Just looking at Tessa made
him feel guilty. She was a frail little thing, and quite pretty, hardly
a walking prototype of valor on the field of battle. She had got her
injury while manning a first-aid post on the Aragon front, having
braved machine-gun fire to attend to a wounded militiaman. Her
ankle had been shattered, and she still walked painfully with a
stick. He found it utterly emasculating, having to defend his principles to a woman who had been wounded in action. His fear that
a similar fate would overtake Clara was overridden by the selfish
thought that nothing short of an injury would induce her to come
home.

"Yes, please. I'm addicted to the stuff. The day we run out of
tea we'll have to abandon Spain to the Fascists. Clara said to tell
you Earl Grey, by the way."

"What else did Clara say to tell me, Tessa?"

"Mmm. Your tone tells me I'd be wasting my breath."

"I'm a pacifist. And after reading some of Clara's recent letters,
I'm more of a pacifist than ever. Healthy young men shot to bits,
dying in agony, being patched up so they can go out for a second
helping. And for what? My father spent months in the trenches
watching lambs being sent to the slaughter while the generals passed
the port. How can anyone fall for it anymore? How can you go out
in conscience, seeing what you've seen, and try to persuade young
men to go to Spain as cannon fodder? Because the Comintern tells
you to?"

He stopped abruptly. Tessa didn't bat an eyelid and carried on
sipping her tea sedately, as aware as he that he was protesting too
much. She had doubtless already written him off as a coward. The
kind of coward who sits at home in safety while his wife—Edmund
always thought of Clara as his wife, even though they had never
married—risked life and limb in the cause of that sacred cow democracy.

"Please don't be sarcastic. Believe it or not, I didn't come here to talk you into anything. I was going to come to see you anyway, whether Clara asked me to or not. What I wanted to say to you was this. I think you should try to persuade Clara to come home."

This unexpected bombshell jolted Edmund out of his torpor of cynicism like a rush of cold air.

"Why? What's wrong?"

"Nothing, officially . . . yet. But there soon will be, I think. We've had three nervous breakdowns already, much tougher specimens than Clara, I might add. Not surprising, really. You might go without sleep for several days in a row, and then have to haul a dead man out of bed so that you can lie down. One day I had to dispose of twenty-three amputated limbs, I won't tell you what I did with them. And then there's the endless, soulless drudgery, trying to keep instruments sterile in the most appalling conditions with hardly any time to breathe between operations. One becomes an automaton. If I hadn't been injured, I think I would have cracked up. I was starting to hallucinate, I knew I couldn't go on much longer, but you can't imagine what a sense of failure it gives you to admit it. Some people would rather die than admit it, and Clara's one of them. That's her greatest strength and her greatest weakness. She's trying to prove something to herself, and to you, I expect. At first I was taken in by it, like everybody else, but lately I've started to wonder about her. I don't think anyone noticed the change, except me, and I only noticed because I suddenly had time on my hands. Everyone's too busy to notice things. She's been behaving rather strangely."

"What do you mean, strangely?" demanded Edmund, impatient at Tessa's soft-spoken prolixity, his mind racing ahead. "Strangely" could mean only one thing. She must have been drinking again.

Tessa put down her cup and saucer, leaned forward, and took hold of both Edmund's hands.

"Brace yourself," she said in the hushed professional tones appropriate to the imparting of bad news. Edmund stifled a surge of irritation. "I haven't told this to anyone else. I know I should have, but one's morals get rather muddled in a war. Listen. In the bed next to mine was a Fascist soldier with a perforated lung. The surgeon had done an excellent job on him, and he was expected to make a full recovery. We were in a side ward because we try to keep enemy soldiers well away from the Republican casualties.

"He was only a boy, of course, and in quite a lot of pain, and it was quite impossible to hate him. Fascist or not. Don't quote me, will you. Anyway, Clara came in very early one morning to give him an injection. She was quite brusque with him, I remember, and jabbed the needle in without much ceremony. Soon afterward he fell asleep, and so did I. When I woke up again, he was dead. I called for help, and within minutes he'd been carted off and some other poor wretch was in the bed. We don't have time to do post mortems, as you can imagine, which perhaps is just as well.''

"Wait a minute," said Edmund incredulously. "Are you trying to tell me you think Clara gave him an overdose, or what?"

"I don't know. I've no proof. But it's a possibility. She's been complaining a lot recently about wasting precious resources on enemy casualties, when the Fascists automatically kill all Republican prisoners. Perhaps they do, but we can't *know* that, and even if they did, no one in their right mind would suggest we do the same. I've begun to wonder if she's in her right mind, that's all."

"Then why don't they *send* her home?" exploded Edmund, getting up and walking around the room in agitation. "How can they let her carry on like that?"

"Superficially, there's no reason to send her home. Superficially, she's coping extremely well. I've never seen her cry, never seen her faint, never seen her vomit, and I speak as one who's done all three. Try to imagine what it's like out there. We're desperately short of manpower, everyone's working around the clock. Nobody gets sent home unless they're incapable of working. And Clara's capacity for work is not in doubt. She's regarded as invaluable, and she knows it. It seems to have given her a sense of . . . of *power.*"

"My God," said Edmund quietly. "So she's killed her first Fascist at last. The comrades would be proud of her."

"Don't be bitter, Edmund, please. You can imagine how difficult it was for me to tell you this. I could be horribly wrong, I could be doing her a terrible injustice. That's why I didn't report it. It would destroy her career, obviously, if it turned out to be true, and even if it wasn't true, mud sticks. But I don't think I'm being fanciful. Afterward, she had a peculiar look in her eyes, and when I expressed surprise that the man had died she got rather flustered. I'm sorry, Edmund. I hope I'm wrong, but either way, she's done enough. She can do just as much good here at home."

"Recruiting people to do exactly what she did? It's all right to kill a man with a bullet or a bayonet or a bomb, but not with a hypodermic because *that's* murder. The sheer hypocrisy of it!"

Tessa pursed her lips and bowed her head, not deigning to comment.

"*How* exactly do you suggest I persuade her to come home?"
continued Edmund, exasperated. "Have you any idea how intractable she can be?"

"Yes, a little. I'm going to try to convince the party high-ups
that we need her here, without telling them what I've told you, of
course. She'd come home if they sent for her all right. The trouble
is, I don't suppose they'll want her. She's no good at public speaking, and she hasn't got a gammy leg to show off, like me. Failing
that, I've got no ideas. Is there anyone else she'd listen to? Any
close friends, or relatives? You're the only person she ever speaks
of."

"No, there's nobody. And even if there was, Clara wouldn't
listen. This war is an obsession with her, it has been from the start.
God. Look . . . I'm sorry I've been so short with you, Tessa. I've
been through every kind of hell since she left. She was upset I
wouldn't go with her. I should have gone with her."

"Why didn't you? You wouldn't have to fight, you know. Paci-
fists can act as ambulance drivers, stretcher bearers, orderlies—"

"Because I would have felt a hypocrite," said Edmund.
"Because I'm not the least bit brave, because I'm deeply suspicious
about what's happening to all these funds we're raising, because
I'm not anti-Fascist *enough.*"

Tessa stood up to go.

"I know you don't trust us, Edmund," she said sadly. "I wish I
could convince you we're sincere."

"I know you're sincere," said Edmund.

It amused Jack to watch Marisa smoking. Lots of shallow, staccato
puffs followed by excessive inhalation, as if she were anxious not
to waste any of the smoke. He always gave her a packet to take
away with her, to give to her *novio,* who, despite his bad chest, or
perhaps because of it, nurtured a craving for English cigarettes.

Recently the shortages had become much worse, as more and
more food-producing areas succumbed to Fascist control, and
black-marketeering was rampant. Marisa had invested in a much
larger handbag, capacious enough to accommodate tins of food, or
whatever other portable comestibles came her way through her foreign connections. Anything surplus to her needs she sold for ex-
orbitant sums without compunction. She had become increasingly
eager to negotiate payment in kind, and to offer mutually advanta-
geous discounts. Extortion came naturally to her, and she conducted it with an ingenuous cunning which Jack found endearing.

Their talking sessions had become his principal source of relaxation; he would miss her when it was all over.

Popular opinion among the press was that it would all be over in a month, the sooner the better, the story was getting stale. The Fascists were closing in relentlessly on the capital, and air raids had further reduced civilian morale. It was generally acknowledged that Madrid would have fallen weeks ago if General Franco had not suddenly diverted his troops to Toledo. The Alcázar was by that time a heap of rubble, brought down at last by heavy artillery bombardment. But the surviving defenders had taken refuge deep inside its impregnable cellars, and had emerged triumphant to greet their liberators—a body blow to Republic pride, and a brilliant propaganda coup for the Fascists.

As soon as Jack heard of the planned Fascist detour, he had gone straight to Toledo, in an attempt to get Rosa and the children out before it was too late. But he had found the apartment empty; like so many others, she had already fled, presumably toward Madrid. Madrid was bursting with refugees; to find her would be next to impossible. But a month had gone by since then, and she had still not contacted him. Perhaps she had simply lost his address . . . He was left with a desolate sense of having bungled things, of having let Dolly down.

Jack himself did not wholly share the fashionable pessimism as to the imminent fall of the capital. According to a loquacious and corpulent Slav he knew only as "Gregory"—one of Marisa's regulars—an unspecified number of "technicians" had been imported from the Soviet Union to "advise" the Spanish government in its time of crisis. A generous gesture, Jack agreed. Almost as generous as the noble offer to transport the vast Spanish gold reserves to Russia, for safekeeping, lest they fall into enemy hands.

And of course, there was always the cavalry, in the shape of the much-vaunted International Brigades, a motley assortment of displaced persons, idealists, misfits and adventurers, currently being trained amid unbelievable squalor in Albacete, and possessed of a collective fervor which had impressed even Jack. The fat man had been delighted at the favorable write-up Jack had given them, which had been only partly tactical. At least the poor bastards had been issued decent rifles, which was more than could be said for the struggling non-Communist militias. If Madrid survived the forthcoming onslaught, the International Brigades were lined up to get the credit. If it fell, the anarchists would undoubtedly get the blame.

Marisa lit another cigarette.

"Don't you agree?" she demanded.

Jack had been miles away.

"What? Please say that again, Marisa. I did not understand."

She sighed comically and repeated herself with precision. Jack's Spanish was much improved these days—Marisa knew very well that he had not been listening.

"That I earn these things honestly," she said. "What right has this man to abuse me, when I help feed his woman and the child? I told Lole, I shall keep such things for myself if you allow him to insult me like this. She has no spirit, she allows this oaf to say whatever he likes. Now that he calls himself a soldier of the Republic, he thinks he has the right to judge others. I hope he will be killed in the fighting."

"He probably will be," Jack assured her.

"Do you think the war will end soon?" she continued anxiously. "I hope it does not end soon. If it ends soon, all my foreign gentlemen will go home. Will you go home, when the war ends?"

"Before, perhaps," said Jack. "Some wars last many months, years even. My paper may send me somewhere else."

"And must you go wherever your paper sends you?"

A good question, thought Jack.

"No," he said. "Only if I want them to pay me."

"Then you must," said Marisa. "If they pay you, then you must."

Her work ethic was delightfully clear-cut. She saw no difference between the way she earned her living and the way he earned his, and perhaps she was right. If they paid you, then you must.

"No," said Jack, to himself.

"No?" echoed Marisa. "Then who will pay you? Are you a rich man, that you do not need to be paid?"

"Not rich." Jack smiled. "But I have no wife, no children. I can afford to be poor, if I choose."

Marisa made her "mad Englishman" face. She found him increasingly droll, and tolerated his eccentric remarks with good-humored equanimity. She resumed her chatter, the usual diatribe against the one thorn in her thick-skinned flesh. Jack had heard it all before, but her repetitiveness had become strangely soothing, a nonstimulative barrier between himself and his increasingly morbid thoughts. She spoke rapidly again, as if knowing the words were familiar to him, reliving her outrage, replenishing it, perhaps even enjoying it.

The sudden disruption to her routine—she was very much a creature of routine—had been viewed immediately as a threat. She had returned home one morning in September—how endlessly she had ranted at the time!—to find her *novio's* sister and nephew in uninvited occupation, and Ramón in the throes of a terminal asthma attack, glorying in the attentions of his long-lost kin. Marisa had taken swift exception to these intruders, especially once she encountered their protector, a big bully of a man who had lost no time in making himself unpopular with his puritanical objections to her profession, going so far as to forbid the child to eat the corned beef she had brought back from the hotel. She had been heartily relieved that they had only stayed a few days, until the union found them other lodgings, lodgings that were a mite too near for her liking.

Still, since Lole's arrival the attic room had been scrubbed from floor to ceiling, the linen had been laundered, and Ramón's ragged clothes hand-washed. It had pleased Marisa to see this well-bred lady acting as her servant, and somewhat mollified the natural jealously she felt at having to share Ramón's affections.

She had no quarrel with Lole, she insisted. And at least Lole was always polite to her. The first thing Lole had done next day was to apologize for Tomás, and humbly ask if her little boy could have some of the corned beef after all. Since then, Marisa had generously donated such tidbits as she thought he might enjoy. She enjoyed giving, or rather enjoyed gratitude, and as yet the novelty value had not worn off. But yesterday—she nudged Jack, whose attention was wandering again—yesterday she had called in to give the child some fine French chocolate, and that big brute had answered the door and sent her away with his usual lack of courtesy. She had eaten the chocolate herself on the way home. Ramón had no taste for it.

"Ramón says this man is a hypocrite. Ramón says he is too mean to pay for his pleasures, and exploits poor Lole instead, because she is poor and has a child to care for. And he is gross! I myself would not go with such a man, however much he paid me."

"Liar," said Jack easily. "You would go with the devil himself, for a price."

"I would charge the devil extra," she retorted indignantly, taking him literally, as always. "I would charge the devil even more than a priest."

For the first time in his life, Josep had a willing, docile congregation; for the first in his life he was working in peace and harmony. And he was bored to tears.

Those weeks as an outlaw, without papers, dodging the Fascist patrols between Vallemora and the Basque border, had been the most exciting of his life. He had traveled on foot, cross-country, by night, filled with an unquenchable, reckless sense of destiny.

Getting to the Basque country had been a challenge; being in the Basque country was not. Fear and risk had been intoxicating, energizing. But their effect had soon worn off. The war seemed remote in this sleepy place; life continued much as it had always done, placid, tranquil and dull. The ordinary populace welcomed their new independence, but were quite detached from the struggle raging elsewhere. This was a land of small farmers, not greedy landowners, a land of cooperation, not a temple to the rich and powerful.

Josep's early hopes of serving as a military chaplain had so far come to nothing. The northern front was quiet, and he had been told that his services were not needed; as a "foreigner" he was still viewed with some suspicion and had been placed under the tutelage of an old village priest, a stolid, narrow-minded sort of fellow who fussed a great deal about the state of the altar flowers and preached platitudinous sermons of stultifying boredom. Josep had been placed with him without consultation, and he probably resented it, but the fact remained that there was little enough work for one, let alone two, among people who came obediently to church, made few demands, and were relatively prosperous.

But at least he had learned something about himself. At last he knew what had been missing from his life, he had discovered the cure for the deep, restless frustration. He had thought for years that it was something sexual, physical, something he would finally grow out of. But he had grown into it instead. Insidiously, inexorably, he had come to crave it like a drug. Danger.

Ramón heard his sister's footstep on the stair, and stuffed his blood-stained handkerchief into his pocket. If she saw it, she would fuss at him again to see a doctor, a prospect he found intolerable. Knowing that his days were numbered was one thing; having some smug weasel with a stethoscope pronounce sentence on him was quite another. When he died, he would die a hero, not a victim.

Marisa now worked in the afternoons as well, having extended her pitch to include the big hotel by the Retiro Park, which was stuffed full of foreign Communists. Marisa approved of communists as being practical-minded, and since "Gregory," the fat Russian, had changed hotels, she had had a natural introduction to this profitable new area. Ramón questioned her rigorously about her recently acquired clientele, and had invented all manner of fictitious pillow talk, which he duly entered in his journal. His pride in Marisa's Mata Hari exploits knew no bounds, but he was careful not to share this pride with Dolores, who no doubt repeated everything to that clod García. She was clearly terrified of the man, and it was best that she knew nothing of her brother's solemn vow to exact revenge for the violations she had suffered at his hands.

"Wake up, Uncle!" shouted his nephew, picking up his hand and banging it cheerfully against the bedcover. Ramón opened one eye and smiled wanly.

"Alas, Andrés, I am very tired today," he said, gazing wistfully at Dolores.

"It's time you got up, Ramón," said Dolores briskly. "I want to change the sheets. Take Andrés for a walk, while I clean up in here and make you something to eat."

The cupboard in the corner was full of Marisa's latest spoils, and cooking a meal for Ramón ensured that Andrés would get a share of whatever was going. Thanks to Tomás and his unshakable principles, Marisa's gifts were less frequent than they might otherwise have been. Dolores had no principles, as far as her son's well-being was concerned. She selected a couple of tins and put down the small loaf she had stood in line an hour to buy.

Ramón creaked out of bed and allowed Andrés to help him with his boot. Then he did the boy's favorite conjuring trick and produced some candy from his tattered trouser leg. Andrés fell upon it with squeals of delight. Dolores confiscated it without ceremony, to be saved for after his meal, and after a few routine wails of disappointment, Andrés pulled his uncle to his feet and dragged him off on their excursion.

Andrés adored his newfound uncle, who had seduced him with a never-ending supply of thrilling stories, recounted with a histrionic flair which had blossomed before such an appreciative audience. On arrival in Madrid, Andrés had been sullen and withdrawn, still grieving for his father; since then, Ramón had served to fill the gap in his affections.

It had started when Andrés had tactlessly asked him what had happened to his leg. Dolores had told him to hush, but Ramón had seized the opportunity to give the boy a brief account of the many injuries he had sustained in the course of his military career. Since then, there had been spellbinding tales of heroism and carnage, some set on the battlefield, some in the bullring, others on tall ships braving the high seas in search of the New World. Luckily Andrés's grasp of historical chronology was rudimentary, as was his notion of the human life span. Ramón had met Christopher Columbus and dined with Ferdinand and Isabella, while finding time to mastermind the Moroccan campaigns, slay innumerable *toros*, and conquer that upstart Englishman Francis Drake.

It pleased Ramón to have male company once again. Andrés was a delightfully callous little fellow, with an insatiable appetite for gore. He loved to hear of the elaborate tortures his uncle had endured rather than release information to the enemy, how he had once removed a bullet from his own thigh with red hot tongs without once crying out in pain. Ramón had the foresight to warn his young protégé that the things he told him were secret, very secret, and that he must on no account repeat them to his mother, or anyone else. This pleased the lad greatly, his chest fairly swelling with masculine pride at the confidence thus placed in him.

Today their walk back from the Retiro park took them past the Gaylord Hotel, just as Marisa emerged from her afternoon shift. Ramón hobbled forward to meet her and automatically took charge of her bag, extracting a packet of cigarettes and lighting one with trembling fingers.

''*Salud,* Andrés,'' chirped Marisa, bending down to kiss him. Marisa had a strong, sweet scent that Andrés rather liked. She smelled like the taste of boiled sweets.

Andrés greeted her politely and looked expectant. Marisa nearly always gave him something. He had all the heartless self-interest of extreme youth, as Tomás had discovered to his cost. The only thing Tomás ever gave him was the occasional ride on his shoulders, which was quite good fun, but he was no good at telling stories and for the most part Andrés found him glum and rather boring. His mother had warned him not to talk about his uncle in front of Tomás, because they did not like each other. Ramón had already explained to him that Tomás was very jealous of him, and Andrés could well understand why.

''I have some American chewing gum for you,'' said Marisa, reclaiming her bag to excavate this small treat. ''Do not swallow it, or all your insides will stick together.''

Andrés knew he ought to keep sweet things for after meals, or save them for when he was really hungry, which was an increasingly frequent occurrence. But without his mother there to admonish

him, the temptation proved too great. He was soon chewing glee-
fully, striding along with one hand in Marisa's and the other in
Ramón's, pulling them forward like a dog straining on the leash,
heedless of Ramón's limp or Marisa's high heels.

Marisa smiled indulgently. The boy's high spirits were infectious; Ramón had been less ill-humored since his nephew's arrival,
and a great deal easier to fool about money. Marisa had been quick
to realize that part of her earnings would be diverted to the impecunious Lole, of whom Ramón was inordinately fond, and she had
taken immediate steps to protect her interests. The fur jacket she
had demanded for the winter was now lined with more than silk;
pounds and dollars provided the warmest insulation of all.

Andrés was torn between a desire to prolong the outing as long
as possible, and a natural inclination toward his supper. But once
he had had his supper, Mamá would take him home, and he hated
going home. He hated sleeping in the kitchen, a dark, stuffy room
with a sloping roof and a bare floor which his mother was forever
cleaning. His mother had changed. In Toledo, she had been good-
tempered and cheerful, but here in Madrid she hardly ever laughed,
and once, to his horror, he had discovered her crying into her
apron. He had never seen her cry before. He had asked her what
was the matter, and she had wiped her eyes and said it was just a
headache. Mamá's headaches frightened him. Sometimes she had
to stop what she was doing and lie down with a wet dishcloth over
her eyes, and he would have to keep very quiet. He could never
remember his mother being ill before.

Because of the headaches, his mother no longer allowed him into
her bed. He had loved to steal into his parents' room and snuggle
in between them, especially in the winter when he woke to find his
nose cold against the sharp morning air. But now his mother's door
was locked against him, so that he could not disturb her sleep, she
said, not that it would have been the same with Tomás there.

It pained him to have to pretend that Tomás was his father. He
longed to boast to the other children that his father had been an
officer, an expert in guns, who had died a hero, who was even
braver than his uncle Ramón. But his mother had warned him that
he must on no account tell anyone his real name. This would be
very *dangerous*, she had said, and Uncle Ramón had agreed.

"Naturally, it comes hard to claim such a coarse fellow for your
father," he had said. "But your mother is right. It is your sacred
duty to suffer this indignity bravely. Often one has to remain incognito in the service of one's country." This had cheered Andrés

immensely. Uncle Ramón was the infallible oracle in a world newly full of strange lies.

When they got back, Dolores had a meal waiting for them, a concoction of tinned meat and beans, a poor imitation of *judías con chorizo,* but the nearest thing she could produce. Andrés quite enjoyed the bright pink rubbery lumps of meat, which his uncle found repellent, generously donating his share to his nephew, with a gesture of finicky distaste. Marisa likewise turned up her nose at this ad hoc meal; Ramón was right, she was getting fat, and besides, she nearly always contrived to eat at the hotel.

Dolores sat with the empty saucepan on her lap, scraping the bottom with a spoon. She took her main meal later, with Tomás, after she had put Andrés to bed. She invariably told Tomás that she had already eaten, to persuade him to accept the lion's share. He was such a big man, and she herself had little appetite these days.

"Good boy," said Dolores. "Now you can have the sweets your uncle gave you." Andrés beamed toothily at Ramón, who smiled back over the rim of his medicine glass. He had to drink a lot of medicine, on account of all his war wounds. He took a big swallow, and choked, spluttering into his handkerchief while his womenfolk patted him on the back.

"Ramón," said Dolores sharply. "There's blood on your handkerchief."

"I cut myself shaving," said Ramón, screwing it up into a ball and stuffing it back in his pocket.

"I shaved you myself," put in Marisa. "Your hand always shakes too much. I never cut you. I am always very careful."

"You should see a doctor about your cough," said Dolores.

"You should see a doctor about your headaches," countered Ramón grumpily.

"Everyone has headaches. Andrés, stop swinging your legs like that. We must go home soon. I have work to do."

"You are always working," complained Ramón, the principal beneficiary of her labors. "You have hands like a washerwoman's."

Marisa, who was now possessed of ten long, red talons, looked pityingly at Dolores's unadorned fingers. Even her wedding ring had disappeared, pawned to buy new shoes for Andrés.

"Wait," she said. "I will make your hands beautiful again."

She produced a jar of cream, a nail file, and a bottle of nail polish, and despite Dolores's protests, proceeded to give her a painstaking manicure. Her nails were a good deal shorter than Marisa's, but her fingers longer, and the final result might have been quite impressive but for the knuckles being nearly as pink as the nails.

"Really Marisa," said Dolores, half-touched, half-perplexed. "This is quite wasted on me."

"Nonsense," said Marisa generously. "You must look after your appearance. You should let Ramón arrange your hair, and use my lipstick and rouge. You may borrow any of my dresses, Lole. Why, with looks like yours, you could make a great deal of money. I could introduce you to some of my gentlemen."

"Marisa!" rapped Ramón. "What are you saying? How dare you speak to my sister in such a fashion?"

"Don't be angry, Ramón," said Dolores. "Marisa is only trying to help."

Marisa shrugged petulantly.

"If you prefer your sister to be poor, that's up to you," she said. "I don't have to share my clients with anyone."

"Thank you, Marisa,' said Dolores. "I appreciate the offer. But I am quite happy with my job at the school."

Ramón grunted.

"Now they have chased the priests and nuns away, they have to pay others to do what they did for nothing. Pah! No wonder they need to steal from honest citizens to be able to squander money in such a fashion!"

Dolores let this remark pass. A recent presidential decree had confiscated the property of all those who had taken part in the insurrection, making a Fascist victory essential to Ramón's unquashable hopes of inheritance. Josep was probably dead by now, he declared, with a poor pretense at regret. He had no doubt paid the price of his folly in courting the affection of heathens. Dolores knew only that Josep's parish had fallen to the Fascists, and had hoped this meant that he was safe—far safer than he would be in the Republic. Always assuming that he had had the prudence to keep his politics to himself . . .

After the news of Lorenzo's death, Dolores had lost all heart for the struggle. She no longer cared who won, she just wanted the war to be over quickly. There was too much wickedness on both sides; both sides were like sharks with ever-open jaws, blindly trawling for innocent prey to assuage their voracious greed.

Every day Tomás reported to militia headquarters for training, and returned full of tales of injustice and dirty dealing. He had not been impressed by his new Russian rifle—not that it was truly Russian, any more than it was new. It was Swiss, a good fifty years old, and a very inferior specimen to that being issued to Communist battalions, so Tomás said. He was itching to be sent to the front, but had to be content to wait for the front to come to him. The front was getting closer every minute, and preparations were already being made for house-to-house defense of the city. Barricades were being erected all over Madrid, although no trenches had yet been dug, due to a work-to-rule by the builders' union.

Dolores had enrolled Andrés at a local school; many had already closed due to the mass evacuation of pupils to the country. But Dolores had been reluctant to send her son away. Her long exile, and Lorenzo's death, had left both mother and child with a morbid fear of separation; she was torn between guilt that she was exposing her son to danger and a stubborn determination not to let him out of her sight, ever again.

To this end, she had applied for part-time work as a teaching aide—a lowly job, but she had not wanted to admit her level of education, fearful of provoking awkward questions. She supervised recreation periods, gathered up exercise books, inspected heads for lice, rang bells, and acted as a general factotum. In recent weeks she had become friendly with Paulina Quero, a Spanish Communist who had been given responsibility for reorganizing the curriculum, following the rout of the religious order who had formerly run the school. Paulina was a great admirer of all things Soviet. She despaired of the Spanish temperament, she said. The advent of Russian military discipline was the only hope for a Republican victory.

''These headaches of yours are very bad, are they not?'' she had said kindly, when Dolores had been obliged to lie down; the next day she had handed her some painkillers.

''I have a comrade working in a dispensary,'' she had said. And then, lightly, ''Would you like to join the party, perhaps? I would be happy to instruct you in our beliefs, if you so wish.''

Her missionary zeal was both ingenuous and sinister. But already it seemed to Dolores that Paulina might be a valuable ally. No doubt she had comrades working in all sorts of useful places.

''Thank you,'' said Dolores. ''I am very ignorant about politics. I would welcome the chance to learn more about communism.''

Every day she became more aware of the precariousness of her position. With the enemy at the gates of Madrid, the witch-hunt for anyone with Fascist connections had reached fever pitch. Her identity as the common-law wife of Tomás García had so far sufficed for the purposes of day-to-day living, but it would not stand up to official scrutiny, if she were ever unfortunate enough to attract it.

Suppose, through some unguarded remark, Andrés revealed their guilty secret? It was one of the reasons she had feared to send him away, to live among strangers. Only yesterday Dolores had switched on her brother's radio, and heard a female politician making an impassioned and inflammatory speech.

"We must identify the families of all known Fascists!" she declared to the accompaniment of the "Internationale." "We must arrest and imprison the wives and children of all those who have plunged Spain into a bath of blood!"

Dolores had felt a shiver up her back. The erstwhile defenders of the Alcázar presumably topped the list of enemies of the Republic.

"The life of every volunteer for the front," continued the speaker rousingly, "must be underwritten by that of the mother or child of a traitor!"

Andrés would undoubtedly be viewed as the child of a traitor. Once again, she felt immeasurably grateful to Tomás. Tomás, who had saved her life and still risked his own in shielding her, who bore her no ill will for her unwitting crime against the people, who tolerated her continuing association with the brother he had just cause to hate, who had no idea that she had robbed him of his wife, that her thoughts strayed to another man every time he made love to her . . .

Poor Tomás. She would make it up to him somehow. One day she would repay him for all his goodness.

"You're just tired, Jack," said Harry Martindale, tipping a generous measure of Glenfiddich into a crystal tumbler. He stretched back in his leather armchair, making it creak slightly under his patrician bulk. Jack stood with his back to him, gazing out of the wide high windows onto the molting trees of Hampstead Heath.

"By all means take some time off, as much as you need. No need to do anything drastic . . ."

He tinkled the ice in the glass as if to attract Jack's wandering attention. "Have a drink and we'll talk it through."

"No thanks. My mind's made up, Harry. From now on I'm on my own. Free-lance, independent, self-employed, whatever you want to call it. I write what I like, when I like, or not at all. And having written it, I submit it to whatever publisher I think will be inte: ested in printing it. Don't take it personally."

'Jack, you're not being fair. How often do I meddle with what you write? Haven't I always—well, nearly always—given you a free hand? Have you ever met another journalist who's had the free rein to write the way you've been allowed to do? I mean to say, that's the way you've built up your reputation, isn't it? *Our* reputation. That's what *Red Rag*'s all about.''

''Precisely. I'm tired of writing in a straitjacket.''

''Straitjacket? That's a most unjustified accusation, Jack. You've always had the broadest possible brief to—''

''I'm not accusing you of anything. I take full responsibility for the hole I've dug myself into. I blame myself, not you. I'll work out my notice, of course. I assume you want me to go back to Spain? The next month should be pretty good copy, a chance to boost circulation before I go. I saw a breadline blown to pieces the day before I left. Bits of dead baby scattered all over the street. But of course, blood-and-guts isn't really my style, as you know. *The Daily Worker*'s rather cornered the market on that.''

''For God's sake, Jack, you don't have to be ashamed to admit you've had enough. I'd feel pretty shattered myself, I daresay, if I'd seen some of the things you've seen. You need a break. Don't go back. I can send someone else or use a news agency. Have a month off. As far as I'm concerned, your Spanish tour is over.''

''No it isn't,'' muttered Jack, as if to himself. ''It's only just begun.''

Martindale blinked rapidly, his fleshy eyelids quivering at the unaccustomed activity.

''I refuse to regard this as final, Jack. You're overwrought, played out. It happens to the most experienced of journalists. I know how sickened you must feel, what with beating your head against a brick wall all this time, but things are beginning to move at last, and you've done your share in making that happen. Now that Labour has formally voted to reject nonintervention, the tide of public opinion is bound to turn. There's been the most tremendous response to all these fund-raising appeals, you know, despite all the pro-Fascist propaganda in the popular press. And now, with the International Brigades, ordinary working people are going to have a personal stake in the struggle, they're going to have sons and sweethearts out there in Spain, fighting in the cause of democracy.''

Jack gave a harsh bark of laughter.

''You're breaking my heart, Harry. Anyone would think you'd been taking my dispatches seriously. You know as well as I do that huge amounts of bona fide donations will be mysteriously diverted to political ends, that the poor saps joining up for the International

Brigades are the victims of a massive Communist confidence trick. Democracy is the most abused word in the dictionary, an infinitely adaptable rallying cry to sanctify whatever dirty deeds are carried out in its name."

"I most certainly don't know any such thing. Good Lord, Jack, anyone would think you were a Fascist sympathizer!"

Jack leaned over Harry menacingly and banged his fist down on the mahogany table, making the whiskey jump out of the glass.

"You see? Dare, just dare, to tell it like it is, and someone will immediately call you a Fascist sympathizer. The chap who discovered the earth was round was accused of being an atheist, wasn't he? Well, you can call me a Fascist till you're blue in the face, but I'm through with writing flat-earth copy about this bloody war."

"And who will you be sending your dispatches to in future?" countered Martindale, rattled now. "The *Daily Express,* perhaps? Perhaps you should base yourself at Fascist headquarters in Burgos, not Madrid. They will make you very welcome there, no doubt . . . er . . . I'm sorry, Jack. I didn't mean that."

He retreated into the depths of his armchair in something like physical fear. The expression on Jack's face was murderous.

"I doubt if the *Daily Express* would be interested in printing the truth, any more than you would."

"Then who will, pray?"

"If I start worrying about that, I won't be able to write anything at all, will I?"

"But . . . but what about money?"

"I was hoping you'd mention that. You owe me quite a lot of it. Perhaps we could settle up before I go back tomorrow. A little goes a long way in Spain."

He produced a typewritten sheet from his inside pocket setting out in minute detail the sum due to him. Harry accepted it between finger and thumb, appalled at Jack's bad form. He had always been dilatory about his debts, a facet of his immaculate breeding.

"I'll send you a check," he acknowledged stiffly.

"I'll take it with me now, thanks," said Jack, handing him a pen.

Martindale made a gesture of truce. He had no wish to part on bad terms, and perhaps find himself vilified in print at some future date. He saw Jack out himself, with fulsome admonitions to keep in touch, calmer now, and beginning to see the light. Something had happened to Jack in Spain, something personal, not professional, something that would no doubt work its way out of his system, given time. All this sudden ranting about truth rang hollow. Jack had never had any pretentions to integrity, his guiding lights had always been political expediency, unabashed prejudice, and cold-blooded ambition. Truth telling was for prophets, a lonely, unpopular, impecunious breed who invariably ended up in the wilderness and were never proved right till they were dead. There was nothing of the mystic or the idealist in Jack: he was a born pragmatist, a natural survivor. Yes, he had got himself into some emotional entanglement or other, fallen in love with some Spanish woman and seen her die needlessly, something of that order. And now he was feeling too involved to take the long view anymore.

He would get over it, given time. They had had professional disagreements before, when Jack had gone over the top on some pet hobbyhorse that just wasn't right for *Rag*, but he had invariably capitulated, albeit with a bad grace, on the grounds that he didn't give a damn either way. Jack was loath to admit that he *cared* about anything, and Martindale had exploited this weakness ruthlessly. This was only a phase, it would pass. It was simply not in Jack's nature to care about anything but himself.

Jack hailed a taxi and told the driver to take him to Pimlico. He had returned at short notice with no luggage, and had been planning to return to Madrid next day. But suddenly the thought of that empty flat, that former haven of solitude, seemed intolerable, and without alighting he redirected the driver to Whitechapel.

He had meant to avoid Edmund altogether. His last letter had made depressing reading. It had come as no surprise to know that Clara had taken her dubious nursing skills to Spain, and to know that Edmund was worried sick about her. What had come as a surprise was that he had not tagged along, if only to keep an eye on her. Or perhaps it wasn't so surprising, perhaps he had seen it as the best way of making sure she went to pieces quickly and got sent home. She was totally dependent on him, despite her attempts to prove otherwise, and lacking Edmund she would seek support wherever she could find it, probably in the nearest bottle. There was a shortage of everything in Spain except alcoholic beverages of the crudest and most corrosive kind. It might reassure Edmund if he offered to take a trip out to the Aragon front to see how she was coping. The prospect filled him with gloom, but it might at least provide material for his book.

Jack had come to the uncertain conclusion that fiction was a sounder medium for truth than so-called fact, but he had no intention of telling anyone about his book until it was finished, least of all Edmund, with his dauntingly highbrow literary tastes. Writing a novel was a pretentious enough business without talking about it in advance.

He could see the light burning in the hall of the little house. Edmund was headmaster now of a school that had improved beyond all recognition. Jack had obliged him early on in his career by writing a scathing piece against the newly imposed means test, which had succeeded in preventing some of Edmund's best pupils from taking up grammar school places. The brightest children, in Edmund's view, were rarely the poorest; they were invariably the ones who were not quite poor enough.

Jack rapped loudly on the door, which was opened instantaneously. No doubt Edmund lived in fear of the telegraph boy. His delight was unfeigned, and filled Jack with shame for so nearly not coming.

He produced a bottle of dusty claret and asked if Jack had dined, and only then did Jack realize that he had hardly eaten all day. He couldn't face going out to a restaurant, and settled instead for toasted cheese and some of Mrs. Townsend's sticky gingerbread, telling Edmund between mouthfuls of his interview with Martindale.

"Well then," said Edmund at length. "Good for you."

"Are you just being a loyal friend or do you mean it? Professionally, it's madness. Harry will probably put the word about that I cracked up on the job, or worse. He virtually accused me of being a closet Fascist."

"Oh, join the club, old man. You're no one till you've been called a Fascist, closet or otherwise. Is money going to be a problem?"

"Not for a year or so. I never could get used to spending the stuff. I've got plenty of things I can sell, if times get hard. Elizabeth gave me a gold watch last Christmas. And in a pinch I can always find some woman to subsidize me."

Edmund's expression did not flicker. Every so often, Jack couldn't resist making some crass remark of this sort, to test him out. But if Edmund knew, he never let it show.

"I asked my father about getting Dolly's little boy out of the country," he said. "He seemed to think the idea was fanciful. But I was thinking if I could convince the Spanish authorities that I was the next of kin . . . "

"Forget it, Edmund. I'm sure I would have heard from the girl by now if she'd reached Madrid. She had my card, and would have contacted me for money, if nothing else. The Fascists have a charming habit of machine-gunning refugees from the air. Let's just assume she's dead, shall we, and the child with her. What's a couple more deaths after all?''

He pushed aside his plate.

"Sorry," he said. "I had a big lunch."

Momentarily Jack lost control of his features. He looked, and sounded, so far removed from his normal nonchalant self that Edmund's first instinct was to divert the crisis, to spare Jack the intolerable shame of self-revelation. Jack was not one to share his troubles; if he encouraged him to do so now, he would have to bear the brunt of his subsequent resentment. And so, like a true friend, he changed the subject, using his own problems to make Jack feel strong again. While Edmund brewed coffee he told Jack, with perfect composure and without comment, what Tessa had said, and waited for his reaction.

"Don't go," said Jack simply, lighting a cigarette, back to his old, hard-bitten self. "You won't be able to persuade her to come home; you'll almost certainly do more harm than good. She can't keep bumping off the patients without them catching her sooner or later. Then they'll just put it down to stress and hush it up pronto and find some important administrative work for her to do at home. Let things take their natural course. As you pointed out, if she were a man, they'd give her a gun and a few grenades and let her kill as many Fascists as she pleased."

Edmund shook his head.

"That's what I said to Tessa. I'm afraid her mealymouthed manner rather brought out the worst in me. But it won't wash, Jack. As you know, I don't approve of killing in any context. If I don't try to do something, then any subsequent deaths will be on my conscience. God knows, I feel enough of a moral outcast as it is these days, without betraying what few principles I have left."

"You can't go rushing out there in the middle of the term. You've got a job."

"So had you, until today."

"That's completely different."

"No, it's not. It's to do with self-respect, for both of us, isn't it? It's to do with facing facts and not hiding behind idealism or cynicism, which are two sides of the same coin, ways of keeping real life at bay. Listen. One of my class of 1928 has just gone up to Cambridge to read chemistry. The parents are very proud of him. They keep a fish-and-chips shop that I daren't patronize because they won't let me pay for anything. Anyway, the mother stopped me in the street the other day, quite tearful, because young John is determined to leave college to go and fight in Spain. And because I spoke once or twice at Clara's Aid for Spain functions, the poor woman seemed to think I was in some way part of the conspiracy. She kept asking me *why* and *what good would it do,* and of course there was absolutely nothing I could say. God only knows what pressure Clara's under out there, but I can't help feeling that if I turn a blind eye to what she's doing, I'm indirectly every bit as responsible as whoever robs that mother of her son. A life's a life, no matter whose it is. That's what I've always believed.''

"It does matter whose life it is," said Jack unequivocally. "Don't kid yourself. The Comintern know it, even if you don't. Foreigners' lives don't count for much, they never have. Nothing like a few homegrown corpses for making people care. Hence the big recruiting drive. Don't fall for it, will you?''

"Don't worry, they wouldn't have me. I'm not politically sound."

"Thank God for that," said Jack. "So, when are we off?''

At Dolores's insistence, Tomás continued the thankless task of seeking news of Rosa. All his inquiries so far had proved inconclusive. Refugees were streaming constantly into Madrid, living in squalid and over-crowded conditions, and there were not sufficient resources to keep adequate records of their identities or whereabouts. Without the proceeds from Dolores's mother's rings, they themselves would have been in some communal shelter, herded together with innumerable others, awaiting their allocation. The money they had willingly paid for preferential treatment would, they had been assured, swell the union coffers for the ultimate common good, but Tomás had not needed to believe this to take advantage of the opportunity. The privacy had seemed cheap at the price, especially now that the strain of recent events was beginning to take its toll of Lole's health.

It pained him to see her grow thin, and her headaches frightened him. But selfishly, he was more concerned about the other symptom of physical malaise, the placid, cooperative frigidity with which she allowed him to make love to her. Her husband possessed her more in death than he had done in life, and had become the most invincible of rivals, one whom he could not see and could not kill.

To his shame, he could not respect her grief. He wanted her more and more, and could not control his wanting, exploiting her reluctance to refuse him, a reluctance rooted in fear. He knew her dreadful secret, he had it in his power to denounce her, denounce her brother, denounce her precious son. And so she would never refuse him anything, which made nothing she gave worth having.

Sometimes he would brood far into the night, while she slept fitfully beside him, imagining that she was hoping for his death in action, that she found him repulsive, that her gentleness and patience and kindness were merely to placate, not please him. A more articulate man might have put such thoughts into words; a more aggressive man might have found release in anger, but Tomás was denied such relief. He harked back to the long, hard week on the road to Toledo, when all things had seemed possible. He had wished her husband dead, and now he was, and part of Lole with him. This did not prevent him from wishing the brother dead too, and even, at times, the boy, a curious child who displayed scant regard for him, who openly preferred the company of his drunken uncle and the whore who bought his love with her ill-gotten gains. He had tried to forbid Dolores to associate with them, but the calm, quiet, puzzled look in her eye had shamed him.

"My brother is sick, Tomás. And Marisa is generous to Andrés. Try to understand."

It was she who retained all the power; he could deny her nothing. He would have died rather than betray her, even though he gave her no such reassurances, given that the possibility of betrayal was unacknowledged and taboo. He would have traded that one life against the whole Republic.

He wondered what excuse she would use if he were to ask her to marry him, an ambition that tormented him daily. She would say that it was too soon after her husband's death, no doubt. Marriage was now an informal affair, a public exchange of intent, not a commercial transaction supervised by some whining priest. It was regarded by revolutionaries as unnecessary, but allowable, a token of mutual fidelity and, from a practical point of view, it made the status of widow and orphan easier to classify. As Fascist troops reached the gates of the city, marriage was becoming fashionable again.

Soon Madrid would stand or fall, and the Republic with it. If Madrid fell, he would either die defending it, or be taken prisoner, or be forced to flee. If Madrid fell, Lole would be quick to reclaim her status as widow of a Fascist officer, anxious to buy her life and that of her son. His sister's words rang in his ears. *Do not be deceived, Tomás . . . she will use you, as I would, as any mother would in her place . . .* And yet that much he could bear. What he could not bear was to cease to be of use, to be discarded as no longer useful. It followed, therefore, that he must not be taken prisoner, he must not flee. If the city fell, he must fall with it, he must die fighting because afterward there would be nothing left to live for . . .

If, on the other hand, the city did not fall, if the Fascists were beaten back, then surely Lole would need him more than ever. Already a frantic witch-hunt was in progress, seeking out the notorious "Fifth Column," the network of spies and rebel sympathizers who were lurking everywhere, infiltrating the unions, the militia and even, it was rumored, the government itself. The fate of these traitors would be grim indeed. If their allies failed to come to the rescue soon, anyone with Fascist connections, innocent or not, would doubtless share that fate. Lole must surely live in fear of her brother's drunken indiscretions, of Marisa's sheer stupidity, of a knock on the door from a *checa* investigator alerted to her true identity. Already a nod was enough to have an enemy condemned, and Tomás had been sorely tempted to goad Ramón—who was careful what he said in his presence—into some ill-judged remark, and thus take revenge for poor Rosa at last. But he could never have borne the reproach in Lole's eyes, and besides, the wretch would hopefully soon be dead without human intervention.

No, he could not ask Lole to marry him now, while the battle was still undecided. Defeat and death went hand in hand; only victory could give him life, assure his prize, make Lole his wife in name as well as in deed, linking her fate inextricably with his, wiping out the specter of the past. Victory would give him back his power and make him strong again. Victory would transform him from fugitive to hero, as much of a hero as her husband. What match was a dead hero for a living, loving one?

Ramón spread out the crumpled leaflet that served as a marker for his tattered notebook. He had picked it up in the street in late August, one of a consignment dropped by nationalist planes.

"*¡Madrileños!*" it read. "The army of liberation is at the gates of your noble city! Prepare to welcome us in triumph and celebrate our glorious victory against the Reds! *¡Arriba España!*"

And now, two interminable months later, the promise was at last to be fulfilled.

He hoped it would not be much longer, for his time was surely running out. His constant fear was that the grim reaper would summon him before the hour of triumph and deny him his longed-for moment of glory. How he had been looking forward to that moment when the *caudillo* himself would pin a medal to his chest and hand him back the keys to his kingdom? What plans he had for little Andrés, for Marisa, for Dolores, poor, ruined, ravaged Dolores, her feeble body plundered nightly by a beast of the fields! Without him, what would become of them all? How would Dolores be able to prove her innocence if he was not there to vouch for her? How appalling if she and Andrés were falsely condemned as the wife and child of a Red! And what of Marisa? The girl was totally helpless without his protection and guidance . . .

Ramón's fictional entries in his journal had started as an escape from reality; they had long since become the only reality. His notebook was proof positive that Dolores and Andrés were merely García's prisoners, that Marisa had been acting loyally under his instructions, extracting valuable secrets from the enemy. His notebook was their passport to freedom, one that would carry his voice beyond the grave. What a tragedy it would be if it was buried with him! Please God he would live a few weeks longer, and yet he knew he could be struck down at any moment, he knew he ought to prepare for the worst. But to whom could he bequeath his one, priceless asset?

He had always ruled out the possibility of confiding in Marisa. She was a lazy, forgetful, scatterbrained creature, who required constant supervision, and lacked the intellect required for such a sacred trust. It would have to be Dolores. Dolores had always been a bright child, and she would be eager to act on any information that might safeguard her child's future. The only problem with Dolores was García. Unaccountably, his sister refused to hear a word against the fellow. When he had turned on her for selling herself to such a man, her eyes had flashed angrily and she had defended him in extravagant terms, saying that he had saved her life and that she could never repay him for all he had done. Such sentiments were founded in pitiful delusion, but there was no telling her, she was as stubborn and unpredictable as ever. No, on reflection he could not trust Dolores. It could well be that García had her in some perverted sexual thrall—she had always been a slave to her passions—and who knew what she might reveal to him in the aftermath of lust?

He pondered his problem unceasingly, coughing morbidly into his handkerchief and inspecting the phlegm for portents of death. If only there were a man he could pass the torch to, instead of two helpless, feckless women. If only little Andrés were a few years older!

Sighing, he stuffed his treasure back into his boot. There was very little room left, appropriately enough, in view of his imminent demise. As he replaced the insole, the sirens began to wail again, and he quickly lifted the loose floorboard to retrieve his gun before extinguishing the light.

He no longer felt fear when the bombs dropped. Better to die by a bomb than from this vile, invasive malady that leeched the strength from his body. He released the revolver's safety catch, opened the window, and parted the shutters just enough to poke the barrel through.

Breathless, he waited, his trigger finger twitching with anticipation, his eyes blinking into the blackness, flooded with a blind sense of power. If the bombs dropped near enough, he would release a couple of bullets into the void, the noise of the shot drowned in the general din. Then next day he would take a stroll to view the damage, taking a personal pride in every casualty, imagining that his bullets had done their noble share, looking forward to entering his latest victims in his ledger. He hoped his chance would come again tonight, so that he might record his feat. "Two more enemies of Spain dead by my hand. ¡Arriba España!" He had, by his own reckoning, disposed of more than twenty such vermin since the bombing started, catching them on the run as they scuttled like rats into their holes.

But tonight he was cruelly thwarted. The sounds of the explosions were too far distant to give him adequate cover; to risk discovery would be a folly, given the important work he had still to do. Disconsolate, he reburied his treasure as the all-clear sounded, and hoped for better luck next day.

Next day found him too ill to move. Marisa returned from the hotel to find him delirious, his forehead burning, his extremities ice-cold. She set to work immediately, lifting him bodily from the bed—he weighed less and less these days—stripping off his damp clothes, and wrapping him in her fur jacket. She rubbed his hands and feet to warm them, and tied a damp rag around his head. He babbled constantly, incoherently.

"My boot," he muttered. "My boot!"

Puzzled, Marisa put it on his foot, hoping that this would somehow comfort him, but he kicked it off in his frenzy and began coughing violently.

Marisa was afraid. He seemed much sicker than usual, and the bottle of fine Russian vodka she had brought him yesterday was still half full, indicating that he had been too weak to finish it. She draped the bed with clean linen, laundered by Lole, and laid him down again, quickly removing her outer garments and getting in beside him, cradling him in her arms.

She wedged his head against her breast and began crooning to him like a baby, while he coughed fitfully, each new spasm sending feeble shudders through his body. The room was bitterly cold, but Marisa had excellent circulation, and after a while, his limbs absorbed her warmth, and the coughing subsided. Marisa joined him in a peaceful sleep, waking at noon to find his fever gone and his breathing normal again. Only when she rose and caught sight of herself in the mirror did she notice that her right breast was streaked with dried blood.

While she boiled water for coffee on the stove she pondered what she should do. Ramón had always decried doctors as cheats and liars, and she dared not provoke another rage by suggesting he submit to one now, for fear of bringing on another attack. In all the months she had known Ramón he had claimed to be at death's door. "I am a dying man, Marisa," he had told her, that very first day, and she had had no reason to disbelieve him. But like any oft-repeated truth, it had ceased to have the slightest impact, it had become as empty as the threat of hell. And now the devil had finally shown himself, striking terror into the heart of the unbeliever.

Perhaps Lole could succeed where she would fail. Ramón set great store by Lole's good opinion, and never lost his temper with her, however much she scolded. Marisa had resented this at first, but had quickly learned the value of using her sister-in-law as a buffer, and thus deflecting his bouts of ill humor away from herself.

She extinguished the stove, leaving the coffee unmade, dressed quickly and walked the dozen blocks to Lole's apartment. Too bad if Tomás was there, her business would not wait. But luckily Tomás was out, building barricades.

"*Salud*, Marisa," said Dolores, smiling, her face involuntarily betraying disappointment as she saw that her visitor was empty-handed. She had just spent two hours standing in line for their rations—a Russian ship had recently unloaded fresh supplies at Valencia—only to find that most of the food had already been claimed by the militia. All she had to show for her pains were two tins of sardines and half a pound of lentils, with the prospect of another long wait tomorrow. Other women had complained angrily that the militia threw away huge amounts of bread each day while children went hungry, and she could only hope that once Tomás saw active service he might at least get enough to eat.

"Is something wrong?" said Dolores. It was rather early in the day for Marisa to be up and about. "It is Ramón?"

Her tone was anxious, but calm, as befits one who had grown inured to bad news. Marisa unbuttoned her dress and displayed the stained camisole.

"He coughed on me in the night. To cough blood is very bad. And remember the handkerchief. I have never cut him while I shaved him. I am frightened. I come to you as a sister, Lole, to make him see a doctor."

Dolores felt sorry for Marisa. For all that she was stupid and shallow, she seemed genuinely fond of Ramón, and no doubt would miss him when he was gone, as indeed Andrés would. She herself no longer felt such sentimental attachment. It pained her to see the depths to which he had sunk, the galloping physical decay that had consumed him, the rotting of his once sharp-witted brain into paranoia and megalomania. But she found it difficult to care, other than by deed. She could wash for him and clean for him and look after him, but she had no feelings left to spare; she was curiously numb these days about everyone and everything, except Andrés.

She shrugged.

"What can a doctor do for him, except make him more afraid? Let him die his own way, Marisa, in his own time. All the good doctors are needed for the front. Why waste your time?"

Marisa was affronted at this callous response.

"How can you be so cruel?" she demanded. "Do you not love him, as I do?"

"I love him, but not as you do, Marisa. How could I love him as much as you?"

Marisa sat down to digest this dubious compliment. Unexpectedly, she began crying, as suddenly and as artlessly as a baby.

"But what will become of *me*, if Ramón dies?" she sobbed, going straight to the point.

"You are young, and very pretty. You will soon find someone else to care for you."

"Pah!" snorted Marisa through her sobs. "You mean a man. What good are men to me without Ramón?"

Edmund was granted two weeks' leave of absence, saying that his fiancée had been taken ill in Spain and he was going to bring her home. He had had to endure an embarrassing level of sympathy, which spurred him to redeem the lie, even though his lack of confidence in success was obvious to Jack, if to no one else. He insisted on putting his affairs in order and making a will before he left, a precaution that struck Jack as morbid but significant. Edmund would come home with Clara, or not at all, and not at all might come to mean just that, literally, even for a visiting civilian.

They traveled for the most part in silence, while Edmund read Trollope through steel-rimmed spectacles and Jack endured the amoebic writhings of his novel, knowing that perhaps he should suppress it now, before it subdivided, that perhaps the growth would prove malignant and ultimately destroy its host. It would be an unfashionable book, a bloody-minded book, a book without a hero. A hero was allowed one fatal flaw, but only one. A fool was not one's idea of a hero. Why should he want to write about a fool? And why should anybody want to read about one?

Perhaps he was wrong to blame it all on Dolly. Perhaps she had only been a catalyst, sparking his real self into life, the dormant, despised self he had thought to supplant long ago, the Jack only she had ever seen, the Jack that suffered, the Jack that scared him. Since his showdown with Martindale, he had felt sticky-winged, disoriented, missing the earthbound safety of the chrysalis, knowing he had embraced a kind of death. What did a moth feel in that suicidal dance around the candle flame? Ecstasy or despair? Perhaps there wasn't any difference.

They traveled overnight from Paris, Edmund retiring early to his sleeping berth while Jack made his way to the third-class compartment. There were bound to be a few volunteers aboard—passportless "day-trippers" to Dunkirk who had inadvertently lost their way and been misdirected to Perpignan, there to be met by darkened buses bound for the Pyrénées. By now they would have had time to discover the restorative powers of cheap French wine, and might, with luck, prove talkative.

The animated conversation in the carriage ceased abruptly as Jack put his head around the door. Volunteers had it drilled into them not to associate openly on the journey for fear of attracting suspicion, although the precaution was quite superfluous at this stage of the trip. The last thing the French authorities wanted was the trouble and expense of deporting foreigners without documentation, who would shortly be leaving the country anyway. So they took "nonintervention" literally, and did not intervene. Still, the subterfuge no doubt added to the adventure.

There was one spare seat in the compartment. Jack sat down in it.

"Excusez-moi," said one of the men, in an atrocious Oxbridge accent. *"Cette siège est déjà prise."*

"Hope your Spanish is better than your French, chum," said Jack, producing a half bottle of scotch from his inside pocket. "Here's to the Republic, eh?" He took a swallow and passed the bottle to the next man, an ill-dressed, thin, pasty young lad who would have failed any army medical worthy of the name.

"Cheers!" he said, taking an enthusiastic swig.

"Who said anything about going to Spain?" said the college type, affecting confusion.

"Come off it, man," jeered a stocky Welshman, reaching for the bottle. "Death to all bloody Fascists." He tipped the bottle back and smacked his lips. "I won't half be ready for a square meal by the time we get there. You a volunteer?"

"No," said Jack. "I'm a jour—that is, I'm a writer. I wanted to ask you why you're going to Spain."

"That's a jolly silly question," put in the egghead, discarding his cloak and dagger. "Why, to fight for democracy of course, what else?"

"You intellectuals make me die, honest you do," resumed Taff. "Don't start him off," he begged Jack. "He's been educating our minds ever since bloody Paris."

"So why are *you* going to Spain?" said Jack.

"Because I'm a workingman, see? Not like him. *He* thinks it's going to be a jolly good lark, what?"

A chorus of raucous laughter greeted this remark. The poor chap was probably a poet, and Jack could only hope he had the good sense not to admit it in present company.

"Don't you worry about getting killed?" said Jack casually, handing around cigarettes. "The Republic's taken quite a hammering so far, by all accounts."

The assembled company treated this question with the contempt it deserved. Getting killed happened to other people.

"I'll say," came a voice from the corridor. "But it's better than dying on the dole. You've got my seat, mate."

Jack turned around and momentarily lost his composure before standing up and holding out his hand.

"Jack!" said Billie Grant. "Fancy meeting you here. Last time I saw you was down the Embankment. Christmastime, weren't it? Must be five, six year ago!" He wrung his hand energetically.

"Billie!" said Jack, forcing a smile. "Good to see you."

"Lads, meet my old mate Jack Austin," boomed Billie expansively, swaying slightly on his feet, and not just with the movement of the train. "Jack writes for *Red Rag*. Doing a piece on us, are you, Jack? *You're* not daft enough to volunteer, I'll bet."

"*Red Rag?*" echoed the poet politely, cocktail party style. The Welshman glowered.

"That piece of Trotskyite garbage," he spat. "Full of bloody lies, it is."

"Almost as many lies as *The Daily Worker*," agreed Jack blandly, "but not half so boring, wouldn't you agree?"

"Here," interjected Billie, towering over the diminutive Welshman and seizing him by the scruff of the neck, "you calling my mate a liar?"

Taff responded to the assault by delivering a hefty blow to Billie's midriff, winding him. Jack caught him as he tottered backward.

"Leave off," said Jack to the assailant. "He's had too much to drink. If you want a fight, you can have one with me. But perhaps you'd better save your energy for the Fascists. You're going to need it, believe me."

The poet sprang to his feet and helped transport the semiconscious Billie to Jack's sleeping compartment.

"Bit of a rough customer, our Mr. Evans," commented his ally, genially. "Takes all sorts. Personally, I rather enjoy *Rag*. All this Stalin worship gets a bit wearisome, doesn't it?"

"I shouldn't say that in Spain if I were you," said Jack. "Your commissar won't like it."

"My what?" said the poet.

PART THREE
APRIL–JUNE
1937

12

APRIL 1937

Josep had been hard put to hide his elation when the northern offensive had at last begun, when his youth and strength and eagerness to volunteer had given him a sudden, long-awaited advantage over native Basque priests who were older, frailer, or less willing. It no longer mattered, for the moment, that he was a foreigner. He was one of eighty-two Basque chaplains, unique in the Republican army, and viewed with undisguised hostility by the anarchist battalions from neighboring Asturias who were now their reluctant comrades.

War had come suddenly to the province of Vizcaya. Thwarted by the successful defense of Madrid and the Republican victory at Guadalajara, the Fascists had switched their offensive abruptly northward, with the objective of capturing the armaments factories in Bilbao and the vast local reserves of iron and steel, as well as cutting off the Basque border with France. A surrender had been demanded and refused; a small town called Durango had immediately been bombed flat by German airplanes, killing over two hundred civilians, plunging the insular Basques into a state of horror and disbelief.

But there had been no surrender. Josep had seized the chance to offer his services, and had been accepted. It had been a blessed relief to do something at last, something that left no time for morbid self-indulgence, no time to brood about the past, no time to think.

For three weeks now he had been in the thick of the fighting, three weeks that made the last seven years seem trivial. He had administered extreme unction to men in their death throes, hearing them curse and blaspheme in agony, crawling on his belly across no-man's-land to utter that final blessing, flirting with death, tempting it, daring it to touch him, because he was half in love with it, because it made him feel alive.

Danger created a unique, protective capsule of its own, shutting out the world, concentrating every ounce of energy he possessed, giving him a purpose, making him whole, transmuting fear into strength. Under fire he remained calm and detached, displaying a suicidal courage; only when he slept did his iron nerve desert him. The days were a blessed respite from the nights, when the anesthesia of constant activity wore off and the gnawing pain drove deep into his soul, the pain of incalculable waste and inescapable defeat. In his sleep he would reenact the horrors of the day, would twitch and sweat and tremble. His dreams were nightmares of torn flesh, of bodies jerking and writhing like netted fish, of senseless, wanton slaughter. He would wake in terror, screaming one word. *Dolores*.

Every day he saw brave young men condemned to death by their dithering, squabbling officers, by the inertia of far-off generals, by internal strife and poor training and inadequate equipment and collective fear that burst open, like an expanding bullet, into wholesale panic. Only a day ago two anarchist battalions had decamped on their own initiative, leaving their Basque comrades outnumbered and unsupported. For the first time Josep had been tempted to take up a dead man's weapon and join the fight himself, to unleash the surge of anger that momentarily overpowered him. Just in time he had realized that his fury would be misdirected. Why punish the enemy for the perfidy of a so-called friend?

"Salud, camarada," said Paulina, embracing Dolores as she emerged from her afternoon class. Discreetly, she slipped a small vial into the pocket of her colleague's pinafore.

Dolores returned the greeting, her fingers closing around the precious object, feeling the familiar stab of hypocrisy. But she suppressed it easily enough. Black-market food, or Red-market drugs, what was the difference? She had leaned to exploit Paulina as ruthlessly as she did Marisa.

Dolores waited in the corridor for her son, and wrestled with the eternal problem of allocating resources. The pills the doctor had prescribed for Ramón were woefully ineffective. Medical supplies were insufficient for the needs of the front, and civilians were well down in the pecking order. Her first duty was to Tomás, now her husband, but Ramón was still her brother, and she owed Marisa something.

She knew only too well from her own experience what Marisa

had to endure. Ramón's savage outbursts and screams of agony
were histrionic as always, but his illnesses were real enough—not
just the syphilis, but the diseased liver, and the wasted lungs. His
continuing survival had amazed everyone; being an invalid all his
life had given him a peculiar resistance to death. Yes, Marisa deserved some recompense. Tomás would never have got his strength
back after losing his leg in the battle for Madrid without the regular,
nourishing food she had so generously shared, even though she
could have sold it at a huge profit.

"I have plenty else to sell," she would say, with a *grande dame*
shrug. "Take it."

Of course, Marisa meant such gifts for Andrés and herself, and
again Dolores felt like a traitress when she robbed her son to feed
her husband, or robbed her husband to ease her brother's pain. She
would never have dreamed of asking Paulina for narcotics, unaware
that such commodities could be procured, but when her colleague
had heard about Tomás losing his leg, she had acted on her own
initiative and spoken to a comrade working in one of the military
pharmacies. Paulina knew that Tomás was a socialist, of course,
but more and more socialists were being drawn toward the party
these days, seeing it as a force for unity, organization and discipline. Had Tomás been an anarchist, she might well have proved a
good deal less sympathetic.

Dolores embraced her son and asked him routinely what he had
learned that day. He parroted various pieces of dogma in much the
same way as she had once recited her Catechism, cheerful as always
at the prospect of seeing his uncle; Dolores always called in on
Ramón after school, and often left Andrés with him for a few hours
while she saw to Tomás.

Ramón rarely went out these days. The bitter winter had proved
too much for him, and the April air was still chilly. Oil for the stove
was always in short supply, and so he spent much of his time in
bed, swaddled in blankets. Watching her son jump onto the bed
and regale his uncle with the usual chatter, watching Ramón's face
brighten, Dolores marveled yet again at how thoroughly he could
spoil his nephew when he had so cruelly rejected his own son. Poor
Rafael. She still cherished the faint hope that he was safe, somewhere, with Rosa and Petra. She dared not mention them these
days in front of Tomás. Tomás would not have wanted to see them
now. Or more correctly, Tomás would not want them to see
him . . .

His physical pain was probably no worse than Ramón's, but his mental pain was excruciating, if only because he was now even more of a cripple than the man he despised most in the world. His huge reserves of strength were still there, turned in upon himself. Selfishly, as it now seemed to him, he had married her the previous November. Dolores knew that he blamed himself for tying her to a cripple. He had wanted to marry her whole and triumphant, but victory had had its price. The battle for Madrid had been won, but at the cost of his left leg, blown to pieces by a Fascist grenade five long months ago.

"How is it with you today, Ramón?" asked Dolores, feeling her brother's forehead.

"Bad," claimed Ramón with a certain amount of guile. "How horribly I suffered in the night! An old war wound, my boy," he added sotto voce to Andrés. "A bullet through the chest from a Moroccan sniper." He coughed wheezily.

Dolores threw open the window to release the fetid air and began boiling lentils on the stove.

"I am not hungry," said Ramón churlishly. "All I require is *sleep.*" He looked at her expectantly. Dolores fingered the vial in her pocket.

"Where are the pills the doctor gave you?"

"Take them with you to school and use them as chalk, for that is all they are."

"Are you really sleepy, Uncle?" asked Andrés, disappointed. He had been hoping for a story, a nice long one, that would delay the hour of going home. He hated going home more than ever now that Tomás was always there.

"Pah! I can go many days without sleep. I have marched for three days without rest or food in my time. Did I ever tell you about the campaign in . . ."

Dolores prepared a meal for Andrés and replenished Ramón's glass. It was Bell's whiskey again, a gift from one of Marisa's Englishmen, and hopefully more wholesome than the absinthe of old. She added a liberal measure of water.

"I will leave Andrés here for a little while, Ramón," she said, handing her son a plate, "while I see to Tomás."

Ramón did not interrupt his flow to acknowledge her departure. She felt relieved that he was clearly much better today, enjoying one of the unpredictable remissions during which he seemed almost normal—normal, that is, for him. There could be no such remission for Tomás. She was glad she no longer had to choose.

Tomás heard her footsteps on the stair and hauled himself toward the door to meet her, the thump of his crutches sounding a mournful drumbeat against the bare floorboards. He had been discharged from the hospital with his stump still suppurating, his bed badly needed for more acute cases. She had seen him scream and curse with pain and rage and frustration, berating himself for not having died, for imposing his living death on her. If it hadn't been for Paulina's help, and the blessed, if temporary respites from constant pain, he would surely have gone out of his mind. The analgesic power of alcohol was sorely overrated, and in any case, Tomás, puritanical as ever, was still too proud to follow the example of his much-despised brother-in-law. But not too proud to swallow the medicine Dolores claimed to acquire legitimately, to pretend to believe what he knew was a lie. Dolores rationed her meager supplies ruthlessly. Given the chance, he might take too much, either by accident or design. Once or twice she had wondered whether she should allow him the means to do so, and been ashamed.

She measured the precious drops into a glass of water, and heard him sigh in anticipation of relief, of a few hours' painless sleep, of purest luxury. It angered Dolores that pain, even now, was bound up as always with poverty. Tomás was not important enough for his pain to matter. She could not believe that a general or a Cabinet minister would have been required to suffer so much, or that drugs were so scarce that powerful men were discharged from the hospital without the means to assuage their agony and give them healing rest. The revolution had been supposed to make everybody equal; but influence and unfair advantage were now more important than ever, as her own experience proved. Paulina was one of the new rich, Dolores one of the new breed of mendicant, willing to convert to any creed to prove herself worthy of alms.

Tonight Tomás would sleep for once, and so would she. There would be some respite from the terrifying rages, the ever-present threat of violence. He had never struck her, controlling himself with a super-human effort, but lately Dolores had begun to fear for Andrés. Tomás had always resented sharing her attention, and no longer troubled to hide it; consequently she allowed the boy to spend more and more time with Ramón, whenever her brother was well enough to endure company. Andrés was becoming ever more unruly and difficult; he had never been a docile child, but he responded best to quiet firmness, not anger. Lorenzo had rarely had to raise his voice to enforce his authority, exacting obedience out of love, not fear. Once so quiet and firm himself, Tomás now lost his temper with explosive suddenness, bellowing at the boy for the slightest misdemeanor, frustrated by his powerless, chair-bound state, waving his crutches at his agile adversary, falling over the furniture as he tried to pursue him, roaring like a wounded lion. And yet Andrés, with the callousness natural to his age and sex, felt not a shred of pity for him despite his mother's pleas and exhortations. On the contrary, he had developed a devilish tendency to provoke, enjoying his new power.

Tomás knocked back the draft in one swallow. He lived in hope of being fitted with a peg leg, but it seemed a distant prospect. Artificial limbs were a luxury, and even if one had been available, it would surely have been agony to wear, forcing the weight of that massive torso onto a stump that stubbornly refused to heal.

Dolores served him soup—the most blatant black-market produce was indistinguishable in soup. She mashed and chopped relentlessly, inveigling Tomás to consume disguised chicken, liver pâté, and once, caviar—for which Marisa had no taste—watching him swallow the nourishing pulp that would surely have choked him had he known its provenance.

Tomás left his meal unfinished, and retired groggily to bed. He could not bear to sleep alone, and so Dolores lay beside him until he dozed off, rubbing his long, broad back, soothing him into oblivion, grateful for the reprieve from lovemaking. She had thought that the pain would diminish his libido, but it seemed to increase it. It had become his only solace, the only way left to him to prove himself a man.

Five years of marriage to Lorenzo, the most diffident and gentle of husbands, had ill equipped Dolores for Tomás's vast sexual appetite. Poor Tomás. He had been so ashamed of his immoderate size, so afraid of hurting her, so aware of his own deficiencies as a lover. But at first none of that had mattered. At first she had found his clumsiness endearing and had met his demands without flinching, welcoming this physical reassurance of his loyalty and love. It had been easy at first to be kind, easy to give him pleasure; her own lack of desire had not troubled her. She was used to not feeling desire. The memory of desire was one that she had consciously suppressed for all the years of her marriage; affection and tenderness could function without it. And with Lorenzo, they had. But Tomás had not been satisfied with that, Tomás had felt cheated. Tomás wanted a passion to match his own, Tomás demanded more than she could give . . .

Tomás, hovering on the brink of sleep, blessed the potion that drained him of lust, that helped him forget. Ignacia had never ceased to haunt him, seeking vengeance from beyond the grave, mocking him relentlessly. He had come near to hating her in life for her insatiable demands, for her coarseness, for the way she had coarsened him. How relieved he had been when Dolores had shown no fear, what bliss it had been to feel her tight around him . . . Too tight. For a long time now, it had felt like rape, even though she never refused him. Her involuntary reflexes all but barred him entry, and despite the false surrender of her body, her mind was still an impregnable fortress, as unassailable as the Alcázar . . .

Tomás shuddered as sleep finally claimed him. Relieved, Dolores got up and crept quietly back into the kitchen. She finished what was left in Tomás's bowl, and added a little more from the pot. She had to keep well, she had to stay strong. Whatever happened, she must not become ill . . .

The first blackout had happened at school, the second in the street. She had put them down to hunger and exhaustion, and begun forcing herself to eat and rest more. Neither Tomás nor Ramón nor Marisa could take care of Andrés if anything were to happen to her. The third time, she had been ready for it, recognizing the buzzing noise and the sudden bitter taste in her throat and the peculiar acrid smell. She had been at a party meeting at the time, and her collapse had quite alarmed Paulina, who had urged her to consult one of her medical comrades. Paulina knew of the wound above her ear, where no hair grew—the result, she believed, of a Fascist bullet, which was perfectly true, in its way.

Dolores had protested that it was nothing, nothing. The thought of having her complaint diagnosed terrified her. She had watched her mother die of a brain tumor, and had begun to nurture a secret fear that she was similarly afflicted, a fear she could not bear to have confirmed. Thereafter, at the first onset of the symptoms she would find some pretext to excuse herself and lie down—on the floor if necessary—until the attack had passed. As for the headaches, she convinced herself that they were getting better, refusing to admit that she had just become used to them, as one gets used to any disability. What was a headache against a lost leg, or a body rotted by disease? What was a headache against universal suffering? Her misery had bred a warped, desperate optimism. It was tempting to block it all out, to believe what was said at party meetings, that all might yet be well.

The theme of these meetings was always the same. The war first, the revolution later. The revolution must be shelved until the war was won.

"All our energies must be devoted to fighting the Fascists,"
Paulina declared. "Those who put the revolution first are playing
into Fascist hands."

Only the Communists could win the war, Paulina said. The anarchists and the Trotskyites were sorely misguided in their revolutionary zeal and in their mistrust of Communist discipline. The
new, unified People's Army, run on the Communist model, was
the only hope for victory. The days of self-governing militias, who
fought or fled at their own whim, were happily over. The gross
mistakes of the first months of the war were gradually being recti-
fied, and the damage done by extremists slowly being healed. The
Communist party was the ally of the ordinary man: it had no wish
to confiscate private property; it represented freedom for all, justice
for all, equality for all. It represented *democracy*. What a pity that
some diehard socialists did not recognize the natural affinity between the two parties, what a pity they had been influenced by those
who sought to encourage disunity, Fascist infiltrators who sought
to destroy the Republic from within . . .

Dolores listened attentively. The Communist viewpoint sounded
quite sensible to her. Unity was obviously essential to the winning
of the war. As for the revolution, it had been sadly discredited. In
Aragon, the revolution allegedly involved anarchists sequestering
small holdings at gunpoint and forcing peasant farmers to cede all
their crops to voracious committees, which gave them back barely
enough to feed their families. These armed men should be at the
front, she was told, fighting the Fascists, not harassing their fellow
workers and slandering Comrade Stalin, the Republic's only ally.
She should not hesitate to report any people who sought to mislead
her so that a more knowledgeable comrade could seek to enlighten
them . . .

At this stage, Dolores would invariably lose concentration, her
mind preoccupied with the problems that awaited her at home.
Tomás's moods, Andrés's disobedience, Ramón's dementia, how
best to stretch that day's rations, how much liquid was left in the
vial, how much longer all this would go on. Then she would come
to with a start, join the applause, ingratiate herself to the best of
her ability, remind herself that she needed all the friends she could
get.

She wiped her soup bowl clean, flung her coat over her shoulders
and went out to fetch her son. The streets were awash with unswept
litter, the fresh spring breeze sending it scuttling ahead of her,
swirling the dust into her eyes. This time she did not get any warn-

ing. The taste, the smell and the buzzing all came upon her simultaneously before robbing her abruptly of all her senses and sending her reeling into the garbage-choked gutter.

"All right for some," puffed Nurse Kelly, helping Clara lift a two-hundred-pound paraplegic into a wheelchair. She put her chubby fist into her apron and drew out a scrap of paper and two envelopes. "Just bring back as much of this as you can carry, love. Leave out the tins if they're too heavy, apart from the condensed milk, that is. And post the letters for me from London, will you? You lucky people," she continued as the orderly appeared, "what I wouldn't give for a whole month's leave."

Edmund smiled politely and wheeled the patient away. He avoided indulging in idle chat in front of Clara, as if to acknowledge her seniority. She was always peremptory and formal with him when they were on duty, although she had carefully managed the schedule so that their shifts coincided.

Clara put Kelly's list in her pocket without looking at it. She would have to send her a parcel. No one knew that she was not coming back, and no one knew why. She had wanted to keep her pregnancy secret as long as possible.

Three more days. She was not sorry to be going, having resented being sent here in the first place. They had made it seem like a special privilege, posting her to Madrid, people had affected to envy her. But by the time she had arrived, the battle for the city had been fought and won. While other former colleagues had subsequently been sent to field hospitals in Jarama and Guadalajara, in the thick of the fighting, she had been stuck here, in a minor civilian hospital, deprived of the numbing overwork that had once been her salvation. It wasn't what she had come to Spain for, and she had wondered, at first, whether Edmund had had a hand in her transfer, doubting it only because she would have preferred this theory to the less palatable truth.

She had been half expecting him to turn up, knowing that the sight of Tessa's injury would frighten the life out of him. When she had refused point-blank to go home, he had volunteered to stay and make himself useful. At first she had been surprised and delighted, triumphant even. But within weeks of his arrival she had found herself banished from the front to this nice, safe billet, and then Edmund had sought and been granted permission to join her. All very convenient. Since then—or at least until recently—she had pleaded relentlessly for a move, without success.

But it was clutching at straws to imagine that Edmund had some-how engineered it all. They would never have let a really good nurse go to waste just to placate a neurotic lover. No, the real reason was that she hadn't made the grade, as usual; they didn't need her, they had sent her here to get rid of her. The only good thing about this place was that she didn't have to waste precious time or resources on bloody Fascists.

They were off duty in ten minutes. The prurient restrictions be-loved of English hospitals did not apply in Republican Spain; they cohabited in a small room on the upper floor of the building, where the staff was quartered. Clara suppressed a yawn. She got tired quickly these days. A bowl of something disgusting in the kitchens first, which she would probably throw up, then bed, together. Bed together had been his trump card, of course; he had got his own way, as usual. Clara's delight at her pregnancy was very nearly as great as Edmund's, even though she was much too superstitious to admit it.

Clara forced herself to swallow the oily mess while Edmund watched her anxiously. This time it would be all right, this time she would prove that she was just as much of a woman as Flora with her two strapping brats or Dolly with her wide-eyed orphan or Kelly with her boring, handsome grandson. Her child would have gray eyes and hair the color of damp sand. It would not be like her. Every time she imagined a miniature replica of herself she would force her mind back to the Townsend family photograph album, only to remind herself abruptly not to tempt fate. Those images of Edmund as a gurgling infant had returned to haunt her last time.

She sat still for a bit, willing the food to stay down. She refused to dine at the hotel with Jack, despite the ever-open invitation, scorning to enjoy food that was unavailable to the natives, despite her loathing of the villainous hospital cuisine. Time enough to spoil herself once they were back home. She had done her bit, surely? At least she had a proper excuse for leaving, not as good as Tessa's, perhaps, but more than good enough.

Edmund slept instantly, his hand protectively over her still flat belly. He still found his daily round, albeit leisurely by Clara's standards, punishing. It took a lot longer than six months to get used to physical work, to acquire the stamina to keep your eyes open long enough to read, or relax, or listen to the radio without dropping off. He had never known mental exhaustion, had never experienced the chronic bodily fatigue that robs one of the power to think. He hated the work, she knew, still fighting a losing battle against his natural squeamishness. He hated blood and pus and shit and dirt, he had an innate aversion to physical contact with strangers. He had never complained but he had never pretended to like it either. It was all he was qualified to do, and he was doing it for her, not for Spain.

Edmund woke to the sound of Clara vomiting into the basin and stiffened. It was a sound he still associated with her drinking. He pretended to be asleep. She hated him to know she had been sick. Then she put on her dressing gown and went out to empty the bowl, shutting the door quietly behind her.

Edmund stretched luxuriously in the hard, short bed. Only three more days. He had found it hard to conceal his glee in his long-awaited triumph. He liked to think he knew the moment of conception: the night of that vicious quarrel, quite the worst they had ever had, when she had finally, after years of trying, provoked him beyond endurance, an endurance eroded by long hours of standing and stooping and lifting and carrying, by bad food and discomfort, by sheer, crippling exhaustion. He had been horrified at himself, not so much because of what he had done, but because he had enjoyed doing it. He had never struck anyone in his life before, least of all a woman, least of all Clara. He had slapped her, hard, across the face in midinvective, making her mouth bleed, which was bad enough, but he hadn't been sorry, which was worse. It had given him such a tremendous sense of release and blind elation that he had immediately done it again, making her cower in terror, and then he had shaken her till her teeth rattled, pressing his hands hard into her shoulders, feeling her bones bruise. The sight of her terrified expression, the trickle of blood running down her chin, the red imprint on her cheek had filled him with a primitive, appalling sense of pride. He had been surprised at himself, surprised that he had not done it years ago.

But not so surprised as he had been at Clara. Clara, sobbing, on her knees, unbuttoning his fly, knowing before he knew that he was erect with a new and inadmissible kind of rage, stroking her cheek against the evidence of his wrath, wetting it first with her tears, and then with her mouth, an unprecedented gesture, and one that she had not repeated since, which made it all the more telling.

He had been too excited to take her with his customary finesse and had practically raped her, not that she had resisted. For once he truly hadn't cared whether she was ready or whether he hurt her or whether he gave her what little pleasure she was capable of. He had quite forgotten, in the last eight years, what it felt like. *That* must have been when it happened, surely, that must have been the moment when the valve had opened, letting him inside.

It must have been then, because the experience had proved unrepeatable. Not the lovemaking itself; he had been quick to try to recapture the moment, to make amends for its imperfections, to compensate for his savagery with gentleness and warmth and endless patience. But it had never been quite the same again. Rage did not come naturally to him, and to have tried to simulate or reproduce it would have smacked of deceit and perversion. And yet the shared memory of it was a new and potent bond. The change in Clara was indefinable, but unmistakable, the change in himself subtle but stable, settled. Neither of them acknowledged it, as if by unspoken agreement, keeping their precious secret safe from each other and themselves.

Jack no longer filed dispatches. The recent pieces he had sent to Harry, out of spite, had not been printed, not that he had thought for one moment that they would be. Luckily, he had not written them for money; his savings, modest by English standards, went a long way in Spain.

Edmund had posted them for him, to his mother's address, sandwiched between screeds of trivia—the amiable censors had long since been pensioned off, and their successors had come forth and multiplied. There was no doubt that Harry had received them, because he had been quick to write back rejecting them, defending his decision strenuously, proving that Jack's accompanying taunts had got under his skin.

Dear Jack,
   Delighted though I was to receive your two pieces, following such a long silence, I have, after careful consideration, come to the conclusion that to publish these particular stories would be ill-timed and counterproductive to the Republican cause.
   I do not disbelieve, of course, what you say, and if it is indeed the case that foreign volunteers are being denied discharge, even on medical grounds, politically harassed, sent to "reeducation camps," and even shot if they don't toe the party line, then that's quite appalling. But however true it is, no one will believe it except the people who support the Fascists, and who would be all too eager to use such claims for their own propaganda purposes. I simply can't allow Rag to be exploited by Fascist sympathizers in such a way, and I'm sure you will understand this.

You dared me in your letter to tell the truth, and I rather resent the implication that I would choose to tell anything else. But in war-time, the truth can be a two-edged sword, as you of all people must know. I can appreciate your wanting to deter other young men from getting themselves into this situation, and I appreciate that the disproportionate number of International Brigade casualties would appear to support your rather crude "cannon-fodder" theory, but it can't serve any useful purpose to say so now that the flow of volunteers has all but dried up.

As for the alleged activities of the Communist secret police in Barcelona, I doubt if many readers would share your sense of outrage. The anarchists and the POUM are clearly obstructing the war effort, and must expect to fall foul of the authorities in consequence, and your concern that the revolution has been betrayed won't, I fear, cut any ice with the great British public.

However, it goes without saying that I would be delighted to have more material from you written on a broader base . . .

Jack wondered what had become of his old friend Billie Grant, who had so rashly volunteered for the International Brigade. He had met him twice since the train to Perpignan. Once, after the battle for Madrid, when he was in understandably good spirits, one of the heroes of the hour (although the Spanish militia had bitterly resented seeing a small contingent of foreigners get most of the glory) and once after Jarama.

The battle of Jarama had been a technical triumph. The vital road between Madrid and Valencia had not been cut, an achievement that was deemed to justify Republican losses on a Pyrrhic scale. Billie put on a creditable battle veteran act in public, but Jack had noticed the rapid blinking, the trembling hands, the slight twitch in the corner of his mouth, and had lost no time in getting Billie drunk, in the privacy of his room.

Billie had spent seven glorious hours on "Suicide Hill," defending an untenable position against constant artillery and machine-gun fire, a veteran indeed among men even less experienced than he, many of whom had never handled a loaded weapon before. Four hundred out of six hundred men had been picked off like sitting ducks, waiting their turn to be slaughtered, playing their part in the brilliant victory. Incredibly, Billie had escaped without a scratch, and was torn between a terrible guilt that he had survived, and a savage, twisted joy that his hated commissar had finally bought it.

It had taken a great deal of Bell's whiskey to bring him to this admission, so thoroughly had he learned to hold his tongue. A commissar's official brief was to maintain the physical well-being and the morale of the troops, and if you were lucky, you got one who did just that. If you were unlucky, as Billie had been, you ended up with a vicious party diehard, a thought-policeman with a nose for bad eggs. And Billie had stunk to high heaven. How he had survived his initial vetting remained a mystery. He was a life-long Labour man, and he hated Fascists, and he had thought, naïvely, that that was good enough. He had no idea, he claimed, that he was joining a Commie outfit, but even some of the lads who were Commies to begin with were getting bloody pissed off with the whole show. If your face fitted, you got sent home with a cut finger and an arm in a sling, to spread the word; if it didn't, you got patched up and sent straight back to the front as soon as you could stand.

"I volunteered, didn't I?" shouted Billie, waving his glass around. "I've done my bit for bloody Spain. So why can't I go home now? Because they're scared of what I might tell the folks back home, of course. They'll keep me in this godforsaken country until I'm good and dead!"

Next morning Jack had personally delivered Billie to his unit on time, having filled him full of black coffee and warned him to keep his big mouth shut. Billie's avowed intention was to desert at the first available opportunity. Jack had told him not to be bloody stupid, he would end up getting shot. Billie had said he would get shot if he didn't desert, sooner or later, so what was the difference? They had parted on rather uneasy terms, Billie embarrassed at his drunken revelations, Jack at his inability to help him. Doing a Scarlet Pimpernel act for disgruntled Brigaders formed no part of his plans. He felt outrage for them as a group, but little sympathy for them as individuals. Jack himself would never have volunteered for anything; he felt sorry for Billie, but thought him a fool. A few weeks later he had received a note:

> *I'm in hospital in Albacete. Shot my right index finger off while cleaning my rifle. Very careless. I'll give your best to your mum when I get home.*

Jack had gone to Albacete immediately, and found Billie in very low spirits. He had been questioned for several hours about the "accident," and had just been reassured that he would be trained to fire his rifle with his left hand, no doubt at a "reeducation camp."

"Can't you bloody *do* something?" Billie had hissed.

"Don't look at me," said Jack impassively. "It's the oldest trick in the book. You didn't seriously think they'd fall for it, did you?"

"Well, I'm not about to go to no bloody correction camp, thank you very much. I'm getting out. I've got it all planned."

And this time Jack had not tried to dissuade him.

And so Billie had, in official parlance, "deserted to the front." Like many other men, impatient at being hospitalized while their comrades fought the Fascists, he had disappeared that night from his hospital bed, determined to find his way, in his pajamas, without money or food, back to his unit. Men had by all accounts accomplished this feat on numerous previous occasions. It was proof positive of the continuing high morale of the International Brigades . . .

This information was relayed to Jack in a deadpan monotone by a medical bureaucrat who had obviously become word-perfect on this particular issue. Jack wondered how far Billie would get before they caught him, how long before Mrs. Grant received a telegram regretting to advise her that her son had been killed in action. He had heard nothing since.

Jack had put Billie to the back of his mind, but he hadn't forgotten him completely. His memory was increasingly full of things he had put out of his mind, like a jam-packed cupboard in a tidy room. Just because he was writing a novel was no reason to clutter his mind. The only way he could stay in control of that heaving mass in his head was to regard it as something separate from himself, incubating and growing inside him, feeding off him, but not invading him, a fetus that would one day leave him, an uncomfortable but temporary burden. It throbbed and swelled and threatened his freedom, but at least it was alive. He could ignore it for hours and still not feel lonely.

He would not be the only person to write a book about Spain. There were other, already established writers in Madrid who sought inspiration at the hotel bar, and Jack was careful to avoid their company. They reminded him of the kind of pampered, pregnant woman who advertises her condition and revels in all the attention. They made him feel like a ravished scullery maid, hiding her shameful burden, envying them their waiting canopied cradles, fearing dismissal and disgrace, preparing to deliver in secret and smother the ill-starred progeny at birth.

And yet he could not have written the book at home. To discourage retreat he had given up his flat and sold his car and returned

Elizabeth's letters unopened, marked "unknown at this address." His only anchor was the growing pile of pages which he declined to discuss, even with Edmund, not that Edmund was up to discussing much these days. He had lost weight, from hard labor and poor diet, and invariably began yawning almost as soon as he sat down. His scholar's hands had grown red and rough, his posture was bent by constant backache, even his speech was different—he took no pleasure in words anymore, choosing them for economy of effort, rather than for maximum self-expression. Jack blamed Clara, as always. Jack saw nothing ennobling about hard manual labor—he had done too much of it in his time to regard it as anything other than stultifying. But Edmund seemed happy enough, now that he had got what he wanted. Perversely, Jack resented Clara more for taking him away than for bringing him here in the first place.

At his insistence, he was giving them a send-off dinner. It was to have been the previous evening, but Clara had begged off at the last minute, claiming some vague malaise connected with her condition. Jack found it hard to picture Clara as a mother, but at least her baby was half Edmund's; his book had no redeeming genes at all, unless you counted Dolly.

His Dolly character had been well disguised at first, but she had grown impatient of the subterfuge, and cast aside her borrowed clothes, and now she did as she pleased. His supposed manipulation of her was as false as it had always been; he lived in constant trepidation as to what she would do next, how she would foil his purpose, elude his control, vanish totally from his grasp. Every time he sat down to write he expected to find her gone; the relief that she was still there induced him to write himself to a standstill, lest it prove to be the last time.

Marisa had discovered him once in the throes of creation, keeping a prearranged appointment that he had completely forgotten. The interruption had occurred at the worst possible moment, and he had yelled at her to get out, before flinging down his pen and calling her back, knowing that he ought at least to pay her. Only then had he noticed that she looked pale and unhappy, and asked her in, afraid that he had upset her.

He hadn't totally believed her latest sob story, not that it mattered to him whether it was true or not. He had duly got hold of some sleeping pills and painkillers for the allegedly dying pimp, wondering all the while how much she would sell them for. It still infuriated Clara that anything, but anything, could be procured on the black market; she clung to her absurd, self-righteous indignation at the new and thriving industries of war. Jack admired Marisa for her enterprise; he hoped she got good and rich out of this bloody mess. At least she was Spanish, feeding off foreigners, rather than the other way around.

Tonight was her regular night, when she left an hour free for him, and he felt bad about canceling the arrangement at short notice. He left a message for her at reception, together with a bottle wrapped in newspaper, and took the metro to the hospital. In deference to Clara's sensibilities, he had found a modest local restaurant where the food would be bad enough not to upset her digestion.

The hospital was out of town, a former nunnery set in its own grounds, which were now a wilderness of weeds and rubbish. Jack waited outside for a good ten minutes before Edmund appeared alone, saying that Clara still wasn't feeling up to it and sent her apologies.

Jack was heartily relieved, and Edmund made no objection to going into the center of town for a decent meal. Jack knew of an excellent place near the park, recommended to him by the fat man, Gregory, which had formerly catered to the gourmets of Salamanca and now operated under new management for the benefit of an even more exclusive clientele.

They took in a couple more bars first, filled themselves up on *tapas,* and gradually lost interest in dinner. Edmund was back in form tonight, witty, cryptic, precise, but tougher, less genial than his old self, a change that had taken place stealthily, but steadily. Abandoning his normal tactfulness, he asked outright if he could have a look at Jack's novel, and Jack had surprised both of them by agreeing, if only because Edmund was leaving next day. Then, apropos of nothing, Edmund suddenly said, "You were in love with her, weren't you?" and for one awful moment, Jack thought he was referring to Clara, that he had found out about, and totally misinterpreted, their liaison. He realized only just in time that Edmund was talking about Dolly.

Jack ought to have shrugged and said something dismissive like, "If you can call it that, given that I hardly knew her," but a maudlin sense of farewell had already imbued the evening with a mood of indiscretion; they were both in the loosened, lucid state that precedes intoxication.

"Yes," said Jack, grinding out his umpteenth cigarette.

"So was I, you know. I was ridiculously jealous of the fiancé. I couldn't do much about it myself, but I kept hoping that someone else would. Not someone like you, I might add. I had a few qualms, I can tell you, when you came along. I wanted her to meet someone like me, who would woo her decorously and marry her. Not someone who . . .''

"Who just wanted to get her into bed," finished Jack, signaling for the waiter to replenish their glasses.

"Did you?"

"Didn't you?"

"I'm not talking about wanting to, Jack."

"Now why would a well-bred convent girl like Dolly go to bed with a penniless lout like me?"

"That day I got home and found you taking tea with her," continued Edmund, undeterred, "cost me more than one sleepless night. She had a sort of animal glow about her."

"I never knew you had such a prurient imagination. Still, I'm flattered. But even if she had taken pity on me, I would hardly admit it, now would I?"

"Why not?"

"*De mortuis* and all that."

"I wouldn't think ill of her, or you. Life's too short not to take what you can from it. Dolly knew that instinctively, I think. She was all-or-nothing by nature. A bit like Clara."

Jack snorted.

"Think about it," said Edmund. "I'm right, you know. The similarity doesn't have to be obvious to be fundamental. Look at you and me. I'm the conventional one, you're the maverick, both of us rigid with self-control. I sometimes think that self-control's the worst kind of dishonesty."

"Let's go back to the hotel," said Jack, "and then you can be as honest as you like."

He had completed some forty thousand words, which Edmund took a couple of hours to read while Jack filled the room with smoke. He had put on his steel-rimmed spectacles, which made him look erudite and owlish, more like the Oxford don he should have been than the humble schoolmaster he had become. He read fast and attentively and didn't comment till he had finished. Then he took off his glasses, and polished them interminably, before saying simply, "Finish it at home, Jack, for God's sake."

"Are you being melodramatic?"

"Do you just leave it lying around here while you're out?"

"Oh, I usually put it under the mattress. They never bother to turn it."

"Then you must have a death wish."

"Don't exaggerate."

"I'm not exaggerating. People will misunderstand it. They'll think you're a Fascist."

"Don't you start. It's crystal clear I'm not a bloody Fascist. I'm just trying to tell the truth for once."

"People who try to tell the truth in wartime generally end up dead. You know what's going on in Barcelona. It's bound to spread. How long before the secret police take over in Madrid? How long before you come home one night to find your room's been searched? You don't think they'll give you a fair trial, do you?"

"I can't write it at home. It would be . . . cheating."

"Jack, you're not responsible for Dolly dying. Write an antiwar book by all means, and don't pull any punches, but do you have to be so specific? Can't you transpose it to another time, another place? Wouldn't it be just as valid and less politically sensitive? You're just begging for people to misjudge you. The wrong people will attack it, misunderstanding it. Assuming anyone's prepared to risk publishing it, which I doubt. Stalin's untouchable at the moment, the show trials have proved it."

"I don't care whether it gets published or not," said Jack irritably.

"There's no point writing something no one's going to read."

"There's no point writing something just to get it published. If I wanted to do that, I'd just ask Martindale for my job back. Do you think I couldn't write a nice, safe heroic tale if I wanted to, and fill it full of sanctimonious claptrap? Lots of nobility and treachery and daring exploits and passionate love and lyrical loss, with everything nice and black and white except for the compulsory bit of gray, so the critics take it seriously? I'm not out to sublimate my male fantasies. My hero—if you can call him that—doesn't kill any Fascists. He just watches a lot of ordinary, innocent, ignorant people die."

"Including the woman he loves, I suppose."

"You'll have to wait and find out."

"Jack, are you saying that you think they should surrender? Are you saying the Republic can't win?"

"It depends what you mean by winning," said Jack.

A bright light was shining into Dolores' left eye. The lids were pried open between finger and thumb so she couldn't blink. She felt trapped, terrified. The hand moved away momentarily before attacking the other eye.

"How long ago did this happen?" asked the doctor abruptly. The hands switched their attention to the scar tissue over her ear. Dolores blinked, her vision still blurred by dancing blobs of light.

"Last July," she said.

Her heart began beating painfully, as the old fear settled on her again. The doctor and the place were unfamiliar to her, and she cursed the good Samaritans who had picked her up and brought her here. She forced herself to reply to all the questions, minimizing her symptoms. She had headaches from time to time and she had fainted twice when she missed meals, and could she go home now because she felt quite well and her little boy was waiting for her.

He was hurting her now, pressing hard against the tender patch, making her feel nauseous. Then he asked her to stand and tied a bandage around her eyes and spun her around a couple of times before telling her to keep absolutely still. Dolores obeyed him, but the room didn't. She felt the floor sway beneath her feet, and staggered to retain her balance.

"You will have to go to a hospital, for an X-ray," said the doctor gruffly. "I will give you a note."

She took it and fled. She kept running, as if fearing pursuit, until she was able to take her bearings, and then slowed down, panting, arriving at Ramón's apartment hot and breathless.

Everything was exactly as she had left it, except the bottle was nearly empty, and both Ramón and Andrés were both fast asleep. She opened the sealed note for the hospital and read it. The Latin words danced before her eyes, filling her with terror, she felt as if she were holding her own death warrant. Methodically, she tore it into tiny pieces. She did not want to know. Once she knew, all hope would be lost. She would not let them pass sentence upon her, she was not going to die. Ignorance was her last remaining bulwark against despair . . .

She took Andrés home, only to return to Ramón's apartment sooner than she expected. In the early hours of the morning she heard a knock on the door and opened it to find a distraught Marisa. Tomás didn't stir, still deep in drug-induced oblivion.

"Lole, Lole! Come quickly! Ramón is dying!"

Dolores flung her coat over her nightdress, took the vial from its hiding place, and slipped out on to the landing, closing the door quietly behind her.

"Oh Lole, the pain is terrible! He did not know me! And he has such a fever! I tried to give him some pills, but he will not swallow!''

She was still dressed in her finery, a tawdry, short, bright pink dress, cut very low and trimmed with absurd feathers. She had come out without a coat.

Dolores took off her own and made Marisa button it all the way up, which she did on the run, stumbling and tripping on her spindly heels, which she eventually took off, racing barefoot through the filthy streets.

Ramón was not pretending this time. He was writhing in agony, screaming for his mother.

''Hush, Ramón,'' said Dolores quietly. ''I will give you something for the pain.''

He gripped her collar and pulled her with surprising force, bringing her ear level with his mouth.

''My boot,'' he croaked. ''My boot!''

Dolores ignored him, freeing herself from his grip and dropping a double dose of the precious fluid into a glass of water. Marisa tilted his head back to receive it and held his mouth open while Dolores trickled the solution down his throat. He gurgled and gagged horribly as he swallowed. Marisa released his head and it fell back onto the pillow.

''My boot,'' he whispered.

Marisa knelt down by the bed and kissed his hand. Dolores picked up her coat from the floor and opened the door. Marisa turned around, her face still taut with fear.

''Don't go yet, Lole,'' she begged. ''Stay a little while. I am afraid to be alone with him just yet. Stay a little longer.''

Her expression was childlike and pathetic beneath the mask of powder and paint. Dolores sat down listlessly while Marisa continued to whimper and caress Ramón. The table was scattered with her latest spoils—a packet of coffee, a stick of shaving soap, a tin of salmon, a bottle wrapped in newspaper . . .

It was printed in English. Idly, Dolores unwrapped it and spread it out on her lap, yawning. She looked for the date and noted, disappointed, that it was several months old. Then she read the headline:

AIR RAID ON MADRID
An Eye-Witness Account from our Special Correspondent, Jack Austin

Marisa turned around, hearing her gasp. Dolores was scanning the words very fast.

"From my room in the Florida Hotel, looking out on the Gran Via, I can see . . ."

"What is the matter, Lole?"

"Jack Austin," said Dolores faintly. Marisa looked at the newspaper and nodded.

"Jack Austin," she repeated, mispronouncing the name. "The Englishman, the one who gives me whiskey for Ramón. Lole, what is it?"

"Nothing. This Jack Austin. Is he still in the Florida Hotel?" Marisa looked puzzled.

"I told you, he gave me the whiskey," she said, indicating the bottle. "Why do you ask?"

"I . . . I just noticed his name on this newspaper, that's all."

She folded it into a small square and put it in the pocket of her coat.

"Lole, you are so pale! Are you sick?"

Jack. Jack, here in Madrid. Jack belonged to London, to the past. He had no right to invade her city, her present, reminding her of things best forgotten . . .

"Lole?"

"I'm just tired, Marisa. Ramón will not wake now till morning. I must go home."

She turned away and quickly left the room, just as she heard the distant wail of a siren.

Jack heard it too. He switched on the light and got out of bed for some water. His mouth was tight from an excess of wine and tobacco and his head ached. He swallowed a couple of aspirin and lay down again, ignoring the rap on his door and the shout to go to the shelters. Bloody waste of time.

Perhaps Edmund was right, perhaps he did have a death wish. But if he did, it was only for show, it was only because he knew he was immortal. It was always the wrong people who died, the good, the brave, the beautiful, the happy, the innocent, those who had something to live for. What satisfaction was there for the gods in culling someone like him, who was indifferent to life's riches, who had nothing to look forward to except the dubious satisfaction of being proved right, too late, like some latter-day Jeremiah? No, he was beneath death's contempt. It was the Dollys of this world who died tragic deaths. He would live to be a hundred unless he did the job himself.

He felt the vibration from some distant explosion and lit another cigarette, watching it burn in the dark. He had switched to a coarse Spanish brand that scoured his throat, giving his tasteless English ones to Marisa. Another bang. Amazing how one got used to it. Would people ever get used to it at home? How long would it take for them to scorn the shelters and carry on making tea, to treat an air raid like a thunderstorm? How many people got struck by lightning, after all? It wasn't courage, just an acquired tolerance to adrenaline. Yes, you got *used* to war, no doubt about it, to the extent that you probably missed it when it stopped. Even Edmund had admitted as much.

"I can't wait to get home, but it'll take some getting used to after this," he had said as he left. "I haven't enjoyed it, but it's the sort of thing we'll tell the grandchildren about one day. It'll acquire a kind of golden glow. It's a bit like school days being the best days of your life. Hell at the time, but something to feel smug about when they're over."

Oh yes, it would be something to dine out on for the rest of their lives. The "I was in Spain" tag was already a highly marketable commodity, especially for a writer. He could make his name if he gave them what they wanted. The darling of the Left Book Club, Jack Austin. He might submit his novel to Gollancz, just for fun. It would be like sending pornography to the Bible Society . . .

The all clear. That hadn't lasted long. He rolled over and went back to sleep.

How could he have slept? It haunted him for years afterward that he could have slept, that he could have proved so utterly lacking in telepathy, so devoid of intuition, so totally self-absorbed. In books people got dreadful premonitions, even in real life they had the grace to claim retrospectively that they had had a "feeling." But he hadn't felt a thing. All he had done was smoke a cigarette and fall fast asleep.

He didn't find out until Clara regained consciousness and managed to give them his name. She had been very lucky, Jack was told. Edmund's body had broken her fall, and a beam had miraculously shielded her against the worst of the cascading rubble, providing her with an air space until they could dig her out. A great pity about her *novio* and the baby, they agreed, but luckily her injuries were superficial. *Superficial.*

She didn't weep. Jack did, for the first time in twenty years, while she held his hand, squeezing it abstractedly, her face whiter than the sheet. Her composure was chilling. She told him, in a deadpan monotone, that they had ignored the siren, because they were making love. The chances of a direct hit were remote, and in any case they were leaving tomorrow. Because they were leaving tomorrow, they had felt quite safe . . .

"Don't cry," she said over and over again, more as an instruction to herself than to Jack. "Please, please don't cry."

Jack struggled to control himself, ashamed, knowing that he was making it worse for her. He must take care of all the practicalities, have the body sent back to England, cable the Townsends. He must take Clara home . . .

He pulled himself together and spoke to her gently, soothingly, telling her he would see to everything, wanting to spare her pain. Only then did the old Clara resurface abruptly.

"I'm not going home," she said. "And I'm not sending him home. He's mine. He's to be buried here, with the baby. I made them keep it. They throw them away when they're that small, unless you ask them not to. Straight down the drain. I made them put it in a jar. We're not going home, any of us. There's nothing to go home to. They're mine, and I want them here."

She was dignified, adamant, but clearly still in shock. It seemed disrespectful to argue with her. Jack nodded, resolving to come back later, and try again.

"It's already been arranged," she preempted him, her voice suddenly harsh. "They bury bodies quickly out here. First thing tomorrow morning. Don't you dare tell the Townsends yet. They'll phone the embassy and put a stop to it, so they can take him away. Don't send the cable until tonight, then it'll be too late for them to do anything. Promise."

Her eyes, dead and opaque with anguish, dared him to betray her.

"Clara, think what you're saying. You're not going to stay in Spain forever. You'll . . ."

"I shall die here, same as they did," she said. "Clever of God, wasn't it, to send a miracle to save me? He's good at little touches like that. But He can't stop me choosing where I die, or how I do it."

"Clara—"

"Oh, don't worry. I'm not going to make it easy for myself. I'm not going to take the coward's way out, like my precious father. I wouldn't insult Edmund by doing *that*."

Her voice was flat again, unemphatic.

"I'll come back tonight," said Jack gently. "I'll show you the cable before I send it."

He bent to kiss her and she gripped his hand with startling strength.

"You're not lying to me, are you?"

"I've never lied to you, Clara. Never."

He forced himself to see Edmund's body before he went, knowing the fantasies of mangled flesh would flay him forever unless he confronted the reality. It was lined up with four other corpses, covered with a dirty gray blanket. There was no blood. His neck had been broken, he must have died instantly. Perhaps that explained it. Jack had not felt him die, because he had not felt it himself. He clung desperately to that thought, shivering with the cold comfort of it. He must take care of Clara. There was nothing else he could do.

Dolores made her way out of the shelter into the thin, cold blur of dawn, Andrés still sleeping groggily on her shoulder. The air struck chill after the rancid warmth of huddled bodies.

She had not been able to rouse Tomás; he had slept through it all. She made coffee—or what passed for coffee—crumbled stale bread into it, adding a precious measure of sugar, and took it to him in bed. He waved it aside irritably and struggled on to his crutches.

"You treat me like an invalid," he grumbled. "I can manage."

He sat watching balefully from his chair while Dolores dressed Andrés, who yawned and complained of a headache—grumbling that he did not want to go to school, he would rather spend the day with Ramón. Tomás began breathing heavily.

"If you are ill, you stay at home, with me," he barked. "If you are well enough to visit your uncle, you are well enough to go to school."

Dolores made great play of feeling her son's forehead and deciding that he was not feverish and being stern. Tomás complained incessantly that she was too soft with the boy.

"Do not be late," he warned her, as she kissed him good-bye, investing the few words with a wealth of meaning. There were male teachers at the school, educated, bourgeois men of her own class, men with two legs. Unwisely, she had lied to him the first time he had questioned her, reading his thoughts, insisting that all the staff were female, only to have Andrés contradict her chirpily. The men

involved were party members who were unfit for the front, although
it remained unclear what exactly was supposed to be wrong with
them.

She managed to catch Paulina in a break between lessons, men-
tioning as casually as possible that Tomás's pain was worse than
ever, hoping desperately that her next ration might come sooner
rather than later. In her moments of despair, she felt fear and resentment that she had become so utterly dependent on Paulina's
goodwill, that she had put herself so totally in her power. How she
envied Marisa her independence! Marisa named her own price,
Marisa felt no shame, Marisa was a professional, whereas she,
Dolores, was merely a bungling amateur. She had sold herself too
cheap, and now she was little better than a slave. How it would
pain Lorenzo to see them now! He had been the kindest of husbands, the proudest of fathers . . .

The thought had come to her in the night, while she huddled in
the shelter, that perhaps she should go to the Florida Hotel and
hand over her son to his real father and beg him to take him to
England, to safety. But it had been the kind of thought that only
flourishes in darkness, that could not withstand the bright white
light of day. For all she knew, Jack was married now, with children.
How could she inflict such a burden on an unsuspecting wife? And
even if he were single, why should he want to accept responsibility,
after all these years, for one forgotten night of folly?

In any event, he could not get Andrés out of the country unless
he obtained forged papers. Forged papers were both expensive and
dangerous, but it remained unthinkable to apply for a permit through
the official channels, to invite the bureaucratic thoroughness that
might unearth her guilty secret.

One of many guilty secrets, one of many lies. She had lied to
Lorenzo, lied to Andrés, lied to Tomás, lied most of all to herself.
That one night of happiness had started the spiral of deceit, denying
her all tranquility, all content. She felt a terrible surge of anger
against Jack, if only because he was ignorant of his crime, because
he remembered her as fickle and faithless, because he was *here*,
damn him. Most of all, because he was *here*.

It was a civil ceremony, conducted in Spanish, and totally unsat-
isfactory from Jack's point of view. He felt a need for ritual, for
grandeur, for a public display of grief, but Clara seemed glad that
it was quickly over. There was no point in glorifying yet another
pointless death.

He spent the rest of the day at the telephone building, trying to get a connection to London. The Townsends would have received the cable by now, and Clara was fretting that they would want to see the grave. She begged Jack to keep them away.

"They'll blame me, of course, and why not. I'm fond of them, Jack. I can't bear it. I can't bear to see his family now. Talk to them for me. Make them understand."

It was Flora who answered the telephone, much to Jack's relief. The vapid coquette had long since grown into a formidable matron, a no-nonsense organizer who ran her household with an iron hand.

She was brisk and matter-of-fact, only a slight tremor in her voice betraying her distress. Everyone else had gone to pieces, so it had fallen to her to cope. Her mother had telephoned her just after breakfast, and was now under sedation. Her father was locked in his study and refused to speak to anyone. Archie had been sent to Thomas Cook to buy the tickets.

Jack spoke very fast, fearful that the line would go dead on him. Surprisingly, she took his point. She agreed that the journey might be premature and that her mother especially wasn't up to it. Clara's wishes about the disposal of the body would have to be respected, whether they liked it or not. Her mother was desperately worried about Clara, she added. The primary objective of the journey had been to bring Clara home.

"Tell her we don't blame her, won't you," she said gruffly. "Edmund wouldn't want us to blame her. I'll talk to Daddy. Phone back tonight, if you can."

Clara discharged herself later that day, against medical advice, but did not protest when Jack booked a room for her at his hotel. She still had a dreadful, chilling calm about her which boded ill. He wished that she would weep and rail against fate, get angry, hysterical, discharge the poison of her guilt, release the pressure of her grief, but it was as if her suffering was so precious that she could not bear to part with any of it. She hid it jealously like a miser hoarding gold. She would count it in secret every day and watch it grow and share it with no one, seeking refuge in a treasurehouse of private pain.

Another long wait at the Telefónica produced confirmation that the Townsend pilgrimage had been postponed. Flora had placed an obituary in *The Times* and arranged a memorial service, and informed all the relatives. There was a letter for Jack with Edmund's solicitors, which they would forward.

It was the longest evening Jack had ever spent. Clara was clearly terrified to be alone, although she would not say so. Jack had food brought up to his room on a tray and made her eat some of it. He tried to encourage her to talk, thinking it might help, but she was beyond his reach. He resisted the temptation of the whiskey bottle, knowing that he could not drink with her, or without her, and told himself selfishly that she would go to bed soon, and leave him alone, and then he would drink himself to sleep. But she didn't move, and it seemed tactless to suggest she do so.

Finally she said, "Have a drink, if you want one. Don't mind me," and given that to prevaricate would have been to insult her, he poured himself a generous measure, and swallowed it quickly, almost furtively. He was unnaturally aware of footsteps in the corridor, of people talking and laughing as if nothing had happened. He wanted to shout at them to shut up and show some respect for the dead. He had another drink.

Still only ten o'clock. This time last night he had been in that bar with Edmund, discussing Dolly. Only the good died young all right. He wished savagely that the bomb had landed on the Florida Hotel, taking him and his wretched novel with it. He was not aware until Clara spoke that he had voiced the thought out loud.

"They had to die," she said. "It was the only punishment that would do, don't you see?"

"Punishment for what?"

"For what I did, of course. *Vengeance is mine, saith the Lord.*" Her tone was flippant, conversational. "I helped myself to a couple of lives, you see. I tried to redress the balance. I might have known He wouldn't let me get away with it. I pushed Him too far this time."

Jack felt a chill up his spine.

"What are you talking about?"

"I killed off a couple of patients in Aragon. Fascists. And now He's got His own back. Proves which side He's on, doesn't it? As if we didn't know."

A belief of God was supposed to be a comfort, not a curse. Jack blessed his own lack of religion, watching Clara's perverted version of it eating into her guts. No point in saying, don't be silly, no point in trying to reassure her, her faith in her own damnation was absolute. Hell was still her spiritual home.

She helped herself to one of Jack's cigarettes and lit it clumsily from his. Her hand was shaking so much that she was unable to guide her cigarette into her mouth, and in the end she dropped it, letting it burn a hole into her skirt. Jack leapt forward to pick it up and threw it in the ashtray.

The minute he put his arms around her, she stiffened. But she let him take off her shoes and lift her on to his bed, and lay there docile, in a waking sleep, while Jack dreamed jerkily beside her.

It was market day in Guernica, and the sun was shining. Josep's blood-stained battle dress was drying in the April breeze, and the loathsome lice had gone. He felt clean for the first time in a month and wonderfully free, enjoying this respite all the more because it was to be so brief.

Not that there was anything to be cheerful about. His unit was retreating inexorably, driven farther and farther back each day by the relentless offensive of Navarrese troops who claimed each new victory in the name of Christ. The irony of his situation depressed him, as did the fearful level of casualties. He had arrived exhausted in an ambulance full of wounded men, bleeding profusely from a flesh wound in his thigh, which had now been cleaned and bound up tight and which would not prevent his return to the front next day. Until then, he was at leisure, and he was determined to make the most of this short-lived respite. He knew that his euphoria was the result of shock and loss of blood, and was glad of this excuse to feel so unreasonably lighthearted.

You would never know there was a war going on, but for the throng of refugees herding together outside the railway station, awaiting transport to Bilbao, which was still deemed to be impregnable, surrounded as it was by fortifications known as "the ring of iron." But for that, and the frantic activity inside the hospital, every inch of corridor filled with injured men, it could have been any other market day, with hens squawking and vendors shouting and women jostling. Jostling a bit more than usual, perhaps, now that food supplies had diminished, but good-naturedly enough, for people here had no experience of hunger.

Last night, in his hospital bed, Josep had fallen asleep to the raucous lullaby of the Sunday night open-air dance, enlivened by the whoops of drunken soldiers who were billeted in the local convent. Preparations had begun to fortify Guernica against attack, much to the dismay of its inhabitants, many of whom would have much preferred to surrender, as a matter of common sense.

Josep had woken to a bright new morning and a whole day's leave. After breakfast he had set off to explore the town and enjoy the sunshine, blithely ignoring the advice to rest his leg. After weeks of crawling and crouching for hours on end, to walk upright, slowly, and for pleasure, was a sensual delight not to be missed.

By noon he was feeling weak and slightly giddy, and he sat down to rest awhile on the stone bench beside the fountain in the plaza, luxuriating in the pure spring air, untainted by the putrid stench of death. He shut his eyes against the sun and dozed off, waking to the sound of a woman singing.

She was standing in the line for water, holding a small boy by the hand and swinging his arm to and fro in time to her song. The child sniffed and whimpered and seemed unwell, and from time to time she bent down and wiped his nose with her handkerchief.

The elderly woman ahead of her padded off lopsidedly, one shoulder weighed down by her bucket, and the girl put a large jug under the trickle of water, lifted her son in her arms, and cuddled him while it filled.

Josep shut his eyes again, opening them reluctantly as the child began crying loudly. His mother needed two hands to carry the heavy jug; he was refusing to walk and demanding to be carried.

Josep stood up.

"I will carry the child for you," he offered.

She beamed her thanks, relieved, but when Josep bent down to pick the boy up he redoubled his angry sobs. His mother sighed and shook her head.

"Please take the water instead," she said, handing over her jug. "He is not well today."

She led the way to her home, chattering all the while. Josep's Basque was still rudimentary, and he found her rapid speech difficult to follow. She insisted on inviting him in and pouring him a glass of wine, which Josep felt bound to accept. There was a photograph of her husband, in uniform, on the mantelpiece, taking pride of place beneath a large crucifix. The juxtaposition seemed ominous. How many more young men would be sacrificed for the sins of others? It was obviously a poor home, and Josep left before the woman could press further hospitality upon him, while her infant, now gurgling happily again, mimicked her wave of farewell.

Josep found a café and ordered another glass of wine. The premises were crowded, the conversation intense, too fast and colloquial for Josep to understand more than the gist of it. There was talk of market traders leaving town early, of troops digging in around the cemetery, and of locals preparing to move out. The Church of San Juan was allegedly being sandbagged, and a machine gun installed in its crypt.

Josep drained his glass and shut his ears. Nothing was going to spoil his day of rest. He had no wish to see the sandbags and machine guns that so fascinated the locals. Such things were too commonplace to hold any interest for him.

The wine helped the muscles in his leg relax. He could feel it restoring the depleted blood in his veins, a supremely secular transubstantiation. He realized that he was very hungry. Guernica had two restaurants, one an expensive place catering to the bourgeoisie, which Josep rejected out of hand, and the other an informal establishment thronged with sheep drovers and cattle dealers, and serving huge bowls of *fabada* at fifty centimos a plate. Josep found a seat and prepared to do the hearty stew justice. The bread was fresh and he washed down a hunk of it with more wine while he waited for his meal.

They were busy, and he had a long wait, enjoying the sense of anticipation. When his brimming bowl arrived, he resisted the temptation to wolf it down, determined to savor every delicious mouthful, chewing it slowly, enjoying the succulent chunks of meat nestling among the beans. Tomorrow's beans would be dry and hard and tasteless; he resolved to enjoy this feast as if it were his last meal on earth.

He wished too late that he had eaten it quickly, gulped and not sipped his wine, made time to fit in a cup of strong, black, fragrant coffee. As it was, his bowl was still half-full when the sudden, panic-stricken exodus sent plates and glasses crashing to the ground.

He heard the explosions, felt them, knew what they must be, and yet he didn't move. He carried on eating, shoveling the food into his mouth while his fellow diners jumped to their feet and fell over one another in their haste to reach the door. His only concern was to finish his meal. It was the only thing that seemed important. Only when his bowl was knocked over did he come abruptly to his senses and notice an old man lying on the floor, moaning, trampled underfoot.

Josep picked him up and carried him out into the street, following his directions to the nearest shelter. There was another massive explosion and the sound of people screaming. And still all he could think about was that bowl of spilled stew.

13

Dolores arrived home with Andrés one evening to find Tomás entertaining guests. Two former comrades-in-arms were home on leave and had evidently succeeded in getting him very drunk.

"There you are, woman," Tomás greeted her. "You are late again. Hurry yourself and prepare some food for my friends."

Andrés gave him a venomous glare, affronted to hear his mother addressed in such peremptory fashion. Dolores hushed him into a corner and told him to play quietly while she put on her apron. It was unusual for Tomás to have visitors, even more unusual for him to drink; of all things he despised drunkenness, especially drunken cripples.

She dared not produce any illegitimate foodstuffs, and there was very little else to eat, just the eternal lentils and a piece of salted cod, barely enough for two, let alone three. She was glad Andrés had already eaten. Ramón had not been hungry, and so he had had double rations again.

The two men had the grace to look embarrassed and began prevaricating, saying that they would eat at home, their families were expecting them. Tomás insisted loudly that they stay, they repeated their excuses, and the bottle was passed around yet again, until finally, with the meal all but ready, they stood up to go, saying that they would call again next time they were on leave.

Tomás fell silent when they had gone. Dolores knew instinctively that there was going to be trouble, she could smell it in the air like gas. Her only thought was to get Andrés out of the house before it ignited.

"Andrés," she said. "Take a little of this to your uncle for me. Perhaps he is feeling hungrier now."

It was a mistake.

"Stay where you are," snarled Tomás. "Why should we share

our rations with that worthless sot? There is little enough to eat as it is.''

''I put extra in the pan,'' said Dolores, ''thinking your friends were staying.''

''Then save it for tomorrow,'' said Tomás. ''My friends are welcome to share our food. My friends are fighting for the Republic. Put that bowl down, boy.''

''No,'' said Andrés.

Tomás reached for his crutches and hoisted himself to his feet.

''I said, 'Put it down!' ''

''Do what Tomás tells you, Andrés,'' said Dolores quietly.

''No!'' shouted Andrés. ''Why should I? *He's* not my father!''

''Thank God for that!'' roared Tomás. ''I may be a cripple, but at least I am not a Fascist, as your father was, God rot him!''

''Tomás!'' interjected Dolores.

''Why don't you tell the boy the truth, Lole?''

''My father was not a Fascist!'' protested Andrés. He had learned at school that all Fascists were evil.

''Then why must you pretend I am your father? Why are you not allowed to mention him? Why are you not allowed to use his name? Because he was an enemy of the Republic, that is why!''

''Tomás, be quiet!'' Dolores opened the door and pushed Andrés out into the corridor, whispering, ''Take no notice, he is drunk. Go, now. Wait with your uncle. I will come to collect you. Quick.''

Her voice was quite calm. If Andrés realized that she was afraid, he would not leave her. He was just getting to the belligerent age when he would have taken on the gigantic Tomás single-handed to defend his mother. Mistrustfully, he went down the stairs, turning several times to look back up at her. She smiled brightly and waved and waited till he had reached the bottom before shutting the door.

''You promised,'' she hissed at Tomás. ''That was low of you. He is too young to understand. How can I explain such things to a child?''

''What difference does it make? You have trained him well to lie about his father, have you not? Are you afraid he will tell your precious new friends the truth? Don't worry, Lole. He is a good liar, that one, like his mother.''

Dolores gritted her teeth, and placed his food in front of him, hoping that it would soak up the effects of the cheap spirits. Tomás lunged with a huge paw and sent the plate crashing to the floor. Without a word she got down on her hands and knees and began scooping the slimy mess back onto the plate. Tomás kicked it out of her hands with his right foot, sending her sprawling.

"I should beat you, woman! You drive my friends away with your miserable face! You humiliate me by not making them welcome! Their wives are at home, waiting for them! My wife is never here! My wife cares only for her spoiled brat and her whining brother and her dead Fascist of a husband! She smiles for that dirty whore Marisa"—he simpered grotesquely—"she smiles for her new comrades, but she cannot smile for me or for my friends!"

He seized the bread knife from the table and inspected the blade. Then slowly, grimacing horribly, he pressed it to his throat.

"*That* is what you would like, is it not, my little Lole? To come home one night and find me dead by my own hand. That is why you provoke me, that is why you make my life a misery, so that you may drive me to despair. Why do you insult me by pretending love? Why do you not admit you hate me?"

He dropped the weapon with a clatter on the floor and began sobbing noisily.

"Hush, Tomás," she said, putting her arms around him. "Do not distress yourself. Of course I do not hate you."

Yet again, she was filled with remorse. She tried to remember him as he used to be. Gentle, kind, wise, dignified, patient, the virtues of a strong man. She had admired and respected him for those qualities, but she had never loved him. And he knew it.

And yet she did not, could not hate him. If anything, she hated herself. She had caused him more anguish than even the loss of his leg. Not intentionally, but inescapably. She had never refused him, but her body always betrayed her, her simulations had not deceived him, he had striven tirelessly to please her until she came to dread his striving, all her muscles contracting in anticipation of pain.

He returned her embrace, wept like a child, begged her forgiveness, berated himself as an animal, entreated her not to leave him, while she comforted and forgave him, as she always did, making herself feel better, making him feel worse.

"I try to love the boy, Lole," he said. "But I know he resents me, as I resent his father. To him I am still, I will always be a stranger . . ."

Again, her mind flew to Jack, Jack the seducer, Jack who was still, who had always been a stranger. Then she looked at Tomás, Tomás her savior, a man whose heart was an open book, a man who loved her. And she clung to the devil she knew.

* * *

Edmund's letter was dated the previous October, prior to his departure for Spain.

Dear Jack,

I hope you will never read this, but I felt it wise to set my affairs in order, knowing that the contingencies not provided for are those that invariably happen. I have made a will, and named you as my executor, a liberty I know, but one that I hope you will forgive. I decided that it was pointless to leave my rather limited assets to Clara, or to my family, who don't need them, so I've left everything to someone to whom they might actually make a difference, one Andrés Montanis, last heard of in Toledo, with instructions that you take all reasonable steps to locate him, at my expense. If he can't be found, then I have left it to you to see that my estate goes to some appropriate orphan relief fund, preferably one that does not concern itself with the politics of the dead parents.

I've also prepared a letter for Clara, of course, explaining what I've done and why. I haven't told you why, because I know I don't need to.

Finally, do it out of love, not duty. I don't want you to feel bad about anything that may have happened in the past, or to feel that you owe me anything. I ask you to do this because I respect you and because you are my friend. I ask you to do it for Dolly, not for me.

                                                          Yours ever,
                                                          Edmund

The solicitors had enclosed a second letter for Clara, conveying Edmund's request that Jack stay with her while she read it. Hers was as long as Jack's was short, and occasionally her face softened and twitched as she read, but still she did not cry. When she had finished, she said, "If you need any money to do as he asks, let me know. You can have all the money you want. But I don't want to be involved."

Jack nodded, still lost in his own thoughts.

"Thank you," she continued stiffly. "For helping, the last couple of days. But I'm all right now. I'm over the worst. I've put in for a transfer, and I should hear shortly. Then I shall be off, wherever they send me, the sooner the better."

Jack said nothing, aware that lectures about going home for a rest and taking it easy for a bit would fall on deaf ears. She folded Edmund's letter and put it away.

"I'll say good-bye now, then," she continued, standing up. "No need for you to nursemaid me any longer. I'd rather move out of here, if you don't mind. I need to be on my own for a bit."

Jack took her hand and held it tight.

"Don't, Clara. Don't shut me out. I loved him too, you know. Can't we be a bit kind to each other?"

"I don't want your kindness," said Clara without rancor. "And I don't want to be kind. We're neither of us kind by nature, what's the point in pretending? It's maudlin and hypocritical. All this is quite bloody enough without getting sentimental about it. If you're going to need money, let's settle up now. I don't want to have to think about it again."

"I'm not going to need money."

"Damn you. Will a thousand pounds do it?"

"I said I don't need it, Clara."

"As you wish."

She opened the door. Jack wanted to call her back, hold her close, comfort her, but what was the point? He had nothing to offer her, except bad memories of shared guilt. *I don't want you to feel bad about anything that may have happened in the past.* He had known, then. It was a relief. It should have made him feel worse, but it was a great comfort, that Edmund knew the worst of him and still saw him as a friend.

"I'm here if you need me," he managed to say, but her reply was predictable.

"I don't need you," she said. "I don't need anyone."

He heard her go off down the hallway and sat down again to reread the letter and the copy of Edmund's will. His estate was larger than Jack would have expected. He had come into some money on his majority, and inherited half a house in Kent from his paternal grandmother in 1933, which had been sold and the proceeds invested. In all, he was worth over ten thousand pounds.

Trying to find the boy would be a labor of love all right, and one that Jack, a pessimist by nature, would not have embarked on voluntarily. And now he had to do it, whether he wanted to or not, for Edmund. No, not for Edmund. *I ask you to do this for Dolly, not for me.* No, not for Dolly either. For himself.

"It's not true, Uncle, is it?"

"What did your mother tell you, my boy?"

"That Papá was killed in action, that he died a hero. And now Tomás says that Papá was a Fascist. Tomás says that's why I can't use his name."

"And why should you care what Tomás says? The fellow is nothing but an ignorant blockhead."

"But Fascists are the enemy of the people. Fascists—"

The door opened and Dolores appeared, breathless. She looked fearfully from Andrés to Ramón and back again. Andrés scowled.

"Andrés," she said. "Tomás is very sick today. He did not mean what he said about your father."

"He said my father is a Fascist. You told me he died for the Republic."

Dolores took her son's hands and spoke very quietly. "Do you think I would lie to you, Andrés? Your father died bravely, fighting for what he believed in. Your father was no Fascist."

"Then why can't I tell them at school?" he said. "I hate being called García! I hate pretending Tomás is my father!"

"Your mother is bound by a vow of silence," interjected Ramón loftily. "Your late father was engaged in work of the utmost secrecy. It must never be spoken of, nor the manner of his death. You must hold your peace."

"Why?"

"You ask why? A good soldier never asks why. Orders must be obeyed without question. You disappoint me, young man."

Dolores flung Ramón a grateful look.

"Your uncle is right. Show you are a man by doing what is difficult."

"It's not true, then? Papá wasn't a Fascist?"

"Your father died for his country, Andrés. Do not insult his memory by asking me that question again."

Andrés's lip quivered mutinously. Dolores had a sudden, fearful vision of the future. If anything were to happen to her, if Andrés had to be placed in foster care, or even evacuated, how long would it be before he confided in some friendly, listening ear that his real name was Montanis, that his father had been a secret agent, and that he had been warned never to tell anyone about him and pretend that Tomás was his father?

She put her arms around her son.

"One day you will understand, Andrés. But until then, you must be brave and do as you are told."

"Don't worry," said Ramón. "I will talk to Andrés, man to man. Leave us alone, Dolores."

His face was flushed, his tone expansive, he was in one of his well-oiled moods when he would say too much. Dolores gave him a warning look, which elicited only an infuriating, mysterious smile. It was almost as if he were enjoying her discomfiture.

"Another time," she said. "Come, Andrés. We must go home now."

"No!" said Andrés. "I want to stay here. I hate Tomás. I'm not going back there!"

"You'll do as I say!" shouted Dolores, gripping his arm and applying several sharp blows to his bottom. "Your father would be ashamed of you, if he could see you now!"

And of me, she thought miserably, frog-marching him home. And of me.

Josep had thought he was used to death. But when he stumbled out of the smoke-filled shelter, crammed with suffocating bodies, with some vague notion of tending the wounded and giving spiritual succor to the dying, he saw that he had no notion of death at all.

The air raid on Fontenar, all those months ago, had appalled him with its indiscriminate slaughter. The sight of his father's burned-out house haunted him still. But Guernica was like a hundred Fontenars, a thousand burned-out houses. Whole streets had been flattened, others blazed from incendiaries, and everywhere there were bodies, broken and dismembered. Not the strong young men whose fate it had always been to fight and die. No longer content with them, the war had now sought out their homes and families, as if to destroy the hive that had once sustained them.

It was very quiet again. He could hear the faint whimpers of people trapped beneath piles of rubble, and men were already passing buckets hand to hand to put out the fires. Josep did not know what to do first. He began crawling into a gap in a mountain of fallen bricks. Somewhere in there he could hear a baby crying. Then he felt a tug at his trouser leg as someone dragged him back.

"You'll kill them," he said. "And yourself. It will collapse. We need supports, ropes, shovels."

The man began giving orders, calmly. People were emerging from the shelters, dazed, coughing and blinded by smoke, to discover the familiar landmarks gone, and unrecognizable corpses scattered piecemeal, littering the streets of their tidy little town. Soon every able-bodied person was engaged in clearing rubble, in passing buckets, in carrying the wounded to safety. Josep helped lift a woman with her throat torn open, a child with one arm hanging by a thread. He ignored the dead. The ritual of giving posthumous absolution suddenly seemed supremely trivial, reducing God to a petty bureaucrat obsessed with spiritual paperwork. God would take care of the dead without his help. He must do what he could for the living.

And all the while he worked, he asked himself *why?* Why this peaceful market town with next to no strategic value? There was a bridge and an arms factory. But the river was too shallow, and too narrow, for the bridge to have any tactical value. And the arms factory was hardly large enough to justify such a devastating attack. No, it must be to terrorize the Basques into surrender. What other reason could there be?

Some of the victims were riddled with machine-gun bullets, slaughtered as they ran for shelter, strafed by low-flying aircraft. There were no stretchers, no advance dressing posts, no field ambulances, all the familiar infrastructure of the battlefield was lacking. Josep lifted bodies single-handed, carrying them into the private vehicles which were already ferrying the wounded to the overcrowded hospital. He tried to be callous, to ignore the ones who were beyond help, whose injuries were so appalling that they would have to die where they lay. But then he came to a body he recognized.

He should not have wasted that precious half minute, a half minute that might have helped save a life. But he did, giving the final benediction, unable to pass by. It was the young woman with the water jug. She had fallen on the run with her child in her arms, a child that would never cry again. Her dress was drenched with bright patches of red, and one of her legs had lost its foot. Her scarf had come off, and her long hair tumbled all around her shoulders as if in sleep. Her face was unmarked, her eyes open and startled, as if she had awoken in the middle of a terrifying dream.

Innocently, unwittingly, this girl had made enemies, enemies she had never harmed, enemies who had nonetheless set out to destroy her, together with her child and the children she would have had. And they had succeeded, triumphantly, snuffing her out like a lamp, snuffing her out like Dolores . . .

Josep had never allowed himself to visualize his sister's death, fearing the anger that would consume his spirit, never allowed himself to mourn her, fearing the devastating power of grief. A priest's love must be diluted, distributed among the many, eschewed in its most intense, rewarding form, the form that engenders the capacity to hate, the primitive need to avenge . . .

For a moment he was paralyzed by inertia, overwhelmed by intense, private pain. But then he heard two sounds, simultaneously. One was the pathetic mewing of two small children, wandering around distracted, hand in hand, looking for their mother. The other came from above. Josep looked up and saw three airplanes, flying abreast, swooping like eagles, the sky behind them dark with their following flock.

He flung himself on top of the children just as a hail of bullets sleeted down from the sky, and lay there, helpless. It had not finished yet. It had only just begun.

"Clara, my dear, I'm so dreadfully, dreadfully sorry."

Dr. Peabody clasped his comrade's hand and squeezed it very tight. He would scarcely have recognized her as the dedicated nurse who had so impressed the Aid for Spain committee, who had once been the backbone of the team in Granazán. She sat like a discarded puppet, shoulders sagging, knees together and ankles apart. Her head was bowed and her eyes wide open, staring at nothing. Everything about her screamed despair. He recalled the letter from her fiancé, pleading with him to transfer her, and wished too late that he had sent her home instead. Edmund had written:

> Clara is not as strong as she looks. She was severely depressed by the loss of our baby last year, which took its toll on her health, and although going to Spain has given her a tremendous sense of purpose, the strain is beginning to tell. However, she absolutely refuses to desert her post, and I'm afraid that if you send her home, she will feel a dreadful failure. I'd be eternally grateful to you if you could transfer her somewhere that will make fewer demands on her, and post me there with her so that I can give her some support . . .

And now that support was gone.

"I'm not asking for any special treatment," said Clara tonelessly. "Just that you get me another posting quickly."

"You shouldn't have discharged yourself from the hospital, Clara. As a nurse you should have known better."

"I feel perfectly all right." She stood up jerkily, as if pulled by some invisible string. "I know you've got patients waiting. I don't want to keep you. I—"

"Sit down, Clara, please. I simply can't allow you to be posted elsewhere in the state you're in. It would be totally irresponsible. You're not fit for work, and that's that."

She shook her head violently.

"I have to work. I want my mind fully occupied, I want to be so busy I haven't got time to think, I want—"

"Clara, you've got to allow yourself to grieve. It's the only way to get over something like this. If you soldier on, you will damage both your health and your sanity. Work is a painkiller, not a cure—"

"Work is all I've got. It's all that's left."

"Please cooperate, Clara. Forget about work and think about your career. You're a good nurse and I don't want to lose you."

"You mean you're trying to use this as an excuse to get rid of me. You mean—"

"Listen to me, Clara, not only as a doctor but as a comrade who respects you and cares what happens to you. You are physically and emotionally on the verge of collapse. You've just had a miscarriage, you're anemic, and you're suffering from shock. And on top of that you've just lost Edmund, and you're blaming yourself for his death. You should still be in the hospital, and I have to insist that you spend tonight in the ward."

Clara stood up, eyes flashing, intending to march out of his office. But she sat down again, giddy, nauseous. Perhaps this was what she had wanted after all. This wasn't sympathy. He was only doing his job. That made it all right. He was only doing his job.

"I'm going back home in a couple of days," continued Peabody implacably. "I suggest that you come with me."

"But I—"

"I'd like Professor Elliott to take a look at you."

The benign Professor Elliot had made his name treating shell-shocked victims of World War I, and his work had since expanded to cover a plethora of psychological ills. He had successfully treated two Aragon-induced nervous breakdowns, who were now reputedly back on the wards, as good as new.

"Professor Elliott? You mean you think I'm about to crack up."

"I mean I don't think you're going to get over this without help."

"I don't want help and I don't want sympathy. I killed Edmund, and that's all there is to it. I killed Edmund and my baby too. Nothing can change that, ever. I don't want excuses made for me, and I refuse to blubber about my private affairs to some medical equivalent of a priest."

Peabody took a deep breath. He had better cable Elliott and

arrange an immediate admission. She was a suicide waiting to happen.

"Clara, remember that you're a nurse. And a nurse can't function in a state of nervous exhaustion. You wouldn't want a patient to die because you'd broken down on the job, now would you?"

She flinched, and looked at him with something like alarm, blinking rapidly.

"What do you mean?" she said sharply. "What exactly are you trying to accuse me of?"

"I'm not trying to accuse you of anything, other than self-neglect. Trust me, Clara. I've seen people in this state before, people who've suffered much, much less than you. There's absolutely no criticism of you intended. We brought you out here, and now it's our duty to take care of you."

She didn't answer for a moment, her mouth working soundlessly, trying to shape itself around the words.

"So . . . if I agree to see Elliott, you promise you'll let me come back?" She was flustered now, babbling. "I've got to come back. Edmund's here. Oh God . . ."

Dr. Peabody patted her hand, congratulating himself on her sudden capitulation. She wouldn't want to come back of course, and why should she. But she'd never admit it till she was better.

Clara swallowed pills obediently and let them put her to bed. She was still bleeding profusely, but she seemed oblivious to her sodden underwear, the dark stain that had seeped through to her skirt. The only part of her that could weep had shed its tears in silence.

It took Jack several days to work up steam. So thoroughly had he convinced himself that Rosa must be dead, and Dolly's child with her, that it required an enormous and conscious effort of will to shake himself free of this gloomy presupposition and get down to work.

His abortive attempt to rescue her, just before the Fascist attack on Toledo, had at least served to confirm that she had had the sense to flee. That was a start. The relief of the Alcázar had involved the usual proscription that accompanied all Fascist victories. The streets of the town had allegedly run with blood; even the wounded in the local hospital had been slaughtered, together with the doctors and nurses. Even allowing for rumor and exaggeration, it remained beyond doubt that the town would have been systematically purged of any known or suspected "Reds," together with their families. Knowing this, Rosa had wisely not taken any chances.

German pilots liked to practice their aim by strafing fleeing civilians, and there was always the possibility that she had met this hideous fate, but it was just as likely that she had quite simply lost his card in the confusion. Perhaps she was in Madrid at this very minute. She mentioned that her brother had gone to Madrid, perhaps she had set out to join him. Certainly it seemed the most likely place to start searching haystacks.

Possibly Rosa had enrolled the child at school, presumably as Andrés García. Not that Jack intended to inquire for him by name. He would need a pretext for his search; the allocation of ten thousand pounds to the six-year-old son of an anarchist might sound just a mite suspicious and attract the attention of sinister and increasingly powerful officialdom, the new and proliferating elite who had taken control of the city since the government's evacuation to Valencia. The friendly propaganda minister Jack had met in Toledo had long since been removed from office, to be replaced with a hard-line Communist. Bureaucracy was now chillingly efficient, and the come-into-my-parlor bonhomie of "advisers" like Gregory did not deceive Jack for a moment. He could not risk confiding in anyone.

He would say that he was writing an article about the new and progressive education system that had replaced the religious brainwashing of old. He would ask Gregory for some introductions, claiming to have a particular interest in elementary schooling. That way he could get inside the classrooms. He would know that child again anywhere. Dolly's mouth, her hair, and most of all, her eyes. One lost child that represented a much greater loss, the loss of everything that might have been his, that might have been Edmund's.

Edmund's lost children were beyond reach, gone forever. All the more reason for him to find this one. The daunting impossibility of the task was an inbuilt incentive. He had never before conceived an ambition that as not calculated, attainable, that had not retrospectively seemed too easy, felt like cheating. He had never feared failure, relying on his sleight of hand to pass any failure off as a success. But this time there could be no pretense, not even the pretense of wanting to fail, of claiming he didn't care, of casting a superstitious curse, like the one he had placed on his novel. It was the first time in years he had wanted something for its own sake; the first time in years he had been prepared to take a risk.

Edmund had never been afraid to want, to feel, to fail. Perhaps that was his hidden bequest. To want was a start. To feel would follow. And to fail would be only too easy. It was the not being afraid that was hard.

People were fleeing from Guernica in droves, fearing the planes would return yet again. The chaos was indescribable, bodies pouring out of the shelters, choking and spluttering, preferring to take their chance in the open rather than risk asphyxiation. Josep picked himself up, covered in dust, to find that both he and the two children were unhurt. Whichever way he looked, the town was in ruins. Surely it was finished now? Surely it was over?

The little girl was about eight, the boy four or five. They were stunned, beyond tears, staring at him blankly. Josep looked around for some likely female to entrust them to so that he could get on with the relief work, but such was the chaos, the weeping, the panic and confusion, that he had no choice but to take charge of them himself. Should he install them in a shelter, in anticipation of another attack? Or should he get them out of town, join the general exodus toward the safety of the nearby caves?

He lifted the boy onto his shoulders and took the girl by the hand.

"I want to go home," she whimpered. "I want my Mamá."

"I will take you home later," said Josep. "We will find your Mamá later. We must leave Guernica now."

"My Mamá is in Mundaka," said the child. "We come from Mundaka. We came with my uncle, for the market."

"Then we must find your uncle," said Josep, seeing a ray of hope. Mundaka was a little coastal town, not far away.

At the mention of her uncle the girl shook her head violently and began to cry. She clung to Josep very tightly. "I want my Mamá," she repeated, tugging his arm. And then she broke free and began to run ahead, showing him the way home, willing him to follow her.

They had been walking for half an hour or so when they heard the planes again. Not knowing what direction they might take, Josep lay on top of the children again until the danger was past. Even at this distance the explosions were deafening, sending vibrations through Josep's body, mimicking the mighty throbbing in his injured leg. The few minutes' respite from walking were enough to lock it solid. When he tried to get up again, he found that he could barely stand.

"You must walk for a little while," he said to the boy. "I cannot carry you any longer."

They had kept close to the river, under cover of the trees lining the bank. Josep knelt down and cupped some water into his mouth, praying for the strength to continue as far as the estuary, where there would be some habitation. He splashed some water on his burning, swollen leg, noticing the bright patch of blood.

"Look," said the girl, pointing. It was the answer to his prayer. It was a boat.

Marisa kicked her shoes off and lay down on Jack's bed. She looked forward to these little rests, especially now that she was working so hard. Ramón insisted that the war would soon be over, which made her determined not to waste a minute of it, but lately she had begun to feel rather tired.

She felt her eyes closing, and sat up on her elbows. He was ignoring her as usual, tapping away on his typewriter.

"Come and talk to me," she pouted.

"You're the one who talks, not me. Go on. I'm listening."

He stopped typing and sat down beside her. She stroked his thigh absently, innocently.

"Why do you not want to sleep with me?"

"Because I prefer to be your friend. How is your *novio?*"

She shrugged grumpily.

"The pills you gave me were no use. Soon I will be alone." And then, taking him by surprise, "Will you look after me, after he is gone? I could stay here, in the hotel, with you, and talk as much as you like. I would not ask for money. When I do not work, I sleep. I should not disturb you."

Jack felt absurdly touched. He opened his mouth to be kind and tactful and evasive, and said merely, "No, Marisa."

"Why not? You said you liked me."

"I prefer to live alone. Perhaps someone else . . ."

She shook her head angrily, as if he had insulted her. Jack didn't know what else to say. How could he "look after" her? In any case, she was more than capable of looking after herself. Or was she? Once Gregory had regaled him with a stomach-turning account of a session with her which he could only hope was lurid fantasy. It had made him feel responsible for her, frightened for her, and now she had asked for help and he had refused it, shrinking as always from personal involvement, wanting only to observe. He had once found her company a relaxant, and now it was proving the reverse. He was allowing himself to be drawn into her sad, sordid, busy little life, a life that should not concern him at all, except as a case study. Her dogged ability to survive and thrive was testimony to the evolutionary ruthlessness of war, the way it atrophied the fat, soft, flabby human traits that fed on peace and plenty. It was that ability that had fascinated him, seduced him into writing about her, forced him to care. He could have put her in a piece for *Rag* with his usual callous detachment, but transmuting her into fiction had made her real.

"I will find somewhere for you to live," he said, anxious to placate her. "And you can come to me for help if you have any troubles. In return . . . I want you to be more careful."

She looked at him oddly, as if she did not understand.

"What I mean is, you must not do anything dangerous, or allow anyone to hurt you, for money."

The look rounded into a mocking, dismissive laugh. She got out her compact and grimaced at herself, applying powder and a thick red smear of lipstick, reverting abruptly from anxious child to hard-faced whore. Then she looked at his watch, stood up, helped herself to a half-empty bottle of scotch and some cigarettes, and snapped them without ceremony into her outsize handbag.

"I must go now," she said briskly. "Can you get me some silk stockings?" Jack grinned, absolved.

"Clear off, you greedy little bitch," he said. "I have to work."

He carried on writing until midnight, and lay wakeful, reviewing his plans for the next day, when he had an appointment at the Education Ministry. Gregory had arranged an interview with the relevant official, who would no doubt subject him to a thorough vetting. His six-month journalistic silence had not been picked up; Martindale had not publicized his resignation, and had resorted to printing secondhand, predictable stuff which bore no byline, and which Jack was quite happy to pass off, implicitly, as his own. Interest in the war had waned a good deal lately and many corespondents had moved on in pursuit of more newsworthy events. The heavy fighting around Guadalajara and the continued bombardment of Madrid had aroused only minimal interest at home; it would take some quite startling new development to jolt the readers out of their customary apathy. He was glad it no longer fell to him to do the jolting.

Marisa had cleaned him out of whiskey again. He had better get some more if he wanted any sleep tonight, he found it almost impossible these days to switch his brain off without a slug or two.

He went down to the bar, intending to take a bottle up to the room. While he was waiting to be served, he spotted Laszlo, the Hungarian photographer, whom he had not seen for several weeks, and felt rather more sociable.

Laszlo accepted a drink moodily, and without bothering to waste time on the normal greetings, launched into a self-castigatory volley about some picture or other he had missed. He seemed to be slightly drunk, although his natural excitability often made it difficult to tell when he was slightly drunk and when he wasn't. Jack wasn't quite sure what he was talking about, but given his tendency to speak in two or three languages at once, that wasn't unusual in itself.

"I not there!" he ranted. "Two days ago I am in France! I get boat across if I knew what going happening! Best bloody pictures of bloody war and I don't get. I here in fucking Madrid!"

Jack nodded sympathetically, curious now. He had been working solidly on the book all day, knowing that for the next few weeks he wouldn't get much time to write. He had been too engrossed to stop for meals, and until Marisa arrived, he hadn't realized the time. He suddenly felt like Rip Van Winkle, and yet the old, built-in fear of looking a fool made him reluctant to admit his ignorance. Luckily, Laszlo did not need interrogation.

"Bombed flat," he continued, shaking a fist. "Three, four hours' bombing. What pictures! The Fascists they say no bombing. Basques set town on fire theyselves! And I don't get no pictures of German Junkers. Bastards! You know why they do this, my friend? I tell you. They practice! How many Guernicas in Spain, in France, in England? They practice! Republic now must declare war on Germany! Britain, France, must declare war on Germany! Fascist lies! No pictures, no proof!"

The news was so incredible that Jack thought there must be some degree of exaggeration. For three and a half hours the small Basque town of Guernica, with fewer than ten thousand inhabitants, had been subjected to almost continuous bombardment by German planes. Hundreds of civilians had perished, crushed under tons of rubble, burned alive by incendiary bombs, suffocated by smoke in the shelters, machine-gunned from the air as they ran for safety; the destruction and the casualties had been out of all proportion to any possible military gain. Popular opinion was that it had been to terrorize Bilbao into surrendering without a shot, leaving its valuable industrial resources intact. But a Nationalist communiqué had already been issued flatly denying that the raid had ever happened.

The town had been destroyed as part of the Basque scorched-earth policy, by the Basques themselves . . .

It was a propagandists' dream, everyone agreed. Public opinion would now be solidly behind the Republic. There was no possible way to condone such a massacre . . .

Practice. Would Germany publicly discredit the Nationalist cause just for "practice?" The frantic denials being issued from Fascist headquarters told their own story. Probably no one had bothered to ask Franco's permission. Hitler didn't much care who won this little war, as long as he won the big one. And practice made perfect.

"Please, Father. Please save my children."

"I am no sailor," repeated Josep. "I know nothing of the sea. Your children might drown."

"My children will surely die if they stay here," said the woman bitterly. "There can be no hope for us now, not after today. This one"—she patted her swollen belly—"has no choice but to share my fate. But Joachim and Inéz have a chance if you help them. Surely you did not save my children's lives only to condemn them to death?"

She began weeping again. For two hours now she had been haranguing Josep without mercy. His relief at locating the children's mother and delivering them to her safely had been short-lived.

"First my husband," she wept, resuming her refrain, "from a Fascist bullet, and then my poor brother, from a German bomb. And now my children too. They would be safe in France. They would be among Basques. You tell me to send them to Bilbao! There they will be trampled underfoot by those who are there before them. Thousands and thousands of children are waiting by the dockside. And even now the bombs are dropping there! I would rather they died at sea than by a bomb! I would not ask this of you, Father, I would take them myself, but for my condition. Look at me! How can I row a boat? Do you think I would beg and plead with you if I could do it myself? Please, Father."

Josep was tired, so very tired, too tired to think. Why would this woman not let him be? All he wanted was sleep, and oblivion.

"It is late," said Josep. "I will give you my answer tomorrow. I . . ." he keeled over dizzily. His wound had bled profusely, compounding his light-headedness, he was speechless from fatigue.

Chastened, she made up a couch for him in the kitchen. It was a humble fisherman's cottage, a few meters from the beach where her late husband's boat, her only asset, was moored. All her hopes were invested in that boat; she had been anxious to show it to Josep and demonstrate its seaworthiness, to convince him of its superiority to the borrowed craft that had brought him to Mundaka.

He lay down on the makeshift bed, exhausted, and tried to sleep. It was silent, but he could still hear the screams, it was dark but he could still see the dismembered bodies. Nothing he had experienced on the battlefield had prepared him for the horror of this day. Was this how war would be from now on? Would it happen again tomorrow, and the next day, and the next? And even if there was a surrender, then what? This poor woman's husband had been an ardent Basque nationalist, and she would no doubt pay the price of his convictions. Whole families were routinely wiped out by the Fascists as part of the rearguard action. Her fears for the children were real enough.

He tried to weigh his chances realistically. The blockade of the Basque coast had been rendered largely ineffective by the presence of friendly foreign vessels, and most of the attention was focused on Bilbao. If he were to get outside the five-mile limit by night, he might evade observation. The real danger was not the Fascist ships, but the weather and the rocks. He could not have understood a navigational map, even supposing he had access to one. Fishermen did not use maps . . .

He was woken by the sound of shelling, as the enemy advance moved inexorably closer. The children were dressed and waiting for him, and a bag of provisions already prepared. The little boy was whimpering, picking up his mother's distress. Josep looked at him, and knew he could not abandon them. Saving lives now seemed more important than merely saving souls.

"Cheer up Joachim," said Josep, lifting him into his arms. "Cheer up. We're going fishing."

"Of course, our roll is falling daily," said the hatchet-faced woman. "Many children have been sent to Valencia, or to the country. Their teachers also. This school will soon close."

Jack felt a wave of despair. This was his tenth school of the day. He had spent six solid hours gaping amiably at rows of seemingly identical children, looking with apparent fascination at class registers, maintaining fatuous conversations with wary teachers who no doubt thought he was on some kind of fault-finding mission. Several of them had assumed he was Russian.

Predictably, there were innumerable children called García. He could spend the next month doing this and getting precisely nowhere. And then what? The same again in Valencia? A tour of every

village in Republican Spain? Which was the more arrant waste of
time, writing his book or finding the child? There wasn't much to
choose between them in the futility stakes, which only went to
prove that he had nothing better to do. Futility was the order of the
day, after all. Futility was the essence of war.

Presumably Rosa would have found work, if she were here, and
so it had seemed worth approaching the CNT, the anarchist trade
union, posing as an admirer who had lost touch. This had proved
entirely abortive. Their membership records were nonexistent, bureaucracy of any sort being anathema to the true spirit of anarchism. Jack had visited a number of factories and other likely
workplaces only to abandon this line of inquiry as counterproductive. Even if anyone had known of her, they would not have admitted it to a stranger. Mistrust was endemic; to admit one knew
anything or anyone might be to incriminate oneself.

When he got back to the hotel, he found a note from Clara in
terrible, shaky handwriting.

Dear Jack,
    *Don't worry, I'm all right. I've decided to take a short break
before going back to the front. I've made contact with Richard
Peabody who is arranging a transfer for me. Thank you for helping. Tell the Townsends I'll write to them eventually.*

                             I'm sorry,
                             Clara

It was the first time she had written to him since the "Wednesday,
two o'clock" days. He had thought then that he despised her, he
had continued to think that he despised her, and yet by far the worst
part of Edmund's death had been watching her suffer. He had woken
up during that dreadful first night and seen her lying there, eyes
open, staring into the dark, and had had to stifle a sudden, shocking, overwhelming impulse to take her in his arms and make love
to her, in a separate attempt to blot out the horror. In some cultures,
the dead man's brother had to marry his widow; perhaps he had
been responding to some primitive urge to offer himself as a surrogate. It had been an emotional, not a physical need, a need that
had appalled him and one that he would never have acted upon.
But it had been undeniable, nonetheless, and suppressing it had left
him with a residual frustration, a feeling that he had failed her.

He tried to remember the last time he had slept with a woman.
It must have been Elizabeth, that night he resigned from *Red Rag*

after he had seen Edmund. He couldn't remember a single detail of the encounter. Sex was a supremely forgettable experience, except when you wanted to forget it. Still, it had been over six months ago. perhaps he should pick up a whore, wear himself out, help himself sleep . . .

No. He had always avoided paying for it. It went against the grain to acknowledge that much need. And if Marisa found out on her professional grapevine, she would doubtless take umbrage. Besides, it was no solution. Easier to do the job himself, not that that was a solution either. What he really needed was companionship, someone to relieve this dreadful, relentless sense of isolation . . .

He went down to the bar in search of Laszlo, or perhaps, more honestly, in search of Thérèse, whose good, colloquial English made for a rather more satisfactory conversation. Jack was glad she was already spoken for, otherwise he might have felt obliged to seduce her and thus ruin any chance of friendship. She was, admittedly, startlingly attractive, with glorious dark red hair, a mischievous pixie face and a deceptively fragile, slender build which belied her agility and toughness. She was also a born flirt; Jack suspected that she deliberately led men on to keep Laszlo on his toes. She was often to be seen standing at the bar, happy to the be the only woman, totally relaxed, totally ruthless. She had a way of touching a sleeve, of lighting a cigarette, of crossing her legs, that was infinitely physical, infinitely suggestive, and yet by all accounts she had never been unfaithful to Laszlo, perhaps because she was passionately jealous herself.

Jack checked out the bar, but as yet there was no sign of either of them. It was still early; with luck they would come down later. He ensconced himself in a quiet corner, got out his pocket dictionary, and set about deciphering the latest issue of *La Batalla*, the official mouthpiece of the revolutionary POUM.

He was on his third drink when Thérèse appeared and made straight for his table.

"Aren't you being rather antisocial today?" she said, indicating the newspaper.

"No, just reading," said Jack, brightening. He stuffed the paper into his pocket and pulled out a chair for her.

"That's what I meant. Reading *La Batalla* could easily be construed as an antisocial act." Her voice sank to a conspiratorial whisper. "I could be an undercover agent for the NKVD and report you to my superiors." She made a throat-slitting gesture.

"How did you know it was *La Batalla?*" asked Jack, amused. He had kept the title page folded inward.

"I recognized the kind of print they use. And I'm sure the secret police would too."

"I wouldn't call the NKVD secret."

"An open secret, then," she said. "What does it say? My Spanish is atrocious."

"The usual. Revolutionaries find it very hard to distinguish between one kind of oppression and another. They fail to appreciate the subtle difference between communism and fascism."

"So do you, evidently."

Jack shrugged. He rarely gave anything away, even to people he trusted. It was unfashionable, not to say dangerous, to be anti-Communist, and although Thérèse affected political cynicism, her French publishers were staunchly pro-Stalin.

"Where's Laszlo?" said Jack, changing the subject.

"In Barcelona, covering the May Day celebrations, hoping for a few riots."

"Why didn't you go too?"

Thérèse made a moue of chagrin.

"Have you had a row?" prompted Jack. Their lovers' quarrels were invariably a public affair, as were their reconciliations.

"I've had a row, yes," she said. "But not with Laszlo."

There was an edge to her voice, and Jack realized belatedly that she had sought him out deliberately, that she was angry and upset.

"What's the matter?"

"The magazine, that's what's the matter. My pictures, *my* pictures, and they credited them all to him! Laszlo was furious too, naturally. But I told him, there's no point in us working together anymore. It's not the first time this has happened. No one will believe I take my own pictures, everyone will think they're his."

She launched into a volley of explosive French while Jack got her a drink.

"I risked my life to get those shots," she continued bitterly, tossing back a man-sized slug. "I wanted to show the markings on the plane, as *proof* of German intervention. But I'm only a woman of course, so I couldn't have done it."

"Of course you couldn't have done it," said Jack, teasing her. "Women aren't brave enough, everyone knows that. So, what are you going to do instead?"

"I'm damned if I'll get myself killed for nothing. Male editors!" She ejected another stream of untranslatable expletives. "I met a female journalist today, an American. She wants some pictures to go with a magazine feature.''

"Which magazine?" said Jack.

"*American Woman*. They're doing a four-part series on 'Women at War.' "

"New exciting ways with chick-peas. How to get those stubborn bloodstains out of your laundry. Blackout for the well-dressed window.''

"Very funny. It's about widows and orphans, you hateful man. Anyway, I said I'd take the job. She pays a lot more than those French bastards. She even gave me an advance.'' She produced a wad of money from her handbag and waved it triumphantly. "Come on, let me buy you some dinner.''

"If you like,'' said Jack easily. "But not here, for God's sake. I know a very expensive place, by the park.''

Thérèse made short work of the rest of her drink and stood up to go.

"Thank God you were here,'' she said with an exaggerated shudder of relief. "I was going insane. The minute Laszlo left for Barcelona they were all lining up outside my door, *comme ça.*'' She mimicked a panting dog with its tongue hanging out. "At least I feel safe with you.''

"What makes you so sure of that?" asked Jack, rather taken aback at this affront to his masculine pride.

"Instinct," she said. "I can tell.''

"Tell what?''

"That you're in love with somebody else," she said, putting her arm through his. "Are you going to tell me about her?''

"Not a chance," said Jack.

Marisa was fond of her little penknife, as she was fond of all the things Ramón had given her. She carried it dutifully in her handbag, and had not liked to offend him by telling him how impractical it was. A razor blade was smaller, sharper, and much more discreet.

She was rarely required to take off all her clothes. Stockings and garters were generally considered to be an improvement on nudity, and so far no one had objected to her charming habit of keeping on her shoes. If anyone had done so, she would have thought twice about accommodating him. One quick tug at the sticking plaster under either instep would release a razor blade, giving her the means to defend herself. She trusted none of them, except Jack.

Her lesson had been learned the hard way. The welts she had

shrugged off to Ramón had been inflicted systematically and savagely when she was bound and gagged, and she had been very
frightened. Since then, she had never allowed herself to be tied up.
In fact, whenever possible she reversed the process, and carried a
number of tasteful scarves and belts specifically for this purpose.

She was not, she would have assured Ramón, afraid of the fat
man, despite his sadistic pleasure in threatening her, his enormous
weight and size, his elaborate quasi-violence. Her relief when each
session ended was not, she told herself, the result of fear. Had she
been truly afraid, she could simply have ceased to oblige him. But
although she would have been delighted to hear he had left the
country, or been flattened by a bomb, she could never have brought
herself voluntarily to turn away such a good customer. He had never
actually hurt her, after all. And she was always extra careful to
avoid any situations where her hand could not reach her foot, or
vice versa. Several times her fingers had strayed nervously toward
the strip of sticking plaster, but nothing had ever come of his little
charades, nor would, if she kept her wits about her. Those soft
chubby hands would never quite close around her throat, the heavy
blows would all be aborted, as long as she demonstrated the req-
uisite degree of terror. As long as she trembled and pleaded for
mercy, he was well content, and as for the ritual with the bottle—
sometimes Manzanilla, sometimes vodka, which she much preferred as being less sticky—that had become positively welcome,
heralding the end of the encounter and another successful transaction completed. Afterward, as she took her bath, she would fanta-
size about cutting off the end of his penis with her razor blade and
ramming the bleeding stump into the empty bottle until it was full
of blood and forcing him to drink it. But still she would not have
admitted that she feared him.

Nevertheless, she approached the imposing portals of the Gaylord Hotel with something less than her normal enthusiasm. She
was very tired again, and wished it was a Thursday, when she might
take a welcome nap at Jack's expense. She stifled a yawn and crossed
the road without looking, narrowly avoiding a cab, which screeched
to a stop, blowing its horn, before discharging its passengers on the
opposite pavement.

Marisa never acknowledged her clients in public. She held back,
watching Jack pay the driver, and was quite unprepared for him to
turn and wave, as did his lady friend. Unaccountably, she found
this irritating, and did not return the greeting, turning her back on
them and flouncing into the hotel without a second glance.

The incident kept floating back into her mind throughout the next few hours. Her work required little concentration, and often she would distract herself from the matter at hand by daydreaming about the future. But lately her daydreams had been bad, the future had loomed not beckoned, she had been searching for a new faith to replace the one she had lost. If Ramón were to die, she would never board that liner, never tour the world, never live in luxury, never know the bliss of idleness. Since that morning when she had woken to find herself streaked with Ramón's blood, she had been seeking some other vision to sustain her; one that might be less perfect but one that had the charm of possibility.

She had asked Jack to look after her with only the vaguest notion of what she meant, her words shaping her unformed thoughts. But now, lying in the bath while the fat man snored, the new images began to gel. One day Jack would take her back to England with him and there she would live the life of an English lady. She would no longer have to work, no longer have to stick razor blades under her shoes, no longer have to obey strangers for money. She would have leisure to sleep and sleep and talk and talk. It would be like being a child again, except that she had never been a child. Like a child, she would be fed and kept and nothing would be required of her. Because he liked her. She had finally come to understand the value of that.

The Frenchwoman represented everything Marisa longed to be. She oozed elegance and charm and wit, she was a native of that magic world that Marisa could never enter without an escort. And now seeing her with Jack had made her jealous. Not sexually jealous, such an emotion was alien to her. If she had discovered them in bed together, she would have accepted it with equanimity, but she did not like to think of them talking together, of Jack liking her, preferring her.

Liking was still a novel concept for Marisa. She loved Ramón, she loathed Tomás, she was indifferent to Dolores, she felt sorry for the boy. As for family, they were family, just as clients were clients. Personal preference did not come into it. But if Jack suddenly had no money or whiskey or cigarettes, she would still want to go and lie on his bed and talk to him. And so . . . she must like him.

She would prove it, to herself and to him. Next time, she would not take his money. Next time she would just take the whiskey and cigarettes. It was a momentous decision, and afterward she felt much happier.

* * *

Dolores looked at the pile of money, speechless.

"Take it," said her brother, with a magnanimous gesture, but averting his eyes, as if he could hardly bear to contemplate the enormity of his gift.

"How did you come by this?" she asked. "Is this Marisa's money?"

"It is my money. I am a man of abstemious habits. I have lived like a pauper these past few years out of choice, not necessity. I knew that times would be hard. Did I not warn you, years ago, what would happen? Did I not predict that we would be stripped of all our land and property, that the day would come when we would be persecuted by the masses? You did not believe me then, little sister. You believed in your world of justice and freedom where all men would be equal, you were foolish enough to believe that it was right to share. Share! Do they share with us? But I will share with you, and with Andrés. My days are numbered, but even if they were not, I would want to see you safe." He put his hand on his heart in a melodramatic gesture, and filled the room with his saintly smile.

"But Marisa . . ."

"Pah! When I am dead, she will be some rich man's mistress. This she will owe entirely to me. I picked her up out of the gutter, I fed her and clothed her and equipped her for the only occupation for which she is fit. She owes everything to me. My first duty must be to my own flesh and blood."

"But . . ."

"I give you this to free you from that animal. Go to Valencia with the boy. Let him report you. The *checas* will never find you once you have left Madrid."

"But they might find you. Remember, Tomás hates you. The only reason he does not denounce you is because of me." She pushed the money back at him. "Thank you, Ramón. But I cannot take it. Keep it. Who knows what may happen? We may need it yet to buy our lives."

"Let him denounce me," said Ramón with a wave of the hand. "I have told my odious neighbors a thousand times that I am of exalted birth. No one believes me, and no one will believe him either. I have posed for years now as a feeble invalid, a wretched drunkard, incapable of conspiracy. Thanks to this disguise, I am beneath suspicion. By all means let him accuse me, hopping here on his one leg to point a finger at a fellow cripple. He will make himself a laughingstock. Think, Dolores. One day, after I am dead, the city will be liberated, and you will be branded as the wife and child of a Red! Have you no care for your son?"

"Ssh!" Dolores looked anxiously toward the door. "Someone may hear you!" She looked at the money again. Perhaps they could just disappear one day, without even telling the school . . .

"I will think carefully, Ramón," she said. "But I know no one in Valencia, I know no one outside Madrid. It is often as dangerous to flee as to stay. And I am not afraid of Tomás. If I flee, it will not be from him."

Ramón heaved a deep sigh of regret.

"I offer it for the boy," he said haughtily. "He is like my own son."

Poor little Rafael, thought Dolores. If Rosa and Rafael were here she would have taken Ramón's money unhesitatingly and handed it over to his rightful heir.

She kissed her brother, noticing his flushed cheek. He had a good color today and seemed much better. He stuffed the money back into his pocket. She had let her chance slip by, perhaps for good. His mood swings were such that he might well think better of his offer, or even deny that he had ever made it. She should have played safe and accepted it, given herself time to think. Had she been rejecting the money, or rejecting what it stood for? She had run and run and run. Perhaps she was tired of running.

"Say nothing of this to Marisa," put in Ramón unnecessarily. "The girl is obsessed with spending. She cares nothing for the future."

"Perhaps she is right. Perhaps there is no future."

Ramón let this remark pass. He could have reassured her that all would be well, but it was clearly not prudent to do so. He had hoped that she would jump at the chance of escape, that she would prove herself worthy of his trust. For a long time now he had suspected that the brute maltreated her—such men always beat their womenfolk—and that she would have learned the error of her ways. But she had miserably failed the test he had set her, confirmed his worst fears. She remained in thrall to García, despite everything, she had proved herself unfit for his sacred mission. Which left only one possible ally . . .

As soon as Dolores had left, he replaced the money safely under the floorboards, smiling at the gun like an old friend. If they ever came for him, they would be too late. It was the only honorable way. Not that he feared torture. For one as inured to pain as he, torture held no terrors. But he would deny them the pleasure of inflicting it. He put the muzzle in his mouth, closing his cracked lips around the smooth cold metal, enjoying the tactile taste of death. He must leave a note before that moment came, naming the boy as his legatee. But he would leave his nephew more than money. He would leave him a priceless heirloom.

Paulina disappeared from the school quite suddenly, without saying good-bye. Dolores assumed she had got a new posting, not that this was officially confirmed. Paulina had been ''transferred,'' a euphemism for both reward and punishment; one did not question the divine will of the party.

Her sudden departure left Dolores without supplies of the pain-killing drug. Paulina had been careful not to name her comrade, nor the dispensary where he worked. Dolores dreaded breaking the news to Tomás.

He had been subdued since the outburst with Andrés, as had Andrés himself, his bright blue eyes betraying a new and formidable adult scorn. Gone were those early, happy, eager days when she had truly felt herself a mother, able to cater to his every need, certain of his love. The bond between them had been prematurely, cruelly severed. He had found out too soon that she was not perfect; he had begun to judge her and find her wanting.

If only she had someone to confide in. If only Josep were here . . . No, that was a selfish thought. If Josep were here, in the Republic, he would be in terrible danger. Every day, she prayed that he had escaped persecution at the hands of his anarchist flock. Every day, she gave thanks that his parish was now safely behind Fascist lines. By now he would have learned of events in Albavera, by now he almost certainly thought her dead. It was just as well. If Josep knew of her present circumstances, he might put himself at risk by trying to join her. If he was still alive, he must stay alive. There had been too many deaths already.

Two more children were missing from school that day, their parents having opted for local evacuation, as perhaps Dolores might have done herself by now, if she had had nothing to hide. The number of pupils was diminishing daily, as more and more parents sent their children off to the country, motivated more by the shortage of food than the bombing and shelling. In any case, now that German planes had destroyed a small town like Guernica, nowhere was safe any longer. Who knew where they might strike next?

She waited for Andrés in the corridor, and asked him brightly about his day, but he was in one of his silent moods. As usual Dolores was preoccupied, not picking up the warning signals until he flung the question at her, taking her completely by surprise.

"Are you going to send me away?" he demanded without pre-amble.

Dolores reacted guiltily, assuming immediately that he wanted to get away, and that she would have to find an excuse for keeping him at home. Several of his little friends had already left, and she knew he hated their dingy lodgings, hated Tomás, and in all prob-ability, hated her too.

"Why? Would you like to go away?" she prevaricated brightly, unsure how to proceed.

But his response was explosive, angry and immediate.

"I won't go!" he shouted. "I won't go! I don't want to live on a farm! I don't want to leave Uncle Ramón!"

"But Andrés—"

"I won't!" Dolores was momentarily speechless. "I won't go!" He was very near to tears. Jumbled, piecemeal, it all flooded out of him, the fear he had been bottling up for weeks now that she was planning to get rid of him, that Tomás would make her send him away, and that once he was gone he would never be allowed to come back.

Appalled, Dolores tried to hold him close, but he shrank from her, fighting not to cry, hiding his feelings of misery and rejection, rebelling, not pleading. Even at six years old, he had too much pride to plead. No, not just pride. He had that strange, evocative Jack-like mixture of confidence and anxiety, his aggression nothing but a front.

He allowed her to comfort and cajole him only briefly before reverting to his normal self-contained self. No matter how much she tried to reassure him, he would always doubt her. Had she driven him to it in some way, or was it congenital, inescapable, beyond her control?

"Andrés," she said firmly. "If I ever sent you away, it would not be to get rid of you, it would only be to keep you safe."

"I won't go," he repeated, calmer now, but implacable.

"You don't have to go. Not yet. But if I ever decide that you must, then you will have to do as I say."

"Then I'll run away," he growled. And then, striking terror into her heart, "Tomás said I mustn't tell anyone about my father being a Fascist, or they'll put you in prison. But my father wasn't a Fas-cist, was he? Was he?"

"No," said Dolores, heart beating. Had Tomás been trying to undo the damage, or compound it? "Just remember, Andrés, your father is Tomás. If anyone asks you, your father is Tomás."

"No, he's not," he muttered mutinously. And then, again, "You won't send me away, will you, Mamá?"

"No," said Dolores, half-defeated, half-relieved. "No, I won't send you away."

She left Andrés with Ramón and set off for home, bracing herself for further trouble from Tomás.

"Paulina has gone away," she told him stiffly. "I don't know anyone else who can help us. You know how scarce drugs are."

She held her breath, waiting for the inevitable accusations: that she planned to sell her supplies; that she preferred to give them to her brother; that she was deliberately withholding them to make him suffer.

"Good," said Tomás quietly. "Now we need be dependent on her no longer."

Dolores was momentarily speechless.

"My pain is much less," he continued doggedly. "Soon I will find work again, in munitions. Then I can feed my family again."

Dolores should have been glad at this unexpected improvement in his spirits. No insults, no anger, no suspicion. He had addressed her civilly, normally, for the first time in months. But all she could feel was unease. This must surely be the calm before the storm.

"Where is the boy?" he continued. "With his uncle?"

"Yes," said Dolores defensively. "I wanted to give you some peace, that is all."

"It is natural to love one's own kin," said Tomás. "I cannot expect the boy to share my grievance. Lole . . . I know you do not love me. I know you despise me as half a man."

"I do not despise you, Tomás."

"I know you fear me. There is no need. Even if you left me, I would never betray you. I would rather you left me, than stayed with me through fear."

Dolores felt her face burn with telltale color. She had spent a day and a night agonizing about Ramón's offer, cursing herself for not accepting it, wallowing in the martyrdom that had replaced her self-respect, finding security in captivity, trying to dress up inertia as tenacity, fear as prudence, guilt as loyalty.

"If I had wanted to leave you, I would have done so by now. As you know, I'm selfish, for myself and my son. If I stay with you through fear, it is because . . . because I am afraid to be without you. Because I am afraid to be alone.''

"I was wrong to insult the boy's father," continued Tomás gravely. "He was a brave man. I was wrong to make you marry me so soon after his death. I will not force myself on you again."

"You have never forced—"

"I am no fool, Lole. Do not treat me like one. I have said my piece. You have made me a weakling with your patience, you have spoiled me like a child. I know you meant well. But now I must learn to be strong again."

His words were oddly threatening, the unspoken accusations uncomfortably near the mark. For months now she had played the victim, but was she really as innocent as she liked to believe? Did she not visit her guilt on him every day with her eternal tolerance, her stubborn stoicism, insulting him with her forgiveness, humiliating him with her chilly calm? Ignacia would have shouted back at him, goaded him into recovery, given him no sympathy, brooked no self-pity . . .

Had she been driving him toward violence to give herself an excuse to leave him? Or had she used him as a scapegoat for her own apathy? Either way, she was ill prepared for the sudden loss of initiative, which left her nervous and confused. Her unease did not dissipate when Tomás saluted Andrés jovially and humored him into a wary response, nor when he kept his word and did not demand his conjugal rights. She remained on edge, disoriented, torn between relief and resentment. To her own astonishment, she lost her temper over a trifle, the next morning, when Tomás accidentally knocked one of their three cups from the table, sending fragments bouncing all over the floor.

Normally she would have knelt down without a word and picked the pieces up, reproaching him with her very silence.

"You clumsy oaf!" she heard herself shout. "Clear it up yourself!"

She saw Andrés looking at her openmouthed, and waited, frozen by her own folly, for the ricochet. But Tomás merely got up and said quietly, "Help me, if you please, Andrés."

She stood dumbly while they set about their task, fighting the desire to cry, hating herself for this unaccountable lapse. She marched Andrés off to school without saying good-bye to Tomás, waiting for the little monster to snicker in delight and applaud her display of ill humor, mentally preparing a suitable rebuke. But he didn't say a word, as if fearing to provoke further wrath.

She returned home that evening contrite, determined to atone, to restore the unequal balance of give and take. But Tomás had beaten her to the giving. The cup did not match the other two, crude pieces of pottery, the cheapest available. He had hauled himself off to the market, located a stall trading furtively in expropriated goods, and picked out an exquisite china cup and saucer, to make her feel at home.

A smiling nurse opened the door of Clara's sunlit room at Professor Elliott's Surrey clinic.

"You have a visitor, Miss Neville. A Mrs. Prendergast."

Clara turned over and buried her face in the pillow. A curse on bloody Richard Peabody.

"I don't wish to see Mrs. Prendergast."

"I'm afraid she's a very persistent lady. And she's brought you some lovely flowers."

"Tell her to make a bloody wreath with them. Tell her to—"

There was a sudden commotion in the corridor, and the door burst open.

"Mrs. Prendergast," began the nurse, placing herself between the visitor and the patient. "Miss Neville doesn't feel well enough to—"

"Oh go *away*," interjected Clara. The nurses here were a flaccid lot in her opinion. "Sit down, Flo."

The nurse, realizing belatedly that the peremptory dismissal was directed at her, marched off in some relief. Flora dumped her flowers in the washbasin and drew up a chair.

"First of all, don't take it out on Richard Peabody," she began without preamble. "Or on that old fossil Elliott. They're only men, after all. You look ghastly. I expect the food here's absolutely vile. I brought you some marshmallows."

She opened the box and helped herself to one, keeping up the charade of briskness. Clara looked at the pink blobs blankly, as if unsure what they were. There was a glassy look about her eyes. They'd probably pumped her full of drugs, but it was more than that. If Flora had ever doubted that Clara loved her brother, she ceased to doubt it then.

She resisted the temptation to take hold of that thin, white, freckled hand and squeeze it, to even imply that she could begin to share her suffering. She swallowed the marshmallow with difficulty. She hated their glutinous texture and sickly taste, but Mummy had insisted that they were Clara's favorite.

"What do you want me to say?" said Clara at last. "That I'm sorry? Well, I'm sorry. You're right to blame me. You're entitled to hate me. There's nothing I can say that can possibly make any difference. I wish you hadn't come. You've only come for Edmund's sake. You've only ever put up with me for Edmund's sake. Please leave me alone, Flo. Please."

"But I've only just got here," said Flora placidly. "I won't stay long, just ten minutes or so, and then I might pop in again tomorrow. Thames Ditton's only a hop. In fact, I thought you might like to come and stay with us for a bit, once they let you out . . ."

"I shall be going back to Spain," interrupted Clara tonelessly. "As soon as I leave here, I'm going back to Spain. Richard promised."

"Oh. I see. Well, it was just a thought. Mummy would have come, but she's a bit under the weather. She sends her best. Everyone sends their best."

Clara took a deep breath.

"Flora," she said hoarsely. "I know you only mean to be kind. But I can't bear to have anything to do with the family. No matter what any of you say, I'd prefer you to hate me, I'd prefer that none of you saw me ever again. I've had about as much as I can take, without your kindness."

"Rubbish," snorted Flora, smoothing her skirt, improvising desperately. Hospital visiting was beastly at the best of times. "I'm not in the least bit kind, in fact I've always been *un*kind, at least as far as you're concerned. I never liked you much, you know. I thought you were bad for Edmund. I used to keep hoping he'd meet somebody else, someone like me I suppose, who'd want to get married and make a proper home for him. I used to make cheap jokes at your expense and be generally spiteful and petty at every opportunity. I didn't realize why I was doing it, until Dolly put me right. You know how Dolly used to come out with things. It was at luncheon one day, I remember, and I made some frightfully witty remark about your hair being the same color as the mashed turnips. And then Dolly said, 'Do leave off, Flo. You're just jealous, that's all.'"

Clara gave no indication of listening, her eyes far away.

"She was right, of course," continued Flora doggedly. "I'd worshiped Edmund since I was knee-high, even though he used to tick me off all the time for being vain and silly. He had lots of girlfriends before you, you know, and he used to bring them home from Oxford on weekends and think no one realized when they crept along the corridor to his room in the middle of the night. I lay in wait for one of them once and shouted boo. He was *furious*. And I was never jealous of any of them, even though the were all a great deal prettier than you, or me, for that matter. He could have married any one of them and I wouldn't have turned a hair. Ah, but when *you* came along, you had to take him away from us, body and soul. He still loved us, he still loved me, but it was never the same after that because he loved you *more*. God alone knows why, I'm sure *you* don't, but he loved you more than all the rest of the world put together. He would have died for you, and now he has, and you've no right to be angry with him for it. And neither have I, neither has any of us. I was so *angry* with him for dying, Clara! I still am, damnit!''

No use. Flora seldom cried, but when she did, there were no half measures. She wept copiously, forgetting about Clara, immersed in her own private fury, jerked out of it only by a long thin wail that filled out into a hideous howl, so terrifying that Flora didn't even try to cope with it herself but summoned assistance, mortified at the effect she had unwittingly produced, horrified by the gaping black hole in the middle of Clara's face and the primitive, animal sounds pouring out of it.

Two nurses appeared instantaneously and one of them ushered Flora hurriedly into the visitors' lounge, where she sat sniffing into her handkerchief, wondering where she had gone wrong. Archie was right, she shouldn't have come. She had done more harm than good. But she had *had* to come, if only to reassure poor Mummy that Clara was ''all right,'' even though she knew perfectly well that she wouldn't be ''all right,'' that she couldn't be ''all right'' or she wouldn't be in a mental home. Part of her had wanted to help, of course, but part of her had needed to witness Clara's suffering and yet another part of her had been working on instinct, almost as if Edmund would tell her what to say, what to do, although of course such a notion was absurd, fanciful.

She could hear screaming now, dreadful screaming like someone being tortured. It probably wasn't Clara. The place was presumably full of gibbering lunatics. Besides, she hadn't said anything that could possibly have upset Clara that much. All she had said was how much Edmund loved her. Perhaps she shouldn't have mentioned the mashed turnips. It had been a pretty tactless remark. Perhaps she shouldn't have admitted that she was angry with Edmund, but she hadn't even realized that she'd been angry with Edmund until that moment. Professor Elliott would be furious with her. They'd only let her in as a special favor, they'd warned her that Clara wasn't up to it, and now they would accuse her of "upsetting the patient" and make her feel an absolute fool. Perhaps she should just leave now, quickly, and telephone later for a bulletin. The screaming stopped, but there was a high-pitched keening noise, bloodcurdling in its intensity, rhythmic, hopeless, a distillation of despair.

Flora put a cigarette into her holder and puffed away at it without inhaling, for the sake of something to do. In normal circumstances she would have brought the children. Children always cheered people up, but of course children were taboo in the circumstances. She persevered for a couple of minutes, and then stubbed the cigarette out. She couldn't bear to sit here a moment longer.

"Please tell Professor Elliott that I'll telephone later," she said to the nurse on the desk. "I have to leave now."

"Professor Elliott is with Miss Neville at the moment. Would you mind waiting a little while longer? He said he would like to see you before you go."

Flora didn't doubt that, and sat down guiltily again. She fell to rehearsing some suitable version of the visit for Mummy. Clara was pale and tearful, but bearing up. Bearing up. That was a good phrase. It was irreproachable to bear up. Edmund, you bastard, how could you do this to us?

"Mrs. Prendergast? Thank you so much for waiting. Could I have a brief word with you?"

Flora followed him into his inner sanctum, regretting now that she had bullied Richard Peabody into telling her where Clara was. Jack genuinely hadn't known, and it was the only thing he could suggest. Peabody at Spanish Medical Aid. What luck, she had thought, that he turned out to be on leave in England. How fortunate that he had persuaded Clara to come home. How clever she had thought herself to have bulldozed her way into seeing her. It was true, she was an interfering busybody. She would end up a cantankerous old battle-ax, like Granny Townsend . . .

Flora waited for Elliott to speak, keeping her backbone ramrod straight, adopting the stern demeanor that had quelled a dozen committees.

"Congratulations, Mrs. Prendergast," said Professor Elliott. "You have succeeded where we experts have failed. You have made Miss Neville cry."

* * *

"I should like you to have a memento of me, Andrés, after I am gone. Do not look so sad. No man can survive as many mortal wounds as I and live to be ancient."

Andrés remained subdued. He did not like to think about his uncle dying, let alone talk about it.

"Say nothing yet to your mother," continued Ramón. "It would distress her. But when the last breath leaves this suffering body, before I am laid to rest, I ask you to remove this boot, and keep it always, in memory of me."

He tapped the dilapidated boot with his stick.

"It will serve to remind you of the injuries I have sustained in the service of my country. Swear to me, boy, that you will respect my dying wish, on your most sacred honor."

"On my most sacred honor," parroted Andrés automatically. His uncle was always swearing him to secrecy.

"On no account must García know of this," continued Ramón. "After I am dead, you must ask for my boot, as a keepsake, and guard it with your life. On no account must you part with it. Will you promise me this?"

"I promise." said Andrés, "but I would rather have your walking stick."

"All my worldly goods will be yours, my son. I intend to make a will in your favor. You may dispose of all my property as you think fit, but not the boot. The boot I charge you to keep forever in memory of me. It may seem a worthless object, but I assure you its value is priceless. On no account must it be lost or destroyed. Swear it."

"I swear it."

"Good boy. Let us return home now. I am very tired."

Andrés looked at the boot curiously as his uncle limped along beside him. It was falling apart, and seemed a poor parting gift. But he had given his solemn promise and he would keep it. In any case, his uncle was not going to die just yet. For the first time in weeks, he had gone out for a walk, and seemed much better. Perhaps Marisa would be home when they got back and would give him some chocolate. This hope inspired him to run on ahead, nearly colliding with Tomás.

"Whoa, boy," said the giant. "What are you doing out in the street on your own?"

"Uncle Ramón is with me," said Andrés sullenly, expecting trouble. Tomás looked surprised.

"I thought he was confined to his bed," he said. And then, raising his voice, "*Salud,* Ramón."

Ramón stopped in his tracks. It was the first time he had seen Tomás on crutches. He stared at him cruelly, his lip curling in undisguised mockery, not deigning to return the greeting.

"Let us cease to be enemies, for your sister's sake," continued Tomás. "We have both caused her enough suffering."

Ramón stared disbelievingly at the outstretched hand. Did this brute who beat and defiled his sister dare to offer him friendship? He took a precautionary step backward, out of range of Tomás's crutches.

"You have wronged my sister, García," he accused him haughtily, in the manner of a nobleman addressing a serf.

"You have wronged mine," said Tomás. "Let us not quarrel in front of the child. If you do not want my friendship, then so be it."

"You mocked me once for a cripple," taunted Ramón, retreating another couple of paces. "And now you are more crippled than I."

"I spared you as a cripple," said Tomás. "If you had not been a cripple I should have killed you with my bare hands. Be warned, my hands are still strong. Come, Andrés."

"Come, Andrés," said Ramón.

Andrés took a step toward Ramón, then hesitated.

"Do not be frightened, boy," said Tomás. "If you wish to go with your uncle, then go. I will come to fetch you later. Your mother is ailing, with one of her headaches."

"Thanks to you, no doubt," spat Ramón. "You may wait in the street when you come. You are not welcome in my home."

Andrés stood openmouthed, transfixed, waiting for Tomás to lunge at his uncle with his customary angry roar.

"Even so, you are welcome in mine, for Lole's sake. You need no longer fear me. Why do you stand so far away? Are you still afraid of me? Go on, strike me with your stick and prove how brave you are. I will not hit you back."

Ramón's lips twitched in fury.

"I would not contaminate myself by touching you. Beware, García. If you ever raise a hand to my poor sister, you will be answerable to me!" He waved his stick in the air. "Do you hear me? I will kill you!"

"Do so," said Tomás. "If I ever strike her, then by all means kill me. As I should have killed you seven years ago."

He swiveled himself around and thrust himself along the street while Ramón sneered and Andrés looked perplexed.

"Did you hear that, Andrés? If that oaf ever lifts a finger against your mother, you are to report the matter to me immediately. I'll send him to hell for it!"

Andrés followed Tomás, confused. He had never seen him hit his mother. But if he did so, Ramón would kill him. Not long ago, the prospect of his uncle killing Tomás would have filled him with delight. He hated Tomás, or had, up to now. And he admired his uncle, or had up to now . . .

His mother was in bed, and Tomás asked him to help prepare her supper. Afterward he put him to bed and listened while Andrés read aloud from his storybook. Then he stretched himself across two chairs and extinguished the lamp.

"I will sleep in here, with you, tonight," he said, "so as not to disturb your mother."

Lying there in the dark, Andrés reached furtively for the precious silver-wrapped delicacy he had saved for bedtime, and unwrapped it stealthily under the covers, his mouth watering in anticipation. Two more squares. He popped one of them into his mouth and let it melt very slowly on his tongue, making it last as long as possible, starring at the dull red glow of Tomás's pipe winking at him in the darkness. Then he slipped out of bed and felt his way toward it.

"What's the matter, boy?" asked Tomás gruffly.

Andrés pressed the sticky treasure into his hand without a word and got back into bed. It was several minutes before Tomás said thank you, and by that time Andrés was asleep.

Josep's leg took a long time to heal. By the time he was able to walk again, the Basque country was in the throes of surrender, leaving him with a miserable sense of having deserted. Nevertheless, his voyage had not been in vain. After three days at sea, the little fishing boat had been picked up by a French vessel, and the two children were now installed with a local family, happily unaware that their mother had almost certainly perished.

Josep had been nursed back to health in a nearby convent. His wound had ulcerated and become infected, immobilizing him, and thereby saving his life.

"You are welcome to stay here, Father," the local priest assured him. "There are many Spanish priests here in France who fled from persecution in the early days of the war. And now many Basque children are being evacuated. You speak Basque, you could be of value. They need priests to work in the refugee camps . . ."

Josep had nodded, but not listened, consumed with lethargy. It

was all over, then. There was nothing left for him to do. He had
lost his family, his job, and now his country too. The thought of
some humdrum sinecure appalled him. He felt isolated, trapped,
impotent, more threatened by safety than ever he had been by danger.

His low spirits troubled his mentor, who sought out one of Josep's countrymen in an attempt to cheer him—an elderly priest,
who had fled to France rather than seek refuge in Fascist territory.

He was a sympathetic old man, and it was a relief to be speaking
in Spanish again. As a result, Josep said rather more than he meant
to. For the first time his anger and frustration boiled to the surface,
he found himself railing against the workers who had killed Dolores, the Fascists who had stormed Fontenar, the Germans who had
bombed Guernica . . . and himself.

"I can't stay here," he said. "I'm young, I'm strong, I'd feel
like a coward."

"Then go home."

"Home?"

"There are safe houses in the Republic. Many priests are still in
hiding."

"I have no wish to accept hospitality at the hands of Fascist
sympathizers," said Josep. "Nor to conduct private Masses for the
rich. I would feel like a turncoat."

"Not all priests who remain in hiding are cowards. Not all of
them are Fascist sympathizers. Things are changing at home, Josep. By banning the Church, the Republic has purged it, strength-
ened it, driven it underground, where it spreads its roots like
bindweed. The Church was corrupt, it needed this ordeal to cleanse
it. The time has come to bring it back to the people. There are
those who risk their lives daily, taking the sacraments to the dying,
saying Mass in secret. If you want to join that fight, the struggle
has only just begun."

"There are other priests who feel as I do? Other priests who do
not support the Fascists?"

"Did you think we were alone?"

"I have always been alone."

"Be warned, Josep, the danger is very great, and the secret police are very efficient. Do not take such a decision lightly. Every
day you would face the risk that someone might betray you . . ."

Josep found this strangely soothing. It was better than betraying
himself.

14

"You ought been there, Jack," said Laszlo, spreading his photographs over the bed. "You ought write about it."

The pictures of the violent street fighting in Barcelona had been taken with Laszlo's habitual disregard for life and limb. Officially, the POUM and the anarchists had been the aggressors, attacking the authority of the Communist/socialist coalition under the alleged instigation of Fascist agents. Unofficially, Jack had no doubt that the revolutionary parties had simply responded to deliberate harassment by the police, carried out with the specific aim of inciting and crushing a riot.

Laszlo was right. He ought to be there and he ought to be writing about it, if only to set the record straight. Helpful and informative communiqués had already been distributed, which would be endorsed and reproduced without question, given that the ultraleft had no champions among the foreign press. The Communists had become the most right-wing party in Republican Spain, friends of the petty bourgeoisie, protectors of private property, guardians of law and order, bulwark against the pillaging hordes of collectivists and armed thugs. The rumor had been put about that the revolutionary factions were collaborating secretly with the Fascists to overthrow the Republic, and ludicrous though the theory might be, there was more than enough circumstantial evidence to support it. The smear campaign had been intelligently conceived and executed, and if half as much strategic energy had gone into fighting Franco, the war might have been over by now.

"How are you going to caption these?" said Jack. "How about 'Spanish freedom fighters strike a blow against Soviet imperialism'?"

"My editor, he supports Russian intervention," Laszlo shrugged. "It will be something like 'Government forces quell riots by extremists'," put in Thérèse cynically. "Why didn't you go to Barcelona, Jack?"

"Too busy," said Jack shortly.

"Still doing your research on schools?"

"Yes."

"Do you need any pictures?"

"No thanks."

"You're up to something," she accused him, exchanging glances with Laszlo. "Don't get yourself into trouble, will you? Be discreet."

"That, if you don't mind my saying so, is the pot calling the kettle black. You're the one who takes risks, not me."

"Not anymore. I leave that to Laszlo now, don't I, *chéri?*"

"I going France," clarified Laszlo. "Catch refugee ship for Bilbao."

"While I take pretty pictures for *American Women,*" said Thérèse, grimacing. "I'm off to Valencia tomorrow. Very exciting."

"See you when you get back, then," said Jack, embracing her. "I'd better get on with some work."

He left them to their packing and went back to his own room, on the opposite side of the corridor. He hadn't bothered to lock it; Laszlo had interrupted him in full flow, eager to show him his pictures, and Jack had left his novel strewn all over the desk. He was getting careless. It would be most inconsiderate to get himself arrested; poor Harry Martindale would never live down the triumphant headlines in the *Daily Worker:* FORMER RED RAG JOURNALIST CONFESSES 'I WAS A FASCIST SPY.' He would be in good company. All but the bravest of dissidents ended up "confessing" to treason. He had better heed Thérèse's advice and be discreet, at least until he'd done as much as he could to find the child. It was as good an excuse for staying alive as any.

He worked till midnight and distributed the typewritten sheets under the mattress, for what it was worth. The precaution seemed melodramatic. He had no reason to believe that he was under suspicion, and if he was, they would plant something on him anyway. *Finish it at home, Jack, for God's sake.* Home. The word was meaningless. He could honestly say he felt as much and as little at home here as anywhere else. There was nobody who missed him, nobody to care for, nothing that mattered except lost causes—his novel, and finding Andrés. All his time was taken up with hopeless endeavor, constant activity leading nowhere, not even to exhaustion. However late he went to bed he would wake up at dawn, pinned down by the crushing weight of suicidal depression. He had loved only two human beings in the world, and now both of them had died pointless deaths while he carried on living a pointless life. The survival instinct was treacherously strong. Just how pointless did a life have to be for you to find the guts to end it? In a year, he would have finished the book, given up the search for Dolly's child, spent all his savings. What then?

In a year there might be a war in Europe. He would be called up, unless he got himself accredited as a war correspondent, a role that he could no longer contemplate. He wouldn't qualify for a commission, not that he could have borne to accept one. If there was one thing worse than taking orders it was giving them. He hadn't sold out that much. It would be back to the bottom of the class ladder, they would teach him to know his place at last. It might be quite a relief. He hadn't beaten them, but at least he had never joined them.

He undressed and poured himself a nightcap, some filthy Spanish brew that guaranteed a modicum of sleep. He tossed it back in one swallow, like medicine, switched off the light, and waited for it to take effect. How you died was irrelevant, it was how you lived that mattered. And there was nothing in his life he could be proud of, no one in his life who would remember him; when he died it would be as if he had never lived. All very maudlin. Still, it made you think. It made you understand why people had children.

"Thank you, Tomás."

It had been thank you, Tomás, and thank you, Andrés, for two days now. They had divided her household tasks between them, working surprisingly well together. Tomás had nicknamed the boy Legs. "I am your arms, and he is your legs, until you are better."

As far as Tomás was aware, Dolores had "fainted" from exhaustion. This time it had happened on her way downstairs, and she had taken a heavy fall. There had been none of the familiar warning signals, just sudden, total blackout. She had been badly bruised and shaken, not least by the knowledge that she had been lucky not to break her neck.

Next time, her luck might run out. Next time she might not recover consciousness. Useless to pretend any longer, it had been like a final, vivid warning. She must protect Andrés. Neither Tomás nor Ramón nor Marisa were capable of taking care of him. If she died, he would end up in a state orphanage, one of hundreds of motherless children, flotsam on the bottomless ocean of war . . .

The time had come to swallow her pride. Tomorrow she would go to the Florida Hotel and ask Jack to take responsibility for his son. It would be dishonoring Lorenzo, dishonoring Andrés, dishonoring herself, sacrificing what little dignity she had left. But she must either suffer that humiliation or live—no, die—with the consequences.

What was it Edmund had said to her that day? *You have a great propensity for folly, young lady.* How those words had rung in her ears! If only she were English. No English girl would have felt so much disgrace. Her upbringing had got the better of her, she was permeated through and through with stupid, Spanish pride . . . -

"Thank you, Andrés." It was a plate of corned beef. Tomás had discovered her cache of black-market goods, but he had passed no comment other than to tell her she must eat to build up her strength. She had already begun to take his clumsy tenderness for granted, to forget the horrific frenzies of rage.

Tomorrow she would go to see Jack. She would weep and grovel and plead, she would tell him that she was a dying woman, that her husband was a cripple, that her child would be destitute without her. And if all else failed, then and only then, she would say, "You told me that I wouldn't get a baby, and I did. You seduced me. It's your fault, your responsibility." It was true, after all, even if it wasn't quite honest.

Father Spinks knocked on Clara's door and entered without waiting.

"And how's my prize sinner this morning?"

Clara looked daggers, turned her head away and shut her eyes. Undeterred, the hospital chaplain pulled up a chair, produced a pouch of tobacco and painstakingly rolled himself a cigarette.

"Please," said Clara. "Please leave me alone."

"You've changed your tune, I must say. Last time I was here you wouldn't let me go. I was here half the night as I recall. There's no gratitude in the world."

"I'm sorry. I was delirious. I don't even remember asking for a priest."

"Nasty business, blood poisoning. Still, if you will go gallivanting in foreign parts. Let it be a lesson to you. You nearly died, you know."

"I know," muttered Clara into the pillow. "I thought I was going to hell."

She opened one eye just a fraction and looked at him through the lashes. He could have been any age between thirty-five and fifty, short, squat, badly shaven, with an air of cheerful seediness, more like a greengrocer than a priest. She felt the same kind of hostile intimacy toward him as she had once felt toward the men she had slept with, men who found her vile and disgusting but who tolerated her because she made it worth their while. Like them, he knew the worst of her, like them he wanted his payoff and would hang around for further pickings. Like them, he had served his purpose and he would have to go.

"It wasn't contrition, just cowardice," she added sullenly. "I want you to withdraw your absolution. I got it under false pretenses. I used you and now I've finished with you and will you please leave me in peace."

"If I could leave you in peace, I would do so with pleasure. As it is, I'd better stay a while longer." He continued licking and sticking placidly, evidently more interested in his ill-made cigarette than in Clara's immortal soul.

How horribly degrading confession was! Even as a child, she had found it an intolerable invasion of her privacy, preferring to invent imaginary sins rather than own up to real ones. She must have gibbered for hours, ranting and raving while the flames got nearer and nearer, her whole body melting with infernal heat. He had kept trying to cut her short but she wouldn't let him, not till she'd told him everything, everything, or it wouldn't count. Years and years of untold, unmentionable, unforgivable things. And then finally, there had been no more to say, and she had felt the oil trickling down her forehead and the soft, cool, soothing words, and before she had time to feel relief she had known, with startling clarity, that it had been a trick, that she wasn't going to die after all . . .

"You're in luck," puffed the priest through a cloud of noxious smoke. "I'm only covering for Father Beavis. He's gone on a pilgrimage to Lourdes. He'd have given you more than three Hail Marys, I can tell you. That's why I came in this morning. To give you your penance. I was going to let you off, thinking you were going to die and all, but now you're alive I have to insist. Three Hail Marys."

His voice was perfectly serious, and yet he couldn't possibly be.

"It's all nonsense, isn't it?" sneered Clara. "At least sackcloth and ashes made sense. I don't believe any of it you know. I was brainwashed. It's true what the Jesuits say. Give me a child before he is seven and he is mine for life. Or at least for death. You're wasting your time."

"Three Hail Marys," he repeated unequivocally. "Then I'll go. I delivered the goods as ordered, and now if you want to be rid of me, you'd better settle up. I haven't got all day."

"Don't be ridiculous."

"Come now, I've got a job to do. Try to see my point of view. Three Hail Marys, and I can move on to my next customer."

Clara laughed out loud in disbelief. He shook his head in mock capitulation. "I can see you drive a hard bargain. All right then, make me an offer."

Clara stared at him for a long time. He remained absolutely poker-faced.

"One Hail Mary," she said.

"Two and a half."

"Two."

"Done. But I want to hear you say them. I don't trust you. Specially after some of the things you told me. Talk about a wrong 'un."

He sat there, calmly puffing, shedding ash and tobacco all over his cassock, patiently waiting.

"What's the matter?" he said. "Forgotten the words?"

With a singsong lack of reverence, she obeyed him, tauntingly, watching him all the while. Halfway through she got a fit of sacrilegious giggles, but recovered herself sufficiently to finish.

"Thank God for that," he said, getting up. "Now you're in the clear. No hell, just a few thousand years in purgatory. See you there, I expect. Meanwhile, anytime you're dying, you'll find my rates very reasonable. It's been a pleasure to do business with you, Miss Neville."

He picked up her hand and shook it. Then he bent down and whispered in her ear, like an off-course tipster.

"Ten bob, and I'll get you off purgatory too. Ten bob for a special-intention Mass with all the trimmings and a plenary indulgence with your name on it."

Clara's lips twitched.

"Five," she said.

"Eight."

"Seven and six."

"Done."

He held out his hand and rubbed his fingers together while Clara reached for her handbag and extracted a pound note from her purse.

"Plus ten percent commission, he added slyly. "I've no change on me. Shall I bring it with me tomorrow?"

"Mind you do," said Clara.

"Don't go, Marisa. Thérèse, meet Marisa."

Marisa hovered in the doorway. Jack and the Frenchwoman were sitting together on the bed, with a pile of photographs between them, and Thérèse's shoes were lying on the floor. It was the sight of the empty shoes that made her decide to stay, despite her hostility toward her rival. Marisa's new high-heeled sandals were killing her, and this was the only room where it was safe to take them off.

"*Salud,* Thérèse," she said with a regal nod.

"*Salud,* Marisa."

The red-haired woman smiled and said something to Jack, which he immediately translated.

"Thérèse says she is sorry, she does not speak good Spanish. She asks your pardon, but she has work to do."

Thérèse stood up. Jack handed her the sheaf of photographs, but she shook her head, and Marisa understood by her gestures that she intended to come back later.

"I will not stay long," said Marisa sulkily, after she had gone.

"Don't be jealous," said Jack. "She is only a friend."

This remark served only to confirm Marisa's worst fears.

"Do you *like* her?"

"Not as much as I like you," said Jack. He picked up her handbag and put some money in it. Marisa took it out again.

"You do not pay *her* to talk," she said. "I do not want your money."

"What's the matter?" he said, perplexed, as she threw the bills on the floor. "Have I offended you?"

"She is beautiful. Will you sleep with her? I do not want her to be your friend."

"I cannot sleep with her because she does not wish it. She loves another man. Please take the money, Marisa."

She waved the bills aside.

"What are those pictures?"

"Work. Thérèse is a photographer. She wanted to show me the pictures she took in Valencia. Would you like to see?"

Marisa shook her head sulkily.

"She has just returned. That is why she came to see me. Why are you angry? Why won't you take what I owe you?"

Marisa softened slightly. His tone was coaxing, apologetic. She was not used to being coaxed, or apologized to. She wanted to explain to him, but lacked the words to do so, even to herself. But she must say something, or he would put the money in her bag again, and this time it would be even harder to give it back.

"I come here because I choose, not because I must. If you pay me . . . then I cannot choose. Keep the money. I will take the other things, but not the money."

He looked at her curiously.

"As you wish," he said. "Do you choose to talk?"

"No. I choose to rest. I am very, very tired."

She kicked her shoes off and lay down on the bed.

"You talk," she commanded. "I like to hear you talk." She stretched out sensuously. "You talk," she repeated. "Tell me a story."

He covered her with the bedspread and pulled up a chair.

"What kind of story?"

"A story with a poor girl who meets a handsome prince. A story with a happy ending."

"Very well. Once upon a time . . ."

Marisa sighed in perfect contentment. How delicious it was to lie here and just listen. She did not have to do anything at all, she did not even have to talk, because he had not paid her. This was luxury indeed. This was freedom. This was far, far better than money . . .

Within minutes she was fast asleep, curled up in a little fetal ball with her thumb in her mouth. Jack had never seen her asleep before, it made her look very young . . . she *was* very young, underneath all the paint, she couldn't be much more than sixteen. After an hour, reluctantly, he roused her, knowing she must have other appointments. She woke with a start, scrambled to her feet, and made a sudden bolt for the bathroom. Tactfully, Jack switched on the wireless. After several minutes she emerged, looking rather pale.

"What's the matter?" said Jack, concerned. "Are you ill?" But she just shook her head. She squeezed her swollen feet back into the tight sandals, and peered in his mirror, applying a fresh layer of lipstick and rouge.

"My *novio* has finished the whiskey," she said, reverting to her usual pragmatism. "And you have still not got me any silk stockings."

Jack laughed and shook his head at her. Marisa stuck out her tongue and teetered off, her skirt clinging tightly round her hips. Jack gathered up Thérèse's photographs and started leafing through them idly. There was a tap on the door.

"At last," said Thérèse, rolling her eyes in outrageous innuendo. "Can I come in, or are you too tired?"

"I'm exhausted. You're quite safe."

She sat down beside him on the bed.

"What do you think?"

"They're very good. I'd very much like a list of the places you visited. I'll be going to Valencia myself some time . . . Research for the book, you know."

"You don't think the pictures are too sentimental?"

"I thought your brief was to break the readers' hearts?"

"It is. But I had to cheat a bit, the children were much too cheerful. It's amazing. Some of them have suffered horribly, and yet they recover so quickly. They arrive in tears and rags and within days they're laughing and playing. I suppose they forget quickly, at that age. These children's homes are very well run."

"I know," said Jack absently. "I visited the one in the Palace Hotel last week."

"More research for the book?"

"Indirectly. The Soviet welfare advisers are very conscious of the *bezprizorny* problem. Vagabond children are a threat to national security. They become the revolutionaries of tomorrow."

"How cynical you are! I see human kindness, you see only politics. Shame on you." She pointed at the picture in Jack's hands. "That little girl was my favorite. I wanted to bring her back with me. Isn't she adorable?"

Jack looked at the wide-eyed orphan and nodded before moving on to the next photograph. He had grown sick of the sight of children lately, but it was hard not to be moved, hard not to care. And then suddenly it was impossible not to care.

"Where did you take this picture?" he demanded, jumping up. "Do you remember where you took it?"

Thérèse looked at it and then at him.

"Of course I remember."

"Write down the address," said Jack.

"Why?"

Thérèse squinted at the photograph, which depicted a pretty young Spanish nurse holding the hand of a winsome, if woebegone child. She smiled knowingly.

"She's not bad looking. Who is she?"

Jack opened his mouth to say something and then thought better of it.

"Never mind who she is. Just write down the address."

Thérèse obliged him, sighing.

"Why are you always so secretive? Don't you trust me?"

But Jack wasn't listening, flinging clothes into a suitcase at random, his brow furrowed, his eyes far away. Thérèse gave a Gallic shrug.

"I assume you're going to visit this children's home?"

"You assume right."

"How long will you be gone?"

"I'm not sure yet . . . Thank you, Thérèse. Thank you." Jack hugged her tight, quite winding her, and kissed her on the forehead. "You're a genius."

She peered at the photograph again before he snapped his suitcase shut.

"I always knew you had a past," she said.

"Mr. Austin has left the hotel."

The desk clerk looked Dolores up and down, not troubling to hide his disdain.

"You mean he has checked out?"

"I did not say that. What is your business?"

"Then when will he be back?"

"He didn't say."

"Do you know where he has gone?"

"I cannot give out such information. If you leave your name and telephone number, I will ask Mr. Austin to call you on his return."

From the undue emphasis he put on the word *telephone*, the man made it sneeringly clear that he knew she did not possess one.

"Might it be tomorrow?"

"Who knows?" he snapped, impatient now. "Journalists are always traveling. If it is important, you should leave a message."

His face lit up suddenly as a red-haired woman approached and handed in her key. He thanked her for nothing, smiling obsequiously. As soon as she was gone his manner reverted instantly from ingratiating to insolent.

"I can only take a message, nothing more. If you cannot write, get someone else to do it for you."

Dolores, who had been limp with anticlimax, suddenly rallied.

"Are your manners only to be bought for money, comrade?" she demanded, adopting the hectoring rhetoric of Paulina addressing a party meeting. The man faltered, taken aback by this metamorphosis.

"I was offering to help," he said stiffly. "Do you wish to leave a message?"

"Not with you," said Dolores, fixing him with a look of icy contempt. "Not with a flunky."

She turned her back and marched out of the hotel, more surprised than he. It was intolerable to be talked down to just because she was poorly dressed! What was the struggle about if not equality? How could that man bow and scrape to rich foreigners and treat a fellow worker as an inferior?

She ought to have been outraged because she too was a lady, albeit in disguise, because she too had until recently been accustomed to a measure of courtesy and deference, but it was not that at all. She no longer thought of herself as a lady, the term had become meaningless. Her indignation was because she was a worker now, and entitled to be respected for what she was, not for what she had been. It had been the merest taste of what Tomás and millions like him had suffered for generations, and yet her blood was boiling. She had paid lip service to political principles in the interests of survival, feeling herself a hypocrite, believing that she did not care who won the war as long as there was peace. It came as quite a shock to discover that she did care. The utopian ideals of her youth had been shattered, but something else had replaced them, working its way into the fabric of her mind, a fierce, involuntary partisanship born of experience, not of optimism.

Yes, a worker deserved respect, but did a beggar? Perhaps she had judged the man too harshly. Wasn't her anxious, abject demeanor an admission that she wasn't an equal? The man's attitude had changed immediately when she stood up to him.

Perhaps it was just as well that Jack had not been there to witness her in such a pitiable state. Jack was not the sort of man to be moved by pity; Jack was no Edmund. He despised weakness, such love as he had felt for her had been for the girl she once had been, proud, stubborn, strong-willed. She would come again tomorrow and the next day, and the next, until she found him. But she would talk to him as an equal, not a supplicant. He would find her changed, but not different. She would prove both to herself and to Jack that she was still the same inside . . .

Andrés was bored. His uncle had been asleep ever since he'd got back from school, and he wished that his mother would hurry up and fetch him. He retrieved the piece of chewing gum he had stuck under a chair seat for safekeeping. It was hard and tasteless, but it was something to do. He sat on the bed and tried to wake his uncle up, accidentally, bouncing up and down a couple of times to no avail. Then he fell to exploring the room. There was a rail with a curtain in front of it, where Marisa kept her clothes, which weren't in the least bit interesting. There was the food cupboard, but there were no sweets, just tins mostly, and bottles and cigarettes. He picked up the walking stick lying by the bed, hoisted it on his shoulder like a rifle, and marched to and fro for a while. Then he took aim and shot a few Fascists, with appropriate sound effects. Still his uncle did not stir. Andrés sat on the floor, mightily fed up. His mother had made him promise not to go out alone. He would have broken his promise if it hadn't been raining.

He began creating a battleground on the floor, using whatever materials came to hand. He stacked his storybooks to give the Republican Army the advantage of high ground, and stood a row of empty bottles on top to represent his troops. Then he looked around for a machine-gun nest. His uncle's boot would do. He positioned it on its side, and pushed a tin inside it, to serve as a machine gun, before deciding that the pepper pot would be better and pulling it out again.

The boot was falling to pieces, and the insole came away along with the tin. Andrés knew he would be scolded for meddling, and pushed it hurriedly back again, but it wouldn't fit. There was something in the way. He removed it again, and found the cause of the obstruction. It was a notebook.

Curious now, Andrés took it out. It was torn and dog-eared and tied together with a piece of string, and on the cover were two words: "Top Secret." Top Secret!

Andrés's excitement was tinged with caution, not to say guilt. If it was "Top Secret," he must on no account look at it. His uncle would be very angry if he did. "You are the only person I can trust, Andrés," he was fond of saying. He fumbled with the shoe and managed to stuff the notebook back into its hiding place, clumsy now with fear that his uncle would wake up and discover what he was doing.

When the treasure was safely stowed away again, he sat pondering his discovery, no longer interested in his military maneuvers. So *that* was why his uncle wanted him to keep the boot. *That* was why he had told him not to speak of it. "You are still too young to understand its value," he had said. "But that humble boot is my most prized possession."

Andrés looked at his sleeping uncle and his chest swelled with pride. Whatever the secret was, he would guard it with his life. What the secret was did not concern him; the fact that it was secret was enough. He was good at keeping secrets.

"I'm discharging myself," said Clara calmly. "I've told Professor Elliott."

"I think he'd rather you stayed a bit longer," said Peabody. "Your illness did rather interrupt things. You had a very close call, Clara. It can't have helped, on top of everything else."

"I think it did. I'm a voluntary patient, Richard. You can't keep me here."

"Remember that we agreed, Clara."

"I remember. But I shan't be going back to Spain now, in any case."

"Oh. Well, that's quite understandable. Even so—"

"Not only that, I'm giving up nursing. So you see, I'm not your responsibility anymore. Your conscience will be clear."

"You're giving up nursing? Why?"

"Because I should never have taken it up in the first place. I shall be staying with Father Spinks for a while, till I decide what to do next."

"I see," said Peabody, disconcerted. A confirmed atheist, he regarded priests as little more than witch doctors, exploiting the sick at their most vulnerable.

"I haven't suddenly got religion," continued Clara, reading his thoughts. "I've had religion all my life, one way and another, and now I want to be free of it."

"With Father Spinks's help?"

"It was his idea. Get rid of the lot, he said, and start again. I'm not terribly bright, as you know, and I've never been much good at thinking for myself. I suppose that's why I joined the party. Communism's just the same as Catholicism, isn't it? Full of unalterable tenets and taboos."

Peabody let this heresy pass.

"Clara, far be it from me to tell you what to believe. Just don't go jumping out of the frying pan into the fire. There are no magic solutions in life. You're at a very low ebb at the moment, and . . ."

"I'll be all right, Richard. I owe it to Edmund to be all right. You've done your bit."

"Well . . . er, we'll be very sorry indeed to lose you, that goes without saying. You were dedicated to the job. Perhaps, after a break, you'll feel able to go back to it. The bad memories will pass and . . ."

She shook her head violently, silencing him, fingering the petals on the massive bouquet by her bedside.

"Another thing. I don't want Edmund's family knowing where I've gone. Just tell them I've gone to stay with a friend and I'll write to them. Will you do that?"

Peabody nodded, understanding. The Prendergast woman was bristling with good intentions, overpoweringly so.

"I've got to learn to live with what I did to them," continued Clara quietly. "I was responsible for Edmund's death, there's no getting away from that. He'd never had gone to Spain but for me. And then I robbed them of their family funeral, I robbed them of his grave, even after he was dead I couldn't bear to share him. And Flora trying to be kind only rubs salt in the wound. They'll kill me with kindness, Richard. I'll never get over it unless I keep away from them for a bit."

Peabody nodded, still full of misgivings.

"Remember, if there's anything I can do . . . You can always get hold of me, care of the party. Don't be ashamed to ask for help, Clara. We owe it to you, you gave us everything you had. Let me know how things go."

"Perhaps. Don't look so worried. I know you meant well, bringing me here, You thought I was going to kill myself, didn't you? I wouldn't have, you know. It would have been . . . too easy."

Josep hurried to the address he had been given, in a working-class suburb of Madrid, where a woman was allegedly dying. He was wearing blue overalls and carrying a bag of tools, which concealed the precious box containing the host for extreme unction. He hadn't shaved, his hands were grimy, and a cigarette dangled from his lips. He gave a casual Republican salute to a passing patrol, which it returned.

A frightened-looking woman opened the door and ushered him inside. The place was a dreadful hovel. Her elderly mother lay on a narrow, filthy bed, her face skeletal, her body riddled with disease. It was genuine, then. There had been, as always, the risk that it was a trap.

Underground priests were classed as Fascist agitators, and if apprehended they could expect no mercy. Once anyone in the movement was caught, it was assumed immediately that he would reveal the names and whereabouts of fellow "Fascists" under torture. Hiding places were changed, fresh papers forged, consecrated hosts quickly swallowed to avoid desecration.

Josep's predecessor had spent a week enduring hospitality at the hands of the secret police before hanging himself in his cell, preferring eternal damnation to the prospect of betraying his friends. On an earlier occasion a young woman, who had regularly taken communion in the kitchen of a Catholic doctor, had turned out to be an NKVD plant; her father confessor had been arrested in mid-Mass and had not been seen since.

Despite all this, there was an ever-increasing demand for Josep's services, even though Madrid was still a long way behind Barcelona, where an influx of Basque refugees had swelled the ranks of closet Catholics. Already there were plans to set up a Basque government-in-exile, which would exert pressure on the Republic to allow the reopening of churches, or at least grant the freedom to celebrate Mass in private. Meanwhile, neither the might of the secret police nor the continuing anti-Fascist paranoia was able to still that buried, trembling faith, seismic and ungovernable in its intensity.

Josep asked for a bowl of water and washed his hands. Then he sat down beside the old woman while she babbled, administering the last rites calmly, soothingly, watching her loosen her frantic hold on life, while the daughter kept telling him to hurry, hurry, her husband would soon be home.

As Josep gave the final benediction, the old woman's fingers released their fierce grip on his, and the room was filled with the sudden smell of death. He pulled the blanket over her face and began packing his accoutrements, without haste, ignoring the sound of heavy footsteps on the stair, and the whimpers of panic from the daughter. The old, familiar, inadmissible thrill was as heady as neat spirits.

"Quick, Father! You must hide."

She pulled back the coverlet and indicated the space beneath the old woman's bed. Josep shook his head. The instinct to hide was treacherous; to hide was to incriminate oneself, and others, and in any case he would quickly be discovered. He had his cover story ready as usual, a wad of lottery tickets in his pocket, a forged union card, a certificate declaring him unfit for the front. All useless, if he showed the slightest fear.

The woman turned her back in confusion as a large man wearing an anarchist neckerchief entered the room and took in the frozen tableau: the sobbing woman, the body covered with a blanket, the unshaven stranger.

"She is gone?" he demanded truculently of his wife, looking at Josep.

She nodded, guilt and confusion written all over her face. The man crossed over to the bed, pulled back the blanket, and saw the smear of oil glistening on the old woman's forehead. For a long time he said nothing.

Josep waited, his face betraying no emotion. The man turned around slowly and stared at him, his lip curling. Josep met his gaze squarely, almost insolently. It was fatalism, not faith, that sustained him. Not to care was the ultimate talisman.

The man crossed to the door and opened it wide, and Josep walked away.

Thérèse had omitted to mention one thing. The address in Valencia she had given him wasn't an ordinary orphanage. It was a home for handicapped children.

Jack sat in the visitors' room, looking out on the playground, watching a variety of maimed and mutilated bodies hurling themselves about with gay abandon, shrieking and laughing, while others in wheelchairs looked on. Dolly's child was not among them.

He looked at the photograph again. It showed four apparently perfect limbs and two huge seeing eyes, there was nothing obviously wrong. Thérèse must have made a mistake. He hoped she had made a mistake, that he would have to telephone her and that she would give him some other address. It had never occurred to him that the child might be damaged. Not all injuries were visible, of course. A lot of refugee children were deaf, their eardrums perforated by a blast. Perhaps he was deaf. If he was deaf, at least it wouldn't show.

After what seemed like hours a middle-aged, motherly woman greeted him pleasantly and ushered him into a small office. She asked after Thérèse and wasted several minutes singing her praises. At last she held out her hand for the photograph. Many people came here looking for lost children, she said. Was he a relative?

"Yes," said Jack, to be on the safe side.

She looked at the picture.

"Then you can tell us his name?" she said.

"Andrés. Andrés . . . García."

"García?"

Wrong, thought Jack.

"His mother may have taken another name," he said casually, adding, "Can I see him?"

"Certainly you can. He knows you well? When did he last see you, and where?"

"With his mother, in Toledo, just before the Fascists took the city. She is dead, presumably?"

"We can only assume so. Well, let us hope he recognizes you. He was found by an army truck several months ago, wandering alone on the open road a few miles from Madrid. We took him to be an orphan. Many refugees were machine-gunned from the air, as you know. We were unable to establish any details, until you came. Andrés—we have been calling him Miguel—has not uttered a word since he was found. He can hear, and he can understand, but he is withdrawn and gets easily upset. No doubt he saw his mother killed, something of that order. Some children are more severely traumatized than others. Perhaps your visit will cheer him. Come."

Jack breathed a sigh of relief. Just dumb. Not even deaf, just dumb. That wasn't too bad, surely.

Dolly's son was in a room with several other children, sitting in a corner by himself, painting. Yes, there was no mistaking him. Her eyes, her hair, her mouth . . .

"He likes to paint," said the warden. "The pictures indicate that he is very disturbed. We could not discharge him to an orphanage, he still needs special care."

Jack stood frozen to the spot, watching. The dark head was bent over the page in furious concentration, the shoulders were hunched, the right hand was daubing furiously. He took a step forward.

"Andrés," he said. "Andrés."

The child did not react at all.

"Let him see you," she said.

Jack walked around to the front of the little desk and crouched on the ground.

"Andrés," he said. "Look at me."

The child looked up and stared at him blankly for a moment before resuming his attack with the paintbrush.

The woman shrugged.

"You say he knows you well?"

"Not well," said Jack. "But I knew his mother very well indeed. In fact, I would like to assume financial responsibility for him. I am sure it would be her wish. I would like to take him back to England. How would I go about this?"

"You mean, adopt him?"

"Yes, if necessary."

She ushered him out of the classroom and back into her office.

"You realize that this child is far from normal? It may be many months before he can readjust to family life. Psychological problems are much harder to treat than physical ones. If a child has no arms, people will make allowances. But Miguel—that is, Andrés—looks perfectly well, and other children, particularly, can be very cruel. If you are serious in your wish to adopt, you will have to satisfy the relevant authorities that you are able to provide for all the child's needs and be a fit parent. Do not imagine that because this country is at war it is an easy matter to export a child. If anything, it is more difficult. Many wealthy, childless couples assume that Spanish orphans are for sale. That is very far from the case. Remember, this is his homeland, the only thing he has left that belongs to him. To uproot him from the country of his birth, where he knows the language and customs, where he is used to the food and the climate, and to take him to England . . . is this really a kindness?"

So she thought he was acting out of kindness. Jack fought back the wave of impatience. What she said was undoubtedly true, but her objections only served to set the wavering, gelatinous idea into solid intent.

"He is young enough to adapt," he said. "And besides . . . he is half English."

"Half English?" She gave him a knowing, quizzical look, and Jack knew immediately what she was thinking. "Are you telling me that you are this child's father?"

"Yes."

"But you were, I take it, not married to his mother?"

"No."

"You have a wife?"

"No."

"You are a single man?"

"If you advise me to acquire a wife to facilitate the adoption, then I will do so. I have the means to care for him, and I am confident that his mother would prefer him to be with his own flesh and blood rather than with strangers, however well intentioned."

She didn't comment, but drew out a folder from a cabinet.

"Perhaps you can kindly tell me the child's date and place of birth. Also details of the mother's name and date of birth. Also details of . . ."

To obfuscate the inevitable verification procedure, Jack claimed
that the child had been born in England. He named the mother as
Rosa García, fearful of stirring up any hornet's nest of Fascist par-
entage. He was in every way informative and cooperative and
charming. Her manner softened. If he could prove that the child
had British nationality, then that might put a different light on the
matter. Had the mother named him as the father on the birth certificate? The authorities would want to satisfy themselves that (a)
attempts had been made to locate the mother without success and
(b) that there was some evidence of paternity. It would be a lengthy
process, obviously . . .

"How lengthy?" said Jack.

"That depends. His mother may be among the many casualties
who will never be identified. On the other hand, the unfortunate
woman may even now be desperately searching for her child. We
have had him here for several months without benefit of a name.
Now that we have this information, we must circulate the details in
the hope of reuniting mother and son. This would, of course, be
the ideal solution, as I am sure you would agree."

"But Rosa must be dead, surely," said Jack, "if the boy was
found wandering all on his own?"

"Not necessarily. She may have been rendered unconscious by
her injuries and become separated from him. Such things are not
uncommon. All the possibilities will have to be explored. May I
ask how he came to be born in England?"

"His mother was in service to a Spanish family, and accompanied them on a visit to England. They dismissed her when she
became pregnant, but she refused my offer of marriage. Shortly
after the birth she elected to return to her homeland, posing as a
widow. I have always maintained the child financially, since the girl
had no family of her own. I came here when war broke out in the
hope of persuading her to return with me, but by this time, of
course, there was another man, and she would not agree. Ever since
Toledo fell, I have been searching far and wide for my son."

"I see. Well, I look forward to receiving the child's birth certificate."

"I will send to England for it immediately."

"There is no hurry. You must resign yourself to a long wait while
the necessary formalities are carried out. Still, this delay will give
you an opportunity to befriend the child. You must understand that
if he does not take to you, then we cannot allow him to be removed,

whatever the other circumstances of the case. The child's interests must come first."

"I will find a hotel in Valencia," said Jack. "You have no objections to my visiting him each day?"

"Now as long as he responds positively. You will have to tread carefully, he is easily frightened. Do you have any experience of children?"

"I have ten younger brothers and sisters. My mother was widowed young, and as the eldest I took on the role of father of the family. All my life I have longed for children of my own. It broke my heart when Rosa left me. I loved them both very much. Forgive me." Jack chose this moment to let his voice break and blow his nose, watching her over the top of the handkerchief.

She nodded kindly.

"Come again tomorrow," she said. "The afternoons are best, after lessons are over. Please be assured that I will do everything in my power to bring this matter to a happy conclusion."

She shook his hand warmly and showed him out.

Jack was dizzy with exaltation. It took several hours of hard thinking to analyze and evaluate the difficulties of carrying out his plan. With hindsight, he should have prepared himself more thoroughly, worked out a foolproof cover story. But until that extraordinary moment when he had seen Andrés again, his intentions had been ill defined. That sudden, fierce determination to have him, keep him, steal him if necessary, had been involuntary, not planned. It had not sprung from sentimentality, nor softheartedness, nor generosity; he did not possess such qualities and never would. And it had nothing to do with Edmund's will. It was the product of pure, unadulterated selfish need, or perhaps greed would be a better word. He had only ever felt this way once before, just once. And this time he wouldn't be cheated, this time he would win. In the meantime, his story could not be proved or disproved; his lies had served to give him a foothold. The tangled web was infinitely less restricting than the straight and narrow cul-de-sac of truth.

The long-winded official "inquiries" might or might not produce an anxious Rosa, who would have to be persuaded and placated. The formalities could drag on for months, while he contended with a vast and cumbersome bureaucratic machine. Meanwhile the Fascists were gaining new ground every day. The Republic might fall before matters were completed, and then what? There would be a wholesale purge of all existing officials, he would have to start all over again . . .

He would have to find a shortcut. Getting hold of forged travel documents shouldn't be a problem, thanks to Edmund's money. As soon as the boy learned to trust him, as soon as he had his confidence, he would ask to take him out for the day. A day was all he needed. By the time they realized he was not coming back, they would be safely over the border . . .

He booked a hotel room for the following night, and caught the train back to Madrid to collect his belongings. Predictably, Thérèse was lying in wait for him.

"Ask no questions and you'll be told no lies," he said implacably. "I'm checking out. I'll be at the Hotel Cristina in Valencia for the next few weeks."

"A double room, I trust?"

Jack smiled enigmatically.

"Poor Marisa," goaded Thérèse. "She'll be inconsolable."

Poor Marisa. Jack's conscience pricked.

"Do you have some silk stockings?" he said.

"Come in, Marisa. Is something wrong? Here, let me help you."

She was laden down with a large box. Dolores took it from her, staggering under the weight, and gestured at her to keep quiet. It was still early, and Andrés and Tomás were still asleep.

"I cannot take this home with me," said Marisa, panting. "Ramón would only drink it all at once. Can you hide it for me?"

The box contained a dozen bottles of whiskey.

"Where did you get all these?" asked Dolores.

"My Englishman has gone away. He left them for me, with this note. Can you read it for me?"

The handwriting was as evocative as scent. Dolores tore the envelope open and stared at what was written inside.

"Well?" said Marisa anxiously. "When is he coming back?"

" 'I shall be away on a job for some weeks. Look after yourself while I am gone, Jack.' "

"Silk stockings!" sighed Marisa, delving deeper into the box. "And some chocolate for the boy. And cigarettes. Ah, you see, he truly cares for me!"

She extracted a stocking reverently from its package and slid it onto her arm, admiring the sheer, shimmery texture.

"He is certainly very kind," said Dolores woodenly. "I will keep the box under the bed for you."

"Twelve bottles," mused Marisa. "Do you think that means that he will be gone twelve weeks?"

Twelve weeks.

"Who knows? Will he contact you when he gets back?"

"Oh yes. He is very fond of me. He has promised to take care of me after Ramón is dead."

"To take care of you?"

"He will take me back to England with him and there I shall live in a house and be a proper lady."

"He told you this?"

"More or less." Marisa smoothed the stocking against her cheek. "Once I am in England, I shall send you parcels, and after the war you may come to visit me in my fine house."

She yawned cavernously.

"You look ill again," she observed. "Do you have a headache?"

"Not in the way you mean," said Dolores, "I just have a lot on my mind."

"You are a fool to stay with that big oaf. When Ramón is gone, when I am gone, who will help you then? You are still young, you should find another man, before it is too late. Think of your son."

"I think of him all the time," said Dolores.

She closed the door quietly, and stared down at her sleeping son. Twelve weeks or twelve days, it might still be too late. She had delayed too long already.

She took a piece of paper and started to write. Then she tore it up and began again. After three more attempts she put it in an envelope, sealed it, and addressed it to Mrs. M. Townsend, 32 Landsdowne Gardens, London, England.

15

Sleep, oceans and oceans of sleep, full of strange and slippery dreams like brightly colored fish darting through the darkness. Clara would wake full of fleeting, fleeing knowledge, knowing that she had learned something but unable to remember it, craving the next journey into the weightless world of oblivion.

Father Spinks encouraged her to lie in bed. It was the best medicine, he said, and in any case she was a lot less trouble asleep than awake, getting under his feet and interrupting his meditations with all manner of sacriligious nonsense. Clara had all the fury of a woman scorned, railing like an unrequited lover against the God who had cast her off; Father Spinks didn't interrupt her—he had to admit she had a point.

"He never lets up, does He?" she fulminated. "First He forces my father to murder my mother. My father had the choice of saving her or me, and the priest said it had to be me, because a baby's life is always sacred. Why is a baby's life always sacred?"

"You tell me," said Spinks.

"Because the only good kind of woman is a virgin, so a mother is no loss. Anyway, my father went along with it, like the good Catholic he was. I got born and she got buried at the age of twenty-two. Then my father thinks to himself, if Helen's life was dispensable, then mine must be as well. Quite logical. So he goes off to Sussex for the weekend and shoots himself with his hunting rifle. Bang."

"How old were you?"

"Two. Anyway, my father got it wrong. My mother's life wasn't worth a bean, but *his* turned out to be sacred, just like mine. They buried him in unconsecrated ground, to make sure that everyone knew he'd gone to hell."

"You can't be sure he went to hell, Clara. You won't know for sure until you get there. So what happened to poor you, after your father dispatched himself?''

"I became rich. I never stood a chance after that. Easier for a camel to pass through the eye of a needle than for a rich little brat to enter the kingdom of heaven. My great-aunt and uncle took me in. I liked my uncle. He was a kind man. Then one day Aunt Mary caught me sitting on Uncle Edward's lap. We were singing our favorite nursery rhyme. 'This is the way the lady rides, trot, trot, trot. And *down* into the ditch.' Am I embarrassing you?''

"After twenty years of hearing confessions, Clara, I've heard it all. How old were you then?''

"Eight. I was starting to quite enjoy it, to be honest with you. It hurt a bit at first, but then that's never put me off things. I thought it meant he was fond of me, you see. Anyway, Aunt Mary soon put a stop to all that. Aunt Mary was a good Catholic, so she didn't like anyone liking it, specially not her husband, specially not *me.*''

"So that's when they packed you off to the convent?''

"Bloody nuns. 'Do you know what hell is, Clara Neville? Hell is more pain than you can possibly imagine. Hell is like being shut into a red-hot iron box, inside a furnace, forever and ever . . .' ''

"No wonder you were so pleased to see me that night.''

"Fear. The whole Catholic faith is based on fear. Well, there's nothing else He can do to me now, not till I die, anyway. He's taken everything. Edmund, my babies, everything. I'm not afraid of Him anymore. I'm not!'' And then, belying her words, "Edmund will be all right, won't he?''

"All right?''

"Edmund was an agnostic. He didn't believe in God. There are special rules, aren't there, for non-Catholics, because they don't know any better. So he'll be all right, won't he? I can't bear to think of Edmund not being all right!''

"Tell me more about Edmund,'' said Father Spinks calmly, ignoring her tears, knowing that sympathy would silence her.

"Edmund? I worshiped him. I love him more than I loved God, that's why he had to die. I hate God. I hate Him.''

"And why did you love and worship Edmund?''

"Because . . . because he was *good*. Because he made me believe in goodness.''

"Well, then. Now we're getting somewhere.''

"Tomás . . . I have been thinking, about Andrés. It would be best for him if I sent him away, until the war is over.''

"No. No. A child should be with its family. I parted from Petra, and now I do not know whether she is alive or dead. Bombs can drop anywhere. You will worry more if he is with strangers and he will pine for you."

"Not strangers. My plan is to send him to England . . . to my aunt and uncle. There are no bombs in England, there is plenty to eat, and—"

"And how will you get him to England? You will have to apply for a permit. You will be asked questions, you will have to lie. And if your lies are discovered . . ."

He did not need to finish the sentence. If her lies were discovered, she would die. But she was going to die anyway, she knew it in her bones. But she could not tell Tomás that.

"I am sure my uncle will find a way. Perhaps he will send enough money to buy false papers. I have said nothing to Andrés yet. He would only get upset at the thought of leaving me."

Tomás sat silent for a moment.

"There is no need for him to leave you," he said stiffly. "Do not separate yourself from your son on my account. You must go to England with him."

"It would double the risk of discovery, if both of us tried to leave. In any case, you are my husband, my place is here with you. And when the war is over, Andrés will return."

"You think that your Communist friends will win the war for us? You are a fool. Caballero's days are numbered. Soon he will be replaced with a puppet. Soon Russians will be ruling Spain. You might as well live among foreigners in England."

"I have told you many times that I would not leave you, Tomás. I am your wife."

Tomás shifted uncomfortably in his chair.

"You owe me nothing, Lole. I wanted you, that was all. I kept you safe because I wanted you, no other reason. I was glad when I got news of your husband's death. I was glad, Lole."

"I knew you wanted me, Tomás. I knew it, and used it. But good has come of it. Where would we be without each other now?"

"Lole . . . why did you not write to your relatives before? Why now? What has changed?"

"Changed?" Dolores looked away. He must not know of her illness, he had enough sufferings of his own. "Well . . . everything is getting worse. The food shortages, the danger. There is talk of another Fascist advance, another bombing campaign."

"There were bombs before, and you did not send him away. And the boy does not go hungry. You go hungry, but he does not. Something else has changed. It is me. It is because I raged at the boy and treated him badly!''

"No! It's not that. Why, he has grown quite fond of you of late. It's nothing to do with you. I should have done this long ago. I kept him with me out of selfishness, because I was afraid of losing him.''

"Lole, listen to me. There is something I must tell you. The boy could have been in England long since, and you with him, but for me.''

"Tomás, I assure you, you are wrong. This plan is recent, believe me, very recent. It is a last resort, that is all, and only for Andrés, not for myself. I have no great love for England, I would never live there from choice. I despise those who desert their country in time of trouble. I have never thought in terms of running away, I—''

"Let me finish. I would rather you heard this from me than from your relatives, who will surely tell you. There was an Englishman. An Englishman visited Rosa, looking for you.''

"What?''

"While we were in Albavera. He came to tell you of your husband's death and take you back to England.''

Dolores looked at him uncomprehendingly.

"He had come to Spain seeking news of you, and had spoken to someone in the government. He told Rosa your husband had been killed in action and gave her a letter for you. I burned it. This is how I knew of your husband's death.''

Dolores continued to stare, speechless.

"But for me, you and the boy could be safe,'' continued Tomás gruffly. "I feared to lose you, Lole. I clung to you, as you clung to Andrés, out of love.''

"Did . . . did Rosa tell you this Englishman's name?''

"I did not ask her. He gave her his card, but I burned that too.''

Dolores shook her head, trying to clear her thoughts.

"When I told you your husband was dead it was no lie. I told myself I would keep you safe, and love you as your husband had done. I told myself there was no harm. I was wrong.''

Dolores felt hot and cold all over.

"I do not ask or want your forgiveness. I ask and want that you leave me, that you go with your son to safety. I have done you a great wrong.''

Dolores turned away from him while she fought for control of her face. She was angry, appalled . . . ashamed. Ashamed at the clumsy innocence of his crime, the studied guile of her own. An excess of love on his part, a lack of it on hers. Which of them had done the most harm?

"It's all right," she said. "I understand."

"I acted out of selfishness."

"And so did I."

"I deceived you."

"And I you."

"But for me, you would be safe."

"But for you, I would be dead! Enough, Tomás, please. That's all in the past now. It's over."

She placed a finger across his lips, not trusting herself to say more. It was all in the past. But the past was never over, never finished with, its tentacles were treacherously long. Edmund or Jack. Which had it been, Edmund or Jack? It must have been Edmund. It must have been Edmund.

"My cousin may arrive suddenly while I am at work," she said, thinking aloud. "Just tell him you are my husband and ask him to wait."

"You are not ashamed to acknowledge me as your husband?"

"I am ashamed of many things," said Dolores. "But not of you."

Slowly does it, Jack had told himself. But slowly didn't do it. The child tolerated him, nothing more. He could tell the staff were unimpressed by his progress. He tried everything. Stories, puzzles, games, bribes. Andrés treated them all with supreme indifference. He would masticate sweets without apparent relish and discard toys after a few minutes' cursory examination. All he wanted to do was paint, and to force him to do otherwise produced sudden, violent tantrums, tantrums that were not so much willful as woeful, full of unspoken terrors.

The boy disliked being touched, and did not respond to humor. More than anything, Jack wanted to hear him laugh. Once he laughed, he would speak. Once he spoke, everything else would follow. There was nothing wrong with his vocal cords, as his screaming fits proved.

Jack had studied the paintings by the hour, trying to decipher their meaning. There were no recognizable shapes or forms, just blobs of vivid color and thick black lines, angry and confused and apparently random. Some long-winded psychologist had already interpreted them in some glibly obvious way, blinding Jack with meaningless science, reducing the boy to a textbook case. Clearly he disapproved of amateur interference but fortunately the principal remained firmly on Jack's side. She had swallowed his attractive story so thoroughly that she even claimed to see a family likeness. Jack had dined with her several times, and had come to enjoy her company. She was disarmingly apolitical, especially when suitably refreshed.

"Theorists and politicians, they are all alike. Always competing, always claiming they have all the answers. I deal in realities. No war is worth what you see here. No war. No principles, no ideals can justify what we are doing to our children. Oh yes, we do it to their children too, given the chance. It is just that they are winning, and so they have done most of the damage. Ah, I am saying too much as usual."

"I won't quote you," said Jack. "And even if I did, I would never reveal my sources. It's the only point of honor we journalists possess."

"Tell me more about Andrés's mother." Pepa loved a good story. Everyone loved a good story.

He called her Rosa, but it was Dolly he described. It was comforting to describe her to a stranger as the lost love of his life, the woman who had spurned him and found another man. He had been wrong to seduce her, he said, but he could not help himself, it had been an act of passion, impossible to regret. But she had been wise not to marry him, wise to find someone kinder and more responsible than he. He had misused her, and she had been right to punish him for it . . .

He had never thought of it like that before, never accepted his share of the blame, never shed the feeling of betrayal, even when he heard that she was dead. It was as if by keeping those angry feelings alive, he could keep her alive as well. But now he could bury her decently, lay her ghost, because a part of her had been restored to him, like an undeserved gift from beyond the grave.

"Blood is thicker than water," Pepa was fond of saying, reminding him of the falseness of his claim. But it didn't matter. If he found out tomorrow that Andrés really *was* his child, it wouldn't make any difference. What mattered was that he was Dolly's, part of her. If they had had a child together, he would have felt the same. He was no admirer of his own genes, neither his looks nor his character were worth propagating. The ideal child would have been a perfect replica of her. And but for his sex, Andrés was very nearly that.

It occurred to him that Dolly might have taught the boy English nursery rhymes, that perhaps he was bilingual beneath the silence.

He racked his memory for the few he had learned in childhood. He sang "Ride a Cock Horse," he intoned "Little Miss Muffett" and "Hey Diddle Diddle," and once or twice he fancied he had sparked off a flicker of recognition, which led him to persist, ignoring the snickers of the other children. But so far that had been the only point of communication, apart from the pictures. And perhaps the pictures were private, perhaps it was intrusive to try to understand them, to presume to analyze another person's thoughts.

His mounting frustration craved some release, and he found it in his book. The manuscript was too bulky to hide anymore, but it hardly seemed necessary, here. The Hotel Cristina was a modest establishment near the bullring, within walking distance of the children's home, and life in Valencia seemed almost normal compared with Madrid or Barcelona. The area was the domain of small tradesmen and a wealthy peasantry, who had managed to survive by cooperating with the anarchists and continuing much as before. The compulsory sale of all produce to the unions was handled by the self-same merchants who had prospered under the old régime, and whose knowledge of export procedures was essential to maintain vital foreign trade. Officially, private commerce had been abolished; but despite routine expropriations and executions, the whole town remained indelibly middle-class and stubbornly disaffected by the war, as if they saw it as an aberration and had resolved to merely sit it out rather than to win it.

It had not been difficult, in this climate of dogged enterprise, to locate a tradesman dealing in forged documents, albeit through a tortuous chain of intermediaries. It was a business, like any other, and clearly a highly profitable one. Jack had cabled Edmund's solicitors for funds, handed over Thérèse's photograph of the boy, and duly collected the goods, leaving Andrés considerably poorer. Life might be cheap in Spain, but liberty certainly wasn't.

"Well, boy? Any more trouble with that oaf García? Your mother is well?"

"Yes, Uncle. Tomás is very quiet. He just sits in his chair all day. He never even shouts anymore."

Andrés had grown to dread these interrogations. His uncle never seemed satisfied with his answers. He had thought he would be pleased to hear that all was well at home, but however reassuring the news he would fall to ranting and raving about his duty as a gentleman to defend his sister's honor.

"You will see him tremble and beg for mercy, Andrés," he

declared. "First I shall slap his face, like so!" He sliced the air. "Then he may choose any weapon he pleases, saber, pistol, or bare hands. Then—"

"But, Uncle, he cannot fight," interjected Andrés, troubled by the prospect of this uneven contest. "He cannot even stand without his crutches. And I am sure he would never hurt Mamá."

"After I am gone, it is you who must protect your mother," Ramón reminded him. "You have not forgotten, have you, about the keepsake I have bequeathed to you?"

"No, Uncle." Andrés went pink at the memory of his unauthorized snoop.

"Good. You must keep it well hidden from García. It is vital that it does not fall into the wrong hands."

"Yes, Uncle."

"My time is drawing near, alas," he continued, gesturing to the child to refill his glass. "I am very tired." He took a big swallow, and fell back on the bed.

Before long the rasping, shuddering breaths commenced. Andrés sighed. His mother had said she would come back for him in an hour or two, after she had finished her shopping, but today it was not raining, the sun was shining, and Andrés did not relish the prospect of yet another long, boring wait indoors. His uncle was not half so much fun as he used to be, and Andrés had grown weary of the diatribes against Tomás. There was something about that huge, quiet, immobile figure that commanded his respect, that was infinitely more awesome than the angry giant who had shouted at him and tried to pursue him, one-legged, around the room.

Tomás never had much to say, but he was very good at listening. His mother was always too busy to listen, and his uncle kept interrupting him, but Tomás was happy to let him talk as much as he liked. Andrés liked talking, especially to a captive audience, and teaching Tomás to read made him feel very grown up.

"I have not your quick brain, boy," Tomás had warned him. "You must be patient." Andrés wasn't patient by nature, and he sometimes got annoyed when Tomás couldn't remember his letters, but then Tomás would say, quietly, "Save your anger for important things. Save your anger for when you need it," and Andrés would be humbled into silence.

The snoring grew louder, deeper. Andrés fidgeted for a few minutes of indecision, and then slipped out of the room. He had been eager to visit his uncle, in the hope of some chocolate and a few good stories, but both commodities had proved lacking, and now he heartily wished he hadn't come.

His mother would be cross with him, but as long as he went straight back home, he would get away with it. He was under strict instructions not to play in the street, although lots of children much younger than he did so. Their mothers didn't mind how dirty they got or how much noise they made, and Andrés sorely envied them their freedom. On one memorable occasion he had got into a fight with a gang of urchins who had tried, unsuccessfully, to rob him of some chewing gum, and had come home breathless, bruised, and keen to relate his adventure. But his mother hadn't wanted to hear his good account of himself, she had smacked him instead. Women did not understand such things, Tomás had told him afterward.

Half-naughty, half-obedient, he left the room against instructions but resisted the temptation to loiter and went straight back home. He ran up the stairs and was about to knock for Tomás to let him in, when he heard voices. Not just voices. His mother was crying.

He hesitated, shifting from foot to foot outside the door. Suddenly he was frightened, frightened that perhaps Tomás *was* hitting his mother, as his uncle repeatedly claimed, that he was going to hear or see proof of it, that he would be duty-bound to tell his uncle, who would challenge Tomás to a duel and kill him . . .

He pressed his ear against the door.

"You and the boy should go to Valencia together," Tomás was saying. "There you would both be safe from the bombing. That way you would not have to send him away to England. Once you send him there, you will never see him again. Your relatives are rich and we are poor. Will you bring him back after the war, to live in poverty with us? Think about it, Lole. You can never have any more children. How can you give your only child away?"

"And what if I were to die?" his mother wept. "What then? You cannot look after him, Tomás."

"And why should you die? You are young. Are you sick?"

"Not sick. Just . . . just tired. You know how unruly he is, Tomás. I cannot cope with him any longer. I am not sick. Just tired."

His mother started crying again. Andrés stood frozen to the spot, unable to believe his ears. England! She had promised not to send him away, and now she was going to send him to *England!*

He wouldn't go. He would run away. Tomás had said that once he went to England he would never see his mother again. Andrés felt his entire world crumble beneath his feet. He nearly opened his mouth and revealed his presence, nearly shouted out loud, "No!

I won't go!'' But prudence prevailed. He stole down the stairs again and retraced his steps back to the Plaza de Chueca, and was sitting gloomily by his uncle's bed when his mother came to fetch him.

"Good Lord,'' said Flora, reaching for Dolly's letter. "And there's Jack telling everyone she was dead. Well I never.''

"I showed it to Daddy, of course, but he says it's not our problem. You know how he is these days. What do you think, darling? Poor Dolly. One must do something.''

Margaret's tone, as always, was vague, but the vagueness had changed from the gentle mist, which had always been part of her nature, to a dense, artificial fog.

"Pamela's grandchild,'' she murmured to herself. "Poor Pamela.''

She sipped her tea with vacuous calm.

"So I thought to myself, Archie will know what to do. Will you talk to Archie, darling?''

"Archie?'' echoed Flora, still reading. "Oh, of course. Leave it all to me, Mummy.''

"Poor, poor Pamela. Such an unfortunate marriage.''

"Steven!'' barked Flora, looking up. "Manners!''

"Please-Granny-may-I-hava-bitta-cake?''

"Of course, darling.''

"May I have a piece of cake too?'' asked Arabella primly, proud of her superior social graces.

"She does so remind me of you at that age,'' sighed Mrs. Townsend. "So neat and polite always. So—''

"Mummy, do you mind if I leave the children here for a bit? I think I'll drop in on Daddy at the office.''

"He'll be terribly cross. Bella, come and sit on Granny's lap.''

"Can I go to see Grandpa too?'' asked Steven.

"No, you will stay here and you will be very quiet until I get back, and you will *not* speak with your mouth full. Understood?''

Flora sallied forth and hailed a cab. Despite her diminutive size, she had a presence that stopped taxis on sight and produced instant sycophancy in the surliest of tradesmen. Her only talent was manipulation, which she had learned at her father's knee and practiced on him still. He might bluster and prevaricate but he always gave in to her in the end, and he would do so now. It was high time that Daddy came out of his shell of mourning and tried to do something positive.

Flora swept through the portals of the Foreign Office and announced that her business with the under secretary was urgent. He had them show her in at once and glared at her across a barricade of gleaming mahogany.

"I suppose it's this Spanish nonsense," he said before she had time to speak. "Infernal cheek. The girl caused nothing but trouble while she was here—and I never wanted to take her in. I knew how it would be—and now seven years later she writes a begging letter. 'My best to Edmund' indeed!"

"Daddy, she couldn't possibly know—"

"If she'd bothered to stay in touch, then she would have known! If she'd known, she surely wouldn't have the gall to impose on us further! It would have been bad enough if Edmund had died for his country, like his uncle, but to die for someone else's country, a barbaric, primitive, uncivilized country, to die for a regime that opposes law and order and religion and common decency . . . I want nothing to do with this letter! The girl's got herself into a mess, and I feel sorry for her, but there is absolutely nothing I can do to help, and even if there were, your mother and I are in no position to go adopting a small boy at our age . . ."

"Daddy, *I* would look after him. I'm thinking of Edmund, not of Dolly, the child is his heir after all. All I ask of you is advice and support. Is there someone at the embassy I should write to? What are the rules?"

"Rules?" he barked. "There aren't any rules. The so-called Republic is virtually a police state, they make up the rules as they go along. Legally, the rules are that Dolores simply applies for a travel permit. *If* she dares. Judging by all the circumlocutions in her letter, she doesn't dare."

"Exactly! Look at this bit. 'Andrés's father, Tomás, agrees to my plan. As you know, we are only poor working people and cannot even afford to pay the boy's fare." And then she signs herself García, not Montanis. She's worried the censors might read her letter, don't you see? She's the widow of a Fascist officer! She can hardly do things through the official channels without the risk of spilling all the beans. Daddy, there must be some strings you can pull to help her!"

"Flora, I repeat, even if I had it in my power to do anything unofficial, I would not. Such maneuvers have a habit of backfiring. Given that your cousin has got so much to hide, she would be well advised to avoid drawing any attention to herself or the boy until the war is over . . ."

"But Daddy, she's ill. She says it's serious, that she's afraid she might even *die!*"

Mr. Townsend rapped his ruler on the desk.

"I remember young Dolores very well indeed. You would agree that she had a tendency to exaggerate? To overdramatize? Worse, to deceive?"

"But that was years ago!"

"Flora, for the last time, I refuse to involve myself in anything remotely illegal and I expressly forbid you to try to meddle on your own account. It may interest you to know that several British passports holders are currently being held in Spanish jails accused of unspecified crimes against the state, and despite all manner of representations from the embassy, there's nothing we can do to help them. Two of them have died of 'pneumonia' in the last month . . .''

"But Daddy—"

"I repeat, I will not embroil myself or try to embroil others in Spanish politics. Diplomatically, the situation is extremely delicate. And if you dare to compromise me by trying to go behind my back or over my head, I shall intervene immediately to put a stop to it. Is that understood?"

Flora opened her mouth to plead and wheedle, but something in her father's face stopped her short.

"This family has done enough for Spain," he said thickly. "I pray to God the whole miserable, evil country is wiped off the face of the earth."

Flora bowed her head.

"I'm sorry, Daddy. I didn't mean to upset you."

She turned to go. She had just reached the door when he called her back.

"Promise me," he said. "Promise me for Edmund's sake that you won't do anything foolish."

"Don't be silly," said Flora innocently. "Archie would never let me."

"We call this tent the Lyceum," Mrs. Pinkney told Clara, parting the canvas to reveal rows of mutinous children with their heads plastered in white goo. "Some of them have got scabies as well, hence the sulfur-baths. Now, now, pet, no need to cry." A little girl was being briskly divested of her long dark hair.

"I'm not surprised she's crying," said Clara brusquely. "Doesn't anyone around here speak Basque?"

"Oh yes. About a hundred adults sailed with the children on the *Habana*. Mostly female schoolteachers and a few priests."

"Among four thousand children? That's not a very good ratio, is it?"

"Well, they'll have to learn English now, obviously. We need volunteers for that as well. The response from local people has been fantastic and Eastleigh Council has been absolutely marvelous. The land was given gratis by a local farmer, and the Boys' Brigades and Scouts worked nonstop to erect the tents. And it's all entirely voluntary. The government wouldn't give us a penny. The Home Office only agreed to give the children entry on condition that they didn't become a charge on public funds. Would you believe, the War Office actually had the gall to charge us for hire of the tents and field kitchens! But luckily donations are simply flooding in. People just can't do enough, especially the Catholic organizations. So, what kind of work would interest you, Miss Neville?"

"If donations are flooding in, can't we do better than tents and latrines and six-thirty A.M. reveille? Does it have to be quite so regimented?"

Mrs. Pinkney looked mildly affronted. Most visitors were full of praise for the camp. Mr. Atlee had been most impressed.

"We have to have discipline," she explained with a tolerant smile. "Some of these children are . . . well, a bit unruly, especially the older boys. They're quite a handful, I can tell you!" She chortled with matronly good humor.

"Perhaps that's because they come from Bilbao, not Bournemouth. Any boy older than twelve has probably been working in an armaments factory or even fighting at the front. They're not used to being patronized by adults. Children grow up very quickly in Spain. That is . . . so I'm told."

"Really? Well, all I can say is that most of them have still got a lot to learn." She dropped her voice to a prurient whisper. "The lavatories, my dear. Simply dreadful. Most of them have never even seen one before. I mean, one has to tell them what to *do*. We keep catching them behind hedges and such. No wonder we've been having such a problem with flies . . ."

"Wouldn't they be better off with families?" asked Clara. "This is hardly a natural environment for children. And all these uniforms, like that scoutmaster chap over there—these children associate uniforms with Fascists."

"It was the Basque government's special request that they be kept to together to retain their national identity," said Mrs. Pinkney. "Personally, I agree with you that it's a bad idea. If they're going to live in England, then they should live together with English children and learn English ways. Still, ours not to reason why. Eventually, we hope to farm them out in largish groups. Various philanthropists have shown an interest in providing accommodations. But it will take time and a vast amount of work. Heaven knows how we'd cope if we'd taken all ten thousand.''

''Ten thousand? So who decided which ones got left behind?''

''Oh, the National Joint Committee was scrupulously fair. The children had to be between five and fifteen, we had to have written consent from the parents, and the applications accepted were in *exact* proportion to the distribution of the different political parties in the Basque parliament.''

''How very comforting for those who were rejected,'' said Clara dryly.

''So,'' resumed her guide, getting back to the subject in hand, ''What kind of work did you have in mind?''

''What's your least popular job?''

''Apart from cleaning the lavatories? No, no, my dear, I was only joking. Several local women have already volunteered for that, you know, people who are *used* to that type of work.''

Clara bit back the sarcastic rejoinder.

''And apart from cleaning the lavatories?''

''Well . . . not too many women are able to live in. Family commitments, you know. And of course, the environment isn't exactly luxurious. We've got two hundred tents, twenty children to a tent, and the Spanish teachers are assigned one to each tent, which leaves half the tents with only part-time supervision. Some of the children are rather disturbed, they do need around-the-clock support.''

''You mean, a sort of tent mother? I ought to confess I refused to join the Girl Guides. And I'm not very good with children.''

''Tent mother? What a charming phrase. It sums it up rather well. As for being good with children—well, it doesn't pay to be too emotional. I'm afraid it's thankless work, most of them aren't in the least grateful and don't seem to appreciate that we're doing what's best for them. You could always try it out for a week, and if you find it too much, then . . .''

''I'd like to think it over,'' said Clara. ''I'll come back again, if I may.''

Mrs. Pinkney beamed encouragingly, and Clara wished that she had been rather less terse with her. She found her fulsome manner an irritant, and yet she obviously meant well. She was the kind of stalwart, middle-aged woman who had time on her hands and was

in her element doing good, who relished that irreproachable brand
of power.

"Whatever you do," Father Spinks had warned her, "do it out
of love this time, not hate. Do something positive you will enjoy,
or don't do it at all." And as soon as she was out of his sight for a
day, she had found herself asking for the least popular job. She
could have said she was a trained nurse, who had served in Spain
for six months, in Aragon and Madrid, and been hailed delightedly
as an expert, found herself coopted onto half a dozen different
subcommittees, with her new colleagues constantly deferring to her
and seeking her advice. It was what she had dreamed of, once, the
recognition and respect that would greet the words "I served as a
nurse in Spain."

But she could not say, "I served as a nurse in Spain," without
adding, "and while I was there I killed two unarmed men in cold
blood because I didn't agree with their politics. Worse than that, I
convinced myself that I was entitled to do it."

Whatever Father Spinks said, however much he absolved her,
however true it was that she had acted under stress, however much
she came to terms with her guilt, it was not a period in her life she
could ever use for her own glorification. She had forfeited that right,
irretrievably, and yet her silence was not a penance. It was being
kind to herself, helping herself forget. To talk about it would have
been unnecessarily painful, and necessary pain was more than
enough.

Her obsessive need to return to Spain had been discredited, the
falseness of her motives exposed. To go back now would be a
retrograde step, it would merely be to justify having gone in the
first place, to prove that it hadn't all been a hideous mistake, that
it hadn't cost her everything but her life. That was why she had left
poor Edmund there, as a hostage, to force herself to return. *Do it
for love, or not at all,* Father Spinks had said. She hadn't gone to
Spain out of love. She hadn't gone there to help others but to resolve
her private problems. It hadn't been courage, just bravado, a defiant
attempt to prove that she was strong, to deny her own inadequacy.

"You've got to learn to love yourself," he had told her. "Until
you do, you can't love anyone else, not properly, and you certainly
can't love God." The notion had seemed absurd, at first. It had been
dinned into her from childhood that the self was intrinsically evil,
requiring constant subjugation. She had always thought of the self
as a trapped genie writhing, imprisoned, inside her mind, tormenting and tempting her toward the relief of vice, mocking her inability

to refuse its demands, reducing her to slavery. Every ounce of energy she possessed had gone in to the fight, even though she knew defeat was inevitable, even though she connived at it constantly, reveling in the hopelessness of the struggle, wallowing in failure.

If she came to work in the camp, in whatever capacity, would she be doing it out of love? She had no knack for children, none at all. Normal women found children endearing. Normal women peered into prams. Normal women had no inhibitions about picking children up and cuddling them and talking to them in silly voices. Even if her babies had been born, she would have found it difficult to behave toward them as other mothers did. She had never been mothered herself, after all.

But then, not all children were lovable. The nuns had deemed her a delinquent, not worthy of love. Some of these children were allegedly delinquent, too, and no wonder. Not very grateful, indeed. "You're a wicked, ungrateful child, Clara Neville!" Perhaps there was some hope for her yet. If she had to do it out of love, then she'd better start with the ungrateful ones, because she knew exactly how they felt.

"Only for an hour," Pepa had decreed. "You may take Andrés out, but only for an hour. Too much excitement may be bad for him."

Jack hadn't argued with her. An hour was a start. Next time it would be two hours, then half a day, then a whole day, and a whole day was more than enough to reach the border.

"*Salud*, Andrés," Jack said cheerfully. He had planned a visit to the railway station to accustom him to the sight and sound of trains.

They had dressed him in a coat that was far too big for him and his eyes were huge and mistrustful under the mop of dark hair. He did not respond to the greeting, impervious as always to his name. They said that the merest whisper of one's name was audible above the loudest din, that the ear was especially attuned to it. Jack wondered if Dolly had given him a nickname, but he had tried all possible Spanish diminutives without success. He had even tried Anglicized versions, like Andy and Drew, to no avail.

Jack held his breath as the child let him take his hand and lead him toward the door. Pepa had emerged from her office to witness the great event and gave him a broad smile of encouragement.

Jack opened the door and ushered the boy out. There was a large garden to cross, and a gate in the middle of a high wall. Jack opened the gate, just as a car drove past. A flicker of interest lit up the boy's features. Jack began to feel more hopeful. Cars and trains.

All boys were supposed to love cars and trains. Cars and trains and airplanes . . .

"Look," said Jack without thinking, pointing. "An airplane." It was one of the much-praised Russian fighters, on a morale-boosting exercise, although the days when people would stand in the street and cheer them were long gone.

He realized immediately how stupid he had been, but the boy would have heard it anyway. It was flying low, showing off, with a great deal of engine noise. Andrés wrenched his hand free, covering his ears, and ran, screaming, back across the gardens to safety, out of range of the machine-gun fire that had rained down on him and no doubt killed poor Rosa.

Jack followed him slowly as Pepa rushed out of the house. It took them a long time to calm him down. He would not allow anyone to hold him or comfort him, shrinking from the slightest touch.

"Do not be discouraged," said Pepa philosophically. "This happened once before, when the children were exercising in the gardens, and it will happen again. It is quite normal. Many children react in this way, but in the end they get over it, and so will Andrés, given time. We cannot keep him indoors forever. Leave it a week or so, and then try again. Patience, my friend."

Patience had never been Jack's forte. Of all things he hated waiting, he was geared to action, to quick results, to deadlines. Failing a deadline, he would set himself artificial time limits—you could get twice as much done that way. If today had gone well, he would have given himself a month, six weeks at most, but now that seemed absurdly optimistic.

He felt angry, thwarted, almost resentful of the boy's refusal to cooperate. Pepa was right, it wasn't a kindness to remove a child from its homeland when that was the only thing it had left. He was doing this for his own benefit, acting out a pathetic fantasy, pursuing a foolish dream. he ought to hand over Edmund's money, pass it off as his own, and clear out, admit defeat, leave the boy to the experts. The whole enterprise was grossly self-indulgent. He'd give it one more month, perhaps two, no more. Or three at the outside. Three more months should finish the book . . .

When he got back to his room, there was a message for him to telephone Thérèse. It was urgent.

He called her back from the phone in the hotel lobby straightaway. The first thought that had sprung to his mind, unbidden, was that something had happened to Marisa.

"Jack? At last. I've been waiting for your call all day. There's a cable for you from England, and the desk clerk didn't like to forward it in case it was important. He can't read English and asked me if I'd phone you. Do you want me to open it?''

"Thanks," said Jack.

There was a sound of paper tearing. Jack relaxed, assuming that it was some belated request from Martindale.

"LEAVING IMMEDIATELY STOP ARRIVING PLAZA HOTEL SOONEST STOP DOLLY ALIVE STOP FLORA. It's dated the day before yesterday." And then, after a moment. "Jack? Did you hear that?"

"I'm sorry," said Jack, recovering himself. "Would you mind repeating that? Its a bad line."

"LEAVING IMMEDIATELY STOP ARRIVING PLAZA HOTEL SOONEST STOP DOLLY ALIVE—"

Jack gripped the telephone very tight.

"Thérèse, will you tell the desk that if a Mrs. Prendergast asks for me to tell her I'm on my way. And will you book me back into the hotel from tonight?''

"All right. Is there anything else I can do? What's going on?''

"Can't explain now. Thanks, Thérèse."

He hung up, flung a few belongings into an overnight case, and ran all the way to the station. He felt no surprise as yet, it seemed entirely natural. Of course she was alive. Of course. How could he ever have doubted it?

He shut his mind to the moment when he would see her again, refused to indulge himself, for fear something would go wrong. Only this time, nothing would go wrong. He would not let anything go wrong this time.

Last time, he had had nothing to give her, but this time he wouldn't come to her empty-handed. This time he would give her more than a gold chain and a little brass bell. This time he would give her her son.

The knock on the door came at one in the morning, making Dolores jump. For days now she had been expecting to open the door to find Edmund standing there; she was sensitized to the slightest sound. But Edmund would never knock like that. She felt a chill of fear.

"Stay here," said Tomás, alarmed, immediately assuming the worst. "Hide yourself. I will see to it."

Dolores shook her head.

"If it's a *checa* investigator, they'll rip the place apart. We must act normally."

Andrés was sitting up in bed, rubbing his eyes. With Tomás towering on his crutches behind her, Dolores opened the door.

"Are you Lole?" said the girl. "Are you Marisa's sister, Lole?"

Her face was contorted behind the mask of paint, she was breathing heavily and had obviously been running. From her tight, gaudy clothes, Dolores could tell she earned her living as Marisa did.

"I am Lole. What is wrong?"

"They have taken her away in a car," said the girl. "There was so much blood! So much blood!"

Dolores flung on her coat.

"I am coming. Tomás—"

"Go to her. I will look after the boy. Take care."

It was the small hours of Sunday morning, and there was no transport to be had. The girl had no idea where Marisa had been taken, so they had to go to the hotel first to find out.

"She was worried about her *novio,*" puffed Luisa. She told me to run and find you. But Lole, there was so much blood, so much blood!"

"Where was she hurt?" asked Dolores.

"Inside," said Luisa hoarsely. "Inside."

The streets were pitch-dark but for a few dull blue lights and the Gaylord Hotel was blacked out. Dolores raced past the doorman and up to the reception desk.

"Where have they taken the girl?" she demanded without explanation.

"What girl?"

"Marisa. The girl who was hurt. The prostitute."

"Prostitute? I know nothing of prostitutes. This is a respectable hotel. There must be some mistake."

"Tell him, Luisa!"

But Luisa seemed to have lost her tongue.

"You must know this girl!" said Dolores, pointing at her companion. "She works here too."

"I do not know all the staff. I have never seen this girl before in my life."

"Lole," hissed Luisa. "Come away. Come away."

"You must have come to the wrong hotel. We have no prostitutes here. Good night, camarada."

Luisa dragged Dolores out into the street.

"It was foolish to come back here," she hissed. "I should have known. They will deny it all. The fat Russian is very important."

And then Dolores understood. Marisa might be more than hurt.

She might not have been taken to a hospital at all, but disposed of to avoid a scandal. Perhaps the driver of the car had "taken her for a ride" to protect the important fat man against embarrassing repercussions . . . Only recently Marisa had told her that one of her fellow prostitutes had "disappeared." People "disappeared" with increasing frequency, and if you were wise you made no inquiries about them, you behaved as if nothing had happened, for fear of attracting the same fate . . .

She blinked into the blackness. Luisa had melted into the night like a wraith; a militiaman had materialized in her place.

"Papers," he said.

"I have none," said Dolores. "Look at me. I have just got out of bed. I have had word of a sick friend and I am trying to find her. Where is the nearest hospital?"

"A woman should not be alone on the street at night. Where is your husband?"

"On crutches," spat Dolores, incensed. "Have you no respect for the wife of a veteran seeking to aid a comrade in distress?"

He scrutinized her for a moment, then jerked his head at her to follow him. The hospital was about ten minutes' walk. Dolores ran inside an asked if a girl had been admitted in the last hour, bleeding profusely, she was her sister.

The nurse shook her head.

"Where else would she have been taken? She had an accident at the Gaylord Hotel, where she works. She—"

Dolores kneeled over dizzily. She must not have an attack now. Not now. The nurse, alarmed, allowed her to sit down.

"You cannot search for her in the blackout," she said kindly. "Wait here while I telephone for you."

It was daybreak before there was any news.

"Your sister is in a unit in the suburbs. There were no beds in the city. She is out of danger. You may visit her."

Dolores nodded, too numb to feel even relief, knowing that it was nothing to do with a shortage of beds. Marisa had been put beyond the immediate reach of family or friends until her condition was known, until she was fit enough to be warned to keep her mouth shut. If she had died from her injuries, there would have been no news, she would simply have vanished without a trace.

The hospital was a somber gray building with the look of a former convent about it, although there was no longer a cross on the roof. A female doctor took her into a cubicle and asked if she was next of kin, and Dolores said that she was Marisa's sister-in-law.

"She has suffered profuse vaginal bleeding," the doctor said levelly. "The injury was no doubt associated with her trade. She has assured us that no other party was involved, and that the accident was entirely her own fault. She has been given stitches and is now comfortable, but she has lost a great deal of blood and should remain here for a day or two. Luckily the baby was not harmed, but bed rest is essential. She is still suffering from shock."

"The baby?" echoed Dolores. "Oh yes . . . the baby. Thank you, Doctor. May I see her now?"

Marisa was deathly pale. She whimpered at the sight of Dolores and clutched her hand very tight.

"What happened, Marisa? Tell me what happened?"

Marisa looked this way and that as if to see if anyone was listening.

"Swear you will not tell Ramón. Swear it. I want him to think I have female troubles. Will you tell him it is just female troubles, Lole? Will you bring him to see me, so he does not fret?"

"I will tell him you have female troubles," said Dolores. "Do not distress yourself."

Marisa beckoned her with a weak wave of the finger and hissed in her ear.

"They have told me if I speak someone will denounce me as a Fascist collaborator. No one must know. But I will tell you if you swear to be silent."

"You need not tell me, then. I can guess."

"I want to! *I must tell someone!* Oh, if only my Englishman was here! I could tell him."

"Do not tell anyone, Marisa," said Dolores. "Tell me, now, if you must, and then be silent. Think of Ramón."

Marisa gestured to her to hug her, and while they were locked in their embrace, she whispered into her hair, she told her about the fat man, and the bottle, and the neck of the bottle breaking, and the blood. So much blood . . .

Dolores patted her and tried to soothe her and waited for her to tell her about the baby, but she fell back onto the pillows, exhausted by the effort of speaking. She left her sleeping, went wearily home, and told Tomás an edited version of what had happened.

"She had a bad hemorrhage. Some female disorder. She wants to see Ramón. I must go and tell him, and then take him there."

"Is Marisa sick?" asked Andrés.

"Yes, but she will soon be better. I am taking your uncle to visit her, so Tomás will look after you today."

"When will you be back?"

"I'm not sure. Your uncle will be worried and he is all alone. I will be as quick as I can. Please be good, Andrés."

Andrés scowled and treated her to one of his accusatory looks. He had been extra difficult these last few days, and yet he had grown excessively friendly toward Tomás, playing him off against her at every opportunity.

"We will keep each other company, eh, boy?" said Tomás, poking him in the ribs. "One day, when you are big and strong, I will sit astride your shoulders and feel how it is to run again."

Dolores kissed them both and left the room, still preoccupied. Marisa pregnant. Poor, hapless Marisa. And the child could be anyone's, anyone's at all, except Ramón's. Anyone's at all, even Jack's. Oh no, not that. That would be too cruel. That would be more than she could bear.

Archie didn't like it at all. He didn't like driving his immaculate Bentley along filthy Spanish roads, and he emphatically didn't like Flora's harebrained scheme about smuggling this child out of Spain on the family passport. She had challenged him to come up with a better idea, but Archie was not a great one for ideas. Useless to mention that the boy was too old to be Steven and the wrong sex to be Arabella, Flora insisted that they would never check such minor details, and in any event no one would ever suspect two respectable English tourists of dealing in contraband children.

The journey out was a dry run, as Flora called it, for their return, which would of necessity be by a different route. She had dressed in deepest mourning, and equipped herself with Edmund's death notice from *The Times,* a copy of the *Whitechapel Gazette,* complete with photograph and obituary, and Jack's fateful cable. When the guards at Port-Bou demanded to see their visa and asked why they were visiting Spain, she burst into tears and began telling them the whole sad story. That they did not understand English did not deter her. She interspersed her narrative with a few well-rehearsed phrases of atrocious Spanish so that they could not fail to get the gist. Not content with that, she insisted on showing them the telegram and the press clippings and a selection from the family photograph album, until they literally begged her to get back into the car and hurriedly waved them through.

"You see?" she said. "Same story on the way back. It works like a charm.

"And suppose the customs men decide to search the car? The child might start jabbering at them in Spanish. If they smell a rat, we'll be done for, we'll be arrested for kidnapping and flung into some filthy foreign jail. Your father will go absolutely berserk . . .''

"Nonsense, he'll sleep like a baby all the way, and they won't have the heart to wake him. I've brought some of Mummy's pills with me. That was the whole idea of coming by car, remember? Do stop fussing. Daddy won't know anything about it until we're safely home. I say, Archie—I've just thought of a super scheme for coming back. What if I were to pad myself out to look nine months' gone? Then if they get the least bit tricky, I can start wailing like a banshee and clutching my lump. They're bound to let us go right away. Men are simply terrified of things like that.''

Archie looked duly terrified.

"Steady, Flo old girl. Don't you think you're rather letting your imagination run away with you?''

"Well, that's better than having absolutely no imagination at all, like you. Don't be such a bore, Archie. Just drive the car.''

The roads, although narrow and in bad condition, were virtually deserted. Nevertheless, they were stopped an alarming number of times, although Flora's mourning outfit and the press clippings and the repeated, pathetic rendering of "We came to see my brother's grave. He died for the Republic" worked like magic. The patrolmen, despite their truculent appearance, were an astonishingly sentimental breed. Several of them looked patiently at all the photographs and scrutinized the incomprehensible scraps of newspaper, shaking their heads sympathetically and muttering condolences. They invariably saw them off with a vigorous Republican salute, which Flora returned with gusto. Archie had the sense to do the same, even though, from a personal point of view, his sympathies were firmly with the Nationalists.

"Sloppy-looking soldiers, if you ask me," he muttered as Flora waved out of the window. "Wouldn't pass muster in the British Army, that's for sure.''

"Don't be such a crosspatch. Some of them are only boys. They've all got mothers, you know. Now, remember what I said. Always stop, whether they flag you down or not. And don't put your foot down so hard when you move off, you'll make them suspicious. You know, perhaps we could get Dolly out as well, in the trunk, she's probably thin as a rake by now. She'd be much better off having treatment for these blackouts in England. I dread to *think* what Spanish doctors are like.''

Archie wiped his brow.

"Easy does it, Flo. No point in pushing our luck, eh?''

"Mmm. You know, if it wasn't for poor Edmund, I'd be quite enjoying this. I do like to think he's watching, don't you? Oh dear."

"Don't cry, old girl. Save it for the next patrol."

"I'd give absolutely anything for a cup of tea. How much longer?"

"Couple of hours. Oh, Flo . . ."

Archie stopped the car and put his arm around her.

"Cheer up, Mrs. P. I'm here. I'm here to look after you."

Flora sniffed and returned his hug.

"Oh, Archie," she said with perfect sincerity, "What would I do without you?"

They spent their third night within striking distance of the capital to avoid arriving during the blackout and set off again early next morning, after an uncomfortable night and yet another inadequate breakfast. As they approached Madrid, the checks became more cursory. The car seemed to invest them with instant respectability—such an aggressively bourgeois conveyance was deemed unlikely to contain anyone subversive, and they were treated with a certain amount of deference, just as they would have been in any other European capital. Flora, who had been expecting gangs of angry workers to pelt them with rotten eggs, was heartily relieved, not realizing that there were precious few eggs to be had in Madrid, rotten or otherwise.

A message was waiting at the Plaza Hotel from Jack.

"I am at the Florida. Phone me as soon as you arrive."

Flora ordered a pot of boiling water to be brought up to their suite, together with two cups and saucers. Sighing with anticipation, she unpacked her Spode china teapot and measured out two large spoonfuls of Fortnum's Superior Blend. The milk tasted rather peculiar, but then that was only to be expected.

While she sipped, she put through a call to the Florida. She had always found Jack a rather odd fellow, but she was heartily glad he was here. Much as she would never have admitted it to Archie, she was actually scared stiff.

She jumped when the phone rang and sprang to answer it.

"Jack?"

"Flora. I'll come over straightaway. You're absolutely sure? There can't be any mistake?"

"None at all. Dolly wrote Mummy a letter asking if we could get the child out of the country. That's why we came. Luckily Steven and Bella are both on Archie's passport, so we brought the car and . . . oh Lord, the phones aren't tapped, are they?"

There was a deathly silence. Flora clapped her hand to her mouth.

The telephone was her favorite hobby, and she used it with unin-hibited relish; it had never occurred to her that those beastly censors might be listening in. How appalling. Such things could never hap-pen in England.

"Jack?"

"You mean . . . she's got two children?"

"Two? I say, Jack, is it really safe to talk on the phone?" Her voice sank to a resonant stage whisper.

"Never mind about that. I didn't realize she had two children. Is there a baby, then?"

"A baby? Hardly. It's six years old. You know, the little boy named in Edmund's will. The one you saw in Toledo, the one you've been looking for. She didn't say anything about a baby. Why? Do you know something I don't?"

There was another long pause.

"Flora," said Jack very quietly. "Can you just remind me of the child's name?"

"His name? Don't you know? It's . . . would you believe, it's gone straight out of my head. Wait a moment."

Flora rummaged in her handbag, spilling out passport, press clippings, maps, pills and boat tickets. Finally she found Dolly's letter folded inside her address book, and began delving anew for her reading glasses.

"Here we are." She scanned her eye down the page. "I had it on the tip of my tongue, but honestly, after three days' travel on these dreadful foreign roads, I'm really not quite myself, in fact—"

"Flora," said Jack almost inaudibly, "Is he called Andrés?"

"That's it!" said Flora, tracing the word with her finger. "Andrés. She always used to say she would call her first son Andrés. Well, how soon can we meet? I've got everything all worked out, but I'd rather not tell you on the phone, obviously."

He didn't answer right away.

"That is, the sooner we get moving the better. No point in wast-ing time."

"Yes," said Jack. "Yes, I'll be right over."

"I say, Archie," said Flora, handing him his tea. "Jack sounded rather under the weather. I'd better send down for another cup and saucer."

Archie extracted a bottle of French cognac from the luggage and gave his wife a coaxing, naughty-boy grin.

"Perhaps he'd prefer something stronger," he said hopefully.

A DISTANT THUNDER 498

shortcomings were tolerable because they did not mirror your own.

16

Ramón was still asleep when Dolores let herself in. The air was thick with tobacco and whiskey fumes and a trapped bluebottle was hurtling around the room in its death throes, droning angrily as it bounced off the walls. She hesitated a moment before waking him. Seeing Marisa in the hospital would undoubtedly distress him, but not seeing her would distress him more. Having spent half the night finding her, she must see the ordeal through, cope with the hysteria and the asthma and the coughing fit and the tears, dose him with just enough alcohol to get him dressed and on his feet.

She tried to rouse him gently, but had to resort to shaking him and shouting, while he cursed and swore, clinging to sleep like a lover.

"Ramón," she bellowed. She was dying to get this over with, to be free to go home and sleep herself. Thank God it was a Sunday. "Wake up!" and then finally, "Marisa is sick!"

He opened his eyes immediately and looked up at her, startled into instant alertness.

"Sick? Someone has hurt her?" He sat bolt upright. "Where is she?"

"No one has hurt her. She was taken ill at the hotel and they took her to a hospital, quite a long way away. There was no space for her in the city. She is asking for you. She is much better now. She said you must not worry."

"You are lying!" snapped Ramón, wide awake with a vengeance, throwing his leg over the side of the bed so that she could fit the caliper splint. "Someone has hurt her. I will kill him. I will find out who it is and go to the hotel and kill him."

"No one has hurt her, Ramón. She has had some female problems, pain and bleeding, that is all."

Ramón's reaction was instantaneous.

"You mean a miscarriage?"

461

"A miscarriage?" faltered Dolores. "What makes you think that? Is she pregnant?"

"She swears not. But I did not believe her. She has not bled for many weeks now. I am attentive to such things. She said it was often so with her. How dare she lie to me!"

"Ramón, I know nothing of any miscarriage."

"Was it an abortion then? These Red doctors mock God with their abortions! It is immoral. It is murder. Has she had an abortion, behind my back?"

"Ramón, I promise you she has not miscarried nor had an abortion. You must not upset her by accusing her of such things. She is very weak. Promise me you will not upset her."

"Life is sacred," declared Ramón. "I told her, if it was so, she must cease her whoring. Many times I have tried to dissuade her from her life of vice, offered to support her. You know I am a wealthy man. Everything she has she owes to me. She has no right to deprive me of a son!"

"Deprive you of a son?"

"I should like to have a son before I die. I had thought to make Andrés my heir, but now that you are sending him to England . . ."

"Sending him to England? Who told you that?"

Ramón pushed past her into the hallway and began descending the stairs with alarming agility.

"Why, the boy himself, of course. Naturally he confides in me."

"But I have never mentioned it to him!" Dolores had to struggle to keep up with him: she had not seen him move so fast in months.

"No indeed. You swore to him that you had no such plans. But he overheard you talking to García. The boy is no fool, Dolores. He takes after me."

It was impossible to talk above the din of the metro, and Dolores kept her peace. Mad people were said to have peculiar powers of perception, strange twisted insights denied to those whose brains were trammeled by rational thought. It was easy to underestimate mad people. Just as it was easy to underestimate children. Marisa and she had made the same mistake. Poor Andrés. How confused he must be! Perhaps she should have told him. But there had seemed no point in upsetting him in advance, and besides she had felt so weak lately . . .

They would allow only one visitor at a time. Ramón went in first while Dolores waited anxiously, expecting a nurse to appear any minute and ask her to remove her brother, he was causing a disturbance. But after half an hour or so, he emerged, head held high, perfectly composed.

"You may go in now," he informed Dolores regally. "Kindly do not tire her."

Marisa was propped up on the pillows. Some of the color had returned to her cheeks, but she looked far from happy.

"Lole," she said, grasping her hand. "He has found out about the baby!"

"What baby?" said Dolores carefully.

"He said the doctors told him!" She began crying.

"What is the matter? Was he angry with you?"

"Angry? No, no. But now he will not let me work. I was sure it was not a baby, but the doctor says it is. I do not want a baby, Lole. I want them to cut it out of me. But Ramón says I must have it!"

She was trembling and Dolores began rocking her to and fro, but the flow of words continued.

"Ramón says that he will treat the baby as his own. But Ramón will soon be dead, and what will become of me then? Oh, Lole, there was so much pain! Is it like that when a baby is born? Is there that much blood? I am so afraid!"

She began weeping into the pillow.

"There's nothing to be afraid of," said Dolores helplessly. "Your mother had all your brothers and sisters, did she not? And she survived. It is not so terrible."

"It is, it is! How she screamed! She screamed for a day and a night when my brother was born. They thought she was going to die, and the baby too, they even sent for the priest!"

"That was in Andalucía. Here in Madrid there are doctors, hospitals, here you will get proper care. Hush, now. If you cry so loudly they will blame me and send me away."

"Don't go away. Don't go. Stay with me. Tell me how it was with Andrés. Was there much pain?"

"It is soon forgotten."

"More pain than with the bottle breaking?"

"Much less."

"Then why did my mother scream for a day and a night? Ramón said it could not happen, as long as I used the bag. But often I was tired . . ."

"Try to rest now."

"You promise not to leave me? You will be here when I wake?"

"I promise."

As soon as she dozed off, Dolores went to find Ramón. He was fidgeting in annoyance at being kept waiting, and evidently in need of refreshment. He declared that he would find his own way home, he had pressing business to attend to.

"By the time my son is born, the war will be won!" he declared expansively, impervious to Dolores's signals to keep his voice down. "By the time my son is born, I will have reclaimed my estate. You will always be welcome there, dear sister. But not García. Think about it."

He strutted off down the corridor, with much flourishing of his walking stick, his posture newly erect. For a man who spent most of his time confined to bed, such sudden energy was startling. Was there any difference between hope and delusion in their power to revive and sustain?

And so Dolores deluded Marisa. She soothed her with lies, promising her there would be no pain, assuring her that Ramón would not die, telling her all the things she desperately wanted to hear. Constant repetition was a tried and tested aid to faith, the politicians knew that, and the Church, and everyone else who manufactured truth. Constant repetition. Gradually, gradually, the drug took effect, lulling both of them into sleep.

Tomás gave Andrés his latchkey and let him scamper on ahead. Hoisting himself up the three steep flights of stairs was a laborious process, and one that he preferred to tackle in easy stages. He hoped that Lole would be waiting for them with good news. He cared little for Marisa, but she had her uses, and without her the full burden of caring for that good-for-nothing drunkard would fall upon Dolores.

Andrés's company had proved exhausting. Lole was right, if anything was to happen to her, he would be hard put to care for the boy. The union had promised him a sitting-down job packing cartridges, alongside women and men deemed unfit for the front. It would be tiresome work demanding nimble fingers and no strength, but it was better than being idle, and once he was independent Lole would feel less responsible for him, she might yet agree to follow her son to England . . .

Andrés ran up the stairs, head down, making guttural warlike noises in his throat. Today he was a bomber pilot, he had been careering to and fro all morning, demolishing Fascist positions. He was ravenous, and he hoped his mother had made some soup. He reached the topmost landing and flew, nose down, along the corridor, ready for the final drop before returning to base.

He stopped in midair. There were three people standing outside the door, two men and a woman. He looked from one to the other in terror. He knew straightaway by their clothes that the dreaded moment had finally arrived, that these were the people from England who had come to take him away. He wanted to turn and run, but his reactions were frozen, he found himself unable to move.

The woman smiled and crouched down.

"Good day, Andrés," she said in a funny accent. The tall dark man with the mustache beamed and nodded at him while the shorter one just stared, without speaking, until the woman whispered something in his ear.

"Where is your mother, Andrés?" he said.

Andrés took a step backward, as if to test that his limbs were still working. Then he turned and ran. He could hear them pursuing him, their footsteps thumping hollowly against the bare floorboards, but he did not look back, his legs moving like pistons, down the first flight, down the second, and bang into Tomás, whose huge bulk straddled the narrow staircase like a colossus.

"Whoa, boy," he roared, startled, almost losing his balance. Undeterred, Andrés dived into the empty space once occupied by Tomás's left leg, and continued on his journey, just as the three adults arrived breathless on the landing above, thwarted by the giant human obstruction. By the time Tomás had swiveled himself around and gone back to the bottom, in order to let them pass, the boy had a clear start. The two men ran off and the woman followed more sedately, her face alert with anxiety.

Tomás watched them disappear, cursing under his breath. One of the men must be Lole's cousin. Clearly they had frightened Andrés in some way for him to have run off like that. The child was totally out of control. Six months ago, he would have trapped him in his arms and carried him back up the stairs like a kicking rabbit. As it was, he might as well have been an old woman, powerless to catch that whirling ball of flesh.

He heaved himself to the end of the street, and looked this way and that, but by this time there was no sign of any of them. Nothing to do about it but to wait. The boy had nowhere to go, except his uncle's, and his uncle was not in, he was with Dolores, at the hospital. He would return soon enough.

Unable to face the stairs again so soon, Tomás repaired to the café on the corner, sweating with exhaustion, and sat down outside, so that he could keep the building in sight. If the strangers returned, he would explain who he was. Clearly Lole had not told her cousin

of his condition, otherwise he would surely have recognized him
and acknowledged him in some way. They were well-dressed, rich
people, people with whom he had nothing in common, people
whom he would have hated on sight had they been Spanish. But
Lole insisted that English rich people were different, that they did
not oppress the workers or allow children to die of starvation, that
there were no Don Felipes, no Father Luises, no Civil Guard, that
the people there were free. He must make them welcome, he must
not make Lole feel ashamed of him.

After twenty minutes or so, the woman reappeared, together with
the man with the mustache. They looked out of place in this poor
quarter, people stood in clusters and stared at them like creatures
from another planet. The woman was dressed all in black. She wore
a black hat with a black net veil coming down over her face. Tomás
had thought she was the cousin's wife, but perhaps she was a widow.
He pulled himself upright and followed them down the street, calling after them.

They turned and looked at him politely but blankly. He asked
them if they were Lole's relatives from England, and introduced
himself as her husband, and told them not to worry about the boy,
he would not go far. But clearly they did not understand. The woman
got out a book and addressed him in Spanish, reading the words
off the page very loudly, but Tomás could not understand her and
had to ask her to repeat herself. She did so, several times, but she
might as well have been speaking English, and then she showed
him the book and pointed with her finger, but Tomás's reading
lessons had not progressed as far as unseen words, and he made an
embarrassed gesture of apology. The man and the woman addressed each other in agitated English, and seemed to be arguing
about what to do. Tomás gestured toward the apartment, indicating
that they could wait there, and eventually they seemed to understand, and followed his labored progress up the stairs. Only when
they reached the very top did Tomás remember that Andrés still
had the key.

Ramón felt full of vigor and youth again. Soon he would have a son
of his very own! This was cause for celebration indeed.

No more would he spend his days lying in his bed, waiting to
die. He felt like a man waking refreshed after a long sleep. How
out of touch he had allowed himself to become! Today he had
noticed for the first time that the city was becoming normal again.
The fashionable bars that had closed down in the early days of the

war had now reopened; well-dressed people were to be seen in the streets once more; offensive banners no longer adorned every doorway. Madrid, like him, had come back to life.

Unfortunately he had come out, in his haste to see Marisa, with only some loose change in his pocket. He would return home, extract some of his hoard, and treat himself to a celebratory bottle of French champagne. Now that people of good quality had come out of hiding—confident, no doubt, that the day of victory was at hand—he would perhaps find someone glad to engage in intelligent conversation. He was full of plans for his son's future, and was eager to discuss them with other cultivated people.

His sickness had been born of despair, his health worn down by the years of living among the rabble. Now he could walk tall again. His son would never see him dressed in rags, never smell the stench of these wretched slums. How good it was to be alive!

He beamed fatuously at every passerby, twirling his walking stick. For the first time in months, he had an appetite. Perhaps he would find one of his old haunts, dine in style, consort with people of quality, share reminiscences about the good old days and look forward to the day of liberation, when the *Caudillo* would lead his victorious troops into the city while people tossed flowers in his path. How delightful it would be to witness the public executions of the likes of García! How grateful Dolores would be for her brother's protection! The days of deprivation would soon be past, a new era of wealth and luxury was about to begin.

How vile this building was! Crawling with bugs, rank with disgusting odors, raucous with coarse voices. His son would walk on marble floors and thick carpets, his son would ride and shoot, his son would have servants whose only function was to satisfy his every whim. Dolores might deprive him of his nephew, but she would have no such rights over his son. This weakness she had for England had been the cause of her undoing. It was there that she had filled her head with subversive nonsense and learned contempt for her own class. How wise he had been not to trust her with his secrets. She was clearly more besotted by this García than ever, so besotted she had allowed him to persuade her to send her only son away. It was just as well he no longer needed the boy. Now that his health had been restored to him, now that he would have a son of his own, now that victory was assured, his worries on that score were over. What a fool he had been to succumb to despair! Did God not always reward the just man?

He stifled a wave of irritation as he discovered his once-favored nephew cowering outside his door, waiting for him. How typical of García to leave the boy to his own devices. Such a man was not fit to be a father. He would send the boy home immediately, his plans for the rest of the day would not accommodate a child of six.

"Good day, Andrés. What brings you here? I am going out again directly, to an important rendezvous which I regret you cannot attend."

Andrés followed him into the room, fighting back the tears.

"Then can I stay here? Can I stay here while you go out?"

"What is the matter, boy? Why are you sniveling? Tears are for women, a gentleman never cries. Speak up."

"Nothing is the matter," said Andrés sullenly, wiping his eyes on the back of his hand.

"Is it trouble with García, boy? Has he threatened you?"

"No. But . . . but I prefer to be with you than with Tomás. Can I stay here till you get back? Please?"

Ramón smirked at the compliment.

"Wait in the corridor while I complete my toilette, child. Then you may await my return. If García should come looking for you, you are on no account to let him in. I refuse to allow that animal to contaminate my studio with his unspeakable presence. Is that understood?"

"Yes, Uncle."

He sent the boy out of the room and took all the money out of his hoard, leaving only the gun. Then he replaced the floorboard and the threadbare rug and allowed Andrés inside again.

"Uncle . . ." began Andrés, his lip quivering.

"Yes? What is it?"

"Uncle, I am afraid."

"Afraid? Of what? A gentleman knows no fear. Are you afraid of García? There is no need. If he should trouble you in any way, he will be answerable to me!"

"When will Mamá be home?"

Ramón shrugged.

"She is attending to Marisa in the hospital. No doubt she will come looking for you when she returns. I myself will not be home till late. I have urgent business to attend to."

Andrés opened his mouth again to speak, but Ramón interrupted him.

"I must make haste, my associates await me. We shall discuss your problems with García tomorrow. Here—" He delved in his

pocket and extracted a five-peseta bill, extending it as a bishop
extends his ring. "This is for you, my boy."

Andrés gaped speechless at this sudden untold wealth and before
he could stammer his thanks his uncle was gone.

He sat for a while examining the bill. It was a lot of money. If
his uncle refused to give him refuge, at least he would have enough
to buy food for several days. He must stay in hiding long enough
for the English people to give up and go home again. He hoped
Ramón would not be gone long, and would give him some advice.
When he had told him of his mother's plan to send him away, it had
been in the hope that he would intervene. But his uncle had been
annoyed to be woken up and had shown little interest in his problem, even when he had asked him what he should do about the
boot. He had started muttering incoherently and fallen asleep again,
and soon afterward his mother had come to fetch him. Yet who else
was there to turn to? He knew that Tomás did not want him to go
to England, he had heard him say so, but he could not hide from
his mother with Tomás.

Perhaps he had better not wait for Ramón. His uncle might berate
him for being disobedient and remind him that orders should always
be obeyed without question. Not long ago he would have trusted
him absolutely, but now there was no one he could trust—except
Tomás, who could not help him. He had best leave now, before his
mother came looking for him. He knew of a disused church where
he could hide, children often played there among the smashed relics
and charred wood. He would stay there until the danger was past.

He opened up the food cupboard and found a packet of dry
biscuits, which he stuffed into his pocket. Then he looked around
the room for other useful things. His uncle had an old walking
stick, which was split at one end, and which he no longer used
since Marisa had bought him a new one. It would serve as a weapon,
in case he had to defend himself. He remembered the gang of rough
children who had tried to steal his chewing gum. They might kill
him for five pesetas . . .

He was just about to open the door when he heard the unmistakable thump of Tomás on his crutches, orchestrated by other, lighter,
footsteps. They had come looking for him already!

He hid himself quickly behind the curtain that protected Marisa's
clothes and stood motionless, inhaling the strong, sweet smell of
cheap scent while Tomás hammered on the door and shouted,

"Andrés? Andrés? Are you in there? Don't be afraid, boy. Let
me in!"

Andrés kept very still, frightened even to breathe. Then he heard Tomás say, "I did not think he would be here. His uncle is with Dolores at the hospital. We had best return home and wait for her there." The ominous sounds went into reverse as the footsteps disappeared into the distance.

Andrés waited several minutes, to ensure the coast was clear, before emerging from his hiding place. His uncle had often spoken of spending days, weeks, under cover in enemy territory, evading the clutches of scouts and raiding parties while he carried out mysterious secret missions. He would show his uncle he was not a crybaby, not a sniveler; he would prove to them all he could take care of himself.

He stole out of the room, closed the door quietly, and crept down the staircase, his ears cocked for the slightest sound. The usual urchins were clustered around the pump and he walked the long way around to avoid them, fearing to be set upon and robbed of his precious assets. Then he ran like hell for the church.

"Jack!" Flora greeted him, relieved. "About time. Any luck?"

"No. I've made inquiries all over the place but no one seems to have seen which way he went. Those alleyways are like a maze. He could be anywhere."

Flora and Archie were both standing in the middle of the tiny room and the big, one-legged man was perched on a narrow chair which looked too flimsy to support his weight. He nodded at Jack and indicated that he should sit.

"He seems to be a neighbor," said Flora. "He had to break the lock to let us in."

"You'd better sit down," said Jack.

"I'd rather not," said Flora squeamishly.

"For God's sake, Flo, it's perfectly clean."

She obeyed gingerly, covering her reluctance with a bright social smile. Archie immediately copied her, depositing himself awkwardly on a low stool.

"What a fearful hole," continued Flora. "How dreadful to think of Dolly living in a place like this."

Jack felt horribly embarrassed by this crass remark, even though the big man clearly didn't understand a word of English. The place was indeed a hole, but no worse than many he had lived in himself. He felt ashamed to be sitting here dressed in smart clothes, patronizing this crippled giant. Jack addressed him in Spanish with great courtesy, asking if he knew where the boy's mother was.

"Dolores is visiting a sick friend," he replied. "She will be home shortly."

"Let us hope Andrés returns before her," said Jack politely.

"The boy is unruly, he gives her much worry. She will be happier when he is safe in England. I try to be a father to him, but . . ." He indicated his stump and shrugged.

Jack's blood stopped flowing. He had to struggle to find the words.

"You are her husband?"

"Her second husband, yes." He looked at Jack steadily. "Was it you who visited Toledo? Was it you who brought word of Lorenzo's death?"

Jack nodded.

"Rosa told her?"

"Jack," interjected Flora. "I'm simply desperate for a bathroom. All that tea. Would you mind if Archie and I went back to the hotel? We'll come back straightaway."

"No need to come back. I'll wait here with Dolly's husband until she gets home, then I'll bring her to the Plaza."

"He's her *husband?*" squeaked Flora, aghast.

"For God's sake, Flo, show some respect."

"So there *is* a Tomás. I thought she was just . . ."

The man nodded acknowledgement at the sound of his name. Flora recovered herself, smiled graciously and extended her hand, gesturing at him not to get up. Then Archie did the same.

"We won't move until we hear from you," said Flora. "I say, Archie, can you find our way back? Some of the people out there looked distinctly unsavory . . ."

"You're safer here than you are in London," snapped Jack, annoyed now. "Do you know the way, Archie?"

"I'll find it," said Archie quickly, ushering Flora out of the room.

"So Dolores got my letter?" resumed Jack.

"No. I destroyed it."

"But why—"

"Listen and I will tell you. Dolores and I escaped from Albavera. Everyone else was killed. We went to Toledo to find her son. She begged me to seek news of her husband. I told her he was dead. It was no lie."

His voice was firm, matter-of-fact, unapologetic.

"I told her nothing of your visit and I swore my sister Rosa to silence. I feared you would take her away to England. I wanted her for my wife. You understand?''

''Yes,'' said Jack slowly, understanding him perfectly. ''Yes, I think I understand.''

''This I have told her, and now I have told you too. I ask your pardon.''

His quiet dignity was unanswerable. Jack was momentarily overcome by a wave of understanding. He would have done the same. No question about it, he would have done the same.

''You are her cousin?'' continued Tomás, eyeing Jack curiously. ''She spoke of you.''

''The lady is her cousin,'' said Jack. ''I am a friend of the family.''

''You are kind to come so far,'' said Tomás. ''How will you get the boy out of the country? To apply for a travel permit might be dangerous. Many questions would be asked. This troubles Dolores greatly. She fears they would find out that the boy's father was a Fascist.''

''The lady has a child the same age on her passport,'' said Jack. ''There is no photograph. It will only be necessary to dress Andrés as a girl.''

Tomás chuckled.

''There is nothing of the girl in that one,'' he said. ''He is a great trial to his mother. But he has suffered much. He has lost his father, and his cousin, and now he must lose his mother too.''

''His cousin?''

''He perished with my sister and daughter when the Fascists took Toledo. That is, as far as we know. We have had no news of them all these months. Many died. My sister's *novio* was a hostage, an anarchist. She would have had to flee. But they pursued them in airplanes, they shot them from the air. Who knows, the same may happen in Madrid. Dolores is wise to send the boy away.''

Jack struggled to control his features. He wanted to leave this room, to be alone, to think, to readjust. But he was trapped now, in a trap of his own making. He dared not even light a cigarette for fear his hand would shake. He cast his mind back to Toledo, to that magic moment when he had seen the dark-haired child. He had barely looked at the other boy, the real Andrés, Dolly's blue-eyed son, he had seen him today as if for the first time. Dolly's blue-eyed son . . .

He was acutely aware of the big man staring at him. He made him feel utterly transparent.

"When I visited Toledo, last September," said Jack at length, choosing his words carefully. "I saw three children. One of them looked just like Dolores."

Tomás gave no sign of surprise.

"Rafael, my sister Rosa's child. Dolores's brother's bastard." He made a gesture of contempt. "Dolores took Rosa and the baby into her own family."

"Rafael is alive," said Jack.

"What?" Obeying a useless reflex, Tomás tried to spring to his feet.

"He is in a children's home, in Valencia. He cannot speak, he could not tell them his name."

"And Petra? My daughter?"

Jack shook his head. Tomás covered his face with his hands.

"Forgive me. This is good news. It is many months since we had good news. Lole will be overjoyed. She loved him as her own."

"*Lole?*"

"I call her Lole. I like to forget that she was once Dolores. I am only a workingman, as you can see." He gestured around the room. "Her cousin was shocked, no doubt, to find her with such a husband. Will you drink with me?"

He waved aside Jack's offer of assistance, swung himself out of his seat and fetched wine and two glasses, filling them to the brim.

"To the Republic," he said. "To freedom."

"To freedom," said Jack.

Tomás took a long swallow.

"So," he said, looking at Jack hard. "You are not her cousin." Jack did not reply. *Lole.* Lole and her big oaf of a one-legged husband. All these months she had been near enough to touch . . . Lole.

"You are not her cousin," repeated Tomás.

"Her cousin? No. As I said, I am a friend of the family."

"You have known Dolores long?"

"I knew her when she was in England, as a girl. I met her through her cousin, the lady's brother. He was killed here in Madrid, in an air raid."

"Here in Madrid? He came to look for her?"

"No. He was working in a hospital. We all thought that Dolores was dead."

Tomás bowed his head. "Dolores will be sad to learn of this. In Madrid, and we did not know it!"

"Madrid is a big place," said Jack with feeling. He began to feel trapped again, the big man's eyes seemed to be boring into him, as if he could read his thoughts. "Should I go and look for the boy in the street? Has he friends nearby, where I can make inquiries?"

Tomás refilled his glass and pushed it toward him.

"You saw three children in Toledo," he said. "You saw Andrés."

"Yes. I saw Andrés." Tomás pinned Jack to his seat with another penetrating look.

"You offered to take him back to England?"

"Yes. I thought he was an orphan. He had lost both his mother and father, and—"

Tomás let out a harsh bark of laughter.

"His father? I am crippled, my friend, but not blind. You take me for a fool."

For a long time they sat staring each other out. Jack was the first to look away.

"I was the blind one," he said. "I was the fool."

"I must get home before dark, Marisa. I will come again tomorrow after work."

Marisa nodded wanly.

"Thank you, Lole. You are a good sister to me. Will you take care of me and the baby after Ramón is dead? The Englishman will not want me with a baby. Now I will never go to England."

"You would not like England," said Dolores. "It is too cold."

"Colder even than Madrid in winter?"

"Not the weather. The people. They are kind people, but cold."

"Like my Englishman?"

"Is your Englishman cold?"

"Yes. He cares nothing for women. He pays me just to talk. I think perhaps he is sick. But he is kind."

"Just to talk?"

"Just to talk. He would be very angry to know what has happened. He cares for me, I know."

"Say nothing," said Dolores. "If the fat man is so important, you must be very careful. Think of Ramón. What will become of him if you are put in prison? Think of me. How will I manage without you?"

Dolores tucked her up like a child and kissed her.

"How do you feel now?"

"Better. It is good to rest. Ramón says I must not strain myself. Ramón says that ladies lie in bed all day until their babies are born. Is it true Ramón has money, Lole? He says he has money."

"He has some money, yes. Do not worry about money now. Try to sleep."

Dolores set off for home, exhausted. Fatigue made her mildly euphoric. He paid her just to talk. The knowledge was like an absolution. Not that she had cared whether Jack slept with Marisa or not, but she was profoundly relieved that it would not fall to her to bring up his child.

She fell asleep in the metro going home, and nearly missed her stop. It was already getting dark, and she was still wearing her nightdress under her coat. Now she need not bother to dress at all, she would prepare an early supper and go straight to bed. She quickened her step. It had started to drizzle, an oily sheen coated the piles of garbage. As she turned off the main road she saw a rat skulking in the gutter. Rats sometimes ate babies alive in the poor quarters. She must make sure Marisa put a net over the crib. She might lose Andrés, but she would have Marisa's baby. That would be some comfort. Tomás was right, she could never bring Andrés back to a life of poverty and squalor. If he went, it would be for good. Whoever won the war, they would always be poor. A victorious Republic might make the rich poor, but it would never make the poor rich.

There would be no war in England. In England they were devoted to peace, safe on their remote island. Whatever happened in Spain, whatever happened in Europe, England would remain apart. Once she had shared the general disgust that England would not help the Republic. But now she was glad, for Andrés's sake, that England cared only for itself.

She climbed the stairs slowly, dragging one foot after the other. Poor Tomás must be as tired as she after a day looking after the boy. Perhaps he was resting, she had better use her key.

She took it out of her purse in readiness as she walked along the corridor and put out her hand to insert it in the keyhole, only to find that the heavy iron lock had been removed, leaving a bare patch of splintered wood. Fearing robbery or worse, she let out a cry of alarm and she flung open the door, her face already full of shock, robbed of its power to react.

"Jack," she said simply, transfixed by those familiar bright blue eyes, the eyes she saw every day of her life, the eyes that had never allowed her to forget. She had expected him to look different, and yet he hadn't changed a bit. The sight of him hurtled her back into the past, it was like a little death, the moment of inescapable truth that only comes at the last . . .

"Dolly."

Jack stared back at her. He had braced himself for the worst, expecting her to be haggard, careworn, unrecognizable. She looked older, certainly, thin and ill, but she still took his breath away. The sculpted shadows gave her face a new dignity, she wore her pallor with pride.

He held out his hand but Dolores did not take it, looking around the room in sudden alarm.

"Where's Andrés?"

"Lole, the patrols are looking for him now. He has run away."

"Run away?" She sank into a chair.

"They say they will soon find him," said Jack. "Now you are home, I will join the search. Everyone is helping. Don't worry. We will find him."

He was speaking to her in Spanish, like a stranger.

"Thank you," she said. "Thank you."

"Flora and Archie are here," he continued, the proper names jolting him back into English. It was strange, hearing English again. "They're in the hotel. When you feel up to it, I will take you to see them."

"Thank you. Thank you. Flora and Archie?"

The question was implicit.

"Edmund is dead," said Jack. "He came out to Spain with Clara to work in a hospital. He was killed in an air raid."

She looked at him blankly for a moment, and then said tonelessly, "Oh. Oh God. I'm so sorry."

"I must go and help look for the boy," continued Jack stiffly. "May I return later?"

Tomás nodded. Dolores did not reply, and Jack left the room quickly, feeling like an intruder.

Tomás reached for Dolores's chair and dragged it nearer his own. She seemed completely numb, her hands were cold and she was shaking. He rubbed her frozen fingers, but after a moment she freed her hands and stood up. She seemed unsteady on her feet.

"I must lie down," she said indistinctly. "I must lie down flat." She walked slowly into the bedroom and shut the door behind her, and when Tomás looked in a few minutes later, he was astonished to find her asleep.

It was very cold in the church, and full of strange noises. Flapping and scurrying, rustling and scratching and whistling. Some of the children said it was haunted by the ghosts of dead nuns, who came there on broomsticks in the dead of night. Andrés crossed himself in an instinctive attempt to ward off evil. He had learned at school that religion was all lies and superstition, but he thought it best to placate the vengeful spirits. He had been glad when Mamá had stopped making him say his prayers at night, for he was a natural heathen. But now he found himself harking back wistfully to the cozy comfort of those bedtime chants.

He had eaten all the biscuits, and now he was thirsty. An expedition to the nearest pump would be dangerous at this late hour, when he might be stopped and asked why he was not at home in bed. Besides it was too dark now to find his way out through the piles of broken timbers and rubble.

His teeth began to chatter and he buried his hands under his armpits to keep them warm. He wondered how his uncle had managed during his secret missions. He must not cry. Only women and cowards cried. Rafael had been a terrible crybaby. He wished Rafael were here now. If Rafael were here it would be easy to be brave. "Don't cry, Rafael," he would say grandly. "Just do as I say and all will be well." Rafael had always taken the role of little brother, even though he was the elder, and automatically deferred to Andrés in all things. It was a bit like having a sister. Andrés had enjoyed looking out for him and fending off the bullies. This would be fun, if there were two of them again. It took two to make an adventure.

His stomach rumbled loudly. He wished now he had saved up all his chocolate for just such an emergency. He shifted uncomfortably on the cold stone floor, and finally managed to doze off, only to wake with a yelp as something ran over his bare legs. Two green beads of light gleamed viciously at him in the darkness, making the hair stand up all over his body. He lashed out violently with his stick, sending the rodent running for cover, but after this unforeseen attack sleep was impossible. Every nerve was sensitized in readiness for the next engagement, and though eventually he ceased to be awake, he did not rest.

"I demand to see a lawyer," demanded Ramón, wiping his chin with his sleeve. "You have no right to detain me here against my will."

"Shut up, will you," rasped a gritty voice from the next cell. "Some of us are trying to get some sleep."

"You'll be dealt with in the morning," sneered the guard. "Now keep your mouth shut up or I'll put you in with *him.*" He jerked his head toward the unseen neighbor.

"But by morning I shall be dead," Ramón protested. "I am a very sick man."

"You can say that again. Mind you're sick into the pail next time, comrade, or you can lick it all up off the floor with your highfalutin tongue."

Ramón was incensed. Such impertinence! No doubt the odious fellow expected a bribe. He felt in his empty pockets for the twentieth time and promptly vomited again.

Robbed! He had been robbed! And these so-called police wanted nothing to do with it, they showed no interest in tracking down the criminal and booking him, in apprehending the vulture who had picked his pocket and reduced him to penury. No, their only interest was in harassing an innocent citizen over one small, unpaid restaurant bill, even though he had offered an IOU and his word as a gentleman that the debt would be settled on the morrow. The arrogance of tradesmen! And now they dared to accuse him of drunkenness! Why, he had not drunk enough to intoxicate an infant. He could not remember exactly what or how much he had drunk, but it was a derisory amount, even though the first bottle of champagne seemed a very long time ago, as did the *tapas* which now festered in the bucket. But however long ago it was—for he had no watch—he was most definitely not drunk. If they would only incarcerate the low scoundrel who had robbed him, then he could settle the paltry bill immediately and be on his way.

"My wife is pregnant," he had informed them. "She may give birth at any moment." But these Communists showed no respect for the family. "How dare you manhandle a war veteran?" he had rebuked them sternly, only to meet with ignorant jeers and insults. It was intolerable. He would definitely take the matter further. As soon as he was out of this vile place, he would write a letter to the President himself, demanding an apology and due compensation and insisting that these ruffians be reprimanded and dismissed without notice.

He would send for Marisa in the morning, when she returned from the hotel, and she would pay them off. Such villains lived on bribes. Then he remembered that Marisa was in the hospital, and was sick again. After that he felt slightly better, and then a great deal worse. As the alcohol deserted his bloodstream, and matter resumed its sway over mind, he began to shake, and then to gasp, and then to fight for breath and scream hoarsely for help, careless now of the volley of threats and abuse from the neighboring cell.

He was blue by the time they answered his frenzied pleas, with his eyes popping bulbously out of his head. There was no doctor on hand, and his distress was convincing enough to persuade his jailers that he might be about to die on them, and thus generate a tedious amount of paperwork. Since the Communists had taken control of the police, each death had to be meticulously accounted for. Deaths now happened out of sight, sanctioned facelessly from afar, and unauthorized "accidents" had become more trouble than they were worth. And so, rather than risk a time-consuming investigation, the guards tore up their charge sheets, hauled the troublesome inmate out of his cell, dumped him in a puddle at the end of the street and left him there to die.

"At last," said Flora, ushering Jack into her suite. "I've been out of my mind with worry." She had hidden her curlers under a pink chiffon scarf and was nursing a cup of strong cocoa. Archie was in the adjoining room, asleep.

"They've called off the search till morning," said Jack. "You might as well go to bed."

"Did you see Dolly?"

"Yes. I didn't stay long. When I reported back to Tomás, she was already in bed."

"Did she look terrible?"

"You would think so, yes. I told her about Edmund. She didn't seem to take it in. We thought we wouldn't tell her about Rafael till after they'd found Andrés. She's had about enough for one day."

"Rafael?"

"The boy I found in the orphanage in Valencia. He's her nephew, apparently, hence the resemblance. Quite a spectacular mix-up on my part. Can I have a drop of that?"

He poured himself some of Archie's brandy.

"Well, it was an easy mistake to make," remarked Flora thoughtfully. "Specially as Andrés doesn't look the least bit like her. Presumably he takes after his father."

"Yes," said Jack, tossing back the drink in one swallow, blushing despite himself, wondering if she had guessed. If she had, she would certainly say so; Flora was much too forthright to be tactful. If she hadn't, he would not enlighten her. Dolly clearly hadn't wanted anybody to know, and her secret was not his to tell.

"So, did you find out anything else?" demanded Flora.

"The husband doesn't seem to know about this illness of hers. I daresay she didn't want to worry him. I hoped perhaps she'd been exaggerating, to try to persuade you to come, but having seen her I don't think so."

Flora shuddered.

"Poor Dolly. We must get her to see a doctor. She'd be much better off in England. I can't imagine what possessed her, marrying someone like that. And so soon after her husband died. I mean to say, less than a year . . ."

"He says she married him out of pity, after he lost his leg."

"He told you that?"

"He told me a lot of things." Jack poured himself another drink and lit a cigarette. "He asked me to try to persuade Dolly to leave with Andrés."

"Oh, absolutely. But how do we get her out?"

"We can't. Not with you, anyway. Specially now you'll have to take two children out, and not just one."

"That's a very optimistic forecast. One of them's run away, and the other one can't go outdoors without having a screaming fit."

"You have to be patient in Spain. Things happen either very slowly, or very suddenly. You have to stop thinking logically. The only way you survive out here is by instinct."

"Are you drunk?"

"Not with booze. Sorry. I ought to let you get to bed."

"Oh for God's sake. I wouldn't sleep a wink in any case. I keep thinking of that poor mite roaming the streets in the dark. Dolly must be frantic."

"I think she's beyond being frantic about things. She's been through rather a lot in the last year by all accounts."

"You seem to have got on with this husband chap remarkably well."

"We turned out to have a lot in common. Get some rest now, Flo. We'll talk again in the morning."

"Perhaps I ought to take one of Mummy's pills. Would you like one?"

Jack shook his head. Flora tipped one back with a grimace.

"How old are your children?" asked Jack.

"Bella's five and Steven's four. But I don't suppose the border guards will go into that, specially if we have them wrapped up in blankets in the back and fast asleep. We're going home a different way, so we don't see the same guards, and I shall pretend to go straight into labor the minute any of them start getting sticky."

She jutted her chin out purposefully and fell to rapid stirring of her cocoa. A ghost of a smile lit up Jack's features.

"You know, Flora, you're the most awful snob, but you're absolutely wonderful in a war."

"Thanks very much. Perhaps I'll have some of that stuff as well." She held out her cup and allowed Jack to lace it. "So how does one go about getting Dolly out?"

"Well, she can't apply for a passport and a visa without lying about pretty well everything—her maiden name, her date and place of birth, her mother's name, her father's name, her father's occupation, and so on, and if anything didn't check out they'd start asking a lot of rather awkward questions. Suspicion is endemic, and whatever you're suspected of, you're automatically guilty until proved innocent. Her marriage to Tomás was a two-minute declaration of intent, one of the early revolutionary ceremonies before the bureaucrats took over. So although Dolores García exists on a ration card and an employment register, she came from nowhere, she's got no history, no credentials. Anyone with anything to hide is assumed to be a Fascist and dealt with accordingly. There are any number of people rotting in prison on all kinds of trumped-up charges, your father wasn't exaggerating about that. So, it would be less risky, in her case, to get out illegally than to try to do it legally."

"You mean, on a forged passport? Can you get hold of one?"

"At a price, yes. I know of a place in Valencia. That's not the problem. The problem will be persuading her to leave."

"Because of her husband?"

"He says she won't leave him. Perhaps she'll listen to you. I'll give you a letter for the lawyers, by the way, so that they can release Edmund's money. I'm sure Archie will know how to invest it. I'm also going to ask them to commence adoption proceedings, for Rafael."

"That's not necessary, Jack. Archie and I—"

"It is necessary, for me. For a long time I thought he was Dolly's."

"But now you know he isn't!"

"It doesn't matter anymore. I'll have to ask her permission, of course, as next of kin."

"Good Lord. You mean you actually *want* him?"

"I suppose I must."

"Well. I would never have credited you with any paternal instincts."

"Neither would I," said Jack.

* * *

"Hush, Lole. All will be well."

Her deep, sudden sleep had been short-lived. She was pacing the floor by candlelight, wrapped in a shawl, her face pinched with anxiety. Tomás had had to restrain her from going out to look for Andrés there and then.

"Ramón told me he heard us talking," she said. "I should have been honest with him. I should have explained. But how could I be sure that they would come? I broke my promise not to send him away . . . I should never have promised. I felt too weak to argue with him. And now . . ."

"He will come home when he is hungry," repeated Tomás. "He has no food and no money. Do not blame yourself. I should have stopped him, but he was too quick for me. Go back to bed. Tomorrow everyone will join in the search and find him for you. And then, I promise, you will have more good news, news that will make you happy again."

"What good news? There is no such thing as good news anymore. And now Edmund is dead as well! Oh, Tomás, if anything should happen to Andrés . . . I can't bear it. *I can't bear it!*"

She began weeping helplessly, her hand on the table. He pulled his chair next to hers and lowered himself into it and tried to comfort her, but there was no comforting her. He had never seen her so distressed, not even when her husband had died.

"I will prove to you there can still be good news, if you will dry your eyes for a moment."

She did not respond, she seemed not to hear him.

"Lole . . . your Englishman has found Rafael."

Still she did not respond. And then, very slowly, she raised her head and looked at him through huge, bloodshot, dark-ringed eyes.

"Listen. I meant to tell you this tomorrow, once the boy was safely home. But to cheer you, I will tell you now. Your dead cousin left all his money to Andrés. A great deal of money. This Englishman searched everywhere but could not find him. But he found Rafael, in a children's home in Valencia. He is well, but still too frightened to speak. They think he saw Rosa and Petra killed. When Andrés is found, the Englishman will take you to Valencia to see him. Then your cousin will take both boys back to England. Her two children are listed on her passport. Does this cheer you?"

Dolores stared at him incredulously.

"But how can he be sure it is Rafael? If he cannot speak, it might be some other child!"

"He says he is sure. He says he remembered him from Toledo, because of his likeness to you."

She waited a long moment before asking her next question.

"Did he see Andrés, before he ran away?"

"Yes. And in Toledo."

She buried her face in her arms again.

"He did not realize, Lole, till today."

She looked up, startled, crimson.

"He thought Rafael was your son," continued Tomás gently. "He saw Andrés in Toledo, and yet he did not see himself. He saw only Rafael, he saw only you."

She would not meet his eyes. She wound her arms tighter than ever around her head as if trying to bury herself.

"You are ashamed, before me? How can you be ashamed, before me?"

"I do not want Andrés to know," she said, her voice muffled. "He will never forgive me. He adored Lorenzo so! He thinks ill enough of me already!"

"If he thought so ill of you, why would he run away rather than leave you?"

"I am a bad mother. I cannot care for him. He will be better off without me. I only kept him with me through selfishness and pride. But I cannot bear that he should think me a whore. I cannot bear it!"

"Calm yourself. Did you love this man?"

"I thought so then. I was very young."

"Then you were no whore. One day Andrés will understand this. And he will understand it better if you are with him. I have asked the Englishman to find a way for you to—"

"No!"

"Lole—"

"I said no! What do you take me for? Do you think I would run away and leave you? Never insult me by suggesting that again!"

"And what sort of love would I have for you if I kept you here? When I burned that piece of paper in Toledo, I thought I loved you, but I did not, not as I do now. Now I love you enough to let you go. How can you refuse the only thing I have to give you?"

"You are my husband," she said stubbornly. "You are my husband, and this is my country, and that is all there is to it. Besides . . ." Her voice trailed off and she began to weep again, exhausted.

She let Tomás persuade her back into bed and lay staring into the dark. Besides. Besides, she might be dead before long. And Jack knew it. She had hesitated before admitting it in her letter to the Townsends, but such had been her fear of rejection that she had played her trump card there and then rather than have to write a second time. After all, she had behaved abominably all those years ago, retreated into her shell of disgrace, and contacted them again only when she needed something. If she had known of Edmund's death, she would have been even more doubtful of a favorable response. And now Jack knew about her illness, Jack knew that Andrés was his son. Now Jack would pity her, and feel guilty about her. Now she had lost every last precious vestige of her pride.

But at least Andrés would be financially independent. Thanks to Edmund, Jack need feel no obligation to maintain her son, his son. Whatever he chose to do, whatever interest he chose to take, it would be voluntary, neither she nor Andrés need owe him anything, thanks to Edmund.

As for Rafael—assuming it really *was* Rafael, and she would not believe it till she saw the evidence with her own eyes—perhaps the money would yield enough for both of them. If not, Flora would surely help. Rafael was nothing to Jack, Rafael could not compromise her. Once they were all safely gone, she could live, or die, in peace.

How much he must have found her changed! Even now he would be thinking, poor Dolly. Poor, poor Dolly. The humiliation of it stuck in her throat. No doubt he despised the slum she lived in, no doubt he thought Tomás an ignorant boor, no doubt he thought she had married beneath her and too hastily, showing scant respect for her dead husband. Well, let him think it. She would not say one word to disillusion him. How glad she was now that she had not found him at the hotel, that she had not prostituted all her emotions, thrown herself at his mercy. At least this way her debt was to Flora and Archie, not to Jack.

As the first daylight seeped in through the shutters, she fell into a troubled, hopeful sleep. Tomás was right, of course he was right. Andrés would come home when he was hungry.

The smell of new bread was intoxicating. Andrés's mouth watered as he handed over his entire fortune.

"What's this?"

The woman behind the counter seemed very big.

"Have you no change, child?"

Andrés shook his head and sneezed. The church roof had leaked all over him in the night.

"Then you must go home again and ask your mother. Sending a child out to buy bread with a five-peseta bill! The woman has more money than sense!"

She turned to the next customer. Andrés stared at the bill she had thrust back into his hand. It was no substitute for food. He had waited patiently outside the shop for an hour before it opened. This unexpected setback was more than he could bear.

"But I cannot go home with no bread!" he wailed. "I am hungry!"

Two large treacherous teardrops blurred his vision and he sniffed vigorously in an attempt to reabsorb them.

He stretched up his hand to the counter again, proffering the useless bill, and let out another earth-shattering sneeze.

"Do not cry, little one," said a voice behind him. "I will buy bread for you."

Andrés waited, relieved, while the woman completed her transaction, and snatched the loaf from her greedily, almost forgetting to say thank you. She shepherded him out of the shop, her hand resting on his shoulder.

"Now we must go home together, to see your mamá, so that she may pay me back. Where do you live?"

But Andrés was too busy tearing the loaf apart and stuffing the cavernous space inside his stomach to answer her.

"Are you new to this quarter?" she persisted. "I cannot remember seeing you before."

Andrés shrugged and tried to wriggle free of his benefactress. Her grip on his shoulder tightened.

"You are soaked through. Why have you no coat? What is your name?"

The woman's voice was soft, her eyes were kind. He was torn between an urge to run away and a craven need for comfort.

"You are shivering. You must dry your clothes and drink; something hot. Come."

She steered him into a narrow side street and through a dark doorway into a small, stuffy room. An old woman rose from her chair.

"Who is this?" she said. "He is wet through!"

The glow from the stove sent out seductive ripples of warmth. A pan of dark liquid was bubbling on the burner. The young woman poured some of it into a bowl and put it on the table, indicating that Andrés should sit down. He put the raggedy remainder of his loaf on the oilcloth cover and held his hands around the bowl for a minute. Then, with fierce concentration, he began tearing off bits of bread and dipping them into the steaming brew, turning each dry morsel into hot, juicy food.

The two women talked quietly in a corner while he ate, and then the old one went out, closing the door quietly behind her.

"What is your name?"

"Andrés," said Andrés, with his mouth full.

"Andrés. Now take off your clothes, Andrés, so that we can dry them in front of the stove, while you drink another bowl of coffee."

The blanket was thin and coarse, but he felt warmer inside now. He lapped up his second bowl and demolished the rest of the loaf. His hunger satiated, the urge to sleep at last was overwhelming. He yawned hugely.

"Lie down until your clothes are dry." said the woman. She pulled aside a curtain, revealing a narrow bed. After a night sitting on wet flagstones it looked soft and enticing. Andrés allowed her to tuck him in. He was safe here. Here the English people would never find him. Here was warmth and food and a bed, and he still had his five-peseta bill. He was under cover at last.

"I had a little boy like you once," she said. "But he was killed."

And she was still weeping softly to herself when the patrolman came to fetch him.

"But what about Ramón?" said Dolores. Tomás sighed. The wretch had lain in the gutter all night before crawling home on his hands and knees. Would that he had died where he lay!

"He has a fever," she continued. "And Marisa is still in the hospital—" The plea was unspoken, but unmistakable.

"Lole, Rafael is more important than Ramón. I will look after your brother, I will do for him whatever you would do. I may hate him, but I love you. If he shuns my help, then it will be a sign that he is well enough to look after himself. Now go!"

"He must not have whiskey with the yellow pills. And—"

"Give me his key, and go," said Tomás. "They are waiting for you."

Dolores stood on tiptoe to kiss him.

"Are you ready, Andrés? Are you ready to come and see Rafael?"

Andrés nodded sullenly, but it was only for show. The sight of Flora and Archie's Bentley, and the promise of a reunion with Rafael, had made the trip to Valencia an outing he would not have missed for worlds.

"Good-bye, boy," said Tomás gravely, shaking his hand. "Remember what I said to you."

András nodded and sniffed.

"Go now, both of you. The key, Lole."

Dolores handed over the key to Ramón's apartment, and took Andrés by the hand. He wrenched it free.

"What's the matter now?" said Dolores, exasperated. "We must hurry, Andrés. The car is waiting."

Andrés stuck out a rebellious lower lip.

"Do as your mother says, boy," said Tomás. "You gave me your word and now you must keep it."

Andrés looked from his mother to Tomás and back again.

"Is . . . is Uncle Ramón going to die?"

"Perhaps," said Tomás gently. "He is very sick. Too sick for you to see him today. I will say good-bye for you. He will understand."

"But . . ." Andrés hesitated in an agony of indecision. He was not to speak of it in front of Tomás, but he trusted Tomás, even if Uncle Ramón didn't. He trusted Tomás more than he trusted his mother. It was Tomás who had treated him like a man, Tomás who had convinced him of his duty to look after Rafael and make sure he got to England safely.

"Rafael will be too frightened to go without you," he had said. "You must give him courage."

He stood irresolute for a moment and then muttered, "I want to tell Tomás something."

Dolores flinched at the hostility in his eyes and left the room without a word.

"Yes, Andrés? What is it?"

"If Uncle Ramón dies, I am to have his boot. The boot with the big sole."

"What?"

"If he dies, it is not to be buried. Will you send it to England for me, Tomás? He made me promise to look after it. It is very important."

"Important? A boot? Why?"

Andrés looked at the floor, hopelessly torn between conflicting loyalties.

"It's a secret. He told me not to tell you. Please don't tell him I told you. I promised."

"Then tell me no more. I will do whatever is necessary, and I will not tell your uncle that you spoke of it. You have kept your promise. Now go. Your mother is waiting."

Andrés sniffed his relief, threw his arms round Tomás's leg in a valedictory embrace and raced out of the room.

A crowd of children had assembled around the car, gaping enviously, and Andrés felt a surge of pride as he climbed into the back seat and inhaled the sensuous smell of leather. His mother immediately began talking in English to the woman with the black hat who was sitting in the front. He craned his neck forward, for a better look at the dashboard. The man sitting next to him smiled and spoke to him in Spanish.

"Would you like to sit in the front, Andrés?" he said, reading his mind. Then he tapped the woman on the shoulder and said something to her, and a few minutes later the car stopped.

Normally Andrés would have scorned to sit on a woman's lap like a baby, but this was an exception.

Tomás wiped the sweat from his brow. The journey to the hospital had left him panting, but he had promised Lole he would do this too, and he would not fail her.

Marisa was sitting up in bed, staring into space. She started in surprise when she saw him.

"Where is Lole?"

"Lole has visitors, from England. She asked me to come in her place."

Marisa lay back listlessly.

"Visitors from England?"

"Cousins. She wrote to them to come for the boy."

"And Ramón?"

"He is drunk, as usual. Lole is seeing to him. She said you are to rest, and not to worry. How is it with you?"

"I have pain when I walk. But it is good to rest."

She sank back into a torpor and proceeded to ignore him. Nevertheless, Tomás waited a while, to regain his breath. A curse on the wretched girl! As soon as her bastard was born, it would be Lole who fed it and cared for it and laundered for it, while its mother went back to her whoring. Best for Lole if she returned from Valencia to find all three of them dead and thus be free to follow her son to safety. Best if Marisa had bled to death, best if Ramón had choked in the gutter, best if he himself had died in battle.

After a while, Marisa began prattling about her baby. It was to have a wicker cradle with a lace canopy, and a silver teething ring, and half a dozen fancy names. Ramón had told her that they would leave Madrid as soon as it was born and reclaim his father's estate, where they would build a big new house and have many, many servants.

"Be quiet, woman," growled Tomás. "If people hear you talking thus they will take you for a Fascist."

Marisa pouted.

"Pah! Is it Fascist to want to live in comfort and to have beautiful things? Is it Fascist to want the best for my child? My child will never work in the fields or go to bed hungry. My child will never walk without shoes! Are such things Fascist?"

"I must go," said Tomás, reaching for his crutches. Her stupidity wearied him. "Be warned, Marisa. Be discreet in what you say, for your own sake, and Ramón's."

She made a face as he dragged himself off. What a misery he was. Poor Lole. He was as strong as an ox, that one, he would live forever. Only the good, like Ramón, died young . . .

Her eyes strayed to the girl in the next bed. Her breathing was shallow, her skin like candle wax, a putrid odor of decay hung all around her. Marisa felt no pity, only curiosity. A surfeit of sleep had left her lazily alert, not to say bored. She wished that Jack were here, to tell her a story . . .

A nurse approached and roused the girl gently, murmuring something in her ear. The girl nodded eagerly and struggled into a sitting position while the nurse propped her up on the pillows. The nurse left the ward and came back a few moments later with a visitor, a young man wearing a blue jerkin and carrying a backpack.

He sat down on the bed and held the girl's hand and began speaking to her very quietly, lowering his head so that she could whisper in his ear. Marisa looked on idly. Clearly he was her lover. He was tall and very handsome, and Marisa found herself staring at him. Not because she found him physically attractive—she had no sexual interest in men—but because she was trying to remember where she had seen him before.

At that moment, he caught her eye, and his expression flickered, as if he had recognized her too. Instinctively Marisa smiled, a professional smile, as if to reassure him that she would not give him away. She did not expect the man to acknowledge her; clients were always embarrassed to encounter her in public. He must have been one of the early ones, he was clearly too poor to afford her present fees . . .

He looked startled by the smile, and Marisa put a discreet finger to her lips, swearing silence, amused by his discomfiture. Then the nurse came back, and drew the curtains round the bed, as if to give the couple privacy.

Half an hour later, the man emerged, and flung Marisa a brief, grateful look before walking quickly away. Marisa watched his departing back without interest, her thoughts already elsewhere.

She had fallen to brooding again on the agonies her mother had endured in giving birth, the bloodcurdling screams that had resounded through the olive groves, filling Marisa with primitive terror. Both mother and unborn child had been near to death, and the midwife, a religious old crone, had sent Marisa's brother to fetch a priest. But the nearest village was a good two hours' walk away across rough, hilly countryside, and by the time her brother returned, the danger was past. Marisa's father had abused the meddling midwife and sent the handsome young priest away . . .

And then Marisa remembered where she had seen the man before.

Jack did not invade the space Andrés had vacated. He kept to one side of the back seat while Dolores looked assiduously out of the opposite window. Archie was doing his best to amuse the boy, changing gear with the child's hand under his and letting him fiddle with the knobs on the dashboard. Flora's capacity for trivial conversation was undiminished by circumstance. She regaled Dolly with endless details of who had married whom while Dolly affected fascination.

"Sylvia Morton—that's Sylvia Trevelyan that was—is as big as a house these days! You wouldn't know her, she's put on more weight than you've lost. You're like a skeleton, Dolly. None of the clothes I brought will fit you."

"The clothes are lovely, Flo. I can easily take them in. You really shouldn't have bothered."

"You're awfully pale. Are you feeling faint? I've got some smelling salts in my bag."

"No, I'm fine."

"You don't look it. In fact, you look perfectly ghastly, doesn't she, Jack? I do wish you'd be sensible and come home."

"Please, Flo. We've been through all that."

"You're just as stubborn as ever."

"And you're just as bossy as ever." Dolores smiled and squeezed her cousin's hand. It was true, she did look ghastly, all the more so when she compared herself with Flora, Flora who had once been jealous of her looks. Flora's perfect pink-and-white complexion was still soft and smooth, her figure curved and womanly and well fed, her clothes and hair as immaculate as always. Sitting here in this car, with Flora, she might almost be back in England again, Flora seemed to carry England around with her like an invisible protective shell.

Jack stole covert glances at Dolores, aware that she was deliberately ignoring him. God, she looked ill. Couldn't Tomás see that it was more than fatigue and worry? But then Tomás saw her every day. No point in alarming him, no need for blackmail. He wanted her to go to England anyway. He loved her that much.

And she did not love him back, so Tomás claimed. But Jack suspected she probably did. Loving came naturally to her; she was as generous with her affection as he was mean with his. The love she had given him long ago had been carefree, unthinking, spontaneous, an overflow of the warmth she felt toward the world in general. For him it had been intense, obsessional, exclusive. Miser though he was, he would have spent his last penny on her; spendthrift though she was, she had given him the merest pittance.

He had been ready to cheat and lie and steal, to do anything to get her back again. Such resolutions seemed unworthy now. Her life was all that mattered. He would cheerfully give her up, never see her again, if only she would live.

In London, Flora would have her installed in some fancy clinic on arrival. The top man would be summoned immediately, no expense would be spared. They would force her to rest and feed her and fill her full of borrowed blood and whatever was wrong with her they would do their utmost to cure. They might succeed and they might fail, but at least she would have the best possible treatment.

In Spain all the odds would be stacked against her. There was a shortage of every medical commodity—staff, drugs, dressings, equipment—everything except patients. Patients there were in plenty. She would have a long wait and low priority, she would be treated by over-worked doctors in primitive conditions, an unimportant civilian in a land where life had become cheap, where death had become routine.

But to use this line of reasoning would be futile. Flora had already done her best and failed, and Jack had no reason to suppose that he would fare any better. Of all the people in the world, she must trust him least of all. She remembered him as a cheapskate seducer, an aggressive young lout with a chip on his shoulder, an unashamed social climber, ambitious, grasping, ruthless, callous and a rotten, lousy lover. She would have forgotten him instantly, but for the child, but because of the child she had not forgotten and not forgiven either. All these years he had tried to be angry with her, never dreaming that she might have cause to be angry with him. He could feel her anger now, radiating toward him, the only point of contact between them.

"Dolly's told me about Andrés," Flora had said crisply. "She wanted to tell me before you did. I told her you hadn't said a word. Quite the perfect gentleman these days, aren't you? A pity you weren't a gentleman then, you swine. How could you?"

It had been a relief to have Flora give him a piece of her mind. He wished that Dolly would do the same, but she wouldn't allow him that much comfort. She was polite and frigid and pointedly avoided being alone with him, as if she could not bear to discuss it.

Jack wondered if her husband had known. If so, she must have been through hell. In prewar, middle-class Spain, the perceived disgrace would have been unexpungable, blighting her marriage and stigmatizing her child. He would have imagined Dolly as a doting, demonstrative mother, but her manner with the boy was curt and strained, and he obeyed her with a very bad grace. According to Flora, Dolly had confessed that Andrés was beyond her control, and certainly he was a sulky little brat. But whether that was due to present circumstances or the shadow of the past was difficult to tell.

Jack watched him dispassionately as he squirmed around on Flora's lap. This was his son. He ought to have felt some surge of fatherly feeling, but so far he had felt nothing for him, nothing at all. This was a stranger who looked like him, nothing more. He shrank from the self-scrutiny of trying to see himself in the boy. Not the physical characteristics, which now seemed too obvious to matter, but the other things, the things that required interest and attention and study. Normal parents found the exercise endlessly fascinating, eager to recognize and magnify family traits and foibles. Normal parents liked themselves enough to want to produce yet another generation. It was supposed to be easy to love your own child, and yet to Jack it seemed infinitely easier to love someone else's, to love a child who could not remind you of yourself, whose shortcomings were tolerable because they did not mirror your own. It had been easy to love Rafael, thinking he was Dolly's. Dolly would have been adorable as a child, affectionate, cheerful and guileless. Rafael hid all those endearing qualities inside the shell of terror, of that he had been sure. He had been determined to bring out the Dolly in him, he had bewitched himself into seeing what wasn't there, and now it was too late to break the spell.

Andrés reminded him horribly of himself at the same age—at any age—cocky and cunning and cold. He had never wanted a child, or so he thought, and yet he must have, if only for a moment. He had wanted to make that moment last forever, and he had. No wonder she still hated him for it, for leaving her with a living reminder of her folly, making it hard for her to love her own, her only child.

"Dolly," he said tentatively.

"Yes?" Her tone was defensive, abrupt.

"I had to tell a few lies at the children's home. I'd better tell you now, so you can follow what goes on."

"Lies?" He almost thought he saw her lips twitch. "Fire away. I'm good at lies."

"I thought he was yours, as you know, and I thought you were dead. The only hope I had was in convincing them I had some rights over the boy. The bureaucracy of adoption is staggering. First of all, they have to satisfy themselves beyond all reasonable doubt that the mother is really dead, then they have to—"

"What lies?"

"I told them I was his father." Jack felt his face and neck prickling with color. "And so life would be much simpler if you would tell them you're his mother. Then they'd be able to let him go. The resemblance alone should convince them, and then you can produce evidence that you're called García, and—"

"And what if he doesn't recognize me?"

"Then we keep going back until he does. The warden is a great sentimentalist. You coming back from the grave is just the kind of happy ending she'll want to believe."

"And I suppose we tell her that we're going to get married and live happily ever after?"

"Something like that. It would cut through all the red tape."

She looked out of the window again.

"All right," she said. "I'll go along with your fairy tale. You've been very inventive, I must say."

"The other thing I wanted to say was . . . you wouldn't have any objection to my adopting him, would you?"

"Who? Andrés?" Her voice was sharp.

"No. Rafael. You're his next of kin, not counting your brother."

"Oh. That's very noble of you."

"Not at all. You know me better than that."

"On the contrary. I hardly know you at all. But it's much too early to talk about that now. First I want to see him with my own eyes, before I believe it's really Rafael. And then—"

"What are you two whispering about?" boomed Flora.

"Just strategy," said Jack. "I'd like Archie to leave the car well out of sight, then Dolly and I will go ahead alone on foot. Even if everything goes like clockwork, we're unlikely to get Rafael out of there today. Then we'll all check into a hotel and debrief."

"Will Andrés mind being left alone with us, Dolly? Does he know any English at all? I would have thought you would have taught him."

"No. It caused nothing but trouble between my own parents. You can only have one nationality in the end. I didn't want him caught between two cultures, like I was."

"Well, he will be now, like it or not. Still, he's young enough to cope, aren't you, Andrés?"

"Andrés looked around noncomprehendingly.

"When do we see Rafael?" he asked his mother accusingly.

"Not today, darling," said Dolly. "Tomorrow perhaps."

"But you promised!"

"I didn't promise today. You must stay in the car with your aunt and uncle and be very good."

Andrés was torn between relief and disappointment. The day he saw Rafael would be the last day he saw his mother. Once he saw Rafael they would leave for England . . . He must not cry. And so he scowled instead.

They left him well engrossed in the contents of the glove compartment, particularly Archie's flashlight. He did not acknowledge his mother's departure, as if to demonstrate his indifference. Jack had a sudden urge to wallop him.

"About the name," said Jack, helping her out of the car. "We'd better tell them that Rafael is his middle name, and you used it all the time at home, but I didn't realize. I hardly knew him, you see." He began talking very fast, horribly embarrassed. "You were a Spanish servant girl visiting London, and I made you pregnant but you wouldn't marry me and returned home. I came to Spain when

the war broke out to try to persuade you to come back to England
with me, but you refused, because you loved another man . . .''

"Well, at least it's nice and easy to remember," she said.

"I'm sorry. I had to tell them something." He risked a look, but
she didn't return it. "Er . . . if we want them to believe our little
story, you'd better take my arm, if you can bear to."

She nodded and took it. He tried to think of it as just an arm,
and not as part of her.

"Try to relax, now. You're stiff as a board. The warden's very
nice. No need to be nervous."

She stood there looking very demure while he told Pepa the
wonderful news, that he had found Rosa quite by chance in Madrid,
that they were reconciled, that she was overjoyed at the prospect of
seeing her long-lost son again.

"I renamed him Rafael, after my late *novio,*" ventured Dolly
shyly. "His real father did not know this."

Pepa nodded, only half-listening, staring at her delightedly.

"Why, he is the image of you, my dear! I would have known you
for his mother anywhere! It is so rare that we reunite a child with
its family, all the staff will be delighted. But . . . but be prepared
for disappointment. He is very withdrawn, he may not respond
straightaway."

"He must have thought I was dead," said Dolores calmly. "I
was badly wounded when the Fascists shot at us from their planes.
I did not regain consciousness for many days. I have been looking
for him everywhere, ever since. May I see him now?"

Pepa led the way. Dolly's grip on Jack's arm tightened. He wanted
to reach out and squeeze her hand but did not dare.

It was the classroom where Jack had first seen him. The rest of
the children were clustered around a big table and looking up at the
blackboard. Rafael was in his usual corner, painting, as always, his
brow furrowed in concentration.

Dolores stared at him from the doorway, and for one dreadful
moment Jack thought that it wasn't Rafael after all. Her face was
the picture of desolation, her eyes were hollow with pain, she
seemed unable to move or even speak. Then she took a deep breath
as if screwing up all her strength and said quietly, clearly, "Rafael."

It seemed to happen in slow motion. His ears pricked up like a
dog's, and then he turned around. Still Dolly did not move. He
stared at her for a moment and she spread her arms wide.

"Rafael."

Jack swallowed hard. The tears were already streaming down Pepa's cheeks but Dolly's composure was absolute. Still she didn't move an inch, waiting for him to respond. When he finally did, it was all in a silent rush, he ran at her and let her lift him into the air and wound his arms around her neck and held on for dear life, as if afraid to utter a single sound and perhaps wake himself up.

Pepa let out a whoop of glee, hugged Jack ecstatically and kissed him on both cheeks.

"I am so happy for you," she sobbed. "So happy for you both!"

Only then did Dolly meet his eye, for the first time in seven years. She didn't speak, but the look was enough to tell him he was forgiven.

Tomás opened the door to find Ramón comatose but still very much alive, judging by the drop in the level of the whiskey bottle. No whiskey with the yellow pills, Dolores had said. Tomás was sorely tempted to concoct a lethal mixture there and then, or smother him where he lay, but he had promised Lole he would look after him, and besides, it would solve nothing.

His eye fell on the boot, lying on the floor beside the bed. Why should he want to bequeath the boy such a repulsive object? It was a secret, Andrés had said, and he had not liked to press him to break faith.

Perhaps it concealed money. Lole had wept to find that Ramón had been robbed of all his savings, savings he needed to support Marisa and the coming child. Tomás knew how it would be. He and Lole would end up subsidizing them out of their meager income, and she would wear herself to a shadow looking after all of them. If there was any money in the boot, he would take it now, without compunction, and keep it, for Lole. Andrés had no need of it now.

He pulled at the loose outer sole, but it concealed nothing, and the heel would not budge. He recoiled at the thought of inserting his hand into the foul-smelling interior, but was soon rewarded as the insole came loose and his fingers reached into the cavity beneath.

He pulled out the wad of paper triumphantly, thinking they were bills, and then stared blankly at the sheets of illegible writing. They were loosely bound together, but the two words on the cover meant nothing to him, they were not ones Andrés had taught him.

Patiently, he sifted through the leaves, in the hope that money might be concealed between them. Then he stopped short, with a sudden intake of breath. No reading skills were necessary to recognize a Falange membership card, the loathsome insignia of yoke and arrows spoke to him loud and clear.

He fingered it thoughtfully. This was quite a find. The Falange had been quick to destroy all their membership records at the start of the war. Other right-wing parties had not been so circumspect. Their members had been hunted down throughout Republican territory, and those who had not fled in time had been captured and for the most part executed. But many Falangists had remained undiscovered and were still actively plotting the downfall of the Republic. The alleged "Fifth Column" had become notorious, and anyone suspected of connections with it was a dead man . . .

He scanned the pages uselessly, wishing he could read. Whatever the words said, they were undoubtedly incriminating. But why should Ramón leave such documents to Andrés? So that a fellow Falangist would know where to find them? The wretch clearly had no scruples to involve an innocent child in treason.

He had always thought of Ramón as a Fascist, but the swine had never once admitted it, careful and cowardly even in his cups. In any event, Tomás would not have denounced him, sorely as he would have been tempted, for Dolores's sake. But now the time had come to be cruel to be kind.

He stuffed the papers back inside the boot, except for the card, which he put safely in his pocket.

"You are a dead man, my friend," he muttered to himself, while Ramón snored on, oblivious. "But before you die, you must get strong again."

He gritted his teeth and set to work to prepare food for his enemy. He made no effort to be quiet, and eventually his enemy groaned and woke.

"What are you doing here?" demanded Ramón, blinking. "Where is Dolores? I demand that you leave immediately!"

"Drink this soup and I will leave with pleasure. I do this only for Lole, not for you, she is not well today. I go now to empty your slops. I shall take the key with me."

Walking on one crutch was hideously slow, but the only way to leave a hand free. Tomás edged his way out of the room bearing the brimming chamber pot at arm's length and negotiated the steps at a snail's pace, fearful of spilling its noisome contents over himself.

On the first landing, however, a passing neighbor took pity on him, and divested him of his burden, returning with it empty a few moments later.

"A pleasure, comrade," she said, waving aside Tomás's thanks. "I can see you are a veteran. Have you taken the vacant room on the top floor?"

"No. I come on behalf of my wife to tend to her sick brother."

The woman's eyes narrowed.

"The cripple?"

"Yes."

The woman spat on the floor.

"I am glad you did not tell me this sooner. Otherwise I might have left you to struggle alone. *Salud.*"

Ramón had evidently not expected to see him back so quickly. He was squatting on the floor, loading a revolver, leaving its underground cache exposed to view. He started violently.

"Get out!" he hissed, pointing the weapon at Tomás. "Get out or I will shoot!"

Tomás kicked the door shut behind him.

"Shoot," he said. "Then shoot yourself as well and prove yourself a man. That way we may rid your unfortunate sister of both of us."

Ramón's hand was shaking violently. Tomás reached out for his second crutch, which was leaning against the doorjamb.

"Shall I turn around so that you may shoot me in the back?" he jeered. With a sudden movement he struck out with his crutch and sent the gun flying out of Ramón's grasp. Ramón sat transfixed, cowering, as if expecting the next blow to be directed at him. Tomás laughed.

"Another time, perhaps, we shall have that duel you promised me. But not while you are still a cringing invalid, not while I am your nurse. Now get back into bed."

Ramón did so, panting.

"You must eat, and then I will go," Tomás resumed calmly, as if nothing had happened.

"I am too thirsty to eat."

"Here is water."

"I am not thirsty for water."

Tomás smiled. He knew all about the crate of whiskey under their bed at home, but the wretch had had his quota for the day.

"Then give me some money and I will buy what you require," he taunted.

"Animal! As if I would trust you with my money! Get out!"

"As you wish. I will return in the morning. I hope to find you dead tomorrow by your own hand. If you have any love for your poor sister, then end your miserable life without further delay."

"The same to you, scum!" yelled Ramón, once Tomás was safely gone. The impudence of it! Leave Marisa a widow and his child an orphan? What would become of them without his protection? What would become of Dolores?

He crawled out of bed again, retrieved his weapon, and put it under his pillow. Then he put a chair in front of the door. García undoubtedly planned to murder him in his sleep. Next time he would be ready for him.

He began to pant again. How dare Dolores give García his key! How dare she leave him at the mercy of his sworn enemy, without funds! Why, he had offered her every penny he possessed, out of brotherly love, and now she had left him without the price of a miserable drink. There was no gratitude in the world . . .

Tomás dragged himself home, thoughtful now. Perhaps he should have picked up the gun, shot Ramón, shot himself. But it had seemed an ignoble thing to do, to kill a sick man and leave Dolores with both deaths on her conscience. No, he must leave her no legacy of guilt.

Three things stood in the way of her freedom—Ramón, Marisa, and himself. Most of all himself. He had been considering ways of killing himself ever since the Englishman's arrival. A fall down the stairs or a traffic accident would be easy to achieve, but not foolproof—the danger would be that he would end up more of an invalid than ever, break the other leg or an arm and render himself immobile. A deliberate act with a knife or other weapon would be obvious suicide, and cause Lole too much pain. And the gesture would be superfluous without Ramón dead as well, as would Ramón's death without his own.

As for Marisa . . . that was a far more delicate problem. He could do nothing to harm a pregnant woman. A curse on all of them, himself included.

"You must make her love you, Englishman," he said out loud. "You must make her love you enough."

Flora jumped out of her seat as Andrés leapt for the door handle and bounded on to the pavement. Thinking he was about to run away again she made a lunge to catch him, but he was too quick for her. Both she and Archie moved simultaneously, scrambling out of the car to give chase. Only then did they see what his sharp eyes had spotted in the distance.

By the time they caught up with him the two boys were scrambling on the ground and squealing over each other like a pair of puppies. Jack was visibly moved by it and doing his best not to show it, but Dolly was like a block of wood, betraying no emotion at all. She ran toward Flora and pulled at her sleeve.

"I'm going to disappear right away, Flo, while they're all wrapped up in each other. Otherwise Rafael will cling. It's best if you get moving as soon as possible. No good-byes. Thank you a thousand million times."

"But Dolly . . . I mean, it's a bit sudden, isn't it? I never thought they'd let him out today."

"They hadn't got much choice, He'd have screamed the place down if I'd left him. Thank God Andrés is here. Give them some of those pills and then drive as fast as you can. I must go. *I must go!*"

She took one last long look at the children and then tore her eyes away and ran off down the street, with Jack in hot pursuit.

"Well, Archie," said Flora, winded but determined. "Let's go to it, then."

She wheeled both boys into the back of the car. Rafael started crying for Dolores, but Andrés took over, whispering things in his ear that seemed to calm him down. Flora produced a large bag of toys and a bag of sweets, slipping two of Mummy's pills in with them. As soon as they dozed off she would put them in pajamas, wrap them up in blankets, and pad herself out, ready for the first patrols.

Archie didn't speak, and for once Flora didn't either. They both knew what each other was thinking. It seemed an awfully long way to France.

PART FOUR
AUGUST
1937

17

AUGUST 1937

"The letters are obviously fakes," said Clara, glaring at her visitor. "I refuse categorically to let these children go."

Henry Jarratt looked uncomfortable, physically, at least. The smoking room at Hambleton Grange, the Neville family seat in Sussex, had been divested of its former opulence; hard wooden chairs discouraged time wasters from overstaying their welcome. All twelve bedrooms had been stripped of their antique furniture and dark, heavy drapes, and converted into bright, cheerful dormitories, now noisy with the hubbub of thirty-two boisterous Basque adolescents.

Jarratt shifted his weight from one ample buttock to the other and smiled at Clara fixedly.

"Miss Neville, may I remind you that the parents' wishes must, of necessity, take precedence over your own? We only ever sought to provide temporary refuge for these children, and we—"

"'We'? Who exactly is 'we'? When *we* took the Basque children in, *your* Repatriation Committee hadn't even been invented. Your members never lifted a finger to help, never donated any funds, and now suddenly you dare to point a moral finger at me and talk about the parents' wishes?"

"My dear Miss Neville—"

"My dear Mr. Jarratt, you were one of the first to speak out against allowing the Basque children entry in the first place, and ever since you've done nothing but circulate lies and whip up public feeling against them. All these questions in the House and scare stories in the gutter press are your doing. None of these children has ever attacked anyone, or stolen anything, or damaged any property—"

"Then all credit to you for their reform, Miss Neville. I gather

503

their record was not quite so immaculate before you took them in. This charming country house of yours is, by repute, a special home for the more delinquent element . . ."

"They were disturbed, that was all. So would you be, if you'd been shelled and starved and shot at and sent away from your family."

"Quite so. And now the time has come to return them to their families. I have seen no evidence to support your view that these letters are forgeries."

"Evidence? It's common sense, that's all. Look at this piece of nonsense here." She donned her reading glasses again, adopting the fierce, school-marmish air that fooled everyone except herself. "This boy's father is a Basque Nationalist. Do you expect me to believe that he genuinely wants his son to 'return home and enlist in Franco's glorious army'?"

"Everyone is entitled to change his mind. Many former supporters of the Republic have come to realize that the only hope for a stable future is to join forces against the Communist threat."

Clara threw the letter back at him.

"Oh, spare me the Fascist propaganda. This discussion is a waste of time. I will not let these children go, and that's final. So sorry I can't help you."

Clara stood up, indicating that the interview was at an end.

"Mmm. I am reliably informed that you *are* letting two of them go. Not that you have any legal right to decide who goes and who doesn't."

"Those particular children are not returning to Fascist territory. Their parents have escaped to Catalonia, and are eager to be reunited with them."

"And what makes you believe that their letters are genuine and that these are forgeries? I would suggest that it is nothing more than your own political prejudices."

"Then I would suggest precisely the same to you. Good day."

"Miss Neville, this is just a preliminary courtesy visit, seeking your cooperation. Far be it from me to tell you the law of the land, but may I point out that you have no legal grounds to detain these children against the wishes of their parents, and that it is the Repatriation Committee's duty to see that those wishes are carried out."

"And what if the children themselves refuse to go?"

"They are in no position to refuse to go. They are here by temporary leave of the Home Office, as refugees, and they would appear to be no longer in danger in their own country. Peace has been restored in Bilbao, and in Santander. Normal family life is now being resumed. The refugee status will ultimately have to be withdrawn, and if necessary the children deported.''

"Peace? You call occupation by enemy forces *peace?* I wish you could have seen how these children reacted when they heard that Bilbao had fallen to the Fascists. They didn't regard it as peace, I can tell you.''

"I heard all about their reactions, dear lady. It was just before you opened this charming establishment, as I remember. They vandalized the loudspeakers for broadcasting Fascist lies, broke out of camp, and roamed the countryside in guerrilla groups stealing food and harassing unsuspecting villagers.''

"That is a gross exaggeration and you know it,'' said Clara, folding her arms. "But I'll let it pass, because it proves my point. Nothing will induce these boys to go home and fight for Franco. Their parents were made to write those letters at gunpoint.''

"Miss Neville, an escort party will be coopted in due course to take the children back to their families. If you will not release them voluntarily, a court order will have to be sought against you. An unnecessary and unpleasant procedure, which I am sure you would wish to avoid.''

"You're bluffing. I'm not the only one to doubt the bona fides of these letters. You'll have a fight on your hands, and not just with me, either. You wouldn't dare remove these children by force. We're pressing for a full investigation into the authenticity of these letters, and if Franco wants to convince us he's genuine, then he'd better allow an independent working party to visit the parents and satisfy all concerned that they wrote these letters of their own free will.''

"I can assure you that relevant inquiries are already being made. But clearly we have no moral right to keep families apart longer than is absolutely necessary, nor to indulge our own political beliefs at their expense. The children are entitled to know that they are likely to be returning home as soon as the necessary formalities are completed.''

"Oh, they'll be told, don't worry. And now I'm afraid I have to ask you to leave. I have a lot of work to do.''

"Of course. Perhaps we could resume our discussion at a more convenient time. I would like to bring back a fellow committee member and interview the children in question. I am sure you would agree that it would be wrong of you to subject them to any negative influence.''

"We don't try to influence them. That's your department. Luckily, they're more than capable of thinking for themselves."

"Splendid, splendid. I'd like to fix a date for next week, with your permission, to come back with Mrs. Jefferson-Smythe. As you probably know, she's very active in child welfare charities and you can have every confidence that she will put the children's interests first. What day would suit you?"

"I happen to be away next week, and I'm not sure when I'll be back. Perhaps you'd like to phone me toward the end of the month. Meanwhile, you won't find my fellow workers any easier to fool than me."

"I see. Very well, then. Mrs. Jefferson-Smythe is most impressed with your work here, she was looking forward to meeting you. She will be disappointed at the delay."

"Please convey my apologies. Now, if you'll excuse me . . ."

"Certainly. Thank you so much for your time."

Clara gritted her teeth and shook the limp, soft hand. She hadn't lost her temper. Not quite.

"Good-bye, Mr. Jarratt. And thank you so much for calling."

"My pleasure. Good-bye, Miss Neville. And bon voyage."

"I beg your pardon?"

"I hear Catalonia is delightful at this time of year."

Clara smiled frostily and showed him out.

"Come in," said Dolly. "Tomás isn't home yet. The factory's been on overtime all week for the new Aragon offensive."

Jack hesitated. It was an established ground rule that she never saw him alone, a fate that he had brought upon himself with her connivance. But the sight of the English stamp on the letter was obviously too much for her.

She tore it open and read it several time before handing it to him.

Dear Dolly,

Notes from both the children attached. They were delighted to get the photograph you sent. It was good to see you looking so much better. We've got in a special tutor so they won't be too much at sea when the term starts next month. They're making excellent progress although obviously they miss a certain person *rather a lot, but I won't dwell on that.*

Everything is absolutely fine, nothing for you to worry about at all. Clara is taking two of her protégés home shortly and will be delivering a parcel full of goodies with our love. I can't say

*any of the things I want to say for obvious reasons, but hopefully
she will say some of them for me.*

> *Love and best wishes from all of us,*
> *Flora*

Andrés scrawl addressed her as "Dear Dolly" and comprised a
couple of lines of English painstakingly copied out under Flora's
supervision. Rafael's missive was limited to a row of kisses and his
name. Flora was always elaborately overcautious, she took a delight
in thwarting those nasty little sneaks who had the nerve to open
other people's mail. As usual, Dolly betrayed no emotion, ever
mindful of the Valencia fiasco. How Jack cursed himself for it now!
And yet how could he regret it?

She had broken down completely as soon as Archie's car was out
of sight, sitting down on the pavement and weeping as if her heart
would break. Jack had had no choice but to take her back to his
hotel and let her recover before they returned to Madrid. She had
been inconsolable. He had felt quite helpless in the face of so much
grief. He honestly had not planned to kiss her, it had been a desperate attempt at comfort, nothing more. It had been a tentative,
gentle, there-there embrace, devoid of ulterior motive; he had done
nothing to solicit that sudden fierce response, nothing to deserve
the equally sudden fierce rejection. She had weakened for all of ten
seconds, tempted him beyond endurance, and then beaten him off
angrily as if for all the world he had tried to force himself on her.
But those ten seconds had been enough to give him hope.

"Will you stay for supper?" she asked, folding the letter and
putting it in her pocket.

"I've already eaten, thanks. How are you feeling today?"

"Fine. I'll be glad when it's all over, of course. I'm looking
forward to seeing Clara and thanking her for arranging everything.
Jack . . . in case the operation fails . . ."

"It's not going to fail."

"Let me finish. I want you to do something for me. No, not for
me." She hesitated before saying slowly, "For our son."

It was the first time she had ever referred to him as such, and the
words sent a shiver down Jack's spine.

"I know he'll be well looked after, thanks to Edmund and Flora.
I'm glad he's financially independent of you, that I don't have to
ask you to support him, even though I know you would, because
that isn't what it's about."

She flung him one of those proud, stubborn looks that made her look like a girl again.

"I've been thinking about this a lot, and it's got to be said now, before it's too late, that's why I asked you in. I want him to know. I want him to know the truth. I want you to tell him, before someone else does."

"No one's going to tell him, Dolly."

"Even if they don't, he'll find out, sooner or later. But that's not the reason. It would be different if his father—I mean, if Lorenzo was still alive. As it is, I want him to know, whatever happens to me, I want you to tell him. Promise me."

He didn't answer for a moment. "We'll talk about it again next week."

"There may not be a next week."

"Do you mind if I sit down?"

She shook her head abstractedly, embarrassed now that the words had been said, withdrawing into her usual frigid composure. She took a chair as far away from him as possible.

"In case there isn't a next week," said Jack. "Do you mind if I say my piece as well?"

"I'd rather you didn't."

"Then you know what I'm going to say."

"Then there's no point saying it."

"I'll say it anyway. Cast your mind back, Dolly. Remember me as I was. You seem to have got the idea from somewhere that I'm a reformed character. Well, I'm not. I haven't changed. I wasn't an altruist then, and I'm not now. I wasn't generous then, or unselfish then, or honorable then, and I'm not now. Everything I've done for your benefit has been for my benefit, there's no difference. So don't waste time appealing to my nonexistent better nature. Don't expect me to do good deeds for their own sake. If you come out of this alive, then you'll have to take the consequences."

"You're going to send me a bill, you mean? Blackmail me with gratitude?"

"You know perfectly well I don't mean that. You don't owe me anything. Clara's the one with the money and the medical contacts, not me. The last thing I want from you is gratitude."

"I can't give you what you want."

"Yes, you can. Tomás would set you free. He's told you and he's told me. How can you make him suffer like you do? What does he have to do to convince you?"

Dolly froze him with a look.

"It's my decision, not his. It's not a question of setting me free, it's not a question of convincing me. How do you suppose I would live with myself, let alone you, if I turned my back on him now? Besides, it's not just Tomás. It's everything. This is my country, this is my war. You're asking me to desert, and I won't do it. I won't run away and leave others to fight my battles for me. Surely you know me better than that?"

"And aren't you deserting your son?"

"That's why I want him to know, can't you see that? A father's a lot more use to him than a mother. He can manage without a mother. He's already a misogynist at six years old. He'll forget me soon enough. Will you do what I ask, or won't you? I have to know. I have to know beforehand."

Like everything she had ever asked of him it was a challenge, not a plea, Jack nodded, defeated, unable to deny her anything, hating the power her illness gave her, the way it robbed him of control, resenting her calm, cold-blooded manner, envying her lack of fear.

"Thank you," she said, brisk and formal again. "Well, I'd better get on with supper. It was nice of you to bring the letter. Good night, then."

It was a dismissal, curt and cruel, and it hurt, it made him angry. Perhaps he should have felt proud at her trust in him, proud of the freedom to acknowledge his son. But he felt cheated. Rafael had been a precious gift, an undeserved bequest; Andrés was a booby prize, a white elephant. If she thought she could pay him off, or punish him, with Andrés, she was very much mistaken . . .

Three months ago he had thought that her life was all that mattered, sworn to himself that he would be content with that, refused to think beyond it. But the resolution had been hollow. If she died a second time he would never forgive her. This time he would take it personally.

Peabody's man had been cautiously optimistic. Excellent, if limited, facilities were available, even in wartime Spain, for high-ranking party members, and Clara's hefty donation to the aid fund had secured Dolly priority treatment in the private wing of a military hospital reserved for important personnel. Clara had taken a ruthless relish in using her money to get her own way rather than buy approval, and had driven a very hard bargain.

Peabody had duly come up with a French specialist as good as anything Flora could have found in Harley Street, who had diagnosed a subdural hematoma resulting from a blow to the skull. Surgery was necessary to remove the clot pressing on the brain, but he had refused to operate without a preparatory program of rest, special diet, and blood transfusions. Dolly had been required to give up work and eat meat every day, and it had been almost painful to watch her cheeks regain their color, her figure fill out, her eyes lose their circles of fatigue. She looked so much better already, it seemed wanton to subject her to the knife, to risk losing everything.

But Dolly herself showed no apparent fear. She had prepared Tomás for the worst, and resigned herself to her fate with infuriatingly fearless pessimism. It was that which made Jack angriest of all. Fear would have been a sign that she wanted to live, that she had something to live for. But she showed none. It was he who was afraid. Tomás who was afraid. Their only relief was in sharing their fear.

"But for this, I would have left her," Tomás had told him. "But for this, I would have gone away. But now I will wait, I must wait. I cannot leave her without knowing. You understand this?"

"Don't leave her on my account," Jack said. "It wouldn't work. She still wouldn't come with me. So don't try to be noble and leave me to take the blame."

He didn't want to win by default. But neither did he want to lose ignominiously. Better to leave her with Tomás than leave her without Tomás. Tomás would be a sop to his pride at least, an excuse for failure. Naturally she felt loyalty to Tomás, a man Jack admired unreservedly, naturally she was reluctant to run off and leave him. He could bear to lose her to a husband. But not to patriotism and principles and pride. Especially not to pride.

Ramón arrived home to find Marisa still asleep. He jingled the coins in his pocket, which woke her up immediately and elicited a sunny welcome-home smile.

"Rouse yourself," he said gruffly, tossing the morning's takings at her. "I have eaten nothing all day."

She picked up the coins and began heating up some mess in a saucepan, chattering between sensuous yawns.

"I have felt so poorly today," she sighed. "I have had such pains."

"Pains? Whereabouts?"

Marisa patted her burden wistfully.

"Your son makes his poor mamá suffer so. I was afraid to leave my bed, but now you are home again I feel much better."

She knelt down and began massaging his leg.

"Have you been out today at all?" demanded Ramón. Marisa shook her head.

"Of course not. You know how easily I tire. Oh, what would become of me if you were not here to support me?"

Ramón grunted. His contribution to the family budget was nominal, but Marisa had felt it wise not to enlighten him as to the subsidies she continued to receive, not only from Jack but from other former clients who were embarrassed to encounter her in the street in her present inflated state. It did Ramón good to go out for a few hours and play at being a pavement artist again, and his absences gave her the opportunity to improve their standard of living.

She had come to enjoy being pregnant, regretting only that it was not a state that could be prolonged indefinitely. A life of licensed sloth suited her perfectly, and despite Ramón's continued testiness and jealousy, he remained totally bewitched by his vision of fatherhood, and perpetually anxious about her supposedly delicate health. In actual fact she had never felt better in her life, being well-fed, well-rested and well-treated, an unprecedented combination.

Since her pregnancy, Ramón had talked incessantly of the imminence of peace and the subsequent restoration of his property. He had drawn up plans for a new house of palatial proportions to replace the one that had been destroyed. It had more rooms than Marisa could count, each of them a shrine to luxury and taste. Every piece of furniture, every picture, every drape and fitting was described in minute detail, an inventory Marisa knew by heart. This elaborate domestic scenario appealed to her even more than the earlier tales of travel, which had entailed rich foreigners lining up for her services. The prospect of working for her living had lost its charm; she much preferred indolence to enterprise.

She still nurtured hopes of going to England, in the event of Ramón's dreaded demise, but tact demanded that she keep such thoughts to herself. To Marisa's mind it was providential that Jack should turn out to be Lole's long-lost cousin. She for one had no doubts that Lole would shortly follow her son to safety, whatever she told that oaf Tomás. When Ramón died, Lole would surely send for her, Lole would take care of her and her baby . . .

And yet, even as she spun these daydreams, she worked busily with her needle, sewing her savings into her fur coat like a squirrel stowing nuts against a hard winter, as if she knew in her heart that Ramón would die in poverty, that she would never go to England, that she would one day be not alone, but alone with a child, which was worse. It did not bear thinking about, and so she thought of more pleasant things while she acted instead, on instinct, as if by preparing for the worst she could stop it happening.

Ramón consumed a few mouthfuls of food straight from the pot, and then lay down, exhausted, while Marisa greedily devoured the rest.

"Lole came today," she said, pouring him a tumbler of whiskey. She had taken to watering it down, a little more each day. "She brought cigarettes, from your cousin."

Marisa had learned to refer to Jack studiously as "your cousin" rather than "my Englishman." In deference to Ramón's fatherly pride, she never referred to her former activities. In Ramón's newly patriarchal mind, those days had never existed. He had plucked her out of obscurity and elevated her to be his consort. Hence any extras that came their way were now from "your English cousin." Ramón displayed little interest in Jack, but he had been ready enough to accept him as kin. Like Marisa, he was far too self-absorbed to be curious.

Ramón tossed back the life-giving brew and held out his glass for a refill.

"Lole looks so much better," continued Marisa placidly, "since the boy went to England. He was a great worry to her."

"Pah! The child lacked discipline, that was all. His own father was an ineffectual fellow, and he had no respect for that clod García. Our son will be brought up in the old way, Marisa, to show respect for his elders."

Marisa nodded sagely. "Poor Lole," she sighed. "She misses him, I am sure. Perhaps she will join him, after the war."

Ramón snorted. "She will never leave García. She is too softhearted. But thanks to me the brute no longer dares to beat her. He knows now that I would tear him limb from limb."

"He quakes when he hears your name," agreed Marisa. "How fortunate for Lole that she has you to protect her!" She leaned her head on his chest and yawned mightily. "Tell me again how it will be when the war is over," she pleaded. "Tell me again how it will be after our son is born."

She liked to shut her eyes while he spoke, sinking into a trance, as if communicating with the oracle. It was as soothing as a lullaby, and as usual it sent them both to sleep.

"I can't possibly take all this with me," said Clara, inspecting the contents of Flora's outsized parcel. "And in any case, it's bad luck. If I take winter clothes, she's more likely to die. It's like buying a layette before the baby's born."

"Clara! Don't be morbid. I thought you said there was a good chance of success?"

"I said she was getting the best possible attention, that's all." She began unpacking the box and dividing the items into two piles. "If you really don't need these things, I'll get someone to pick them up from you. There are plenty of other god causes besides Dolly."

Flora watched helplessly. Most of the items were brand-new, not castoffs, the result of a special expedition to Harrods. It had quite taken Mummy out of herself.

"Here, let me do it," she interjected, as Clara subjected a tin of smoked oysters to a look of withering scorn. "I thought they would make a change," she said defensively. "And I wanted to send things that would cheer her up. Don't be such a bore."

"You're quite incurably frivolous, Flo. But you're right. I am a bore." Clara replaced the oysters and suppressed a smile at the jar of bath salts. Dolly probably hadn't had a bath in months.

"Not quite such a bore as you used to be," conceded Flora. "And I'm not quite as frivolous, either."

Flora poured tea and Clara sat with Rafael on her knee. He was a docile child, and had started to speak again, not that he had a great deal to say for himself. Steven and Arabella sat to attention like two small soldiers, displaying well-drilled manners, while Andrés slouched and scowled and scattered crumbs. Archie had just had to spank him, on Flora's instructions, for bullying Steven again. Despite the bright missives Flora sent to Dolores, there was absolutely no love lost between Andrés and the junior Prendergasts, and Flora was beginning to regret her rash undertaking to bring him up as her own. After all, as Archie kept saying, he was Jack's responsibility.

"How young do you take delinquents?" quipped Flora, with a sideways glance at the cuckoo in her nest. Andrés glared, as if aware they were discussing him.

"Is it that bad?" Rafael sneezed all over Clara's collar and she used this excuse to slip him gently off her lap.

"Well, naturally we didn't expect it to be easy. He was bound to feel very unsettled. But I must admit we got rather more than we bargained for."

"Now you know what Jack's mother had to put up with," said Clara dryly. "No wonder she was glad to see the back of him." She returned Andrés's glare, poked her tongue out at him, and provoked a reluctant snicker.

"I was much worse than that," said Clara airily. "I tried to set fire to the house once."

"Good Lord," said Flora, alarmed.

"It's harder for him, of course," continued Clara, enjoying Flora's horrified expression. "He can remember his parents. I can't say I envy you. Give me my adolescents any day."

"Do tell Dolly he's pining for her. I don't like to worry her in the letters, but I think she ought to know he's not settling. Rafael's a sweetie, everyone adores him." She dropped her voice to a whisper. "Jack ought to adopt Andrés instead. It's the obvious solution."

"Jack's quite incapable of bringing up either of them," said Clara. "I daresay he'll think better of it once he gets back home. It's easy to get carried away in Spain."

Flora nodded with feeling. The heady excitement of the rescue mission seemed a very long time ago, and now she wanted the perfect order of her life restored.

Clara prepared to take her leave. "We'll send you a wire, of course, to let you know how the operation went. I'll be gone at least two weeks, perhaps three, I've got quite a busy program. Some of the children would like to get back into Spain, if I can find foster homes for them in the Republic."

"What on earth for? Surely they're better off in England?"

"They don't see it like that. The average fifteen-year-old Basque boy wants nothing more than to go back and enlist. Especially now that the pressure's building up to repatriate them back to Fascist territory. I'd like to preempt that, if possible. There's a Basques-in-exile organization in Catalonia that should be able to help."

She talked enthusiastically about her project while Flora feigned interest, anxious to delay her departure as long as possible. Not that Clara had offered much direct reassurance, but at least with Clara she didn't have to pretend that all was well, with Clara she could drop the confident, coping front, if only because she knew that Clara would see through it. Clara had the doughtiness of one who had been to hell and back, a journey that had left her with an air of omniscience, half-spiritual, half-pragmatic. Flora did not attempt to analyze the change in her, but she respected it. She had always avoided disagreeing with Clara; now she was happy to defer to her instead. The difference did not show, superficially, but it was fundamental. It was the nearest she would ever get to loving her, but it was near enough.

Clara was right, things looked very different in Spain. Spain was another world, its air thick with all manner of strange passions, just being there seemed to rob one of one's sanity. The escapade had been short and thrilling; the aftermath looked set to last indefinitely.

Flora felt quite desolate as she waved Clara good-bye, succumbing to a bout of self-pity which lasted a good five minutes. The children were in the garden, playing, and she stood looking at them through the French windows, grimly anticipating trouble. Andrés was standing aloof from the others as usual, contemplating his next act of sabotage. When she saw him from a distance, like now, or watched him sleeping, her heart went out to him. But close to her, awake, he drove her to distraction. Not that it was his fault, of course. The poor lamb was unhappy, that was all, and not just unhappy, angry as well. He cried for his mother in secret, emerging from the lavatory with red-rimmed eyes, and yet he never mentioned her. It had been all Flora could do to get him to copy out those little notes she included with her letters. The Spanish tutor who came in each day had done her best to reassure him, but Andrés still felt himself unwanted, betrayed, abandoned. The only warmth he showed was toward Rafael, as protégé and fellow victim. He refused to let him out of his sight, terrified to lose his only ally in a hostile, alien world.

Flora sighed as Steven let out a howl of protest and steeled herself not to intervene. There was nothing to do but to sit it out and hope for the best. In the meantime, she had better hide the matches.

Tomás lurched to a halt, extracted a coin from his pocket, and tossed it into Ramón's open shoe.

"Lole will be away for a while," he informed his brother-in-law. "Her cousin is taking her to the country for a rest. She asked that I tell you."

Ramón picked up the coin and hurled it back at the donor, furious to be caught unawares with his foot exposed and his chalks in his hand.

"To the country? Pah! More likely he has persuaded her to leave you. What a fool you are, García. Take your money. You will need it when you no longer have my English relatives to support you."

"I work for my living, as would you if you had any pride. There is plenty of work for the likes of us. You could be packing ammunition for the front instead of begging from your fellow citizens. Or perhaps you have no wish to support the struggle. Perhaps you are a Fascist in disguise."

Ramón flinched and looked involuntarily to the right and left. "How dare you accuse me thus? What proof have you? Am I not a poor man? You can see I am dressed in rags. How could I be a Fascist? Have a care, García, or I will sue you for slander.''

Tomás threw the coin back at him. ''From one poor man to another, then. And death to all Fascists. Death to all Fascist *spies.*'' He spat on the ground, smiled menacingly, and continued on his way.

As soon as he was out of sight, Ramón pulled on his boot hurriedly and scrambled to his feet, trembling. Not that he was afraid. Fascist spy indeed. It was nothing but an idle threat. García had been bluffing, in the hope of frightening him into some indiscretion. He was acting under union instructions, of course. He had no brain of his own . . .

He limped home, seething, reaching deep into his pocket for the cold comfort of his gun. Since Tomás had discovered its hiding place, he carried it with him at all times, in readiness against attack. He had been sorely tempted to shoot García down like a dog, but to have done so would have been to incriminate himself, to play into enemy hands. They had no proof, no proof at all. All his odious neighbors were Reds through and through, and yet none of them suspected him, because he was only a poor cripple. In the early days he had been unwise enough to let them know he was well connected, that he was a man of property who had been swindled and fallen on hard times. They had laughed and jeered and refused to take him seriously; the local urchins aped his walk and took him for a drunken lunatic. And he had borne these insults, seeing their value. As a crippled, drunken lunatic he was beneath suspicion. It was indeed a masterly disguise.

He was more than a match for an imbecile like García. But the fellow tried his patience sorely. How delightful it would be if Dolores deserted him and followed her son to England. Than he need have no compunction about taking his revenge at last. García had plotted the downfall of the family, murdered his father, defiled his sister, blackened his good name, engineered his banishment and disinheritance. He would not rest till he and his kind were wiped off the face of the earth.

He arrived home puffing with indignation, and lost no time in recording the incident in his journal, with appropriate embellishments. García was a Red agent, who had been sent to spy on him. Luckily, like all Reds, he was a bumbling fool, and he had had no difficulty in feeding him false information and thus outwitting him. Nevertheless, he would have to be eliminated at the earliest opportunity. His name already topped Ramón's death list, but he underlined it several times for good measure. After this, he felt a great deal better, and drank a toast to victory, rather too fast, provoking a violent coughing fit which punctuated the dog-eared page with bright blobs of red.

By the time Marisa returned, perturbed to find him home before her, he had graduated from euphoria to morbid despair.

"I am a dying man, Marisa," he reminded her feebly, and for the next few days he declared himself too ill to step outside the safety of his door.

Barcelona had changed. An air of bourgeois respectability had replaced the heady atmosphere of revolution, and the big hotels were back in business, ready to lick your boots for money just as much as ever. Clara was glad to be able to avoid them, for the hospitality that greeted her was overwhelming. She spent each night with a different family, to avoid giving offense, and numerous invitations awaited her return after her visit to Madrid.

It hurt, giving the children up, despite her satisfaction at reuniting them with their parents. She had come to love them, in her own fashion, a gruff, undemonstrative kind of love, the kind of love that suited adolescents, that was no good with small children or men. She knew now what she would do after the war. And she knew that she would do it out of love, not hate. She knew that Edmund would be pleased.

Both the boys she had brought back came from Catholic families. Clara was surprised at the openness with which they continued to practice their faith. Various religious artefacts adorned their humble apartments, and when she expressed surprise at this, and asked if it was not dangerous, their response was swift and belligerent.

"The Republic must allow the Church to be reestablished," one of the children told her gravely, translating the vehement words of his parents. "We Basques in exile must put pressure on the Catalan government to lead the way. Already it has begun to ignore what is going on, knowing that it cannot prevent it. Soon the rest of the Republic will follow suit. To persecute the Church is bad propaganda. It helps the Fascists."

To demonstrate their point, they took Clara with them to Sunday Mass in a neighboring apartment, a well-attended affair, with some twenty people taking Communion. The priest wore no vestments, and the kitchen table had been draped with a white cloth to serve as an altar. Clara found the experience refreshing. Despite her technical reconversion to the faith, her unorthodoxies were legion—a healthy sign, Father Spinks had claimed, with his usual disregard for dogma. She still found the atmosphere in church oppressive, she retained a puritan mistrust of excessive trappings, and had yet to conquer her phobic aversion to the smell of incense. The simple practicality of the ceremony appealed to her; for once she felt able to join in the responses without feeling a fraud. Despite the airy assertion that there was no danger, a lookout remained outside the door and below, in the street; this precaution enhanced her sense of occasion.

Clara could not understand the sermon, but her wandering thoughts were captured by the sudden mention of her name. All eyes turned to look at her and there was a burst of clapping. Afterward, the priest shook her hand and thanked her in broken English for all her valuable work.

"Many of these people would be glad to look after children whose parents are behind Fascist lines," he said. "Will you be staying long in Barcelona? They would be pleased to receive you in their homes."

Clara explained that she was going to Madrid, but would be back shortly.

"My late husband's cousin is having surgery. I must stay until she is out of danger." Then, on impulse, she added, "She is a Catholic. She is being treated in a Communist military hospital. She may wish to have the last rites before they operate. Are their priests, like yourself, in Madrid, who would visit her?"

"There are priests like myself everywhere. I will arrange for someone to make contact with you. Write down your name for me, and your address in Madrid."

Jack had made a reservation for her, and Clara scribbled the details onto a piece of paper, which the priest read several times before destroying it.

"Don't worry on my account." said Clara, interpreting this gestures correctly. "I'm still a member of the British Communist party. They wouldn't dare touch me."

"Of course not," said the priest, smiling, seeking to reassure her, making her feel a fool.

"Can we go to your hotel first?" asked Dolly unexpectedly. The hospital was some thirty miles east of Madrid, and Jack had ordered a car to take them door to door. "When I was working," she continued hurriedly, "I used to use the showers at the school, and I know perfectly well they'll scrub me from top to toe when I arrive, but . . . would you mind if I had a bath, before we go? I'd feel so much better if I was properly clean. It's poetic justice, I know, me asking you for a bath."

It was the first time she had ever referred to the past, even obliquely. Jack noticed that she was rather pink.

"Be my guest," he said lightly, anxious to minimize her embarrassment. "But the water's not always very hot, I'm afraid."

He told the driver to drop them outside the Florida and wait. She followed him demurely up to his room and made straight for the bathroom, and the years fell away as he sat and smoked and listened to the splashing behind the closed door. This time she didn't sing, and this time she would drain all the water away. And this time he wouldn't dare lay a finger on her; she was more inaccessible now than ever she had been then. This might be the last time he would ever be alone with her, in a few days he might even lose her for good, and yet despite that, or because of it, he was powerless to exploit the situation, unable to risk a final irredeemable rejection. And she knew it.

Afterward it would be different. Afterward there would be nothing he wouldn't risk. But for now she was safe, quite safe, safe enough to risk being alone with him and linger naked in his bathroom and torment him with her nearness. It was poetic justice all right.

"Will you be much longer?" he called after an age. "I told the driver to wait."

"I'm washing my hair," she shouted back. "Send him away for an hour."

He went downstairs, gave the man a tip and told him to come back later, and was on his way back to the room when he bumped into Thérèse in the corridor. She had just got back from New York, where her work on widows and orphans had won her an award.

"Jack!" she greeted him. "How are you?" She kissed him on both cheeks.

"Fine. Did you have a good trip?" Normally he would have been glad to stop and chat, but today he was in a hurry, and it showed.

"Fine. You seem *distrait*. Is anything wrong? How's the novel?"

"Finished," said Jack, truthfully enough.

"Good. Now perhaps you'll stop being so unsociable. Come out to dinner with us tonight."

"Sorry, Thérèse, I'm doing something this evening. Another time, perhaps."

She treated him to her mischievous feline smile. "You can bring her with you, if you like," she said. "I saw her getting out of the car just now. *Ravissante*. What happened to that pretty little nurse in Valencia—the one in the photograph? Did you break her heart, or did she break yours?''

Jack managed a mysterious grin, which didn't quite come off. "I'll tell you about it some other time," he said.

"Secretive as ever, aren't you? You're driving me insane with curiosity. What's her name?"

She jerked her head toward his room. Jack wondered if Dolly could overhear.

"I've got to go," he said. "Tell Laszlo we must get together soon."

Thérèse stood jingling her keys for a moment and looking all-knowing, before heading back to her own room. So distracted was Jack by this encounter, that he was even less prepared than he might otherwise have been for the sight of Dolly, swathed in towels, sitting on his bed, pulling his comb through her long wet hair.

"Sorry," he said. "I'll go down to the bar for a bit while you dress."

"No, don't do that," said Dolly quietly. She held out the comb. "I haven't washed it for weeks, it's full of tangles. Would you mind?" Her manner was quite matter-of-fact. He hesitated, took the comb from her, sat down on the bed beside her and started pulling it through the long, knotted strands, making her wince.

"Do you remember that day I had it all cut off?" she said. "I looked a perfect fright."

"Don't fish for compliments," said Jack.

"Have I changed much?"

"You're older, that's all."

"I'm only twenty-five. I suppose I look like a real old hag. It must have been quite a shock, seeing me again."

"Of course it was a shock. But you don't look like an old hag and you know it."

"I used to think I didn't care what I looked like. But it's easy not to care when you look all right. The uglier one becomes, the vainer one gets. Ridiculous, isn't it? As if they'll care whether I've got clean hair or not. I expect they'll shave it all off anyway."

"Your hair is still very wet. You'll catch cold. I'd better go down for some more towels."

"No. No, don't go. Jack . . ." She offered him her hand and he took it. It was ice-cold. "I'm frightened."

It was the first time she had owned up to fear; it seemed a good sign, a sign that she wanted to live.

"That's only natural. Anyone would be. But you'll be in the best possible hands."

"It's not that. I'm not frightened of dying. At least, I suppose I must be, but I've had to learn to live with it. Every time I black out, it's like dying. It sort of loses its impact. After a while you start thinking you're immortal. I suppose that's what I'm frightened of. Living. Living hurts."

Jack flung down the comb, exasperated, and seized her by the shoulders. "It makes me so bloody angry when you talk like that. You'll live and like it. Don't enough people love you to make it worth your while? What more do you want?"

She took a deep breath and hitched up the towel. "Don't take this the wrong way. I do want something, actually. I want to be like we were, just once. Can you understand that?"

Jack froze, certain that he had misunderstood her. "Like we were?"

"I don't care if it's all the most utter disappointment, I'd rather it was. These things grow in the memory, I know. But anything would be better than all this pretense. I'm not trying to start anything, I'm trying to end it. I think it would be easier for both of us."

Jack shook his head slowly, not believing his ears. She took the negative gesture literally.

"Damn you. It was just like this the first time, or rather the last time. I practically had to beg you, as I remember. There!"

She flung the towel aside and dared him to look away, unable to hide her transparent terror that he would not want her. Jack shut his eyes. "No," he heard himself saying. "No."

She flinched, as if he had slapped her, and covered herself up.

"Of course it will be utter disappointment," he said, keeping his voice hard, cold. "It's bound to be. That's the whole point, isn't it? Just once, that's all, to get it out of the way, so I've got no chance. Just once, so that you can convince yourself you've got no regrets. No."

She flung him a look of undiluted venom, stalked off into the bathroom, and crashed about inside, emerging moments later fully dressed.

"We can't go yet," said Jack. "I sent the car away for an hour. *Don't look at me like that.*"

He pulled her onto the bed and hugged her tight while she fumed and wriggled and abused him in gutter Spanish. Her anger was like a balm, he would have happily let her beat him black and blue. And her tears were even better.

She had always talked too much, by her own admission, and she
did so now, saying more than she meant to, things she would never
have said if he had let her have her way. Jack had always thought
that words were useless between lovers, but they had their place,
their very inadequacy was potent, telling.

And so he said all the things he should have said seven years
before, feeling giddy with the relief of it, letting her prompt him
into total exposure, doing the same to her, leaving nothing unspoken, nothing denied, and everything still to do.

It was like an exchange of vows, though none was given. Quite
the reverse. Nothing had changed, she told him, sadly. But for Jack
that was the beauty of it. Nothing had changed.

Clara plumped up the pillows with professional briskness and cast
a critical eye around Dolly's private room.

"It's horribly gloomy in here," she remarked crossly. "They
might have put you somewhere brighter. I noticed an empty room
on the other side of the corridor with a view over the gardens. I'll
get them to move you."

"Oh, please don't bother," insisted Dolly, still examining the
contents of Flora's parcel. "This is like Christmas. I don't see how
I can ever repay you for all you've done, all of you. Bath salts!"

"I told Flo to be practical but she wouldn't listen. I'm afraid I
had to leave half the stuff at home. So, how are they treating you?"

"Oh very well. Doctor Jannet seems to think I'm ready, anyway.
I was worried they would put it off."

"You're still rather thin. Hasn't Jack been feeding you?"

"I've got meat coming out of my ears. I feel so guilty about it.
Everyone else living on scraps and me being fattened up like a
goose."

"Don't feel guilty. The people who matter don't go short of
anything, in wartime or any other time, believe me."

"That's what Jack said. It made me feel worse. Why should some
people matter more than others? Money and influence shouldn't
make any difference. That's what the war is about. And now . . ."

"Money and influence will always make a difference and equality is all humbug."

Dolly looked quite startled. Clara smiled. "I haven't really
changed my views. I still believe in equality as an abstract concept,
but I don't believe it exists, yet, in the Republic or Russia or anywhere else, and it probably never will. The ideal is still worth
striving toward, but meanwhile, money helps, and the more money,

the more help. Poor Richard Peabody's putty in my hands at the moment. I'm pretty cross about this room, though. I shall take him to task for shortchanging me.''

"Clara . . . tell me honestly. How are the boys?''

"I told you. They're fine.''

"No they're not. It's Andrés, isn't it? Please don't try to spare my feelings. I'll only imagine the worst.''

"Very well then. He's being a perfect little monster and driving them all around the bend, which is only to be expected. It's utterly vile being a child at the best of times, let alone in a strange house in a strange country. Everyone telling you what to do, no rights of your own, being passed around from pillar to post . . . How did you feel when they sent you away to England?''

"That was different.''

"No it wasn't. Your mother thought she was doing the best for you.''

"And my father was glad to see the back of me! Oh. I see what you mean.''

"There you are then. And of course he's inherited Jack's bloody-mindedness. Flora's doing her best, but he doesn't fit in. He'll never be a Prendergast. He needs you. You've got to go home.''

"This is my home.''

"Rubbish. Don't make the mistake I did, Dolly. People first, not places, not politics, not principles. People. The people you love are all that matter.''

"I love my husband,'' she said quietly.

Clara folded her arms. "You love your son. You have to choose.''

"I know. I've chosen. Andrés has a father. Tomás has nobody. He's already lost his wife and all his children and part of himself as well. I'm all he's got left.''

"Andrés hasn't got a father. Jack's not cut out to be a father, specially not to a difficult child like that. You're just making excuses. If it wasn't for Jack, you'd leave Tomás like a shot. You don't trust your own motives, that's all.''

Dolly squirmed visibly. "That's not fair.''

"But it's true, isn't it? God, what guilt does to people. It's not love that makes this bloody world go around, it's guilt, and I should know. Life's short, Dolly. You're suffered enough. And so have Jack and Tomás and Andrés. So have we all. Think about it.''

"I'll think about it. Afterward.''

"That's cheating.''

"That's superstition.''

Clara sat down on the bed. "Talking of which, do you want a priest?"

"What?"

"In case you die. Do you want a priest?"

"A priest? Here?"

"Don't worry, he'll be in plain clothes. There's a network."

"A Republican priest?"

"Of course. Well?"

Dolly thought for a moment.

"It would be a bit hypocritical," she said. "I'm not sure if I believe anymore."

"It can't do any harm. Just in case all that poppycock about hell is true, it's best not to take any chances."

"But . . . won't it be dangerous?"

"Only if one of us turns him in. I'm meeting him at the hotel tomorrow. I can bring him with me."

Dolly shrugged. "All right," she said uncertainly. "It was kind of you to think of it. I never realized that you . . ."

"Oh, I'm not exactly a model Catholic. But I muddle along. One has to have something. It's not as good as love, but it helps. Flora's started trying to matchmake, poor door. As if anyone could ever replace Edmund. Oh, Dolly, don't cry. I didn't mean to upset you." She gave her a brisk squeeze. "My bedside manner was never up to much. Stop sniveling, there's a dear, or you'll start me off as well. I'd better go. Try to get some rest. See you tomorrow with the speakeasy padre. Try to dream up a few juicy sins in the meantime."

She soothed the bedcover and rearranged the items on the bedside table. Then she said, "You know, you can get over anything, in time, except regret. Regret is cold and dark, like a shadow over everything you do. Don't make the mistake I did, Dolly. Don't spend the rest of your life saying, 'If only.' "

Dolores shivered. The room was cold and dark, despite the bright summer sun outside, with only one small window behind the bed which looked out on a brick wall. Regret was like that, it blocked out the sun. Regret was lost opportunity, unfinished business, unrectified error, regret was being too late. It had hung over her life like a shadow and now, against all the rules, she had been given a second chance. The price was high, but then it was bound to be. Nothing worth having came free, least of all happiness. Happiness cost you everything you had.

* * *

At long last Marisa emerged from the apartment and waddled off down the street, a shopping basket over her arm. Tomás waited until she was out of sight before hauling himself up the stairs to Ramón's room. He rapped loudly on the door.

"Who is it?" yelped a strangled voice.

"Tomás. I must speak with you."

"Go away." Ramón fumbled for his gun and pointed it at the closed door.

"I come only to warn you. It is all the same to me. I do this only for Lole's sake. On your own head be it."

"Wait." Ramón got out of bed and pressed his ear against the door. "To warn me of what?"

"Let me in and I will tell you."

"There is no need for you to enter. I can hear you."

"So can all your neighbors. I come to warn you against danger. Do you want your neighbors to know what danger I speak of?"

Ramón opened the door a fraction and poked the barrel of the gun through the gap.

"I am armed," he said. "I will not hesitate to defend myself."

"I am unarmed. Save your bullets. You will need them soon enough. May I pass?"

Trembling now, Ramón opened the door, still pointing his weapon.

"Put that away," said Tomás. "I will not speak with a gun at my head."

Ramón put the pistol under the pillow and sat down on the bed. "Speak then. I am listening."

"Is it true," hissed Tomás, "that you are a spy? That you are one of the Fifth Column? Is it true?"

Ramón felt his throat tighten. "Of course not," he gabbled. "What use would the Fifth Column have for me? I am only a poor cripple. I am a dying man."

"I am glad to hear it. But can you prove your innocence? There are those who would denounce you."

"Who? Who dares say this about me? I demand to know!"

"What does it matter? They are watching you. I come to you as a brother, to warn you. It is useless for you to flee, they will follow you. But if you can prove your innocence, then no matter." He turned to go.

"Wait. How can I prove my innocence? What do they say about me?"

"That there are secret documents hidden in this room, or on your person. That you receive and pass on information to the enemy."

"How do they know this?"

"The secret police know everything."

"But it's not true!"

"Then they will find nothing. I am glad. For if they found anything, assuredly Dolores and Marisa would be in great danger. I care nothing for you, but I would not like to see them tortured and imprisoned as your associates. I am relieved to know that the accusations are false."

"Of course they are false!" squeaked Ramón, fighting for breath. "I am a patriot. I love my country. Who dares spread such slander about me?"

"Who? It is the talk of the neighborhood, my friend. I am surprised it has not reached your ears. Everyone is waiting daily to see you arrested and taken away. Have you been out lately?"

"Out? No. I have been too ill."

"If you had been out, you would have found that people crossed the road to avoid you and refused to speak to you. If you had been out you would find yourself barred from every café, you would find that no shopkeeper would serve you, for fear that they too might fall under suspicion."

"You lie! You are trying to frighten me!"

"If I lie, go out now and prove that I am lying. You will soon see that I speak the truth." His voice sank to a murmur. "A man in our block was taken away last night. I heard him screaming for mercy. We all knew he was a spy. I forbade Lole long ago to speak to him. The wretch is probably dead by now. Good riddance. I must go. I take a great risk in coming here. I do it only for Lole, and the girl. *Salud.*"

"Get out!" shrieked Ramón. "Get out with your filthy lies! You are trying to trap me! I admit nothing!"

"If you are innocent, you have nothing to fear. But be prepared. They will search everywhere. They will slit the mattress, they will lift all the floorboards, they will rip the seams of your clothes. Why, they may even pry open the soles of your shoes! They are very thorough. I am glad you have nothing to hide, brother. I am glad you have nothing to fear."

Ramón reached for his gun. "Scum! You dare to spread lies about me! It is you who have denounced me falsely. You! You! I should kill you now. You are no better than vermin!"

"Kill me then, and be tried for murder. Would I denounce my wife's brother? Would I put her at risk? We would all be tainted with your crime. And how should I denounce an innocent man?

You misjudge me, as always. Well, will you shoot me now, or can I go?'' He turned his back on Ramón and pulled open the door. "Now I may sleep easy again," he said. "I feared greatly for Lole and Marisa. I will not trouble you again.''

Ramón slammed the door behind him and locked it. He was shaking from head to foot, his breath coming in shallow gasps. He knew! They all knew! Who had betrayed him? Had he spoken in his sleep in that vile jail, perhaps? Had some neighboring felon overheard him and informed on him as the price of his own freedom? How long had they been watching him?

It was true, all the neighbors had been shunning him of late, particularly that old crone on the second floor. He had long suspected that she was in the pay of the secret police, and now he had proof. And only last week the local ruffians had pelted him with stones in the street. They all knew! Why had García not warned him before? Why, even now they might be on their way to arrest him and search for evidence to support their trumped-up charge. He was innocent! Innocent! He had never received nor transmitted information, all he had done was keep a diary, for no other eyes than his own, and now this private document was to be seized and used against him!

It was outrageous that his personal property should be threatened in this manner, that he should be forced to dispose of a family heirloom, a history of his life and times for the benefit of future generations. And yet he had no choice. The ultimate sacrifice must be made. Not that he feared the secret police, nor any other Red, but it was his duty to defend Marisa and Dolores against danger. If the Reds found out the truth about their activities, their lives would undoubtedly be forfeit. What need had he of a diary? When the day of liberation came he would recreate his testament from memory. All the facts were crystal clear in his mind. The secret information Marisa had extracted from Russian advisers, the indignities Dolores had suffered at García's hands in the service of her country, everything. He was no more than a humble scribe; it was they who were at risk, not he. He had no choice but to protect them, whatever the loss to himself. Let them search the place from top to bottom, they could not ransack his memory!

Unless . . . He shuddered. No. They would not torture a cripple. He was a poor man, a dying man, they would search and find nothing and then they would leave him alone, and no doubt take revenge on their informant for misleading them.

His fingers flapped and floundered as he unlaced his boot and removed its contents. He flung them onto the stove and watched tearfully as the flames consumed his epic. García had robbed him of his fortune and his reputation, and now, not content with that, he had forced him to destroy his last remaining asset. He thought to mock him, but one day he would pay the price for having crossed him thus!

Hearing footsteps on the stair, Ramón poked impatiently at the burner, sending a shower of red-hot embers all over the floor and burning his hands as he scooped them up and returned them to the fire. He was sobbing with terror by the time they broke down the door, an army of sour-faced men with black raincoats and heavy boots and Russian revolvers who filled the tiny room to bursting. He tried to find the words to protest his innocence, but there was no breath there to fuel them, his mouth opened and closed uselessly while the sweat trickled into his eyes.

Thank God Marisa was here. He clutched her hand tightly while she stroked his hair and sponged his forehead, as if she could protect him from this ravening horde. He watched them out of bulging, glazed eyes as they tore the furniture apart, ripped up the floor, reduced Marisa's wardrobe to shreds. Soon they would advance on him, search the bed, strip him naked, demand to know where he had hidden the object of their quest. He uttered an animal cry of terror and hid himself under the bedclothes, seeking refuge in the pungent darkness. It was Marisa they wanted, Marisa! Let them take Marisa, let them take Dolores, but let them leave him alone!

"What is it, dearest?" cooed Marisa, peeping under the covers. "There is nothing to fear. Here, drink some of this."

She held the cup to his lips and he sucked at the rim blindly like an infant pulling at the nipple. Only as the warmth returned to his ice-cold veins did he risk opening one eye.

"Have they gone?" he croaked.

"Who?"

"The men. The secret police. The men García sent to take me away."

"I saw no men. When did they come?" She looked around the room absently. "You must have been dreaming."

"You stupid girl!" exploded Ramón. "Do you realize we are in terrible danger? Do you not realize that our days are numbered? You must deny everything, everything. They have no proof!"

Marisa smiled and continued to stroke his hair. There was no danger, she assured him. Of course she would deny everything, of course they had no proof. The men had gone now and they would not come back.

"I was too clever for them, Marisa!" he gabbled. "They found nothing! I told them nothing! I did not betray you!"

"Of course you did not. Rest now. I am here. All is well."

He shuddered in relief and gradually the clutch of his fingers loosened as he sank into oblivion. Marisa was glad for him. His dreams were far less troubled when he slept.

"It was kind of you to come," said Clara, opening the door to her visitor, momentarily taken aback. Father J—no names were ever used—was strikingly attractive, in a typically Spanish, Dolly-like way, and not remotely spiritual-looking. He looked exactly what he pretended to be—an ordinary workman, with a firm handshake and a leathery tan and solid, muscular physique. Priests were invariably either weedy or corpulent in Clara's experience. This man, like the impromptu church in Barcelona, seemed like a breath of fresh air.

"I am pleased to meet you, Miss Neville. I have heard a great deal about your work with the Basque children."

"You speak very good English."

"Thank you. I learned it as a child. Your cousin is English?"

"Half English, yes. I should explain, the hospital is Communist-run, and—"

"Most hospitals are. The Communists are very efficient. Your cousin will be in good hands."

"I thought we could say you were a relative. A brother, perhaps."

"A cousin. It is less easy to check. Do not worry on my account. I have papers, and if there are any questions I will answer for myself. Hospitals rarely present us with a problem. More and more nurses are ex-nuns, you understand. The Republic wisely chose to 'rehabilitate' them, rather than waste their medical training."

He took a seat as requested, perfectly relaxed. There was not a whiff of subterfuge about him, nothing to attract suspicion. His disguise was more than skin-deep, it had obviously become second nature. Clara's nervousness evaporated, his confidence was tangible, infectious.

"When is your cousin expecting us?"

"I have ordered a taxi. It should be here shortly. So . . . there is no danger?"

He shrugged dismissively.

"Less than formerly," he said, his voice betraying something like regret. "The authorities are starting to turn a blind eye. There is talk of reestablishing the Church. For political reasons, obviously."

"That should upset the Vatican nicely. If it hadn't been for the persecution of the Church, I'm sure the Republic would have won the war by now. It alienated people terribly at home, and in France it deprived them of allies."

"Perhaps. But the Church had a lot to answer for. Let us hope it has learned from its mistakes. Your cousin's operation, is it serious?"

"She has a blood clot pressing on the brain, the result of a head injury. The chances are quite good, but there's always the risk she won't survive. She's quite philosophical. Too philosophical."

"She has lost the will to live?"

"Not exactly. But death is an easy way out of one's problems, isn't it? I just hope that having the last rites doesn't reconcile her to dying."

"The survival instinct is strong," he said. "I will do my best to encourage it. The last rites are only symbolic, in any event, a mere formality. Absolution comes from God, priest or no priest."

"You really believe that?"

"I have seen too much death to believe otherwise. Priests like to exaggerate their own power. My function is to reassure, nothing more."

"You don't believe in hell?"

"I believe absolutely in hell. I have seen it. Hell is here, on earth. Hell is what men do to one another, to themselves, not what God does to them. Men credit God with their own cruelty, their own desire for vengeance, their own inability to forgive. And the Church credits Him with its own pettiness, its own intolerance."

Clara blinked back the sudden prickle in her eyes. The slightest thing still set her off; imagining God as someone rather like Edmund, sacrilegious or not, was the bedrock of her newfound faith. Father J had trodden unwittingly on highly emotional ground.

"Forgive me," he said. "Did I say something that distressed you?"

"No," said Clara, blowing her nose hurriedly. "What you said was a comfort. I'm sorry, I—"

The telephone rang to announce the arrival of the cab. Clara indicated by a gesture that she was quite all right now, and led the way briskly downstairs, mortified by her sudden maudlin lapse. She half expected him to resume their truncated conversation in the car, to assume a priestly right to pry, but he remained silent, as if respecting her right to do likewise. He was disconcertingly detached and self-contained, and yet his presence was curiously consoling. It was as if he had understood without being told, as if he had suffered too. It was like an unacknowledged bond of shared, private pain.

On arrival at the hospital Clara introduced Father J to the sister on duty as Señora García's cousin.

"No visitors," said the nurse. "The patient is not to have any excitement before the operation."

"But she's not having surgery till this afternoon . . ." began Clara, perturbed, already bristling for a professional argument. Father J touched her sleeve.

"Please, sister," he said. "I have come specially. She is expecting me. If she were to die . . ."

He produced a devastating smile, reducing the nurse to blushing confusion, and after some token prevarication, she led him away.

Clara found Jack in the waiting room, pacing the floor.

"They wouldn't let me in to see her," he exploded. "Something must be wrong."

"They probably decided to sedate her early, that's all. The last thing she needs at the moment is you upsetting her."

"What happened to the priest?"

"Ssh. *He* managed to talk his way in. You probably rubbed them the wrong way. Sit down, for God's sake. You're making me nervous."

"Are you sure this Dr. Jannet knows what he's doing? He's been 'unavailable' all morning. Talk about an ivory tower."

"Do be reasonable, Jack. There's nothing more he can say. Strictly speaking, he shouldn't discuss the patient with you. Medical ethics. You're not even a relative."

"The patient? We're talking about Dolly, for God's sake!"

"Jack, I can hardly breathe in here. Your lungs must be like charcoal." Clara flung the window wide to release the thick fumes of anxiety. Jack lit another cigarette.

"How much of it is soft soap, Clara? And how much of it is to cover their own backs? 'The chances are good but there's always a risk.' It's meaningless. Why won't doctors ever give a straight answer? What do you think, honestly?"

Jack's normal sangfroid had deserted him; in any other circumstances it would have been gratifying to see the mask drop so completely, revealing the real person underneath.

"Jack, I'm not a doctor. I'm not even a nurse anymore. I can't possibly give you an opinion, and even if I could it wouldn't be worth having. Do shut up for a bit."

Jack shut up. But the habit of extorting information, of assembling and analyzing all the facts, was a hard one to break. Knowledge gave an illusion, at least, of being in control. Ignorance and incomprehension were his oldest enemies, and it frustrated him to confront them yet again, to be denied the ability to understand and judge for himself, to be at the mercy of experts. The medical profession deployed more platitudes even than politicians, there was an all-purpose, ambiguous response for every question and no answer was ever given that could compromise them later. Their bland, carefully worded assurances filled him with mistrust, his only allies seemed like enemies. He had already scripted the postoperative scenario in which they offered their sincere condolences and claimed they had done everything possible, with himself powerless to prove otherwise, while Clara nodded politely and thanked them for nothing.

What did it matter to them whether she lived or died? Death was their stock-in-trade, they couldn't possibly care about individual patients. If they did, they'd be nervous wrecks. No doubt they were as cynical about their profession as he was about his own, as detached about the body on the table as he was about the events he wrote about. They had to pretend to care of course, just as he did, in the interests of their own credibility. Meanwhile, Clara's hard-edged flippancy did nothing to improve his attitude; she was one of Them.

"Good thing you weren't around when the baby was born," she commented dryly. "You'd have worn a hole in the floor."

"Perhaps you'd better shut up as well," snapped Jack. "You're as much of a callous bitch as ever."

He squeezed her arm to nullify the insult. She was driving him mad with her studied nonchalance, but thank God she was here.

Clara sat counting her rosary beads, heedless of the comings and goings in the waiting room. Then, without haste, she crossed herself defiantly, like a schoolgirl making an obscene gesture behind the teacher's back.

"Does that really help?" asked Jack gloomily.

"Yes, it helps. As long as you don't expect it to work."

"What about faith?"

"Faith is not expecting it to work. If it worked every time, you'd be doing it too, and faith wouldn't be worth a bean."

"And how do the comrades feel about your reconversion?"

"I haven't been 'reconverted,' not in the way you mean. And all the comrades are interested in is my money. They're quite happy to tolerate my little eccentricities as long as I keep coughing up. How did you get on in Valencia, by the way?''

Jack produced a British passport from his pocket, embellished with the photograph he had taken of Dolly ''to send to the children.'' It purported to belong to one Miss Angela Fraser, schoolteacher, and bore relevant entry stamps and a Spanish visa issued in London. Clara examined it and whistled.

''Pretty good,'' she said. ''So it should be, considering how much it cost.''

''I'll pay you back,'' snapped Jack, putting it away.

''Don't be ridiculous. It was cheap at the price. Better than scaling the Pyrénées by night or stowing away in the trunk of Flora's car. Long live bribery and corruption.''

''Don't say anything to Dolly,'' said Jack shortly. ''She'd jump down my throat if she knew. She still says she won't leave Tomás.''

''So she told me. What's he like?''

Jack didn't answer straightaway. ''He's the only man I could bear to lose her to.''

''Mmm. Flora was appalled. Made him sound like King Kong with poor Dolly as Fay Wray.''

''That's exactly what Flora would think. He's big, all right, in every sense of the word. Just as well I haven't got a decent bone in my body or I might be tempted to do the honorable thing and let the best man win.''

''All's unfair in love and war. Flora wants rid of Andrés, you know. It's not working. Andrés has been bullying Steven half to death. Were you a little thug at that age?''

''Probably.''

''Flo's a great believer in biology. She lives in hope you'll take him off her hands. I can just see you playing with toy train sets and taking the little bastard to Lord's. No, it's Dolly he needs. That's your trump card. You want to make the most of it.''

''I don't want her to come for Andrés,'' said Jack. ''I want her to come for me.''

Dolores was feeling pleasantly drowsy. She had woken up that morning in a state of acute trepidation, with a racing pulse, and they had promptly drugged her into false tranquility. She heard a noise and opened one eye, and realized that she was already asleep.

''Josep,'' she murmured, enjoying the dream. ''Josep.''

But Josep didn't answer. Josep was staring at her, as if he didn't recognize her. No wonder. They had shaved all her hair off, she was completely, horribly bald. She put her hand to her head in a gesture of apology. Poor Josep. He looked so upset . . .

"Josep," she said. "It's all right. It'll grow again. Josep, please don't cry . . ."

She reached out to him and his arms closed tightly around her, crushing her. And then she felt something between fear and relief as she tried to wake up and couldn't. It wasn't a dream, then. She must be dead. She must be dead and Josep too. She must be in heaven.

"Dolores," he kept saying over and over again. "Oh God. Oh God. Dolores." He shook her gently. "Wake up, little sister. Wake up. It's me. *Wake up!*"

Slowly, groggily, she came back to her senses. At first it was impossible to speak, impossible to do more than cling to each other and weep. It was as if they had entered another world, one without the need for questions, for explanations, for anything but joy.

But once the words started flowing, they were unstoppable, in Dolores's case at least. Josep reduced the last tumultuous year to a few short sentences, while his little sister, garrulous as ever, embarked on the longest confession of her life.

"But can't you try to persuade her?" said Clara. "For Andrés's sake?"

Josep shook his head. Jack sighed and looked at his watch. The operation was taking forever. Something must have gone wrong.

"It would be a waste of time," said Dolly's brother. "Dolores is very obstinate. Telling her what she ought to do tends to produce the opposite effect."

"I don't want you to try to persuade her," put in Jack irritably, flaying Clara with a look. He could feel Josep's eyes upon him again, candid, perceptive, judgmental, and experienced another wave of unadulterated, instinctive hostility.

He should have felt overjoyed, for Dolly's sake, that she had been reunited with her much-adored brother, and perhaps he would have been if the much-adored brother wasn't a bloody priest. He had been closeted in there with her for hours, right up to the moment when they wheeled her off, and Jack had not the slightest doubt that he had given her a lecture about the sanctity of marriage and the turpitude of living in sin. Dolly would have told him everything, of course; the thought of it embarrassed Jack horribly, leaving him morally naked. And then, quite apart from that, priests were all terribly keen on eternal life and reaching the pearly gates as soon as possible. She had enough of a death wish as it was, without talk of rewards in heaven . . .

"Can I speak to you in private?" said Josep suddenly, standing up. Jack shrugged.

"If you like," he said ungraciously, bracing himself for a sermon. He wished the fellow were wearing a dress and a dog collar, it would make it easier to dismiss him. It disconcerted him that he was quite so masculine. He felt as if he had just been invited to step outside.

"You two stay here," said Clara, jumping up. "I'll wait in the staff room." She left Jack looking defensive and belligerent. The expression on his face was so typical of Andrés that she had to suppress a smile.

"Well?" said Jack, not meeting Josep's eye. "I suppose she told you all about me?"

"Not at all. Dolores is very loyal to the men in her life. I know as much about you as I do about Lorenzo or Tomás, which is very little. But I know a great deal about my sister, if only because we're very much alike. Too alike. I would feel compromised telling you about Dolores. But I'm prepared to tell you about myself, if that's any help."

"Look, I know Dolly's a Catholic, I know she's a faithful wife, I know she's full of unshakable principles. I understand all that. But—"

"Forget about her virtues. Vices are much more interesting—and relevant. My vices, of course, not hers."

Jack fell silent, curious now.

"She . . . sorry, I. I'll start again. One, I am very stubborn. Even when I know I'm wrong, I don't give in with a good grace. Instead, I try to convince myself I'm right. It's a form of pride."

"Go on," said Jack.

"Two, I tend to act on impulse. In fact, that's the only way I can act. I find it hard to plan, to think ahead. It's a form of sloth. But throw something at me suddenly, and I'll make a decision quickly."

"What are you saying?"

"Three, I can't resist a challenge, and I can't bear to lose. Put something beyond my reach, threaten to take something away from me, and I'll fight for it. It's a form of lust. I use danger as a kind of spiritual aphrodisiac, and if I wasn't celibate I would love the kind of woman who had the same effect—one I could never be sure of, one who stretched me to my limits, one who forced me to risk everything I had.''

He paused while the words sank in.

"That's all," he said. "Now you know all about . . . *me.*"

Jack looked at him properly for the first time and recognized the look in his eye, the look that epitomized Dolly at her most seductive. It was a dare.

"One more thing," added Josep, grasping Jack's hand and crushing it to a pulp. "I'm also very strong."

Jack was sitting by her bed. He was holding a bunch of red-hot blooms and whispering, "I love you, Dolly." She was young again, life pointed a finger to infinite possibilities. Then she blinked and Jack was gone, the room was dark and gloomy, only a thin ray of light hitting the wall opposite her bed. She felt afraid.

Life. She had got it back. She could see, she could hear muffled noises in the corridor outside. And her head ached.

And then it all came flooding back to her. Josep. Josep saying, be true to yourself, Dolores. Don't try to decide what's right or wrong. Just be true to yourself. And she had felt such peace, such overwhelming peace. Suddenly the decision had seemed so simple; it had come to her without pain like a revelation, requiring no conscious thought.

She had made up her mind to leave Tomás, to follow Jack, and she had not even used her son as an excuse, she had not even tried to disguise her defection as duty, she had thought she was being honest with herself. The mystic proximity of death had opened her eyes, and blinded her, to the truth.

Because the truth was not an absolute. The truth was complex, contradictory, many-faceted. Peace came in shutting your eyes to half of it, in seeing only the part you wanted to see. Truth was full of conflict, truth divided hearts and minds, truth was the emblem of war. Being true to yourself was not simple at all, it was a lifelong battle, an impossible attempt to resolve the irresolvable.

What was it Clara had said? *If it wasn't for Jack you'd leave Tomás like a shot.* Yes. That summed it up perfectly. She could go with Jack and be true to herself. She could leave Tomás and be true to herself. But the central paradox was inescapable: however compatible those two truths might seem, *she could not do both.*

"You have a visitor," they told her, and she shut her eyes, knowing and fearing what they would see.

He had not forgotten. He had brought the bunch of bright red flowers, and he said it again, very clearly this time, so there should be no doubt about it, "I love you, Dolly."

And then she told him.

18

"Jack is waiting outside to see you," said Josep.

"Stay with me, please." Dolores removed her scarf, revealing a bandage surrounded by a week's growth of stubble.

"It won't work, you know," said Josep mildly.

"What won't work?"

"Trying to look ugly. It'll take more than that to frighten him off."

Dolores gave an exaggerated sigh. "I'm not eighteen years old anymore, Josep. I know my own mind now. You told me it was something I had to decide for myself, and I have. In any case, you're a priest. You can't possibly be suggesting that I leave my husband."

"I didn't suggest any such thing. I know you better than to suggest anything."

"I wish you'd talk to Jack. I wish you'd make him understand. Where are you going? Josep, I want you to stay! I don't want to see him alone."

"Dolores, I can't protect you from Jack forever. And I can't keep coming here to see you, not now that you're out of danger. Until the government officially changes its policy, I'm a Fascist agent, and if anything were to happen to me, I don't want you to be implicated."

Dolores nodded miserably. "I'm sorry, Josep. I've been terribly selfish. Of course you mustn't keep taking risks on my account. But where can I reach you?"

"It's best if you don't know. In any case I might have to move, suddenly, at any time, I might even have to leave Madrid. If a cell is penetrated, everyone scatters. You must accept that, and you mustn't worry if you don't hear from me for a while."

"Josep . . ." She caught hold of her brother's hand. "I've been thinking. You wouldn't consider coming to England too?"

"To protect you against Jack?"

"Of course not," said Dolores hotly. "You're in dreadful danger here, you just said so yourself, and—"

"Listen to me, Dolores. I hate cruelty and killing and destruction, I hate what all this is doing to our country. But . . . the war fulfills a need in me. In some ways, I dread peace. That's a terrible admission, I know. But when I think of wearing a cassock and having a parish again . . . I wonder if I could ever go back to it. I wonder if it could ever be enough after this."

"You mean . . . you might give up the priesthood?"

"I'm not sure. It's a big decision to make. Like you, I hate admitting I've made a mistake, and like you, I find it hard to do anything in cold blood."

He gave her one of his knowing looks. Dolores blushed. Josep had always been able to see right through her. Thank God Jack couldn't.

"I have to go now." He bent to kiss her and hugged her very tight. "It may be a little while before I can come again. Are you quite sure you don't want me to go and see Ramón?"

Dolores shook her head violently. "He's obsessed with inheriting the estate, it's all he thinks about. He's convinced himself that you're dead and that everything will pass to him. If he knew you were alive, he'd be furious, he'd be more than capable of betraying you. Promise me you'll stay away from him!"

"Calm yourself, Dolores. Very well, I promise."

"Look after yourself, Josep, for my sake. Please don't take any foolish risks!"

"Don't worry about me. And if for any reason you change your mind about going to England . . ."

"I won't—"

". . . Clara has contacts in Barcelona who will know how to trace me through the network. And if anything happens to me,"— Dolores clung to him very tight—"someone will get word to you, and you're not to grieve. I must go, little sister."

He gently extricated himself from her embrace, blessed her, and quickly left the room.

Jack was waiting in the corridor outside.

"I'm going to stay away for a while," Josep told him. "She's hidden behind me long enough. I think she's well enough to cope without me now. Remember what I said."

The two men embraced.

"Take care," said Jack. "It would break her heart if anything happened to you."

"You took the words straight out of my mouth," said Josep, smiling.

Jack felt quite bereft, not to say anxious, as he watched him walk away. Ever since Dolly had given him her decision, a week before, she had never once allowed him to see her alone. Clara or Josep had always been present much to his chagrin. But now he almost wished that they were here. Everything depended on him now, he was all on his own.

To win her he had to risk losing her; in testing her, he had to prove himself. The temptation to hang around Madrid indefinitely, hoping to wear her down, was the coward's way out, and would put unfair pressure on Tomás, who saw himself as the obstruction, who couldn't begin to understand that it was much, much more than that . . .

"I want to go home," Dolly informed him peevishly as soon as he walked in. "Tomás needs me. I feel perfectly all right now."

"Only because you've spent the last week being sensible. You've got to be sensible a bit longer. And Tomás is managing perfectly well without you. You can see for yourself when I bring him here tomorrow to visit you."

"I'm bored," she continued grumpily. "Specially now Josep and Clara have gone. I expect you are, too. There's really no need for you to visit every day. I wish you'd go back to Madrid."

"Very well then. I'll go back tomorrow night with Tomás. I'll come back to collect you when they discharge you, of course. Meanwhile, you can always send word to my hotel if you need anything."

"I won't need anything. I told you, I'm perfectly all right. When . . . when will you be going back to London?"

She addressed the question to the counterpane, avoiding his eyes as usual.

"As soon as you're safely home. In fact, I've got no choice. I'm running very short of funds, and now I've finished my novel, it's time I started taking it around."

"Oh. I didn't realize you were poor again."

"I haven't earned anything for the best part of a year while I've been working on the book."

"What's it about?"

"The war. Well, not exactly. The war was just a pretext."

"A pretext for what?"

"For writing it. You have to have an excuse for writing anything. The subject's just something to hide behind."

"You mean, it's about you?"

"Inevitably. Among other things."

"I'd like to read it. Will you send me a copy, when it's published?"

"I don't think that would be a very good idea. I wouldn't like to get you into trouble. It's certain to be banned in Spain, whoever wins the war."

"Why?"

"Because it tells the truth, I hope. Which will probably mean that no one will want to publish it, and I'll have to go back to washing dishes at the Empire Court."

"You can always go back to being a journalist."

"I think I'd rather wash dishes. It's more honest."

"What about the rich wife idea?"

She didn't forget much, thought Jack. He affected to give the question serious thought.

"I don't know about rich. But I suppose I'll have to marry someone, so they'll let me adopt Rafael."

She began fidgeting with the corner of the sheet. "I don't want the boys separated," she said. "It's been preying on my mind. Clara says that Andrés is acting up. She says that Flora wants to get rid of him."

If it was a hint, it was well disguised. Her tone was accusatory rather than plaintive.

"Nonsense. When I telephoned Flora to tell her you'd pulled through, she said that Andrés was settling down extremely well. Rafael too. As for separating them, they can see each other as much as they like, that goes without saying. Clara's just trying to pressure you into coming home, that's all. She means well, I daresay. But it's not fair on you, and it's not fair on Tomás. Don't give it another thought. The boys will be all right, I promise you." He smiled reassuringly. "After all, it's not forever. After the war, we can always send them back to you."

Dolly shook her head. "I can't imagine 'after the war,' I can't think that far ahead. I don't want to cling to a dream, I have to be realistic. In any case, it's not fair to let them settle down and get attached to people then uproot them again. Better for them if it's permanent."

She blew her nose hurriedly. Jack fought the temptation to comfort her, to take the false passport out of his pocket and show it to her, to tempt her with plans and possibility. He wanted to talk her into it, here, now, while she was still weak and vulnerable. And yet if he did, it would prove nothing, except that she loved her son.

He nodded sagely instead. "Mmm. Perhaps you're right. I can't tell you how much I admire you for making such a difficult decision, Dolly. I know how heartbreaking it must be for you. So I won't mention the children again, except to say that I'm sure you're doing the right thing."

"Thank you." Her voice was cool.

"What's the matter? Have I said something wrong?"

"No, of course not. Thank you for understanding. Thank you for not badgering me. Thank you for everything. Do you have an address for Clara in Barcelona? I must write and thank her properly."

Jack wrote it down in his diary, tore out the page, and put it under her water pitcher.

"If there's nothing else you want, I'll leave you now. Dolly . . . please don't be so stiff and formal with me. I know you're worried about hurting my feelings, but there's really no need. I respect your decision, I respect Tomás, I respect your loyalty to him. I knew all along you would never run out on him. He deserves you. I don't."

She didn't comment, controlling her features pretty well, but not quite well enough, filling Jack with grim satisfaction. This wasn't what she wanted at all. She had been banking on him arguing, she had expected him to blackmail her; she hated him being noble and decent and stiff-upper-lipped. She liked him better as he really was, persistent and unscrupulous and greedy. He took her and squeezed it placatingly.

"The best man won." He sighed, twisting the knife, enjoying the frozen, unconvincing smile, returning it warmly, leaving her without a backward glance.

Josep had told him all he needed to know. Dolly would never know what she really wanted till she thought she was about to lose it. She needed to be threatened, stretched, forced to take risks. And she was strong enough to take it.

"It is as well Lole is not here," Tomás told Jack gravely. "By the time she gets back home it will all be over. She will be greatly distressed. Better for her if he were found dead in the gutter. Better for her if I killed the wretch myself."

"Are you sure about all this?" said Jack, puzzled.

"There is no doubt. Two men came and questioned me this morning. I told them I knew nothing. But clearly someone has denounced him, which is not a surprise. It will be tonight, for sure. They always take people at night. Therefore please do as I ask. Take the girl with you to visit Lole. She is a simple soul, and I would not like her to be there when they come to take him. Who knows? Suspicion may also fall on her."

"Take her with me? Aren't you coming too?"

"We have been asked to work this weekend, to supply the army in Aragon. Besides, if Lole saw me, she might read my face. I am a bad liar. She must on no account know that Ramón is in danger. She would want to go to the prison and plead for him and put herself at risk. It is all for the best. Once her brother is gone, it will be easier for you to persuade her to leave. As for me . . ."

Jack felt a flicker of unease. "Don't," he said. "Don't . . . do anything stupid. What I mean is . . ."

Tomás smiled and shook his head. "You take me for a hero, perhaps? Do not be deceived by this leg. If I had been brave enough to take my own life, I would have done so long ago. Besides, I would never leave my death on Lole's conscience. I was going to say, as for me, my health is much improved. I no longer need a nurse. It is pity that has kept her with me, not love. And soon there will be no more need for pity. So be patient, and all will be well. Now go and fetch the girl, and do not bring her back until tomorrow. You will find her still at home, she sleeps till noon."

The factory whistle summoned the next shift. Tomás hauled himself to his feet and grasped Jack's hand. "Give my love to Lole," he said. "Tell her you have seen me strong and well. I must go."

He left some coins on the table, waving aside Jack's attempt to pay, and left the café, vigorous despite the crutches. Jack watched him through the window as he crossed the road and disappeared through the factory gates, pondering this latest development. The activities of the secret police had indeed been stepped up, and a vigorous campaign mounted to weed out Fascist sympathizers. A new counterespionage agency had been established under the grandiose title, *Servicio de Investigación Militar*, popularly known as the SIM, and rumor had it that over six thousand personnel were employed in Madrid alone to seek out dissenters and deal with them summarily *pour encourager les autres*.

Jack's only concern was for Marisa. He felt no pity for the luckless Ramón, knowing him to to be a millstone around Dolly's neck. According to Tomás, his accusers claimed that his apartment was stuffed full of Fascist propaganda, in which case he was either suicidally brave or incredibly stupid . . .

More likely incredibly stupid. Jack's mind flew to his novel. Now that things were heating up he had better get it out of the country quickly, before it was too late. He had balked at asking a fellow journalist to take it home, for fear he might be searched and arrested, and had for some weeks been cultivating an embassy official, with an eye to the inviolability of the diplomatic bag.

He'd better collect it right away and deliver it to his contact, before he went to fetch Marisa. He'd be no use to Dolly or the children or anyone else if he disappeared into a Spanish jail . . .

He hurried toward the hotel, assailed by a sudden harrowing vision of a ransacked room and a welcoming party of witch-hunters. It was with some relief that he found his completed manuscript undisturbed, layered between his clothes in a suitcase he kept ready packed. He locked it, pocketed the key, and sauntered out of the hotel with it, trying to look casual. Then he made straight for the embassy, emerging ten minutes later empty-handed, lighthearted, and possessed of a brilliant idea . . .

Marisa seemed flustered to see him on home ground, but made him welcome nonetheless, as did Dolly's brother. Jack had to endure a solid hour of blustering, priming him liberally all the while, before he could get Marisa out of the stinking hole.

"It was good of you indeed, cousin, to take my poor sister to the country. Who can say what bestialities she suffers at the hands of the vile brute who has seduced her? I beg of you, take her to England. After the war is over I will be in a position to support her. I will write you an IOU now for any expenses you might incur. You have my word as a gentleman."

Marisa sat quietly, accepting all this nonsense at face value, not speaking unless she was spoken to and gazing at Ramón with apparently unfeigned adulation.

"You do not mind that I am going to see Lole?" she inquired timidly. "I have never been in a car."

"I regret only that my health prevents me accompanying you," continued Ramón, accepting a refill. "The country air would be most invigorating. Alas, I am a dying man."

Jack made appropriate noises, and wondered absently where Ramón had hidden his store of Fascist pamphlets. Had he been sane and sober and English, Jack would undoubtedly have loathed him. As it was, he could not help feeling sorry for him, if only for Marisa's sake and because he was Dolly's brother. He would undoubtedly "confess" to his crime all too readily, not that it would do him any good.

"Well, we had better be on our way," said Jack, standing up purposefully. "I hope to see you again, cousin, before my return to London."

"I am at your disposal," declared Ramón, rising out of his chair and bowing stiffly. "We must dine together before you leave. My regards to my poor sister."

Marisa wisely displayed some reluctance to leave him, but he waved her protests aside and called her a foolish child. Jack hoped he had left him enough scotch courage to see him through the night.

"Did Lole truly ask for me?" she asked, reveling in the novelty of the car ride, adding cheerfully, "Is she sick?"

"She was. She is in the hospital but she is better now. Tomás cannot visit her, he has to work, he thought you would be a comfort to her."

"I cannot leave Ramón for too long," she said, adding wistfully, "you can see how ill he is. We are very, very poor."

Jack stuffed some money into her bag. "I am sorry I cannot give you more," he said. "I will send you something for your baby from England."

"You are going back to England?"

"Soon, yes, I must."

"And will Lole go with you?"

"She says not."

Marisa seemed relieved. "I would come with you, but for Ramón. Will you send for me one day? When Ramón is gone, I will be all alone."

"Perhaps, one day. After the war."

Jack felt a stab of guilt. Tomorrow, if Tomás's information was right, Ramón would be gone, and what would become of her then? He pushed the question to the back of his mind.

"You are so ugly, Lole!" Marisa greeted her tactlessly, falling upon Flora's *marrons glacés*. "What have they done to your hair? Did you have a fever?"

"I thought Marisa would be company for you," explained Jack. "Given that Tomás couldn't come." The excuse sounded false, even to himself. Dolly seemed troubled, asking repeatedly if Tomás was all right, and when this subject of conversation had been well and truly exhausted, she retreated into suspicious silence, ignoring Marisa's chatter and Jack's small talk and eventually saying she was tired and wanted to be left alone.

Jack took Marisa to a restaurant, too preoccupied to notice the fascinated stares of the other diners. She was enormous already, although she insisted that the baby was not due for a long, long time. The baby would be born after the war was over, when Ramón was better. The baby belonged to a chimerical future, it had nothing to do with the present. She was poorly dressed—none of her finery fitted her now—but she had compensated with an excess of lipstick and rouge and cheap jewelry, and never went anywhere without her fur coat, however hot the weather. All eyes were riveted on them throughout the meal. Jack was too engrossed in his private thoughts to notice.

Eventually Marisa yawned and declared herself to be very, very tired. Jack paid the bill and took her back to his hotel, a small, suburban establishment where he had booked her a room. He lay awake for most of the night, working out his plan. In a week or so, Dolly would be discharged from hospital. That gave him plenty of time to talk Thérèse into helping him. A long soulful tête-à-tête over dinner should do the trick; she had always been insatiably curious about his love life, he shouldn't have too much trouble seducing her into cooperating. But timing was crucial. Once Dolly was installed at home again, it would be much, much harder to pull off. He would have to tell Tomás, of course; he owed him that much . . .

He got up early, leaving Marisa to sleep late, and arrived at the hospital to find Dolly sitting up in a chair, fully dressed.

"What are you doing out of bed?" said Jack.

"I want to go home," she said. "I have to go home straightaway. I haven't slept a wink all night. Something's wrong. I know it. Something's happened to Tomás."

She was white with anxiety.

"Of course nothing's happened to Tomás. If you're worried I'll go back to Madrid this minute and check that he's all right. You can't possibly leave the hospital yet, you're still very weak and—"

"I've had all that from the doctors. Can we go now? Tomás promised he would come to see me. I don't believe he's got to work, it's just an excuse. I'm afraid . . . I'm afraid that he's going to do something silly."

"Something silly?"

"To make me go to England with you. I'm afraid he's going to . . ." Her voice tailed off.

"Kill himself? He wouldn't do that, Dolly. He told me as much. He wouldn't want to leave his death on your conscience. He loves you too much for that."

Jack was tempted to tell her the truth there and then, if only to put her mind at rest, but of course it wouldn't put her mind at rest. She would just get into a worse state than ever, worrying about Ramón . . . His mind flew back to Marisa. What the hell was he going to do about Marisa?

Jack left Dolly alone while he sought out the doctor on duty, who proved harassed and less than helpful.

"I've already done all I can to dissuade her," he said. "I've told her we can't be responsible for any postoperative complications. But no, I can't drug her as you suggest. It would be an assault. If she chooses to discharge herself early, there's nothing I can do to stop her. I've given her an appointment for next week, for a checkup, and—"

But Jack was no longer listening, assailed with a sudden overwhelming sense of now or never.

"Can I use your telephone?" he said. "I have to make an urgent call to Madrid."

Thérèse was still in bed.

"Jack!" she greeted him crossly. "What time is it? You know how I hate mornings."

"I want you to do something for me," said Jack.

"Evidently." She yawned.

"I want you to go to the desk and ask them for the key to my room. I'll phone them in a moment to give them authority. Then . . . are you listening? It's important."

"Can I have a cup of coffee and call you back? I'm still half asleep."

"This will wake you up."

It did. He spoke rapidly, anxious now to burn his boats. It meant telling the story rather more baldly than he had intended, but this was no time to be coy.

"Well?" he said at last.

"I'm appalled. You're a bastard, Jack. You're a lying, cheating, scheming bastard."

"Does that mean you'll do it?"

There was a long, agonizing pause.

"You really love her, don't you?"

"Enough to risk losing her."

"Which is all you deserve." She let out a long, disapproving sigh of reluctant capitulation. "All right, you horrible man. You'd better hang up straightaway, before I change my mind. And Jack—"

"Yes?"

"Bonne chance."

"It'll take more than luck," said Jack.

Under normal circumstances, Tomás would have enjoyed the evening. His comrade had made him more than welcome, and two others had joined them for wine and cards, filling the small room with warmth and comradeship.

They were all disabled, including Manuel, his host, who had lost an eye at Guadalajara and resumed his former position as leader of the local branch of the UGT. He had done much to improve the morale of other veterans working in the factory, campaigning for better terms of employment, devoid of pity for himself or others and as committed to the struggle as ever.

Listening to Manuel, Tomás could almost believe in victory again. Listening to Manuel he was able to stifle his doubts about the sinister foreign influences at work in his country and the betrayal of the revolution. In Manuel's view, the Russians were there to be used and later discarded; once the war was won they would all go home and good riddance to them. Meanwhile they were a necessary evil, to ensure a continuing supply of arms. Manuel's hatred of Fascists was such that he would have allied himself with the devil against them.

"More wine, Tomás," he urged him. "What ails you? He misses his wife," he informed his other guests. "And no wonder." He dropped his voice to a suggestive whisper. "For myself, I would gladly trade a leg for a wife like Lole."

There was a roar of ribald laughter.

"Do not speak to me of Lole tonight," said Tomás gravely. "For I must do something that will cause her great pain. That is why I came here this evening. It is something I cannot undertake alone. It is something I would rather avoid altogether, but my duty to the Republic must come before family feeling."

He paused for effect, waiting while they all looked at him expectantly. Then he put his hand in his pocket and put something on the table. There was a general sharp intake of breath.

"Yes," he said sadly. "It belongs to my wife's brother. Now you understand why I am heavyhearted."

Manuel picked up the card, bright-eyed, his lip curling at the sight of the hated emblem of the Falange.

"But you have no choice!" he exclaimed, volatile as always. "You must denounce him. These Fifth Columnists are everywhere, they put the whole city, the whole Republic in jeopardy."

"I cannot denounce him. Lole would never endure the shame of it. You know she has been in poor health, I fear such a disgrace would kill her. If only the wretch would die! She would not weep for him then, she would see it as a release. He is half-crazed with drink and syphilis. It would be better to kill him than denounce him. That way Lole would be spared the shame of knowing her brother was a traitor."

There was a silence.

"Then kill him," hissed one of his comrades. "What difference does it make? The secret police will kill him anyway."

"You are right," said Tomás sadly. "But it is hard to kill a man who is sick. That is why I have shared my knowledge with you. So that I would not weaken."

"If it troubles you so much, then you need not do the deed yourself," suggested one of the other men. "Leave it to us."

But Manuel shook his head, automatically assuming the role of leader.

"To kill him would be too merciful. That way he will avoid torture. Under torture he would reveal the names of his associates. Who knows how many of them there might be? No, Tomás, you must be strong. You must turn him in."

"If it was your wife's brother," said Tomás, "is that what you would do?"

"Think of the shame of it," muttered the third man. "And besides, it might bring Lole under suspicion. We cannot ask Tomás to put his wife at risk."

Manuel looked around the table and then, piercingly, at Tomás.

"Very well. Tomás did not have to tell us this. He trusted us by so doing. Therefore the decision must be his alone. As long as the Fascist does not go free."

There was a murmur of assent.

"Then I must do the deed myself," said Tomás. "But on no account must Lole know of this. Best if he is found dead in the gutter somewhere, with no marks on his body. Then she will put it down to drunkenness. Only recently he was carried home unconscious. She would suspect nothing."

"Then it is settled," approved Manuel. "Let us go now and do what has to be done."

"Wait," said Tomás. "I dare not kill him at home. A neighbor might see us carrying the body away. There would be talk, and Lole might come to hear of it. No, I must lure him out of the house, into the street, and then I will kill him under cover of darkness and leave him, till the patrols find him. But there must be no blood. I will kill him like so.''

He demonstrated a chop to the back of the neck.

''Very well. Where will you take him?''

''Wait for me in the old laundry. When you see us enter, hold him fast, and I will do the rest. But wait till we are safely inside, so he cannot escape us.''

This suggested plan met with appreciative nods and grunts. The erstwhile laundry, along with all the nearby houses, had been reduced to ruins in an air raid, and would be completely deserted.

''Another thing,'' said Tomás. ''He may be armed. He may carry a knife, or even a gun. There is some risk. If this troubles you, then I must act alone.''

This suggestion was treated with contempt.

''Have we not all seen battle?'' demanded Manuel. ''Have we not all been wounded? You insult us, my friend.''

''Nevertheless, I must warn you. If any of us is killed or wounded, we must never reveal what really happened. We must agree that the assailant came at us out of the dark and deny all knowledge of who it was. Otherwise, the truth will all come out, Lole will suffer more than ever, and we ourselves may be arrested and tried. Agreed?''

''Agreed.''

The fever of battle was upon them again, their injuries forgotten in the eagerness to strike another blow against the enemy.

''Your wife will not be disgraced,'' repeated Manuel solemnly. ''Her honor, and yours will be protected. You have our word.''

Four fists knotted together in the center of the table.

''Very well then,'' said Tomás. ''Let us go.''

His comrades made their way to the agreed rendezvous while Tomás set off for Ramón's apartment. He turned the key in the lock quietly and struck a match into the gloom, lighting the candle by the door. Ramón was leaden with drink, stupefied; Tomás hoped he would be able to rouse him.

With difficulty he bent down and picked up the boot lying on the floor and satisfied himself that it was empty, that nothing remained that might later implicate Lole or the girl.

He looked down at the hated, haggard, handsome face and slapped it repeatedly while it twitched and groaned. He was about to pour cold water over it when Ramón suddenly sat bolt upright, eyes staring straight ahead, instantly awake.

''Be quick,'' said Tomás. ''You must hide yourself. Take your gun and follow me.''

"What? Follow you where?" Ramón blinked rapidly in the half-light and felt under the pillow for his weapon. "Is this a trick? I am innocent, I tell you, I have nothing to fear, nothing to hide! Do you take me for a fool? I will not follow you into some trap! Get out!"

"So be it," said Tomás. "But I am unarmed, as you see. I could have taken your gun while you slept and shot you where you lay. But if you think it is a trick, then by all means stay in bed and await your visitors in comfort. My conscience is clear. For the last time, then, *salud.*"

"Wait. Stay where you are. Don't move."

Ramón scrambled out of bed, sniveling with terror, unsuccessfully trying to fasten his caliper splint while keeping his weapon pointed at Tomás.

"Fool," said Tomás mildly. "You have nothing to fear from me. But you may need your gun yet, in case they give chase. They are less than five minutes away, and getting nearer every second. I will count to twenty and then leave, whether you are ready or not. I have no wish to share your fate."

Ramón snarled like an angry dog, threw down the gun and laced up his boot with surprising deftness. He was already fully clothed, he rarely troubled to undress.

"Do not trifle with me, García," he spat. "Or I shall have great pleasure in killing you and avenging all your many wrongs against my family."

"Then pray your aim is true," said Tomás calmly. "Pray your first bullet strikes me dead, for remember, I am still strong." He lifted one long crutch and brandished it. "Be warned. I am a patient man, but you try me too far with your insults and ingratitude. Make haste now."

Tomás led the way down the rickety staircase and made great play of waiting and looking into the blackness before venturing out into the street.

"Luck is with you," he hissed. "It seems they have not yet arrived."

Ramón held back in the doorway. "Are they watching? You said they were watching the house."

"They cannot be everywhere at once. You must take cover until they cease looking for you. It could be for days, or even weeks. I will bring you food and drink, but only for your sister's sake. How it pains me to save your miserable skin!"

He swung himself along the darkened street, while Ramón kept close, as if trying to hide behind his massive bulk.

"Where are we going?"

"To the old laundry, where the bombs fell. No one goes near there, never fear. The whole street has been evacuated, the buildings are unsafe, even the patrols do not bother to check it. It is the ideal place for you to lie low. Wait."

Tomás stopped suddenly. They were near enough now. Nearer would be too near.

"Wait. I think I hear something."

He turned around to face Ramón, who was shaking with terror, his face ghostly and ghastly in the moonlight.

"What can you hear?"

"I can hear someone laughing," said Tomás. "Listen."

There was a long moment of silence, punctuated only by Ramón's heavy breathing.

"I can hear nothing."

"Then you are a fool. I can hear laughter, long and loud. Are you blind, as well as deaf? Can you see this?"

He leaned on one crutch and held up the Falange membership card while Ramón opened and shut his mouth soundlessly, like a fish.

"Yes, you are a fool. In a few moments, they will come for you. In a few moments I will have my revenge. In a few moments you will wish you had never raped my poor sister, you will pray that you had not disowned her child. In a few minutes you will be a dead man. Can you still not hear laughter?"

Ramón began shaking violently, spittle spurting from his mouth, looking this way and that, too afraid to stand still, too afraid to flee.

"Coward!" continued Tomás. "How glad I am that I will see you die. They promised me they would let me watch while they torture you. They promised they would let me watch while they pull your teeth out and twist your shriveled balls off your putrid body and made you eat your own shit. And all the while I shall laugh. The last thing you will hear, Fascist, is the laughter of a free man."

The first bullet produced a mighty roar of diabolical joy. The second did not silence it. Even when the giant lay motionless on the ground, Ramón could hear his laughter, emptying his gun into the prostrate body in a vain attempt to gag his tormentor.

The end was merciful, and cruel. He saw nothing as the shapes ran toward him out of the darkness, he did not feel the swift blow to the back of his neck, but heard the laughter all the way to hell.

Jack told the driver to go slow, to minimize the effect of the potholes. Dolly was very pale, her face white against the dark scarf that she had pulled forward over her vanished hairline, although she kept insisting that she felt perfectly well, just worried.

Halfway back to Madrid they had to stop to allow Marisa to disgorge her breakfast, but not before she had spewed a good portion of it over Dolly. Jack got out and made Marisa sit in the front in his place, and she spent the rest of the journey with her head out of the window, groaning theatrically.

"I'll drop you both off at my hotel," said Jack, dabbing Dolly's skirt with his handkerchief. "You can clean up and rest while I go to the factory and make sure Tomás is all right. I telephoned a friend of mine to ask her to look after you while I'm out. Anything you need, let her know."

On arrival at the hotel, Jack called Thérèse on the reception telephone. The desk clerk affected not to recognize Marisa, who seemed glad to be back on familiar territory, craning her neck toward the bar in search of former patrons. A moment later Thérèse appeared. She greeted Marisa as an old friend, shook hands with Dolores, and embraced Jack.

"You two look exhausted," she said, taking Jack's key. "Don't worry, Jack, I'll take care of them for you."

But Marisa seemed less than delighted to have Thérèse as her hostess.

"I will go home now," she said to Jack, with a sideways look at her rival. "Ramón will be expecting me." She kissed Dolores and made as if to leave.

Jack put out an arm to stop her. If Tomás was right, Ramón would be in jail or dead by now. If Tomás was right, it might not be safe for her to return home.

"Stay with Lole, and have lunch in the hotel," he said.

"Ugh! I cannot eat. I still feel sick. I will walk part of the way with you."

Jack hesitated, seeking inspiration. "If you feel sick, you had better rest for a while. You look tired."

"I can rest at home. Ramón will be worried. I must go."

"He won't be worried," said Jack desperately, cursing her, cursing his better nature. "I'll call in on my way to the factory and tell him you'll be along later. Besides . . . Thérèse has some silk stockings for you.''

"Silk stockings?"

"Silk stockings," said Jack.

"Silk stockings," echoed Thérèse brightly, picking up her cue.

"And if you wait till I get back, I will bring some English cigarettes for you to give Ramón."

It worked. He waited till they were safely in the lift before leaving the hotel. He looked at his watch. Assuming the worst, he'd have to do something about Marisa. So he'd better find out the worst.

"We'll wait in Jack's room," said Thérèse, addressing Dolores in English. "I use mine as a darkroom, I'm afraid it's not very comfortable."

She led the way along the corridor, twirling Jack's key. But his door was already ajar.

"Typical," she said, shaking her head. "The cleaners are always forgetting to lock the doors. The security here is very bad."

She flung the door wide, clapped her hand to her mouth, and dissolved into horrified French.

The room was in chaos, the floor littered with Jack's belongings, every drawer spilling its contents, even the bed stripped of sheets and blankets.

"Oh dear," said Dolly vaguely. "Poor Jack. I hope they haven't stolen anything valuable. Had we better call the police, or should we wait till he gets back?"

Magpielike, Marisa began picking up items from the floor. But Thérèse stood rooted to the spot and pointed, horrified, at Jack's suitcase, which was lying open, empty on the bed.

"Quick," she said. "Into my room."

"What?"

"Do as I say. They might come back. Hurry!"

She pushed them out into the corridor and hustled them into her room.

"Lole," burbled Marisa. "What's happening?"

"Do you know where Jack has gone?" demanded Thérèse of Dolores. "We have to warn him not to come back to the hotel."

"What?"

"That was no burglary, *cherie*. They knew what they were looking for and they found it. I warned him about the secret police. I warned him this would happen."

"Lole," persisted Marisa. "What is she saying?"

Dolores took hold of Thérèse's hand and gripped it fiercely to stop her own shaking.

"The secret police?" she said. "Is Jack in danger of some kind?"

"Danger?" Thérèse gave a hollow laugh. "You knew he was writing a novel, did you? Well, evidently they knew as well. I told him he was getting careless, but he wouldn't listen to me. We've got to get word to him to stay away."

Dolores sat down, weak at the knees. What was it he had said about his book? That it would be banned in Spain, whoever won the war, because it told the truth . . .

"Once they read it, he'll be a dead man," continued Thérèse. "The SIM translators will already be working on it, we haven't got much time. Now, where is he?"

Dolly sprang to her feet. "I'll take you there," she said.

"No," said Thérèse firmly. "You're not well. I'll ask a couple of friends to look for him."

Weakly, quickly, Dolores gave the address of Tomás's workplace. While Marisa plied Dolores with unanswered questions, Thérèse spoke to someone on the telephone in rapid French which Dolores could not follow. Then she slammed the phone down and said, "They're leaving immediately. As soon as they find him they'll take him to the British Embassy. The NKVD can't arrest him there . . . Are you all right?"

Dolores was sitting motionless, rigid. Marisa had her arms around her and was gabbling at her in Spanish, in a vain attempt to extract information.

"What if they were waiting outside for him?" said Dolores. "What if they're following him?" She covered her face with her hands.

Thérèse put her arm around her, conscience stricken. If she'd realized how ill the poor girl was, she'd never have agreed to do this . . . too late now.

"I promise you, we'll find him," she said confidently. "I promise you. The embassy people will protect him. They'll make arrangements to get him out of the country, and then—"

"And then he can never come back," said Dolores. "He can never, ever come back."

"You are looking for the cripple?"

Jack turned to face the taunting, cackling voice. An old woman was grinning at him through toothless gums.

"Yes. Do you know what has become of him?"

Another head popped out of a neighboring door, and then another. Suddenly the entire corridor was party to the conversation.

"He is dead," the crone informed him cheerfully. "And not before time."

"Dead? In prison?"

"In the gutter. He stank of drink. They say he fell down senseless and banged his head. The patrols have taken him to the morgue. It is no loss."

Dead in the gutter, drunk. *Better for her if he died,* Tomás had said. *Better for her if I killed him.* And now he had, he must have. That was why he hadn't come to the hospital, why he wanted Marisa out of the way . . .

Aware that all eyes were on him, Jack hurried down into the street. He should have guessed. Tomás had done his old enemy a kindness if only for Dolly's sake. Tomás would have killed him quickly, mercifully, sparing him unspeakable tortures at the hands of the secret police, sparing Dolly worry and distress. Poor Marisa. Poor bloody Marisa . . .

Jack set off toward the factory, lost in thought. He must tell Tomás of his plan. If it failed, Tomás would have beaten him fair and square, he wanted him to know that. This would be the last time he would see him, whatever happened. Whatever happened, this time tomorrow he would be in France, with or without Dolly . . .

He hung around outside the factory till the whistle blew for siesta and watched the workers stream out. The stream reduced to a trickle, but Tomás did not emerge. Jack accosted a straggler and asked for Tomás García.

"Who are you?" the man demanded suspiciously. "What is your business?"

"I have a message from his wife," said Jack. "Is he here?"

The man jerked his head.

"Come with me," he said. "You had best speak to Manuel."

Manuel turned out to be a sinister-looking individual with bad teeth and an eyepatch.

"Tomás's wife, Lole, is sick," Jack told him. "I need to speak to Tomás urgently. Lole has been asking for him."

"Tomás is not here."

Jack felt a wave of anxiety. Perhaps Tomás's crime had been discovered, perhaps he had been arrested . . .

"Then where is he? At home? I have to find him. What's happened?"

Manuel scrutinized him for a long time before replying, as if assessing his bona fides.

"You have known Tomás long?"

"I am a relative of his wife. I am working in Madrid as a journalist." Jack produced his credentials and waited while Manuel pretended to read them.

"It is as well you came," he said at length. "Better than Lole hears such sad news from a relative."

"Sad news?" Jack caught his breath in alarm. Oh no. Surely not. Tomás had sworn he wouldn't kill himself, he had sworn he would never do that to her . . .

"Tomás dined with me last night and left toward midnight. Two other comrades stayed on to play cards. A few moments later we heard shots in the street below. We ran out immediately and found Tomás lying in a pool of blood, riddled with bullets."

Jack was overcome with horror, and relief, the selfish relief that it hadn't been suicide. He could never have lived with that . . .

"But who would want to kill Tomás?"

Manuel shrugged. "You understand, my friend, that there are many traitors in this city. Every day innocent workers are murdered by Fascist agents. Every day bodies are found in lonely places, shot to pieces and mutilated. This is why the search for the Fifth Column has been stepped up. Who knows how many such vermin there may be? Be assured that Tomás's death will not go unavenged. Even now the police are investigating likely suspects. Someone will be brought to trial, never fear. His death will not have been in vain if one more Fascist is unmasked and apprehended."

"But . . . was Tomás with you all evening?"

"Yes. He came home with me after work. He has been lonely without Lole this last week. Tell her that the union will take care of her. And please give her this."

He placed a dog-eared envelope in Jack's hands.

"We passed around the hat this morning, when the news was announced. Just a token, you understand. She was a good wife to him, and he fought bravely for the Republic. We will not forget that."

"Are you quite sure that Tomás was with you all evening?" repeated Jack, thinking of Ramón, conveniently dead in the gutter. He felt strangely detached, he felt like a reporter again.

"Why do you ask?" The one eye looked at him shiftily.

"Why would the Fifth Column want to kill Tomás? Could it have been . . . to avenge one of their own?"

"I do not understand you."

"I think you do. Lole's brother was also found dead last night. Did Tomás kill him?"

"Tomás was with me all day, and all evening. You insult his memory. Would you have his wife think him a murderer?"

"Certainly not," said Jack.

"Then you will say nothing of this to her. You must say nothing to her. It would pain her to think that her brother was a traitor."

"Was her brother a traitor?"

The man spat on the ground and walked away. It was as good an answer as any.

Heavyhearted, Jack made his way to the embassy. Tomás dead, Ramón dead. She would have come with him anyway. All this elaborate planning and scheming, and she would have come with him anyway. He had risked losing her, he had forced her to choose, and all for nothing . . .

He got the false passport out of his pocket and looked at it. He couldn't leave without her, not now. If she wasn't at the embassy waiting for him, he would just have to confess, eat humble pie, admit his deception. He would say to her, "I'm sorry I tried to trick you. Come home, for Andrés's sake. There's nothing to keep you here now." And she would come. He had been prepared to fail, and now he couldn't fail. She would come with him anyway, for all the wrong reasons, and victory would taste like defeat . . .

And what if she was already there, waiting for him? What if she said the words he longed to hear? What if she said, "I know you can never come back to Spain. I know this is my last chance. Take me with you?" Tomás would have been glad. Tomás would have given them his blessing and absolved them of guilt. Tomás was dead. He would have to sully the glory of that moment by telling her that Tomás was dead . . .

Yes, Tomás was dead. But not in vain. Not in vain.

"No news is good news," said Thérèse with a covert glance at her watch. Jack should have telephoned by now, damn him . . .

"No news is bad news," snapped Dolores unexpectedly, the cliché irritating her out of her trance. She got up and started pacing around the room.

"I was so complacent," she muttered angrily, "Such a coward. I knew Jack wouldn't give up. Whatever I said, whatever he said, I knew he'd find a way. But I wanted to keep my hands clean, I didn't want to have to *choose*. And now it's too late!"

"Choose?"

"Josep was right. I hate making decisions in cold blood. I hate admitting I've been wrong. Everything I've done in my life has been done in the heat of the moment, and I've stuck to every single mistake like glue. If I'd agreed to go with him months ago, this would never have happened! If Jack dies, it will be my fault . . .''

"He's not going to die," repeated Thérèse, fascinated now. Clearly Jack hadn't told her the half of it. Playing Cupid indeed. She had accepted a supporting role in *une petite comédie,* but it wasn't a comedy at all, it was a full-blown melodrama . . .

"And if your friends find him? If they get him to the embassy, what then? How will they get him out of the country?"

"I don't exactly know. Probably they'll give him some kind of temporary diplomatic status to get him as far as the border."

"So he'd be quite safe?"

"There's a war on, remember. Nobody's safe. The secret police are a law unto themselves. There's nothing to stop an accident happening between here and the frontier, a car crash or a trigger-happy patrolman. Such things have been known. It depends how dangerous they think he is."

"Dangerous? But what's so dreadful about this book of his? It isn't pro-Fascist, surely?"

"Hardly. It's anti-Stalin, which is a much, much bigger crime. If there's one thing the Communists hate more than Fascists, it's left-wing romantics like Jack."

"Jack? A romantic?"

"A romantic," repeated Thérèse with feeling, just as the telephone rang.

Dolores sat down abruptly, her eyes huge. Marisa, curled up on Thérèse's bed, wriggled in her sleep. Thérèse picked up the phone, listened for a moment and put it down again without speaking.

"They've found him," she said with a sigh of all too genuine relief. This had gone on quite long enough. "He's at the embassy. You can stop worrying. He's all right, Dolores. He's all right."

Dolores closed her eyes and buried her head in her hands, her shoulders shaking. Thérèse sat down beside her and put her arm around her, appalled, enthralled, still unsure whether she had played the fairy godmother or the wicked witch.

"Relax, *cherie,*" she murmured. "No need to worry. Relax now."

She did not relax. Her body was as taut as a wire. She seemed, if anything more agitated than before.

"I'll go alone to the embassy now," said Thérèse carefully. "I must see if there's anything I can do to help. Do you want me to give him any message?"

"No," said Dolores, jumping up. "No message. I'm coming with you. I have to see him before he goes."

There was a sudden, sensuous snore.

"You'd better tell Marisa," said Thérèse, pointing.

"Oh God. Marisa."

Dolores shook her awake and spoke to her rapidly in Spanish. Marisa's eyes opened wide and she began shaking her head. Dolores seemed to be trying to talk her into something, but to no avail. The girl began weeping and pleading, with Dolores becoming more and more impatient. Finally she turned to Thérèse and said, exasperated, "We're wasting time. She'll get hysterical unless we take her with us. I shouldn't have told her. I shouldn't have told her. But I'm sick of lies."

"What have you told her?"

"Never mind," said Dolores. "Let's go."

Marisa clung to Dolores like a child, as if afraid to let go. It was not like Lole to be angry with her, it was not like Lole to be unkind. For the first time Lole reminded her of Ramón in one of his black rages when she dared not speak to him and she felt afraid of her, of everything.

She did not know what was going on, only that it threatened her. She could not understand why Lole had to go away now, this minute, for good, why she should tell her to say good-bye to Ramón and Tomás for her, why she made no apologies or promises, why she would not explain.

"But what will I tell Tomás?" she had pleaded, fearing to be the bringer of bad news. But Lole had just said that Tomás would understand. It required no intelligence nor powers of analysis for Marisa to know that Lole wanted to be rid of her. A few hours ago, she would have gone home quite happily, but once she smelled danger and double-dealing, her most primitive instincts had taken over.

"Don't leave me, Lole!" she had wailed, infantlike. "What will become of me?" And for a moment she had thought that Lole was about to hit her, her eyes were bright and strange and terrible, but at the last minute she had given in, with the same noisy sigh she used to sigh at her disobedient son.

But once they arrived at the embassy. Marisa began to wish, belatedly, that she had done what she was told. The waiting room was dark and cheerless, and Lole kept talking to Thérèse in English, like a foreigner. Marisa was used to foreigners, she had made her living out of them, but for the first time she felt herself a stranger in her own country, isolated among people whose language she would never understand.

Marisa operated on feelings, not thoughts, and her feelings were contradictory. Half of her wanted to follow Lole, Lole who understood things, who would tell her what to do, who would look after her and her baby. And half of her wanted to stay with Ramón, Ramón who lived in a world where she was a princess, Ramón who would die in a world that cared nothing for her, a world that was nonetheless her home. Harsh reality made a final assault on all her hopes and dreams, its edges lost in a blur of fear.

"Hush," said Lole, gentle again, coaxing her, fueling her mistrust. "Don't cry. I'm sorry I was angry. But if I go, I cannot take you with me. You have Ramón. You will have your baby. Think of them. Don't make this hard for me. Please go home, Marisa. Please."

Marisa looked into the pleading, treacherous eyes, and then suddenly her baby kicked her, prompting her response.

"No," she said.

"Please be patient, Mr. Austin." The embassy official dipped his pen in the inkwell and carried on writing placidly in neat, slow, meticulous script. "I quite appreciate your anxiety, but these things take time. Now, if you'd kindly fill out these forms in triplicate . . ."

"Did you hear what I said?" asked Jack. "I said it was a matter of life and death."

"My dear chap, it always is. Once the necessary formalities have been complied with, then—"

"Formalities? Shall I tell you what will happen while you're complying with your formalities? My fiancée will die, it's as simple as that. Go into the waiting room and ask her to remove her scarf. Go on. They couldn't do anything for her. Her only hope is a London teaching hospital, and she can't get out of the country safely any other way. If she applies for a travel permit, she'll end up in jail. Her late husband died defending the Alcázar and her brother was a known Fifth columnist. Don't you understand? This is her only hope, and every minute counts. What do you expect me to do? Go out and buy the lady a forged passport?"

"A forged passport? Good gracious, no. We would never countenance giving such advice."

"I'm glad to hear it. You are authorized to perform the ceremony, I take it?"

"Mr. Austin, please calm yourself. I have the greatest sympathy with your fiancée's plight. I will do everything I can to expedite the matter. In the meantime—"

"In the meantime," said Jack, "I'm going to start sending cables. I'll have every newspaper in England telling the whole sad story. I can see the headlines now: HEARTLESS BUREAUCRAT GOES BY THE BOOK. I'll send them some lovely photographs of that shaved head of hers, I'll send them copies of the medical reports. I should think they'd be interested even if she wasn't half English. And of course it's quite irrelevant that her uncle's an under secretary or that her cousin is Lady Clara Neville. It's a good enough story without all that, don't you agree? Now, will you please do as I ask, today, now, right away, or is there going to be a *meantime?*"

Jack recognized the look in his eyes, the look of an old Etonian faced with a parvenu, privilege pitted against brute force, power against the people. Come the revolution, thought Jack, the sooner the bloody better.

"I can't promise today, now, right away, without seeking higher authority. And I would remind you that if we bend the rules, it will be out of compassion, not intimidation."

"I'll tell the lady it won't be much longer, then. This waiting isn't doing her any good, she's supposed to avoid any form of stress. It would look rather bad if she died on the premises, don't you think? Do you have a private room I can take her to, somewhere quiet where she can lie down?"

"Mr. Austin, in case you didn't realize, this building, like every other embassy in Madrid, is crowded with people seeking political asylum. No, I do not have a private room, this is not a convalescent home. I will, however, allow the lady to wait in here while I . . . er . . . complete the formalities."

Dolly came in on Thérèse's arm. Her face was pinched, white; it told him absolutely nothing.

"I must get back to Marisa," said Thérèse. She gave Jack a look midway between abject admiration and downright disapproval, and left them alone.

"What's happening?" said Dolly immediately. "Can they get you out of Spain?"

"They're fixing up some documents and arranging an embassy car. Don't look so worried. I'll write as soon as I get home, and

I'll keep you posted about the boys. I'm sorry about all this. It was nice of you to come to say good-bye."

"I haven't come to say good-bye."

Jack kept his features absolutely expressionless.

"I want to come with you. That is, if it won't make things harder for you. If you still want me to. If it's still possible."

"Why do you want to come with me? What's changed?"

"Nothing. Nothing's changed. What's the matter? Don't you want me to come?"

"Of course I do. The children need you."

"Stop it. Stop it. You know what I'm trying to say. You've won. Don't make me spell it out. And don't you dare say, "What about Tomás?" Don't you dare even mention him, don't you dare mention Ramón or Marisa or Marisa's baby. I warn you, if you mention any of them I'll walk right out of this room this minute and not come back. I mean it."

He was overpowered by a heady sense of déjà vu, of Dolly standing in that little room in Bayswater and saying, *After all it cost me to come here, you're just going to let me go? Well, don't expect me to come back again, damn you!* He had been terrified of her then, and he was terrified of her now. She had forbidden him to mention Tomás, and now he had to defy her.

"There's only one safe way I can get you out of the country," he said. "and that's on a British passport."

He put his hand in his pocket and felt the forgery between his fingers, steeling himself to take one final risk, to tell one final lie.

"Well?" she said, impatient with him now. "Can you get me one?"

Jack took his hand out of his pocket, empty.

"Only by marrying you," he said. And then, "Will you marry me, Dolly?"

"But I'm already married!"

He tried to tell her, but he couldn't say it, he could only look at her till she understood, and then he let her put her arms around him while he wept without shame.

"Ramón wouldn't want you to weep for him," said Dolores gently. "He died peacefully. He's out of pain now."

But Marisa was weeping for herself. She howled nonstop all the way to Barcelona, oblivious to the luxury of the embassy limousine. From time to time she would rally briefly, wipe her eyes on her fur coat, and sit up and take notice, like a posttantrum toddler, only to dissolve abruptly into tears again, while Dolly and Thérèse, mostly Thérèse, took turns comforting her.

They arrived in Barcelona the next morning. Clara was staying with a family in Barcelonetta, a poor quarter inhabited by dockworkers, and Jack had cabled her to expect them. Marisa protested loudly at the prospect of being abandoned to a stranger, but Clara, well used to difficult adolescents, didn't bat an eyelid.

"She's just frightened, that's all," she said above the din. "No wonder. She's hardly more than a baby herself. She'll be fine once I fix her up with a family. Now be on your way. The sooner you get Dolly home the better."

They left a wailing, waving Marisa with a thousand promises they could not keep, and which hopefully she would soon forget. Thank God for Clara, thought Jack, relieved. She was looking almost happy these days. Perhaps doing good was doing *her* good, at last.

The border guards, seeing the CD plates, waved them through after a cursory glance at the passports, and at Perpignan Jack and Dolly alighted and the car turned around again.

"Thanks for everything," said Jack, sotto voice, kissing Thérèse good-bye. "You were brilliant."

"You are a wicked, wicked man, Jack Austin. You don't deserve her. I feel sorry for her, really I do. Send me a copy of your novel, won't you?"

"I'll send you a bound volume of rejection slips. Still, at least it wasn't a total waste of time."

"And what are you going to tell her if it's published?"

"I'll tell her to read it," said Jack.

They traveled by train to Paris, where Dolores collapsed into bed, exhausted, and slept like a rock, Jack sitting watching her like a sentinel. She woke early to find him slumped in a chair, still fully clothed. Her wedding nights had never been auspicious.

She shut her eyes for a moment, thinking of Lorenzo, thinking of Tomás. Then she opened them and thought of Jack. She could think about Jack with her eyes wide open, love him with her eyes wide open. With Jack there was nothing to hide.

She reached out for his hand and he woke, startled, and looked back at her and smiled. His eyes were as bright and blue as ever and just as full of secrets. She would discover them slowly, one at a time. With luck it would take forever.